KRAKEN RIDER

BOOK ONE • KRAKEN RIDER Z

DAVID ESTES +
DYRK ASHTON

Wraithmarked
CREATIVE

KRAKEN RIDER Z
Book One of *Kraken Rider Z*
Copyright © 2023 by Dyrk Ashton & David Estes. All rights reserved.

This book is a work of fiction. Names, characters, places, and incidents are either a product of the author's imagination or used fictionally. Any resemblance to actual events, locals, or persons, living or dead, is entirely coincidental. All rights reserved. No part of this publication can be reproduced in any form or by any means, electronic or mechanical, without expressed permission from the author.

Editor: Taya Latham
Cover Illustration: Daniel Kamarudin
Cover Design and Interior Layout: STK·Kreations
Art Direction: Bryce O'Connor

Trade paperback ISBN: 978-1-955252-68-3
Ebook ISBN: 978-1-955252-59-1

Worldwide Rights
1st Edition

Published by Wraithmarked Creative, LLC
www.wraithmarked.com

THE LAST SKY MARSHALLS

Sky Marshall Slan hai Drogo raised his sword, gleaming with runes of golden light. With the other hand, he clenched his gauntleted fist. A flight of enemy dragon and rider pairs dropped from the sky, crushed and smoldering. The mighty dragon he rode upon, Sky Marshall Mogon, reared in the air and slammed his wings together, sending an additional twenty pairs tumbling and broken from the strength of the wind. Another flap of his wings, combined with a roar, and enemy ships capsized, risen on a massive wave, and crashed into those behind them.

The battle raged all around, the air choked with smoke and fire, molten lava and shards of ice, cannon fire, spears, javelins, and arrows. Knights and magickers swarmed the sky as far as the eye could see, engaged in the grisly work of death. Below, a thousand ships clashed, cannons blasting, hulls splintering, decks and sails ablaze.

Mogon roared to rally the much-depleted forces of Tosh and their allies and charged once again into the fray. Drogo swiped the air with his sword. A great arc of flame sliced through enemy dragons and riders alike while also splitting a warship in two. With another deafening roar from Mogon, a dozen dragon and rider pairs and a half-dozen ships burst into flames.

Blinking from one place to another to take the enemy by surprise, streaking with the speed and heat of a comet, the pair wreaked havoc on the Luftoo Empire's forces, both in the air and on the sea. And yet it wasn't enough. As their core burned low, spears and arrows penetrated their Shield and protective aura to pierce flesh and scale, fire scorched them, ice stung them, their armor melted under streams of lava, and cannon fire cracked their bones.

Racked with agony, the sky marshalls surveyed the field of battle.

Of their own Dragon Corps, only a few hundred of what had been thousands of rider and dragon pairs remained, and the combined navies of Tosh and the kingdom's allies were nearly ruined. Steaming bodies and burning ships choked the sea. The waves peaked red. Screaming riders and dragons fell from the sky like rain.

The sky marshalls alone had slain thousands of the enemy and destroyed a hundred of their ships, but the forces of the Luftoo Empire were vast beyond reckoning. By all accounts, the battle should be over and the war lost. But Drogo and Mogon had not scratched, clawed, and suffered to progress faster and farther than any of their peers to lose now.

"*We must*," Mogon spoke through their bond so only his rider could hear. His voice was choked, but not from the smoky haze that hung in the air.

"*I know*," Drogo said, wishing it weren't so. Wishing they had more time. Another life to share, another yoke to carry.

"*I don't want to lose you.*"

Drogo fought back the emotion that swelled within him at the gravity of his dragon's words. "*And you won't, not ever. You will carry me into the skies until fire rains from the heavens and our world is but a steaming ember. Even then, I'll persevere within your memory, like a haunting ghost. Don't think you will ever be rid of me so easily.*"

Mogon roared a bitter laugh. "Then let us fight to the last, so our memories are full and satisfied."

"To the last," Drogo agreed.

He tore an arrow from his shoulder and wrested a javelin from his hip. Mogon ripped a lance from his chest with his toothy maw. Heedless of their own lives, they fought on, waiting for the penultimate moment before reaching for a secret and terrible power they'd hoped never to have to use. Those witnesses who survived the event refused to speak of it in the days that followed. And those who perished under its force... well, the dead tell no secrets.

Nevertheless, the enemy was destroyed. The war was won. Their kingdom would remain free. The cost, however, was dire.

Drogo and Mogon's core had burned out, their bond severed like a cut string. Drogo screamed and slumped in his saddle, Mogon loosed a keening cry, and the Sky Marshalls of Tosh plummeted into the burning sea, never to rise again.

They were the last of the sorcerers, both true knights *and* true magickers, and the only pair to reach high-level Black Titan Class in a generation, a feat yet unmatched in the decades since. The last of the Arch Mages, and the youngest officers in the history of Tosh to hold the rank of Sky Marshall. Now they were gone.

This is not their story, but that of a far more unlikely hero and the even unlikelier beast he rode upon, their bond built of love and sacrifice, and an enduring hope that life could be more than it appeared at first glance. From humble beginnings, even the unlikeliest can become champions, and, perhaps, even gods.

Our story begins eighty years later, on an ordinary day, not so different from any other. It also happens to be the day our heroes first met...

PART ONE

CHAPTER 1

"Hurrah!" Zee cried, clinging to the harness of his pig, Midge, as she ran along the rocky shore. Out off the coast was a ship, not often seen in the rocky waters on this side of the remote key where Zee lived. He wondered if maybe they were surveying the coastline after last night's earthshake. The trembling of the earth was a regular occurrence in that region of Tosh, but last night's had almost knocked him out of bed.

The pig veered toward the water. "Not so close, Midge!" he shouted. She obeyed with a begrudging grunt. "Do you see the flags? That's one of His Majesty's Tradeships. It's a galleon, with cannons and harpoon guns—and dragons!"

Two of the beasts, larger than the largest horses, swooped through the air closer to shore, riders on their glistening backs. Zee recognized their armor and saddlery. They were dragon knights and officers in His Majesty's Dragon Corps—true guardians and heroes of the realm.

"That green dragon with a silver belly is a Greatwing," Zee explained to Midge with bubbling enthusiasm. "They fly fast and really far. The smaller white one is an Ice Diver. They can dive into the water and catch things to eat. They can't stay under for long, though, because dragons have hollow bones, you know."

If the pig did know, or care, she didn't show it.

To hoots of encouragement from its rider, the Greatwing chased a flock of fat gulls and blasted them with a streak of flame. The air shimmered yellow around the dragon and rider, and the pair shot forward without the dragon flapping its wings. It snapped up the cooked birds with its long mouth, bristling with dagger-sharp teeth. Yellow light flashed as the rider touched her chest with both hands, and she was suddenly holding a fishing net in one hand and a line attached to it with the other.

The dragon swooped low and the knight flung the net to drag swiftly through the water. When the dragon flew back up, the net was full of flopping fish. The knight swung it up as if it weighed nothing and wrapped the rope around a post on her saddle.

"That's the best way to catch fish, ever," Zee exclaimed.

The Greatwing swooped closer to shore and flew along the beach. The knight saluted Zee while the dragon eyed the pig hungrily. Midge oinked with concern. The dragon grinned and rocked its wings before heading back out toward the Ice Diver.

"Hello!" Zee waved with enthusiasm. "Look at their shiny silver armor, Midge. That means their bond rating is Silver Class. That's pretty high." He pointed to the other pair, whose mail and helm were polished blue-gray. "They're Iron Class."

The sharp dorsal fin of a sheel cut along the surface of the water, its silver-black body undulating through the waves while it searched for prey. The Ice Diver swooped and blasted it with a jet of ice particles. The sheel bobbed to the surface among chunks of ice and the Greatwing shot a gout of fire, thawing and cooking it, setting the water around it bubbling. The Ice Diver snatched the fish out of the water, but the Greatwing bit down on the sheel's tail. Together they tore it in half and swallowed the pieces. The riders shouted at one another, laughing, and veered back toward the ship.

Zee couldn't wait to tell his ma and da. He wanted to be a dragon rider more than anything. Da would say, "It's all right to dream, but dreams don't feed the pigs or pay the king's taxes." Ma would say, "To dream is a beautiful thing." Zee wasn't sure what that meant, exactly, but he liked it.

In his excitement, Zee began to wheeze and struggle for breath. He retrieved an old parfume decanter and squeezed the bulb to spray mist into his mouth, inhaling sharply, then concentrated on calming himself and controlling his breathing like Ma had taught him. Eyes closed, he drew air through his nose and blew out through his mouth, deep and slow. He felt his tension ease and his airways clear. Soon he could breathe normally again.

Zee's heart was gripped by a fist of yearning as he watched the dragons fly away. His gaze wandered to where the ocean flowed onto and retreated from the beach like fingers of water scrabbling endlessly ashore, grasping with futility to crawl upon the land. To grab him and drag him to the depths. And yet, something about it called to him, hypnotic and desirable…

He scratched absentmindedly at his chest through the light cloth of his long-sleeved shirt, then realized what he was doing. "Stop it, Zee," he reprimanded himself, repeating his ma's words. "You'll just make it worse." Still, he rubbed his neck and adjusted his scarf.

He sighed loudly. He'd better get his head back in the dirt, as his da liked to say. Time for work.

The beach looked different from yesterday. The earthshake last night must have been stronger than he'd thought. It had knocked some things about in the house and set the pigs to squealing but done no real damage. It'd been a long time since the last big one, and from what Zee had heard about that, this didn't come close to it. Still, familiar stone formations were broken, and ridges of sand and rock were heaved up where they hadn't been yesterday. More than he'd ever seen, in all his seven years.

He slid off Midge's back and set to combing the shore, gathering things for his mother to use in her medicines, like rutroot and walloweed, as well as things to eat. There wasn't always enough to eat. They couldn't eat the pigs, they were worth too much. Midge wasn't for eating or selling. She was for riding and pulling the cart to town. She also helped Zee find things by rutting in the sand.

Zee caught a crab for crabby soup. It was a little skinny thing, but

Ma would use it to flavor soup. He also gathered kelpy, slogs, and winkles, altogether making a slimy mess that he put in sacks and oilskin pouches strapped to Midge's back.

They stayed well away from the water's edge. He reminded Midge again when she strayed too close, and again, the pig grunted and obeyed. Zee's parents gave him his independence for the most part. He *was* seven years old, after all. But one rule was hard and fast. "Inviolate," his da called it. Don't go near the sea, and never, under any circumstances, was Zee to swim in the ocean, or even wade in the tide pools.

Zee sang part of the little song his mother had taught him.

"Don't go near the water
Stay away from the sea
The riptides and the monsters
Will be the end of me."

As far as Zee knew, everyone in Tosh learned similar rhymes from a very young age.

"The ocean is full of dangers
Your distance you must keep
Terrible toothy creatures
Wait hungry in the deep."

And all of them involved krakens.

"Most fearsome of all is the kraken
King monster of the sea
When the kraken comes arising
Even dragons flee."

Zee couldn't imagine dragons being afraid of anything, and Da recently confessed to him that no one had seen a kraken in a thousand years, if they weren't a myth to begin with. The other dangers were real, though. Only really brave or crazy people swam in the ocean around Tosh, or anywhere else that Zee knew of. His ma would have a heart attack if she thought he even considered it. Out of love and respect for her and Da, he'd never tried. A good healthy fear and sense of self-preservation had something to do with it, too.

"Don't go near the water
Stay away from the sea
The mighty monstrous kraken
Will make a meal of Zee."

"Hey!" Zee shoved the greedy pig's snout away from a scraggly patch of king's balm and jerked the torn shoots from her slobbery mouth. He stuffed the plants in a sack, then heard something that struck him silent and still.

A little sound, strange and heartbreaking, like a baby bird was drowning. Midge's ears stiffened and she cocked her head toward a broken outcropping of sharp black rocks.

Zee swiftly tied his sack to her harness. "Come on, Midge. Something needs our help!" He ran to the tumble of black stone. Ignoring scrapes from the sharp rocks, he scrabbled up it with purpose.

This could be his chance to be a hero. Like a real dragon knight of the realm, with his trusty dragon, Midge.

He came to the crest of the rocks, wheezing again, and peered over.

CHAPTER 2

In the sweltering sun was a muddy pit, like a tide pool but drained into a crack in the earth, with broken stone around it. Two torn-open eggs, similar to tortle eggs, but black, oval-shaped, and almost as big as Midge's head, lay in the mud. Beside one of them was a creature Zee didn't recognize. Much like a squid or octopod, with multiple arms, but different. Midge, who had found an easier way around, nudged it with her snout. Shining blue carcass-flies buzzed up as it flopped over, dead.

Zee gulped and tears formed in his eyes. He was too late. But then the arms of another one of the things squirmed weakly in the mud.

Zee scrabbled down the rocks to where the pig snuffled at it. "No, Midge, don't eat it." Midge backed away with a grunt as Zee slopped through the sucking muck. He poked the little creature with a stick of driftwood, but it didn't react. Then he heard the gargling peep again, same as before.

A third egg was mostly buried in the mud. Its surface undulated from feeble movement inside. Through a split in the shell, a tiny mouth peeped with fright.

Zee was frightened as well. He shouldn't have been going anywhere near these things. They could be dangerous. Poisonous even. But they were in trouble and needed help. Zee's help. Heroes had to be brave.

He set his little jaw, mouth drawn down in a determined frown, and went to his knees next to the egg. "It's okay. I'm here to save you."

He dug at the mud and tugged on the egg until it came loose with a sucking sound. "Oh, you're heavy."

The creature let out another peep as Zee slid the egg out of the watery hole. Zee hesitated again, then crooked his fingers into either side of the rip in the shell and pulled. It wasn't easy, like trying to rip kelp or wet leather. Zee grunted with effort, and the split widened. Two little arms with rows of suckers along one flat side each forced their way out and reached for Zee. The creature peeped louder.

Zee set to the task with more ardor. "It's okay little thing, I've got you." It was even more difficult to tear at the egg with the creature grasping one of his arms, but Zee finally pulled the baby free and held it out in front of him. And a strange baby it was.

It had a gray and cone-shaped shell, with ten wriggly arms protruding from its base (Zee counted them out loud). Several of the arms wrapped around Zee's arms, holding tight. Not tight enough to hurt, just to secure itself, seeking safety and comfort.

Zee turned the thing this way and that, inspecting it for injury—and trying to figure out what it was. "Where did your mouth go? Where's your face?" he asked. "If you even have a face…"

As if in reply, more of the creature pushed itself down out of the shell, then a horizontal lid popped open, and a bright green orb of an eye shoved out, looking right at Zee.

"Eee!" Zee squeaked. Only the grip of the thing's arms kept him from accidentally dropping it.

"Eee!" the thing squeaked, hanging on tighter so it wouldn't get dropped.

Recovering from his fright, Zee held the baby nearer to get a closer look. A nictitating lens slid down from over the creature's eye, leaving it clearer and brighter. The creature blinked, pushed itself farther out of its shell, and another eye opened. It had an octopod-like brow, a bump for a nose with two slanted slits for nostrils, and a wide mouth with rubbery lips. It blinked again and stared at Zee.

"Hi… *thing*." Zee inspected it more closely. The shell had a slight corkscrewing ridge from bottom to top. Small nubs of the same color as the shell were randomly placed on its surface. He tilted the baby back, then up, then turned it all the way around. No more eyes opened, but the creature rotated its ocular orbs to keep him in sight the whole time, even when he pointed the tip of its cone-head at himself.

"That's nifty," Zee said. "Handy when swimming, I'll bet."

Midge grunted, seeming as fascinated with the creature as Zee was. One of the baby's eyes swiveled to Midge and the baby peeped again, showing stubby triangular teeth.

Cautiously, the little creature probed out toward Zee's face with two of its arms. Zee didn't flinch, though he grimaced when the slimy things touched his cheeks. Surprisingly, they were warm to the touch. The creature cooed, and Zee didn't protest when it reached with more arms and pulled itself closer to nestle against his shoulder and chest. Its head, or head-body, more like, vibrated as a little rumbling sound flowed through it. To Zee, it sounded like a cat purring, and his heart swelled.

A soft slap in the mud drew his attention to the other baby that was still alive. It gurgled pitifully, and Zee's swollen heart nearly broke.

He gently pulled the one he'd saved from the egg away from his chest. "We need to get you two out of the sun. And I bet you're hungry."

* * *

Zee huffed and wheezed, what muscle there was in his skinny arms and legs burning. He'd trudged over a mound of rock and made his way down the other side, a baby squiddly-thing under each arm. He laid the weak one in the water of a clear tide pool farther away from shore in the shade of a cluster of pom trees. The creature livened up a little but didn't open its eyes.

Zee used his lung-spritzer to ease his breathing while the other baby, the one he'd saved from the egg, squirmed under his arm. He leaned close to the water, but the creature was reluctant to let go. "It's okay. I'm not leaving you." Not yet, Zee thought, as he checked the sun sinking from late afternoon toward evening.

"Fear the shore in the day time
A dangerous place to be
But night time is the fright time
The darkness you must flee."

Sea creatures crawled onto the beach at night. Hungry, venomous, and toothy things. Zee had seen the tracks of their dragging bodies, claw prints in the sand, and the slime trails they left behind. Some of them were pretty big.

That's why he'd chosen this pool, a hundred feet from the shoreline, fed with fresh seawater from an underground fissure in the rock. He'd never seen any creature tracks near it or anyone else come here. Rarely did people come to this remote stretch of rocky, inhospitable shore.

The baby allowed itself to be submerged and finally let go of Zee's arms. It settled on the shallow sandy bottom near the edge with just the pointed top of its shell sticking out, looking up at him from beneath the surface.

Midge had followed, and Zee offered the baby some slogs from one of the oilskin sacks. It gobbled them down, humming with a strange sound that resonated in the water. The creature's big eyes followed a silver minny that swam around it. On the minny's third pass, the baby snapped open its mouth much wider than Zee would have thought possible, causing a rush of water to suck the fish in. Though he offered slogs to the other one, Zee couldn't get it to eat, nor did it seem interested in the fish, which made him sad. He hoped it would survive the night.

Zee spent much of the afternoon eagerly catching minnies from other tide pools with a small net Da had made for him and dumping them in the pool with the baby creatures. Some he kept in a water sack to take home for salt-drying and soup. He also buried the baby that had died, saying a solemn prayer to Postune to look after it in the great Sea of Heaven.

It was only when he heard Ma's bell ringing from over the rocky dunes and up the steep slope that he realized what time it was.

"Oh, no." He was crouched at the edge of the pool, watching the baby thing swim clumsily around. "I'm sorry, but I have to go."

The baby swam to the edge in front of Zee, where it used its rubbery arms to pull itself out until its face was above the surface.

"You'll be okay here for the night," Zee assured it, hoping it was true. "I'll be back tomorrow, I promise." The baby blinked at him and held out one of its arms. "I'm sorry," Zee said, "I haven't introduced myself." He took the curled end of the arm in one hand. "My name is Zee Tarrow." He shook the arm gently. "And over there is Midge, Queen of Pigs." Midge grunted from where she snuffled in the dirt for bitter pom fruits but didn't look up.

The baby looked to Midge, then back to Zee, and peeped.

Zee's face scrunched. "'Peep' isn't much of a name." He thought a moment. "I think I'll call you Jessup. How does that sound?"

The creature peeped again, which Zee took as affirmation.

"All right then. Hello, Sir Jessup. It's very nice to meet you." He shook Jessup's arm again to make it official. It occurred to Zee he had no idea if the thing was male or female. Or maybe both or neither at all. But as the creature gazed back at him, Zee got a strong feeling it was a boy, and that would do for now.

The bell rang again.

Zee hopped up. "I really have to go. I don't want to make Ma cross. I'll be back as early as I can in the morning." He scratched at the cloth of his home-sewn pants, frowning at the thought of leaving Jessup and his sickly sibling alone for the night. He'd briefly considered taking them back to the house but had quickly decided that wouldn't be a good idea. In fact, after some deliberation, he'd decided not to tell his ma and da about them at all. At least, not yet.

He hated the idea of keeping a secret from them, but Da was very practical. He might decide these things could be good to eat. Or maybe they were rare, since Zee had never seen one before, not even in the market or the fishers' fresh catches at the docks. They could be worth something. They might even be considered a delicacy. In that case, Da would surely sell them to help the family and the farm. Zee's da wasn't a bad man at all, he just always put family matters first.

"You be careful down here, Jessup." He waved a stern finger at the creature, which looked up at him with its big green eyes. "Don't go crawling out." Zee eyed the pool and pointed to the center. "In fact, you and your brother should hide under those deeper rocks for the night if you can, okay?"

Jessup blinked and peeped.

"Okay. Have a peaceful night. Don't let the kraken bite." It was a silly saying, Zee knew, but it came naturally since his ma said it every evening when she tucked him into bed.

He trudged up the slope to where Midge waited, then looked back down at Jessup and waved, calling out, "See you soon." He climbed onto Midge, and they trotted off toward home.

* * *

Jessup watched the boy and his mount disappear over the rocks that rimmed the pool. He pushed himself up in an attempt to see them still, but they were out of sight. His lips moved as he made little sounds, until he formed a word that sounded very much like "Zee." Then he lowered himself beneath the surface, blew some bubbles, and went to drag his sibling beneath the rocks in the center of the pool.

CHAPTER 3

Midge ran up the steep winding path from the coastline, Zee leaning forward and hanging on tight. They crested the slope, ran past the ramshackle sheds and the pigpens Da had built, then around the rickety barn, Midge kicking up dust all the way. The two scrawny chickens they owned squawked and scattered as Midge skidded to a halt in the barnyard.

"Hi, Ma. We're back!" Zee slid off Midge, cheeks flushed, and began untying his bags.

Ma stood from where she was tending her herb garden. "Zepiter's feathers, Zee." She wiped her hands on her apron and rested them on her hips. "What in the great wide sea have you and Midge been up to?"

He was filthy, and so was the pig. Midge was one of the few animals that Da let him name—officially, anyway, since Zee had secretly named most of them—saying you should never name an animal you weren't going to keep because it would hurt too much when they had to go away. Zee hadn't yet learned that lesson. He had named the baby creature he'd saved. He wondered if that had been a mistake.

Zee looked down at himself, only now realizing the extent to which he was covered in mud and dust. "Um...," he said, flustered. "We gathered some good stuff today. Midge found sprigs of king's balm!"

"Looks like you both had to wrestle slop monsters in the Land of Mud to get it."

Zee tried to wipe the mud from his pants, only managing to smear it and get it all over his hands. "Sorry, Ma."

She flashed him a stern look, tinged with worry. "You didn't get near the water?"

"No, ma'am!"

She took a deep breath and blew it out, shaking her head, then smiled and trod toward him. "You get yourself cleaned up. Midge can take care of herself."

"Okay." Zee hated to worry his ma. "Here's the king's balm." He handed her the sack.

She took it and tussled his hair, then scowled at the filth that came away on her hand. "I'll get the rest of your catch. Off you go to the sprinkler."

"But I can help—"

"Shoo!"

"Yes, Ma." He also hated to make more work for his ma. She toiled from before sunrise to well after sunset every day. Not just cooking and cleaning, but mending clothes, which he and Da were particularly hard on, taking care of her garden and making tinctures, pastes, powders, and salves to sell to merchants in the market. What she made didn't fetch much coin, but every little bit helped. It hurt his heart to see her so tired every night, so he tried to help in any way he could. It looked like today he'd failed—though he had, he recalled, saved a couple of baby creatures from almost certain death.

With that thought in mind, he scratched his trusty mount between the ears. "Thank you for your help today, Midge." The pig grunted and Zee sprinted around to the back of the modest three-room house.

Other kids took baths, he knew, but Ma and Da insisted they all use the sprinkler that Da had rigged behind the house to trickle rainwater from a tub on the roof. "Why soak in your own juices when you can rinse them away?" Da said.

Zee stripped off his clothes and dumped them on a bench before Ma came around to check on him, as he knew she would. His lungs tightened again, and he scratched at the body rash he always bore while he calmed his breath. The rash had been with him for as long as he could remember.

He tried not to scratch too much, and Ma had developed an ointment of kelp goo, aloishus, and salt that eased the itch and reduced the redness. When he was younger, before Ma perfected the salve, he'd dig at his skin so badly he would bleed, and he had scars all over his arms, legs, and torso, some light, some dark and deep, as if he'd been attacked by wild beasts. He remembered how bad it was before the salve, the itch terrible and incessant. Now it stung and burned mightily, but he'd grown more accustomed to the constant irritation. He tried harder to bear it without showing discomfort, too, and never complained any more. He didn't want his ma and da to see him suffering, it pained them so. Besides, he'd heard stories that dragon knights endured terrible burns and other grievous wounds in battle but would still keep fighting. If they could do that, he would bear the pain and irritation the best he could.

His thoughts were interrupted as Ma came around the corner with a fresh bar of lard soap. "Here you go. Now get in there and scrub up good."

"Yes, Ma." Zee hopped under the spigot and pulled the rope, dousing himself, then rubbed the soap in his hair.

Ma scrutinized the rough red patches on his skin, running over with muddy water. "Rinse real well and dry up when you're through. I'll fetch the ointment."

"Thank you, Ma," Zee replied, downhearted she had to see it. He was old enough to put the ointment on himself, though she often insisted, and he couldn't reach his back anyway.

He scrubbed himself with a natural sponge from the shore, careful not to rub too hard on the more afflicted areas of his skin, which would make them burn worse.

Da trudged out of the sparse woods behind the house with an armload of firewood. "Hail, Sir Zee!"

Zee splashed the soap from his eyes, beaming at the nickname. "Hi, Da!"

Zee's da paused, peering at the dark water that pooled at Zee's feet before trickling away in the shallow trench dug just for that purpose. "You and Midge do some wallowing together today?"

"Oh, um, we were just busy combing the beach, as usual."

"I hope you found something good." Da stepped to the lean-to at the back of the house to stack the wood. "By the looks of ya, it was quite an adventure."

Zee grimaced, then tried to hide it by scrubbing the gray suds in his hair. Once again, it bothered him to keep the secret of Jessup and the other strange little creatures from his parents. But he did have something to tell—

"There was a ship in the bay, Da, and dragon knights!"

Having completed his stacking of the wood, Da pushed up with a groan, his knees creaking. "You don't say?"

"I swear it on Postune's seaweed beard!" Zee replied, making an exaggerated sign of a trident over his heart.

Ma came around the corner carrying another set of clothes for Zee. "Dragon knights, you say? You'll have to tell us more over dinner."

"Okay!" was Zee's enthusiastic reply, rinsing off with a pull of the rope.

Da chuckled as he clapped his hands to clear the dust from his palms. He and Ma knew there was no shutting Zee up once he got talking about dragons and riders.

"Let's get you finished up, now," Ma said, placing the clothes on a bench. Da stepped up and held the rope while Ma scrubbed through Zee's hair to help with the rinse.

Zee shivered with the chill and sputtered through the water. "You think they had squires on the ship? If not, maybe they need one."

Da and Ma traded a look, part amusement, part sorrow. "Maybe they do, son," said Da, "but you know only fancy folks with loads of money and fancy little words in front of their surnames get to squire for knights and go to the Citadel for training and bond with a dragon. We ain't got neither of those."

"I know." Zee suddenly felt bad about bringing it up again. It wasn't his parents' fault they weren't rich and didn't have a "mon," "si," "jal," or some such before their last name. Only the highborn had them. There were some merchant families who had gotten very wealthy without them, though. "Maybe one day we'll have money. One can always hope, right, Ma?"

Ma rubbed Zee with a towel, rough and quick on his head, then dabbed more carefully at his body. "Yes indeed, one always can, Zee, and should."

Da added, "As long as it's a practical hope."

Zee grabbed the towel. "I can do it Ma."

"All right. Such a big little man you're getting to be."

Zee wasn't big at all and he knew it. He was small for his age, and skinny. Sometimes people would gape at him when he spoke to them, surprised he could talk so well for his size.

"Then I'll scrub my clothes in the creek and hang 'em to dry," Zee volunteered, tugging on his pants.

Ma tossed his dirty clothes on the stones under the trickler and pulled the rope. "Let 'em soak awhile." She helped him tug a fresh shirt down over his head. "We'll do that later."

Zee frowned, plopping down to put on his boots. Then he brightened. "I'll go feed Midge and the others, then." With that, he hopped up and ran off around the house.

"Tie your boots!" his ma called after him.

"Yes, Ma!" he shouted back without slowing.

* * *

Da shook his head. "Tires me out just watching him."

"He's a spritely one," Ma said with a smile of motherly fondness. "Even with his rash and breathing problems."

Da chuckled, then lowered his tall slim frame to sit on the bench next to the weathered teak table he'd built and wiped the sweat from his forehead. "He doesn't get his energy from me, that's for sure."

She sat next to him, her smile shifting to sadness. "He doesn't get it from either one of us, Jad Tarrow, and you know it."

Da took her hand. "I know it, Seela."

She placed her hand on his. "We'll have to tell him, one day." The lines of sorrow on her face grew deeper, and her voice grew softer. "I only pray that he understands what we've done for him, when he also realizes what we've done to him."

Jad reached his arm around her and held her close. "He will, Ma," he said, followed by a troubled sigh. "One day."

* * *

Zee chattered all through their supper of crabby-minny soup and fried root crisps, describing the ship he'd seen and its rigging and the knights and dragons and their armor in great detail, gesticulating wildly with his arms the whole time.

While helping his ma with the dishes, his mind returned to the little creatures he'd found that day, and how they'd be down by the shore at night, all alone. He thought about Jessup especially, and his big, googly eyes.

He realized he'd stopped halfway through drying the dish in his hand when his ma said, "You feeling all right, Zee? You haven't said a word in almost a whole minute."

"I'm fine, Ma," he replied, then added, "I'm just tired and thinking about the dragons," wincing inwardly at the lie.

* * *

Ma applied ointment to the worst areas of Zee's rash while he sat on the edge of his bed. "What's this, then?"

Zee craned his neck back and tried to see the area high on his left chest muscle she had touched. All he managed was to cross his eyes and make a silly face. "I can't see it. What's it look like?"

"Let's see." She got up from her stool to fetch the oil lamp closer.

Zee ran his fingers over the small area on his chest. It felt rough, like sandstone.

She sat back down, handed him an old cracked mirror, and held up the lamp. "Here you go."

Zee angled the mirror so he could see the spot. It was light gray and roundish, about the size of the tip of his finger. "I don't know what that is, Ma. It tingles a little, but not like when I have a new rash coming on. It doesn't hurt or anything."

She felt around it. "Did you hit yourself on something or touch anything you wouldn't normally?"

Zee scrunched his face in thought. "I don't think so." Then he sat up straight as he realized something.

"What is it?"

Zee scrambled to think of what to say. "I, um, was up by the pom trees. Maybe there was something there, like itch-weed." It wasn't exactly a lie, but it wasn't the whole truth either.

She cocked her head and he tried to look as innocent as possible. She took a deep breath. "It doesn't look like itch-weed, and it isn't red around the edges. It could just be the start of a wartlump or a type of moley. If it's not painful, we'll just keep an eye on it." She set the lamp and mirror on top of the plank shelves where Zee's clothes were kept. "Into bed with you."

She'd tucked him in and kissed him on the forehead. "Have a peaceful night. Don't let the krakens bite."

"Good night, Ma," he said with a smile.

After she'd blown out the lamp and closed the door to his tiny room, Zee let out an exaggerated "Phew!" It was true he didn't recall touching anything like itch-weed. With his rash, he was especially careful not to get near anything like that, and his ma had taught him to recognize all the poisonous plants in the area.

He did, however, pick up a weird squiggly octopod thing and its sibling and carry them around. Could he be allergic to Jessup? Then again, if he was, he should have it all over himself. It wasn't very strong reasoning, but it was enough to dampen his fears some.

He stared out the window at the two moons that watched over night on the watery world of Zhera, gently touching the patch on his chest and worrying about Jessup and the other baby creature. The patch felt warm but in a pleasant way. It comforted him and even helped him bear the sting and itch of his rash, which never ceased entirely, even with a fresh application of ointment.

When he finally fell asleep, he was disturbed by dark dreams about all manner of sea beasties creeping up on the tide pool where he'd placed the little creatures he'd saved.

CHAPTER 4

Zee sat upon Midge at the top of the rocky rise that sloped down toward shore, watching over his shoulder in nervous anticipation as the morning light brightened. He'd risen early, gobbled down his breakfast, and run out of the house before he usually did, leaving his da chuckling and Ma shaking her head.

As soon as the crown of the sun's bald head peeked above the hills, he slapped Midge on the shoulder and thrust an arm in the air. "Take flight!"

Midge couldn't launch herself into the air like a dragon, of course, but she did her best by bolting down the slope. Zee cried out as he nearly tumbled off, but caught himself and hung on while they wound their way down, burlap bags and oilskin sacks flapping at the pig's sides. Midge knew exactly where Zee wanted to go, and took the shortest route to the tide pool where they'd spent most of the day yesterday.

She skidded to a stop at the top of the rocks near the pool, nearly toppling Zee forward this time. Zee slid off, knees shaking, but instead of being angry or frightened, he was flushed with excitement. He hugged Midge around the neck. "Good pig!" Midge grunted and snuffled off to rut for more pom fruits.

Zee picked his way down to the pool and peered into the clear water.

"Hello? Jessup? Are you awake?"

There was no sign of the babies, causing Zee to worry all the more. Then Jessup poked his gray cone-shaped head out from beneath the black rocks at the center of the pool and shoved out his eyes. He caught sight of Zee and peeped under the water, then reached out with his arms and extricated himself from the tight space.

Zee grinned and waved. "Good morning!"

Jessup sat on his arms under the water, blinking up to him. Zee moved closer to the edge and leaned over. "I can't come in after you. I'm not allowed to go in the water. You'll have to come to me." Jessup cocked his head. Zee beckoned with his hands. "Come on. It's okay."

Jessup shuffled along the bottom with a squirmy-armed waddle, then stopped, appearing to be thinking about something, puffed out his cheeks, and floated up until his shell popped to the surface like a cork. Zee watched in amazement as Jessup wriggled awkwardly with his arms, then got the hang of treading water and pushed himself up until his face was out of the pool. The little creature grinned at his accomplishment.

"That's great!" Zee cried. He waved his hands toward himself in encouragement. "Come on."

Jessup paddled to the edge and with more determination, pulled himself farther out. Then he tipped and fell over backward with a peep, where he flailed about, half in, half out of the pool.

"Hang on!" Zee crouched and snatched hold of an arm. "I've got you!" The creature wrapped Zee's wrist and allowed himself to be lifted and tipped up into Zee's arms.

Zee sat back with Jessup in his lap. "There you go, safe and sound." The creature stared up at him, making little gurgling sounds. "Did you have a good night?"

Jessup blinked wide and said, "Zee!" The sound of it gave Zee such a start he cried out and nearly slipped into the water.

Zee sputtered, "You can talk?"

"Zee!" Jessup said again.

Recovering from his shock, Zee asked, "Can you say anything else?"

"Midge!"

Midge jerked her head up and stared at the little creature.

Zee was overcome with joy. "That's amazing! What else can you say?"

"Zee!"

Zee giggled. "That's a good start, I guess. I'm going to talk all the time so you can learn some new words."

Midge's eyes fell on Zee, the look on her piggy face practically communicating *nothing new there*.

Zee peered into the pool once more. "Where's the other one?"

Jessup gurgled softly, the sides of his mouth turning down and the lids of his eyes lowering in the outer corners. A sadness rose in Zee's chest, emanating from his touch with the creature on his lap, and he knew the other baby was dead.

A bell later, Jessup had pulled the limp body of his sibling out from under the rock and dragged it to the edge of the pool, where Zee had fished it out of the water with a piece of driftwood. Now Zee shoved the sharp end of a marker made of sticks lashed together with vines in a crude rendering of Postune's trident at the head of the grave where he'd buried it next to the one that had been dead when Zee found them, beneath the cluster of poms. Jessup watched quietly from where he clung to Zee's back, peering over Zee's shoulder. Like he'd done before, Zee commended the little creature's soul to the Sea of Heaven. They returned to the tide pool and Zee proceeded to gather tasty things for Jessup to eat, which cheered the little fellow up quite a lot.

* * *

A small skinny boy, a little ten-armed sea creature, and a pig, scrounged through the stony sand of the beach, as had become their daily routine after Jessup had been fed each morning. Jessup shuffled along on his arms, moving much better than he had early on. His head, or body, though Zee figured it was both, was oversized for his limbs, and at first he'd fall over with a squawk quite often. It was an effort to squirm his legs under and right himself, so Zee'd had to tip him back up on many occasions.

Jessup was becoming more adept at swimming, too. He could tuck his legs forward, then fan them out and shove them back in the water to push himself, but he'd also learned to hold them behind him and wave them to move more evenly and faster. When he wanted a burst of speed, he'd shoot a jet of water out his bottom between his legs, stirring up the sand. Round and round the tide pool he'd go, humming under the water.

Zee spotted the telltale spout-hole of a particularly tasty find and shouted, "Clammys!" He knelt and proceeded to dig with a sharp stick.

Jessup slithered an arm into another watery hole in the sand. "Zee!" he cried. "Jessup found thing!"

Zee turned from where he was brushing sand off the clammy he'd dug up, still amazed at how quickly Jessup was picking up words and putting them together. There was still plenty for him to learn, though. "Jessup found *something*," Zee corrected.

Jessup nodded with his whole head-body. "Yes!"

Zee chuckled. "What is it?"

With a grunt, Jessup tugged his arm free and held up his catch. Gripped in the curl at the end was a rotted perchy, the tail-end of it mostly spine and rib bones. "Fish!"

"Ew!" Zee exclaimed, then seeing Jessup's disappointment, said, "I mean, 'Oh!' That's very nice, but I don't think we need it today. Is that all right?"

Jessup looked perplexed, then held it out to the pig. "Midge! Fish!"

Midge snuffed at Jessup's prize but shook her head with a snort and backed away. Jessup held the fish to his nose, sniffed, then popped the whole thing in his mouth. Zee fought between laughing and gagging at the crunch and slurp of Jessup chewing the nasty thing.

Jessup swallowed and patted his shell above his eyes. "Yummy!" He got a serious look on his face and repeated his version of what Zee had told him when it was time to get to work. "Head back in dirt."

Zee's lips spread in a smile as Jessup turned and continued his waddling beachcombing with a diligence to match Zee's own.

There were few other children in the area where Zee lived, and his family couldn't afford to pay for the only school in town, several miles away on the other side of the key, so Zee had no friends other than Midge. Now he had Jessup too. He hadn't realized how alone he had been until Jessup came along. He felt oddly calm around the little creature, in stark contrast to his usual high-speed self, mind whirling all the time, and sometimes he imagined he could sense Jessup's emotions and even hear—no, feel—what Jessup was thinking. On a few occasions, he swore Jessup reacted to what he was about to say before he said it, while the words were still forming in his mind. He put it down to his overactive child's imagination and happiness at having rescued this strange creature he was becoming so incredibly fond of.

Zee watched his little friend shuffle over the sand, the gray patch on his chest warming with the thoughts of their friendship. The pleasant feeling spread through his heart and stomach as Jessup turned and smiled at him, then surged with elation when the little creature pounced on a small crabby.

"Got you!"

* * *

As they often did at the end of a day, Zee sat on a flat rock overlooking the sea, singing to Jessup while flinging stones to skip on the waves. Today it was the simple rhyme his mother had sung to him since he was a babe in the cradle, the mantra that helped keep him safe from the dangers of the ocean. Jessup hummed along and chimed in with the last word of every verse—or one of his own making—which never failed to make Zee grin.

"Don't go near the water
Stay away from the sea
The riptides and the monsters
Will be the end of—"

"Zee!"

*"Fear the shore in the day time
A dangerous place to be
But night time is the fright time
Before then you must—"*

"Flee!"

*"The ocean is full of dangers
Your distance you must keep
Terrible toothy creatures
Wait hungry in the—"*

"Deep!"

*"Most fearsome of all is the kraken
King monster of the sea
When the kraken comes arising
Even dragons—"*

"Flee!"

*"Don't go near the water
Stay away from the sea
The mighty monstrous kraken
Will make a meal of—"*

"Jessup!"

"Very good!" Zee complimented. "You're a better singer than I am."

Jessup chuckled to himself, a highly gurgling sound that made Zee grin. "Zee silly." He picked a stone off the pile between them and flung it wildly. It flew straight up, then came back down to bounce on the edge of the rock in front of him and plop into the water below Zee's dangling feet.

"You're getting better," Zee encouraged.

"No!" With a determined frown, Jessup took up another stone.

Zee felt the dogged resolution, tinged with anger, that his little friend exuded when trying to accomplish something that frustrated him.

Jessup wound back an arm and threw again. Zee ducked as the stone spun past his head.

"Be careful!"

"Sorry, Zee."

"It's fine, don't worry, but try throwing from the side, like this." Zee made the sweeping motion slowly, then picked up a stone. "See how I hold it? Now watch me." Jessup watched carefully as Zee threw, sending the stone skipping across the waves.

Jessup took another stone, practiced a side-arm throw slowly, then took a deep breath like he'd seen Zee do when he was concentrating on something, and threw. The stone didn't go far, but it skipped twice.

"Hurrah!" Zee cried, thrusting his fists into the air. "You did it!"

"Jessup skipped!" The little creature waved all ten arms. "Hurrah!"

"Yes, you did." Zee placed a hand on Jessup's shell. "Now I want to show you something." He took Jessup by the base of the shell and lifted him into his lap. "You're getting heavy."

"Heavy Jessup!"

"And bigger, too." The creature had indeed increased in size over the last few weeks. His shell had become harder too, while the little nubs that rose from its surface and the ridged spiral that corkscrewed up from its base to where a point in the form of an arrowhead was taking shape, had become more pronounced. Sometimes at night, instead of sleeping under the rocks in his pool, he would corkscrew himself into the sand at the bottom, using his arms to unscrew himself in the morning.

Zee reached into his shoulder bag, made from a grain sack, and retrieved a lacquered wooden box, which he set down in front of them.

Jessup pointed with one of his arms. "What's that?"

Zee laughed. That phrase had been Jessup's favorite thing to say for almost a week. He'd point at something and say, "What's that?" Zee would explain, then he'd point at something else and say it again, then something else, over and over again, with a desire to learn that matched Zee's own. Even Zee would become exhausted answering all Jessup's questions. That phase had passed for the most part, but Jessup was still curious as ever.

"It's my treasure chest. My da made it for me. It's where I keep my treasures." He opened the lid.

"Ohh," Jessup exclaimed. "Pretty."

Inside was a collection of crystals and smooth shiny rocks, colorful seashells and bits of sea fan, tiny fossils, a shiny brass belt buckle, a couple of malformed pearls, and other trinkets.

"These are all things I found on the beach," Zee explained. "I keep it hidden under my bed because you have to keep treasure chests secret, you know. Otherwise pirates might steal them."

"Secret," Jessup said softly, then climbed down off Zee's lap for a closer look. He poked through the items carefully.

"I found an old king's coin one time. Ma said it would have been enough to buy more pigs and maybe pay for schooling so I could learn to read, but Da is an honest man, and all real treasure that's found on land belongs to the king. He took it to town and gave it to the lord governor's men."

Jessup uncovered something in the box that caught his eye. "Ohh…" He had to use suckers near the tips of two arms to lift it out. He stared at it wide-eyed as it gleamed in the sun. "What's that?"

"It's a marble. People play games with them." The ball of glass was clear with swirls of all the colors of the rainbow. Zee had always marveled at how anyone could make such a thing.

"Pretty marble," Jessup said, then popped it into his mouth.

"Hey!" Zee admonished. He held a hand down in front of the little creature. "Spit it out." Jessup swiveled his eyes up at him. "It's not good for you. It would probably make you sick."

Jessup spat it into Zee's palm, along with a generous amount of baby-creature spittle. Zee wiped the marble and his hand off on his pants.

"Sorry, Zee," Jessup uttered, and Zee could not only see the remorse on his face, he felt it in his heart.

"Don't be sorry. It does look like something tasty," Zee said. He lifted a loop of cord from his neck up and over his head. A pointed black object hung from it, smooth and lustrous from being polished in the sea. "Here's another treasure. Da says it's a dragon tooth. He drilled a hole in it so I can wear it for good luck."

Jessup touched it gently. "Shiny dragon tooth."

"It's my favorite thing I ever found on the beach."

"Favorite?"

"Yup," Zee replied with a smile. "Except for you."

Jessup had to think about that, but then his expression brightened. "Favorite Jessup?"

Zee grinned. "Very favorite Jessup."

Jessup lifted several of his arms toward Zee, grinning to himself. "Very favorite Zee."

Zee lifted him into his arms and held him close, the warmth of the spot on his chest spreading through his body. The spot had grown to almost the size of a king's copper, its surface rougher, and it was turning darker gray. His mother treated it with ointment like she did his rash and said nothing, but he could tell she was concerned about it. He'd even heard her talking to Da in whispers, saying she hoped it wasn't a more dangerous manifestation of his lifelong condition. It didn't itch and wasn't spreading all that fast, so Zee didn't worry too much. "Worry is only suffering over something that might never happen," his da would say.

"Even though it's a secret," Zee said, "I wanted to show you my treasure chest because you're my best friend, Jessup."

"Best friend Jessup."

"And best friend Zee."

They sat together watching the ocean, the only sounds the splashing waves, a warm breeze through the pom trees, and Midge snuffling in the sand. The bell rang from home, and Zee had to go. Parting each evening was heartbreaking, but they were both tough little fellows, and there was always the promise of seeing each other the next day.

CHAPTER 5

The third weekend since Zee had found Jessup came, and it was market day. Zee hated to leave Jessup alone for so long, but he'd promised to come to the beach when he and Da got back that afternoon. Zee was excited, too. If he could figure out how to ask his questions without raising suspicion or giving Jessup's existence away, he was going to see if he could find out exactly what kind of creature his little friend was.

It was just before sunrise as Da hitched up Midge and Boaris, an older male hog even larger than Midge, whom Zee had also been allowed to name since he was kept for breeding. The two older hogs led four half-yearling pigs to pull the cart. Zee helped pack and load Ma's tinctures and powders, along with some teak chairs Da had made to sell.

Ma often went with them, but she wanted to stay and get some house-keeping done. She handed them their packed lunches, kissed them both on the cheeks, and waved them off.

Da promised to bring her something special, at which she frowned and shouted after them, "Don't you spend any coin you don't have to, Jad Tarrow!"

Da pretended he didn't hear her and winked at Zee.

It took a while to cross the key, what with the pigs' slow pace and

Da unhitching them partway to get a drink and wallow in the shallows of a pond to cool themselves. It also afforded a last chance for Zee and his father to clean them up before they arrived at market. Wiping them down and spreading oil over their bodies to make their hides shine, Zee realized how much he missed Jessup already, like an empty space had been left in his heart.

The market in the central square of the small coastal town of mon Tontuga was already set up, but the stalls and tables weren't as crowded with customers as they had been last time.

"Where is everybody, Da?" Zee asked.

"Tax time is coming," Da answered with a touch of defeat. "Folks don't have as much coin to spend this time of year." When Da saw the distress on Zee's face, he forced cheer into his voice. "Don't worry your little head, son. It's not a boy's concern. Your ma and I have been saving up."

That put some pluck back into Zee's mood—as did the cry of gulls and the sight of masts rising from the port at the edge of town. "Can I, Da?"

His father smiled. "Like I could stop you. Try not to talk the sailors' ears clean off. They need them, you know."

Zee grinned back. "Okay, Da. I'll try." He grabbed his shoulder bag and clambered down from the cart. He patted the bag. "Got my lunch. Meet you at the auction at one bell after midday?"

"As always, and don't you be late. Your mother would worry something fierce."

"I'm always on time. Sometimes early!"

"Come to think of it, you are. Forgive my lapse in memory."

"Oh, Da." They had this conversation every time they came to town. He backed away, waving. "Good luck!"

"Who needs luck? I've got pigs!" With that, Da slapped the reins like he was driving horses. "Yah!" The pigs grunted and trudged forward. Da pretended like he was being thrown back by a sudden burst of speed.

Zee laughed and watched them go, then turned toward the docks, considering his mission to find out what kind of creature Jessup was, and took off at a run. Every time Zee's parents brought him to market he'd slip away to question anyone he could about ships and the sea, but especially about dragons and Triumf's Citadel Academy, the most elite and only school for riders in the kingdom of Tosh.

Zee strode along the wharf, keeping an eye out for a likely sailor to approach. Most sailors were happy to tell yarns, especially after a few cups of grog. Then his breath caught at the sight of shining armor over a blue quilted aketon that could only be worn by a dragon knight of the realm. She and her squire sat at a table on the outdoor deck of a saloon.

The knight looked right at Zee, and his knees went weak.

"You all right, lad?" she asked. "Never seen a knight before?"

Zee swallowed and forced himself to speak. "Only from a distance."

She pointed toward his neck. "What's that you have there?"

For a moment Zee feared his scarf had come loose and she'd seen his rash. His hand flew to his neck, and he realized his necklace was hanging outside his shirt.

"My da says it's a dragon tooth, sir."

The woman's squire, a boy of fourteen or so, glared at Zee with disdain. "A lady knight is to be addressed as ma'am, boy. Have you no couth?"

Zee took no offense at the squire's scornful manner and responded innocently. "I don't know what 'couth' is, but I might like to have some."

The knight chuckled, and the squire snorted. She shot him a look that wiped the derisive sneer from his face. "Manners, Tem."

"My apologies, ma'am."

"I'm not the one you should be apologizing to."

The squire balked, but under the stern gaze of his master, he nodded formally at Zee. It was apparently as much of an apology as he was willing to give, and it pained him to offer that.

The knight beckoned Zee closer, indicating with a hand toward his necklace. "May I see it?"

Zee gulped, tucked his scarf tighter to the skin of his neck, then stepped onto the deck.

She lifted the tooth. "It's a dragon tooth, all right. From a Rock, I'd say. One of the smaller teeth from the bottom jaw near the middle." She let it drop back against his shirt. "That's quite a prize."

Zee beamed with joy at having his treasure verified by a real knight. He tucked it back under his collar.

"Thank you, ma'am."

"What's your name, lad?" the knight asked.

"Zee Tarrow, ma'am." The scorn returned to the eyes of the squire. Zee knew why. There was no fancy little word in front of his last name.

"Have you had your midday meal?" the knight inquired.

Zee patted his shoulder sack. "Ma packed me a lunch."

"Perhaps you'd like to save it for your next meal. Pray join us in our repast. We have plenty and can always order more." The squire squirmed at the invitation, but the knight paid him no attention.

Zee grinned. "Thank you. That is very kind."

To the squire's obvious discomfort, Zee climbed up on one of the chairs. His chin barely cleared the tabletop, so he tucked his knees under himself.

The knight introduced herself. "I'm Dame Zara mon Toomsil, Knight Chevalier of His Majesty's Dragon Corps, assigned to His Majesty's Tradeship Fleet." She held a hand toward her squire.

The squire looked down his nose at Zee. "And I am Temothy jal Briggs, Esquire." A raised eyebrow suggested Zee should recognize the name. He didn't.

Flushed with excitement and hardly believing his grand luck, Zee responded. "It's an honor to meet the both of you."

"You see," Dame Toomsil said to Tem, "Zee Tarrow here has couth to spare." Her voice hardened. "Now fix him a plate."

Tem jal Briggs's face turned red as he tore a leg off one of the glazed seaducks on the platter and placed it on a plate, along with boiled tubers and jellied redberries. He appeared to resist flinging it at Zee before sliding it across the tabletop, then handed over a knife and fork.

Zee waited, utensils in hand, not sure if he should begin.

Dame Toomsil took a bite, then noticed Zee wasn't eating. "Go ahead. We've already started."

Zee tasted the seaduck. It was so delicious he had to force himself not to shovel it in. Still, the squire seemed put off his meal just from watching him. The knight had no such compunction and ate heartily.

The saloon proprietor's tray rattled as she stopped short at the sight of what could be considered a street urchin sitting at one of her tables—with a knight of the realm, no less. "Is everything all right here, Dame Toomsil?"

The knight took a healthy swig of her wine. "Why wouldn't it be?"

Realizing her mistake, the proprietor said, "I… was just wondering if I could bring you anything else."

"Zee Tarrow, would you like something to drink?"

"A small cup of water would be lovely," Zee replied.

To the proprietor, the knight said, "A goblet of sweet-wine for the young gentleman."

"Right away, ma'am." The woman sped off.

"I've never had sweet-wine," said Zee.

"I'm sure you'll like it." She leaned closer and lowered her voice. "And I wouldn't drink the water here if I were you."

"Oh." Zee had never eaten at an establishment like this before, so he had no idea. "Thank you."

She set to her meal. Zee inspected her raiment with admiration then awe as he caught sight of the band of green satin scales that circled her wrist.

"What do you think, now that you've seen a knight from a closer distance?"

Zee jumped at her voice, then swallowed so as not to speak with his mouth full. "You are glorious." She grinned and his cheeks turned red. "Ma'am," he added. His gaze returned to the wristband of scales. "Is that your dragonbond?"

She pulled up her sleeve and turned her wrist so he could see that the wide band of scales went all the way around. "You know what this is, then?"

"I do. Well, only from what I've been told."

"And what have you been told?"

Zee took a deep breath and repeated what he'd heard from old sailors and townsfolk, his eyes shining with excitement. "After a dragon accepts a rider at the academy, and if they are truly compatible, a bond develops between them and a band of the dragon's scales will grow on the rider's wrist, proving to the world and Zepiter they are one, bonded for life. The longer a rider and dragon pair are together, the stronger they get, developing more Abilities, and the wider the band grows. Some older riders have scales all the way up to their elbows!"

Dame Toomsil's lips curved on one side at Zee's youthful enthusiasm. "Well said, and entirely correct." Her gaze returned to her dragonbond, and she gently touched the scales. Her voice brimmed with affection. "It was the greatest day of my life when the bond was complete and Peloquin's scales fully encircled my wrist; an honor beyond anything I had ever imagined."

Zee's gaze went from her dragonbond to her armor, then back to her dragonbond. "Were you flying near the beach on the other side of the key a few weeks ago?"

"I was."

"I saw you!"

"That was you? The boy on a pig?"

Tem choked on a bite of seaduck.

"Are you all right there, Tem?" Dame Toomsil asked, perfectly aware of why he'd choked.

Tem held up a hand and swallowed, then cleared his throat and wiped his napkin across his lips. "I'm fine, ma'am."

Zee answered the knight's question. "Yes, ma'am, that was me and Midge. You and that other knight and your dragons were amazing."

"Thank you."

"I remembered that one of the dragons was a green Greatwing, and the scales of your bond are the same, and the knight wore Silver Class armor, just like yours."

"That's very observant of you, Mr. Tarrow."

Zee giggled. "No one ever called me that before. Mr. Tarrow is my da."

"And so are you. If you worked on a ship, that's what you'd be called all the time, even at your age."

Zee looked over her armor again. "I saw you use some of your Abilities. I bet you're high-level Silver Class."

"Thank you kindly, good sir," she said, making Zee blush again. "But Peloquin and I are medium level."

"Medium-level Silver is still very impressive, if you ask me."

"We have some work to do before we achieve high level. Progression becomes more difficult as you rise through the classes."

"Then you can progress to Gold," Zee said with enthusiasm. "Then White Titan, Red Titan, and Black Titan!"

"That would be quite a feat," she replied with a chuckle. "No pair has achieved Black Titan Class since Sky Marshalls Slan hai Drogo and Mogon, who are gone these last eighty years and more."

"The Heroes of Tosh," Zee exclaimed. "They're legendary!"

"The Terrors of Tosh," said Tem derisively.

Dame Toomsil said, "They have been called that as well."

"Why would anyone call them that?" Zee asked.

"Let's just say they used some unconventional methods in their last battle and leave it at that."

"Okay." From the tone in her voice, Zee could tell he shouldn't push the issue. "But they did save the kingdom, right?"

"They did. The forces of Tosh and our allies were greatly outnumbered. If it weren't for them, we would be under the rule of the Luftoo Empire today." Her eyebrows lifted in regard. "Drogo and Mogon were surprisingly young when they achieved Black Titan Class and held an almost unheard-of high level at the time of their deaths. Both of them were not even thirty when they passed."

"Wow," was all Zee could manage to say. Thirty seemed pretty old to him, but learning anything new about Drogo and Mogon was a rare treat.

"Tosh may have no Black Titans," the knight continued, "but we do have three Red Titans. The king and his dragon are a low-level Red Titan pair. The academy's commandant pair is high level, as are the deans of magicks. And the commandants and deans not only hold the highest classes in Tosh, they are the last remaining of the pairs who fought beside Drogo and Mogon in the last great war. You'd never know it from looking at them. Higher bond ratings extend lives beyond those of normal people, and dragons naturally live longer than human beings anyway."

"I've heard about that," Zee said. "I'd love to see them in battle,"

Dame Toomsil chuckled. "Be careful what you wish for, Mr. Tarrow."

He had learned so much already, Zee tried not to be too much of a pest for the rest of the meal. He ate more and spoke less, but that didn't mean he didn't ask a few more questions. He just couldn't help it.

Dame Toomsil didn't seem to mind. She spoke easily, encouraged by his innocent inquisitiveness, as if she had all the time in the world—which Zee found out she practically did.

"Several days after you saw us flying near the shore our ship ran aground on a rock where one shouldn't have been, thrust up by the recent earth-shake," she explained. "We wrested it free, but the damage was too severe to continue sailing. Peloquin and I flew to call on oartugs to bring us around to the closest shipyard, which just happens to be here in mon Tontuga. Repairs are almost complete, and we should be ready to sail within a day."

"Thank Zepiter," Tem said under his breath.

The effect of the ointment Zee's ma had applied to his rash that morning was beginning to wear off, and the sting and itch to return. With a great force of will developed over years of suffering with the affliction, he refrained from scratching or even rubbing his skin through his clothing. He had to leave soon, though, and finally worked up the courage to ask, "Do you know of any knights that are looking for a squire?"

Tem snorted once again. Dame Toomsil shot him a glance that slapped the smirk from his face, then answered Zee as sympathetically as possible. "You are much too young, yet. The minimum age is thirteen, though most are fourteen, like Tem, when they begin. It's also extremely competitive."

Zee hid his dismay the best he could. He knew she was really saying that a boy with no money and a name like Tarrow had no chance. When he'd first learned that, he'd only let it get him down for a short time. He was determined he'd get there, one way or the other. He just had no idea how.

And so, it was with delight he heard her add, "There have been exceptions, however. Those outside of the system, so to speak, have been granted squirehood and even acceptance into the academy directly, if deemed particularly worthy."

"Really?"

"It's very rare, but it does happen."

Zee beamed with hope.

It was with joy in his heart that he climbed off his chair to take his leave. His face glowing with appreciation, he performed an awkward salute. "Thank you again, ma'am. I will never forget you."

Dame Toomsil raised her goblet. "Somehow, I have a feeling I won't forget you either, Zee Tarrow."

Zee grinned, cheeks pinking, then turned and ran down the wharf.

* * *

Temothy jal Briggs dropped his scowl as his master turned back to him. "Begging your pardon, ma'am, I'm only asking for my own education, but is it within a knight's purview to give false hope to the peasantry?"

Dame Toomsil's features darkened. "Here are two lessons for you, young squire, *for your education*. First, a good and proper knight never uses the term 'peasantry.' Second, it's a knight's highest duty to give hope to all who need it, regardless of wealth or status, and those without either, most of all."

Tem jumped as she slammed her hand on the table to drive her point home. He sat up straight. "My sincerest apologies, ma'am. Lesson learned."

"I doubt it," she grumbled, taking another drink of her wine. "And make a note to remind me later that we need to have a talk about your manners."

Tem gulped.

CHAPTER 6

Spirits soaring like a dragon in flight, Zee skipped along the wharf. He couldn't wait to tell his da that he'd had lunch with a real Dragon Knight. Da was going to be so surprised. And especially about how sometimes people did get into the citadel academy, even without money or fancy names. Zee just had to prove himself worthy, somehow.

He stopped short. "Oh no, I forgot to ask about what kind of creature Jessup is." He'd been racking his brain for days, trying to figure out how to pose his questions without arousing too much attention. If someone suspected Zee actually had the creature and started asking questions, he didn't know what he'd do. He didn't like lying, and worse, he was terrible at it. He couldn't imagine lying to a dragon knight, anyway. Somewhat eased from the worry at having missed an opportunity and further considering how he was going to broach the subject of what Jessup was, Zee continued along the wharf until a high-pitched roar stopped him in his tracks.

Out over the harbor, a white Ice Diver dragon approached the docks, a knight rider on its back. It screeched again and swooped, snatching a toona from the bay, then carried it straight to a ship raised out of the water and propped on beams on the wharf ahead of where Zee stood. The ship wasn't one of the great lumbering tubs of the tradefleet or warships of the

Navy, but a mid-size trading vessel, built to haul goods at speed and with plenty of armaments to defend itself or even capture pirate ships.

The beast dropped the vigorously flopping fish on the main deck, to the surprised shouts of several sailors, then flapped out and around to the perch deck at the back of the ship, higher than the quarterdeck where the wheel resided behind the forward-placed mizzenmast. Longer and wider than the poop deck on a regular ship, the perch deck was designed specifically to accommodate dragons on His Majesty's Tradeships and larger private tradeships that could afford to pay for dragon protection. Warships in His Majesty's Navy had more space for dragons, and dragon transport ships even more, with special holds for them below as well.

Zee eyed the dragon and rider, both of them outfitted in shining blue-gray armor that designated them as Iron Class, then turned his attention to the silhouette of the galleon and realized they were the dragon and rider he'd seen flying with Dame Toomsil, and this had to be their ship. At the other side of the perch deck the Greatwing, which must have been Dame Zara mon Toomsil's beast, Peloquin, was lying on his belly, long neck curled upward, chin held at his chest as he dozed, either unaware or uncaring of the other's arrival. The green of his scales was exactly like Dame Toomsil's dragonbond wristlet.

The knight patted his dragon's neck and dismounted. His squire ran up the stairs from the quarterdeck and began removing the dragon's saddle and harness.

Zee caught his breath as he saw the carved figurehead at the front of the ship. All the figureheads Zee had seen were dragon heads, wild gods, naked sea-people, or old kings of Tosh. This one, however, had a beast that looked like Jessup.

Well, not exactly, but pretty close. It had a cone-shaped shell like Jessup's, and multiple wavy arms clinging back to the prow. Zee counted them out loud as he walked closer, his excitement rising. Ten arms. Just like Jessup. The ridges on the shell of its head were different, running from bottom to top instead of in a spiral, and they had serrated edges like Da's crosscut saw. Its eyes were smaller for its size, too, and more menacing, and its mouth, thrown open in a silent shriek of attack, was packed with fangs.

Someone bumped into Zee, staggering him. An old man stumbled forward, dropping one of the sacks of groceries he was carrying in his arms.

"Watch where your standing boy. You'll get a body killed!"

"I'm very sorry, sir." Zee scurried to stuff spilled vegetables back in the sack, then placed it with the others in the man's arms.

The man seemed perplexed by the swift amends. "Thank you."

He turned to go, but stopped when Zee pointed and blurted out, "Excuse me, sir, but do you know what that is?"

The man gazed at the figurehead. "It says right on the ship, there."

Zee saw the lettering painted in chipped golden script, but swallowed and fidgeted, shuffling his feet. "I... I can't read it, sir."

The old man's eyebrows lifted and he said in a kinder tone. "It says HMT *Krakenfish.*"

"Krakenfish..." Zee's thoughts whirled as he tried to grasp the prospect. Could Jessup possibly, against all odds and common sense, be a baby *kraken*? The most feared creature of legend and myth in the whole wide world? Could krakens be *real?*

When he looked back up, the man was walking away, shaking his head. Zee felt faint, and he began to wheeze. He was reaching into his pocket when he was grabbed from behind and yanked back between stacks of empty barrels, leaving his lung-spritzer to drop in the dirt.

* * *

A hand clamped over Zee's mouth as he was dragged deeper between the barrels. Zee was so shocked he didn't struggle.

A young voice said in his ear, "Don't shout. We're not going to hurt you, okay?" The hand was pulled away from his face.

Zee spun on the ground and scooted away until his back was against a barrel. He struggled for breath, the shock and fright having further exacerbated the constriction of his airways.

Three children faced him, dirty, in ragged clothes, and emaciated. The one that had grabbed and spoken to him was a boy of about fifteen, the other two a boy and girl with similar features to the first, crouched and clinging to each other, maybe eight and nine years of age. All of them had greasy hair and flea bites on their arms and necks. They also appeared to be just as frightened as Zee was.

Seeing Zee's difficulty breathing, the older boy held his grimy palms toward his captive. "We don't mean no harm. We're just…" He glanced at the other two. "We were wondering if you could spare any coin for us to get something to eat."

Even as he fought for breath, Zee took in the children's condition and the haunted looks in their eyes. He recalled the grand meal he'd just eaten and the lunch his mother had packed for him, then tried to speak, but the empty barrels he'd been dragged between were suddenly flung away with a crash and clatter. The children cringed back as the light of the sun fell on them, then a shadow.

Dame Toomsil stood with her hand on the haft of her sword, glaring at the group. "Mr. Tarrow," she said firmly. "Are you well?" Seeing his difficulty breathing, she knelt and held out her hand. "I believe you dropped this." His lung-spritzer lay in her open palm. He took it and tried to blow off the dust, but his lungs were too weak. He wiped it on his shirt, then sprayed it twice into his mouth, inhaling at the same time.

She stood as another voice sounded from the other side of the space. "Well, well, what have we here?" came the haughty tone of Temothy jal Briggs. "Criminals, in mon Tontuga?"

The older boy pleaded. "We're not criminals, sir, I swear!"

"Stowaways, from the looks of them," said Dame Toomsil.

Tem grabbed the two younger children and yanked them to their feet. "Come here, you scumsuckers."

A mad terror gripped the older boy. He jerked a rusted table knife from his waistband and screamed, "Leave my brother and sister be!"

Zee watched in shock as the stowaway leapt. Tem just had time to release the children and block the knife before the boy slammed into him and both went tumbling back. They shoved barrels away and surged to their feet.

The boy attacked with a ferocity Zee had never seen, swinging wildly with the knife. Tem's expression and movements were calm and focused. He blocked and dodged, then caught the boy's wrist and twisted viciously until bone snapped, and the knife dropped. Tem threw an elbow into the boy's jaw, snapping his head back, then spun and flung him over his shoulder, slamming him to the dirt. The younger children shrieked as Tem twisted the boy's arm behind his back and shoved a knee into his spine.

Sweat glistened on Tem's forehead and mocking sneer, cruelty glinting in his eyes. "Won't be trying that again, will you, scumsucker?" He wrenched the boy's arm, causing him to cry out. The younger children wailed and clung to each other.

"That will do, Squire," Dame Toomsil ordered. Tem eased his torturing of the boy but kept his hold on him, scowling like a petulant child who'd been scolded. "Fetch the city guard." To the boy Tem held, she said, "You won't try to run, will you, lad." It wasn't a question.

The boy sobbed, face down, spittle dribbling in the dirt. He shook his head. Tem was reluctant to release his victim but let go and shoved up as if pushing away from a pile of dung.

The knight helped Zee to his feet and stooped to lay a hand lightly on his small shoulder. "Are you sure you're well?"

"Yes, ma'am. Thank you."

"My duty," she replied. She pulled his scarf back up to cover the rash on his neck. "And my pleasure."

Zee clutched at his scarf in embarrassment. He stood straight and looked back to the other children as if she'd seen nothing.

The tussle had raised such a ruckus that villagers and sailors were shouting for the city guard, and the guard's whistles and pounding boots could already be heard.

Zee felt like he was going to cry—for the gentle kindness of the knight and for the children who'd only wanted something to eat. Begging was forbidden in mon Tontuga, and everywhere else in Tosh, as far as Zee knew. But they hadn't tried to steal. They did the only thing they could think of—ask for mercy from another child. Someone like them. If they were stowaways, though, the punishments were harsh. Zee had heard stories of ship captains tossing them over the side on the open sea when they were caught.

He forced down the lump in his throat. "What will happen to them?"

Dame Toomsil's hard look fell upon him, but her expression softened, and she looked away without answering.

Zee reached into his shoulder sack and stepped to the younger children, who cowered. "Take this," he said, holding out his wrapped lunch. They looked back at their older brother, who sat clutching his broken wrist to his chest, tears streaking the dirt on his cheeks, awaiting his fate. The girl timidly reached for the wrapping, then snatched it from Zee's tiny hands.

The children tore at the food, shoving it in their mouths. The girl tossed a tuber to her older brother. He let it fall in the dirt in front of him as city guards marched in.

* * *

Out on the wharf, Zee stood next to Dame Toomsil watching the guards lead the children away. Their feet dragged on the flagstones from weariness and malnutrition, and they put up no resistance.

Zee had never known that kind of poverty existed in Tosh. He knew what hunger was from when times were hard on the farm, but nothing like what he'd just seen. How could the king and the lords allow such a thing in their own land? There was nothing he could do about it, though. He was just a kid. But he wished he could.

His eyes moved to the figurehead on the ship and his attention shifted back to his purpose in coming to the docks.

"Ma'am," he asked, "is that really what a kraken looks like?"

"No one knows," she replied, "but it's close to how I've seen them depicted on tapestries in the halls of Triumf's Citadel."

"Have you ever seen anything else that looks like that?" Zee immediately worried he'd said too much.

If he'd piqued the knight's interest, she showed no sign of it. "Octopods, I suppose. And squids." She pointed at the figurehead. "You'll notice, though, that krakens are portrayed with ten legs instead of eight. A nautilus has many legs and a shell, but they are very different." She gazed at the kraken carving as if it was the first time she'd seriously considered it.

Zee had never seen a picture of a kraken, and the stories and songs just described them as huge and vicious, with nasty chomping teeth for eating ships and people and lots of octopod arms. It never occurred to him that the gentle little creature he'd secreted away on the shore near his home could be one. He couldn't believe Jessup would hurt anyone. And what if he wasn't really a kraken, but something else? Something harmless? People might not believe that, though.

Then and there, he vowed to continue to keep Jessup a secret and to protect him with his life. At least until Jessup was big enough to take care of himself, whenever that time might come. A cold hole opened in his heart at the thought of Jessup shuffling into the sea and swimming away, forever. They hadn't been parted for a whole day, and Zee already missed him terribly.

"Is something bothering you, lad?"

Zee wiped the wetness that had creeped into his eyes and swallowed down the strange loneliness that filled his chest. "No, ma'am. I'm okay."

"Would you like us to escort you home?"

"My da is at the livestock auction. It won't take me but a few minutes to get there." He glanced at the clock on the tower of the dockmaster's building. Zee may not know how to read, but he could tell time. "I'd better go."

He darted off without thinking, then stopped himself and turned back. "Thank you again for helping me, and for lunch, and for…" His eyes went to where the children had been led around a corner down the wharf and finally to the figurehead on the ship. "…everything."

"Be well, Zee Tarrow."

"You too, ma'am." He turned but stopped once again and looked back. "Dame Toomsil?!"

"Yes?"

"Is it true that dragons can talk, just like people?"

"It is true, yes."

"Oh..." Zee gawped. "Um, have you ever heard anywhere... Could krakens talk?"

Stepping to the knight's side, Temothy jal Briggs smirked at the question, eyeing Zee with contempt. "That's impossible. Krakens were dumb, vicious beasts." Dame Toomsil raised an eyebrow, unsettling him. "So I've been told."

"Not that I've heard, Mr. Tarrow," the knight said. Zee's face drooped in spite of himself. She added, "But you never know."

Zee's expression brightened. He saluted her as he had done at the end of their lunch, and she saluted back.

* * *

The knight watched Zee run off down the wharf. "Curious boy, that one."

Tem huffed. "That's one way to put it. He's diseased as well. I saw his neck."

Dame Toomsil, over a head taller than her squire, looked down at him. "And you'll never mention that again, will you?"

Defiance flashed on his features, then melted under her stern gaze. "No, ma'am."

She looked back along the wharf, eyes narrowed in thought. "He hides it well, but he has suffered much. Something you have not endured a day in your life, young squire. It builds a certain strength and character." She turned back to him. "As your master, I will do everything in my power to help you build some yourself."

Tem's face went white as she turned and strode toward the ship.

* * *

Sprinting to get to the livestock auction in time, Zee said to himself, "What a day!" His da wouldn't believe this story. Well, he would, but wouldn't he be amazed.

As much as he looked forward to telling it, his most abiding desire was to get back to the shore and see Jessup. And the little creature wasn't just his best friend anymore. Jessup was a *kraken*.

CHAPTER 7

"Da! Da!" Zee shouted when he saw his father, then quieted and slowed as he approached. Jad Tarrow was hitching two of the four young pigs they'd brought back to the cart behind Midge and Boaris; the chairs his da had made were still in the back, and worry creased his da's brow.

"What's wrong, Da?"

Jad forced a smile and rubbed Zee's head. "Nothing, son." He lifted Zee onto the cart's bench. "Let's go see your ma."

They weren't far out of town before Zee's da finally relented under the boy's mournful stare. "All right, enough with the gloomy face. The auction didn't go as well as I'd expected, is all." Zee glanced to the chairs in the back of the cart, unsold. "Don't worry your little head." He reached into a sack between them and pulled out an oblong fruit with orange markings. "Look what I got for your ma."

"A peachpear! That's Ma's favorite."

Da bobbed his eyebrows and grinned with mischief, producing another from his bag. "And one for just you and me."

"Wow! Are you sure?"

"Of course." He teased, "Unless you want me to toss it to the pigs."

"No way!" Zee grabbed it from his da, laughing, the troubles on his mind forgotten.

"Now tell me about your day."

While Zee regaled him with the tale of his lunch with a real knight and the incident with the stowaways, his da cut thin slices off one of the peachpears with his pocketknife for them to share. The fruit was cool and sweet and delicious on Zee's tongue. He wondered if Jessup would like it, then chuckled to himself. Of course he would. Jessup would eat anything.

Da reacted with appropriate delight at hearing about the knight and dragons, but after learning what happened with the stowaways, he told Zee to stay close the next time they went to town. Zee agreed more quickly than he should have, partly because he was still shaken by his run-in with the starving children, but also because he still felt remorse for not saying anything about Jessup or revealing what he'd learned about him on the docks.

Jessup. His friend, the kraken. His heart leapt at the thought of seeing him.

The cart hadn't come to a full stop in front of the house before Zee hopped off and hurried toward the shed to gather Midge's riding harness and his beachcombing sacks.

"Where are you off to?" his da called after him.

Zee spun to walk backward as he spoke. "I haven't done my shore chores today."

"You can take a break from combing today, son. I think you've earned it after your day."

"But," Zee sputtered, "there's still plenty of daylight left." Worried he was appearing too desperate, he straightened. "And it's my duty, to the family."

"You are a most honorable boy." The voice was his mother's, who stood in the open doorway of the house wiping her hands with a towel. "But don't you think Midge could use a rest as well?"

Midge grunted and sighed a pig's sigh.

Zee hadn't thought of that. Midge did look tired after her travels to and from town. He squirmed with the desire—the *need*—to see Jessup. "I'll walk. It won't take long."

His da said, "Don't you want to tell your ma about your exciting day?"

"I will, at dinner."

Zee's ma narrowed her eyes at the position of the sun, then at him. "I'm sorry, Zee, but the beach will have to wait until tomorrow."

Zee's heart fell, and the emptiness in his chest grew deeper. "But..."

"No 'but' today, either. Help your da with the pigs, then get cleaned up and come help me get dinner ready."

Zee fought hard to slow his breathing and heartbeat, to quell the tears that tried to form in his eyes. He took a deep breath to still the quiver he knew would try to enter his voice. "Yes, Ma."

Da watched him closely, then said, "Hey, Ma!" He lifted the peachpear from the bench and held it up for her to see. "Look what Zee brought you."

Zee inhaled another unsteady breath, then forced a smile and a laugh. "No, I didn't. Da did."

Da tossed the fruit, and Ma caught it.

"My favorite!" she exclaimed. "I do adore peachpears." She rubbed it with her towel to make it shine. "We'll share it at dinner."

"That one's just for you, Ma," Zee said. "We already shared one."

"You did, did you?"

Da half grimaced, half grinned at Zee.

Ma tapped her foot in mock disapproval. "Seems to me, you each only had a half, and for me to have a whole to myself wouldn't be fair."

"Fair's got nothing to do with it, Ma," Da protested, striding to Zee and putting a hand on his shoulder. "We wouldn't hear of it." He winked at his son. "Would we, Zee?"

Catching on, Zee replied, "Nope!"

Ma propped her hands on her aproned hips. "Listen here, you two—"

Da pressed his hands to Zee's ears and said overly loudly, "We can't hear you!"

"Jad Tarrow!" Ma protested.

Da let go of Zee, pressed his hands to his own ears and began to sing, "La dee da! La dee da!"

Zee joined in, covering his ears. "La dee da!"

Da continued to sing, taking the collars off the younger pigs and leading them toward the barn. Zee gripped hold of Midge and Boaris and followed, grinning back at his ma.

Ma shook her head and smiled, though she was trying not to. "You searascals!"

* * *

For all Da's encouragement and Ma's attempts to keep him occupied, Zee's retelling of the events of the day at dinner wasn't as enthused as it normally would have been, no matter how hard he tried to hide his distress. He'd promised Jessup he'd go see him after they returned from the market and hadn't kept his word, but more than that, it hurt to be away from Jessup for so long, right in his chest.

He went to bed early in his tiny room. He considered sneaking out the window, something he'd never done before, and shuddered at the thought. That's what bad children did. And worse, it was night. He sang softly to himself.

"Fear the shore in the day time
A dangerous place to be
But night time is the fright time
The darkness you must flee."

So many things ran through Zee's little mind he was unable to sleep. Sorrow and guilt, but also excitement at having learned Jessup could be a kraken. His skin itched, too, and the rough gray spot on his chest tingled unpleasantly.

Jessup was always thrilled to see Zee, just as much as Zee was to see him. Jessup wasn't a pet, though. He was Zee's best friend. Zee wanted it to be that way forever, but deep down he worried Jessup would grow too big for the pool and have to take to the open sea, his true home. Zee's greatest fear was that he'd swim away one day without a word and never come back.

Until that fateful day came, Zee resolved with all his heart to do what was best for Jessup and not for himself. Dragon knights had to be selfless and do everything they could to help better the lives of others. Selfishness had no place in the king's Dragon Corps.

Out loud, he said softly, "I'm sorry I didn't come see you today, Jessup. Ma and Da wouldn't let me go to the shore. I hope you're okay."

An odd warmth reduced the chill of longing in his heart, the unpleasant tingle in the patch on his chest ceased, and the pain in his chest subsided. Eventually, he drifted into fitful slumber.

* * *

"*Zee!*"

Zee shot up in bed, suddenly awake and in a panic. Jessup had called to him. He heard it. And his friend was in trouble.

Zee jolted as the little creature's voice came again. "*Zee!*" Now he was certain he heard it, though not with his ears. The voice was in his head.

He rubbed his eyes and looked around to make sure he wasn't dreaming. Blue and silver light streamed in through the small window in his room, the dual moons of Zhera, full and bright.

The cry came again. All caution flew from Zee's mind. He had to help Jessup. Right then, and always. It was the only thing that mattered. He threw off his blankets and leapt out of bed, then realized he had to be quiet so as not to wake his parents. As quickly and silently as he could, he tugged on his clothes and boots, softly repeating, "I'm coming, Jessup, I'm coming."

* * *

Zee fell on his pell-mell run to the beach, but leapt back up, rubbed his gritty and scraped palms on his pants, and kept running.

Jessup's cries grew more plaintive and filled with terror.

"I'm coming!"

He hadn't fetched Midge for fear the pigs would squeal and wake his ma and da. His lungs screamed so painfully he had to use his spritzer, but he never slowed. As he grew closer, the rough patch on his chest throbbed with heat.

He finally heard Jessup's cries with his ears as he rounded the rocks, and skidded to a halt at the sight of beasts descending upon Jessup's pool. And not just any beasts, but massive leones of the sea. A whole pride of them. Sea leones were similar to seals Zee had seen sunning themselves on the rocks and frolicking in the sea on occasion, but these only came out at night, and they were huge.

The creatures' long fangs slavered, clawed fins scraped on the stone, flat tails slapped the ground, and water flew from their manes as they shook their heads.

The largest among them entered Jessup's tidepool, just its massive chest and fins taking up half the pool. It crept toward Jessup, who was pressed against a rock on the inland side, half out of the water.

Taken by terror, Zee shouted and threw a stone at the monster. It bounced harmlessly from its side but startled the beast. It whirled, splashing water from the pool, and hop-dragged itself out toward the beach.

Breathing fast, heart beating wildly, Zee felt a sense of relief and ran to the edge of the pool. "Are you all right?"

Jessup nodded, and the warmth of his gratitude filled Zee's chest. Then Jessup's eyes went wide, and he shouted in his tiny, gurgly voice, "Zee! Monster!"

The big sea leone had turned back. Seeing only a small boy, it growled and stalk-flopped toward them.

"Oh, no…" Zee cast about for anything to use as a weapon. Why hadn't he brought a pitchfork, a bush knife, anything?! Gazing in terror at the sheer size of the creature, its thick hide and long teeth, and the dozen others that followed it, Zee knew no weapon would help him against them. Still, he would defend Jessup with his life. He'd made a vow, and he wasn't going to break any more promises.

He snatched up another stone and strode around the pool to face the creature. "Get back!" he shouted, flinging the stone.

The beast ducked, and the stone struck its mane with no more effect than if a fly had landed on it. Then it raised its massive head and roar-barked at Zee. The others took up the barking cry, bobbing their heads. The sea leone crept closer, predatory intent gleaming in its eyes under the light of the moons.

The rough patch on Zee's chest burned hotter. His hand shot to it. The heat helped him focus and gave him strength. He could feel Jessup's fear in his stomach—but not the little kraken's fear for himself. His fear for Zee.

Zee stood his ground before the oncoming beast, having made up his mind. "Take me!" he shouted, looking up into the massive face of the sea leone, which was nearly as big across as Zee was tall.

It glared at him with bulging eyes, then roar-barked again, louder and longer than before, blasting Zee with hot breath that reeked of fish.

A tear ran down Zee's cheek. Fear tried to take hold of him, to make him run, to crumple him to the ground. But he stood where he was. For Jessup. For his friend.

He'd wanted to be a dragon rider, even a knight. Maybe this was close enough. He had kept his vow and would die with honor. He closed his eyes and accepted his fate without fear or remorse. He couldn't help wondering how bad it would hurt, but it didn't matter. It wouldn't last long.

He heard the beast shuffle closer, felt its hot, huffing breath on his face, ruffling his hair while it sniffed at its meal.

But nothing happened.

Zee opened his eyes. The creature was staring at him, tilting its enormous head in an odd fashion. It sniffed him again, shook its head violently, mane flying, then huffed deeply and pushed itself back and away on its clawed front fins.

Zee's fear was replaced by confusion. Could it smell his rash? Did it think he would make it sick if it ate him? If so, why hadn't it just knocked him aside and gone after Jessup?

The pride of sea leones was silent except for their heavy breaths and the shuffling of their bodies as they dragged themselves toward the ocean, peering back on occasion.

"Zee!" The voice wasn't Jessup's. It was Jad Tarrow's.

Zee whipped around. An oil lantern swung wildly on the steep winding path where Da was running down the rough rocky slope.

"Where are you, boy?!" There was anger in his father's cries but terror too.

For a fraction of time, Zee thought he should hide, but that would have been even more wrong than sneaking out of the house and coming to the shore at night. He couldn't make his da worry any more than he already had.

"I'm here, Da! I'm okay!"

Da made his way toward Zee's voice, abandoning the path to shove through shrubs, nearly twisting his ankle on the stones. He ran straight to Zee, gasping for breath, his face glistening with sweat, a wild look in his eyes, with a rusted harpoon gripped in one hand. His shirt was unbuttoned and torn, and he had scratches from his reckless descent to the beach. One of his boots was untied. He set the lantern to tilt on a rock, staggered to his knees in front of Zee, and grabbed him by the shoulders. "What are you doing, Zee? On the shore? At night! Do you know what state your mother is in? She's out of her mind with worry! It was all I could do to make her stay at the house in case you came back!"

Emotional turmoil ripped through Zee. He'd thought nothing for them. Only for Jessup. Only for his own honor. He stood silent, his face clouded, and tears welled in his eyes.

His father shook him again. "Zee—!"

Da stopped short, staring over Zee's shoulder at the shoreline. "Are those leones of the sea?"

Zee turned back to the shore, wiping tears from his eyes to see more clearly. He couldn't answer for fear that speaking would set him to sobbing.

Half in the surf, under the light of the two moons, the pride of sea leones watched them, then turned and shuffled into the sea.

"Never in my life have I seen them in this part of the kingdom or even heard of them coming here," Da said. "What could have possibly brought them here, and tonight?" His anger and fear returning, he said to Zee, "They could have killed you, Zee. What were you thinking?"

"I..." Zee swallowed to gain his voice. "I scared them away."

His father gawped. "You? Scared away leones of the sea?"

"Yes, sir."

Da flustered. "You... why... I..." Tears came to his eyes. He grabbed Zee and stood, lifting him, crushing him in a hug, and sobbing. "You bad, terrible, wonderful boy. If anything had happened to you..."

Zee hugged him back, head on his shoulder. "I'm sorry, Da."

Da released him from the hug and held him with one arm. "We need to get you back to your ma."

He stooped to retrieve the harpoon, then leaned toward where he'd set the lantern. "Take the light, lad."

Zee lifted it, and as they turned, its glow fell on the tide pool.

Jad Tarrow froze at the sight of Jessup's cone-shaped head, the creature's octopod brow and big green eyes held above the surface of the pool while Jessup treaded water. Jessup's eyes went even wider at being sighted. He peeped and dropped into the water.

Da's head turned slowly to Zee, disbelief written on his features. "What in Postune's heavens was that?"

CHAPTER 8

"You're staying home today, Zee Tarrow." Ma set his breakfast of porridge and boiled tubers on the table in front of him. "No argument, no complaints, you hear me?"

Zee had expected that would be the case, but it still hurt to hear it. "Yes, Ma."

She wiped her hands on her apron and crossed her arms. "No pigs, no shore, just helping me here at the house. Your father is still in a terrible state."

At seeing that Zee was on the verge of tears, her fierce disposition softened. She took him by the face with both hands, looking into his eyes. "Then, we will never speak of this again. All right?" A shaky sigh escaped her lips. She looked like she might cry herself. "My precious boy." She kissed him on the forehead, holding her lips there, then stood quickly, sniffed, and rubbed her face. She went back to busying herself at the stove.

Zee was an emotional wreck, torn between worry and love for Jessup and his love for his parents. He felt terrible about what he'd put them through but was positive he had done the right thing. Hadn't he?

He'd risen late, having been exhausted by the night's adventure and crying himself to sleep, then slept more soundly than he had in weeks. Da had already left, taking Midge, Boaris, and the cart. Zee didn't want to push his ma more than he already had, so he hadn't asked where.

Zee glanced at his ma, but her back was still turned. Trying something new, he consciously reached out to Jessup, asking if he was all right.

For a moment, nothing happened, then warmth swelled in his chest, and he heard his friend's voice.

"*Jessup okay.*"

Zee had to stifle a gasp so as not to draw Ma's attention, then said, "*Are you sure?*" A feeling of more warmth, along with comfort and safety, answered to the affirmative.

Jessup asked, "*Zee okay?*"

"*I'm all right. But I can't come see you today.*"

After a pause and a sense of sadness, an answer came. "*Jessup know.*" Then gratitude flooded Zee's heart, and Jessup said, "*Zee save Jessup. Jessup thank Zee.*"

"*You're welcome, Jessup. It's my duty, to my friend.*"

Joy flowed into Zee, then the warmth faded, and the connection was gone.

* * *

Jad Tarrow hesitated at the door to the office of Mayor Tremon sen Dios, going so far as to lean his forehead on the cool carved wood to calm his inner turmoil. He and Seela had talked it over. They were doing this for Zee's protection and, hopefully, to improve the family's financial situation, especially with tax time coming. It was the right thing to do.

But if that was true, why was he having so much trouble going through with it? He took a deep breath and pushed.

Mayor sen Dios looked up from his desk as Jad entered, then lowered his glasses on his long narrow nose. "Jad Tarrow. I'm surprised to see you here, though not at all displeased. I have not forgotten it was you who turned in a king's coin you'd found on the beach, when most would have kept it for themselves. The rogues." He removed his glasses and leaned back in his chair, fingers working at the end of his long mustache. "My clerk tells me you may have some news of import."

Jad pulled off his hat and squeezed it in both hands at his chest. He and Seela had discussed how to present the information, and for Zee's sake, they felt it best to leave him out of it. He tried to get his nerves under control, but spoke quickly in spite of himself. "I've found something on the shore near my home, honorable Mayor. Eggs, you see. The day after the last earthshake. Something hatched. It wasn't until I was in town for the auction yesterday that I had any inkling what it might be. I discussed it with Ma—my wife, Seela—and we felt I should bring the information to you straightaway."

He wrung his hat, his knuckles white, and forced himself to speak more slowly. "We were hoping it may have some value, maybe in the form of a reward or finder's fee?" The mayor began to look suspicious. "Though we would never insist upon such a thing," Jad hurried to add. "If it is what I think it might be, it could be of interest to not only you, honorable Mayor, but also the governor, and maybe even the king."

The mayor leaned forward. "The king, you say?"

* * *

Zee worked hard for his ma, trying not to think too much about Jessup and what he had done to upset his parents so badly. He scrubbed the floor on hands and knees, cleaned the windows, wiped down the walls as high as he could reach while standing on a chair, climbed up and dusted the rafters, then proceeded to clean out the pigpens with the child-sized pitchfork his da had made him because Zee had kept pestering to help—all under the watchful eye of his mother.

Zee didn't mind helping. His ma and da always worked hard. It was part of who he was. They'd taught him the value of hard work, for character, strength of body and mind, and instilled an ability to take joy in even the most menial, difficult, and distasteful jobs. And stinky ones, like cleaning up after pigs.

The hardest part was the pain of missing Jessup, the heartache of scaring his parents so badly, and the guilt that he'd told his parents how he found Jessup, and that he'd been spending the days with him. He'd been so overwrought, he even told them what he thought Jessup might be, even after he'd sworn he wouldn't. He hadn't told them the little creature could talk, though, and insisted Jessup was gentle and not at all dangerous.

Then, in the middle of a late lunch, Zee felt a stabbing pain in the gray patch on his chest and the harsh swell of fear in his gut. The bowl he was drinking broth from fell from his hands to clatter and spill on the table, causing his ma to jump where she sat stripping leaves from yellow branch twigs for her tinctures.

"Zee Tarrow!" she shouted.

His eyes went to her. "Ma…" The pain came again, nearly doubling him over. He wasn't ill, though. He'd felt this pain before. Jessup was in trouble again, only this time, it was worse.

Zee reached out to his little friend, silently calling his name, asking him what was happening. Jessup didn't answer.

* * *

Jad Tarrow stood next to the mayor on a rise of stones looking over the tide pool, biting his nails, glancing occasionally up the slope where his home was.

Mayor sen Dios said, "You've done the right thing, Jad Tarrow, and a service to your governor and king. If this creature is indeed what we think it could be, it is a danger to all the good people of Tosh." Greed glinted in his eyes as he tugged at the end of his mustache. "And perhaps, quite valuable."

"Do you truly believe it could be a kraken, Your Honor?"

The mayor lifted a finger to his lips, indicating for Jad to speak more quietly. "I have no way of knowing, of course. Perhaps no one does, but Governor jal Briggs has access to scholars who might. He has already conveyed as much in a message delivered to me via carrier gull and is most eager to see the creature for himself. Either way, it is very rare, whatever it is, and Governor jal Briggs, too, believes King mon lin Phan will be very interested in it once it is properly identified."

Behind them, city guards held the reins of nervous horses and tended to fidgeting mules hitched to a cart and a covered wagon.

The scene before them would be comical if Jad wasn't so worried about how Zee would feel about what he had done. A group of men and women, strong dockworkers from the looks of them, with long wooden digging paddles, were trying to retrieve the creature Zee had told him and Ma he'd named Jessup. The little beast was proving too fast and wriggly for them. Peeping and squeaking, it had thwarted every attempt to scoop it from the pool.

The mayor shouted, "Go in after it, you fools!" The dockworkers balked at the idea, but one of them slipped and fell in anyway. "Good man! Now grab it!"

The man hesitated, then grunted and dove after the creature. Jessup shot away with another peep.

The mayor shouted again. "All of you, in!"

Some stepped down carefully, others jumped feetfirst. The deepest part of the pool came up to their chests. They peered into the silt-stirred water. A large barrel-chested man spied something beneath the surface, then plunged in with a roar.

When he came up, Jessup was in his hands, flailing his arms and squeaking frantically. The man roared with triumph. "Got ya!" Arms slapped his face, but he hung on to Jessup's shell with strong hands. Switching to a different tactic, Jessup grabbed hold of the man's head and pulled himself to suck the bottom of his shell and base of his arms—basically his butt—right to the man's face.

The man staggered back, thrashing his arms, unable to breathe. Two dockworkers rushed to his aid, taking hold of Jessup and trying to pull him off.

The mayor chuckled. "The little fellow is a fighter, I will give him that."

The dockworkers tugged, succeeding only in dragging the big man forward in the water. Suddenly Jessup let go, sending them all flying back and splashing into the drink.

One of them came up sputtering, still hanging on to the wriggling creature. Jessup used his arms on the woman's wrists to turn the base of his body to face her, then shot a spray of dark blue ink at his attacker's face.

"Gah!" the woman cried with a mouthful of ink. She let go and fell back into the pool with a splash, then shot up, spitting and sputtering, her skin stained blue.

"Oh, my." The mayor chuckled. "It can ink like an octopod!"

The barrel-chested man glared at the water, still rubbing his face where Jessup had hold of him earlier. "You little shadfish!"

He and another man plunged down and came up grasping Jessup once more. Jessup cried out with a shrill squeak.

"Do not harm it!" the mayor ordered. "Anyone who damages the creature will have their wages withheld for a month!"

The men grunted while doing their best to hang on to the squirming beast.

Jessup sucked his face up into his shell, tensed the arms coiled on the men's arms, and went still. The men eyed him with surprise and no small amount of suspicion. For good reason, as it turned out.

Zig-zags of blue electricity danced on Jessup's shell, then shot down his arms, zapping the men. They cried out, their hands flying from the creature, and tumbled back into the pool. Jessup dropped into the murky water.

The mayor clapped his hands together. "And it shocks like a zap-eel! Fabulous!"

The dockworkers scrambled and splashed out of the pool to stand soaking wet and heaving for breath.

Jad stood agape. This was what Zee considered a "pet?" He was now more convinced than ever he and Ma had made the right decision. The thing was definitely dangerous. How Zee had grown so attached to it, so much as to risk going to the shore at night and facing leones of the sea on its behalf, he hadn't a clue.

The mayor shouted back to the guard by the mules. "Did you load the loop-poles, like I told you?"

"Yes, Your Honor!" He hurried to the back of the wagon.

Three of the dockworkers by the pool, including the big man with the barrel chest, were now armed with long wooden poles with a loop of thick rope at one end, threaded back through eyehooks on its shaft so the loop could be pulled taut. They used them to probe the water.

"Be gentle with it, you buffoons!" the mayor instructed. Without looking at Jad, he said, "These poles are used on ships to aid in docking, as well as to retrieve floating objects from the sea, you know."

Jad did know but didn't answer.

The mayor twisted the end of his mustache, pleased with himself. "It was my idea to bring them."

Jad still said nothing.

The dockworkers made failed attempts to ensnare Jessup, then finally the big man roared with satisfaction. Straining to hold the rope tight, he lifted Jessup, who peeped and struggled against the loop that encircled him. Two dockworkers hurried to the edge of the pool with a sturdy barrel. Jessup tried to zap again, but the electricity wouldn't travel up the rope or wooden pole.

"Gently!" the mayor reiterated.

The big man shoved the pole into the barrel, loosed the rope, then gave the pole a shake and yanked it out. Jessup clunked to the bottom. The woman who had been inked, the skin of her face still stained blue, slammed down a circular grate and fastened it in place.

The mayor shouted, "And the water!"

Jessup peeped as buckets of seawater from the pool were poured through the grate.

The mayor clapped dust from his hands, as if he'd done the work himself. "That does it." More loudly, he said to the others. "Make haste! We mustn't miss the ship!"

* * *

Zee struggled in his mother's arms. "Jessup!"

The burning itch of his skin, the stabbing pain in his stomach, cold press on his heart, and searing heat and sting of the rough gray patch on his chest were absolute torture. Far worse than he'd experienced last night. But the worst of it was that his little friend wouldn't answer him.

Seated on a bench in front of the house, arms wrapped around her hysterical son, Seela Tarrow was beside herself, tears of anger and fear streaming down her reddened face. "Zee, please, control yourself!"

"Let me go, Ma! Something's happening to Jessup!"

"I don't know what in Postune's coral gardens you're talking about," she replied, "but you're obviously having a breakdown of some sort." What she was thinking, however, was, *how could he know?*

"No, Ma, it's Jessup!"

Seela Tarrow's arms burned from hanging on to him. She squeezed her eyes and took a deep breath. Shouting was obviously not going to work. "Please, Zee. Your father will be home soon and we'll get this straightened out. I'll prepare some tea to make you feel better."

Zee settled down, though his breaths came in tiny heaves. The frantic nature of the terrible feeling in his chest had decreased somewhat—but the fear was still there, and mounting.

Ma reached into his pocket and retrieved his lung-spritzer. "There, there, good boy. Such a good boy." She sniffed, trying to hold in her fear for her only son. The happy and gentle boy who had brought her so much joy when she'd thought she would have none. "Open," she said. He complied, and she sprayed the mist into his mouth. Two more times she sprayed, Zee inhaling with each. His lungs began to clear, and he breathed more deeply.

"Ma, please," he pleaded. "Let me go to him."

His mother sobbed and pressed her face to the side of his head. "Oh, Zee. Dear, dear Zee."

The neighing of horses, clopping of hooves, and rattle of wagon wheels came to them from a distance. Dust rose over the slope where Zee knew the widest of the paths to the shore was.

Zee stiffened as men riding horses appeared, followed by a cart loaded with dockworkers and pulled by mules. Behind it was a covered wagon—

and somehow, Zee knew, his friend was in that wagon.

"Jessup…," he gasped softly.

Using all his strength, he jerked free of his mother's arms. He sprinted toward the barn, leaving his ma pushing herself up from where he'd tugged her to nearly fall in the dirt.

"Zee Tarrow!" she cried. "Come back here this instant!"

Zee heard her, but he wasn't stopping for anything or anyone. They'd taken Jessup, and he was going to get him back.

CHAPTER 9

Holy Zhera made the earth of a shred of her skin, the sea with a single tear, and the heavens from a breath. A drop of her blood gave rise to the first being. She disappeared into the cosmos, leaving her children, Zepiter and Postune, to complete her creation.

They tore the first being in half. With his half, Zepiter made humankind for the land, and with a shoulder bone created the dragon so they could also rule the skies, grow stronger together, protect each other, and never be alone.

Postune cast her half upon the waters, and from its decay were born the murfolk and creatures of the sea.

—*The Creation Scrolls,* King Daled ja Tallack's Revised Edition

Jad Tarrow strode up the dusty path from the shore to where it leveled at the edge of his property. He sighed, placed a folded piece of paper in his breast pocket, then hefted the bag of coin the mayor had given him. It was enough for him, Ma, and Zee to live comfortably for a year. If he used just half of it to invest in more livestock and tools, maybe even a horse or a mulie, much longer than that. They could hire a tutor for Zee so he could learn maths and reading and have a better life.

The beat of cloven hooves and a shout from Ma snapped his head up. "Jad! Stop him!"

Midge barreled toward him, Zee clinging to her back. His son was red-faced, as if he'd been crying, but his jaw was clenched, and his eyes burned with determination.

A panicked thought hit Jad like a blow to the head. *He knows.*

"Get out of my way!" Zee shouted with a rage Jad had never seen in his son.

Shocked as he was, Jad lunged to grab Zee, but the pig swerved, and Zee cried, "Get away from me, you traitor! Liar!"

Jad caught himself on his knees. His son wouldn't listen, but the pig was well trained. "Midge, ho!" he cried. Midge just lowered her head and put on more speed, dust flying beneath her hooves.

Watching his son disappear over the rise, a crack opened in Jad Tarrow's heart. *Traitor. Liar…*

Breathing hard, Seela grabbed him and pulled him to his feet, her face contorted with terror. She, too, had been crying. Jad's heart cracked a little more.

She shook him. "He knows, Jad! I don't know how, but he knows!" She looked desperately down the road, then back. "You go after him, right now!" She realized what she was doing, let go of his shirt and placed her hands on his chest. "Please. Bring our son home."

Jad looked back to the barn. He could try to ride Boaris but had little faith even the big boar could carry him for long. He took Seela by the shoulders and kissed her on the forehead. "I will, Ma. I promise."

And Jad Tarrow ran.

*　*　*

"I can't believe Da did this," Zee fumed out loud, to himself as much as to Midge. None of the townsfolk who hustled out of their way could hear him anyway, as softly but forcefully as he spoke, and as much noise as the pig's squeals of warning and pounding hooves made.

As frantic and riled as he was, he slowed Midge from a run. He didn't want to cause too much of a ruckus. He wasn't sure how he was going to get Jessup back, but he figured he'd better not attract the attention of the city guard in case it was something they wouldn't approve of.

Midge was breathing heavily, her rib cage expanding and contracting beneath him, but she hadn't slowed the entire mad dash over the key and kept up a swift trot to the dockyard. Zee didn't know how he was so sure that's where Jessup was being taken. Jessup still wasn't answering his silent calls. Only the sickness in Zee's stomach and the burn of the rough patch of gray skin on his chest told him Jessup was still close, still afraid, and near the docks.

He searched this way and that, then saw the wagons and horses stopped at the end of the last and largest pier. He spurred Midge forward, then leapt off when they arrived. Out on the pier, dockworkers in wet, muddy clothes were pushing a handcart with a violently-sloshing barrel up a loading ramp to a ship.

The mayor of mon Tontuga was there as well. "Carefully, you lackwits. If you spill it, I will have your hides!"

Jessup was in that barrel, Zee could feel it. He ran to the pier but was blocked by a wall of city guards.

"No access to the pier, lad, by order of the mayor," one of them said.

"You don't understand!" Zee cried. "My friend is on that ship!"

"Your friend?" another guard asked. "What's their name?"

Zee struggled for an answer. He'd nearly blurted out "Jessup," but that would do him no good. He looked at the ship, then back along the wharf, then back to the ship. It was the HMT *Krakenfish*. They'd finished the repairs and put it back in the water.

"Dame Zara mon Toomsil," he said. "Silver Class Knight Chevalier of His Majesty's Dragon Corps."

The guards snickered. The second one to speak responded, "Is that so?"

"Yes, sir. I had lunch with her and her squire just yesterday."

"I see," the guard said with a disbelieving smile but a ready answer. "Dame Toomsil and the other rider are out with their dragons, hunting for the beasts' weekly meal. Perhaps when she returns, if the ship hasn't already set sail, we'll ask if she will see you."

Zee froze. "Set sail?"

"Indeed. The ship is scheduled to leave port this afternoon."

"Where are they going?"

They snorted. "The city guard are not privy to such information, lad. Nor would we tell you if we were. This is the governor's business and, by proxy, that of the king himself."

Zee's mouth opened and closed wordlessly, then he bolted in an attempt to shove his way between the guards.

He nearly got through, but with a surprised, "Whoa, there!" they grabbed him and pulled him back.

"I must get through!" Zee cried. He tried again, but this time they were ready and stopped him easily. One woman took three long strides and set him on his feet on the wharf. Kicking and struggling as he was, he fell on the ground. She backed to her place in the line of guards and held one hand out in an attempt to pacify him. "Don't make this worse than it has to be, boy. You're going to have to wait."

Zee shoved to his feet and dragged his sleeve across his face to clear his teary eyes and running nose, then ran to the edge of the wharf beside the pier and shouted. "Mr. Mayor! Your Honor!"

In the distance, the mayor turned, head tipped forward to peer over his spectacles.

"You have to give him back!" Zee shouted. "He's my friend!"

The guards looked at each other, chuckling in amusement.

"Please!" Zee cried. "He's frightened. You don't understand!"

The mayor didn't understand, nor did he care. He spun back and strode up the ramp.

* * *

"Captain lon Bomba," Mayor sen Dios said to a man in a uniform slightly too small for his large frame. The captain turned from where he was overseeing the placement of the barrel on a lift to the hold. He had a cruel set to his dark eyes, which were placed too close to his broad nose, and a scar across his chin.

"Dios," the captain spat. He stalked forward to glower down at the shorter man. "You had better have that bill of lading."

The mayor nearly stepped back but held out a folded document, hand trembling, then swallowed and cleared his throat. "Signed by the governor of Akhtar Province, Lord Commander Farig jal Briggs, and delivered by carrier gull."

The captain opened it roughly. His lips moved silently as he read.

The mayor pointed at the document. "To be delivered posthaste to the governor's castle dock—"

"I can read, Dios," the captain rumbled through gritted teeth, leaning threateningly, crushing the document in his fist. This time the mayor did step back. "This will put me even further behind schedule, but it will be done."

The mayor began to speak, but Ion Bomba spoke over him. "Now get off my ship." The mayor backed away. The captain roared at the mayor's hired hands as well. "All of you. Off!"

The captain's sailors moved toward the mayor and his crew, some with hands on swords and belted knives.

The mayor retreated down the ramp, the dockworkers tripping over each other behind him.

The captain turned back to glower at the barrel as the lift was lowered. On the other side of the hatch, an older man, broad of shoulder but stooped, leaned on his cane, intently watching the barrel descend. From inside of it came a splash and a frightened peep.

The captain's eyes lifted to the man and narrowed dubiously, as if he didn't want to ask but was compelled to. "What do you make of it, surgeon?" he said gruffly, like it was a challenge.

The surgeon's eyes didn't leave the barrel. "It's not identified on the bill of lading?"

"I wouldn't ask if it was, now, would I?" the captain replied.

The surgeon finally tore his eyes from the barrel, lifting them to gaze at the captain from beneath thick and overly long gray brows. One of his eyes was crystal gray, the other cloudy beneath a scar that bisected the hedge of an eyebrow above it. His gaze was altogether unsettling, but the captain glared back. "Then I'm certain I have no idea." The look on his face as he gazed back down into the hold betrayed something else, and the captain knew it.

"Damn you to Zepiter's blazing fires, surgeon."

The surgeons lips tipped in a mocking smile. "Again?"

The captain snorted. "Again, and always."

A deep grating roar drew their eyes to the sky over town.

Raising a hand to the crew that was lowering the lift, the captain ordered, "Hold!"

* * *

Fretting where he stood next to Midge, gripping her harness with one hand, Zee jumped at the roar.

Two dragons circled, one higher than the other. The lower dragon, with shining blood-red scales and forward-facing horns, shouted in a deep guttural voice, "Clear yourselves!"

Townsfolk and dockworkers who'd been drawn to the pier by the arrival of the wagons and the odd parcel to be loaded on the king's tradeship scattered out of the way.

Though Dame Toomsil had confirmed that dragons could speak, knowing something and experiencing it firsthand were two different things altogether. Zee had to close his mouth and shield his eyes against the dusty wind whipped up by the dragon's wings as it settled on the wharf.

Zee had never seen this kind of dragon, but he knew from descriptions it was a Royal Crimson. It was more sturdily built than Dame Toomsil's or the other knight's he'd seen, and heavily muscled. Royals were the strongest of the dragonbreeds and frighteningly swift in the air for short bursts, though not very maneuverable or well suited for long-distance flights. They were deadly brutes in battle and preferred by many dragonriders, especially those who served as special guards—or in this case, a Lord Commander. And the man's mail shirt and helm were shining white. He and his dragon were White Titan Class. They had to be one of the most formidable pairs in the kingdom. Dame Toomsil had told Zee there weren't more than fifty White Titan knight pairs in all of Tosh. He also wore a colorful green sash trimmed in blue. Zee didn't know what the sash was for, but he figured the man must be pretty important.

The dragon lowered itself to its belly, and the White Titan knight dismounted with swift aplomb.

The second dragon flapped down and landed near the first. It was also a Royal, but an Ebon, with satin black scales, larger than the red dragon, and its horns and the mane of spines on its neck gleamed red. Upon it was a knight in golden armor.

The White Titan knight spoke quietly to his dragon but said nothing to the guards as he strode toward them in his tall riding boots, throwing his cape over his shoulder.

The Gold Class knight followed closely at his side and just behind. "Lord Commander Governor Farig jal Briggs, coming through!" he shouted. The city guards parted for them without question, then closed ranks again.

Zee was right; the man was important. Zee had never seen a White Titan Class dragon and rider, let alone the governor of their province. Then Zee noticed everyone else was gawping as well, their attention drawn by the arrival of the governor and the dragons. He gazed along the pier, setting his mind to a crazy and dangerous plan. "Midge, stay."

She grunted in reply, then watched him slip past a stack of crates at the edge of the wharf and climb down to the timber braces beneath the pier.

CHAPTER 10

Quietly as he could, Zee struggled along beams and through cross braces attached to pylons that supported the pier. He watched the dark water below, trying to keep thoughts of something toothy lunging out at him away. As scrawny as he was, Zee was a good climber. At least he didn't weigh much. It was tough going, nonetheless, the wood barnacled and slimed with algae closer to the water's surface, rough and splintered above. He swallowed, trying not to think about slipping and falling in as he made his way toward the ship.

* * *

On the pier, Governor jal Briggs strode up to Mayor sen Dios.

The mayor was the first to speak, his voice a stutter of surprise. "My Lord, I did not expect to see you here."

"Am I not allowed to visit a town in my own province, Mayor sen Dios?" Briggs replied.

"Of course, Lord Governor, at your pleasure."

Dame Toomsil's squire, Tem jal Briggs, trotted down the ramp with hope in his eyes, but also no small amount of trepidation. "Greetings, Father. It is good—"

"Temothy," the governor interrupted. "Are you hale and hearty?"

"Yes, Father, I—"

"Well met, then," his father interrupted again. "Your mother will be glad to hear it." Governor Briggs turned back to the mayor, dismissing his son. "I would see this prize you have promised me, Dios, and my dear Hutson wished to stretch his wings." The governor raised an eyebrow. "Unless, of course, I am not welcome."

The mayor's jaw bobbed before he replied. "Of course, milord. You are always welcome. Follow me, please."

They stepped up the ramp. Tem stood silent, face fallen, as his father brushed past without so much as a second glance.

The mayor stopped at the top of the ramp. "Permission to come aboard, Captain?"

The governor swept past him without waiting for a reply.

* * *

Zee's meager muscles burned, he cut his hands and tore his pants, but he persisted, for Jessup's sake. He would endure this, and much more, for his best friend.

Voices and clomping footsteps came from above. Shadows flitted across slats between the planks. Something splashed in the water beneath him, startling him and causing him to slip from where he shimmied on a timber. He nearly fell in but clung upside down with arms and legs wrapped over the beam. Hanging on for dear life, he saw Midge, her ears up and forward, watching him from the edge of the wharf as if ready to jump in after him if he fell.

He crawled along beneath the beam until he came to the next cross brace and used it to wrestle himself back on top. He waved back to Midge to let her know he was okay. She shook her head, ears flapping.

Zee could see the long hull of the ship through the timbers. Almost halfway there. His rash prickled something fierce, but he couldn't scratch it for fear of letting go. The sense of Jessup in his gut drove him on. He set his teeth and whispered. "I'm coming, Jessup, I'm coming."

To distract himself from the discomfort and fear, he softly sang his shoresong.

*"Don't go near the water
Stay away from the sea
The riptides and the monsters
Will be the end of me."*

He tried not to look down as he went, but out of the corners of his eyes he caught movement of dark things and flashes of scales beneath the surface, some thick and sluggish, some darting.

Through sheer will and determination, he finally found himself even with the loading ramp. Footsteps sounded down the ramp, and Zee held his breath at hearing the voices of Mayor sen Dios and Governor jal Briggs.

"I have called for the appropriate scholars," said Briggs. "The creature is small and not at all pleasant to look upon, but I must admit, it is promising. Well done, Dios."

The mayor blinked at the rare word of praise from the governor, cheeks glowing. "It is my great pleasure, milord Governor."

Zee watched them through the cracks in the planks, like giants towering above him.

"While I am here," Briggs said, "I would like to discuss the upcoming collection of annual taxes in your district."

"I am at your service, milord." They strolled a short distance up the pier, continuing their conversation.

Zee breathed in relief and loosened his grip on the beam he clung to. He muffled a cry, having slid his hand along the beam and stabbed a spine of wood into his palm. Wincing, he pulled it out with his teeth, wiped his hand on his grimy pants, and continued his arduous crawl beneath the pier.

* * *

Jad Tarrow jogged along the wharf, drenched in sweat, breathing hard, legs aching from his long run from the far side of the key. He cupped his hands to his mouth. "Zee!" Gulping for air, he turned to a man at the door of a tackle and bait shop. "Have you seen a tiny lad, only yea high, wearing a scarf?"

The man frowned in thought. "I don't believe so."

"He may have been riding a pig."

"Ah, yes." The shop owner pointed down the wharf. "He headed that-a-way."

"Much obliged!"

* * *

Past the ramp, two thirds of the way along the ship, Zee poked his head from beneath the pier. Heavy ropes secured the ship to posts, one of them passing close to an open gunport. Taking a deep breath and praying to Postune no one looked his way, Zee grasped the rope and pulled himself out from under the pier. His boot caught on a peg. He pulled but only managed to slip his foot out. He made a mad grasp for the laces, nearly losing his grip on the rope, and missed. He caught himself, but the shoe splashed into the water.

The sound of the splash wasn't loud, but then the surface below him roiled, churning loudly as sea creatures fought for the prize.

Zee clung to the rope in terror.

Two dockworkers stood from where they were securing the top of a crate to peer in the direction of the sound, but a loud squealing at the base of the pier drew their attention away.

Zee stared in amazement as Midge plowed through the line of city guards, spinning them and knocking them down. Up the dock she ran, going out of her way to bash into dockworkers and sailors alike, drawing the attention of everyone on the pier. Only the railings kept them from being flung into the bay. Curses and cries filled the air.

Zee realized Midge was purposefully causing a distraction—and he'd better not let it go to waste. "Good pig," he said softly, marveling at her bravery and good sense. "Thank you, Midge." He strained and shimmied up the rope, hanging beneath it.

The mayor watched the mad hog in horror, but Governor Briggs looked on with an amused sneer. Midge doubled back before coming close to where they stood, raising a new set of cries, then looped around again.

A dockworker raised a hammer, another an oar, but the pig swerved and dodged, sending them flying as well.

"Be careful, Midge," Zee whispered. But he was having troubles of his own. When he finally came to the height of the gunport, his face was red with effort, his muscles on fire, and his grip on the verge of failing. He gritted his teeth and reached, but his fingertips slipped from the sill. A second try missed as well.

Midge continued to wreak havoc on the pier, bobbing and weaving, knocking dockworkers and guards to the heavy boards or sending them leaping out of her way. The mayor, having clambered atop a crate to escape the rampaging pig, yelled and blustered, trying to restore order. The governor snickered at the chaos caused by the wild hog.

Zee swung himself so he rocked back and forth on the rope. He missed the sill again but redoubled his efforts, swung harder, and caught it with one hand. With tremendous effort, he loosened his grip on the rope with his legs and caught the sill with the other hand as well. Straining with all he had, he pulled until he just had the rope pinched between his ankles. He shoved his elbows into the port, let go with his legs, and let them swing free.

* * *

Shouting dockworkers ran toward the ship, Midge charging behind them. They split up and slipped past the governor's knight, who stood his ground and drew his sword. Midge skidded to a stop.

The man's lips parted and curved up at the corners, showing far too many teeth. "My beloved mount, Presley, would love to meet you, my dear pig." Midge backed up as he stalked forward, all the while keeping an eye on Zee in the shadows of the ship beyond.

Kicking at the planks, Zee tugged himself, huffing and grunting, through the gunport. When at last his feet, one shoed and one bare, slid into the darkness, she spun and bolted toward the wharf.

* * *

Jad Tarrow jogged along the wharf on tired legs, searching frantically for his son. A squeal and a shout, and Midge was running toward him, a young city guardsman waving his hat behind her, cursing the rogue hog.

The pig halted in front of Jad and looked up at him. "Midge?" She grunted in reply.

The guard slowed, heaving for breath. "Is that your Zepiter's bane of a hog?"

Jad wasn't sure he should claim her if she'd caught the attention of the city guard, but he couldn't afford to lose her. "She is, Constable. I'm very sorry." He took hold of her harness.

"Keep the cursed beast locked up, then. It nearly knocked half the dockworkers into the bay."

Midge grunted and lunged toward the guard, who jumped back.

Jad held on to her harness, surprised by her behavior. "I will, sir, and I'm truly sorry," he said with more urgency. "She's very protective. Have you seen a young boy with a scarf?"

"I have." The guard frowned. "He was with that hog, in fact. Last dock up."

"Thank you!" Jad set off down the wharf at a run, hanging on to Midge, who ran alongside. The young guard stepped clear as they passed, then donned his crumpled cap and followed.

* * *

Zee squeezed past a cannon mounted on a carriage and crawled to peer along the gun deck. He'd never been on a ship before. It smelled of wood and salt water, old rope, oil, and gunpowder. There were rectangular openings with netted rope railings along the center of the deck floor and in the ceiling above. Wooden grates that normally covered them had been tipped up, and crates and sacks of goods were being lowered through. There was no one on the gun deck, but shadows of sailors moved above, and he heard the sounds of movement below.

Zee crept toward the steps at the stern, then heard footsteps on the treads and conversation rising from below. Panicking at the thought of being caught before he could find Jessup, he hurried to the rope netting that served as a railing at the end of the nearest opening. He scrambled under and froze, clinging to the ropes at floor level. Right below where he hung, two sailors were storing coils of line. Two more sailors stepped up onto the gun deck from the stairs but thankfully proceeded upward on a ladder.

Zee's grip began to slip. *Please go away, please*, he silently pleaded to the sailors below. Luckily, they did, moving through a bulkhead to another part of the ship. Zee's grip failed as they closed the door and he dropped with a squeak of fright.

Zee extricated himself from a tangle of ropes, rubbed his head, then glanced around while using his spritzer to ease his breathing and allowing the burn to recede from the muscles of his aching limbs. The room smelled of musty leather, rusted iron, and old salty wood. Thinking back to what he'd been told while badgering sailors, he figured he must be in a storeroom above the hold.

He listened but heard only distant, muffled voices and soft clunks of merchandise being stowed. He was terribly afraid, felt lost, and questioned his mad decision to climb aboard the ship—but the sense of loss and fear for Jessup returned, and the warmth in his chest increased, as did the prickle of the patch on his chest.

Zee grunted with determination. His friend was here, somewhere, and he was going to find him. He crept to the door, listened, then opened it a crack. No one was there, but he suddenly got a feeling Jessup was close. He thought he could even tell which direction. Following the tug in his chest, he wound through barrels and around braces to a set of stairs and descended.

Zee peeked around the corner at the bottom of the steps but pulled back quickly as more sailors finished placing a crate and walked toward him. He held his breath, wondering if he should run back up the stairs. They stomped past, caught up in conversation, without a glance in the direction of the stairs.

The threat past, the pull and tingle of his patch drew him from the stairs to the right. The large room—part of the hold, Zee guessed—was stocked tight, with aisles between stacks of tethered crates and barrels.

It was lit only by dusty light from a grate above and a single lantern that swung softly from a hook on a beam. He made his way between crates to one corner, then heard a small splash and a miserable peep.

"Jessup?" he said softly as he rounded a stack. There in the corner, sitting on a pallet and tethered to the walls, was a barrel with the tips of Jessup's arms reaching through the round iron grate at its top.

Zee stifled a cry of elation and ran to climb onto a crate so he could peer down into the barrel.

Holding himself above the surface was Jessup. The creature's fearful voice sounded in his mind. "*Zee! Jessup stuck!*"

"*Jessup!*" Zee replied mentally. "*It's going to be okay. Don't worry. I'll get you out.*"

* * *

Jad arrived at the pier to a gathering crowd. He gaped at the dragons sitting on the wharf. As he secured Midge to a post with a rope that hung there, he saw a green dragon and a knight in silver mail land on the perch deck at the back of the only ship docked at the pier. There was no sign of Zee in the crowd, so he approached the guards, who eyed Midge warily.

"Excuse me, but I'm looking for my son, Zee." Sheepishly, he added, "He was riding that pig."

"I see," said the ranking guard. "And your name?"

"Jad Tarrow, sir."

"I'll be issuing you a citation, Mr. Tarrow, for allowing that beast to roam free and endanger the good people of mon Tontuga. There may be reparations for damage." One of the guards ran her hands over a rip in the coat of her uniform.

Jad tapped the bag of coin that bulged in his pocket. "I will gladly pay, sir, but—"

"That won't be necessary, Sergeant." The guards parted at the sound of someone approaching behind them. "Jad Tarrow, is it?" said Lord Governor jal Briggs, his guard knight just behind.

* * *

Zee pulled at the latches on the lid, but they were too stiff for him to move with his small boy's hands. He sighted a rack of tools on the wall, including several pry bars. "*Hang on,*" he told Jessup, then fetched one.

While prying at the first latch, Zee said. "*Why didn't you answer me before?*"

The tone of Jessup's voice changed, and Zee was surprised by the sense of regret that Zee had come. "*Danger for Zee.*"

The latch popped, and Zee moved to the next. "*Don't say that. It's okay.*"

"*Not okay,*" came Jessup's high mournful voice. "*Jessup danger for Zee.*"

"*No, you're not,*" Zee rebuked. "*You're my friend. This is what friends do.*" Jessup watched him with his googly green eyes. The second latch snapped open. "*You'd do the same for me, right?*"

Jessup's reply came with an earnestness Zee felt right in his heart. "*Yes. Jessup help Zee. Always.*" Zee gulped down a sob at the conviction that spread through his chest from his little friend.

The third latch popped, and Zee gripped the grate. Jessup let go and floated at the surface of the water. Zee tugged, straining. It was stuck. Zee used the pry bar, but it still wouldn't come loose. He wedged a foot against the barrel and pried with all his weight and strength, groaning. "Come. On...," he grunted.

The grate let loose with a shriek of iron on wood. Zee flew back into a stack of small crates with a cry. The crates, not yet lashed against the movement of the ship at sea, crashed down. The grate flipped into the air, banged off a beam above, then clattered to the floor, where it spun like a coin.

Jessup pulled himself to the lip of the barrel and clung there, watching the spinning grate with wide eyes. The grate clanged down, bounced, and clanged again before lying still. Jessup turned to Zee, his mouth hanging open and eyes even wider.

Someone shouted from a deck above, then more shouts rose from fore and aft.

Zee sat up. "Uh-oh..."

CHAPTER 11

Jad had seen the governor once before at an annual Zepiter festival in town, from a distance. He'd never thought the man would actually be speaking to him. He whipped off his hat and knelt clumsily on one knee. "Milord."

"Please, rise."

Jad hesitated but pushed to his feet.

"From what your esteemed mayor has told me, Mr. Tarrow, it is I who should bow to you." Governor jal Brigg's tipped his head and made a flourish with his hand.

Jad balked at the gesture but did not miss the amused condescension in the man's eyes.

"Under my direction, the mayor has rewarded you for your service today in the form of a tax levy waiver and a payment of coin, has he not?"

"He has, and very handsomely, milord Governor."

"No one can say their governor is not generous and kind to peasants who are truly loyal."

Jad bristled at the term "peasant," but said, "It is my pleasure, milord, to serve my governor and king."

The governor tapped his chin in thought. "You're the man whose son found the king's gold coin on the beach last year, correct?"

"Yes, milord. And it is in search of my son that brings—"

"Did he discover this creature as well?" Briggs interrupted.

Jad struggled with the honesty engrained in his character. "He did not, milord," he lied. "My son knows nothing of it."

Shouts of alarm arose from the ship.

Jad's heart sank. *Oh, no. Zee, what have you done?*

* * *

Zee scrambled to his feet and snatched up Jessup. The little creature was still getting bigger and heavier, but being able to hang on with ten arms helped. The voices of alarm grew louder.

Zee sped through the cargo to the stairs he'd come down, but footsteps sounded, and shadows fell over the staircase at the top. He darted away and back to a ladder.

"Here, move around," Zee instructed while pushing Jessup so he clung to his back and shoulders. Zee clambered up as the sailors tromped to the bottom of the stairs.

"Oy!" One of them pointed. "Get back 'ere, you!"

Zee pulled himself up off the ladder, then slammed the hatch down and slid the hook into place to secure it. Jessup whimpered as more shouts arose from an adjoining cabin and the sailors below banged on the hatch. Zee hurried up the next ladder to the gun deck.

Thankfully, the gun deck was still empty of personnel. Zee breathed a small sigh of relief and ran to the port side of the ship where it was docked to the pier. Looking out a gunport, however, he realized there was no way they could escape that way. The pier swarmed with sailors and city guards.

Zee heard alarmed voices of men and women on the ship, and a loud curse. Someone shouted, "The creature has escaped!" Muttered cursing and quick shuffling steps followed. "Search the ship!"

Zee turned to starboard, the side of the ship open to the harbor, and the open gunports there. Zee couldn't escape that way. But Jessup could.

He ran to the port farthest from the stairs and crouched between the cannon and bulkhead, hiding himself from the rest of the deck.

"Come on," Zee said quietly, pulling Jessup back around front of him. "You have to go in the sea, Jessup. There's no other choice."

"Zee not go in sea!"

"No, I can't, but you can."

Zee lifted Jessup to the port, but Jessup clung to his arms.

"Jessup not leave Zee."

"You have to. Who knows what they'll do to you. They might kill you if you stay."

Jessup's eyes grew wide and his arms tensed. "Why they want to kill Jessup? Is Jessup bad?"

"No, you're not bad. Please, never think that. It's just that they don't understand." Zee struggled with how to tell him the truth about what kind of creature he was. After everything he'd said about the dangerous beasts in the ocean—and the most dangerous of them all. "Jessup, I think you're a kraken."

Jessup's eyes grew wider, and his mouth fell open. "Jessup? Kraken?"

"Yes, and now they think so too. They don't understand. They think you're a monster."

Sounds of the search came closer. Someone stomped down the stairs from the main deck. "Please, Jessup, you have to go now."

Jessup's voice grew softer. "Jessup afraid."

Zee's eyes grew wet with tears and a lump formed in his throat. He was afraid too, but he wasn't going to let that stop him from saving his friend. "Remember the song I taught you, in case you ever had to go in the water?"

Jessup nodded, and Zee sang softly.

"Swimmy, swimmy, in the sea.
Swimmy, swimmy, and be free.
Just be careful, watch the deep.
Keep eyes open, safety keep."

Jessup said the rest with him,

"*Swimmy, swimmy, and survive.
Swimmy, swimmy, stay alive...*"

"That's it! But don't go back where I found you. They'll look there. Go far away, okay?"

Jessup made a noise that sounded like a sob and pulled close to embrace him. Zee's tears dripped down his shell.

Zee pushed Jessup back to look him in the eyes and spoke aloud. "Do this for me, Jessup, please. I want you to be free."

Jessup blinked big wet eyes. "For Zee. For friend." Zee nearly broke down sobbing, but lifted Jessup with a grunt and the little creature reached to the port.

On the outside of the ship, Jessup's cone-shaped shell and eyes cleared the port but he clung there high above the water. If a creature such as Jessup could gape and whimper, that's just what he did.

Zee started at a shout.

"Stop right there, ya li'l bastard!"

Zee peeked over the barrel of the cannon. On the other side of the ship, at the far end of the deck, a rough-looking sailor with muttonchops, buttons popped open over his bulging gut, and a peg leg, pointed a boat hook.

"That's the property of Lord Governor Briggs!"

Zee ducked back down as the man started clomping his way around to the starboard side, calling to the crew. "He's on the gun deck, ya sea-cretins!"

Zee pushed at the base of Jessup's shell. "Jessup, let go." Jessup whimpered again. "We'll see each other again someday, I just know it."

The man clomped closer, grumbling curses.

Zee sensed resolve from Jessup forming in his chest. His little friend said, "Jessup know, too," then launched himself out over the water.

Zee shoved his head through the gunport. A profound sense of loss flooded him and he nearly swooned as Jessup splashed down and disappeared below the surface, but the sailor's shouts and a jab in the shoulder by the boat hook brought him back to his senses.

"Ya shad-shite carpie!" the man cursed at him. "There'll be Postune's scaly hells to pay for that!"

The boat hook tore Zee's shirt as he scrambled under the barrel of the cannon to the other side. The big man stepped to block his escape, then lunged in to grab at Zee's leg, but Zee pulled himself back under the cannon, leaving the sailor wedged and cursing. Zee scurried away from the cannon.

More cries came as sailors slid down ladders and ran up to the gun deck. Zee glanced around, frantically seeking a way out. Once again, the only escape was down. He dove under the netting that edged the opening to the lower decks, where he just managed to catch the ropes and swing himself to the top of a high stack of crates.

A sailor in the room cried an alarm and stepped to a lower crate to climb up to Zee. Just as he reached out, the crate broke under him, sending him crashing onto another sailor who was pushing into the tight space.

While they cursed and shoved at each other, Zee swiped the tears from his face, leapt to the top of another stack of crates, then over the heads of more shouting sailors to a high pile of grain sacks. He lost his footing and tumbled down the other side. A sailor snatched at him but only got his scarf as he darted away. Another ripped his shirt with a grab, but Zee was small, quick, and emboldened by his success.

He'd rescued Jessup. He'd saved his best friend.

Through the deck he ran, room to room, weaving this way and that, leaving in his wake sailors crashing into cargo, knocking heads, and swearing as only sailors can.

* * *

Jad Tarrow feared the worst as he watched Governor Briggs stride up the loading ramp, the mayor tripping behind him. Somehow, Zee had snuck onto that ship. Jad knew it. He chewed his lip in mounting despair. He dared not say anything. Zee might escape. As long as he didn't go into the sea...

* * *

Dame Toomsil removed her riding gloves and handed them to her squire. "What's happening here, Tem?" She place her hands on the interior rail of the quarterdeck and looked down to the main.

"I don't know, ma'am. I mean, they loaded something for my father—Lord Governor Briggs, I mean to say—then a ruckus was kicked up below."

The disturbance below decks grew louder as Governor Briggs stomped to the top deck. "Captain, report!"

The captain glared at him. He turned to his quartermaster, a giant of a man, even taller and thicker than the captain, wearing belts of leather crossing his hairy chest and attached to his breeches. "Mr. Corl!"

"Aye, Cap'n." Corl strode to a stairway to the lower decks, bellowing, "What in Postune's bloody fins is going on down there?!"

As he peered into the darkness, Zee shot out between his legs and slid across the deck. Corl spun back in surprise. Sailors on deck cried out. More came charging up the stairs. The first mate bounced off Corl's broad back, knocking those behind her back down the stairs with a chorus of shrieks and foul language.

Zee rolled to his back and stared up at the glowering bearded face of the captain.

"A stowaway," the captain growled, then raised a boot, and stomped.

* * *

Zee squeaked and rolled, escaping the booted blow.

He leapt up and ran around a mast, then against the rail away from the dock, wheezing hard, eyes darting like a cornered rabbity. He could barely breathe, and his strength was waning fast.

"That's Zee Tarrow!" said a white-haired sailor Zee recognized as Mr. Trib. Trib had been glad to spin tales of dragons and the sea when slurping ale. His congenial mood was gone now.

* * *

From where he stood at the top of the ramp, Governor Brigg's eyes snapped to Jad down on the pier.

"Zee!" Jad made to move toward the ramp, but the governor's knight flicked his sword so the light of the sun glinted off its blade. City guards grabbed Jad by the arms.

"You must let me go to him," Jad pleaded. "Please, sir!"

The knight just sneered.

* * *

Another sailor on deck pointed at Zee and shouted. "He's diseased!"

Zee's hand clapped to his chest, realizing his shirt was torn open and his scarf gone, leaving his rash, scars, and patch of gray for all to see.

"Don't touch him!" another warned.

A rope snapped tight around Zee, pinning his arms to his body.

A cruel, gruff voice gloated, "No need." Corl croaked a laugh and hoisted Zee into the air on the end of an extra-long loop-pole. Its length barely bowed under Zee's weight. Zee kicked and tried to cry out, but his lungs burned, his breathing further constricted by the tightness of the rope.

"Zee!" Zee's eyes turned to the pier where his father struggled against two city guards. A knight laid the tip of a sword on his da's shoulder. Da ceased to fight, but the look on his face…

Zee's anger at his father drained away, replaced with shame and remorse, as well as fear for his da's safety. He wanted to shout that he was sorry, but all he could managed was a soft wheeze. "Da…"

The first mate scrambled back up the stairs from below. "The lord governor's cargo has escaped, Captain. The boy let it loose!"

The captain roared his rage and stomped over to stand next to Corl, glaring at Zee. "No one boards my ship without permission, and never has a thief laid a hand on my cargo!" He grabbed the pole and shook it violently. "Where is it, boy?!"

The best Zee could do was open and close his mouth, then shake his head.

The big sailor with the peg leg who'd found Zee and Jessup said, "Escaped into the sea, Captain. He shoved it through a port."

The captain roared again, grabbing the rope on the pole and cinching it tighter. Zee squirmed as the roughness of the line grated on his skin, his rash erupting with further agony. His vision blurred as he fought to breathe, sucking shallow, insufficient breaths.

"He can't breathe!" Jad Tarrow shouted, thrashing in the grip of his captors. "He has a condition!"

Zee saw the knight cuff his da across the mouth, crumpling him to his knees.

The ship's surgeon, roused by the activity below but having thought best to ignore the mad antics of the sailors, now came up the stairs. He inspected the boy dangling high above the deck, taking in the rash and the gray mark on his breast.

"A condition, ay?" the captain said. Cruelty gleamed in his eyes as he pulled harder on the rope. Corl chuckled low in his throat.

The lord governor approached. "Captain? If I may?" By the tone of his voice, it wasn't a request.

The captain grunted and eased his grip on the rope.

"Young man," the governor called to Zee.

Zee squeezed his eyes shut a few times, trying to focus.

"I am Lord Commander Farig jal Briggs, governor of this province, and you have interfered with the transport of my personal property. The penalties for these actions are severe." He put on an air of caring. "However, I can be lenient. Can you call this creature back to you, as a man would call a dog?"

Zee shook his head firmly.

"Do you know where it's going?"

In spite of his condition, Zee mouthed the word, "No."

The governor sighed dramatically. "Captain, do what you will."

"A dip in the bay will loosen his lips," growled the captain. "Mr. Corl!"

Corl marched to the rail and swung Zee out over the harbor.

A frantic cry came from Zee's da. "No!"

Zee writhed and kicked as a primal fear took him. Not the sea. Anything but the sea!

Corl and the captain sneered. No more questions, no options. Zee was swung down and plunged into the dark water.

* * *

A panic like Zee had never known seized him. The water was disgustingly warm. All sound dulled. Through the wavering surface above, he saw the sneers of the captain and quartermaster at the rail and the faces of sailors leering down at him.

He was plunged deeper into the darkness. Shapes darted at the edge of his vision, then came closer. Tiny salt-ranhas, all toothy mouths, and a slim cooda with a narrow snout full of fangs. He wanted to scream, but to do so was to die. The cooda made a glancing attack, tearing at what was left of his tattered shirt and nicking his arm. Zee struggled and kicked, his salty tears lost in the salt water. The undulating silver-black body of a young sheel, its wide mouth open to reveal rows of jagged teeth, lunged out of the darkness.

A flash of gray shot through the water. The point of Jessup's shell slammed into the sheel's gills, and Jessup discharged a pulse of blue electricity. The sheel recoiled, twitching.

Jessup's voice sounded in Zee's foggy mind, calling his name. The little creature clung to him, slapping the cooda and ranhas away. Jessup pulled at the rope, gnawed it with his teeth, but it was too thick.

With what consciousness Zee had left, he said, "*No, Jessup. Go, far away. Live a happy life.*" He wasn't sure what he was saying, but it made sense at the time.

"*Jessup save Zee!*"

A buzz rose in Zee's ears, and colored lights danced in his eyes. The pounding of his heart subsided and a great peace settled on his mind, overwhelming the sense of Jessup's panic, as well as his own. The seawater caressed Zee's skin, soothing the itch of his rash until it was completely gone for the first time he could remember. The gray patch on his chest pulsed with heat, but it was a pleasant feeling. Jessup's telepathic cries faded away. Zee closed his eyes. He'd be all right. Jessup would be all right.

And yet, Zee's body knew he had to breathe. His eyes and mouth popped open and he sucked in the salty brine of the sea.

* * *

The governor and mayor had joined the captain and Corl at the rail, one with a cold expression of inquisitiveness, the other fretting.

Bubbles burst to the surface.

"You've killed him," the mayor said, aghast.

"Maritime law, my good mayor," growled the captain. "Well within my rights."

"But… just a boy…"

"Haul him in, Mr. Corl." The captain clapped Corl on the shoulder and turned back.

Corl heaved on the pole to lift Zee high for everyone to see, to be a lesson to all, then nearly dropped it at what met his eyes.

Gasps from the crew spun Captain lon Bomba back around.

At the end of the pole, dripping wet, Zee wasn't dead. He wasn't human, either.

CHAPTER 12

Gills lifted rhythmically on either side of Zee's neck. More opened and closed between his expanding and contracting ribs, leaking seawater. His hands twitched, revealing webs of skin between his fingers. His toes had elongated, spread, and were also webbed. His skin was the same color as before, but his rash was gone, leaving the scars from scratching, the cuts from fish bites, and the gray patch on his chest plain to see.

* * *

The guards kept their grip on Jad as he pushed himself up to his feet on the pier, eyes red from sobbing, face wet with tears. At the sight of Zee he sobbed in relief—and dismay.

* * *

The captain gaped at the surgeon, who had an expression of more than scientific curiosity. There was also awe.

"Murfolk," the surgeon breathed. "One of the people of the sea…"

"I'll be shaddamned!" the captain roared, clapping himself on the thigh. "The shadbrat's a flapping mur!" He spun to Governor Briggs, challenge flashing in his eyes. "And by all the laws of the sea, he is mine."

Briggs looked as if he might draw his sword and cut the captain down, but controlled his temper, conceding to the maritime law of finds as it applied to murfolk. He spun and strode to the top of the ramp on the other side of the ship and glared down at Zee's da.

Zee tried to shout. Water gushed from his mouth instead of words.

"Bring in our prize, Mr. Corl," said the captain.

The quartermaster backed from the rail and swung the pole to drop Zee roughly onto the deck. Zee struggled to breathe, forcing water from his lungs through his mouth and gill slits.

The surgeon knelt next to him, setting his cane on the deck, and grabbed at the loop that still held Zee. "Remove this shorking rope, Mr. Corl!"

Corl grunted, unsure if that was a good idea. Like most people of Tosh, he'd probably never seen one of the murfolk. Few had.

"Now," the surgeon commanded, "unless you'd like to lose this prize for your captain as well!"

"Do it," Bomba confirmed.

Corl loosened his grip on the rope. The surgeon tugged the rope off, turned Zee on his back, and placed a rough, long-fingered hand on his chest. "Breathe, boy. Breathe."

Zee forced the water out with a great gush and a cough. He took a deep lungful of air, kept breathing, deeper and more freely than he could ever remember. He lifted his hand to clear the water from his eyes, then looked at it with more surprise than the others had shown when they'd seen him lifted from the water. He sat up quickly, gaped at the webbing between his fingers and the lung slits between his ribs, then gave a strangled cry as he touched the flaps on his neck.

As he continued to breathe the air, the webs retreated from his hands and feet, and the gill slits closed until they could no longer be seen, and his feet returned to human form. Zee ran a hand over his ribs, then realized the rash was gone, and with it, the itch he'd lived with all his life.

His eyes, filled with fear and childish wonder, met the surgeon's. "What's happening to me?"

Governor Briggs's voice rose before the surgeon could answer. "Your son knew nothing of the creature, ay?" He shot an accusing glance at the mayor, who stood next to him. "It appears we have been deceived by this Jad Tarrow."

Zee leapt up at hearing his father's name. "Da!"

The surgeon grabbed him by the shoulder and gave a quick shake of his head.

"But, my da…"

"Come," said the surgeon. He pushed himself up on his cane and limped across the deck, holding Zee by the wrist. Sailors stepped back and stared as they passed.

The mayor cleared his throat, drawing the governor's attention to the townsfolk crowded along the wharf at the end of the pier, and they did not look pleased. Some knew the kingdom's laws of land and sea, but all recognized torture and attempted murder of a child when they saw it.

"Nevertheless," said Briggs, shifting his tone, "my ship has its prize."

"The king's ship, milord," the captain amended from behind him, "under my sovereign command."

Fury flashed over the governor's features, but he knew better than to challenge the king's law—at least not in front of a crowd. Still, there was defiance in his reply. "Under lease to me, Captain, governor of all Akhtar Province."

The captain scowled.

Zee had to stand on tiptoes to see over the rail. A lump formed in his throat at the sight of his da held tight by the guards.

Back to Jad, and loud enough for the crowd beyond to hear, Governor Briggs proclaimed, "I am nothing if not a reasonable and generous man. You may keep your levy waiver and your coin, Jad Tarrow."

Jad breathed heavily, looking from Zee to the governor.

"This murlad, however," Briggs continued, "is hereby taken in lieu of my expected prize, conscripted into the service of His Majesty Brevor mon lin Phan's Tradeship Fleet and the HMT *Krakenfish*, as a ship's boy and hull scrubber."

Jad's jaw bobbed without words. He swallowed to clear the knot in his throat. "Is there nothing I can do, milord?"

"Perhaps the captain would take you in trade. Are you murfolk as well, Jad Tarrow?"

Jad blinked raw eyes, then shook his head.

"Then there is nothing you can do." The governor's gaze became harder. "And he is not, and never was, your son."

Zee's da shook with rage. He pulled at the guards, but they held him tighter. By the look on the face of the knight, he wanted very much for Jad to resist further so he could cut him down.

Though held by the guards, Jad managed to pull the sack of coin from his pocket. He stared at it, shaking it to hear the tinkle of gold. With a burst of strength, he tore one arm free and flung the sack out into the bay. Onlookers gasped. The water roiled as creatures fought over the boon dropped in their midst, thinking it something good to eat.

The knight drove a fist into Da's stomach and a guard threw an arm around his neck from behind.

"Da!" Zee cried.

"City guard!" Governor Briggs commanded. "Escort this man out of town, and make certain he does not return until after this ship has sailed."

They drug Zee's da back down the pier, listless and silent, his anger replaced by despair.

"Da!" Zee shouted. "I'm sorry! Da, please!"

The governor and knight's dragons roared as the guards dragged Jad off the pier. The crowd cried out at the sound and pushed farther away but Zee's da didn't even look up.

Captain Bomba shouted to the crew, "Heads up, you scallywags! We have a new ship's boy." To the first mate, he said "Ms. Tammet, have a tiny hammock set up in the berth." Turning to the ship's carpenter and smith, he instructed, "Mr. Loris, fit him for weights and secure them. We'll not have this prize swimming away. Mr. Corl, prepare the ship. We sail in a bell's time."

Crew got to work finishing the loading of merchandise and supplies, securing the hold, and readying the ship to sail.

The captain stepped closer to Zee—but not too close—and inspected him like he was prime livestock just obtained at auction. "Surgeon, give him a thorough looking over. Make sure that rash we saw is nothing to worry about." He said nothing about the wounds from Zee's encounter with the creatures in the bay.

"I will tend to his injuries as well," said the surgeon, not missing the oversight.

"That too," the captain replied offhandedly. "He'll need to be hale and hearty for what I have planned for him."

Zee looked from the captain to the surgeon and back. "What are you going to do with me?"

The captain backhanded him across the face with his beefy knuckles, nearly knocking him from the surgeon's grasp.

At the rail on the quarterdeck, Dame Toomsil glowered, but said nothing. She made her way down the steps to the main deck.

Zee's cheek stung and his head rang. The captain leaned closer, a vein on his greasy forehead throbbing. "You'll not open your filthy fish-trap in my presence without first asking for permission to speak and receiving it." Zee nodded quickly. "And you will at all times address me as 'Captain, sir.' Understand?"

"Yes, Captain, sir."

The captain grimaced at the knuckles he'd hit Zee with and wiped them on his jacket, then met the disapproving gaze of the surgeon. "He's a quick learner. I think we'll get along just fine." He sneered back at Zee. "If not, there's always the lash."

The surgeon glared at the captain, unintimidated. He squeezed Zee's wrist. "Come, lad."

Zee stopped as they passed the knight on the way to the doorway to the stairs below. She glanced at him, then looked away to gaze sternly along the ship.

"Dame Toomsil?" Zee pleaded softly.

She replied without meeting his eyes. "The captain is within his rights according to the king's law, and I have a sworn duty to uphold it."

Zee blinked back tears as the weight of his plight, whatever it really meant, truly hit home. He looked to the wharf where his da dragged his feet, head down next to Midge. A guard shoved him to keep him moving. From the shaking of his shoulders, he was crying.

"I'm sorry, Da," Zee whispered "I'm so sorry." He sniffed and started toward the door, but the surgeon held him back.

The surgeon stepped close to the knight and spoke quietly. "Is it your duty to uphold the law, or to do what's right?"

Her features squirmed with conflict, but she said nothing.

Zee looked up to where Temothy jal Briggs leaned on the rail of the quarterdeck, the dragons of the ship's knights above and behind him on the perch deck watching the proceedings with silent interest. Tem's eyes went from his father to Zee. None of his previously fixed expression of haughty superiority remained.

* * *

Jad Tarrow pulled his sleeve across his raw eyes, trying to control his ragged breaths. This is what he and Seela had feared since they'd found Zee mewling on the beach, washed up after a storm, and decided to care for him because they knew to leave him to the sea would mean his death, and they could have no children of their own. Zee was the reason they'd moved to the secluded farm and hid what they knew Zee to be, even though he suffered so.

Such a sweet, innocent boy. They'd kept the worst of the world from him. The cruelty, and the pain. He was about to learn just how hard and cruel it could be. And it was all Jad's fault.

Jad Tarrow's heart broke that day, as did his wife's when he later told her what had happened, never to mend again.

CHAPTER 13

Zee sat on the edge of a table in the cramped infirmary, absentmindedly feeling the rash-free skin of his forearm and gazing at his fingers where the webbing had been. The surgeon applied salve to his scratches, bandages to his deeper wounds, but Zee hardly noticed. It was like it was happening to someone else. He barely felt the prods and pokes as the surgeon inspected his skin, hands, and feet.

He'd lost his home, his family, and his best friend. The sense of it all was sinking in fast. The emptiness at the thought of never seeing his ma and da again. Or Jessup. The warmth in his chest and heat of the gray patch at Jessup's proximity was cooling. To add to his misery, his dragon-tooth necklace was gone. And he could breathe underwater. Or had he dreamed that?

The fear for the future hadn't yet begun.

"What's this then?" The first mate, Ms. Tammet, held Zee's pants in one hand, the lung-spritzer in the other.

"It's for my breathing." It sounded to Zee like someone else was answering. "I have a condition."

The surgeon took the old parfume decanter. "Do you know what's in it?"

"No, sir. My ma makes it."

The surgeon sprayed it in front of his face and wafted the mist to his nose. "Hmm…" He unscrewed the top, dabbed some of the liquid onto his finger, tasted it. After a moment of deliberation, he tipped a few drops on his tongue and sloshed it around. "Sea water, if I'm not mistaken. Strained for impurities, I'd guess, and with a hint of lyptus oil." He screwed the lid back on and set the spritzer down.

The surgeon felt Zee's ribs and placed a stethoscope on his chest. "Breathe in. Deeply, please."

Zee did, and marveled once again at how easy it was.

"And out. Keep breathing."

After several breaths, the surgeon moving his stethoscope to different areas of Zee's chest and back, he pulled the stethoscope from his ears. "The sound is different from what I'm used to hearing, but quite clear. Your ribs seem to be more flexible than those of humans as well." Before Zee could respond, the surgeon continued. "This rash you had, do you know its cause?"

"No, sir."

"And you've always had it?

"Yes, sir. My ma made an ointment that helped the itch and redness, but it never went away."

"Until now."

Zee brushed the rash-free skin of his belly with his fingertips. "Yeah."

Zee didn't flinch as the surgeon examined the roundish patch of rough gray skin on his chest with a long, thick finger. Zee noticed the scars on the man's hands, then the deep creases on his weathered face and crow's-feet at the corners of his eyes. He stared at the surgeon's one milky eye with a scar below that cut up through his bushy eyebrow above. He'd be a scary-looking pirate of a man if it weren't for the crystal-clear inquisitiveness and deep thoughtfulness of his good eye.

"And this?" the surgeon asked, regarding the gray patch.

"I don't know what that is, sir. I haven't had it long."

The surgeon gently scraped the tough gray area with a fingernail. "It's not scale or the lepsy. I'd say it's safe, though we'll keep an eye on it."

The first mate scrutinized the patch skeptically.

Zee looked directly at the surgeon. "What happened to me in the water, sir? Is there something wrong with me?"

The surgeon watched him a moment. "No, lad, you're just different from most people, is all."

Zee recalled what the surgeon had said when he'd seen him lifted from the bay. "What's a murfolk?"

The surgeon's good eye seemed to sparkle. "Something rare and wonderful, lad. Rare and wonderful indeed." His face became grave. "Though in this day and age, it does not come without a cost."

* * *

The surgeon led Zee along a short hall, his cane tapping on the floor. The first mate trailed behind them. Sailors pressed against the wall, staring at Zee, some of them scowling. The surgeon opened the door to his quarters.

The first mate said, "I have my orders, Doctor. The gilly is to be oriented and fitted for weights straightaway."

The surgeon stared down at her. Tammet was not a small woman, but the surgeon struck an imposing figure when he straightened on his crippled leg and squared his shoulders. "Perhaps the next time you come to me with an affliction from one of your visits to a less-than-reputable establishment at port, Ms. Tammet, I may find there is no remedy other than to burn it out with a hot iron."

Tammet paled. "Just... don't be long, then."

The surgeon ushered Zee through the door and closed it behind him.

The quarters were not large, but Zee's mouth hung open at the collection of items that packed the railed shelves lining every inch of the walls. Rocks and fossils, creatures floating in bottles of liquid, feathers, bones of strange beasts, but mostly books.

Zee touched book covers, marveling at the embossing and strange symbols. He jumped and pulled his hand back as the doctor spoke.

"Do you like books, Zee Tarrow?"

"I might, sir, but I don't know how to read."

"Is that so?"

"Yes, sir. My folks neither." Pain stabbed at his heart. Would he ever see them again?

"First of all," said the doctor, moving to half sit on the edge of a small desk piled with books and scattered with trinkets, paper, and quills. "My name is Drall tak Aenig. You are to call me Dr. Aenig."

"Yes, sir. I mean, Dr. Aenig, sir."

Zee caught sight of a globe attached to a stand. He approached slowly, hand reaching as if on its own. He stopped himself and looked to the doctor.

"Go ahead, it won't bite."

Zee wiped his fingers on the rough wool of the ill-fitting pants he'd been given from the ship's stores, then turned the globe gently. The entire world of Zhera, right there at his fingertips. Zee knew Zhera was almost entirely ocean, but to see it like that… The island kingdoms that scattered its surface looked insignificant in comparison to the vast blue of the sea.

The doctor stopped the globe and pointed to one of the little patches of land. "This is Tosh." He moved a fingernail along the writing on the area of brown and green. "That's what this word says."

Zee leaned closer. "Tosh."

"And here"—the doctor pointed with a quill from his desk—"is mon Tontuga, where we are right now."

Zee tilted his head in amazement. The world suddenly seemed so very huge and so very small, both at the same time.

Dr. Aenig pulled a folding canvas stool from a peg on the wall and set it up in front of his desk. He patted the seat, pulled a book from the shelves, and squeezed around to the other side. While Zee sat, the doctor eased into his chair with a groan, stretching his leg out beneath the desk.

Aenig tapped the cover of the book, the movement shifting his sleeve so that Zee noticed stains of red on the frayed and graying edge of the cuff buttoned snuggly to the man's wrist. Zee wondered why the doctor hadn't rolled up his sleeves to examine him.

"This is the only text I have that makes any mention of murfolk, the people of the sea. Even in all my travels, I have learned very little about them, though I've met a few on other ships. They aren't a talkative lot, though they can hardly be blamed for that."

"Why don't they like to talk?" Zee asks.

The doctor frowned and breathed a sigh through his nose. "Murfolk are exceedingly rare. For the longest time they were considered a myth. Then, twenty years or so ago, one was found wandering on a beach in a daze. Over the years since, more were discovered rolling in the surf, barely alive, or found hiding among the population in remote coastal villages. All were young, sometimes only infants, and had washed up on shore after a recent storm."

Zee's mind reeled. "You mean… is that what happened to me?"

"Most likely, yes."

"Then… Ma and Da aren't my ma and da?"

"They absolutely are, in spirit, which is the only way that truly matters."

That comforted Zee in a way, but he had to ask, "Where did I come from?"

Aenig spread his hands. "No one knows. Beneath the sea. Somewhere."

Zee sat stunned and silent.

"But now the mystery of your rash and breathing condition is solved. The murfolk can live on land, breathe the air, and pass entirely as human, except every so often they must return to the sea, even if briefly. It was the sea that cured you, Zee. Your true home."

Tears formed in Zee's eyes. "But… Ma…"

"I'm assuming your mother knew, and she's obviously a skilled healer. She figured out how to soothe your skin and ease your breathing problems without having to resort to submerging you in the ocean, which would have revealed your true form. She did that to protect you, Zee. So did your father."

"So people wouldn't know what I was?"

"And, I would guess, so you didn't either. So you wouldn't feel different, out of place, any more than you already did, perhaps. I'm sure they would have told you eventually, but you're still quite young."

"I'm seven."

"Well, yes…"

"Is it a bad thing to be a murfolk?"

"No, but it comes with a heavy price." Dr. Aenig considered before continuing. "By law, all murfolk are subject to seizure and conscription into service on ships of the realm. The youngest will do the work of a ship's boy or girl, but all are tasked with the work for which they are best suited. Difficult and dangerous work."

Zee's eyes darted about as he thought on that, then back to the surgeon. "In the water?"

"Deep-sea retrieval, crew rescue, underwater light repair, and scrubbing the hull."

"Oh… For how long, sir?"

The surgeon's features twisted uncomfortably at having to deliver the news. "It is a lifetime service, lad."

* * *

"Shut yer hole, gilly-boy!"

Zee flinched as a sailor jabbed his canvas hammock with a broom handle. He didn't know which sailor it was, and he didn't care. Curled up high in one corner of the berth, he rubbed his little fists in his eyes, trying not to cry. Or at least to cry more softly.

It was all too much to take in. Far too much. What he was. What he was to become. Everything he knew and loved was gone. Ma and Da, the farm, Midge, maybe even his dreams of being a dragon rider. All gone. And, somehow, the worst of all was losing Jessup. An indescribable loss, in body and spirit.

Zee placed a hand on the gray patch, which was now cool to the touch. The sense in his gut of the little creature had cooled as well, leaving a chilling void.

"*Jessup?*"

No answer.

Zee held in a sob. Would he ever see his friend again? Would he ever *have* a friend again?

He fingered the chains coiled and locked around his wrists, rubbed a heel at the ones on his ankles, and shifted in his hammock in an attempt to find a more comfortable position amid the chains locked at his waist. There was no more comfortable position.

"Even a gilly can't swim long with that much weight, so don't even try it, boy," the ship's carpenter, Loris, who was also the blacksmith, had told him. "You'll sink to the bottom, and something will make a meal of you." Just the thought of being alone and lost in the open sea terrified Zee, so he wasn't sure why they bothered.

All the lamps in the berth but one were extinguished. Zee furrowed his brow in the darkness. When he'd had lunch with Dame Toomsil, she'd said sometimes the least likely people could be accepted to Triumf's Citadel. Under special circumstances, and if they proved themselves worthy. Zee figured he was definitely under special circumstances, and decided then and there, even with all that had happened to him, this *would* happen for him. He'd cling to his dream of being a dragon rider and never let go. He would prove himself worthy, no matter what.

"You never know what the fates might have in store for you," his da would say. "What seems bad can swap to the good. What seems good can swap out to bad. Personally, I think it's kinda up to us."

Zee held on to that with all he could, let the heat of it grow and warm him and give him strength. Postune knew he needed something. He'd work hard, make himself stronger, and grow bigger. Even under these circumstances, if it was possible to make himself worthy, he was going to do it, or die trying.

To the soft movement of the ship, creaking of lines, muffled sounds of the night shift above, and snores of sleeping sailors, Zee wept silently until he could cry no more, and finally drifted off to sleep.

* * *

"*Swimmy, swimmy, in the sea.*

Swimmy, swimmy, and be free.
Just be careful, watch the deep.
Keep eyes open, safety keep."

The silver-blue light of Zhera's moons faded as Jessup swam deeper, singing the little song Zee had made up just in case Jessup ever had to go into the sea. He kept close to the bottom, eyes swiveling in vigilance, acclimating himself to the sounds of the ocean. Looking, listening, feeling out for danger.

A sheel circled in from the darkness. Jessup squeaked, blew out a cloud of dark blue ink, and dove into a narrow canyon in the coral. He kept going, winding his way through and swimming deeper.

"*Swimmy, swimmy, and survive.*
Swimmy, swimmy, stay alive."

Jessup added his own lines to the song.

"*To see Zee again.*
To see best friend…"

PART TWO

CHAPTER 14

Ten Years Later

There can be no doubt the boy has suffered, working the worst jobs on the ship, suffering harsh treatment, being harassed and, perhaps worse, simply ignored. The most difficult and dangerous of his assigned tasks is scrubbing the hull while at sea. Each time he goes down, there is a chance he won't return, at least not whole and alive. And yet, he has, every time.

* * *

Zee stood at the rail in his swim trunks, gazing over the sea while Loris checked the heavy chains what wrapped his wrists, waist, and ankles, then prepared a nearby capstan wound with cable.

The HMT *Krakenfish* had been approaching Tosh from the north before dropping anchor. The island was too long for Zee to see its full expanse, but his gaze was locked on the fading landmass to the east. At the far end of the island would be the key where he'd spent his youth, the house where he'd once lived and, he hoped, where his ma and da still did. Home. Below the secluded farm would be the rocky shore where he'd found Jessup and spent the best weeks of his life. It seemed like a lifetime ago. Someone else's life. A story he'd been told. A dream. One day he would see it all and his parents again. One day.

As hard as Zee's life had become, he'd never regretted the decision to save Jessup, and knew he never would. For months he'd tried to reach out with his mind to his little friend, to ask Jessup if he was all right, and just to see if he could. Jessup never answered. Never a twitch did Zee feel in the patch on his chest, which had grown very little over the years, and the feeling of Jessup's presence had chilled to a cold hollow in Zee's heart. A hollow that persisted to this day.

One of the dragons spoke gruffly to a squire who was shining armor on the high perch deck at the back of the ship. For a moment, Zee expected to see Dame Toomsil with her dragon, Peloquin, and their squire, Temothy jal Briggs. But, no. Representatives of Triumf's Citadel Academy had come to announce Tem's acceptance seven years ago, at the completion of his three-year squireship. Tem had turned seventeen, the requisite age for first-year cadets, and been taken to begin his training. Dame Toomsil did not take on a new squire, and she had been transferred to another ship several years ago.

Zee watched the dragon criticizing the squire's work. How it moved. The muscles rippling beneath its scales. The twitch of its mighty wings. The regal curve of its neck. Though he saw dragons every day now, and they would have little to do with him, he'd never lost his fascination with them, nor his desire to ride one and to be a knight of the realm.

Corl barked orders to the crew, who were busy scrubbing the decks, polishing the rails and brass fittings, and touching up paint. In two days' time academy representatives would be arriving again, this time for the squire who was shining armor above, Derlick don Donnicky, who had reached the end of his three-year squireship. The captain wanted the ship in pristine condition.

Derlick's eyes met Zee's and they shared in a nod. Of all the people on the ship, Derlick had been the most decent to Zee since Dame Toomsil had left, other than Dr. Aenig. They were the same age, would converse about dragons and squireship, and sometimes spar together down in the hold when no one else was around. He was the closest thing Zee had to an actual friend and colleague. Zee was certain Derlick would be accepted by the academy, and wished him well.

Loris clipped a cable to the chain at Zee's waist then tapped his shoulder, letting him know the rig was ready. Zee climbed to balance easily on the rail, breathed in deeply, then blew it out and held his breath, ready to suck in salty water as soon as he hit the waves. He took one more look at the island kingdom in the distance, then dove gracefully into the sea, producing nary a splash as he slipped beneath the waves.

* * *

Mr. Tarrow remains short for his age, and slim, but what muscle he has is hard as iron, forged through a decade of hard labor forced upon him by cruel masters, and arduous training he forced upon himself in the wee bells of the night. The scars from an affliction of his youth are now layered beneath many others. Some from terrible wounds inflicted by teeth of creatures of the sea while scrubbing the hull or on deep retrieval dives, others caused by accidents, and more from axe and dagger of marauders who nearly took the ship. The most wicked, however, were inflicted by the quartermaster's whip, for a petty crime I am certain Mr. Tarrow did not commit.

* * *

Zee jabbed at the base of the barnacles with his chisel, cracking them away from the hull. Seawater flowed in through his mouth and nostrils, out through the gills on his neck and along his sides as his rib cage rhythmically expanded and contracted. Breathing in the ocean was more natural for him now than breathing air had ever been.

He rolled his shoulders to work out the ache, reached hands marred from barnacle shards and bites from fish into the pouch attached to the coil of chain at his waist, and retrieved his scraper. Moving the tool forward and back, pressing hard, he worked to clear the debris from the area he'd chiseled. When he was finished with the scraper he'd use a holystone, either hard pumice or harder sandstone, depending on how tenacious the remnants were, to scrub the hull smooth.

It was grueling work, but Zee had never had a problem with hard work. "If a job has to be done, best to get it done and do it right," his da used to say. "Especially if you ain't got a choice." After all this time, the words of his father still came to him often, and he cherished them.

* * *

When Zee was barely nine years old, our carpenter, Mr. Loris, was thrown overboard in a fierce storm on a darkest of nights. While Loris sank, tangled in line, dazed and being dragged down by his tool belt, the crew shrieked and fumbled for lifebuoys and poles. All but Zee Tarrow, who without prompting clipped a line to his waist and dove after the carpenter, a man who had been most cruel to our young murman, swam deep, then tugged the line to be hauled in.

* * *

A slim cooda dashed after a shining saltperch. In an instant, Zee had his stinger out of its loop on his belt of chains and jabbed the attacking predator. Blue light sparked from the stinger, the fish thrashed and twitched, then was still. He watched it sink in the water. As expected, a larger fish shot in and gobbled it up.

The curious saltperch circled closer. Quick as a striking sheel, Zee snatched it with his hand, then bit it behind the head to cease its struggles. He returned the stinger to his belt and continued scraping away at the hull while finishing his fishy snack. Discovering his ability to catch small fish and stomach eating them raw had helped keep him healthy in spite of the meager meals provided to him on the ship. Dr. Aenig also snuck him extra food from the galley when he could.

* * *

I was able to revive Mr. Loris, alone in the infirmary and in my own way, of which all on the ship remain ignorant.

Earlier this year, another crew member was caught high in the rigging of a broken spar with a line around her neck. Even with the heavy chains Zee is made to wear at all times, he was first up the ratlines to free her. As far as I know, neither she nor Mr. Loris thanked the boy, though they no longer harassed him, and more than once their cold glares or a well-placed fist silenced the jeers of their mates.

Mr. Tarrow has also seen the ship boarded by pirates of the most heinous nature and engaged in the bloody battle that ensued. He not only survived, he fought alongside his crewmates with honor, aplomb, and a cold fury that surprised us all.

Through it all, the boy's spirit has remained indomitable. He has never lost his humble and generous nature or his sense of wonder, and his lifelong dream to be a rider burns as bright as ever.

* * *

Zee paused, listening while peering into the haze at the edge of his vision and scanning the depths. His hearing was better here, his eyesight sharper, especially in the dark, both in and out of the sea. With the nictitating lenses he could deploy, he didn't even have to blink. He'd also seemed to develop a heightened sense of impending danger. He was rarely surprised by a predator, large or small, and his terror of the sea had long since been replaced with a healthy vigilance.

The ocean brightened around him, and he looked to the shoal they'd anchored near. Multicolored fishes flitted among bright corals in sunlight that beamed between clouds high above. A sea tortle flapped by calmly. With all the terrors held by the sea, and Zee had seen plenty, there was peace and beauty here as well.

* * *

He still has his secrets, but I feel I have come to know Mr. Tarrow well. His character, and his will. The frightened boy who came to us, the weak, sickly, illiterate child has grown into a powerful, skilled, and confident young man who knows only the wisest kind of fear.

For my small part, in the periods of time Zee could spare from his duties, I have taught him to read, basic maths, natural science, history, and geography. Since his arrival, I have devoted myself to learning all I can about murfolk, going ashore at every port to seek out books and ask questions of scholars, and passing what I learned on to Zee. The records are scarce and the accumulated knowledge limited mostly to legend and speculation, but one theme persists. All the stories about the murfolk also involve tales of krakens, the ancient terrors of the sea.

Now I know why...

* * *

Zee finished scrubbing as far as he could reach from his current position. He tapped three times on the cable with the chisel. On deck, the carpenter or another sailor who had taken his place pulled Zee starboard three feet, where he began work again.

The cable formed a loop that stretched around the ship, passing through pullies with cranks on capstans that were mounted to iron tracks against the railings of the ship—the same rig Zee had seen the captain and Mr. Corl use to keelhaul a crew member caught stealing from the captain's quarters. Zee kept the hull so smooth, it had taken four passes for the man to die. Zee had been horrified, but it was only one of many atrocities and violent deaths he'd seen in his years aboard the *Krakenfish*.

The cable pulled again, and kept pulling. Zee hadn't tapped it, but he stuffed his tools in his pouch and gripped the cable, preparing to be drawn to the side of the ship and lifted back to deck, though he didn't know the reason. He was suddenly jerked to a stop.

The skin on the back of Zee's neck tightened and the hair stood on end. Danger lurked in the sea. He spun in the water, seeking its source. When he spotted the long sleek shape approaching at speed from the side of the ship away from Tosh and heard its terrible shriek, it wasn't what he'd expected. It was worse.

Seadragons weren't related to dragons, he'd been told. Rarer than other sea serpents and larger, they had heads similar to a dragon's and bodies like a snake, with four short, winglike fins. They were vicious beasts, with no more brains than a sheel, twice the hunger, and none of the caution.

Zee had seen one once before. He'd even had a hand in slaying it with a harpoon cannon. That time, however, he'd been on deck and the beast had been nowhere near the size of the shrieking terror that was heading straight for the ship.

CHAPTER 15

Dr. Aenig whipped around at the shrill whistle of the lookout.

"Seadragon!" the sailor high on the mainmast cried, pointing north. Another rang the quarterdeck bell in alarm. Sailors poured up from below deck.

Captain lon Bomba stepped out holding a chicken leg like a club. He flung it into the sea, ripped off his bib, wiped his greasy hands on the jacket of his uniform, and snatched a spyglass from one of the watch.

The seadragon's undulating body humped through the waves, approaching fast. It was easily as long as the ship itself.

"To the cannons!" the captain ordered.

Sailors scrambled to positions, and dragons were saddled and harnessed, all with swift and practiced efficiency.

"Bring Mr. Tarrow up!" Dr. Aenig shouted. The carpenter and another sailor heaved at the crank on the cable rig.

With a roar, the dragons took to the air. The first of the cannons, including a swivel cannon on the main deck, fired and missed. The dragons dove toward the threat, a Royal Crimson spouting flame, but the serpent submerged with a splash from its whipping tail.

* * *

Beneath the surface, the seadragon's eyes gleamed upon Zee as it barreled toward him. Zee steeled himself, stinger in one hand, cable held in the other. Attached to the cable as he was, he had nowhere to flee and nowhere to hide. He'd have to save himself in the open water, and alone.

Mouth full of swordlike teeth gaping and forked tongue reaching, the serpent lunged. Zee jerked himself up against the hull to avoid the snapping jaws, but a horn on the serpent's head slashed his thigh, and he was slammed into the hull. The creature's speeding body pummeled him against the ship as it rushed past. The water was blasted from Zee's lungs, and his skull pounded against the hard wood.

* * *

Aenig steadied himself against the sudden lurching of the ship.

The captain roared to the crew, "Keep your wits about you and your eyes peeled!"

Corl leaned over the rail, peering into the water. "Does anyone spy the beast?!"

The seadragon burst from the sea and launched itself over the rail. Corl tumbled back with a cry, barely avoiding the creature's jaws. Its long thrashing body sent sailors flying as it slithered fast across the deck, shrieking as it went.

Loris leapt out of the way, but the other sailor at the cable rig wasn't so lucky. The serpent crushed him in its jaws, taking the capstan with it and snapping the cable. It crashed through the rail and dove toward the sea.

Aenig spied the cable breaking loose, dropped his cane, and dove the best he could with his lame leg. He scrambled to grab the cable, cursing as it eluded his grasp.

A sailor swung his axe at the length of the beast as its body scraped along the deck, but his blade barely scratched the monster's scales. Its tail slithered through the broken rail, and the monster was gone.

Aenig cried out as the frayed end of the cable slipped through his fingers and slid over the rail.

* * *

Zee shook his head to clear it. It did nothing to reduce the throbbing of deep bruises all over his body and only increased the pain that stabbed through his skull. He closed his eyes and breathed in deep, purposeful breaths, just as he had when he was a child and suffered from his breathing affliction. The sharp jab of broken ribs caused him to gasp. He could barely move his right arm due to damage to his shoulder, and the wound from the seadragon's horn stung terribly. Worst of all, he recognized the deep ache of internal injuries.

His eyes snapped open at the sound of a something heavy hitting the water. The seadragon plunged back into the sea at the side of the ship, spitting out the body of a sailor and the broken capstan.

Zee stared at the end of the shredded cable sinking slowly, then began to swing down and away from the hull. Realizing what had happened, he returned the stinger to its place on his belt of chain and grabbed the cable with both hands. Gritting through the pain, he pulled himself along it toward the opposite side of the ship where it still hung from the surface.

Hand over agonizing hand, he made his way along the hull. Then the other end of the cable came loose from above, and he began to sink.

* * *

Riders shouted as they and their dragons caught sight of the beast. The Royal Crimson swooped closer to the surface, scorching it with fire. Most sea beasts they'd encountered would retreat upon seeing dragonfire. Not this one. The serpent shot out of the water, jaws snapping. The dragon tucked its wings and rolled, evading the attack, but received a glancing blow. It tumbled and nearly hit the waves while the serpent snapped at the dragon's wings. The dragon of the other pair, an Ice Diver, blasted the serpent with ice, turning the side of its head frosty white. The serpent shrieked and dove.

* * *

As strong a swimmer as he was with his webbed hands and feet, Zee had no chance against the weight of the thick chains on his wrists, ankles, and waist, let alone the length of cable locked to his belt. Through the water above, distorted images of the dragons searched the sea around the ship.

The serpent circled and fixated on Zee once more.

Hard as he fought, as grave as his circumstances were, his injuries and fatigue sapped his strength and his sight began to dim. Then he realized the sea itself was darkening from above. Muffled thunder rumbled through the water, followed by a distant roar.

* * *

Dr. Aenig pushed himself up on his cane, gazing toward the east end of the island of Tosh. Black storm clouds had formed where moments before there had been none. The storm grew quickly, heat lightning flashing—and it was moving swiftly toward the ship. A great roar vibrated through the ocean, like that of a pod of whales and a squadron of enraged dragons combined. With it came a wind that nearly blew him off his feet.

Holding his cap to his head, Captain Bomba took labored steps, leaning against the gale, to grip the ratlines where the surgeon steadied himself.

He shouted over the wind as the storm grew closer, shutting out the sun. "As if the biggest and most ill-tempered Postune-damned seadragon I've ever laid eyes on wasn't enough. What is this fresh terror, surgeon?"

"I'm afraid I can't help you there, Captain."

"You take me for a fool, surgeon?"

"You know I do."

Bomba scowled. "You must have a guess."

"I do not," the doctor lied. He did have a guess, but only a guess, and a preposterous one at that. He said no more.

Bomba grunted, preparing a coarse retort, when the storm reached them, black as night. Waves and wind rocked the ship, causing it to buck and heave. Seawater splashed over the rail. The roar came again from the deep. Closer. Louder. And lightning flashed.

* * *

Lightning flickered on the surface above, strobing the depths in eerie luminescence, and a roar shook Zee to his bones. In a fever dream of half consciousness, a warmth Zee hadn't felt in a decade swelled in his gut, and the rough gray patch on his chest tingled. Then a voice intruded into his mind.

"*Jessup is coming, Zee. Friend is coming.*"

The voice was deeper than Zee remembered, but… *could it be?* An approaching darkness took shape at the far reaches of his vision. Large, crackling with zigzags of blue electricity, and moving fast.

"*Jessup?*"

A rushing sound in the water and the seadragon shot toward Zee from below, mouth gaping wide. The massive speeding shape collided with the serpent with a concussive whump, followed by a shriek and a roar.

Zee spun violently in the wake and became tangled in the cable as he sank. He fought to stave off the oblivion that threatened his consciousness, and the world went white.

* * *

The ship lurched and shook as it was slammed from beneath. Drenched and in terror, the crew hung on for their lives.

Dr. Aenig swiped the brine and soaked hair from his eyes. Roars and shrieks came from below the surface, on this side of the ship, then that, then below again. Bomba cursed as he clung to the ratlines. As bolts of lightning illuminated the waves, they caught brief glimpses of dark, octopod-like arms wrapped around the seadragon; a flash of a gray, thorned shell; and thrashing that sent up spouts of seawater.

Bomba looked on in disbelief. "Postune save us all."

The ship was struck again, harder than before. The crew cried out. Blue light flashed in the deep. There came a monstrous keening cry—then nothing.

The lightning diminished to soft flashes high in the sky and the wind slowed, but the darkness remained.

Dr. Aenig glanced about, scanning the calming sea for any sign of the creatures—and for Zee. With a groan of creaking timbers, the ship began to tip forward.

In a flicker of heat lightning, the doctor caught sight of a thick, suckered arm slung over the forecastle. Then another writhed up over the rail next to it.

The captain saw it too. "No…"

The arms pulled, and a great weight tipped the ship farther. Aenig and the captain clung tighter to the ratlines and hung with feet slipping beneath them. The crew screamed, scrambling to catch hold of something, anything, some sliding on the deck toward the bow of the ship to slam into stair rails, masts, and the forecastle wall. The dragons, driven to the perch deck by the storm, dug their claws in to keep from sliding off, their knights hanging tight atop them as the back of the ship rose out of the water.

The forecastle rails splintered beneath the weight of the beast. A gray, thorned shell rose over the forecastle deck, then a great green eye beneath a massive octopod brow glared upon them.

Bomba gaped in terror. "It can't be…"

"It is…," Aenig replied.

Bomba screamed, "Kraken!" He waved manically at the crew. "Attack, you sea-cretins!" None of the crew were in any condition to fight. He screamed back at the perch deck. "Dragons! Repel the beast!"

The dragons hesitated, working up the courage to do battle with a monster they instinctively feared but had always been told didn't even exist.

"Wait!" Aenig shouted.

Another arm was lifted above the bow. It uncoiled slowly, then gently deposited the body of Zee Tarrow on the deck.

A voice like the sea itself rose from an unseen mouth below the shattered rail of the bow. "Save friend. Save Zee."

All on the ship were stunned to silence.

Aenig was the first to recover, and the only one to move. He lowered himself to the main deck and let loose of the ratlines, allowing himself to slide to the stairs at the fore.

"Surgeon!" Bomba shouted. "What in Postune's hells do you think you're doing?!"

The doctor ignored him, straining to raise himself on the stair banister and step awkwardly across the steps, now nearly horizontal.

He stopped, staring down the inclined deck into the eye of the beast. Of all the horrifying sights he had seen in his life, never once had he laid eyes upon a kraken. No one had. He had no doubt, though—this was a kraken. Alive, on their ship. *And it knew Zee.*

That thought, and the sight of Zee, battered, unconscious, and barely breathing, gave him strength and courage. He let go of the banister, using his palms and heels to slow his sliding descent, until he lay next to Zee, staring up into the eye of the one true beast of the sea.

He swallowed, dried salt stinging his throat. "I'm a surgeon. I will help him."

The creatures eye narrowed as it studied him. "Promise, surgeon?"

"I swear to mighty Zepiter and great Postune, and in the name of Zhera herself, I will do everything in my power to heal him."

After brief speculation, the beast pulled even closer. "Jessup will be watching, surgeon." It took an effort of will for Aenig not to cringe back. The kraken began to lower itself, setting the ship to rocking.

Aenig shouted, "Wait!" The creature paused, then raised up to look once more at the doctor. "Jessup. Is that your name?" There was suspicion in the kraken's eye and he remained silent but did not leave. "Why are you doing this?"

"Zee is best friend," Jessup answered as if it was obvious. "Zee saved Jessup."

Aenig watched, incredulous, as the beast lowered itself into the water. With great care, it let the bow ease up until the ship rested, rocking gently, and the kraken disappeared into the sea.

* * *

The carpenter kicked open the door to the infirmary and rushed in with Zee's limp body bundled in his arms. Dr. Aenig followed, the captain behind him. Corl and several mates also shoved in. A dozen crew crowded in the hall, craning for a look.

There were murmurs from the crew in the hall.

"A real live kraken…"

"...saved Mr. Tarrow..."

"...saved the ship..."

"Never in all my years..."

Aenig pressed a hand to Zee's pale and damp forehead, checked his pulse, then his eyes, which were rolled up in his head. He gently probed the deep purple bruising on Zee's ribs and lower abdomen, then grabbed the lock that held the coil of chain at Zee's waist. "Get these damnable things off him!"

"Absolutely not," Bomba commanded.

Aenig turned on him. "I cannot treat him properly under these conditions, Captain!"

Bomba scowled.

"I'll do it," said the carpenter.

The captain frowned more deeply. "Only if you fancy a dance with Mr. Corl and the cat-o'-nine tails, Mr. Loris."

Aenig growled. "Do you want to lose your precious hull scrubber merely for fear he might escape, in his condition? On deck, you called upon Postune to save us all. She may have done exactly that. What will you do to help save this boy?"

The captain grumbled, then acquiesced. "All right!"

Loris said, "I'll get the keys," and bolted out of the room, shoving crew out of the way as he went.

* * *

The last of the chains jangled to the floor. Aenig tied off the catgut he'd used to stitch a gash in Zee's scalp, then spun to the room. "Everyone, out!"

"You can't mean me," said Bomba.

"Especially you."

Bomba growled, "You just make sure that gilly lives."

"I'm doing everything I can, Captain. Now, out."

Bomba swiped a hand at the others. "You heard the man!" He groused as he pulled the door shut, "Bastard thinks he's captain now."

* * *

In the hall, Bomba slammed the door and turned on the crew. "Back to work, you lot. There are repairs to be done." He grabbed Tammet and another sailor as they began to move off. "Not you two. Stay right here and make sure that gilly goes nowhere."

"Aye, Captain."

The captain glared at the door, clenching his fists, then spun and stomped down the hall behind the scurrying crew.

* * *

Aenig leaned on the table where Zee lay as peaked as a whitefish, breathing in short, gasping breaths that grew weaker by the minute. He looked at the lad with grave concern, but also wonder, then sighed, half groaning.

Truth was, Aenig hadn't done everything he could to save Zee, and the boy was fading. His expression squirmed with inner turmoil. The boy was worth it. More than worth it. Perhaps essential. And he had made a promise—to a kraken, no less.

He limped to the door, jerked it open, and shouted at the nearest mate. "Tammet, go to the kitchen and get me eels. Two buckets full."

Tammet stared blankly.

"Hurry!"

"Aye, Doctor!" Tammet spun and sprinted down the hall.

Aenig shouted after her, "Live eels, mind you!"

* * *

Tammet hurried in with a bucket in each hand, sloshing water. "There were only enough eels for one bucket, the other is sea slogs. The cook wasn't happy."

"The cook be damned. That will have to do. Put them there and take your leave. Quickly."

Tammet set the buckets near the table and rushed out the door, closing it hard behind her.

Aenig eyed the squirming buckets of sea life.

He would try, for Zee's sake. He just hoped he still had the power to accomplish the task.

The doctor held his hands out over the buckets and rubbed them together as if washing them in the air. He closed his eyes and set his jaw, all the while taking deep, even breaths. He reached out with his mind and spirit. An old feeling returned as he drew elements of Empyrean deep into what was left of his crucible. Mining it. Refining it. Forming it. Once it was fully processed, he sparked it to life, feeling the old power flow through him. When he opened his eyes, he was pleasantly surprised to see golden light swirling over his fingers and palms. The residual power of creation, left over from the world's forming. It was a tiny ember compared to what he was once able to conjure, and his crucible was withered and weak, but he prayed it would be enough.

He muttered arcane words—an incantation the magickers at the citadel would never teach their students or use themselves, even if they knew it. Red light, licking the air like flames, limned the golden glow of his hands, wreathed in black shadow. A forbidden power, deeper, and darker. Continuing his incantation, thin tendrils of red reached from the creatures in the buckets to his hands. The eels and slogs writhed, then thrashed wildly, splashing water over the floor as the tendrils throbbed and grew brighter.

Aenig drew the power to his hands. The red began to consume the gold like crimson fire. With it came an icy chill he remembered well—and abhorred, so cold it burned at his soul.

He moved his hands until they hovered over Zee. "Young Mr. Tarrow, forgive me." He slammed his palms onto Zee's chest.

* * *

The mates in the hall jumped as the door thumped behind them and a wind of blackness mixed with red and golden light blasted through the crack beneath it. They gazed at each other in shock, then thrust open the door.

"What was that?!" Tammet shouted.

Aenig was hunched over Zee, leaning on the table edge, his hair hanging down over his face, drenched in sweat.

Tammet stepped in cautiously. Steam rose from the buckets on the floor. Inside, the eels and slogs were black and shriveled in a slop of inky goo.

"What happened to those?"

The surgeon turned his face to her, exhaustion lining his grayed, feral features. "I'm sure I don't know, Ms. Tammet. Perhaps bring me better ones next time?"

On the table, color returned to Zee's cheeks, and his breathing was steady and deep.

* * *

A match sparked and the flame of the desk lamp glowed in Dr. Aenig's quarters. The surgeon slumped back in his chair, pinched his nose, and rubbed his face. Though the method he'd used to heal Zee had been far weaker than he could once perform, it had taken far more out of him.

He poured himself a snifter of brandy, took a generous swig, then retrieved the letter he'd been writing from a drawer. After setting a dish of red wax on a heating stand, he inked his quill and continued writing.

Upon completing his task, he signed it:

With all sincere urgency,

Dr. Drall tak Aenig
Ship's Surgeon
HMT Krakenfish

Aenig retrieved a stamp from a hidden and locked box. He folded the letter and affixed a family seal he hadn't used in many decades, then placed it in an envelope, addressed it, and sealed it with the stamp of the ship.

CHAPTER 16

The rough gray patch on Zee's chest prickled, stirring him from deepest sleep, and a pleasant warmth spread through him. A voice came to him in his mind. "*Zee okay?*"

Zee's eyes snapped open. "Jessup?"

Posted inside the infirmary door, Tammet jumped, dropping her mug of morning grog to crash on the floor. "You're awake," she uttered. She ran from the room. "Doctor! He's awake!"

The voice came again. "*Zee?*"

"I... ohh..." Zee groaned out loud at the pain in his ribs, gut, and limbs as he sat up, then winced, placing a hand on his bandaged head. He looked himself over, at the bruises and wraps, then grimaced as he bent his elbows, then knees. "*I'm pretty beat up, but I'm all right, I think.*" Then the full realization of who he was speaking to hit him. "*Jessup? Is that really you? I thought it was a dream!*"

"*Zee is okay. Jessup go now. No more trouble.*"

"*What? No, please stay!*" Zee felt Jessup's relief flood into him through the invisible tether that connected them. He didn't want to go. Zee threw off his sheet and swung his legs over the edge of the table. "*Wait, what trouble?*"

Dr. Aenig hobbled in on his cane, then stood staring at Zee as if he couldn't believe his eyes. The surgeon looked haggard, like he hadn't slept in days, but smiled and came closer.

"How are you feeling, Zee?"

"Aching, but—"

"Can you walk?"

"I think so."

The surgeon helped Zee steady himself as he lowered his feet to the floor. "Good, good. Now you must come with me." He handed Zee a pair of his best pants and a new white blouse. "Put these on, quickly now."

* * *

They hurried down the hall. Even with the pain and stiffness of his injuries, Zee felt stronger, lighter. He was still in a daze as the memories of what had happened when the seadragon attacked came back to him—that it was Jessup who had struck the beast, that his childhood friend was actually here—so it was only then that he realized his chains had been removed. He touched his waist in amazement, checked his ankles, and stared at his wrists, the skin callused, scarred, and stained from years of being shackled. They'd used more and heavier chains as Zee had grown and only taken them off to put more on. Now they were gone. "What's going on, Doctor?"

"Your little escapade with the seadragon, and especially your manner of rescue, have caused quite a stir."

"How long was I asleep?" The quarterdeck bell rang above. "What's happening?"

The surgeon stopped at the bottom of the steps to the main deck and turned to look down at him with a glint in his good eye. "You were unconscious for two nights and a day, but you're mending well. And the citadel is coming."

Zee had almost forgotten. Representatives from Triumf's Citadel Academy were coming to inform Squire Derlick don Donnicky if he'd been accepted into the academy or was to be relieved of his duties and sent back home.

Dr. Aenig led the way up the stairs.

Zee winced and raised a hand at the brightness of the morning sun as he followed Aenig onto the main deck. A shadow passed across the bow. He lowered his hand. It was a dragon. One of many. More than Zee had ever seen. They soared through the air, fully armored knights on their backs, all around the ship and out over the water.

He spun slowly in astonishment. On the glassy sea were ships of His Majesty's Navy. Dozens of them, in a perimeter several hundred yards across around the ship, with cannon ports open, guns at the ready, and harpoon cannons manned on decks. But why?

"Jessup…" They were here because of the kraken. Fear for his friend gripped him. The feeling in his stomach grew warmer, more taut, as if an invisible line tugged at his core, and the patch on his chest heated. Jessup was close.

A call came from the crow's nest, and the quarterdeck bell rang out the signal of someone approaching in the distance. Bells rang on the other ships as well. On the perch deck, the riders and dragons drew to attention, armor gleaming. Squire Donnicky stood rigid and nervous as he awaited judgment, peering at the sky in the direction of Tosh.

Three specks appeared through low clouds, off the coast of the island nation. The representatives from the citadel were approaching.

"Tarrow!" The captain's gruff voice made Zee jump. Bomba stomped up to gaze down at him. "It's about time you were up and about."

"Yes, sir!"

Bomba thrust a hand over the deck. "Join the crew, then!"

The crew was all on deck, dressed in their finest, which meant their shabby clothing was at least freshly laundered and pressed, but they weren't in formation yet—and all of them were staring at him.

Zee swallowed and looked to the doctor, who nodded. He went to lean on a set of ratlines, grimacing at the lingering pain from his injuries. He noticed the condition of the rails. They'd been hastily repaired from damage taken during the seadragon attack, Zee assumed.

He reached out to his old friend. *Jessup, are you all right?*

"Jessup okay."

"Where are you?"

"Swimming, not far."

"Good. Don't go anywhere, okay?"

"Jessup stay."

A tingle beneath Zee's shirt brought his hand to the patch on his chest, and he smiled at the warmth that surged in his heart. He could sense his friend was nervous, but also happy to be nearby. *"Thank you."*

Zee watched the three dragons approach. Other dragons parted before the new arrivals, some falling into formation to escort them.

Zee had seen this ceremony before—though with nowhere near this many dragons, and no ships. First, when they came for Tem. He'd been accepted after the academy's Academic Board considered reports of his service from Dame Toomsil and, Zee assumed, because of his name and status. His father was a White Titan Class lord commander, after all, as well as a governor.

Twice more the citadel had come for squires during Zee's tenure on the ship, taking them to embark on the next step in their lives' adventures. To be chosen by a dragon to bond with and be trained as riders in the hopes of becoming knights of the realm. Each time they soared away over the glinting waves, Zee had watched with wistful yearning. As unrealistic as it was, he still dreamed of being a knight.

Zee's gaze roamed over the crew. People he'd spent years of his life with, and none of whom he'd ever really gotten to know. The two other cabin boys who had never spoken a kind word to him, now promoted to sailors in their own right. Loris, the carpenter, and the lookout, whose lives he'd saved. The scowling captain and cruel Mr. Corl.

After all the years he'd spent on the ship, one thing hadn't changed much since his childhood. He still had no real friends, and when he had someone close, they eventually had to leave.

At least he'd had Donnicky, and before him, Dame Toomsil. She'd taught Zee how to use a sword, knife, and hatchet so Tem would have a sparring partner, much to her squire's chagrin, then continued his training after Tem left.

Then there was Dr. Aenig, who'd given him everything. He was more a mentor than a friend, but he'd bestowed upon Zee the ability to read, knowledge of the world, and even hope. Other than the fact that Zee was one of the murfolk and Aenig was clearly interested in them, Zee didn't know why the man spent so much time with him or treated him so well, and perhaps he never would. Still, Zee would be forever grateful.

"Attention!" the captain roared. All the crew but those manning the guns ran to their places in formation. Zee headed for his usual position at the back, but Loris and old Mr. Trib pushed the sailors next to them to the side to make room for him in the front line. Zee was surprised by the uncharacteristic show of respect but took the space between them and stood at attention, ignoring his aches and pains.

The dragons from the citadel drew nearer, one with the blue-and-gold banner of the academy flapping on a spear shaft that rose from the back of the rider's saddle, which was typical of these occasions. But the dragon and rider pair in the lead…

The knights, dragons, and squires on the perch deck stiffened to even greater attention. Murmurs arose from the crew. The dragons from the academy circled the ship, and with a sharp intake of breath, Zee saw why.

The lead dragon, a Greatwing with silver-green scales, was larger than other Greatwings he'd seen. Shining red barding adorned her chest, and she wore a red helmet fitted between her horns. The rider was not in combat armor, nor the drab uniform normally worn by an academy admissions representative. Instead, he wore a blue dress uniform and a red mail vest festooned with medals and ribbons, with two sea stars on his shoulder plate.

This was no ordinary representative or dragon knight, but Peleus ran Aureosa, a Daimyo General, Red Titan Class, and the commandant of Triumf's Citadel Academy.

Zee watched in slack-jawed reverence as the commandant landed on the perch deck, the ship's dragons and knights pressing back to make room. One of the other representatives landed there as well, and the third flew to the front of the ship to alight on the forecastle. Both were Gold Class lord commanders, fully armored and armed.

Zee looked to Dr. Aenig, who stood among the mates behind the captain, calm as could be, hands clasped in front him, holding his cane. The surgeon's eyes met Zee's, revealing nothing, then returned to the perch deck.

Together, the commandant dragon and rider pair struck an imposing image. Not only were they in one of the highest positions at the academy, reporting only to the superintendent, equal to the dean of academics and the dean of magicks, and in charge of all military training and discipline, their Red Titan Class made them one of only three pairs that held that threat level in the entire kingdom.

As the man dismounted, the knights and squires saluted crisply while their dragons lowered their heads. Commandant Aureosa saluted back, and his dragon nodded. The commandant and his dragon spoke briefly, then he went to greet the ship's knights and their squires, including Derlick don Donnicky. All the while, the captain and crew waited at attention on the main deck.

Commandant Aureosa made his way down the steps from the perch deck to the quarterdeck, followed by the knight armored in gold, then down more steps to the main deck. He appeared to be in his sixties, though younger than Dr. Aenig, but it was difficult to tell. Riders who advanced to bond ratings as high as his lived longer than normal people.

Aureosa set foot on the main deck, followed by the Gold Class knight who had also landed on the perch deck. The Gold Class knight who had landed on the forecastle joined them.

The captain saluted the best he could, which wasn't very well. "Welcome aboard, Daimyo General Commandant. It is a great honor to receive you on the HMT *Krakenfish*. The admiral sent me a message by carrier gull after I reported the attack to him and, of course, the kraken that I found."

Aureosa's stern features revealed a hint of amusement. "That you found, is it?" He headed toward the rail.

The captain huffed and stepped quickly to keep up with the man's long stride. Dr. Aenig followed as well, along with Corl and the mates.

"Why, of course," Bomba said. "It took all the might I and my crew could muster to fend off both a particularly large and ill-tempered seadragon *and* a kraken, but we accomplished it with brave aplomb." He leaned closer, speaking in a conspiratorial tone. "We've come across more rare beasts of disproportionate size and disposition of late. It's unnatural, if you ask me."

"I didn't ask, but thank you, Captain. I'll make a note of it." The commandant placed his hands on the hastily repaired rail and looked out at the waves. "You're certain the kraken is still here?"

"We believe so, sir. We hear a rumble from below now and again, a terrible sound, and its monstrous shape is seen moving in the depths." Bomba glared at the water. "We would have dispatched the demon, but the admiral ordered us to leave it be. I have no idea why."

The commandant's dark amber eyes fell on the captain. "Because I asked him to."

"I… of course, Commandant. My apologies."

The commandant's brow knit in contemplation as he gazed at the sea, then he removed his hands from the rail and addressed the captain while looking over the mates. "I would speak to your surgeon. A Doctor…" His voice trailed off as his eyes fell on Aenig, his eyes widening ever so slightly.

Before the captain or commandant could speak, the surgeon stepped forward, reaching out his hand. "Daimyo General Commandant, sir, I am Drall tak Aenig, ship's surgeon, at your service."

The commandant collected himself and shook the doctor's hand. "Aenig… of course."

"May I propose we retire to my quarters for conversation and a glass of wine?"

"I believe that would be in order. Thank you, Doctor."

Aenig gestured to the stairway that led down to his quarters. "This way, please." One of the knights in gold opened the door for them.

The captain's face burned with indignation. "This is highly irregular."

The commandant peered down his nose at the man, one eyebrow with a burn scar raised high. "Is it, Captain?"

Bomba flustered. "I... suppose not, Daimyo General, sir." The commandant turned to follow Aenig below. "Will you be staying for lunch, sir?" the captain asked. "We've prepared—"

"My apologies, Captain, but I'm needed back at the academy as soon as possible."

"Yes, sir, of course, sir." Bomba fumbled another salute, sweat beading on his ruddy face.

When the door had shut behind Aenig, Aureosa, and the citadel knights, Bomba cursed and wiped his sweaty hands on his jacket. He glared at Corl, who shrugged.

Zee had no more idea what that was all about than they did. All any of them could do was wait. Corl ordered the crew to return to their ease, so Zee went to the rail and looked down at the sea, hoping for a glimpse of Jessup. He knew it was best that his friend stay out of sight, but he could still talk to him.

"*Jessup?*"

"*Zee, you okay?*"

"*I'm fine, though I'm not sure what's going on. Are you all right after fighting with the seadragon?*"

"*Jessup fight worse monsters than seadragon.*" Zee could sense that his friend was smiling. "*Jessup talking to Zee. Seadragon dead.*"

Zee chuckled. He wasn't sure how to best broach the subject, so he just asked, "*Do you remember when I told you what you are, on the ship?*"

A moment passed before the answer came. "*Jessup is a kraken.*"

Zee tried to sense how Jessup felt about that, but he couldn't tell. "*Those silly songs we used to sing were wrong. Krakens aren't bad. Not all of them, anyway. You're not bad.*" Somehow, Zee could tell that his old friend was amused, somewhere in the deep. "*What?*" he asked.

"*Songs not silly. Jessup still sings them to feel better, to remember Zee. Songs not all wrong either. 'When the kraken comes arising. Even dragons flee.' That part true.*"

Zee laughed softly. "*Do you remember when the men put me in the water after I came for you on the ship?*" Zee felt Jessup's anger rising. "*It's okay, don't worry about that now, I'm talking about when I changed.*"

"*Zee breathed with gills like fish and grew webby hands and feet like froggy. Zee had them when Jessup brought Zee up from sea after killed seadragon.*"

"*It's because I'm a murman,*" Zee explained, "*one of the murfolk, the people of the sea, not a human like everyone else.*"

"*Good, they are bad people.*"

"*They're not all bad. Some of them have helped me a lot.*"

Jessup seemed to think that over. "*Surgeon is good? Helped Zee?*"

"*Yes, very much.*"

Jessup's concern seemed to dissipate entirely. "*Okay.*"

Zee couldn't help the smile that spread across his face. "*I can't believe you're really here!*"

"*Jessup can't believe either.*" The joy they shared through their connection bloomed.

"*How did you find me?*"

"*Jessup felt Zee was in trouble.*"

"*Wait, where were you?*"

Jessup didn't answer.

"*You stayed, didn't you? After I told you to leave and never come back.*"

"*Jessup left for long time, went deep and far. Saw many things. Fought many fights. Survived. But... comes back sometimes, hoping to see Zee.*"

"*You* are *a bad kraken.*" In spite of the admonishment, Zee was grinning, and he could tell Jessup was too.

"*Bad kraken. Not sorry.*"

Out of the corner of his eye, Zee glimpsed a couple of sailors staring at him as if he was crazy and realized he was giggling like the seven-year-old kid he'd been when he and Jessup used to romp on the beach. He cleared his throat and forced a fake scowl until they turned away.

While everyone else waited impatiently for the commandant and doctor to reemerge from below, Zee and Jessup passed the time telling each other what they had been doing since they'd last seen each other. Zee could feel Jessup growing angry when he explained the kinds of duties he'd had aboard the ship, so he tried to make it sound less grueling, his shipmates less cruel.

Zee learned that life had been no easier for Jessup than it had been for him, comprised largely of hunting for food, avoiding ships, hiding from predators until he'd grown large enough to fend them off, and fighting for his life.

Zee asked, *"Have you seen any murfolk like me in your travels?"*

"No murfolks."

"Any other krakens?"

A sadness seeped to Zee from his big friend. *"No krakens either."*

"That doesn't mean there aren't any, just that we haven't found them yet. We'll look again, one day. I promise."

That cheered Jessup up. *"One day."*

* * *

Bomba paced the deck, becoming increasingly irritated as the time passed, and it was over a bell before the door swung open. The crew rushed back to formation, then saw it wasn't the commandant but one of the citadel knights.

"The commandant requests the attendance of Mr. Zee Tarrow," the knight announced.

Zee turned back from the rail. "Me?"

CHAPTER 17

Bomba glowered at Zee, who stared back in shock. "You heard the man, hull scrubber. Hop to it!"

Zee gulped, patted his shirt and trousers to straighten them, then hurried across the deck.

Bomba stepped to block his path and spoke with soft menace. "Be careful what you say about your captain in there, gilly. Wouldn't want the Daimyo General to get the wrong impression."

"I'll try not to speak of you at all, sir," Zee replied, caught off guard.

"Oh, you will, boy. And it will be glowing praise. Understood?"

"Yes, sir."

The captain stepped aside. "Hurry, then. Mustn't keep the commandant waiting."

The knight followed Zee as far as the bottom of the steps. "They're in the surgeon's quarters. You know where it is?"

"Yes, sir." Zee headed down the hall. The other knight was posted at the far end. Whatever the commandant and Dr. Aenig were discussing, they didn't want to be interrupted or overheard.

Zee's mind spun as he wondered what the commandant wanted to speak to him about, and he doubted very much it had anything to do with

Captain Ion Bomba. All he could think of was that it had to be about Jessup, and that worried him.

He smoothed back his hair at the doctor's door, took a deep breath, and knocked. He was bid to enter, and went inside.

Aureosa stood with his back to the book shelves at the left, a wine glass in his hand. He'd unbuttoned the top button of his shirt and rolled up his sleeves. The shining silver-green scales of his dragonbond went from his wrist all the way up to disappear beneath the sleeves below his elbow. Dr. Aenig stood behind his desk. Zee waited, frozen, until the commandant spoke.

"You must be this Mr. Tarrow your surgeon has been telling me so much about." Zee looked to Dr. Aenig, who gave him an encouraging nod.

Breaking his stunned silence, Zee snapped to attention and saluted crisply, just like Dame Toomsil had taught him. "Yes sir, Daimyo General Commandant, sir!"

Aureosa looked amused but also impressed by Zee's perfectly executed salute and proper address. He saluted back. "At ease, lad." Zee dropped his hand stiffly to his side. The man indicated a stool at one corner of the desk. "Please, take a seat."

Zee swallowed, his throat painfully dry. "Yes, sir." He sat while the commandant seated himself in a folding chair near the other end of the desk. Aenig eased into his own chair.

It took all Zee's concentration not to fidget under the commandant's scrutinizing gaze. The man took a sip of his wine, then sat back in his chair. "The good doctor here has told me quite an astonishing tale, Mr. Tarrow."

"He has?" Zee croaked. His eyes met Aenig's, who only smiled at Zee's anxiety.

"A tale of a young boy who snuck onto one of His Majesty's Tradeships and released a small creature taken as a prize for a local lord governor."

"Oh..."

"A boy, who, as it turned out, was actually one of the rare murfolk. A murman who, ten years later, was saved by an oddly similar creature, albeit much larger. In fact, Dr. Aenig, and the captain and crew, are absolutely certain this beast was none other than a kraken. Not only that, but the surgeon says his name is Jessup."

Zee stared at Aenig. He trusted the doctor as much as anyone he had ever known but had never spoken to him about Jessup, and Aenig had never asked. "How…"

"He told me," the doctor said, "when he placed you on the forecastle deck, bedraggled and half dead, and asked me to help you."

Zee could only stare as the doctor poured a finger of bingberry brandy in a tumbler and slid it toward him. Zee lifted the glass and downed the sweet liquid in one swallow. He grimaced, but was thankful for the wetting of his throat and the warmth that spread after the burn subsided.

"So it's true," said the commandant. "You know this creature."

"Yes, sir, I do," Zee said. Aureosa watched him expectantly. "I found him on the beach near my home when I was seven years old and named him Jessup. He's… my friend."

"Are there others of his kind?" the commandant asked.

"Not as far as we know, sir. I asked him, and he says he looked but found none." Zee stiffened, realizing he'd just revealed he could communicate telepathically with a kraken. For some reason, neither the commandant nor Dr. Aenig seemed surprised.

"That is not unexpected, I suppose." Aureosa scratched his chin. "You can speak to him, then?" He touched his temple with a callused and scarred finger. "Here?"

They *had* noticed. It felt wrong, revealing his secrets about Jessup after keeping them for so long and swearing he never would. But it was also oddly elating to be able to share. "Yes, sir." The commandant and Dr. Aenig exchanged glances. "But we had no contact after the day I let him loose. Not until he came to save me." Tears welled in Zee's eyes. All the lonely years he and Jessup had been separated, then his friend had risked discovery, maybe even his life, to save him. And he was still here, waiting.

"Could you speak to him now, while sitting in this cabin, from this distance, through the bond?"

Embarrassed, Zee quickly wiped his eyes. "I could, sir, but… wait… the 'bond'?"

Surprise registered on the commandant's features. "You didn't know?"

"I…" Zee's voice trailed off as he slumped on the stool, jaw slack at the revelation. Bonding was something he'd only thought happened to people and dragons, and even then it was something not just any of them could do. Some cadets and dragons had to leave the academy because they couldn't find a suitable bondmate.

"You've already told us you can communicate with each other telepathically," the commandant stated. "That is something only dragon and rider pairs can do when bonded, sometimes not fully until the bond is complete. Do you also sense his presence, a warmth, here?" The commandant placed his hand below his own heart.

Zee nodded, staring as he tried to wrap his mind around what the man was saying.

"If he is content, you can feel it. The same if he is troubled or in danger."

Zee met the man's gaze. "Yes, sir."

"I'm guessing it's the same for the kraken. According to the doctor's testimony, he came to you, from a distance, in your most dire need."

Dr. Aenig said, "After what I now know and have seen, Zee, I have no doubt that the mark on your chest is the sign of your bonding with the kraken, just as the scales on the wrist of a rider are the physical manifestation of their bond with a dragon. It's even the same color and texture as the beast's shell."

"But…"

"Have you noticed," the doctor continued, "since he came back to you, less than two days ago, it has grown?"

Zee fumbled with the buttons of his shirt. He ran his fingers over the patch. It felt thicker and perhaps larger, but placed as it was on his chest, it was hard to see. He looked to the doctor.

Aenig continued, "It has also begun to take a shape." He placed a book

Zee recognized on the table and slid it toward Zee. It was one of the old books on kraken lore they had read together, the first book the doctor had used to teach Zee to read. Just children's stories, Zee thought. On the cover, pressed in flaking gold foil, was a symbol Zee had always thought was the sun. A circle with ten curved points. The points were each slightly different, and it occurred to Zee, instead of flames on the sun, they could be arms…

The doctor indicated a dressing mirror on the wall behind where Zee sat. Zee stood and turned to gaze at it, his mouth suddenly very dry again. Reflected in its surface were the doctor and commandant watching with knowing fascination. And on his chest… though the points, flames, *arms*, on the circle were shorter, the patch had indeed taken the shape of the symbol on the cover of the book. The sign of the kraken. He had a krakenbond.

Zee sat heavily on the stool. He slowly spun the stool to face Dr. Aenig, remorse and shame mixing with his shock. "I'm sorry I never told you about Jessup before now, sir."

"Think nothing of it, Zee. You wished to protect him."

"Exactly, sir. I promised myself I would never speak of him, for his own safety. I had figured out he was a kraken and was afraid of what people would do to him—were already doing to him."

"I completely understand."

"We could communicate, knew what each other felt, even then."

Aureosa paused as he raised his wine glass to his lips. "At such a young age… That is unprecedented among humans and dragons." He took a deep breath. "We are in uncharted territory here, however. Who knows what a murman and a kraken are capable of."

"Who knows, indeed," said the doctor, giving Aureosa a questioning look.

The commandant knitted his brow in consideration. He set his wine glass on the desk and sat straighter in his chair, eyes on Zee. Penetrating amber eyes that Zee felt looked right into his soul.

"Mr. Tarrow." The commandant's voice had suddenly become more authoritative.

Zee sat straight. "Yes, sir."

"It's my understanding that you have always wanted to be a dragon rider."

Zee was blindsided by the statement and took a moment to answer. "Yes, sir. More than anything."

"I'm afraid that's impossible."

Zee's heart sank.

"However, how would you feel about the possibility of training to be a *kraken* rider at Triumf's Citadel Academy, the first in the history of the Kingdom of Tosh?"

Zee gaped, his mind whirling at the very thought of it, then finally found his voice. "I think…. I mean, I would, sir. Very much."

"I may be getting ahead of myself, and I want to make myself very clear. This must be presented to the board and passed by majority vote. You and the kraken will have to come to the citadel so the board members can see for themselves that he truly exists and is willing before it can even be considered, otherwise I will have an even more difficult time making my case. Is that acceptable?"

"Yes, sir, that only makes sense. When would we leave?"

"As soon as possible, today."

"Today…" Zee's head felt light. He took a deep breath to gather his wits. The feeling faded but did not go away entirely. "I'll have to ask him first, sir. Jessup, I mean."

"Of course. We have never taken a cadet into service, person or beast, without them expressing an explicit desire to do so. I wouldn't dream of attempting it with a kraken." The commandant raised one eyebrow, and a corner of his lips curved up.

As shaken as Zee was by what the commandant had offered, it took him a moment to see the humor in the statement. He emitted a nervous laugh. "Yes, sir."

"Could you ask him now?"

"Um… yes, sir," Zee stuttered. "But, would you mind if I asked him in person? I haven't seen him yet, you see…"

"I wouldn't have it any other way." The commandant stood from his chair. "I'd very much like to see him myself."

* * *

Zee proceeded down the hall in a daze, Dr. Aenig at his side, the commandant and one of the Gold Class riders in front of him, the other behind. He looked up at Aenig who, for the first time in all the years Zee had known him, actually winked. Before Zee could respond, they were moving up the stairs and onto the deck.

The crew was hustling back into formation, and everyone was staring at him—Captain Ion Bomba with fierce scrutiny. Zee wasn't surprised, since he'd never seen the captain look at him any other way. Somehow it didn't have the same effect it once had. In fact, Zee found it almost comical. Bomba turned his dour gaze upon Dr. Aenig, who ignored him entirely.

Commandant Aureosa shouted to the crew, "At ease!" Then his voice carried over the ship and to the dragons in the air nearby. "Stand down. Take no action unless expressly ordered to do so!"

On the quarterdeck, signal flags were waved and the bell was rung to pass the order to the Navy armada. Acknowledgments were received from the decks and crow's nests of the surrounding ships.

Dr. Aenig leaned down and spoke close to Zee's ear. "Call to him."

Zee closed his eyes and spoke to his friend. A tense moment passed, long enough that Zee wondered if Jessup was going to answer.

Then a deep reverberating roar rose from beneath the waves. The surface of the sea rippled at the sound, the deck shivered, droplets of water dancing on its surface, and loose fittings rattled in place. Crew members backed away from the rail.

To Zee, it sounded like music.

A dragon roared off the port bow. The watch in the crow's nest pointed, shouting. "There! Bearing oh nine hundred, straight off port!"

Zee ran to the port-side rail. Aenig followed, his cane tapping on the deck, as did the commandant.

Just inside the perimeter of the ships, a dark shape beneath the surface approached the HMT *Krakenfish*. A giddy elation that Zee hadn't felt in ten years rose in him.

A thorny gray shell partially broke the surface. Zee couldn't help the grin that spread on his face. His little friend had gotten bigger. A lot bigger, and gnarled spines stuck out where the smooth knobs used to be on Jessup's baby-shell. Zee gripped the rail in anticipation.

The captain shouted, "Remember, you scum, do not fire upon the beast unless ordered!" He grumbled under his breath, "Commandant's orders."

The tension of the crew, knights, and dragons was palpable. The shell submerged, the shadowy figure slowed, then paused, thirty feet off the port side.

Zee reached out to his childhood friend. *"Jessup?"*

The darkness rose. An arrowhead-shaped point two feet across at the base broke the surface, and kept rising. Straight up Jessup came, his cone-shaped, thorned, and whorled gray shell stained in algae, barnacled, and scored with marks of claws and teeth from battles fought. Some of the spines were broken. Zee felt a twinge of sadness for what his friend must have gone through since they'd last seen each other. His life had not been easy. Just like Zee's.

When the base of the shell broke the surface, it stood nearly twenty feet tall. The shell tipped back and the kraken's octopod brow and eyes rose above the waves.

Jessup's eyes swiveled as he scanned the sky and the ship, then he caught sight of Zee, and his big green eyes brightened. He rose higher, pushing his nose-slits and wide mouth out of the water—and he was grinning. Even with the triangular serrated teeth that lined his mouth behind thick, rubbery lips, to Zee it was a beautiful sight to behold.

Jessup spoke in a deep and gurgling but intelligible voice. "Hi, Zee."

The crew gasped and one of the dragons cried out in surprise. "It speaks!"

Zee wasn't listening to them. He leapt to the rail and dove.

CHAPTER 18

Zee swam to Jessup and did his best to hug him, arms out, cheek pressed to the kraken's great wide face. Warmth flooded through him. The pain and stiffness left him and he felt an elation he'd never known. Similar to what he'd felt when he and Jessup were younger, but deeper, stronger, and more joyous.

Jessup coiled the end of an arm around him, lifted him out of the water, and held him close. Jessup's body hummed with a deep vibration that thrummed through him. The kraken was purring.

The captain shouted in protest, but when Zee turned back to the ship with tears of joy in his eyes, everyone else stood astounded and staring. None moved to retrieve the captain's murman. Not even Corl.

* * *

A touch of awe crept into Commandant Aureosa's voice. "And there it is. The kraken of myth and legend." He looked to his dragon, who had craned her regal neck up on the perch deck to peer down at the spectacle below. She returned his gaze with equal amazement.

* * *

No one was more moved by the sight than Dr. Drall tak Aenig. Bittersweet tears trickled through the creases of his cheeks. He remembered that feeling. What Zee and Jessup were experiencing now. Unlike Zee, though, the dark pit of emptiness in the doctor's soul would never be filled again.

* * *

Jessup held Zee out to get a better look at him. *"Where are Zee's murman gills?"*

"*They only open when I need them. I can still swim without them, or my webby hands and froggy feet.*"

Jessup grinned. *"We go now?"*

Zee was taken aback. He hadn't considered that. The chains were gone. They could just dive deep and swim away, right now. No one could stop them. Away from the hardships of the ship. Off on a new adventure, a new life, together, completely free, in the sea.

But, then what? Where would they go? What would they do? He eyed the ships and dragons. Would they be hunted, pursued to the end of their days? How would the dragons and Navy catch them, though? A kraken and a murman could stay underwater forever. And never see the sky...

Zee's thoughts and emotions were in turmoil. *"Actually, there's something I need to ask you. See that man at the rail, the one in the uniform and red vest?"*

"Jessup sees."

"That's the commandant of Triumf's Citadel Academy."

"Jessup remembers academy. Dragon rider school. Zee wanted to go there."

"That's right. He's asked if I'd like to attend the academy." Zee sensed the mixed feelings swirling in Jessup's mind. *"To train to be a kraken rider."*

Confusion added to Jessup's thoughts. *"Kraken rider?"*

"Maybe the first one ever. I'd need a kraken to ride, though."

"Zee mean, Jessup go too?"

"That's the idea. What do you think?"

Jessup looked to the commandant, eyes narrowed. *"Zee trust him?"*

"I trust Dr. Aenig, and I believe this is his doing."

Jessup looked to the rail. *"Surgeon? Man with one eye next to commandant?"*

"That's him."

Jessup studied the man, then his expression relaxed. "*Doctor is good man,*" he said as a matter of fact. After more consideration he added, "*Long shadow.*"

"What do you mean?"

"*Sad. Darkness. Not sure. But he has been friend to Zee?*"

Zee could feel Jessup's deliberation. "*He has.*" Zee sniffed. "Our *friend.*"

Jessup's grin returned. "*Jessup has hoped that Zee be able to go to academy and ride dragons.*" His green eyes gleamed with pride and joy. "*This is better.*"

"So, you'll go with me?"

"*Jessup go anywhere with Zee.*"

Zee shot his fist in the air. "Hurrah!" He caught sight of the commandant and Dr. Aenig watching them from the rail. He cleared his throat, saluted, and addressed the commandant. "Sir, Daimyo General Commandant, sir!"

Jessup swiveled his eyes to Zee, then lifted an arm from the water and held it over his brow to salute as sell.

"Astonishing," Aureosa uttered. He returned the salute, then crisply dropped his hand.

Zee whipped his hand down, following formality. Jessup imitated his move, his arm slapping up a great spout as it hit the water, splashing Zee.

Zee swiped the brine from his face and tipped his head to Jessup. "Sir, this is Jessup. He's... the kraken... sir." Zee winced at his ridiculously obvious statement.

"I've never seen a kraken before, Mr. Tarrow. I'll have to take your word for it. It is a pleasure to meet you, Mr. Jessup."

In an attempt to recover what dignity he might have left, Zee said, "Say hello to the commandant, Jessup."

Jessup blinked his plate-sized eyes, then said in his deep gurgling voice, "Hello, Commandant, sir."

More exclamations arose from the knights, dragons, and crew.

From what the commandant had learned from Dr. Aenig and Zee, he should have expected the kraken could speak aloud, but apparently to hear it address him directly, and properly, was another matter. Recovering his military bearing, he said, "Mr. Tarrow, have you put the proposal to Mr. Jessup?"

The captain frowned. "What proposal?"

Aureosa ignored him.

"Yes, sir. We accept."

Jessup nodded, nearly dunking Zee in the sea.

"Very well, then," the commandant replied.

Bomba said, "Accept what?"

Aureosa turned to regard the captain as if he was something one would want to avoid stepping in, then strode to the quarterdeck stairs, up, and to the center of the rail. The Gold knights from the citadel followed and stood near.

Aureosa gazed over the crew, who drew to heightened attention. "On behalf of the Academic Board and the Board of Visitors of Triumf's Citadel, I would like to welcome Derlick don Donnicky, Esquire, to the Dragon Corps Academy." The crew cheered and applauded. The ship's knights clapped Donnicky on the shoulders, and the younger squire congratulated him.

"We will be leaving straightaway." Aureosa paused, then announced, "Mr. Tarrow and Mr. Jessup will be coming with us."

Gasps and murmurs spread through the crew. The ship's knights glanced at each other in confusion. Donnicky frowned.

Bomba's face grew more red, veins bulging on his forehead. "Commandant, sir! I have forgiven the offense of attending the surgeon instead of myself, the captain of this ship, but this! By all maritime law, the gilly and the beast are mine!"

Corl and the mates took an apprehensive step away from the captain as visible golden power pulsed from the commandant, shimmering in the air around him. Above and behind him, his dragon had the same golden glow. She raised her regal head with a growl. Yellow light flared in her eyes, and smoke seeped from her nostrils. She gave her wings a short but swift flap. The gust sent the captain's cap flying and the crew staggering back. The ship jolted as the sails snapped taut.

Mr. Trib, the sailor manning one of the starboard harpoon cannons, flinched, and the slow match he'd been holding brushed the touch-hole filled with gunpower. He slapped at it, trying to put it out, but the cannon fired. The noise was deafening, its report echoing off the wall of ships in the distance while the smoke cleared.

"Hold your fire, Zepiter damn you!" shouted Aureosa.

Signal crew on the quarterdeck waved flags and rang the bell to convey the message to anyone in the armada who might have gotten the wrong idea.

Bomba glared at Mr. Trib.

The old sailor seemed to shrink in on himself. "It was an accident, I swears!"

Only then did they see the harpoon stuck in Jessup's shell, with Zee gaping up at it. The point of the projectile had just penetrated the surface, and the thin cable attached to its shaft hung loose between where it stuck and the cannon.

"Jessup, are you all right?" Zee asked.

"Jessup okay." But the kraken was not amused.

He snaked an arm out the water. A bony spike, short but sharp, pushed out from the center of each sucker. Jessup wrapped the arm around the cable, and yanked.

The harpoon cannon tore from its bolts, crashed through the rail, and splashed into the sea. Jessup tugged the harpoon out of his shell and dropped it, letting it all sink.

Zee gaped. "Oh…"

Jessup watched the ship with narrowed eyes.

"Mr. Tarrow!" Aureosa shouted. "Mr. Jessup! I offer my sincerest apologies, on behalf of His Majesty's Dragon Corps and His Majesty's Navy." He glared at the captain. "And especially, His Majesty's Tradeship Fleet." His dragon lowered her head and growled at the crew, the flames that licked from her nostrils reflecting in her golden eyes.

"You were saying, Captain?" Aureosa continued.

The redness drained from Bomba's face and sweat poured from his brow. "Nothing, sir, Commandant, sir."

"Something about this being your kraken?"

The captain sputtered. "I was terribly mistaken, Commandant, sir. You're welcome to it."

"You forget your station, Captain, besides appearing to have little control over your crew." Mr. Trib shrank further under his glare.

Bomba gulped and went to one knee, smoothing back the sparse greasy hair on his head. "Of course, Daimyo General Commandant. My most sincere apologies."

"By maritime law, you will be properly compensated for your conscription contract with Mr. Tarrow." One of the Gold Class knights with the commandant reached into a satchel attached to her dragon's harness and tossed a sack of coins to the main deck, within Bomba's reach.

The captain's greed nearly overpowered his good sense, but he jerked his hand back before it could creep all the way to the sack.

"Thank you, Commandant. You are most generous."

Aureosa addressed Zee. "Mr. Tarrow, I suggest you pack your belongings."

* * *

It was tradition for anyone leaving service on the ship to shake hands with the crew. A duffel bag slung over his shoulder, Zee followed Squire Donnicky down the line. When Zee had tried to congratulate his friend, Donnicky had given him a cold stare and turned away, leaving Zee with a hand outstretched and unshaken. After Zee recovered from the rebuff, he admonished himself for having been so naïve as to think someone like Donnicky would ever be a real friend to him. Now that the squire had been accepted into the academy, and in light of the fact that Zee was also traveling to the citadel, Zee saw that their relationship had been predicated on Donnicky's superiority alone. Now that his status was threatened in the slightest, the squire wanted nothing to do with Zee.

Donnicky received claps on the back and kind words of good luck. The best Zee got was a brief handshake from Loris, the carpenter. Others were hesitant to touch him. No surprise there. That came when he reached Captain Bomba.

Bomba scowled down at him, and Zee was certain that was all he would get from the man. Then the captain reached out his hand. "You've done a fine job here, gilly. Your service will be missed."

Zee hardly believed what he'd heard. The captain had said Zee's service would be missed, not Zee himself, and called him a gilly, but it was the closest thing to a compliment Bomba had ever given him. "Thank you, Captain." Bomba grunted in reply and stalked out for a better view of the higher decks at the back of the ship.

Last in line was Dr. Aenig, standing with his cane at the foot of the stairs to the quarterdeck. He wished the squire good luck, then turned to gaze down at Zee with his one good eye, an inscrutable expression on his lined face.

Zee reached his hand to the man who had done so much for him, and had somehow arranged for this as well. Not only had he made it possible for Zee to leave conscripted service on the ship, but Zee was also going to the academy he'd always dreamed of. It wasn't assured he'd be accepted, but still. A tightening in his throat made it difficult to speak. "Thank you, sir. I don't know how I will ever repay you."

The surgeon took his hand. "Don't thank me yet. And you can call me Drall."

Zee blushed at the kind informality. "Thank you, Drall."

"Whatever may come, be strong. Work hard. Give it everything you have, and more." The surgeon pulled him closer, as if to embrace, but spoke softly next to his ear. "Reach deeper than you could possibly imagine. Farther than you ever have before. Only at the moment of most dire need will more power come to you. The greatest potential lies with those closest to defeat. The most high will be those with the noblest intent, perhaps most aligned to the divine will of Zhera herself."

The doctor released him. Zee could only stare back.

Dr. Aenig's lips curved up in a smile, a knowing look in his good eye. "Show them what you've got, Zee Tarrow. I believe in you."

"I… thank you, sir."

"I have a parting gift." Aenig pulled a duffel from his shoulder and handed it to Zee.

Zee took it, beaming with gratitude. "You shouldn't have."

"Probably not, but take it anyway."

Zee opened the flap to see a long waterproof bag made of layers of oilskin, its top edge rolled tight and secured. "What is it, sir?"

"Much less than you deserve, but there's something in there we were going to study next. Perhaps you'll have better luck with it than I have." He leaned closer and lowered his voice. "Keep it close." He leaned back, eyeing Zee sternly.

"I will, sir." The doctor had taught him that, other than stories to scare children or for general entertainment, serious study of murfolk and krakens was frowned upon by the general populace, and especially the powerful Church of Zepiter, the official church of Tosh. If Aenig had acquired a new book about murfolk, Zee couldn't wait to read it. "Understood."

A lump formed in Zee's throat as he put the duffel onto his shoulder. "Thank you, again."

"Now be off with you. You've been nothing but trouble and a drain on my precious time."

Zee smiled and shook the man's hand again. For a moment, he didn't want to let go. He looked over the ship and the crew. He was happy to be leaving, but he'd grown up here, with these people. Other than his childhood memories, he didn't know anything else. For better or worse, this had been his home for most of his life.

Now his life had been set on a drastically new and different course. Whatever it held for him, he would embrace it with everything he had.

And now, he had Jessup.

He sighed deeply and met the doctor's gaze with a smile. "Aye, sir."

He released his mentor's hand and proceeded up to and across the quarterdeck, then up to the perch deck.

"Mr. Tarrow." Commandant Aureosa indicated over his shoulder to his dragon, who had a passenger's saddle rigged to her back behind Aureosa's. "You may ride with Vandalia and me, if you wish."

Sitting on a similar rig behind one of the Gold knights, Squire Donnicky glared at Zee.

Vandalia grunted, scrutinizing Zee, head held high on her arched neck, looking down her long snout. All dragons were amazing to Zee, but Aureosa's was particularly glorious, intimidating and oozing power.

Aureosa chided her. "He does look quite heavy. Are you worried you may not be able to carry him all the way to the citadel?"

"Please," she scoffed, smoke puffing from her nostrils. "I could carry ten of those little things to the north ice and back if I wished."

To Zee, Aureosa said, "That's as much of a 'welcome aboard' as you'll get from Vandalia. Up you go."

Conflicting desires pulled at Zee. All his life he'd wanted nothing more than to ride a dragon, and his chance had finally come. But…

He stepped closer to the port-side rail and looked down at Jessup, who waited patiently, watching. "Thank you, sir, but I'll go with Jessup." He cleared his throat and raised his voice. "If that's okay with you, Jessup."

Relief and joy swelled in his chest from his friend in the water, making the decision more than worth it. That and the fact that thousands of people of Tosh and from many other nations had gotten to ride dragons. How many had ever ridden a kraken?

"It's okay with Jessup," the kraken replied through a wide rubbery grin.

Zee removed his shirt and boots, then stuffed them into the duffel that contained all of his meager worldly possessions. He handed the bag to one of the Gold knights, who stood with a hand outstretched to receive it. It would be safer with her than in the water, and definitely drier. He patted the bag given to him by Dr. Aenig. "I'll hang on to this one, if that's all right."

When she didn't insist, he thanked her, then dove over the rail.

* * *

Zee treaded water a few yards from the beast. "Permission to board, Mr. Jessup?"

Jessup let out a snort that sprayed droplets over Zee. "Permission granted."

Jessup raised an arm to help him. Zee sprang from it and climbed Jessup's shell with dexterity earned by years of climbing lines, masts, and ratlines. He settled above Jessup's brow, feet on two spines, hanging on to two higher spines.

Vandalia lowered her head down next to the commandant's shoulder. "It speaks, *and* it has a sense of humor."

"*That's one thing it has that you haven't,*" he replied through their bond.

She harumphed. "*It has many things I do not. Like a hideous ugliness and arms like worms. But it still cannot fly.*"

"You cannot swim."

"*Swimming is for fishes.*"

"By that logic, flying is for birds."

"*I will bite you.*"

"*No you won't.*"

The commandant ran a hand along her neck, then called down to Zee. "We'll travel at appropriate speed for your mount and circle around if need be. Try not to lose sight of us."

The kraken said, "Jessup knows the way to citadel island."

"You do?" asked Zee.

"Jessup went to see it. For Zee."

Zee smiled and patted his shell. "I appreciate that, but you shouldn't have. It could have been dangerous."

"It was dark."

"In that case," said Aureosa, mounting his dragon. "Perhaps we'll follow your lead."

* * *

Zee looked over the ship that had been his home, and his prison, for over half his life. He'd survived, grown stronger, and learned much, which was something. Now he was leaving. Whatever awaited him, he was going to Triumf's Citadel Academy, even if it wasn't assured he would be a cadet. No matter what they had planned for him and Jessup, it could never be more difficult or dangerous than what he'd experienced on the HMT *Krakenfish*. He waved to the surgeon with the deepest gratitude. Aenig waved back, then gave him a crisp salute.

The commandants and Gold knights took to the air. Vandalia circled tight over Jessup, and Commandant Aureosa shouted down, "Lead the way, Mr. Jessup!"

"Aye, sir!" Jessup replied.

Zee made no attempt to suppress the grin that spread across his face as Jessup made his way toward where the ring of ships was opening for them to pass. He looked back at the long octopod arms waving beneath Jessup's wake, to the sides at others that pulled up and pushed back in even, practiced strokes, altogether propelling them smoothly forward at the same speed the ship had cruised on calm seas.

In the sky, many of the other dragons fell into formation, the commandants in the lead. Vandalia's long, graceful wing stroke put them all to shame. Others flew in flights of five at their flanks, another flight ahead, and another behind. A Silver Class knight from the citadel flew close to the commandants to receive orders, then soared off ahead toward the island. Sent to deliver the news that a kraken and a murman were on their way to the citadel, Zee figured. Wonder, confusion, joy, and trepidation all churned within him. He could tell that Jessup was feeling the same way. His chest warmed and his krakenbond tingled pleasantly as they comforted each other, setting off on a new course in their lives, wherever it may lead. Whatever may come, they were together at long last. Salty tears mixed with the salt water of the sea that misted Zee's face in the bright sun and warm breeze.

And he was riding a *kraken*.

CHAPTER 19

Zee breathed deeply of the briny air as they swam several hundred yards away from shore, following the coast. The HMT *Krakenfish* was gone from sight behind, but a half dozen Navy ships cruised along with them, farther out to sea.

Several of the knight pairs who had been patrolling the air by the ship flew closer, the dragons conversing while glancing openly at Zee and Jessup, their expressions somewhere between awe, fear, and disdain—as much as Zee could tell from the expressions of dragons, anyway. Dame Toomsil had told him early on that rider and dragon pairs shared all rank, privilege, and station. She and Peloquin were both Silver Class Knight Chevaliers, and together they were a Silver Class Knight Chevalier pair. Peloquin had tolerated him, even spoken to him on occasion, and was never rude or condescending, but the other dragons assigned to the ship had acted as if he wasn't even there.

Zee repositioned himself on Jessup's shell, which didn't make the most comfortable seat. It could be a long trip, and Zee was sure he'd be sore when they arrived. "How long do you think it will take for us to reach the citadel?" he asked.

"Bells."

"Yes, but any idea how many?"

"Many bells. Citadel is on island, on other side of Tosh."

"We're going to have to work on your accounting of time and distance."

"Jessup would like to learn."

Zee watched the dragons high in the sky. The double rows in V-shaped formation flew easily behind the commandant, moving lazily back and forth so as not to outpace them.

One of the flights at the starboard flank was practicing formation and maneuvering techniques, corkscrewing up into the sky. Another flight was climbing, banking, and diving in a single line, then swooping up again, tracing a figure eight in the sky. The thrill of watching them never abated, even after all the years that had passed.

He wondered if he would be frightened being so high up, at the mercy of a beast that could chuck him off with a buck and a tip. He'd do it anyway, without hesitation.

"Zee could have ridden on dragon," said his big-shelled and ten-armed friend. "Jessup would understand."

It was as if Jessup knew what Zee was thinking—which shouldn't surprise him. It had seemed that way from the very first day they'd met. That felt like a whole other lifetime, long ago. But also, together with Jessup now, like just yesterday.

"I might get another chance. Right now, I wouldn't want to be anywhere else in the world than right here."

A purr rumbled through Jessup, then he asked, "Zee want to go faster?"

"How fast can you go?

"Faster."

"Okay, we'll work on your reckoning of speed, too. Show me what you've got."

"Climb to back of shell."

Zee glanced over the spiny shell, then climbed around the base to the opposite side. "Is this good?"

"Jessup think so."

"We'll probably have to do some tests, but let's try this out for now."

To Zee's surprise, Jessup's spines retracted into his shell, all but the ones Zee was leaning against and hanging on to, which Jessup had left out for him. "That's fantastic," he remarked to himself. "Less drag in the water, too."

Jessup tilted his shell forward so his face was in the water with the shell's point above the waves like the prow of a ship. Zee felt a shudder through the hard surface on which he sat, like water was rushing deep inside.

Jessup contracted the length of his arms and pulled them forward. "*Zee ready?*"

"*Sure, let's*—WAH!" Jessup shot forward with tremendous acceleration. Zee's fingers slipped from the spines and he flew backwards, flipping head-over-heels to splash into the gushing wake.

Zee tumbled underwater in a powerful surge, but righted himself and snatched the strap of the duffel containing the waterproof bag Dr. Aenig had given him as it slipped from his shoulder.

Jessup jetted away, arms held straight back behind him, water shooting from the center of his lower body. Then he stopped, arms blooming out like flower petals, then rolled and tipped up to look back at Zee through the water.

"*What happen, Zee?*"

"*I fell off!*" There was no anger in his voice, just excitement and surprise. Zee surfaced. Jessup surfaced as well and paddled toward him.

Zee slapped the water with his palms. "That was incredible!"

* * *

"What happened?" Commandant Aureosa watched down over Vandalia's shoulder as she circled back. The other dragons turned as well, maintaining formation.

"Mr. Tarrow fell off."

"What were they doing?"

"The beast suddenly shot forward. Quite swiftly."

The commandant watched Zee swim down and around the kraken,

then surface to converse with him. "Do you remember our first flight together, Vandalia? After we were paired and the bond began to take hold?"

"An unforgettable thrill."

"They're feeling that now."

"They are already bonded."

"You believe so, too?"

"They have been for some time," Vandalia said. "But they've been separated. The bond hasn't had a chance to grow until now."

"A murman and a kraken, naturally paired, and bonded. I wonder what they could accomplish, for better or for worse."

"I, for one, would like to see it. For better, or worse."

"Even if the kraken is dangerous, better to have it on our side than any other. Do you think we can convince the board?"

"I can be very convincing, as you know. And Mr. Tarrow comes with quite the recommendation."

"Yes…" The commandant's eyebrows knit. He shook his head as if still not believing it. "Remember, we're sworn to keep that to ourselves."

"Of course." They continued to circle, observing the exhibition below.

* * *

"I'd almost forgotten about your water chute, Jessup!" Zee finished tying the duffel strap to one of Jessup's spines.

"Jessup's water what?"

Zee slipped back into the water and paddled along while the kraken swam slowly, inspecting his friend's arms. They'd grown longer in relation to his body than they'd been when he was a baby, each of them about thirty feet long when contracted to be pulled forward, forty when pushed back and stretched out.

"Your siphon," Zee answered, returning to the surface. "It's also called a hyponome."

"Er…"

"You used it when you were a baby, to squirt water out the back for a quick burst of speed. Octopods have them too. It's like a tube that can be contracted down its length."

"Where Zee learn so much?"

"Dr. Aenig. We studied anatomy of sea creatures, among a lot of other things."

"Studied big words."

"I'll teach you if you want, as much as I can. Do you still draw the water in through your nose and mouth?"

"Yes, but these are better." Using the tips of two of his arms, he pointed to two areas on either side of the front of his shell, just about halfway up.

At first Zee couldn't see anything but crescent-shaped creases in the shell, closed half ovals roughly a foot and a half across. Then they opened at the flatter end and pushed out to form scoops. "Wow," Zee exclaimed. "I bet that makes a big difference."

"Jessup have more." He pointed to the back quadrants of his shell on the same level. "Only open back ones when all the way under water."

"Why?" Zee recalled sitting on the beach with Jessup while Midge snuffled in the sand nearby, then uttered, "Oh...," with a childish grin.

Zee had passed gas, said, "Excuse me," then giggled. Little Jessup's eyes had gone wide, then he'd taken a deep breath, grimaced, and forced out a drawn out, flapping expulsion of air that ended with a squeak. Zee's mouth had hung open in shock—and respect. Jessup had giggled, then the two of them had laughed until Jessup fell over in the sand, wriggling his arms helplessly.

Zee grinned at the much-grown Jessup. "I get it. Pass wind."

"*Big* wind."

"Storm wind."

"Hurricane."

Zee laughed, wiping brine and tears from his eyes. Jessup's laugh reverberated through the water.

When they'd recovered, Jessup looked his friend over. "Zee does have fish breathers for underwater, and froggy hands."

Zee chuckled. "I do, but they're called gills and webbed hands." He lifted a foot above the surface and wiggled his enlongated toes. "I even have webbed feet."

"Jessup remembers seeing them when Zee was put in water by bad men, but thought maybe had dreamed it." He thought for a second. "How fast Zee go?"

"I don't know, to be honest. Let's see."

Zee puppy-paddled in the direction they'd been heading. Jessup swam along beside him, a frown forming on his big kraken face. With Zee's slim but muscular build and murman attributes, he wasn't swimming all that slowly, but still.

"Zee kidding?"

"Yes, Zee's kidding," he said with laugh, and broke into a faster froggie-stroke.

Jessup watched, then his voice rumbled in Zee's mind. *"Faster."*

Zee felt the mark on his chest tingle but thought little of it. It was doing that often since he and Jessup had been reunited. He began using a front crawler stroke, nearly leaping from the water with each powerful movement.

Jessup increased his speed to keep up. *"Faster."*

The warmth in Zee's chest from Jessup's presence increased, and it felt to Zee like he did swim faster. It was probably because he was trying harder so he could impress his friend—and, he realized, he'd never swum without his chains on. Not once, in his entire life. It was liberating in a way he'd never experienced before. Exhilaration filled him from head to webbed toes.

"Faster, friend Zee."

Zee's chest and gut heated more. He dove beneath the surface. Jessup submerged his eyes to watch. Using a porpus kick—which Zee only knew the name of because he'd described how he swam underwater to Dr. Aenig—he did go faster.

"Faster!" Jessup said in encouragement.

Zee set his face in determination, turned on his side and sped through the water using his fastest stroke, undulating his body in a fishie kick. The connection between him and Jessup seemed to grow stronger. Faster and faster he went, zipping through the water, until he reached a threshold he could not break.

He pulled up and rose to the surface, where he forced the water in his lungs out through the gills on his neck and along the ribs of his heaving chest. "Yes!" He spun to find Jessup, eyes and mouth above the water, grinning. "What do you think?"

"Jessup think Zee is tiny."

"Tiny compared to you!" He paused. "Well, and dragons. And pretty much everyone else."

"Zee swims faster than other people."

"I would hope so. I *am* one of the murfolk."

"Fast tiny murfolk."

Zee grinned. "I'll take that as a compliment."

"Jessup remembers when Zee was giant." He spread two of his arms wide above the water. "Very big Zee."

"You were a baby. I've grown, too, just not as much as you. Now you're the giant!"

"Jessup doesn't feel so big."

"No?"

"Ocean is *big*."

Zee scanned the vast horizon, then submerged and swam slowly. The coral bottom below swarmed with colorful fish, tortles, small sheels, and cooda. Farther out, turquoise water shot with rays of the sun near the surface grew darker blue as it stretched on forever, dropping to blackness in the depths. "*Yes, it is.*"

A sensation tingled on the back of Zee's neck. "*Jessup...*"

"*Zee...*"

They both felt it. The kraken submerged, spines shooting out to snap into place on his shell.

Zee barely saw it at first, so swiftly did it move through ravines in the coral. The surface of its body shifted to mimic the colors and patterns of its surroundings.

Zee had spotted other predators in the water from atop Jessup's shell, but they'd all beat a hasty retreat upon seeing the kraken. Not this one. He'd seen its kind before, and barely gotten out of the water with his life. A hammerhead orcapod.

Zee considered how large the creature was, at least fifteen feet long. Its skull had a wide crossbar with its eyes on the ends, and it undulated like an eel, though it had eight slim arms like an octopod. He barely had time to recall their enormous mouths with rows of razor-sharp teeth or that orcapods always hunted in packs and realize this one appeared to be alone when he was snatched by the ankle and dragged with incredible speed into the depths and out to sea.

Zee struggled as the orcapod pulled him fast through a field of kelp. More than a dozen more orcapods swarmed above.

Jessup roared as they attacked him, darting in and biting, evading his much larger arms. Their bites did him no harm, but that was not their intent. They had their meal. They just needed to distract the kraken long enough to escape with it.

Zee curled his body to tug at the orcapod's arm with his hands, but it was too strong. He let go and kicked at it with his free foot, but it held, the beast dragging him deeper. Another orcapod shot in, mouth wide. Zee pulled with his caught leg and curled away. The new attacker sank its teeth into the arm of the beast that held him, and Zee was free.

The orcapods circled, pale eyes watching. The largest of the pack attacked. Zee flipped in the water and caught hold of its wide hammerhead. His arms were nearly wrenched from the sockets, but he hung on for his life.

The creature bucked and twisted, trying to shake him off. Others chased after them. One lunged in. Zee ducked, avoiding its teeth, but one side of its head rammed him with a glancing blow. Zee's hold began to slip.

Jessup roared again and charged toward Zee, ignoring the pack that harried him. The orcapods were swift and agile, biting hold of his arms to be dragged along with him.

Jessup wasn't able to catch them, but help came to Zee in another, unexpected form. His krakenbond burned hot, and heat swelled in his chest. Heat and strength, like when Jessup had encouraged him to swim faster, but even more intense this time. Zee could feel his friend's anger as well, but more than that, there was supreme determination and focus. The will of a kraken. To be stronger, to be faster, to fight and survive.

Zee squeezed his legs around his mount's body and gripped its hammerhead tighter. Gritting his teeth, he arched back and pulled, steering the beast toward the surface.

Jessup turned his attention to keeping the others away from Zee. An arm snapped out like a whip, knocking one to float, twitching, upside down. He took out a second with another whip-strike. Wicked claws, like those of a cat, folded out from the tips of his arms, and the short, sharp spikes extruded from his suckers. His multiple arms moved in coordinated attacks—raking his claws across their hides, coiling around them and crushing them. One bit hold of the end of an arm. He yanked it to his mouth, smashed it with his teeth, and swallowed it whole.

An orcapod swimming alongside Zee angled in to bite him. He threw himself to the side, wrenching the head of the one he was riding, rolling it in the water. The attacker pulled up just in time, having nearly bitten into its packmate's belly.

The beast in Zee's grip attempted to dive again. Zee shifted his grip to grasp the ends of its head, digging his nails into its eyes, and tugged upward. In a frantic rush to escape the pain, the beast put on greater speed. Zee caught sight of another orcapod gaining on them.

Zee pulled again. The brightness of the surface flared as they shot up out of the water. The power of his krakenbond heated more, and it was as if time slowed to a crawl.

The other orcapod flew out of the water after them, arcing straight at Zee, enormous toothy mouth gaping. A flicker of shadow, a dragon's cry, and the beast was snatched out of the air.

Vandalia yanked the beast higher, her talons sinking deep into the predator fish, then flung it into the air and loosed a torrent of fire.

Jessup's roar reverberated and a pulse of blue lightning flashed beneath the waves.

Sailing high on the back of the orcapod, Zee felt even stronger, like he could tear the monster's hammerhead right off—and he nearly did.

The beast's head twisted in his grip, the flesh at the base of its skull wrinkling and tearing, and its spine snapped. Zee kicked away from it, flipping backward, and dove into the sea.

Stunned, Zee floated beneath the surface, looking up at the wavering sparkles of sunlight on the waves. How had he done that? He'd never felt so strong. Been so strong. It thrilled and terrified him at the same time. And now it was gone. He barely managed to paddle to the surface.

Something blocked the vision of one of his eyes. He felt for it and pulled it away. The wrap Dr. Aenig had used to bandage his head. He touched the gash and felt the stitches, but there was no pain in the thin ridge of flesh, and no blood showed on his fingers.

Commandant Aureosa's voice pulled Zee from his reverie. "Mr. Tarrow! Are you hurt?!"

Zee turned in a slow circle, treading water, taking in the aftermath of the battle. A mist rose from the waves. Torn and crushed orcapods floated belly-up, steam rising from their bodies. One was charred to a crisp.

Dragons dove and circled. An Ice Diver blasted a twitching orcapod with ice, freezing it in a tiny iceberg. The closest was Vandalia, Aureosa leaning over in the saddle with concern and incredulity on his face.

"I'm all right, sir!"

"And Mr. Jessup?"

The heat Zee'd felt had cooled and a quick pang of fear stabbed at him. Then he felt Jessup's presence and the rush of water below. His friend rose out of the sea next to him. An arm gently pulled Zee close.

"Jessup okay, sir."

Aureosa ran a hand over his face and appeared to be considering something astounding. Zee wondered if it was because of the attack, or what he'd seen Zee do. Zee still couldn't believe it himself.

Vandalia said, "Perhaps you should ride with us now, Mr. Tarrow."

For Zee, it wasn't even a consideration. "Thank you, ma'am, but I'll be all right. I'll stay with Jessup, but no more swimming today." She puffed smoke from her nostrils, but did not protest.

"Are you well enough to proceed?" Aureosa asked.

Zee and Jessup's eyes met and an unspoken communication passed between them. "Yes, sir." He put a hand on Jessup's shell. "We can go faster now, too."

Aureosa gazed at him for a moment. "We'll be ready to move out when you are." He and Vandalia soared higher, the dragon loosing a screech to rally the other dragons to them.

"Jessup glad Zee is not hurt," said the kraken.

"I'm glad you're okay, too. I see you can still produce electricity like a zap-eel. Good thinking, using that when I was out of the water."

"Jessup didn't know if it would hurt Zee."

Zee's brow furrowed. "What did you do, Jessup?"

"What does Zee mean? Zapping?"

"No. You made me feel stronger. More than that, I *was* stronger. A lot stronger."

Jessup thought a moment. "Jessup doesn't know. Just trying to help Zee fight bad fish."

Zee considered. "Okay. We'll figure it out, somehow."

He climbed up on Jessup's spines, then around to the back, speaking as he went. "They're called hammerhead orcapods, by the way."

"Bad fish," Jessup repeated.

"That works, too."

Zee's other bandages were in tatters. He settled into his place near the base of Jessup's shell at the back and pulled them away to reveal only pink marks where he'd been injured by the seadragon, even the long stitched one on his hip and thigh where he'd been gored by the monster's horn.

His bruises were gone. How had he healed so quickly?

The dragons circled high above. "We should get going. We don't want to keep Commandants Aureosa and Vandalia waiting."

"Zee ready?"

Zee gripped the spines. "Zee ready."

Jessup retracted all of his spines except the ones Zee clung to. "Jessup start slower this time."

"Good idea," Zee replied. He was going to hold on tighter, too.

* * *

Vandalia and Aureosa observed the smooth, rhythmic movements of the kraken's arms as it sped through the water, the point of its shell cutting through the surf like a ship's prow.

"The bond appears to be much stronger than we'd expected," said Aureosa. "And I'm certain they've never forged."

"There is great power between them," Vandalia replied, "but it's raw, and Mr. Tarrow doesn't know how to control it."

"That's why the academy exists," the commandant replied. "To teach them discipline, proper forging technique, and control."

"For humans and dragons, Peleus. No one knows how to train a murman and a kraken."

"Can it be that different?"

Vandalia remained silent as they watched the kraken's arms move below the surface, waving together behind it, then blooming out and shoving back while it propelled itself forward with a stream of water that gushed beneath the surface. Jessup would begin to slow after a hundred yards or so, then repeat the motion.

"I'd say they're traveling at close to fifty knots," said Aureosa.

"Impressive," Vandalia replied. "If they can keep up this pace, we'll be at the citadel in no time."

CHAPTER 20

Zee marveled at how fast Jessup swam, and it didn't seem that his friend was tiring in the slightest. The dragons could fly more rapidly, but this was far faster than the HMT *Krakenfish* could sail under the best of conditions.

Then he realized the Navy ships were keeping up with them. On the perch deck of the nearest ship, a man in a blue robe with a golden sash and a beret was slowly waving a wand. A dragon sat on its haunches behind him, pushed up on its front legs, slowly flapping its wings in time with the waving of the wand. The sails were full and taut, far more than the wind off the ocean could do.

"Magickers...," Zee uttered, then sent his voice to his swimming friend. *"Hey Jessup, there are magickers on the Navy ships conjuring wind to make them go faster. They're moving as fast as we are."*

"What is magickers?"

"Knights aren't the only types of bonded pairs at the academy. There are also magickers. They have higher magick affinities and go through different training because they're more suited to defense and healing than fighting, which is what knight pairs are best at. There aren't as many of them as knights, but they learn how to conjure barriers to protect ships and knight pairs, make potions and elixirs,

cast spells, create wards, and enchant things. Apparently, they can make ships go faster too."

Positioned for speed as he was, Jessup's eyes were below the surface and he couldn't see what Zee was talking about. *"People who wear dresses, have funny hats and little sticks?"*

"You could put it that way. The hats are called berets, the dresses are robes, and the sticks are called wands, but how did you know?"

"Jessup has seen them with dragons on ships."

An uncomfortable thought occurred to Zee. *"You never had any trouble with ships, did you?"*

"No trouble. Just sneaking to look at night. Zee said stay away, but Jessup wanted to look sometimes."

Zee breathed with relief and replied with a smile. *"Sneaky kraken."*

"Sneaky Jessup."

"Do you remember when I couldn't find you at the tide pool one morning, then you yelled from up on the rocks behind me?"

Zee felt his friend chuckle through his shell. *"Zee jumped high and almost fell in water."*

"And you laughed so hard you actually did fall off the rock."

"Those were good days."

"The best."

Having slowed while they were talking, Jessup picked up speed again. Zee sat with the sun on his face and the wind in his hair, perfectly content for the first time in ages.

He couldn't remember the last time he'd done so little for so much time. On the ship, unless he was sleeping—and he had shorter nights than the rest of the crew—every day was filled with hard physical labor, cleaning the latrines, scrubbing the deck and hull, and myriad of other tasks. When he wasn't working, all his time was spent studying with Dr. Aenig, training with Dame Toomsil and Tem, or practicing sword forms and strikes and exercising on his own. After the knight had left the ship, he'd sneak out of his hammock every night and find space in the hold where he'd train for a few bells on his own. This span of inactivity felt odd. It made him anxious. He took deep breaths to settle himself, like his ma had taught him so long ago to help with his breathing condition and resist the urge to scratch his rash. He didn't have those problems anymore, but he used the technique often to calm himself when he was irritated, endure the pain of an injury, or focus his mind on his training.

"*There is pass*," said Jessup.

The dragons angled toward shore and began flying over land above an opening in the cliffs.

"*That's the Strait of yon Siddoway. It runs through the narrowest part of the island, about twenty miles. We never went through it on the ship. Only Navy ships and small tradeship ferries are allowed.*"

"*Krakens allowed?*"

"*Looks like it. This one, anyway.*"

A dragon flew down to circle a Navy ship exiting the strait. The ship maneuvered to give the kraken a wide berth. One of the ships that had been escorting them entered the mouth of the strait, most likely to clear the way and warn other ships they were coming through.

Zee said, "*We should slow down.*"

"*Zee come to front?*"

"*Good idea.*"

Jessup decreased their speed and tipped his shell up.

Zee climbed around and settled in place above the kraken's brow. "*We're getting good at this.*"

Jessup tipped his shell back further to lift his face above the waterline. "Zee and Jessup make good team."

"Yes, we do," Zee said with a grin. "The best murman and kraken team in the world."

"Only murman and kraken team in world."

"Well, there is that. It doesn't mean we can't strive to be the best we can be, though, right?"

"Zee always right."

Zee laughed. "Oh, my friend, if you only knew."

Jessup chuckled.

Knights and their dragons stood atop the cliffs on both sides of the mouth of the strait, peering down at the strange sight below. Members of His Majesty's Marine Force crewed large cannons as well, pointing and shouting to each other. Zee was relieved to see the cannons remained aimed out over the sea and not at them.

The air became thicker and warmer as they entered the gap. The tall, dark cliffs contained more battlements manned by more marines, some with horses, others with enormous drakes and piles of boulders to drop on enemy ships.

They kept the ship ahead in sight and matched its pace. Ships slowed and moved closer to the cliffs, their crews gawking at the passing sea monster of myth with a small man perched on its shell. Most were clearly amazed, but some cringed back in terror and made the sign of Zepiter over their hearts. Others scowled with hate in their eyes. Ships coming toward them on their left did the same. One pilot became so distracted he ground his ship against the stony cliff wall, raising cries from captain and crew.

Dragons from the citadel flew ahead to keep the peace and reassure the crews, but Jessup remained vigilant and cautious.

Zee projected comfort to his big friend as much as he could. "It's all right, Jessup."

"If Zee says so," the kraken replied, not entirely convinced.

"We can't blame them. Until just now, they didn't believe you even existed, and if you did, you'd be vicious and terrible and want to eat them."

"Jessup would not eat people or dragons. Smell yucky." Zee laughed. "Jessup can be vicious and terrible, though."

"We'll let them keep thinking that."

That pleased Jessup. He growled at a particularly aggressive-looking captain and his crew, sending ripples across the water and vibrating their ship's hull. Zee smiled and waved at them as they stepped back from the rail.

Zee had lost track of the bells when the cliffs began to recede and the air became fresher on an incoming breeze. First came terraced rice paddies, then cultivated fields and pastures for livestock, humble homes and grand estates, then villages becoming closer together until they were a cramped sprawl. Then the grand coastal city of da Chmilenko came into view. The capital of Tosh. Though he had never been allowed to leave the ship, Zee'd seen major cities from port but never the capital of his own kingdom. He soaked in every detail, trying to imprint it on his mind forever.

Four concentric walls of white stone encircled the city like tall stone serpents, one within the other. The walls, as well as the buildings, grew grander as they proceeded up the rise of the mountains. The highest structure of them all was the gleaming white castle of the king.

"There is pretty castle," observed Jessup.

"You've seen it before?" Zee replied.

"Jessup has seen many cities in many places."

Spires and parapets of shining ivory stone speared the air. Colorful flags and banners flapped in the breeze. Dark Royal Ebons and Royal Crimsons of the King's Guard perched on walls and towers with knight's on their backs, while others patrolled the skies. The grandeur of it, the power it represented, struck Zee with reverence and admiration.

The strait widened and a low mist obscured their view of what lay ahead, though the sky above remained clear. Zee climbed up higher on Jessup's shell to look back at the grand port of the capital and the city and castle that rose behind it.

The waves picked up and the coastline spread away to either side. Jessup sped up as their dragon escort gathered back into formation overhead, heading out to open sea once more. Zee continued to gaze at the castle until it, too, was lost in the mist.

Jessup called his name, bringing him out of his reverie.

He turned, still high on Jessup's shell, holding on to the point at the top. "What is it?" Moments later they emerged from the fog. "Oh…"

In the distance ahead, a dark landmass thrust severely from the sea.

The mountains of Triumf's Island. Home of da mon si Triumf's Citadel Academy for His Majesty's Dragon Corps.

CHAPTER 21

The features of the island became more defined as they approached. It looked much like a king's crown fashioned of rough, dark stone. All around it, dragon knights and cannons were placed on leveled areas of the peaks, wide stone walls between them. More pairs soared the air, individually and in flights, their scales and armor glinting in the sunlight. Five sharp mountains thrust into the sky at one end.

Aureosa and Vandalia circled down within shouting distance. "Follow us, Mr. Tarrow!" said Vandalia. "We're going into the harbor. Once through the gates, proceed to the beach next to the docks."

"Yes, ma'am," Zee shouted back. "Thank you, ma'am!"

They rose and flew ahead. The rest of the knights flew over the high walled cliffs.

"My gods, Jessup," said Zee, his stomach in knots. "I can't believe we're actually here."

"Jessup can't believe it, too."

The entrance into the harbor came into view, its opening between the tips of two curved stone promontories that reached out into the sea like arms. Zee's jaw hung slack at the sight of enormous statues carved into the stone at the point of each promontory. Dragons rearing up, mouths open in silent roars, their armored riders thrusting swords to the sky. Their inside wings connected to form a great arch high enough for the tallest mast to pass underneath. At the base of the promontories were two massive towers with iron gates several stories tall swung inward between them. Carved into one tower were the words "Be Strong," in the other "Be Brave," together the slogan of the Dragon Corps.

Inside, the harbor was far larger than Zee had imagined, the pass they had come through the only access to the sea—and Triumf's Island was more than an academy. It was an entire port and military base. Nearly a full armada of warships and quite a few armed merchant ships were docked or anchored. The wharf bustled with activity. There were warehouses, cranes, long barracks, and a town as large as mon Tontuga, maybe larger.

The gate where they entered was near one end of the wide harbor. Straight ahead was a beach that sloped to a plateau, then hills that rolled to the base of the mountains, all marked by paths, streams, and one small river. The island was roughly oval in shape, with a ring of high ridges and walls all the way around, right up to each side of the cluster of mountains at one end. Dr. Aenig had told Zee that Triumf's Island was an ancient volcanic caldera that formed a natural fortress. A gravel road led up to the academy campus, which was comprised of multiple stone buildings. At the center of the campus sat the citadel itself. The largest building by far, and the oldest, built all of gray stone. It had towers like might be seen on a castle, but the citadel had been designed centuries ago as a fortress. Flags flew from the towers and walls.

Already, people were crowding toward the beach.

Zee took a deep breath. "Everything's going to be fine. Don't be nervous."

"Jessup not nervous. Zee nervous?"

"No, I'm fine."

"Zee lie."

Zee chuckled. "Yeah, Zee lie."

"Jessup lie too."

Zee thought for a moment. "If they want to see a kraken and a murman, we might as well give them a show." He explained his thoughts to Jessup.

"Zee think this is good idea?" Jessup asked.

"Maybe not, but let's do it anyway."

Zee felt Jessup perform a mental shrug. "Okay."

* * *

From Vandalia's back, Commandant Aureosa watched the boy and his kraken swim into the harbor, then submerge. "Hmm. What do you suppose they're up to?"

Vandalia circled around, peering at the water with her superior dragon eyesight. "They're still there, just under the surface, moving toward the beach."

"Let's proceed, then."

Vandalia landed on the beach and walked forward on the rocky sand. The Gold knights, including the one carrying Squire don Donnicky, landed near them. A crowd was gathering on the subtle rise above the beach. They spoke in loud but conspiratorial tones. The school year had not yet officially begun, but most of the cadets and new recruits had already arrived. Half of the recruits already had their heads shaved for Basic Military Training, which they would endure for their first sixteen weeks at the academy. Some stood together with their instructors, while the new dragon recruits grouped behind them and off to the side.

Normally the place would be buzzing with activity: instructors screaming orders at the minnies and duckies, which was what the fresh human and dragon recruits were called, and returning cadets training on their own with swords or on their dragons in the air, but word had spread. A kraken was coming to the citadel.

The surface of the bay humped, spines breaking the water, bringing gasps from the crowd. The beast submerged again, then all held their breath as the kraken rose.

* * *

Jessup drove his shell straight up out of the water as they neared the shore,

Zee at the top gripping the arrowhead-shaped peak. Zee lowered the nictitating lenses that protected his eyes while underwater, then forced water out of the gills on his neck and ribs, which vanished while his hands and feet returned to human form. He gaped himself, as shocked by the crowd as the spectators were of what had just appeared in their harbor.

People and dragons packed the area, and the arrival of the kraken had caught the attention of all in the basin. New recruits sat with jaws dropped in the middle of having their heads shaved. A crew of second-year cadets paused in setting up a long barracks tent on a hill. Third- and fourth-year cadets froze in weapons training. Young dragon recruits glared or stood with their long toothy maws hanging open.

With cold realization it occurred to Zee that he wasn't wearing a shirt. That was something he'd never thought about on the ship. Half the crew worked shirtless much of the time, and they were accustomed to seeing a murman with scars all over his body. Even his gills and webbed hands and feet failed to draw a second glance on the *Krakenfish* after his first few weeks on ship. This was an entirely different situation, and one he was not prepared for. He steeled himself to the fact that he'd have to wait until he was on shore and could ask the Gold knight for his duffel bag.

Jessup's voice startled him. *"Do not be ashamed, Zee."*

A comforting warmth flowed through him, and the tightness in his chest waned. He wasn't yet fully accustomed to Jessup's presence and sense of what he was feeling, but it was quickly returning to how it once was between them. When he felt whole and truly comfortable with himself. And now his friend was older, more experienced, and wiser. *"Thank you, Jessup."* He stood straighter and held his head high. Jessup was right. He had no reason to be ashamed of who or what he was, no matter what anyone else thought of him. Again, he said, *"Thank you."*

* * *

Sallison anh Batcu stood among the newly arrived squires, strong arms crossed over her chest, gazing at the kraken in disbelief. Her father had sent a message that a kraken and murman were on their way to the citadel.

She'd had no reason to doubt his messenger, but the words didn't prepare her for the actual sight of the beast. It was… impressive. Though that didn't quite describe it. Awesome and terrible is what it was.

But what really drew her gaze was the murman. Due to her father's station, she'd seen murfolk on a few occasions, but this one was different. The others had been meek, would never meet anyone's eyes, and only spoke when spoken to. This young murman was small in comparison to humans his age, like the others she'd seen, but he stood straight, had steel in his eyes—and his scars…

"Holy cowfish," came the voice of the lumbering ox of a recruit next to her. All Sallison knew about him was his name, Jondon dil Rolio, which she'd learned a few minutes ago while they sat next to each other getting their hair sheered from their scalps, and that he stood taller than any of the other recruits and outweighed her by at least a hundred pounds. In spite of his size and their unfamiliarity, she elbowed him. "Ssh."

"What?" Jondon asked with surprise.

She spoke sternly but quietly out of the side of her mouth. "You don't want to get into trouble on your first day, do you?"

He glanced around, then was visibly relieved that no instructors were near enough to have heard him. "Sorry, Sallison. Thanks."

"Ssh," she expressed again.

"Right," he uttered.

Sallison's attention returned to the murman. He had more scars on his small wiry frame than anyone she'd ever seen, some of which looked like they'd been earned in battle. He'd lived a hard life, even harder than the others of his kind she'd met, and she'd have bet he'd seen things, done things, knew things, the others hadn't. And this murman had a kraken.

The beast swam forward to the beach and crawled up with its front arms on the shore. At least twenty-five feet tall out of the water, it towered over Commandants Aureosa and Vandalia. Some at the front of the crowd stepped back instinctively.

The young murman climbed down to stand on the sand, where he paused, then said something to one of the Gold knights who had arrived with the commandants. The knight tossed him a small duffel bag. Steadily, confidently, he retrieved a shirt and pulled it on, down over the scars and strange gray mark on his chest.

Sallison's father had told her to stay away from them but asked her to watch them carefully—as if she wouldn't have enough to worry about as a lowly minny preek at the academy. Somehow, though, she didn't think keeping an eye on them would be a problem.

* * *

Zee stepped from one of Jessup's arms to the beach, only to suddenly realize he hadn't set foot on land in ten years. The grit felt odd beneath the soles of his feet, and he would have sworn the ground was moving. It wasn't, of course. He'd heard the sailors speak of having to regain their "land legs" after long periods at sea, but he never expected it to be like this. He swallowed the queasiness that rose in his gorge and stood straight, trying to convince himself he wasn't swaying. When he was nearly certain he wouldn't fall down, he spoke to one of the Gold knights. "Please, ma'am, may I have my bag?"

Zee tried not to fidget and cover himself with his hands and arms while he waited for the knight to toss him his duffel bag. With supreme will to stay on his feet, he retrieved a shirt and put it on as confidently as possible. He nearly yanked it when it stuck on his wet krakenbond but managed to maintain his cool and sighed internally with relief when it was finally in place.

Vandalia stepped closer. Aureosa leaned forward and spoke softly for only them to hear. "Welcome."

"Thank you, sir," Zee replied, then returned his attention to the crowd.

Among those gathered at the fore were faculty and staff wearing robes of Dragon Corps blue with colored sashes, as well as what looked like upper-class cadets in green robes. All of them wore berets and were making an attempt at looking casual but held their wands at the ready. More magickers.

Though their Abilities were more suited to defense, protection, and healing, the more advanced magicker cadets, and especially the higher-rated magicker faculty, could form barriers of power around Zee and Jessup, making it impossible to defend themselves or escape should things go wrong. Their wands were a foot and a half long, sharply pointed at the end, and had short cross guards. They not only focused their power and directed their Abilities, they supposedly could punch through armor as well.

Seasoned knight pairs and more magicker pairs rode the sky, keeping a close eye—some of them wide in amazement—on the monster in their midst.

Monsters, Zee corrected, counting himself. Few of the people here would have ever seen one of the murfolk before, and none a kraken. Besides the shock in their eyes, Zee could see something else as well. Anger, disgust, and fear.

The crowd parted for a group of dragon and rider pairs approaching on the road from the citadel. Some rode upon their beasts while others walked beside them. They didn't come all the way down the slope to the beach, but they drew closer than the crowd. Some looked like civilians but dressed in the finest clothing, with the sashes of governors and senators. By the uniforms, ribbons, and insignias worn by others, Zee figured they were some of the highest-ranking members of the citadel's administration and staff.

One man at the head of the group stood apart from the others in his appearance. He was the tallest of them, wearing a grand white robe, with black hair streaked with gray in a topknot and a braided beard. He looked to be of similar age to the commandant, the two of them being the eldest of the group.

The crimson embroidery on his robe, his blood-red sash, and the horizontal red badge with two hash marks meant he was mid-level Red Titan Class, and his shoulder boards marked him as a four-sea-star Magi General—the highest authority in his order.

"Is that Mihir han Wanchoo, sir?"

Aureosa looked surprised that Zee knew, though he shouldn't have been. The highly esteemed dean of magicks at the academy was well known across the kingdom. "He is."

What at first appeared to be a lump of armor with thick golden scales on Wanchoo's shoulder lifted a narrow snout and sniffed in Zee and Jessup's direction.

"I've only seen drawings in Dr. Aenig's books, but that looks like a quemara." The creature fluttered its wings, and a short flame shot from its pointed nose. "It *is* a quemara. I've heard they're very rare, and come from somewhere very far away."

"Amoxtli is the only one I've ever seen," said Aureosa as he dismounted. "I'll only be a moment." He went to greet the newcomers while Vandalia stayed nearby.

* * *

"Then it's true, Peleus," said the woman in the lead, Emir General Lora aye Hyooz, Gold Class knight and superintendent of the academy. Her vest was golden mail, and her shoulder plate sported three sea stars. She peered through the lenses of her black-framed spectacles at the kraken and murman.

"As strange as it is to say, Ma'am Superintendent, yes."

Dean Wanchoo said softly, "Absolutely fascinating."

"Have we anything to fear?" asked a man with dark, closely cropped hair and a short, pointed beard, Philliam sim Tooker, a one-sea-star Earl General and the dean of academics.

"Would I have brought it here if I believed it was a threat to you or anyone else, Philliam?" the commandant replied.

From where he sat on his dragon, Tooker looked down in suspicion. "You might, Peleus. You just might."

* * *

Commandant Aureosa started back toward Zee, and Zee caught his breath as he spotted a familiar face in the crowd off to the side. Dame Zara mon Toomsil. Her scale mail was now gold instead of silver, and her shoulder plate showed she'd been promoted from Knight Chevalier to Knight Commander. He wanted to go to her but didn't think it would be proper. She returned her gaze to Jessup. Maybe later, he hoped.

Upon arriving next to Zee, Aureosa turned back to the crowd, his commanding presence hushing them. "Cadets, recruits, staff members, and esteemed colleagues, may I present Mr. Zee Tarrow, of the murfolk." He paused, then announced more loudly, "And Mr. Jessup, the kraken!"

Silence was the only reply. Zee and Jessup exchanged nervous glances. Zee gathered his resolve and raised his hand. "Greetings."

Many in the group seemed surprised Zee could speak, but when Jessup raised an arm in the air and said, "Hello," it was as if someone had slapped them all with cold fish.

The commandant narrowed his eyes at the new recruits, cadets, and military training instructors. "They will be treated with due respect during their stay, however long that may be." He let that sink in, then said more loudly, "Understood?"

It was like the spectators were suddenly released from a state of hypnosis, their military discipline returning in a flash. Except for the dignitaries and higher-ranking members of the administration, they all snapped to attention and saluted. As one, their voices rang over the harbor. "Yes, sir, Daimyo General Commandant, sir!"

The commandant gave them a moment to further remember who they were—members and future members of His Majesty's Dragon Corps. "All right then." He returned the salute. "Carry on!"

Instructors shouted at those under their command to get back to work. The crowd scrambled, and all over the basin people returned to their duties. The members of the administration, dignitaries, and upper-level faculty gave Zee and Jessup a last, long look, then turned and headed back toward the citadel. Dame Toomsil hung back a moment, watching Zee and Jessup, then followed the others.

A young staff instructor, however, marched straight toward Zee, a fierce scowl on his face, hand on the pommel of his sword. He paused to salute

Commandant Aureosa, who returned the honor. It took a second, but Zee realized he knew the man. Temothy jal Briggs, Dame Toomsil's old squire.

Tem was even taller now and his frame more filled out with muscle. The red scales of a dragonbond fully encircled his left wrist, he wore the bars of a Knight Chevalier, and his mail was silver, his badge with two hash marks denoting mid-level. If Zee had once been able to nearly hold his own with the squire in sword training, he'd have no chance against the knight who stood before him.

"Hi, Tem," Zee said, taken by surprise. "What are you doing here? And Dame Toomsil?"

Tem fixed him in a furious stare, but a glance back at the commandant swiftly took the edge off his foul demeanor. Still, he spoke as if it defiled him to do so. "I am assigned as an assistant instructor of the sword for the academic year, overseeing the cadet instructors. Knight Commander Toomsil will be a lead instructor of the sword."

He looked Zee over, then up at Jessup. Seeing the kraken from this close, his bearing faltered, then returned as he brought his attention back to Zee. "Why you are here at the citadel is beyond me, but also beyond my station, and therefore none of my business."

Zee could tell Tem wasn't happy about it, though, and badly did want to know why they were there.

Tem jabbed a finger at Squire don Donnicky, who still sat on the back of one of the representative's dragons. "You! Minny scum! What are you waiting for? Maybe one of your daddy's servants to help you down from the big bad dragon?" The squire paled. "Get your slimy bass-butt down here!"

Donnicky hastened off the dragon, dropping his bag and pitching forward in the sand in the process. "Unbelievable," Tem groused.

Zee fought to keep from smiling at Derlick's distress. He was pretty sure the squire had never been spoken to that way in his life. Zee had endured it every day on ship.

The squire leapt up, cheeks flushed, brushed himself off, then ran to stand at attention before the staff instructor and threw a salute. "Sir! Squire

Derlick don Donnicky reporting for processing, sir!"

Tem leaned forward, screaming in the young man's face. "You call that a salute, Minny Docklicker?!" Donnicky winced at the butchering of his name and the spit that flew in his face. "And you're no squire. You're an insignificant Minny now. Lowest of the low, your value only that of prey for the bigger fish of the sea."

"Sir, yes, sir!"

"You won't last a week!"

"Sir, yes, sir!"

"Are you ready to fail, scumsucker?!"

"Sir, yes, sir!"

Tem leaned closer and Donnicky realized his mistake. "I mean, sir, no, sir!"

Tem thrust a hand toward a line of other recruits on a nearby hill. "Then get your worthless minny self to processing, Docklicker, ASAP!"

"Yes, sir!" Donnicky dropped his hand from his brow and started toward the line, then remembered he'd left his duffel in the sand.

Tem shook his head as the squire ran back to get it. "Minnies..."

Zee had heard that Basic Training was extremely difficult. For their first sixteen weeks at the academy recruits were screamed at, humiliated, and driven to exhaustion every day without enough sleep and little time to relax. To Zee, that sounded like every day of his life for the past ten years—and students of the academy, recruits or cadets, didn't have to wear chains locked to their bodies all day and though punished if they got out of line, they were never whipped.

Commandant Aureosa said to Tem, "A moment of your time, Knight Chevalier MTI Briggs?"

"Of course, sir." Aureosa and Vandalia led him a short way up the beach to converse. Aureosa appeared to be asking Tem questions while glancing at Zee on occasion. It made Zee nervous.

Donnicky ran up next to Zee, clutching his duffel and confused. Realizing how close he was to the kraken, he quickly rounded to Zee's other side. There he stared at Jessup, then frowned at Zee.

"This was meant to be my special day, Tarrow," he hissed. "Not some circus with a performing gilly and his demon from Postune's hells."

Zee paused a moment, then looked him square in the eyes. "You want to tell the demon that?"

Fear flitted across Donnicky's features, then he scowled and stalked toward the other new recruits.

"I could tell him for you, if you wish."

Donnicky stiffened to a stop, then hurried on his way.

Zee regretted his response immediately. He'd never spoken to anyone like that on ship. Then he felt the ire emanating from Jessup and saw him watching Donnicky. His friend had a temper, and it affected Zee. He'd have to be careful about that.

"*It's okay, Jessup,*" he said. "*I shouldn't have said that. We don't need to be making enemies, at least not so soon after we got here.*"

"*Jessup doesn't like him. He is basshole.*"

Zee had heard every curse and foul name a person could be called while working on the ship, but Jessup had been alone in the ocean for ten years. "*Where did you learn that word?*"

"*Zee said it once, when Jessup was little.*"

"*I did not.*"

"*Did.*"

It was certainly possible. He'd heard his father say it plenty of times when he didn't know Zee was listening. "*Okay, maybe I did, but it's not a nice thing to say about someone.*"

"*He is not nice person.*"

"*No, he's not, but please don't say things like that out loud.*"

Jessup let out a small sigh, which wasn't so small coming from a kraken.

Jessup was right, though, and shaddammit, he was not a demon. He was a big, sweet fellow and Zee's best friend. A real friend, unlike Donnicky had been. He turned to Jessup, looming up behind him. He supposed he could imagine how others might see him as pretty frightening, though. He *was* a kraken.

"*We'll show them,*" Zee said to his friend. "*We'll be the greatest rider and beast they've ever seen.*" If they were accepted, that was.

A flapping of wings sounded up the beach and a stout brown Rock dragon landed hastily. Its rider, a burly man with broad, sloped shoulders, a bald head, and a prodigious black beard leapt from its back. Together they hastened toward Zee and Jessup. The man would be scary in appearance if not for the look of joyous wonder in his eyes. The dragon also stared up at Jessup, equally enthralled. A cadet landed on her dragon and hastened behind them, carrying a clipboard and quill.

Commandants Aureosa and Vandalia returned, and Zee saw Tem berating a group of huddled minnies as he strode toward them.

"Zee Tarrow," said Aureosa, indicating the bearded man, "this is Knight Commander Kareem eh Mahfouz, Beastmaster of the Citadel." He placed a hand on the dragon's shoulder. "And Mildrezod, of equal rank and position."

Mahfouz and the Rock dragon finally closed their mouths and tore their eyes from the kraken. The man took Zee's hand in both of his and shook it rigorously. "It is a great pleasure to meet you, Mr. Tarrow."

"And you, sir," Zee replied, entirely unaccustomed to anyone being glad to meet him. The man became suddenly more interested in Zee and began squeezing his forearm, then his shoulder.

Zee wasn't sure how to react, but the Rock spoke in a matronly voice. "Greetings, Mr. Tarrow. Welcome to Triumf's Island."

"Thank you, ma'am. It's an honor to be here."

She eyed the beastmaster, who was feeling Zee's neck like a doctor checking for swelling. She cleared her throat, brown smoke puffing from her wide mouth. "Excuse Beastmaster Mahfouz's manners. Or lack thereof."

Mahfouz realized what he was doing and stepped back, holding up his hands. "My apologies, Mr. Tarrow. I'm an aficionado of physicalities, you see. I've never had the opportunity to observe one of the murfolk at such close proximity."

"He's very excited," Mildrezod added, "if you can't tell."

"Again, my apologies."

"It's all right, sir," Zee replied. He put a hand on one of the arms Jessup had folded in front of himself. The top of it came up to Zee's waist. "This is Jessup."

The beastmaster stared up at the kraken. "It is magnificent…"

"Mahfouz!" Mildrezod admonished.

"Sorry! He—*you*, are magnificent, Mr. Jessup."

Jessup's eyes swiveled to Zee. "'Magnificent' is good?"

Before Zee could answer, Mahfouz clapped his hands and rubbed them together as if he couldn't wait to get them on the beast. "Oh my, yes, Mr. Jessup. Very good."

Mildrezod said, "It means tremendous, beautiful even, in a striking and dramatic sort of way."

"Oh," said Jessup. "Thank you, sir."

Mahfouz held up his hands, palms forward. "May we approach, Mr. Jessup?"

Jessup looked to Zee, who shrugged, then replied, "Okay."

Mahfouz stepped up and slowly laid a hand on Jessup's arm. He breathed in sharply, then slid his hand back and forth on the kraken's thick hide. "He's warm, Mil!"

To the terrified cadet with the clipboard, Mildrezod said, "There's your first note, Beastmaster Apprentice Terlani. Krakens are warm-blooded."

The cadet tore her eyes from the kraken. "Yes, ma'am." She scratched at the paper on the clipboard with a pencil.

Mildrezod asked, "Do you surface to breathe, Mr. Jessup, or can you breathe underwater as well?"

"Jessup can do both, ma'am."

"Amazing." Mildrezod looked to their apprentice to make sure she was still writing.

"His hide appears to be incredibly tough," said Mahfouz, "with thick pebbled skin. Quite unlike a typical octopod, yet it retains significant elasticity."

Jessup didn't flinch as the beastmaster poked at his arm, but Zee asked, "*You okay with this?*"

"*Jessup fine.*" The corners of his mouth stretched upward. "*Jessup 'magnificent.'*"

Zee grinned. "*Yes, you are.*"

Aureosa, who had been watching with interest, said "Mr. Tarrow, I'll leave you and Jessup in the beastmasters' capable hands." He climbed into his dragon's saddle. "Vandalia and I have important matters to attend to." To Mahfouz, he said, "Knight Commander, we'll send someone to fetch you and Mildrezod for your report." Mahfouz was so enthralled with Jessup's nose-slits he didn't respond.

Mildrezod shook her head. "I'll remind him."

"Thank you," said Vandalia.

"Excuse me, sir," said Zee. "What about Jessup and me?"

"We'll be back with an answer as soon as we can," was Aureosa's only reply. Vandalia took to the air and flew toward the citadel. Zee's anxiety returned twofold.

CHAPTER 22

"Preposterous," grumbled Senator Ralf san Cubberly. "We've been summoned to an emergency meeting of the Admissions Board, for this?"

"I only received the letter yesterday morning, Senator," Commandant Aureosa replied. "With the new academic year starting soon, time is of the essence."

Philliam sim Tooker, Dean of Academics, said, "You can't be serious."

"Deadly serious, Philliam," Aureosa replied. There was no rancor in his voice, but the set of his features made his sentiments clear.

Comments rumbled among others in the room.

"This is unheard of."

"A murman and a kraken, at Triumf's Citadel Academy?"

"A *dragon* riders' academy."

"And the boy has such a low name."

High in the largest tower of the academy, the Board of Admissions, including six of the highest-ranking members of the Academic Board and the seven members of the Board of Visitors, most of them riders themselves and graduates of the academy, were seated equally spaced at a grand round table. Their dragons sat behind them, each pair's voice considered as one and together holding one vote.

The boardroom took up the entire floor of the tower, its walls of gray stone hung with banners colorfully embroidered with emblems of the academy's cadet wing, fighter groups, and squadrons. Inlaid at the center of the table was the emblem of the Dragon Corps, a crown with the wings of a dragon, its carved insets of shell shimmering under the light of a majestic chandelier.

Aureosa leaned back in his chair, elbows resting on the arms, and steepled his fingers, but it was Vandalia who spoke, seated on her haunches behind him, her regal head high over his shoulder. "We're merely proposing a motion to consider the prospect before the esteemed members of the Board of Admissions."

Dean Tooker's dragon, a wide-bodied Rock, huffed in indignation.

"You're mocking us, is what you're doing, Peleus," Tooker retorted. He shot a look at Superintendent Lora aye Hyooz. "You agreed to this?"

She met his gaze steadily. "I have learned enough that I would like to hear more, even if I've not yet decided one way or the other. And if I were to consider it, so must the board, in case it comes to a vote."

Academy Chaplain Antoon oh Connor said, "Pardon the interruption, but why would we consider such a thing?"

"To put it bluntly," said Vandalia, "it's time we faced a difficult truth. The military might of Tosh, though still renowned throughout the known world, is not as mighty as it once was."

Board members scoffed.

"That's absurd," said Senator Cubberly.

Superintendent Hyooz rapped her mallet on the table. "Order, please."

The room quieted.

Mihir han Wanchoo, Dean of Magicks, leaned forward, hands clasped on the table, consternation on his face. The members of the board gave him their full attention. "Through the dragon and rider bond, all of us draw our strength and Abilities from the residual golden power of Zepiter, our creator. This we know. The cold hard truth, dear colleagues, is that either that power is waning, and has been for centuries, or our ability to utilize it fades. Either way, it amounts to the same thing. We are not as strong as we once were, and we grow less so with each passing year. I fear it is the same with our allies."

More grumbling rose from the group.

"We must face the facts," said Aureosa. "The academy can barely scrape together a hundred new recruits each year, for a full cohort of merely four hundred. When Wanchoo and I were here before the last great war came upon us, the dormitory mounts housed a thousand strong. In elder days, they were filled with thousands of dragons and riders. We now use a fraction of their capacity."

"Today there are but three Red Titans in all of Tosh," said Wanchoo's dragon, a venerable white Ice Diver named Venkatarama. "In our day, there were over a hundred. We also had nearly twenty Black Titans, though only Slan hai Drogo and his mighty Blue Tasarabat, Mogon, ever reached high level. Now we have no Black Titans at all."

There were nods of reverence at the mention of Drogo and Mogon, as well as a few fleeting scowls.

"Wanchoo and I were younger than Drogo," said Aureosa, "third-year cadets forced to graduate early at mid-level Bronze Class and enter the war not fully prepared, so dire had our situation become. We followed Sky Marshall Drogo and Mogon into that final and fateful battle. We were outnumbered ten to one on the open sea. The loss of riders and dragons alike was nearly catastrophic—but we won."

"We all know the history," said Senator Em ell Spencer. "We appreciate your sacrifices and many still mourn the loss of Drogo and Mogon, but what does this have to do with the murman and kraken?"

"Peleus, Mihir, Rama and I," said Vandalia, "along with Drogo and Mogon, are looked upon as having been part of a greatest generation, yet our predecessors of a century before would have put us to shame. More importantly, and this is not meant as a boast on our behalf or a slight to anyone here, none have progressed as quickly or as far since. We are weakening in numbers and in strength."

A tempest of protests whirled about the table.

"We have been at peace!"

"We maintain exactly what is required."

"Let us not forget, the cost of training and maintenance of the Dragon Corps is no small expense."

Aureosa said, "What if such a war came upon us today, at this very moment, in our current condition?"

Dean Tooker opened his mouth to speak but closed it with a frown.

"The sea has ever been a dangerous place," Aureosa continued, "but we've all heard the reports that larger and more aggressive beasts have begun to prowl the depths and attack our ships with greater frequency, some not seen in these waters, or anywhere else, for a century. Mr. Tarrow and the kraken were attacked by a sizable pack of hammerhead orcapods just today on our way here, right off our coast."

"They are usually only seen in cooler waters," said Cubberly.

"What was the outcome?" asked Dean Tooker.

"The boy and the kraken killed them all." Aureosa let that sink in, then continued. "There have also been a steady rise in earthshakes, increasing in strength, and storms of unprecedented force. Ships have been vanishing without a trace, more with each passing year. And not just ours, but those of our allies as well."

"You're speaking of the Wraiths," snorted Senator Cubberly. "Phantom pirates on ghost ships that appear out of the fog to take vessels and slaughter their crews, leaving what few who survive so petrified with fright they cannot speak or babbling crazy. Bah! Nothing but tall tales spoken by nattering fishwives."

"Don't be so certain," said Venkatarama. None attempted to argue.

Aureosa said, "Be that as it may, there is no denying that trade routes are being disrupted, and treaties are becoming contested. Tensions are rising between the allied kingdoms. There have been confrontations on the sea that nearly came to blows. Our forces are spread more thinly with each passing month as ships are assigned more knights for protection. Yet no one speaks of it. It's time we did." Aureosa turned to Dean Wanchoo.

Wanchoo stared at the table as if looking beyond it and dreading what he saw. "There is a darkness rising in the world, my friends. Venkatarama and I have felt it. A tingle at the back of the neck and a chill of dread in the heart. We know not its source or purpose, yet we sense a great threat is coming."

Venkatarama added, "It may already be upon us."

"Until two decades ago," Wanchoo continued, "the murfolk were a myth. Now they are among us. They are few in number, and we know little about them, but they're as real as any of us sitting at this table. Now we have been delivered a kraken, free of the foul taint that weighs upon our senses. We cannot but believe these events are related, in some way beyond our sight." His gaze passed from one board member to the next. "This must not be taken lightly, nor judgment made without great consideration."

"Honored colleagues," said Aureosa, "if we are to push our cadets to greater heights, to challenge them as they never have been before, if war is coming, perhaps from a threat of unknown source, scope, and power, and if the ancient terror of the sea is as formidable as the stories tell us, perhaps a kraken is exactly what we need."

"I would also add that the murman and kraken are already bonded," said Vandalia. "It began when the kraken was a hatchling and Mr. Tarrow just seven years of age."

Board members looked up in surprise.

"Seven?"

"That's unheard of."

"So are krakens," said Vandalia.

None had a response to that.

"This could give them an advantage over the other cadets," said Librarian Taya lon Greylock, a magicker specializing in scholarship.

"All the better to challenge the others," Aureosa responded.

Dean Tooker said, "Our traditions of training must not be compromised."

"Adjustments would have to be made considering their affinity for the sea and ours for the air, but I assure you they would be held to the same high standards we expect of all our cadets."

Senator Spencer cleared her throat. "Has the boy squired, Peleus? Not in all the history of the academy has anyone been admitted without having completed their squireship."

"And who would he squire for, Senator? Unless you happen to know of another kraken rider in the kingdom." The commandant looked around the table. "Any kingdom?"

Superintendent Hyooz broke the silence that followed with a rap of her mallet. "Commandants Aureosa and Vandalia have proposed a motion that the murman, Zee Tarrow, and the kraken, Jessup, be considered for admission to the academy for training as rider and beast."

"Seconded," came the voice of Venkatarama.

"Should the motion pass," Hyooz continued, "we will review the application materials he has prepared and hear applicable testimonies. Only then will we ask for a vote on whether they should be admitted. Any objections before we proceed?"

A glowering figure with a well-groomed mustache and beard lay his hands on the table. "Before we waste more of everyone's precious time, I am compelled to raise a formal objection."

"Proceed, Governor jal Briggs," Superintendent Hyooz replied.

"If this murman is indeed one Zee Tarrow of the HMT *Krakenfish*, by all rights, the kraken belongs to me, Lord Commander Farig jal Briggs, Governor of Akhtar Province." His Royal Crimson snorted in support behind him. Board members grunted and more than a few eyebrows were raised.

The superintendent said, "I have been briefed on the possibility of this claim, and the only written document that exists is a bill of lading for shipment of an item that is left unnamed. Unless, of course, you have another?"

Governor Briggs scowled.

"If you wish to have the kraken," said the commandant, a smile quirking on his lips, "go and take it." Briggs's features faltered and his dragon shuffled where it sat. "You'll have to do it yourself, of course, without incident," the commandant continued. "We could not sanction otherwise."

Briggs fumed but kept his temper in check and his voice steady. "I will send word to my full guard and retainers. The beast will have no choice."

"And bring all the might of your personal forces to Triumf's Citadel Academy? I doubt the board would sanction that." Some members glared at the governor, others shook their heads, and a few suddenly found a bit of fruit from the serving plates particularly interesting.

A tall, slim man cleared his throat quietly. He was the only member of the board other than the chaplain who did not have a dragon, but his pointed silk cap and shining blue gown spoke to his position. All attended him with respectful attention. He spoke softly and with impeccable calm, but anyone hearing it would say his voice carried tremendous authority, even if they didn't know he was Davis han Ashura, vice vizier to the king. "Neither would His Majesty."

Briggs raised his gloved fist as if to pound the table, but thought better of it and rested his palm on its polished surface with fingers spread. He spoke in an even tone, but his outrage brewed underneath. "The gilly set it free after it was found ten years ago on one of the beaches of my province."

"A province in the sovereign nation of the king, Governor jal Briggs," the vice vizier reminded him.

Briggs's nostrils flared as he stared at the table, then his expression changed in a flash to one of gracious amicability, and he looked to the vice vizier. "You are correct, of course, Vice Vizier Ashura. My apologies."

Superintendent Hyooz gazed around the table. "Anyone else?"

Chaplain oh Connor said, "I must make the board aware of where the High Clergy might stand on such a proposal, or I have failed in my duty as designated representative of the Church. The Creation Scrolls are clear about the difference between humans and dragons and murfolk and creatures of the sea. Merely speaking in this manner could be considered blasphemy, and to act upon it construed as heresy."

More murmurs arose from the group, a few making the sign of Zepiter over their hearts.

Superintendent Hyooz said, "Thank you for voicing your concerns, Chaplain. We are all familiar with the Creation Scrolls and have taken them to heart since childhood, as have countless generations before us. Nevertheless, unless there are any other objections, I must call for a vote to hear the commandants' proposal." No more objections were raised. "All in favor, raise your hand and say aye."

Aureosa was first to speak, hand raised. Wanchoo followed, then Librarian Greylock. Chaplain Connor abstained. The others hesitated until Vice Vizier Ashura tipped his palm up and spoke in favor, then acquiesced, with Governor Farig being last.

"The ayes have it. Commandants Aureosa and Vandalia, please proceed."

* * *

Jessup held several arms out in front of him while Mildrezod inspected the short spikes that protruded from the center of each of his suckers, then the larger, more wicked claws he had folded out at the tip of each of the arms. She called out descriptions of her findings for the beastmaster apprentice to record.

Meanwhile, Beastmaster Mahfouz climbed Jessup's shell, examining the spines. He let out a low whistle of appreciation. "You have impressive defensive capabilities, Mr. Jessup."

"Thank you, sir," Jessup replied.

Mahfouz reached for the arrowhead-shaped point at the peak of Jessup's shell. Blue electricity zapped to his hand, giving him a jolt. He jerked his hand back with a cry. "Holy Zepiter!"

Zee winced. "I'm so sorry, sir! I should have told you about that, but I didn't know it would do it involuntarily." Jessup apologized as well.

Mahfouz shook his hand out. "That's perfectly all right, Mr. Jessup. I should know better than to be careless with a kraken." Mildrezod chuckled. Mahfouz mumbled as he climbed down, "Fascinating. Absolutely fascinating." When he reached the ground, he spoke to their apprentice.

"The kraken can produce a shock like a zap-eel, Cadet Terlani. Be sure to note that."

"Got it, sir."

The hail of a dragon drew their attention toward the citadel. A Greatwing lit on the sand, Dame Toomsil in the saddle. Both dragon and rider gazed at Jessup as he retracted his spikes and claws and tucked his arms back.

Zee couldn't help grinning at the knight who had helped him so much on the ship. "Good greetings, Dame Toomsil."

"Hello, Zee."

"I bet this is the last place you ever expected to see me."

"With a kraken, yes. Otherwise, not particularly."

Zee felt himself blush at the gesture of confidence.

She turned her attention to Mahfouz and Mildrezod. "Beastmasters, the board has requested your presence."

"You were there?" Zee asked.

"I've had my say, yes."

"How's it going?" Mahfouz asked.

Dame Toomsil hesitated. "It's... going."

Zee swallowed anxiously.

"Hello, Peloquin," Mildrezod said to Dame Toomsil's dragon, rather awkwardly. "It's good to see you."

Peloquin appeared to be caught off guard. "And you, Mildrezod."

Dame Toomsil and Mahfouz exchanged glances and shared in shaking their heads. Zee wasn't sure what was going on, but it appeared there was something between the dragons. Or they wanted there to be something. Or one of them did, anyway.

Mahfouz climbed up on his dragon. "Come along, Mil."

"All right, all right." After a final glance at Peloquin, she took a running leap and flapped toward the citadel.

Peloquin watched her go, then turned back to see Zee staring at him. A scowl formed on his toothy dragon mouth. "What?"

"Nothing, sir. It's just good to see you both."

Dame Toomsil said, "It appears much has happened since I left the *Krakenfish*, Mr. Tarrow." She looked back to Jessup. "And you have a new friend."

"An old friend, actually."

"So I've been told."

Zee introduced Jessup and greetings were exchanged.

Dame Toomsil glanced toward the cadets training on the field in the distance. "I should get back to my duties." She hesitated, then Peloquin carried her closer with a few steps. "Zee…"

"Yes, ma'am?"

Conflicted emotions twisted across her features, but all she said was, "Good luck." Then to Jessup, "To both of you."

"Thank you, ma'am," Zee replied, while inwardly trying to figure out what she had really wanted to say.

She smiled, but it looked forced. Peloquin took off and flew toward the training fields.

"Nice lady is worried," Jessup observed, watching them go.

"I thought so, too," Zee replied, anxiety churning in his gut.

"Are Jessup and Zee in trouble?"

"I don't know." He leaned back against his old friend. "I guess we'll just have to wait and see."

What if they decided to send him back to the *Krakenfish*? Would they try to keep Jessup? Send him away? Some of the administrators and their dragons hadn't looked very happy at the arrival of a kraken—the *existence* of a kraken. Could they try to kill him? Was that what Dame Toomsil had wanted to say? Was she trying to warn them?

Hot resolve flashed through him. He would never let that happen. And he would never to go back to wearing chains. He and Jessup could be across the bay and deep in the open sea in no time. They'd fight to get there if they had to. Zee would fight for Jessup with all he had. He'd die for his friend. And, he realized, if it came down to it, he'd kill for him, too.

* * *

Mahfouz stood in front of his chair at the board room table and Mildrezod sat behind as they finished their report to the group.

"All in all," said Mildrezod, "We'd say the kraken is a truly magnificent beast."

"He appears to be in good health," Mahfouz added, "and of surprisingly temperate manner, in spite of their reputation. Mil and I are in agreement. As beastmasters of the citadel, we are willing to take responsibility for Mr. Jessup's care should he and the murlad be accepted."

Superintendent Hyooz glanced around the table. "Any further questions?" Board members displayed pensive fidgeting and frowns of deliberation, but no one spoke. "We've now heard from all who are listed and read the letter from the ship's surgeon, which brought the murman and kraken to the commandants' attention in the first place."

Dean Tooker waved a hand dismissively, nearly tipping over his wine glass. "Who is this Dr. Aenig who speaks so highly of the murman and recommends so adamantly that the academy break all tradition and protocol? Why should we take his word seriously?"

"Having spoken to him at length," answered Commandant Aureosa, "I believe him to be highly intelligent, well educated, and in earnest." He was replying to Tooker, but his eyes were on Dean Wanchoo.

Wanchoo gazed at the doctor's letter while absentmindedly tracing the broken wax seal with a finger. He looked up, returning from whatever thoughts had been running through his mind. "Yes, yes. I would not dismiss the surgeon's testimony so easily."

Chaplain oh Connor spoke in a cautionary tone. "However the vote comes out, I am required to make a full report to the Church."

Vice Vizier Ashura's response was delivered calmly but was no less cautionary. "Whatever the outcome, I will be making a full report to the king."

Many in attendance shifted uncomfortably in their seats. The powerful Church of Zepiter and the Crown had long worked together for the benefit of the kingdom, but there were occasionally disagreements that created tension between them.

"Should Commandant Aureosa's proposal fail to pass," said Governor Briggs, "having a rogue kraken roaming the seas, let alone a bonded pair, is a risk we cannot accept. We must destroy the beast, and possibly the murman as well." Several members were clearly uncomfortable with the idea. Others nodded in agreement.

"You make a valid point, Lord Commander," Vandalia responded, "and one that Peleus and I have also considered, but there is an alternative."

"As a point of order, however," Superintendent Hyooz interjected, "these are issues to be discussed after the vote, depending upon the outcome."

Briggs acknowledged her statement with a tip of his goblet.

Senator Cubberly picked at his fingernails. "A murman and a kraken, cadets at the citadel…" He leaned back in his chair, still gazing at his hands. "We'd be the laughingstock of all our allies."

"The laughingstock, Senator," said Aureosa, "or the envy?"

Board members exchanged glances, considering.

Superintendent Hyooz tapped her mallet on the table. "Respected colleagues, I propose a vote to accept or refuse the admission of the first murman and kraken in the known history of Triumf's Citadel Academy. Do I have a second?"

CHAPTER 23

Jessup's big eyes swiveled side to side, tracking Zee as he paced back and forth in front of him. It was only partly because Zee was nervous, though. Mostly he was trying to get his land legs back.

"Zee looks drunk."

Zee stopped short, having to hold his hands out to keep himself from swaying. "How do you know what drunk means?"

"Jessup watch people on beaches at night sometimes. They walk funny and say 'drunk' or 'pissed.'"

Zee grimaced. "Do I look that bad?"

Jessup thought about it. "Zee didn't fall down."

"Ugh." Zee put a hand to his stomach. "It does feel a little like the one time I got drunk on the *Krakenfish*. They were handing out grog after taking a pirate ship."

The rhythmic splash of oars drew their attention to a small oarbarge making its way toward shore, piled with baskets of cabbages and sacks of potatoes. Painted on the side of the barge were the words, "hiu Gregg Produce." The rowers watched the kraken with eyes wide and mouths open, but the grizzled old man at the bow just frowned. The flat bow of the barge beached not ten yards away.

The old man called to Zee. "Hoy, lad! That a kraken?"

"Yes, sir," Zee replied.

"It ain't gonna try and eat us, is it?"

"No, sir."

He appeared satisfied by that answer, stepped from the boat, and hefted a sack.

Jessup said, "Kraken not hungry today. Maybe tomorrow."

Zee gaped up at him. "Jessup!"

The old man just dropped the sack on the beach and shrugged. "Won't be here tomorrow. You eat anybody you like."

Jessup grinned.

The man turned back to where the four rowers still sat staring. "You heard the beast. It ain't hungry, but them recruits will be. Get to unloading!"

Unconvinced, they all climbed out on the side away from Jessup, two of them having to climb over the goods to get there, and proceeded to unload the boat.

"You need some help?" Zee asked.

"Nah," the man said over his shoulder as he hefted another sack. "These young'uns gotta earn their wages somehow."

* * *

"Listen up, minnies!" shouted a third-year cadet instructor. "I need volunteers to do some hauling!"

Sallison anh Batcu stood in line with other newly arrived squires, waiting to pick up their training uniforms and towels. Like the others, she'd been watching the murman and kraken down on the beach and the oarbarge with supplies being unloaded. Unlike them, however, she stepped forward right away. "Recruit anh Batcu, reporting for duty, ma'am."

"Now there's some Dragon Corps initiative," said the cadet. "What about the rest of you lazy good-for-nothing slug-slimers?"

Everyone knew you should never volunteer in the military. It went badly more often than not, especially in Basic. Sallison didn't care. She hadn't done it out of a desire to distinguish herself or to be of service, either. If they were going to the beach, she'd get a closer look at the kraken and murman. Her father *had* asked her to keep an eye on them, after all.

* * *

Zee felt uncomfortable just watching the old man and his crew unload the boat and not helping. Jessup could probably just pick the whole thing up and dump it. Which, on second thought, might not be the greatest idea.

A dozen recruits strode from the Basic Training processing area. The cadet instructor with them shouted, "Double time!" and they began to jog.

All the minnies had their eyes on Zee and Jessup, but two in particular caught Zee's attention. Leading the group was a muscular young woman with dark eyes, running with ease. While the others looked frightened, angry, or amazed, she appeared to be intensely interested. Right behind her was a recruit Zee would have sworn was even bigger than Corl, who wore an expression as if he was seeing ghosts.

They headed straight to the boat, hefted sacks and baskets, and began the march back, all under the gruff direction of the instructor. The young woman with the dark eyes hung back, glancing at the instructor to see if she was watching.

She trotted closer, then stopped and gazed at Zee, then Jessup, then back at Zee. "Greetings," she said.

Zee was taken aback, but managed an awkward, "Hello."

Jessup looked back and forth between the two of them, then also said, "Hello." She stared up at him, her expression difficult to read.

After an uncomfortable pause, Zee asked, "Can I help you with something?"

She cocked her head at him. "No. I just wanted to meet you. Zee Tarrow and Jessup, right?"

"Yes, ma'am."

She snorted. "I'm Sallison anh Batcu, and I'm sure as heckfish no 'ma'am.'"

"All right, Sallison. It's good to meet you."

"Batcu!"

Sallison winced. The cadet instructor stood farther up the slope with her hands on her hips, and she did not look happy. Sallison turned to head toward the cadet, but paused. "Good luck."

Zee opened his mouth to thank her, but she was already sprinting up the slope with what had to be twenty-five pounds of potatoes under each arm. Zee wished he could run like that. Right now, he could barely walk.

The cadet instructor ran alongside Batcu, screaming in her ear. "And for that, you'll be peeling those taters for a week!"

Jessup said, "Sallison is nice lady."

Zee wasn't sure what to make of her. "I suppose."

"Pretty, too."

Zee's gaze snapped to his big friend, finding him smirking. "What?!"

* * *

Zee slid from where he sat on one of Jessup's arms as Vandalia and Aureosa approached from the citadel, followed by Beastmasters Mahfouz and Mildrezod, as well as Dean Wanchoo upon a regal-looking Ice Diver. Knights and magickers who'd been keeping an eye on the murman and kraken flew closer to circle above. Others gathered on the rise above the beach.

Zee spoke silently to his friend. *"Be ready, Jessup."*

"Jessup ready." It was all that had to be said between them.

Farther out on the grounds, new recruits, instructors, and cadets watched surreptitiously while pretending to go about their business. Dame Toomsil and Tem observed from the edge of the training fields.

The trio of dragon and rider pairs landed on the beach, and Vandalia stepped to the fore. Commandant Aureosa wore a scowl, then straightened in the saddle and made a declaration for all to hear.

"Zee Tarrow, it is the position of the majority of the Admissions Board that you will not be accepted for rider Basic Training at Triumf's Citadel Academy at this time."

Zee's heart fell at the crushing news.

"Mr. Jessup," the commandant continued, "it is also the position of the majority of the Admissions Board that you will not be accepted for beast

Basic Training at Triumf's Citadel Academy at this time."

Zee didn't know what to think or how to feel, other than a deep sense of defeat. Surprisingly, the feeling he got from Jessup was more composed than he would have expected, until his friend also saw and felt a rising tension among the knight and magicker dragon and rider pairs that had been keeping an eye on them.

At first Zee expected the worst. He and Jessup would have to fight their way out. Then he realized they were as afraid of how he and Jessup might react as he was of the actions they might take. They viewed the bonded murman and kraken as a serious threat. Zee took strength in that. He relayed that feeling to Jessup through the bond, and felt his friend's confidence growing.

"However," Aureosa added quickly, appearing to sense the tension himself, "we would like to offer you an alternative, positions as maintenance contractors for His Majesty's Armed Forces. Your value, Mr. Tarrow, is obvious, and an aquatic beast of such strength and intelligence as Mr. Jessup could prove of great benefit to the base here on the island. Your compensation will be in line with contractors of your abilities and experience, and housing will be provided. The labor is demanding, but you are no stranger to that, Mr. Tarrow, and I can assure you the bells and working conditions will be more fair than what you experienced as a conscript on the HMT *Krakenfish*."

Zee looked to Jessup and spoke through their bond. *"Not what I expected, but what do you think?"*

Before Jessup could answer, Commandant Aureosa said, "May we approach?"

Zee was surprised he would ask permission. "Of course, sir."

Aureosa dismounted from Vandalia and they stepped to Zee and Jessup, followed closely by Beastmaster Mahfouz and Mildrezod, Dean Wanchoo with his quemara on his shoulder, and Wanchoo's dragon.

Zee couldn't help staring at Dean Wanchoo, and the quemara that dozed on his shoulder.

The group came close, and Aureosa spoke more softly. "You recognized Dean Wanchoo earlier, Mr. Tarrow, but may I formally introduce Magi Generals Mihir han Wanchoo and Venkatarama, Deans of Magicks."

Realizing he'd been staring, Zee hopped to square his feet and saluted. "It's a great honor to meet you, Magi General Deans." Jessup saluted as well.

The Ice Diver dragon nodded and Wanchoo saluted back, then clapped his hands together and held them there, a wide grin spreading across his face. "It is my great honor to meet you both." He gazed up at Jessup. "It is an auspicious occasion to lay eyes upon a kraken, one I would never have dreamed to experience."

Venkatarama said, "And to meet the murman who has bonded with him. Auspicious indeed." Zee blushed, further embarrassing himself.

The quemara shook itself and snorted, little flames flickering from its nostrils. Wanchoo said, "And I must not forget Amoxtli. She can be cranky, but is quite gentle once she grows accustomed to someone new."

The creature reminded Zee of an armored dillo, though slimmer, and its scales gleamed shining gold. It narrowed its eyes at Zee and stretched its neck to sniff at him, appearing not to like what it smelled. It cocked its head at Jessup, then leapt from Wanchoo's shoulder, spreading thin golden wings, and flew straight at him.

Jessup grunted in surprise at the sudden approach of the bold little creature, but it swerved and flew up around his shell.

"Don't be concerned, Mr. Jessup," said Venkatarama. "She is quite harmless, usually."

Jessup's eyes swiveled to Zee, who could only shrug. The quemara landed on the point at the top of his shell.

Mahfouz watched with concern. "Oh... I—"

Mildrezod shouldered him, cutting him off.

Jessup looked to Zee again. Zee could tell what he was thinking and said silently, *"Don't you do it."* Jessup sighed.

The quemara emitted several high-pitched squeaks.

"Interesting," said Wanchoo. "Amoxtli has already taken a liking to you, Mr. Jessup."

Confused, Jessup said, "Okay."

Commandant Aureosa chuckled, then sighed deeply and addressed Zee.

"I'm sorry to have gotten your hopes up, lad. Many on our board keep their heads in the sand, blind to the possibilities. They are stubborn and resistant to change."

"You should know, however," said Dean Wanchoo, "not everyone voted against you."

"Yes, indeed," Mildrezod added.

Mahfouz gestured toward Dame Toomsil and Tem. "Dame Zara mon Toomsil gave you a glowing character reference, as did her former squire."

Aureosa said, "We're not giving up just yet."

"Oh…" Zee replied. That they had all supported him was both humbling and an honor. Tem had also spoken well of him, which was surprising, and odd. Hearing that he and Jessup might still have a chance of getting into the academy filled him with hope and determination.

"What do you think of our offer?" said Aureosa. "I can assure that you will be safe here. You have my word."

Vandalia tipped her head to Jessup. "Both of you."

Aureosa spoke more quietly. "We here would like to help you with forging as well. We have to be very careful, however, and can't be seen to be directly involved. Understood?"

"Yes, sir." He looked to Jessup, then back. "What's our alternative?"

Vandalia said, "If the two of you took to the sea, we'd do nothing to stop you. There are others, however, in high positions, who wouldn't be as understanding. You would never be allowed to return, and most likely attempts would be made to drive you away, or worse, if you were seen anywhere near Tosh."

Zee and Jessup spoke privately through their bond.

Jessup thought a moment. "*Safe is good. Jessup can work.*" A side of his big mouth tipped up and he repeated what Zee would say when they'd start their beachcombing so long ago. The words Zee had learned from his da. *"Time to get our heads back in the dirt."*

Zee smiled, pleased that Jessup remembered. All day he'd been mulling over the attack by the hammerhead orcapods, and what happened to him when he was swimming and Jessup was encouraging him. He shouldn't have been able to swim that fast. He definitely shouldn't have been able to nearly twist the head off a fully grown hammerhead orcapod. The power that had come over him, channeled into his muscles, his bones, his very being. It had come from Jessup. But, Zee was convinced, it also came from inside himself. He and Jessup were truly bonded, and that's what it was like. He wanted desperately to learn to control it, and to a greater degree, he wanted more of it.

The academy was his best chance to accomplish that, but this seemed to be the most suitable alternative. Besides what the commandants, deans, and beastmasters were offering, he could watch the cadets and learn, and he and Jessup could train on their own. The words of Dr. Aenig came back to him. *"Show them what you've got, Zee Tarrow. I believe in you."* Aenig had contacted Aureosa, and the commandant had listened. They'd been rejected by the board, but Zee would show them. He'd prove he was a real rider—a kraken rider—whether they wanted him or not.

He stood at attention and gave the commandant his and Jessup's answer. "We'll stay, sir. Thank you."

Aureosa looked pleased and relieved. "I'm happy to hear that."

Dean Wanchoo turned to the pairs who were standing guard. "You are all dismissed."

The knights and magickers glanced at each other in hesitation, but saluted, then flew off to their regular duties. Zee looked to the rise where Dame Toomsil and Tem had been standing, but they were already gone.

Aureosa said, "Give us a few weeks, and we'll work something out to get you the instruction you need."

"We can do that, sir."

"The question now is where to put you two while the staff makes arrangements for more permanent lodging."

"Jessup and I would like to stay together," Zee replied. "If that's possible."

"Of course. That rules out a hotel." Aureosa glanced at the others.

Mahfouz seemed to be discussing something with Mildrezod through their bond, then said, "We may have just the place."

* * *

Commandant Aureosa and Dean Wanchoo watched Zee and Mahfouz walk along the shore toward the port and town, while Mildrezod led Jessup out through the harbor in the same general direction.

"We'll need to keep a close eye on them," said Wanchoo. "I can only vaguely sense the nature and level of their power, but their bond is as strong as any I've felt. Unchecked and untrained, they could prove a danger to themselves and others, even if it is not intentional."

"Agreed," Aureosa replied.

"Will you write a letter to the surgeon?"

"I will. In fact, I intend to maintain correspondence with him, if he is willing."

"I believe that would be wise." He placed a beefy hand on Aureosa's shoulder. "Come, my friend. We have future riders of the realm to educate." From Wanchoo's shoulder, the quemara squeaked and blew out a tiny flame. "Even Amoxtli agrees."

* * *

Zee enjoyed the tour through the port and town, and Mahfouz was an enthusiastic guide, but the walking itself was miserable. The ground still felt like it was moving with every step. It made him queasy, and his legs wobbled. He asked Mahfouz how long he thought it would take Zee to regain his land legs.

"Some recover within bells or minutes," Mahfouz replied, "others it can take several days, even a week or longer. How long were you at sea?"

"Nearly ten years, sir."

"You never once stepped foot on shore in ten years?"

"No, sir."

Mahfouz let out a low whistle. "After that amount of time, I just don't know."

That didn't comfort Zee much. His legs were tired and shaking. He'd run on the ship when working on deck, but it was never more than short sprints, and not that many in a row. He was determined to recover as quickly as possible, to get his land legs back, then build his stamina and leg strength. He'd never make much of a cadet if he could barely walk straight, let alone run for physical training.

They made their way out of town, past the lumberyard, foundry, and woodworking shops, and continued along the shore. After the over mile-long trek, they came to a stretch of old shacks at the edge of the water, each with a rickety wooden dock attached. Jessup was waiting in the water next to one of the docks, and Mildrezod sat atop the rocks piled on the slope of the shore near the shack.

Mahfouz held a hand toward the shack with a gleam of pride in his eyes. "This one is mine. It's not fancy, but it's right on the water, relatively private, and the roof doesn't leak. You're welcome to it until we come up with something better."

"What do you think, Mr. Jessup?" asked Mildrezod.

Jessup waved a couple arms in the water as if testing it. "Okay with Jessup, ma'am."

"The harbor gates are closed at night," said Mahfouz. "Nothing larger than a small sheel can slip through the bars, and the harbor is patrolled by knights regularly throughout the day. It's as safe a place as you'll find anywhere in the sea."

Inside the shack, to one side was a cot with real sheets, a blanket and pillow; in the corner a small table with a chair, lamp, an alarm clock, and a pitcher and basin for cleaning up. Piled to the other side were fishing poles, netting, broken oars, and old buoys.

"I stay here on occasion when on the outs with the missus," said Mahfouz.

"Which is more often than he'd like to admit," added Mildrezod, her head poking in through the open door.

There were knotholes in the walls, and light cut through seams between the planks, but it was a palace compared to a threadbare hammock on the berth deck of a ship packed with smelly, snoring sailors.

Zee set a sack he'd been carrying on the table and placed his duffel on the bed. "This will be great. Thank you, sir."

Mahfouz handed him another sack. They had picked up food for Zee's dinner and breakfast on their way through town, as well as a bar of soap and some lamp oil.

Exiting the shack with Zee, Mahfouz said, "We'll leave you lads to it. As the commandants said, someone will meet you and Jessup here tomorrow morning at oh eight hundred bells to direct you to where you'll be placed for employment."

Zee spied a dragon carrying an armored knight flying down to perch on a boulder about a hundred feet away.

"They'll probably have someone watching at all times for a while, just to make sure you're up to no mischief," Mildrezod informed him.

"No mischief, ma'am," Zee replied.

"That's somehow disappointing," said Mahfouz. "Not even a little?"

Zee smiled. "Maybe a little. But nothing bad."

"That's better."

"Now Mahfouz," Mildrezod admonished, "don't be encouraging them to get into trouble on their very first day."

"Who's encouraging?" He climbed into the saddle on Mildrezod's back. "A lad his age should enjoy his youth."

"Like you did?"

"Definitely not like I did. Then he *would* get into trouble." With a raised hand, he added, "Good night, Mr. Tarrow, Mr. Jessup."

Zee and Jessup responded in kind, Mildrezod took to the air, and soon the beastmasters were passing over the town and out of sight.

Zee turned to the knight, still sitting on his dragon, and waved. Jessup waved as well. Both dragon and rider looked surprised, but the knight awkwardly raised a hand. Zee figured he should put them at ease as much as possible. He did plan on getting up to a little mischief, but it would have to wait until after dark. With the long summer days, the sun hadn't yet reached the jagged horizon at the west side of the island. There were still a couple bells of daylight left. His stomach grumbled, reminding him he hadn't eaten all day.

He sat on the dock, feet dangling in the water, chatting with Jessup while eating his meal. Jessup had said he wasn't hungry. He only ate once a week or so. That made sense to Zee. The dragons on the ship would only fly out to snatch fish from the sea every few days. Though Jessup was bigger, he could probably eat a lot more at once, and with no worry of it weighing him down.

Zee realized he hadn't actually spoken to Jessup about what a dragonbond was, or in their case, a krakenbond. When he explained it, Jessup wasn't surprised. To him, it was only natural that he and Zee were bonded that way, which pleased Zee more than he could say.

Ships maneuvered in the bay, the shouts of their crews echoing across the water. Knights changed guard on the high seawall that rimmed the harbor. Sounds floated from the port and town. Even with all the activity, the setting felt peaceful, which was something Zee had rarely experienced on the ship.

"I know this isn't exactly what we wanted," he told Jessup, "but I still can't believe I'm here, and with you. All in one day, from being alone, scrubbing the hull of the HMT *Krakenfish*, to Triumf's Island with Jessup. Life is funny, isn't it?"

"Zee is funny," said Jessup.

The reply caught Zee off guard, and he laughed. Then his mood sobered. "I didn't think I'd ever see you again."

"Jessup always knew he would see Zee."

The warmth from their bond swelled in Zee's chest, and his eyes began to tear up. He took a deep breath and wiped them away. Part of him wanted to relax there with Jessup all evening, but his life had been nothing but work on the ship, training with Tem under the tutelage of Dame Toomsil, then on his own, and studying with Dr. Aenig. He was already getting fidgety. The ever-present desire to better himself, to learn, grow stronger, and to be a cadet, was fiercer than ever.

He looked to the knight and dragon on guard, then scooted closer to Jessup and spoke through their bond. *"We need to sneak out and get the bag we hid at the bottom of the harbor. The one Dr. Aenig gave me. Any ideas?"*

Jessup thought for a moment, then flashed a mischievous grin. *"Jessup will swim down and get it while Mildrezod leads him to where Zee and Jessup will stay. Then Zee and Jessup won't have to sneak back to get it."*

"Er… what?"

Jessup opened his mouth and lifted his big flat tongue, revealing the bag tucked underneath it.

"Oh… Oh!" Zee laughed. *"You crafty devilfish! Mildrezod didn't suspect anything?"*

Jessup ducked his mouth underwater and retrieved the bag with the tip of an arm, then snaked his arm through the water and lifted it to set the bag on the dock at the cabin door, out of sight of the guards. *"Dragons can't see very far below the surface. Jessup is crafty devilfish."*

"Yes, you are." Zee laughed and kicked the water, splashing his friend. Jessup slapped an arm down, the resulting geyser drenching Zee.

Zee sputtered, wiping his face. "I should know better than to get into a splash fight with a kraken."

Jessup answered with a grin.

Dusk approached night, and a great creak and rumble drew their attention to the harbor entrance in the distance. The enormous gates swung ponderously closed, moved by massive chains on sets of turnstiles turned by muscular Royal Ebons and their riders. Great latches were dropped, which flashed with golden light as they locked into place. Zee marveled that they must be secured by not only iron but magickal wards as well.

Thoughts of magick and dragons and Jessup and bonds spinning in his head, Zee told Jessup he'd be back later to say goodnight in person, grabbed the duffel, and went inside to see what Dr. Aenig had given him.

* * *

By the light of the oil lamp, Zee opened the duffel and the long waterproof bag inside it, finding four items wrapped in oilskin to protect them further from the sea. The first he unwrapped was his stinger, the tool he had used to protect himself when scrubbing the hull of the *Krakenfish*. Zee smiled at the man's thoughtfulness, but his appreciation grew even more when he opened a small sack of coin. He dumped it on the bed. It may not have been a fortune, but it was more money than Zee had ever seen. As a conscript on the ship, he'd been paid a king's copper a week and got no share in the bounties distributed to the crew. It had seemed like a lot to him, certainly more than he'd ever had, and since he couldn't leave the ship, he had nothing to spend it on. He'd saved it all and brought it with him. What the surgeon had given him was much more than that. He hoped it wasn't all the money Dr. Aenig had or a large part of his life savings. Either way, he vowed he would pay the man back one day.

Another package contained a stack of blank paper, an ink well, and several pencils and quills. Zee had always used the doctor's for his studies. Such a simple thing, but it filled his heart with gratitude.

He unwrapped the last package and his breath caught in his throat. It was a book, as he had expected, but one he had never seen on Aenig's shelves. It appeared to be very old, the cover made of a thick, dark green material, and stamped with gold foil on the front was the impression of a webbed hand. The hand of a murperson.

He placed his hand on the impression to compare them, and watched in wonder as the webs formed between his fingers, something that only happened when he was in the sea. The heat of his bond with Jessup swelled inside him, and his krakenbond began to tingle. He tore his hand away in surprise, breathing heavily.

Jessup's voice came to him through their bond. *"What is happening, Zee?"*

"Did you feel it too?"

"*Jessup felt warm inside, from Zee.*"

"*That's our bond. It happened when I touched a book Dr. Aenig gave me.*"

"*What is a book?*"

Zee slapped himself on the forehead. Of course Jessup wouldn't know what a book was. "*I'll show you.*"

Zee went outside and held the book up in the clear light of Zhera's twin moons. "This is a book. People read them for information or pleasure."

"*Are we bonded with book?*"

"I... don't think so. But it could have something to do with bonding."

"*Zee read book and see.*"

Zee chuckled. Jessup liked to joke around, but he could also be extremely pragmatic. "I'll do that and let you know what I find out."

"*Okay.*"

Back inside, his hand had returned to normal and the intensity of the bond had faded, but a slight tingle of the krakenbond remained. He slipped his hand under his shirt and touched the rough gray patch on his chest, then quickly stepped in front of the old shaving mirror that hung on the wall behind the washbasin, pulling his shirt over his head.

That morning Dr. Aenig had pointed out that the krakenbond had grown in the short time Zee had been reunited with Jessup, but now it was even larger, and the ten arms had lengthened, spreading farther over his left pectoral. He stared, wondering if the book had done that, or if it had grown throughout the day without him noticing. He placed his hand on the book again. The webbing grew between his fingers, the warmth returned, and the tingling of his krakenbond increased, but he didn't see the bond growing. Removing his hand once more, he wondered if the bond between him and Jessup was making up for the time they'd been apart.

He hurried into the chair at the table and moved the lamp to see the book better, trying not to let his excitement get the best of him. It could be a book of fiction or old myths, like the others he'd read. He'd be happy if it was a detailed murfolk history—but he hoped it was a handbook about murfolk and kraken bonds, maybe even a forging and progression manual.

The forging of Empyrean from the Aether was critical to growing stronger and faster, developing Abilities, and progressing through levels and classes. Zee knew very little about it other than dragon and rider pairs did it on a regular basis to increase their power and advance.

He held his breath and opened the book. Inside the front cover was a slip of stationery with handwriting on it. Zee recognized the surgeon's familiar scrawl, and a lump formed in his throat.

To Zee,

Never forget who you are, and always believe in what you can be.

Yours truly,

Drall

Zee knuckled the moisture from his eyes, then flipped to the first page. He released his breath with a frown, which grew deeper as he turned more pages. He checked the middle of the book, then near the back. All of the pages contained strange, unfamiliar symbols. Now Zee understood why Aenig said he'd hoped he and Zee could figure it out together.

It could be a language, perhaps a language of the murfolk, but the symbols were of random sizes, bunched in odd arrangements on the page. It looked more like a code. Zee had no idea how to translate a language, but he and Aenig had done some code deciphering exercises, games really, and he knew a few approaches to cracking them. Solving it would be harder without the surgeon's help, but he had no choice. He took up his new writing supplies.

Bells later, he'd filled sheets of paper and gotten nowhere. He saw the time and realized he'd stayed up much too late.

Frustrated, Zee went outside to check on Jessup, who asked how the book was going.

"It isn't," Zee said. "It's gibberish."

"What is gibberish?"

"Something that makes no sense."

"Zee will figure it out. Zee is smart tiny murman."

"Not smart enough, apparently. Maybe you should give it a try."

"Jessup can't read. All writing is gibberish."

"That's something else we can work on if you want. I don't know if dragons read, but I don't see why you couldn't. Would you like to learn?"

"Jessup likes when Zee teaches him things."

"All right then, it's a deal." Zee held a hand out over the water.

Jessup lifted the tip of an arm to Zee, who took it and they shook on it.

Zee considered staying outside with Jessup for the night. Maybe even underwater. He'd never slept in the sea before but saw no reason why he couldn't. Tonight he needed to get a good rest, though, and didn't think it would be wise to experiment. Tomorrow would be a big day. The beginning of a whole new life. It wasn't as a new recruit at the academy like he'd hoped, but he was still going to train every chance he got, harder than he ever had before. And now he had Jessup and a bond to progress. He was going to do everything in his power to make sure they were ready.

Thinking about tomorrow made him excited and scared at the same time. He reached out through the bond to sense how Jessup was feeling. He was calm, even content. Zee let it flow through him and it helped settle his nerves.

"Will you be able to sleep out here?" Zee asked.

The kraken yawned, his mouth a dark cave with teeth. It would be a terrifying sight if the beast wasn't his best friend. "Jessup can always sleep."

"Glad to hear it. Goodnight, my friend."

Jessup rumbled with contentment. "Good night, friend Zee." Jessup sank into the water, settling on the bottom, until only the tip of his shell could be seen.

Back inside, Zee wound the clock like he'd done with Dr. Aenig's a hundred times, and set it for oh seven hundred bells. He would get four bells of sleep, but that was as much as he ever got on the *Krakenfish*, and rising at seven would be a luxury he hadn't known in a decade. His frustration over the book had subsided and he settled into the most comfortable bed he'd known in ages. Jessup's calm infused him, relaxing his mind and body. The earth still felt like it was swaying beneath him—or wasn't swaying, which was equally foreign to him. Instead of dwelling on the odd sensation, he imagined it rocking him to sleep.

PART THREE

CHAPTER 24

Zee finally got the stubborn bolt threaded into the brace of an oartug rudder when he heard the ring of a heavy bell. Even underwater it rang loud and clear. For a moment he thought about the bell his mother used to ring for him to come up from the beach or in from the barn for dinner, and he missed her and his da terribly.

Zee's supervisor, Androo Cobbling, tapped him on the shoulder and pointed to the surface. Their shift was done for the day. The man wore a diving helmet with an air tube that went to a pump on the surface, something Zee never had to worry about.

Zee held up a finger for him to wait, then retrieved a wrench attached to his tool belt with a line and tightened the bolt. Together they headed for the surface.

As timing would have it, Zee and Jessup had started on the first day of the workweek. Today was the fifth day, and now they would have two whole days off. Not only that, they worked just nine bells a day, and had a whole bell for lunch. It felt incredibly strange to have so much time of his own, but he'd been putting it to good use.

He'd finally regained his land legs and was running every morning before work and again in the evening. "Running" might not be the right word for it, but he'd worked up to a slow jog, and even that was grueling. He would sneak close to the Basic Training fields on occasion and watch the new recruits. He still couldn't run as fast or as far as the least of them. He was better at the other exercises they had to do, though, thanks to the work he'd performed and the daily routine he'd put himself through on the ship. He could do as many pushers and crunchers as the best of them, and more pullers than anyone he'd seen.

Jessup would go to the beach with him and practice walking on land. It was a struggle for him, having to coordinate all those big flopping arms, but he was getting much better at it. He'd learned that if he tightened and contracted his arms, then lift himself a few feet and curved them back, he could shuffle along faster than Zee could walk. The skin of his arms was flexible but incredibly tough, and the suckers that ran along the bottom of them were built for rough work. Even walking on coarse stone didn't harm him. He could use his sucker spikes for more traction, too, when he wished.

A few times when they were out, they'd spotted a small Ice Diver with spectacularly bright white scales running as well. One of his front legs was shorter than the other, with a clubfoot. Up and down the beach he'd go, bounding as fast as he could on his good front leg until he seemed completely exhausted. They kept their distance so as not to frighten him, but admired his grit and determination. Though he wore a dragon recruit's breastplate, he was always training alone, and they wondered what his story was.

Zee and Jessup also swam in the harbor, testing their bond, seeing what they could do and pushing their limits. After the first three days, knights no longer came to stand sentry near the shack or follow them if they went anywhere other than to work, and no one challenged them when they left the harbor to swim in the sea. All they got was a reminder to be back before dusk from one of the guards at the gate. Mostly all they'd learned so far was they were definitely stronger and faster when together, and if they really pushed themselves, it felt like their strength and speed would increase. They also discovered they would lose that extra strength and speed the farther apart they got from each other, until they were their normal selves. Normal for a kraken was still pretty incredible, though.

In the evenings, Zee taught Jessup the alphabet, scratching out letters on the flat rocks near the shack with soft limestone, and Zee continued trying to decode the book Aenig had given him, but he still had no luck. He'd get to a point where he thought he was close, but when he looked back, he'd swear some of the symbols had changed. After each session he was ready to give up on it for good, but the next day he'd be right back at it.

Workers laughed and joked all along the docks, all heading in one direction. They were generally a well-tempered but serious bunch, and Zee noticed the change.

"What's everybody so happy about, Androo?" he asked his supervisor. It felt odd to call anyone older than him by their first name, especially someone he worked for, but everyone he worked with insisted on it. Androo was responsible for acclimating him to working on the docks and trying out various jobs to see what might be the best fit. There were military technicians that worked on the ships, but the majority of labor at the base was done by civilians employed by a contractor. Most of them were just regular folks like him. Well, not murfolk, but very few of them had fancy names like the wealthy and influential families in the kingdom.

"Today is payday," Cobbling answered, "which means tomorrow is our first day off for the weekend, which means tonight most of this rabble will be crowding the taverns and spending a good chunk of their wages on drink."

Zee shook his head and grinned. Nine-bell days and two days off every week. He couldn't get over it. He hadn't even known jobs like that existed.

Zee stepped up to where Meik Tabacchi, general manager of the contracting firm Zee had been assigned to, sat behind a table out front of his office, handing out bags of coin and crossing names off a list. Behind him, a member of the Marine Force Military Police leaned against the building, looking bored. Apparently there was little worry about being robbed on base.

Tabacchi leaned back upon sighting Zee. "If it isn't Zee Tarrow, our resident murman. How was your first week on the job?"

Before Zee could answer, Cobbling stepped from behind him in line. "He's a hard worker and speedy, Meik. He hasn't complained once, which is more than I can say for the rest of this lot." A few of the closest workers laughed. "And he's shaddamn good at everything I've tried him on. Best hull scrubber we've got, handy with any tools I give him, knows basic woodworking, and never shirks the most crab-crap of labors I force upon him."

"Maybe I should give him your job."

Androo laughed and slapped Zee on the back. "Give me a promotion, and it's all his."

The difference between the way these people interacted with each other and the way the sailors on the ship did was like night and day. There was camaraderie and joking on the ship, but most of the time everyone was tired, angry, or afraid. Zee was sure the captain and Corl had a lot to do with that. Fair treatment and good leadership counted for a lot, and Zee had liked Meik Tabacchi and Androo from the first day he met them. Zee would have to remember that if—no, *when*—he became an officer in the Dragon Corps.

Some of the workers had given him the eye or whispered when he first started working with them, but most all of that had abated already in the short time he'd been there, and no one had challenged or insulted him directly. After their initial curiosity, fear, or indignation wore off, most of them treated him like any other worker with a particular set of skills. His most prominent skills, of course, being able to breathe in the ocean, swim faster, and see better under water than anyone else.

Tabacchi shoved two small pouches of coin toward Zee. Zee picked them up but noticed everyone else was only getting one. Some bulged with more coin than others, but no one had two.

Tabacchi answered his question before he could ask it. "That's for the week. One for you and one for Mr. Jessup." Reacting to Zee's blank expression, he added, "If we had a dragon in our employ, you can bet your barnacled sea bottom we'd be paying it too. And from all reports, that monster of yours can do the work of three cranes and four tugs in half the time. I might even have to give him a raise, shaddammit."

Cobbling chuckled and nudged Zee, clueing him in that Tabacchi was paying Jessup a compliment and only partly joking.

"Thank you, sir," Zee replied. "I'll be sure to tell him."

"You do that. Now, get your beast settled and meet me and a few of the lads, including Cobbling here, at the Blind Pig for a pint."

Zee just stood there. Did the boss just invite him to join them for drinks?

"The Pig?" said Cobbling. "I prefer the Bucket."

"The Dripping Bucket smells like piss."

"That's because people piss themselves. It means they're having fun."

"You go to the Bucket and wet yourself, then. Zee and I will be putting a few back at the Pig with dry britches."

"Are you buying?"

"First round."

"All right then," Cobbling responded, then turned to Zee. "See you at the Pig? You've earned it."

Zee didn't know what to say. No one but Dr. Aenig, Dame Toomsil, and Derlick don Donnicky ever wanted him around on the ship, and certainly not for recreation. Now these people wanted him to spend time with them, just drinking and talking?

"Thank you very much for asking, sir," he sputtered, "but I'll need to speak to Jessup." There was also his evening training to do, and he still hadn't solved the mystery of the murfolk book.

"No harm nor foul if you decide against joining us," Tabacchi responded. "You keep working like you are, and the invitation is always open." Zee turned to go. "And Zee, enough with the 'sir,' lad. It makes me feel old."

"You are old," said Cobbling.

"Shut it, Androo, or I'll have that coin back quicker than a dartfish."

Cobbling snickered.

Zee said, "All right, Mr. Tabacchi, no more 'sir.'"

"For Zepiter's sake, boy, it's Meik!"

* * *

More military police sauntered casually on the wharf, a few chatting with town constables, so Zee felt perfectly comfortable counting his wages as he walked. He came to a complete stop when he peered into his sack. It was more than he had earned as a conscript on the ship in a year. And Jessup's pay doubled that.

Zee may not have been a cadet, but he couldn't believe his good luck. Once again his thoughts returned to Dr. Aenig, the man who had made this all possible, and again vowed he would seek him out one day, pay him back the coin the surgeon had given him, and hug the man.

Up ahead, half submerged near the shore between two piers, Jessup lifted a rectangular boulder the size of a horse cart and placed it among the others he'd laid on the bank already.

Atop the bank stood a sturdy crane of wood, steel, rope, pulleys and chain, and a couple more of the big blocks of stone. Two operators leaned against the rig, chatting and watching Jessup work.

"It's about time, Zee," Mickal rot Fletcher said as Zee approached. "He never quits until you show up." He offered Zee his flask. "Have a nip?"

"No, but thank you, Mickal." These men had already given him the 'sir' speech when he first met them. "Is he still doing well?"

Robhat Hayes puffed his pipe and jabbed the stem down the slope. "That beast will put us out of a job."

"There's plenty of crane work to go around, Hat," said Fletcher. "We don't have to work so fast when riprapping, and he'll keep the folks at the quarry plenty busy. It's a win-win if you ask me."

"True enough," Hayes replied, taking Fletcher's flask and throwing back a swig. He grimaced and coughed. "Is that varnish remover?"

Fletcher sniffed the flask and took another drink. "Maybe."

Zee hadn't bothered greeting Jessup when he approached. They each always knew when the other was near. "You ready to go, Jessup?"

"Just two more," said Jessup, reaching for the next stone.

"How many is that today?"

"Seventy-three. Plus these last two will be seventy-five."

"That's just this afternoon," said Hayes. "And it took him some time to unload the stone from the ferries after lunch."

"Jessup docked four ships this morning," added the kraken, "helped load two, and caught one big sheel that snuck in through the gate."

"You've been busy," Zee replied. Not only did Jessup seem to enjoy working, he was making tremendous progress with his counting and math.

Jessup laid the next stone. "Jessup likes busy."

Zee sensed someone approaching in the air and was already turning when Mildrezod called out, "Ahoy! Mr. Tarrow!" After only the short time he and Jessup had been back together, he'd noticed he was able to feel the presence of other bonded pairs when they were within a certain distance. He'd known other dragon and rider pairs could do it, but to realize he could feel it himself had been a surprise. He could tell it was stronger or weaker in different pairs depending on their class and level, but he had a hard time discerning between them if there were more than two pairs close together.

Mildrezod landed far enough away to keep from blowing sand in their faces and strode to them. From her back, Beastmaster Mahfouz greeted the crane operators, then said, "Your new quarters are ready, Mr. Tarrow."

"I wouldn't call them 'new,'" said Mildrezod. "But they seem fit for a young murman and a kraken."

"We think you'll like it," Mahfouz added.

CHAPTER 25

Having retrieved his belongings from the shack, Zee and Jessup followed the beastmasters out of the harbor and along the coast toward where the range of five mountains rose at the far end of the island. As they drew closer, Zee observed that they were different from the mountains of Tosh, more like giant shards of rock thrust into the air.

They rounded a point of land and headed toward the base of one of the mountains. Dragons and their riders flew in and out of rows of cave entrances on the upper half of each mountain. Four of them were dorm mounts, the fifth reserved for meeting rooms and faculty and staff who didn't live in the village. He shouted nervously up to Mahfouz, "We're staying with cadets?"

"Not exactly. They occupy the upper tiers of the mounts. No one will bother you down here."

Just above the waterline, beneath a deep ledge, was a wide opening to a cave. Mildrezod flew straight in, her wings not even coming close to grazing the outer edges.

Jessup paused at the slope of stone that led up to the entrance until Mildrezod called out from the darkness.

"Come along. It's perfectly safe."

They climbed the slope and entered to discover a cavern much wider and taller than the cave opening. Just inside, the stone stepped down to a lake filled with seawater, large enough for a half dozen Jessups to lounge with plenty of room to spare. The ceiling was free of stalactites, and the cavern had the look of having been carved out of the mountain as opposed to naturally formed.

On the far side of the lake, stone slanted gradually to the floor of the remainder of the cave. Waiting there were not only Mahfouz and Mildrezod, but Aureosa and Wanchoo and their dragons as well. Even from that distance, Zee could feel their power. More than any of the other pairs they'd come close to since arriving at the citadel. The power of Red Titans.

Though taken aback by their unexpected presence, Zee managed a well-executed salute and proper formal greeting. "Daimyo General Commandants Sir ran Aureosa and Dame Vandalia! Magi General Deans Sirs han Wanchoo and Venkatarama, sirs!" His voice echoed in the large space. Jessup saluted as well.

"Hello, Mr. Tarrow, Mr. Jessup," said Aureosa. "You don't need to salute us or greet us so formally, you know. You're civilians, now. In fact, people will think it's odd."

Zee was put at ease by Aureosa's casual manner. "People already think we're odd, sir, but thank you for letting us know."

Jessup proceeded into the water, which was plenty deep for him to swim freely, and crossed to the interior side, where he slid his front arms to wrap them in front of him on the shore.

The cave floor looked to have been recently swept and the walls wiped down. There wasn't a cobweb in sight. They had entered near one end of the cave, and it extended farther to the left along the lake. Neatly placed against the curving wall near this end were bedroom furnishings and a table with chairs.

On the walls were Empyrean lamps infused with power by magickers. They bathed the interior in yellowish light. Captain lon Bomba had one in his quarters on ship. Saying "fos" would light them, and "skotadi" would put them out. Of all the wonders of the cavern, his eyes were drawn most strongly to a shelf of books.

Aureosa and Wanchoo dismounted from their dragons, and Zee climbed down from Jessup.

"We hope you find these accommodations to your liking," said Vandalia.

Jessup gazed around the cavern. "Jessup likes. It has much room, and a little sea for swimming."

"We would call it a saltwater lake, but I'm glad to hear it," she replied.

"It's wonderful, thank you," Zee said. The shack had been a big step up from a rope hammock on a ship, packed in with other sailors like smelly sardines, but this felt to him like the bedchamber of a king. "What is this place?"

"No one knows, to be honest," said Aureosa. "There are dozens of them, all around the base of the dorm mounts. Many are collapsed, and all but a few have been blocked up for as long as anyone can remember. The ones left open have been used for storage in the past. It took some doing to get this one cleared. It's now yours and Jessup's for as long as you require it, compliments of His Majesty's Dragon Corps."

"I don't know what to say, sir. Thank you."

"You're welcome. We hear work is going well, and you and Mr. Jessup are exemplary additions to the maintenance and construction teams at the docks."

"Thank you, sir."

"We also hear you've been watching the cadets and doing some training on your own," said Dean Wanchoo.

"You know about that?" Zee was worried they might not approve, but by their reaction, they felt the opposite.

"There isn't much that happens on this island these two don't know about," Mahfouz said with a sly grin.

"I'll keep that in mind, sirs."

Jessup was eyeing the quemara, which gazed at him intently.

"Weird thing is watching Jessup," he said to Zee through their bond.

"It's a quemara, and her name is Amoxtli. You know that."

"*Weird thing.*"

"*After all the creatures you've seen in the ocean. Are you afraid of it?*"

Jessup huffed silently through their bond. "*Like Zee used to say, 'Don't be silly.' Jessup not afraid of—*" He flinched as Amoxtli leapt from her perch and flew toward him. She flapped in a circle around his shell, then landed on one of the arms he had coiled on the shore in front of him.

"*You sure about that?*" Zee asked.

Jessup didn't answer right away. "*Jessup is just cautious.*" He paused. "*There is a strange feeling about it. Jessup's not sure...*"

Wanchoo said, "Amoxtli is drawn to power, Mr. Jessup, or it's potential. You must be a mighty beast indeed."

Zee smiled up at Jessup. "See?" Jessup frowned.

"What will you and Mr. Jessup be doing next to occupy your time when you aren't working?" asked Venkatarama.

"We'll continue to train and get stronger, sir, and we'd like to start forging but we don't know how."

Venkatarama's gaze shifted to Vandalia.

"That would be the natural next step for a bonded pair," she said. "We said we would help you, but you must understand it is forbidden for humans and dragons to bond outside of the academy, let alone forge. An unsanctioned dragon and rider pair caught forging or practicing Abilities as they obtain them can be separated, banished, or worse."

Mildrezod caught the look of distress on Zee's face and said, "The laws don't say anything about murfolk and krakens, however."

"They do not, which is how we've been able to successfully argue that Mr. Tarrow and Mr. Jessup be allowed to stay in spite of their unsanctioned bond. There are some, however, who are already making noises about wanting to have that law changed to include their kind."

"To change such a law would take quite some time," said Aureosa. "Still, to actively engage in aiding an unsanctioned pair to forge could have consequences for all involved."

Vandalia said, "We're telling you two this so you understand why it's not a good idea for us, in our positions, to train you directly. We also have significant demands on our time and are seen often, at all times of the day, all days of the week, particularly during the school year."

Zee was disappointed, but neither he nor Jessup wanted to get them in any trouble. "We understand, ma'am."

Beastmaster Mahfouz said, "Even if someone were to risk guiding a murman and kraken pair in the forging process, we don't know how they'd begin. Humans and dragons forge Empyrean, the residual power of their creation by Zepiter. No one knows for certain what a murfolk and kraken might forge."

"There are theories..." Wanchoo tapped his upper lip. "While there may be consequences to aiding them in forging, I don't see any reason why we couldn't have a look at the core of a bonded kraken and rider pair that hasn't forged."

Venkatarama said, "It could also help us figure out how to proceed in finding them help."

"Not to mention be something no one has ever seen, as far as we know," Wanchoo added.

"If we can see it at all," said Vandalia.

Dean Wanchoo said, "Would you mind, Mr. Tarrow? Mr. Jessup?"

"I don't know what you mean, sir."

"Of course you don't, begging your pardon."

"I mean, I've seen Dame mon Toomsil and Peloquin and the other dragon and rider pairs forging on the ship. They looked like they were meditating. Dame Toomsil wouldn't tell us exactly what they were doing. Not even her squire, Tem. She said it was only taught after Pairing Day and the bonding ceremony at the academy and could only be done by bonded pairs, anyway. She did have us meditate and think about Empyrean sometimes, though. She said it was good for our aura."

"Quite right, and very prudent of her. Forging can be difficult at any time in a pair's progression. It's also safer and less strenuous when done with others."

"She said that too."

"The secrets of forging are passed down through oral tradition to bonded pairs only in cadet training, early in their first year," said Commandant Aureosa. "There is no written instruction. Some have been known to take notes, but they're required to turn them in before graduation. It's forbidden to carry them beyond the academy walls or even to share them within."

Zee was disheartened, but replied, "I understand, sir."

Wanchoo said, "I don't believe we're bending rules too much by telling you at least the basics of what happens when a rider and beast are bonded." He looked to the others, who had no objection.

"Every living being has an aura, the power of life, you might say. When a pair is bonded, their auras, some say their very souls, become shared and grow stronger. Within this shared aura, a space is formed we call a crucible. The crucible contains natural amounts of Empyrean from both the rider and beasts auras, though unprocessed, or unforged. Once the crucible is fully formed, pairs can begin forging what is called their core. The core is the source from which they draw their enhanced power and Abilities, and it is primarily through forging a larger and stronger core that pairs obtain higher levels within classes and progress to higher classes. You're familiar with levels and classes, yes?"

"Yes, sir, I think so. The lowest class is Sand, which is a rating for individuals only. It's based on their individual aura as well as fitness and skill levels, I believe. Like all the other classes, it has three levels, low, medium, and high. The next class is Tin, but only bonded pairs can obtain it. Beyond that are Lead, Copper, Bronze, Iron, Silver, and Gold, and then the three Titan classes, White Titan, Red Titan and Black Titan."

"You're more well informed than I would have expected, Mr. Tarrow, though I should have known better."

Jessup's voice sounded in Zee's head. *Told you. Smart tiny murman.*

Zee tried to hide a grin, which he was pretty sure just made him look gassy.

"Would you mind letting us have a look at your crucible and core?" Vandalia asked.

Jessup spoke in Zee's mind again. *"Why they so excited, Zee?"*

Zee could feel it too. They were eager to see Zee and Jessup's core. It made sense, since they had never seen the core of a murman and kraken before, but it seemed to go beyond that to a kind of hope. *"Aren't you excited?"*

"No."

"You are, too. I can feel what you feel, you know."

"Okay. Maybe a little."

Zee chuckled inwardly.

Jessup said, "Is okay with Jessup."

"It's all right with me, too," said Zee, "but how do we do that?"

Wanchoo beckoned with his hand. "Amoxtli, come." The quemara grunted in protest but fluttered to land between the horns on Venkatarama's head. To Zee and Jessup, Wanchoo said, "It's quite simple, if not as easy as one might think. For beginners, it would be best if you were in contact with one another."

"All right." Zee climbed up to sit on one of Jessup's arms, his back against Jessup's chin—or where his chin would be, if he had one. He crossed his legs and rested his hands on his knees like he'd seen Dame Toomsil do when she and Peloquin were forging.

"Well done," said Wanchoo. "First you must try to calm yourselves and clear your minds."

Zee thought for a moment, then closed his eyes and spoke to Jessup through their bond. *"Do you remember how I used to take deep breaths to help with my breathing? It was as much about calming myself down as anything else, letting the mist from my spritzer do its work, but I also used it to keep myself from scratching at my rash when it really itched."*

"Jessup would do it too sometimes. Breathe with Zee."

"I remember, and that seemed to help me even more than when I did it myself. It must have been because of our bond. Let's try it."

Zee took a slow, deep breath in through his nose, held it a moment, then out just as slowly through his mouth. On the second breath, Jessup joined in, and though the quantity of air he breathed in and out was far greater and rustled Zee's hair, they were soon in perfect sync. After only a few breaths, Zee could feel not only himself but also Jessup relaxing, and any lingering worries faded away. The sensation cycled between them, then became one shared state.

Wanchoo must have felt it too, because Zee heard him speak softly, as if to himself. "Fascinating…" After a moment, he said in a soothing voice. "Now continue to maintain this state while looking inside yourself together, as one. Seek your crucible and the power within it, feel for its contours and substance, and bring it to light in your minds' eyes."

Zee reached with his mind, exploring inside himself. If their core was there, it had to be beyond normal sight. He needed to search and see with a different sense, the bond itself.

Zee didn't know exactly what they were looking for, but he sensed something in his chest below his heart, though not in his chest, like it existed in another dimension. He focused on that, and Jessup's attention followed. He could hear Jessup's heartbeat slow further, then settle in a rhythm like the distant beat of a massive drum, though it beat within himself as well. Speaking softly between them, he uttered, *"Okay, crucible, where are you?"*

The familiar warmth of the bond Zee felt so often in Jessup's presence swelled in his chest. The feeling wasn't stronger than he'd ever felt, but somehow clearer and more defined. He concentrated on peering into it. A distinct and finite spherical space appeared and hung there in his mind as clearly as if it existed right before his eyes.

"Oh…," came Jessup's voice. *"That's in us?"*

"I believe so," said Zee, equally amazed.

Jessup's voice was infused with joy. *"Our crucible. Zee's and Jessup's. Together."*

The wonders of the bond never ceased.

Rapt in the moment as he was, Zee would have jumped when Wanchoo spoke again if the man's voice wasn't so pacifying. The dean must have heard Jessup and Zee gasp when they saw their core. "The hardest part is done, and in record time for a first visualization. Now feel out for the presence of each of us here. I know you can. Then wish for your core to be revealed to us. It might help to speak the word 'reveal,' even if silently to yourselves."

Zee and Jessup both spoke softly but aloud. "Reveal."

Now it was the others in the room who gasped. Wanchoo uttered, "It *is* true..."

Zee and Jessup opened their eyes. Hanging in the air before them was a roughly circular white ring approximately eight feet across. Within it floated a dense cloud of sparkling particles like glowing blue embers floating in a void, or stars in the darkest and clearest night sky. The particles moved and floated within the cloud, which spun very slowly.

"What is it, sir?" Zee asked. "Is something wrong?"

They all just stared. Finally, Wanchoo spoke, though as if in a trance. "My apologies, Zee. It's just that we are witnessing something no one has seen in known history. The crucible and core of a bonded murman and kraken. And it's not filled with yellow Empyrean obtained from the Empyreal Plane, as ours are, but blue Marisean..."

"Marisean? Is that a bad thing?"

Deans Wanchoo and Venkatarama grinned, as did Commandants Aureosa and Vandalia. "Not at all," said Wanchoo. "It's magnificent. Miraculous, even."

"I don't understand, sir."

"According to myth and legend, Empyrean is the residual power of Zepiter, left over from when Zepiter created humans and dragons from one half of the first being. It's what gives us life and enables us to bond and progress. It exists in the Aether, which is all around and within all living things, since all life is magick, and most of all in humans and dragons. But only through the bond can we sense and forge it.

"It has never been known if murman and krakens were able to bond at all—if they even existed. Some say it would be impossible and to speak of it is heresy, even though today we know for a fact that murfolk exist and now at least one kraken as well. Based on remnants of other ancient texts and drawings contained within them, however, there are seekers of deeper truths who have theorized that if murfolk and krakens did exist, they may have been able to bond, and if they did, they would draw not on the golden power of Zepiter, but on the power of their own creator, Postune, that it was called Marisean, and it could be blue. Though we do not speak of it publicly, all of us here are among the believers."

"You, Mr. Tarrow and Mr. Jessup," said Vandalia, "have just proven us to have been right all along."

Wanchoo added, "There is nothing more edifying for scholars than to see their theories justified and beliefs verified, and beyond even that, the broader implications are—oh my..."

There were more intakes of breath as the slowly spinning cloud of blue motes revealed a ribbon of yellow that curved roughly from top to bottom. The edges were clearly defined, the two colors of particles remaining entirely separate but existing together.

Mildrezod muttered, "That, is unexpected..."

"What is it, ma'am?" Zee asked.

It was Aureosa who answered. "Empyrean."

"In the core of a murman and kraken..." said Vandalia.

"Even among the theories I just explained," said Wanchoo, "it has never been considered that murfolk or krakens could access Empyrean. The natural auras of humans and dragons are comprised entirely of Empyrean."

"As far as we know," Mahfouz interjected.

"Correct, as far as we know. Empyrean is all we human and dragon pairs can see, and all we have been taught exists. Because of this, we see only the Empyreal Plane when we look upon the Aether, and from that mine only Empyrean ore into our cores and there forge it. It has therefore been thought that, if murfolk, krakens, and Marisean existed, they'd only be able to mine and forge Marisean. Based on what we see in your core, you and Jessup should be able to see both the Empyreal Plane and the

Mariseal Plane and perhaps forge both types of ore."

"Have we ever known of a human and dragon pair that could use Postune's power?" asked Mildrezod.

"Nowhere in the records we have seen," said Venkatarama, "going back a thousand years."

"What about older records?"

"They were lost, the same time as the original Creation Scrolls."

Gazing at the cloud in their crucible, Zee asked, "Sirs and ma'ams, how did the Marisean and Empyrean get in there?"

Vandalia said, "Simply from living. Small amounts seep into your crucible from your natural auras."

"I'm wondering..." said Aureosa. "Perhaps Zee has Empyrean in his aura because he has lived on land with humans from a very young age. Breathing the air, eating human food."

"And because they were bonded and their crucible began forming when young," added Vandalia, "Jessup has had it too, for quite some time. They have developed not only a tolerance for it, but the capacity for using it. Perhaps even more fascinating, the two energies do not cancel each other out but seem perfectly stable in a single crucible."

"And a quite sizable crucible it is," said Venkatarama, "especially considering they have never forged."

"They've been bonded for a decade. It's possible that a crucible expands with time, even without active forging."

Mildrezod said, "And Mr. Jessup is quite a large beast."

"There is that," said Vandalia. Zee and Jessup exchanged glances, intrigued but also perplexed by the conversation.

"What does all that mean, though?" Zee asked.

Aureosa tore his eyes from their crucible and looked at Zee as if he'd forgotten he was there. "I don't know, Mr. Tarrow. I honestly don't know."

He looked to the others, who shook their heads in agreement.

Wanchoo said, "It's nothing to worry about, just a fascinating anomaly. I've no idea what the practical significance might be."

"It gives us much to think about," added Venkatarama. "Thank you for letting us perceive this wonder."

It was still weird to Zee to be thanked by someone of such status and power. And a dragon, no less. "It's our pleasure, sir." He gazed at their core. "Is there any way for you to tell what class or level we are?"

"That would only be possible if you had begun forging, and even then it would just be an estimate. Only an official assessment could rate your threat level accurately."

Wanchoo said, "And with Marisean, let alone a dual Marisean and Empyrean core…" He tapped his chin as he pondered. No one else had anything to add.

"There is one serious practical matter," said Aureosa. "You must not reveal your core to anyone else."

"Yes, sir."

Wanchoo said. "To hide your core, simply look into it as you did when you revealed it, then imagine dropping a curtain over it. You can think of or say 'hide,' if it helps. It should become dark even to you."

Zee and Jessup tried it, and after a few attempts found they could hide their core and reveal it with ease.

"You two are quick studies," said Vandalia. "Very well done."

Aureosa said, "Now that we know you have Empyrean in your core, I'm much more enouraged we can figure something out to help you with forging." He strolled to the bookshelves. "I hope you find these useful, Mr. Tarrow." He pulled one out, seemingly at random. "Dr. Aenig said you have a fondness for books."

"I do, sir. Thank you."

Aureosa put the book back and returned to Vandalia's side. "We will leave you and Mr. Jessup to get settled, but before we go, there will be a full combat training exhibition in Triumf's Theatrum tonight, if you and Mr. Jessup would like to attend. It's free and open to the residents of the island."

Zee checked with Jessup, but the answer was an enthusiastic, "We would love to come, sir, thank you!"

CHAPTER 26

After following the road a short distance from town, Zee and Jessup passed through an open gate to the academy training fields. The second year cadets, or twosies, as they were often called, on guard duty tried not to openly gawp at the kraken but didn't succeed very well.

Zee had spent the time before leaving for the combat exhibition showing Jessup their pay and explaining coin and what it was for.

"Hmm," Jessup had uttered. It had felt to Zee as if he was thinking about something else, and had been about to ask his friend what it was, but Jessup had asked if they could count it. After counting their pay three times to make Jessup happy, Zee had washed up and changed clothes.

He straightened the collar on the new shirt he'd bought during the week with some of the money he'd gotten from Dr. Aenig. Though the shirt, his trousers, and shoes were all new, clean, and respectable, he still felt out of place among the other townsfolk taking the path to the Theatrum—and who were giving the murman and kraken plenty of space.

Zee regretted not being able to meet Cobbling and Tabacchi at the tavern. As much as he'd like to have gone, though, an opportunity like seeing a full combat exhibition in Triumf's Theatrum had to come first. He hoped Meik had meant it when he'd said the invitation was always open.

Commandant Aureosa had told him that anyone from the base and village was welcome to travel the roads and paths of the academy grounds to attend training events. Zee had been thrilled to hear that. He'd watched the new recruits in training from afar, but he wanted to see and learn as much as he could. That was the reason he and Jessup were walking the distance to the arena even though they could have swum around to it more quickly. They would still make it in plenty of time for the beginning of the matches. The walk was good training for both him and Jessup, too.

The training field was well over a half mile across, and even longer. It was marked off in sections, each designated for a different kind and level of training. Closest to town and farthest from the citadel building was where the new recruits lived and trained during the Basic Training phase of their first year. They all shared a long white barracks tent and took meals out in the open at rows of tables. It wasn't mealtime yet, though, and they were all still hard at work.

A group of twenty-five recruits came running along the road, driven by shouting cadet instructors, lecturing them in military organization, discipline, and honor while they ran. They all gaped when they saw Jessup lumbering up the road and moved out into the grass to go around them, but the instructors quickly recovered and continued their harassment of the recruits once they'd passed.

A familiar voice caught Zee's attention. Dame Toomsil approached from the field. Zee saluted. "Hello, Dame Toomsil, ma'am."

"Hello, Mr. Tarrow, Mr. Jessup. You don't need to salute me, you know."

"So we've been told, sorry," Zee replied.

"Don't be sorry. Old habits are hard to break, and as far as habits go, that's not a bad one. Where are you headed?"

"To the main arena to watch the combat exhibition."

"I just finished instructing a foursie sword class and am headed there myself. Peloquin is in the harbor teaching second-year dragons advanced ship-riding etiquette and will join me there. I'll walk with you, if you don't mind."

"That would be wonderful, thank you."

They continued on their way, exchanging pleasantries about how things were going with her position at the academy and Zee and Jessup's work at the port. Zee spoke and listened carefully when she spoke, but his head turned this way and that, attention clearly divided between their conversation and the activities of the Basic Training recruits.

Dame Toomsil noticed his distraction and told him that early in Basic they focused on physical training and discipline. They hadn't even started weapons training yet. There was no specific regimen for knights to follow in training their squires, so the instructors here had to determine the level of their skills and train them accordingly, bringing those who were lacking up to speed. Most of the training was run by second- and third-year cadet instructors.

"The minnies—the new rider recruits—wear tan training uniforms. Those that pass Basic and become first-year cadets wear yellow. Second-years wear orange, third-years red, and the fourth-year cadets wear purple. Their assessment badges and cadet armor display their level and rank. Only graduates are allowed to wear the royal blue of a knight."

They came upon a group of minnies being forced to belly-crawl in ill-fitting training armor and wearing full pack through a shallow ditch of sloppy mud with thorny brambles growing out of it. It smelled terrible and stretched for a hundred yards. Human and dragon cadet instructors yelled at them to go faster, and some of the dragons were blasting flames over their heads to make them stay low, even catching some of the brambles on fire.

"As you know all too well," Dame Toomsil continued, "essentially all of our cadets come from well-to-do and influential families. Much of the approach to Basic Training is designed to teach them they aren't above pain and suffering. A knight must know adversity and have a level of humility." She lowered her voice. "Though you wouldn't know it from how most of them behave." A hint of a smile appeared on her lips. "I doubt you would have a problem in that regard, Zee Tarrow, and you should take that as a compliment."

"Thank you, ma'am."

"There is also a practical element to an activity such as the trench crawl. There are times when riders and their dragons are separated in battle over land and have to survive. A rider must be prepared for the worst."

Jessup watched the recruits in the trench. "Jessup wants to do that."

She chuckled. "We'd have to make a bigger ditch." The look of longing on Zee's face was clear to see. "You wish you were training with them, too."

"I do."

"I wish you were as well, to be honest." She gave him a knowing look. "And I'm not the only one."

"Thank you. Everyone has been so nice to me here. I have to admit, it feels strange."

An instructor shouted for recruits to keep moving in the ditch, and a dragon blasted a particularly broad swath of flame over their heads.

Dame Toomsil said, "They wouldn't be as nice to you if you were in there."

To Zee, even that didn't look so bad.

* * *

Sallison anh Batcu power-crawled on her belly through the muck of the trench, wearing a determined grimace and passing recruits who whined and moaned. Searing flames drove her down, face in the mud, then she was up and moving again. She shouldered past a recruit in her way, ignoring his snooty complaints, and came up next to Chirt sim Nabbit, a thin but wiry recruit and the smallest in the Basic Training cohort. Under her breath, Chirt was cursing three recruits in front of her, side by side and blocking her way.

Sallison wasn't so quiet. She slapped the boot of the recruit in the middle. "Move it, you sea slogs!"

Derlick don Donnicky glared back. "Shove a slog where the sun doesn't shine, Batcu. We're moving as fast as we can."

"That, I believe." She elbowed Chirt, said, "Come on, Nabbit," and proceeded to crawl over the top of Donnicky.

Chirt shoved her too-large helmet up out of her eyes, grinned, and followed.

"Shaddammit, Batcu!" Donnicky complained.

A cadet dragon instructor roared, "Shut your slimy fish-holes! You want the enemy to find you?" She shot flame over them. Sallison pressed into Donnicky's back, taking the brunt of the heat.

"Ha!" cried Donnicky.

Sallison scrambled over his head, making sure to shove his face into the mud as she went.

Donnicky dug stinking muck from his eyes, and spit. "What the shells?!"

Chirt pushed his face back into the mud as she followed Sallison. "Serves your right, you cocky conkhead," said Chirt, dragging her feet over his helmet.

"Gah!"

Having witnessed Sallison's move, a third-year cadet instructor announced, "Now there's some minny initiative! Anyone who catches and beats Minny anh Batcu to the finish gets a mile taken off their evening run!"

Some of them were encouraged by the challenge, but most just moaned in defeat. Sallison had proven herself to be near the top of the cohort in strength, speed, and skill, having been rated at mid-level Sand Class in her first individual assessment, and she was in the upper range of mid-level at that. Most of the others hadn't reached Sand at all yet, though that wasn't uncommon this early in Basic. Sallison and a few others were the uncommon ones. She was also quite open with her disdain for arrogant highbreds.

"Don't let them beat you, Batcu," said Chirt.

"Hadn't planned on it," Sallison replied.

Her attention was caught by the kraken watching from the road, and the murman who stood next to him with Lead Instructor of the Sword, Dame Zara mon Toomsil. There was no mistaking the look of longing on Zee Tarrow's face. Crazy as it seemed, he wanted to be down there with them, slogging through the muck. He really did want to be a knight.

Well, she did too. She powered forward, ignoring the burn of her muscles, stench in her nose, and grit of mud in her teeth, leaving Chirt behind.

She came upon Mehmet can Yasso, lying there with his forehead in the mud, breathing hard. Chirt wasn't ranked high in the cohort due to her size and lack of upper-body strength, but Mehmet, nearly as short as Chirt but also soft and round in the middle, was currently dead last.

Sallison's hard demeanor softened. "Come on, Mehmet, you can do this. We're almost halfway there."

"I can't," came the recruit's defeated voice from the mud.

"Are you crying?"

"No," he whimpered.

She slapped the back of his helmet. "Get going, Minny. You don't want your brother to see you like this, and especially not your sister."

He jerked his head up and scanned the banks of the ditch. "Are they here?"

"I don't know, but they could be, any minute."

Mehmet began to crawl. "Okay. I can do this. I can do this."

"That's Zepiter's spirit. See you at the finish line."

"Thank you," he said in earnest.

She crawled on ahead. Mehmet's brother was a twosie here at the academy and his sister a threesie, both at the top of their classes. He had a lot to live up to. It didn't help that his brother and sister were cruel snobsnails, like most of the cadets at the academy.

Sallison came upon Jondon dil Rolio. As was no surprise, he'd kept to the side so as not to impede anyone with his bulk. That was just the way he was. Politeness might be a virtue, but the lack of a ruthless competitive spirit could prove his downfall if he wanted to be a knight. The largest of the recruits in their cohort, Jondon was incredibly strong but carried extra weight, was slow on the run, and not very quick with a sword. At the moment, he'd also gotten his backpack snagged on briars and was unable to reach them.

"Hi, Sallison," he greeted her, beathing heavily but relatively cheerful, as usual. "I thought you would have passed me ages ago."

"They made me and a few of the others go last." It was because of her high placement in the cohort so far, but she wasn't going to rub it in. She tugged the briars free of his pack, glad of the gauntlets on her hands even though they were heavy and full of mud. "What would you do without me?"

"Lie here and die of starvation, probably."

She snorted. "You could eat mud."

"I've already eaten plenty." He wrinkled his nose. "I think there's more than mud in here. Smells like dragon dung."

"We'd be lucky if that's the only kind of dung they throw in here," she said as she crawled ahead.

He sniffed the muck. "Ew."

* * *

Zee's head swiveled as he continued along the road with Jessup, trying to take it all in. New dragon recruits marched in drill training, being yelled at just as much as the humans, their instructors calling them "waddling duckies" and "belly-crawling worms," among other things. All of their instructors were cadet dragons, with only a few accompanied by their bondmate human cadet. Another group of dragons was running sprints out to a post and back. Zee had never seen dragons run like that before and marveled that they were quite good at it, their legs built and moving very much like those of horses, just sturdier.

"Dragons are made for flying," said Dame Toomsil. "They grow tired after some time, but it comes easy to them. Running is a more efficient method of conditioning, though they don't like it much."

Jessup let out a big kraken sigh. "Jessup can't run."

"You're built even more for swimming than dragons are for flying," said Dame Toomsil.

Zee said, "We'll figure out something, Jessup. You're already walking better than you were a week ago." An old memory brought a grin to his face. "And much better than when we played on the beach when you were a baby."

Jessup chuckled. "That is true."

Zee noticed Dame Toomsil watching them with an expression of amusement and added, "He fell over a lot," he added.

"Jessup was little," the kraken said in his defense.

"He was about the size of a small water pail. A pointy water pail, with lots of arms."

"Tiny murman," Jessup retorted.

Dame Toomsil grinned and shook her head. "I'm still a bit in shock that krakens even exist, to tell you the truth. And they talk. And here I am, walking with one who's joking about his youth with a murman. Wonders indeed never cease." Zee smiled, and she continued. "You two are wonders. Don't let anyone tell you differently. Do you hear me?"

Zee and Jessup both said, "Yes, ma'am," at the same time, then said, "Thank you" simultaneously as well.

"Are you doing that on purpose?" Zee asked Jessup.

"No," the kraken replied, then thought for a moment. "Maybe."

"It's the bond," Dame Toomsil interjected. "Dragons and riders do it all the time."

"That's a good thing, then," said Zee.

"It's certainly not a bad thing."

The atmosphere changed drastically as they passed beyond the Basic Training area into the cadet training field. Gone were the insults, roars, and chaotic nature of Basic, replaced by orderly drills, rhythmic clack of training swords, and firm but supportive comments. Faculty and staff instructors provided oversight, but cadets of various years trained together and most of the orders and advice came from the cadet instructors from higher classes to those in the lower.

Groups of bonded dragons and riders worked on further developing their bond Abilities. One pair would blast fire at another, who would block it with their Shield Ability, then fire back in turn. Greatwings and Royals threw Fireballs, Ice Divers shards of ice, and Rocks spewed dragon ambergris lava, while their riders flung spears they snatched from their Keeps.

Groups of five pairs called flights, the smallest unit of pairs in the cadet wing, flew close together in the air, practicing their formations. More clashed in light combat training while magicker cadet and instructor pairs circled them. Two pairs dove too close to one another and collided harder than they should. Their wings became tangled and they began to fall. A magicker instructor thrust his wand forward and a Platform of translucent yellow light appeared below them, slowing their descent until they righted themselves. They flew apart, saluted each other, and continued as if nothing had happened. Other flights raced in the air, flying through a course of globes of light that floated at various distances and heights, conjured by magickers.

At the sound of Dame Toomsil's voice, Zee realized he'd been watching with eyes wide and mouth hanging open. He clacked his mouth shut as she spoke.

"These fields are used for light combat. Heavy combat takes place in simulation fields. Most of those are farther out toward the dorm mounts. There, Simulation Artefacts create areas for virtual combat. It looks and feels real, including injury and pain, but no damage is done, and any fatalities are false deaths."

Zee stared at her. "You use real weapons? And fire, and Abilities?"

"We do."

"But no one gets hurt. How is that possible?"

"Magick." She shrugged. "It's the same with the Orb of Assessment."

"What's that?"

She waved along the road. "I'll show you."

They followed the road to the citadel. The old fortress was simple but still grand. Honor guards stood at the main entrance, and knight riders sat upon their dragons on the towers.

They continued along one side of a path that encircled an enormous courtyard. Detailed statues of kings and heroes of old lined the path, all astride their dragons. One in particular caught Zee's attention. It was larger than many of the others, and the rider was smaller in comparison to the truly impressive looking dragon. Zee read the engraving on its base. "Sky Marshalls Slan hai Drogo and Mogon. The Heroes of Tosh." Zee frowned as he noticed the statue appeared to have been vandalized over the years, then cleaned up and repaired. He could still make out one deeply scratched word where the mortar used to fill it had worn away. "Traitors."

Perplexed, Zee stepped closer. The detail on the statue was incredible. He perused the copious bars and ribbons carved onto Drogo's chest, recognizing all but one. The badge that designated the pair's type was neither knight nor magicker, but something else. There was a sword, like the knights' badges, but also a wand, like the magickers.

He was about to ask Dame Toomsil about both the defamation of the statue and the badge when she said, "This is where assessments are carried out." A cadet squadron comprised of five, five-pair flights stood in formation to one side of the courtyard, waiting their turn to be assessed. "At the beginning of each year, the cadets stand before the Orb to have their assessment badge and armor enchantments checked and recalibrated. There's rarely a discrepancy, but enchantments can degrade over time. The badges sense a pair's level and class and display them whenever they change. They change color when a pair reaches a new class and trigger the armor of rider and beast to change as well."

A cadet pair approached a simple structure in the shape of a half dome, like an apse in a church, the inside surface inlaid with a mosaic of colored glass. Within it sat a stone plinth, above which floated a round and faceted crystal the size of a person's head, glowing with dim white light.

"That is the Orb of Assessment." They stopped to watch as a magicker announced the name of the rider and dragon to the Orb and stated they were reporting for assessment.

The Orb grew brighter, then spoke in a strange resonating voice while words appeared in the air as if written by hand in flowing cursive on an invisible chalkboard.

Rider: Davide das Beneme
Beast: Wenard
Rating: Bond

The Orb began to turn slowly and the color of its light changed to yellow, which projected out to play over the dragon and rider, who shivered at its touch.

"Does it feel strange?" Zee asked.

"The only way I can describe it is a sense of a scrutinizing intelligence inspecting you inside and out, and like ants crawling over and through you, especially in your crucible and core. It's not a bad feeling, but yes, it is strange."

"How does it work?"

"Some say the Orb contains the spirit of an Arch Mage who was in charge of assessment thousands of years ago and consented to have their conscious soul placed in the crystal as they lay dying of old age. Others say the Arch Mage was trapped against their will. Still others say it is a window to another realm that allows greater beings to peer into this one for the sole purpose of assessment, or that it is an aspect or avatar of Zepiter himself. Some believe it is simply a machine. The truth of it is, like the Simulation Artefacts, no one truly knows. The only thing we're sure of is they were made by more enlightened minds than our own, long, long ago."

The Orb did not speak, but the categories and ratings were written out in the same cursive letters, one after another.

Class: Copper
Level: Medium

Magick Affinity: Copper
Aether Capacity: Copper
Type: Knight
Potential: Gold

The Orb spoke again. "You may reveal your core." Its color shifted back to white and it dimmed.

A spherical area appeared, floating before the pair, much like Zee and Jessup's. The core was solid instead of an amorphous cloud like theirs, though, all of glowing yellow Empyrean, perfectly round, and close to six feet across. This pair's crucible, the band of white outside the core, was no thicker or denser than Zee and Jessup's had been, though.

Jessup said, "They have a little sun."

"It does look a bit like that," Dame Toomsil commented. She looked to the sky. "Speaking of the sun, we should keep moving, we don't want to be late."

CHAPTER 27

Triumf's Theatrum was even larger than Zee had expected. It looked like everyone on the island could attend and only a quarter of it would be filled.

Zee, Jessup, and Dame Toomsil had followed a wide, stone-paved path from the citadel along the inside of the high ridge that ringed the island, toward the base of the mountains, then through a gated tunnel that passed through the cliffs. After a short walk on a wide trail that overlooked the sea, they'd come upon the academy's main arena.

The Theatrum appeared as if it had been scooped out of the side of the mountain at this end of the five-mountain range, with curved coliseum seating carved into its slope right down to the sea. Cadets pairs flew in orderly spirals of squadrons and flights to take places on the upper and middle tiers, which were basically wide curved steps designed to accommodate dragons. Mounted faculty and staff arrived as well. Among them Zee spotted Tem seated upon a shining Royal Crimson. It was the first time Zee had seen Tem's dragon. She was a majestic and muscular beast. Tem caught his gaze, scowled, then looked away.

Unmounted faculty, staff, and villagers filed past Zee and Jessup on the path, giving them a wide berth, to the lower tiers where the seating, aisles, and steps were the proper size for people. Practically everyone, including the dragons, gaped, frowned, or gazed in keen interest at the kraken and murman in their midst. One flight of third-year cadets sneered more openly than others, nudging each other, pointing, and whispering derisively.

Zee had always been able to suppress the ire that rose in such situations, but he found it difficult this time. He glanced at Jessup, who stared at the cadets with eyes narrowed. It was Jessup's anger he felt, on top of his own, and the kraken's was stronger. Only by focusing on his breathing was he able to quash it. Jessup seemed to sense what he was doing, and his anger abated as well.

Still, Zee couldn't quench the cold anxiety of being at the center of so many people's attention. He'd been the object of stares and ridicule before and never let it bother him, but like the day he'd arrived on the island, this was a lot of staring.

Jessup didn't seem to care about the scrutiny, but he eyed the long stairs up to where the dragons were seated. To both Zee and Jessup's relief, Dame Toomsil led them a shorter distance down to a terrace off to the side where they could watch comfortably, be out of the way, and not have Jessup's bulk blocking the view of anyone seated behind them.

Centered against the Theatrum's base was a much larger terrace, built out into the sea, with a short jetty that thrust farther into the waves, a circle of stone at the end. Several Navy warships floated in the sea, their decks lined with spectators.

On the jetty, magickers were setting up a strange apparatus. It had lenses and mirrors on multiple metal arms, dials and switches on the front, and on a metal pedestal at its center sat a crystal of the same material and size as the Orb of Assessment. Over a dozen of the same type of crystal, though smaller, were being placed in holes on the pedestal. In spite of its complexity, the apparatus looked surprisingly sturdy.

"That's the largest of the Simulation Artefacts at the citadel," Dame Toomsil explained. "The others are integrated into the simulation fields."

As the magickers further prepared the Artefact, the hundred or so recruits jogged in to a cadence shouted by their cadet instructors, then filed into rows just below and to the left of where Zee and Jessup stood. They had changed clothes and all of them were wearing their caps—or lids, as they were called in the military—but they apparently hadn't had much time to clean up. They were still sweaty and many had mud on their faces. None of them sat until they were ordered to. They all looked relieved to be off their feet, but soon quite a few were whispering and gazing up at the murman and kraken.

A cadet instructor noticed and shouted, "Keep your guppy eyes forward and carpie mouths shut, minnies!" They obeyed, but Zee noticed the young woman with dark eyes he'd seen on the beach, Sallison anh Batcu, seated in the back row next to the giant recruit who'd been with her, sneaking a look back at him. The expression on her face was hard to read, but for some reason Zee felt more embarrassed than angry or anxious. A small recruit seated at her side opposite from the giant recruit nudged her shoulder, pointing toward the jetty, and she turned away.

The cohort of over a hundred new dragon recruits flew overhead and up to the middle tiers, being berated by their cadet dragon instructors as they went. So many dragons. Even those of the same breed were individuals of different color variations, sizes, horn placement, and eye colors. Among them was the bright white Ice Diver Zee and Jessup had seen on the beach, small in size even compared to other Ice Divers. When he landed, he held his clubfoot against his chest.

Zee knew very well what it felt like to be stared at, so he turned away. He was still curious though, so he asked Dame Toomsil about him.

"That's Fennix. This is his last chance to become a cadet. If recruits don't pass Basic the first time, they get two more attempts to return the following year to try again. He's actually a prince of a small but highly respected tribe of Ice Divers, and one of the best fliers I've ever seen."

Zee felt bad for the dragon, and he sensed empathy for him from Jessup as well. But there was an intensity and resolve in the gaze of the little white dragon that Zee admired. Fennix was intent on beating the odds and becoming a cadet, just like him and Jessup. Zee hoped he'd make it.

Zee returned his attention to the amphitheater. More cadet pairs arrived until it looked like everyone from the academy was there. They wore sashes designating their groups, with stripes for their squadrons and flights, each cohort seated together. Navy sailors and marines had gathered to watch as well. The sight was colorful and grand.

"This event must be a pretty big deal," he said.

"It is, for some," Dame Toomsil answered. "Just routine for others." She held still and silent for a moment, then peered up into the seats. "Peloquin is here. I must go to him so we can prepare." She laid a hand on Zee's shoulder. "Enjoy the exhibition."

"Prepare?" Zee asked, but she was already striding away up the steps.

A threesie cadet instructor stepped up onto a seat below the recruits and shouted, "Stay seated, but listen up, minnies!"

They all sat up straight.

"Our focus thus far has been on conditioning and discipline, and this will continue, but tomorrow you will begin weapons training as well. The greatest weapons in your arsenal, however, will be your beast itself and the Abilities you develop through your bond, if you're lucky enough to pass Basic Training and be paired. The defensive aura you'll develop once bonded will help protect you and your beast, but you'll also need to fend off enemies and take them down yourselves. You will be training with javelins, spears, bow and arrow. A lance can be quite effective under certain conditions, but your training with the lance will not begin until, and if, you pass Basic Training, become a cadet, and are paired and bonded. For close combat, you will learn the sword, shield, dagger, and if you are so inclined, the boarding axe. The techniques will change considerably when you're riding in the air, but the basics are a necessity.

"There may also be times when you're dismounted and must fight on land and, more likely, in the sea—in which case, you must be able to swim powerfully. Ideally it would be left for the marines, but you may be called upon to board ships and search lower decks or to be involved in incursions inside buildings where your beast cannot go. Therefore, you'll also be instructed in grappling and other hand-to-hand combat. Be assured, all that we have and will put you through is for your own good. To help you to stay alive—and of course, continue to fight for your beast, your fellow pairs, the Dragon Corps, and your king. And in doing so, you fight for your friends and families back home, and the entire nation of Tosh.

"You're here today to see for yourselves the results of rigorous training and dedication. It might even inspire some of you to work a little harder, knowing that one day you, too, could be a dragon rider of the realm, if you want it bad enough."

The instructor gazed over them with a hard look in her eyes. "What do you say? Do you want to be dragon riders?"

As one they shouted at the top of their lungs, "Ma'am, yes, ma'am!"

"Let's hear it, then!"

"Hurrah! Hurrah! Hurrah!"

"Pitiful, but you will do better. For now, keep silent, stay sharp, and learn."

Zee wished more than ever he was among them.

"Watch yourselves," came the voice of a female dragon.

Zee was hit by a gust of wind, and turned. A Royal Crimson landed on the cliffs next to the terrace where Zee and Jessup stood. She clung there with her claws, then climbed along the face of the cliff to the terrace with ease. Temothy jal Briggs slid from the saddle and strode toward them.

Zee wondered why he hadn't felt their approach. Tem and his dragon were Silver Class. Zee should have easily sensed their power as they flew near. Maybe it was because there were so many other bonded pairs in the amphitheater, but he still couldn't feel the power of their bond, even this close.

Zee held back the inclination to salute as Tem came up to stand beside him. "Hello, Tem."

Tem faced the main terrace below. "Mr. Tarrow."

"What are you doing down here?"

Tem gave him a haughty look, then faced forward again, clasping his hands behind his back. "Watching the exhibition, same as you."

Through the bond, Jessup asked if he could slap Tem. Zee suppressed a laugh. *"Probably not a good idea. At least, not right now."*

Jessup breathed a small "Harrumph," then spoke to the dragon. "I am Jessup, ma'am."

The dragon seemed taken aback, then replied, "I'm Knight Chevalier Timandra, Assistant Instructor of Tooth and Claw. I'm pleased to finally meet the kraken I've heard so much about and seen working at the docks."

"Jessup is pleased to meet Timandra, ma'am."

Zee grinned at how well Jessup was adapting. He leaned to introduce himself. "My name is Zee Tarrow, ma'am."

"It's good to meet you as well, Mr. Tarrow. I've heard much about you." Tem kept his eyes forward but cleared his throat softly. A corner of Timandra's mouth turned upward. "This is your first exhibition, I take it?" she asked Zee.

"Yes, ma'am."

"You're in for quite a show. I will warn you, simulated combat can be rather brutal."

"Thank you for letting us know, ma'am. We'll keep that in mind."

Tem shuffled slightly, as if uncomfortable with his dragon having a conversation with the two of them. Timandra gave him a look and puffed smoke from her nostrils. It appeared to Zee they were speaking through their bond, and she wasn't pleased with whatever he was saying.

Out on the jetty below, a magicker flipped a lever and the main crystal of the Simulation Artefact began to glow. As it grew brighter, the dozen crystals that had been placed in its base lit as well, then floated and zoomed out over the water to form a roughly circular area approximately two hundred yards across, the nearest crystal only a few yards from the end of the jetty. The mechanical arms tipped to face them and began to spin slowly around the base.

The magicker at the controls flipped another lever. Beams of light shot out of the smaller crystals, straight up into the sky and down into the sea. A turn of a knob and the light of each beam spread to the next crystal at both sides until they met in between. The light of the beams dimmed as they spread out, and all together they formed a barely visible, twelve-sided barrier.

Members of the crowd pointed to the sky and everyone began to cheer. Commandant Aureosa and Dean Wanchoo glided down to the main terrace on their dragons and dismounted.

"*Where is weird thing?*" Jessup asked through their bond.

Zee knew exactly what he was talking about, and he didn't see Amoxtli either. "*I don't know. Probably back in Dean Wanchoo's quarters. Why, do you miss her?*"

Jessup scoffed. "*No. Why would Jessup miss quemara-thing?*"

"*She seems very fond of the big strong kraken.*"

Jessup smirked and shook his ponderous head. "*Zee is silly little murman.*"

The crowd quieted as Aureosa took the steps to a stone dais and stood behind a podium with the symbol of the Dragon Corps carved on its front.

He gazed over the crowd, then cleared his throat. "Welcome, everyone, to our first combat exhibition of the school year." His voice was loud enough for all to hear, a function of the strength of his and Vandalia's bond. "I'm certain these matches will entertain, as well as provide a valuable educational experience for our cadets and new recruits. Watch carefully, young riders and beasts, and young cadets-to-be."

As one, all the cadets, including the dragons, roared, "Hurrah! Hurrah! Hurrah!" The sound echoed off the cliffs and rolled out over the waves.

"For our very first match," Aureosa continued, "we have a fourth year pair, Cadet Wing Commanders High Mountain ber Sakai and Saralin. Cadets, please take the field!"

Every cadet in the stadium leapt to their feet, cheering and applauding. Above and to one side of the highest seats a sleak Greatwing flew out of a tunnel, its rider holding up a hand to the crowd below.

As the pair flew to circle outside the simulation arena, a translucent screen of light took form above the Simulation Artefact. The pair's stats appeared on the left side.

Rider: High Mountain ber Sakai
Beast: Saralin
Rating: Bond

Class: Iron
Level: Mid

Magick Affinity: Lead
Aether Capacity: Silver
Type: Knight
Potential: Red Titan

Tem said, "The Simulation Artefacts are linked to the Orb of Assessment. They not only display a pair's statistics, but the Orb can reassess them through it as well."

Zee was surprised that Tem had made the effort to explain something to them.

Aureosa announced their opponents, a flight of fourth-year cadet pairs called the Dreadbats and one of their squadron's fourth-year combat magicker pairs.

More cheers rose from the crowd as they exited one after another from a tunnel high on the opposite side of the stadium from where the wing commanders had emerged, the loudest from the squadron and group to which they belonged. Their stats appeared in a row to the right of the wing commanders. The knights were all high-level Bronze or low-level Iron Class, the magicker high-level Bronze.

"Six on one doesn't seem very fair," said Zee.

"The wing commanders are at the top of their class and therefore the entire cadet cohort," Tem said. "They reached mid-level Iron Class at the end of their third year, usually a fourth-year achievement. It's part of the reason they were chosen to lead the cadet wing. They also possess excellent leadership skills and are masters of both micro- and macro-level combat tactics. They shouldn't be underestimated."

"They're already on the verge of leveling up to high-level Iron," Timandra added. "This match might just help them do that. At this rate, they could be Silver Class by the time they graduate, a rare feat by any standard."

Tem pulled a spyglass from his belt and handed it to Zee. "Watch closely."

Zee took the spyglass gently, amazed that Tem would offer. He was also aware these devices were very expensive. "Thank you." He'd learned that his eyesight was better than anyone's in darkness and under the water and was even better when Jessup was close, but out of the sea and in the daylight, the benefits were minimal. He raised the glass to his eye.

While the flight and magicker pairs flew around the ring in formation, the wing commander pair flapped to the center of the arena and hovered there, appearing extremely composed. They took a deep breath together, then let it out slowly.

Aureosa shouted to the combatants, "Noble cadets of the citadel, spark your cores!" Zee felt the power of their cores igniting, even from this distance. "Be strong," said Aureosa. "Be brave!" He paused as the riders leaned over their saddles. "Begin!"

Instead of charging straight in to attack, the flight split into a set of three pairs and a set of two, the magicker pair staying to the rear of the two pairs, before pounding attack Ability projectiles at ber Sakai and Saralin. The wing commanders did not retreat or put up a Shield. Instead, they appeared to smear across short distances in quick bursts, avoiding the projectiles, the Greatwing dragon blasting a tight beam of intense fire at one set of opponents while ber Sakai hurled Fireballs with both hands at the other. Shields of light flared yellow and the pairs used Burst and Haste to avoid the attack while attempting to stay together. Zee had to adjust the spyglass for a wider field of view just to keep track of all the action.

Timandra said, "The wing commanders are using Shift to move, a very difficult Ability to control, and Saralin is employing her Stream projectile Ability. Both take significant amounts of Empyrean. Stream can drain the core of an opponent of equal class very quickly and be devastating to a protective aura, but it also uses large amounts of their own core."

The wing commanders took a few hits, but each was blocked or deflected by a flare of their aura, and with each Shift they rose higher, staying above their opponents. It didn't take long for the Shields of the flight pairs to dim under the wing commanders' onslaught, even with the extra Shielding from their magicker. Instead of pressing the attack, however, ber Sakai and Saralin finally activated their Shield and spiraled gradually upward. Three opposing pairs attempted to maneuver around them to a higher position above, but the wing commanders continued moving higher, using Shift or Burst when necessary.

The attackers continued to fire at them, hammering their Shield with Missiles of fire and ice and Geysers of molten ambergris lava. After a short time, light flashed across the wing commanders' Shield, causing ice, lava, and built-up ash to be loosed from its surface and drop away. The attackers were forced to use their Shields or evade the falling debris. Saralin drew her head back, then thrust it forward with a roar, combined with a single great flap of her wings that knocked the attackers back, some of them tumbling. Zee grimaced at the volume of the roar.

A dragon was struck in the wing bone by a hunk of hardened lava. It screamed and the pair toppled to splash in the sea, where they flapped helplessly in the water. Many in the crowd groaned. Others cheered.

"Blare and Windstorm at the same time," Timandra commented. "Extremely difficult, and very taxing on the core."

Tem said, "They're not going for a quick win, though, but intentionally draining their core to push themselves to their limits. That will give them their best chance to level up from this match."

Though Tem and Timandra seemed to be casually analyzing the match in the course of conversation, Zee listened closely and committed everything to memory. He sensed that Jessup was paying close attention as well.

The wing commanders dove in pursuit, Saralin Streaming fire into their foes while ber Sakai drew heavy long spears from his Keep and flung them one after the other, using Shift to hop side to side as they went.

One of the riders was skewered by a spear, right through his physical shield. The dragon had not been hit, but its cry was a heartrending wail. It flapped out of control, shrieking, until it passed through the wall of the arena. The spear vanished and the rider sat up in the saddle with a shout. The dragon got control of itself and flew to the main terrace where it landed and crumpled to its belly, sobbing. The rider slid weakly from the saddle and embraced the dragon around the neck, shoulders shaking in grief.

Timandra said, "There is no death, no wound from sword, spear, or beast, that hurts more than losing a bondmate."

"It's like having your heart and soul ripped out through your chest by an icy hand so cold you feel like you'll never recover," said Tem.

"Many of those who experience it in real battle never do."

Tem placed a hand on her neck and held it there.

Zee didn't know what to say. He looked to Jessup, fearing to imagine what it would be like to lose him. Jessup met his gaze, reached out with the narrowed end of an arm and laid it lightly on his shoulders. Both returned their attention to the arena.

Just in time, as it turned out. The magicker pair was flopping limply down from the heights, both dragon and rider skewered by a spear thick as a fence post and fifteen feet long.

"Impressive," uttered Timandra. "Even lower-class magickers are exceedingly hard to kill due to their enhanced defensive and healing Abilities."

"The wing commanders timed it perfectly," said Tem. "The magicker pair was paying more attention to the defense and healing of the flight pairs than themselves. They allowed themselves to be distracted and their own Shield to flicker."

Zee lifted the spyglass back to his eye. Saralin appeared to be having trouble staying airborne, while ber Sakai slouched behind his shield, sword in hand, breathing heavily. Their remaining opponent pairs shot forward, throwing everything they had at them.

The wing commanders were struck several times, their aura flashing dimmer with each strike. Saralin tucked her head back and drew her wings together in front of them for protection, though she somehow remained floating there, and no Shield formed. Zee was sure they were done for.

"Watch closely," Tem said, narrowing his eyes at the action.

Saralin suddenly threw her wings back tight against her flank while ber Sakai leaned forward and thrust out his sword. The wing commanders flashed bright as the sun and shot toward the oncoming pairs like a comet.

Their opponents had no chance. Shields flared, but ber Sakai and Saralin passed right through them, the pairs bursting into flame as they passed.

Dragons and riders alike shrieked as they fell, immolating, to splash into the waves.

The living flame that the wing commanders had become went out. Saralin was able to slow the pair's descent but couldn't keep them from landing in the water, where she swam slowly toward the terrace. Her rider slumped forward, one hand on her neck, patting her gently with the other.

The crowd was up from their seats and roaring.

Commandant Aureosa announced, "End match! Victory goes to Wing Commanders High Mountain ber Sakai and Saralin!"

"That was every bit as impressive as I expected it to be," said Timandra.

"What was that?" Zee asked, in awe.

"An Ability called Phoenix," Tem replied. "They've been practicing it in secret all summer. That's the first time they've used it publicly, as we were hoping they would. It's usually an Ability only White Titans can manifest, and very few of them, at that. At the cadet wing commanders' class, it wouldn't do much damage to a Gold Class pair or higher, but against these fourth-years, it's devastating."

"They also drained their core dangerously low using it," said Timandra.

"Which I'm sure was their intent. But to have that much awareness of how much forged Empyrean they had in their core and exactly how much it would take to activate the Ability took tremendous focus and skill."

Zee watched in fascination as the walls of the simulation arena rippled and bright light washed through it, occluding the view. When it dimmed, all wounds had been healed, armor and weapons mended, and lives restored. All in the water rose out of the sea on sheets of light, completely dry. They coughed, breathing heavily as they recovered from their ordeal.

Once all the combatants had gathered on the main terrace, "Reassessing" blinked above the columns of stats. Two of the flight pairs had gone from low- to mid-level Iron Class, and the magicker pair from high-level Bronze to low-level Iron. They hooted with joy. The other stats had remained the same—including ber Sakai and Saralin's. They took it well, nodding and waving to the crowd. When they were done waving, Saralin reached a wing around her rider and held him close.

"They still didn't reach high level," said Tem.

"It's disappointing but not a surprise," Timandra replied. "It's still quite early in the school year."

"They have to be extremely close, though."

Off Zee's questioning look, Timandra said, "It becomes more difficult to progress with each new class. I would be surprised if the others there on the terrace advance any further this year, which is fine. High-level Iron is usually the furthest anyone gets in their four years at the academy."

Tem said, "Commandants Aureosa and Vandalia and Deans of Magicks Wanchoo and Venkatarama haven't advanced even a level in decades, and I don't believe it's for a lack of trying."

"What would they have to do to advance?"

"For the commandants, combat with more advanced opponents," said Timandra. "The deans would need to support knights in combat against the same. But that's the problem. There are none in Tosh, or any other kingdom, as far as we know. They'll often take on many White Titans at a time, but nothing has worked."

Tem said, "Forging takes up more time at higher classes as well, since their cores are so much larger."

"There are artefacts and potions that will enhance a core's power and Abilities for a brief amount of time, but there's nothing we know of that will speed progression. As far as we know, there are no shortcuts."

"Anything special that could help them level up in Red Titan Class or break through to Black Titan is only spoken of in myths and legends. They might exist, but they must be exceedingly rare and difficult to obtain if those two haven't found them."

Zee's attention was drawn to the cadet flight and wing commander pairs rising from the stage below and flying over the audience toward their seats. He recalled something that occurred to him during their bout.

Before he could voice it, however, Jessup spoke. "They attacked too close together."

Timandra and Tem turned to him, as did Zee. That's exactly what Zee was thinking. "I thought so too. Even if the flight pairs didn't know the wing commanders had the Phoenix Ability, they shouldn't have held such a tight formation during their final attack. If they'd spread out more, one or more of them might have survived. The wing commanders were so weak after they used Phoenix, they might have been beaten." Jessup grunted in agreement.

Tem said, "But if they had spread out, the wing commanders might not have used Phoenix and tried another attack."

"They were hidden behind Saralin's wings, preparing the Ability," said Timandra.

"They could have felt the auras of the attacking pairs, or even used Tracking, and known exactly where they were."

"Unless one or more of their attackers were Occluding their core."

"Hmm. That's possible. I guess we can't know unless we ask them."

"Which we should."

"Agreed."

Timandra addressed Zee and Jessup. "Very acute observation, gentlemen. Are you sure you haven't been trained in combat strategy?"

Zee nearly blushed. "No, ma'am. Jessup has lived in the sea for ten years and had to fight to stay alive. I've just read a lot of books, and seen how fish hunt in the sea, including how smaller predators can take out much larger ones by working together."

"If I recall correctly, Dame Toomsil taught you a few things," said Tem, a hint of a smile touching his lips. "And your sparring partner of a few years was quite talented."

Tem had never smiled when speaking to Zee on ship, always acting like it was beneath him to interact with him at all. Was this a different Tem than he'd known years ago? Zee decided he'd see if he could find out. He shrugged. "He was okay, I guess."

Timandra chuckled.

Tem's eyes widened, then narrowed.

Zee didn't back down. "How did you get stuck down here with us, anyway?" Zee asked.

"We're not 'stuck' anywhere."

"Dame Toomsil told you to come, didn't she?"

"She most certainly did not."

"So you just wanted to hang out with your old buddy Zee for old times' sake?"

The dragon snorted, and Tem forced away the smile that snuck through on his stern features. "You do know that I am a Knight Chevalier in His Majesty's Dragon Corps, and you scrape barnacles off ships."

"All that means is you actually have no authority over me, since I'm a civilian." Zee smiled, holding his gaze.

Tem stared at him, then looked toward the arena and crossed his arms. "Unbelievable." Timandra laughed under her breath. Tem shot her a look. "You're no help whatsoever." The dragon just grinned.

CHAPTER 28

The sun was setting, thin clouds on the distant horizon brimming with color. The walls of the arena somehow remained transparent even as the area grew progressively brighter, illuminating it bright as day. Empyrean lamps lit up over the stage and throughout the amphitheater.

Zee and Jessup had watched match after match, completely enthralled but paying close attention to strategies, various Abilities and what they were called, and the observations that Tem and Timandra made on the bouts. At the end of each match, all combatants and equipment were made whole again by the wash of white light through the arena.

"Is the Simulation Artefact actually healing them and fixing damage?" Zee asked.

"No one can be certain if it does that," Timandra replied, "or if it's all just an incredibly elaborate illusion. The terror and pain certainly feel real enough."

Tem said, "We do know you can't put the injured or dead inside and reverse their condition, so the theories lean more heavily toward illusion. It won't fix wrecked ships or ruined objects that are placed in it either. The arena can only affect what happens within it."

Superintendent Lora aye Hyooz strode onto the stage from where she'd been sitting with her dragon. The crowd hushed as she stood behind the podium. "We have something very special in store for our final match this evening. On one side, the citadel's own Daimyo General Commandants Peleus ran Aureosa and Vandalia, and Magi General Deans of Magicks Mihir han Wanchoo and Venkatarama!"

As she spoke, their stats appeared on the screen. Both pairs were Red Titan Class, mid-level, with Black Titan potential. Wanchoo and Venkatarama's magick affinity was significantly higher than the commandants', though, and their type was magicker as opposed to knight.

The crowd roared, then broke into a united, "Hurrah! Hurrah! Hurrah!"

Aureosa, Vandalia, Wanchoo, and Venkatarama all bowed.

"This will be a sight to see," said Timandra excitedly. "I would love to be pitted against them in a simulation match, but in a real battle, I'd fly away as fast as I could with my tail between my legs."

Tem said, "And I'd be screaming, 'Faster, Timandra! Faster!'" They both laughed.

Zee had never heard Tem laugh other than with scorn, and he laughed with them. "I've been dreaming of seeing Titan Class knights in battle for as long as I remember."

"This is the way to see it," said Timandra. "Not too far away, but safe from danger."

Tem said, "The commandants and deans of magicks have been a team for a very long time. If they were pitted against a low- to mid-level Black Titan pair, I still might not bet against them."

Superintendent Hyooz announced they would not be fighting cadets but a flight of full-fledged knights: four low- and medium-level White Titan Class pairs and a medium-level Gold Class pair, accompanied by a mid-level White Titan combat magicker. Each pair flew from a tunnel above the amphitheater as their names and ranks were announced, the crowd cheering, and their stats appeared in columns above the Simulation Artefact. The last pair to fly out was Knight Commanders Zara mon Toomsil and Peloquin.

"Oh...," Zee uttered. "That's what she meant when she said she and Peloquin needed to prepare."

Tem whistled and Timandra roared with enthusiasm as they passed by overhead.

Still clapping, Tem said, "She and Peloquin won a particularly competitive lottery to participate in this match. They're very close to reaching high-level Gold and are hoping it will push them closer."

"Do pairs only level up when in combat?" Zee asked.

"You can level up anytime," Timandra replied, "but levels are really just a measure of progression toward your next class."

"Class is different," said Tem. "A class up happens most often during or after periods of stress, like in combat, or after a forging session, but Timandra and I have progressed while simply training. When you've mastered your Abilities well enough and your crucible and core are ready, whether nearly empty or full, it just happens. And when you advance to a new class, you feel it."

Zee said, "What's it like?"

"Like nothing you've ever experienced," Tem replied. "An overwhelming feeling of power and joy, like being one with the universe and indestructible."

Timandra added, "The sensation is brief, but when it passes you know you're stronger, faster, and, oddly enough, even healthier. It's hard to describe."

"Thank you for trying," said Zee, smiling up at her.

Back out in the arena, the commandant and dean pairs circled each other as if on an afternoon pleasure flight, chatting casually. Zee imagined they were plotting what terrible things they were going to do to their opponents.

The flight of knights circled the arena, evenly spaced, with the magicker pair sticking closer to Dame Toomsil and Peloquin.

Superintendent Hyooz ordered the combatants to spark their cores. The power that struck Zee left him breathless. Hyooz raised a hand, then chopped it down with a shout. "Begin!"

The flight pairs didn't charge in to attack but constricted their circle until they were inside the arena walls, continuing in the same formation.

The commandants and the deans hovered in place beside each other, the deans slightly higher and facing the opposite direction.

Without changing their flight pattern, the attackers all began firing at once. The speed and power of their strikes was far beyond anything they had witnessed in previous bouts.

For a few moments, the pairs at the center simply let the attacks strike them. The yellow light of their protective auras was far thicker and brighter than any of the others Zee had seen.

White-hot balls of fire, red-hot boulders, and Missiles of ice, all the size of a carriage, shattered against their auras. Geysers of fire, ice, and lava flowed around them. Spears and arrows broke or ricocheted away. Their auras didn't seem to be reduced at all by the barrage that struck them from every side.

Finally, the deans threw up a Shield to cover themselves, several feet thick and so broad it would have been difficult for any of the flight pairs to move around it swiftly, and Aureosa and Vandalia began their attack.

The attack Abilities they used weren't much different from the others Zee had seen, though they were faster and looked far hotter. The White Titans' Shields were impressive, but they were blown back by Beams of white-hot fire and dense, speeding Fireballs that struck like oversized cannonballs. They used Burst, Haste, and Shift, moving nearly faster than the eye could follow, to avoid the blasts. Zee was happy to see Dame Toomsil and Peloquin holding their own, avoiding strikes as well as the White Titans, though the flight's magicker pair was shielding them more than the others.

Then Venkatarama turned his eyes on the White Titan magickers, Wanchoo gave his wand a swirl, and a bubble of golden light surrounded them while also trapping Dame Toomsil and Peloquin.

"Testudo Globe," said Timandra. "Knights can't attack from behind their Shields, but magickers can cast Shields and healing Abilities through their own. Testudo Globe, however, completely cuts off all Abilities. Not even Aureosa and Vandalia could harm them while they're in there, but the pairs are trapped and can do nothing but watch. Their flightmates could try to weaken it by firing upon it, but that's risky. If Wanchoo and Venkatarama dropped it suddenly, they could wound or kill their own team members."

Tem said, "Toomsil and Peloquin could also attack it from inside, but only with sword and spear. Dragon projectiles would harm them more than help."

"How long can Wanchoo and Peloquin hold it?"

Timandra snorted. "At their class, with the size of their core, and against just four White Titans, as long as they'd like, I'd imagine."

The deans dropped the larger Shield that protected them and erected a Testudo Globe around themselves. At the same time, Aureosa and Vandalia threw up their own Shield and Streaked straight at the White Titan pair closest to the arena wall, a comet tail of yellow light in their wake. Their Shield collided head-on with the Shield of the opposing pair. In a blast of light, the White Titans were knocked out of the arena. It took them a moment to figure out what had happened, then the rider hung his head and they flew around the arena toward the main stage.

"One down," said Tem. He turned his head toward Zee without taking his eyes off the arena. "That Ability is called just what it looks like. Streak. It's an advanced form of Burst or Haste, much faster, and they can travel much farther."

In another Streak, the commandants were across the arena, Aureosa having drawn a lance from his Keep. It pierced the Shield of another White Titan pair, the lance's tip stopping only a foot away from the rider's chest. The rider drew her shield and sword from the pair's Keep and held the shield to her chest while hacking at the lance.

The other White Titan pairs rushed to her aid. The commandants' Shield appeared behind them, blocking the attack, then Aureosa and

Vandalia Shifted forward. The White Titans' Shield Ability shattered. The lance pierced through the rider's shield, aura, and chest while Vandalia seized the dragon's neck in her jaws and broke it.

The crowd gasped as one.

"Two down," said Timandra as the bodies splashed into the sea. "A kind death, truth be told, to kill both rider and dragon at once."

The commandants turned to hover in the air behind their Shield, facing the remaining White Titans.

* * *

Seated among the new recruits, Mehmet can Yasso looked on in horror. "I don't think I can do that."

"What's that?" said Chirt sim Nabbit, the small recruit who had crawled over Donnicky with Sallison anh Batcu in the trench. "Kill people and dragons, or die a horrible death?"

"I'm sure I can die a horrible death, and probably will." He swallowed. "The killing..."

Sallison kept her eyes forward. "It's what we're being trained for, Mehmet. You know that." Her tone wasn't cruel, just pragmatic.

The giant of a young man, Jondon dil Rolio, nudged Mehmet with his elbow. "Maybe you'll be a magicker type. That way you could defend and heal people instead of attacking them."

Mehmet's voice was weak. "I'd like that very much, but only five percent or less of any new class qualifies to be a magicker." He looked down at his hands in his lap. "It would probably be best if I just dropped out right now."

Sallison's eyes snapped to him. "Don't say that. It's exactly what they want. Why do you think they're having us watch this exhibition so early in Basic? They want us to quit."

"I think it's inspiring," said Chirt.

"So do I, but they want anyone with doubts out now." Sallison risked the wrath of the cadet instructors by leaning forward to see Mehmet around Jondon's girth. "Mehmet, look at me. You quit now and you'll prove what your brother and sister say about you. You don't want that, do you?"

Mehmet didn't look up but shook his head.

"You can do this."

Mehmet met her gaze. "I can do this." He didn't sound entirely convinced.

Sallison smiled in encouragement. "Good, now shut up and watch the match."

Mehmet sniffed and returned his attention to the arena.

* * *

Zee lifted the spyglass back to his eye for a closer look at Aureosa beating at the Shield of a White Titan pair with his sword while standing in his stirrups. The blade of his sword was rimmed in flame, and each strike was doing serious damage to the opponents' Shield, opening gaping gashes and causing it to dim and flicker, then crack. The White Titans dropped their ruined Shield and the dragon blasted great gouts of ice at Aureosa and Vandalia, but it vaporized into steam on their aura.

Vandalia swatted at the other dragon's head with a wing and Aureosa leapt from his saddle straight toward the rider, sword swinging. The rider had just enough time to raise his own sword and shield, but the flames of Aureosa's sword flared brighter and sliced through them, cleaving the rider's head from his shoulders.

Aureosa's leap carried him over the rider and dragon, and he began to fall.

Vandalia spat a tiny white ball of fire at the dragon, which hit it squarely in the chest, then dove while the beast ignited. By the time she'd Streaked to catch Aureosa on her back, the White Titan pair were just blackened bones and molten armor dropping toward the sea.

"Three down," said Timandra.

"Holy Postune," Zee breathed, lowering the spyglass.

Tem glanced around. "Careful with that. Most people at the academy don't approve of appeals to Postune or even curses in her name."

"Sorry," said Zee. "It's a sailor thing."

"May I?" said Tem, holding out his hand.

"Of course." Zee gave Tem's spyglass back to him. Looking through the glass was starting to give him a headache, anyway.

In the arena, Wanchoo and Venkatarama dropped the Testudo Globe that surrounded Dame Toomsil, Peloquin, and the White Titan magickers. Both pairs shot toward the action, but the magickers were halted in mid-air, trapped in another Globe. No sound could be heard, but the magicker dragon was obviously roaring in frustration, its rider shaking her fist and yelling.

Aureosa and Vandalia Streaked and Shifted in the arena, randomly blasting the two knight pairs that remained in the fight with fire and burning spears.

"They're toying with them," said Tem. "They have been the entire bout."

Zee was surprised to hear that, having thought the commandants had been putting their all into the fight. "Are Red Titans really that much more powerful than White Titans?" Zee asked. "It's just one class difference."

Timandra said, "By standard progression measurements, pairs of each class are about two times stronger than the one before them. Directly corresponding with that, their core is about two times larger in volume. Now consider how that multiplies up through the classes. White Titans have rather large cores to draw from, making them stronger, healing them even during a battle, giving them great energy and speed, and powering even more potent attacks—and Red Titans have twice as much as they do."

"That in itself is one thing," said Tem, "but also remember that the commandants and the deans have far more actual combat experience than any other living pairs in Tosh and have been forging for decades longer than most. All that time, strengthening their crucibles and growing their cores, while at the same time, mastering their Abilities and developing the most efficient use of their forged Empyrean to power them. So no, Red Titans aren't necessarily all that much more powerful than White Titans and should have more trouble against four White Titan Class pairs and a Gold Class pair, all being protected by White Titan combat magickers. These particular Red Titans, however…"

Tem let his voice trail off, but Zee understood. With all that power and talent, he marveled that they still hadn't reached Black Titan. Just how strong did a pair have to be to get there? It also occurred to him just how frightening a Black Titan pair must be.

The commandants Streaked past a strike from Peloquin toward the last White Titan pair, but instead of attacking them straightaway, they stopped twenty yards short. Vandalia started flapping her wings, her body vertical, head up and tail down. The movement of her wings and her aura blocked the assaults of the White Titans, and whenever Toomsil and Peloquin tried to attack, Wanchoo would tip his wand and throw a wall of yellow light up between them. After several attempts, the Gold Class pair gave up and flew in slow circles, gathering their strength.

Tem said, "You'll notice no one has tried to attack Wanchoo and Venkatarama. Against those two, it would be a complete waste of their core."

Vandalia's wings blurred and the air before her whirled in a vortex. She breathed hot Cinders and Ash into it until it looked like a small, dark tornado with spinning red embers caught in it. A small, dark tornado that grew and grew.

The White Titans tried to escape, but their Streak was no match for the Red Titans', and the Tornado, which was a Red Titan Ability, went everywhere with them. The whirling wind became so strong the White Titans were sucked into it, where they spun in the dark whirling ash and crimson glow.

Vandalia suddenly threw down her wings. The Tornado vanished to reveal the White Titan pair, scoured, burned, and mangled. Only after they had splashed into the waves far below did the commandants turn to face the last remaining knight pair, Dame Toomsil and Peloquin. Wanchoo and Venkatarama dropped the wall that separated them.

Zee realized he was holding his breath as the remaining pairs traded blows in swift succession, and forced his lungs to work again.

The commandants pursued the Gold pair relentlessly, forcing them to use every evasive technique they had, then fought them head-on, letting their Shield take blow after blow of Toomsil and Peloquin's strongest attacks. Not once did they give their opponents a chance to rest or recover.

Finally, the commandants hit them with a spinning Pinwheel of flame that cut like a saw blade into the Gold knights' Shield, causing it to collapse. Toomsil and Peloquin evaded the Pinwheel, but the commandants closed in. Aureosa threw Fireballs with his hands until their opponents' aura protection failed. Dame Toomsil could barely hold her shield up, and Peloquin was having a hard time keeping them in the air, yet still they fought, she with her sword held high and he with a weak Stream of fire.

Vandalia flapped once and she and Aureosa Streaked backward, easily increasing the distance between them and their attackers. She floated there in a vertical position once more, but this time Aureosa held his hands together as if praying. Vandalia did the same thing with her wing tips.

Tem yelled, "Cover your ears!" at the same time as the Basic Training cadet instructors.

Dame Toomsil and Peloquin recoiled, then caught themselves as they realized what was coming—and that there was absolutely nothing they could do about it.

The commandants separated their hands and wings, then violently clapped them together.

A small sun exploded in the arena, accompanied by a report like a thousand cannons going off at once.

Zee blinked spots out of his eyes as the sound echoed through the stadium, then took a sharp inhale of breath at the sight of Dame Toomsil and Peloquin, crushed and crisped black, dropping to the ocean with smoke trailing behind them.

"Thunderclap...," Tem breathed. "I've heard how it's done, but never seen them use it."

The crowd sat in stunned silence while the fallen knights bobbed on the waves, steam rising from their charred bodies.

"That has to be hard to watch," Zee said to Tem. "I know it is for me."

Tem said nothing for a moment. "I only pray I never have to see it in reality." He and Timandra exchanged glances.

Aureosa stared at the results of their most powerful Ability, his expression inscrutable, then Vandalia flew them to join Wanchoo and Venkatarama near the White Titan magickers, the single remaining pair of the opposing flight. Wanchoo made a curt wave of his wand and the Testudo Globe around the other magickers disappeared. For a moment, the White Titan pair stared at the commandants and deans, then the rider saluted and they flew out of the arena toward the stage.

"End match!" shouted Superintendent Hyooz. "The victors, Daimyo General Commandants Peleus ran Aureosa and Vandalia, and Magi General Deans Mihir han Wanchoo and Venkatarama!"

Once more light washed into the arena from the walls to heal, resurrect, and lift the fallen combatants. The crowd gave them all a standing ovation, the dragons roaring in appreciation.

Once they had gathered on the stage, their stats once again appeared on the ethereal screen above the Simulation Artefact. One White Titan knight pair had advanced to medium level. Dame Toomsil and Peloquin went from mid- to high-level Gold, while their potential changed from Red Titan to Black Titan. Grinning, Dame Toomsil raised a hand, and Peloquin slapped it with his nose.

Zee said, "Now they're just one progression away from White Titan."

"It won't be easy to achieve," said Tem while applauding, "but I'm very happy for them."

Timandra said, "It may have seemed cruel, but Aureosa and Vandalia did their best to give them a good fight and the greatest chance at advancement."

"And as painless a death as possible," Tem added.

Superintendent Hyooz thanked everyone for attending, and the crowd prepared to leave. Zee continued to watch Aureosa, who was speaking to each pair he and Vandalia had fought and shaking hands.

"*We'll be that strong one day, Jessup,*" Zee said through their bond.

"*No,*" Jessup replied. Zee looked to his friend, who was staring intently at the stage. "*We will be stronger.*" He met Zee's gaze. Zee took a deep breath, then tipped a determined nod.

Timandra cleared her throat, which was especially startling coming from a dragon. "What are you two talking about?"

"Nothing important, ma'am," Zee responded, a little too quickly.

She eyed him, then Jessup. "You don't know how to forge, do you?"

"No, ma'am," said Jessup.

She watched them both as if trying to read their thoughts, which Zee was pretty sure she couldn't do.

Tem said, "I'd completely understand if you wanted to, but the last thing you two need right now is to get yourselves into trouble. Having you here has already put the commandants and deans of magicks in a delicate position. You can't be caught forging."

"We know that," said Zee. "We'd never want to get them into trouble."

Tem squinted down his nose at him. "Why is it you call Timandra 'ma'am,' but you don't call me 'sir'?"

Zee thought for a moment. "Because she's a dragon, and you're Tem."

Timandra chuckled while Tem glowered from beneath the brim of his cap. Tem tipped his head toward the path leading to the citadel. "Go swab a deck or something."

"Yes, sir?"

"That's... better?"

Timandra chuckled again. "Now, off with you both or this big beast will be in everyone's way."

"Thank you, ma'am," Zee replied. "Thank you both." And he meant it. He looked over the crowd full of dragon and rider pairs, then once more out over the arena. The walls of light had vanished and the smaller Simulation Artefact crystals were floating back to the machine on the terrace. "This has been an incredible experience."

"Our pleasure," Timandra replied.

Tem said, "Well, hers, anyway."

Timandra snorted and shook her head.

Jessup thanked them both, and he and Zee headed up to the road along the cliffs.

Zee was more inspired than he'd ever been. He and Jessup had work to do, a lot of it. He had to keep training, harder than ever, but most important, they had to begin forging.

Unsurprisingly, Jessup was of the same mind. *"We need to forge, Zee."*

"I know. We just have to figure out how. And not get caught."

CHAPTER 29

Zee leapt off Jessup as they reached the floor of the cavern and strode to the bookshelves. Jessup crawled out of the water behind him. Zee scanned the titles. He wanted to read them all, and he would, but what he really needed now was something, anything, that would help them figure out how to forge. Nothing looked particularly promising. There was a set of academy handbooks, one for first-year cadets and another for Basic recruits, but those had been in Dr. Aenig's collection as well. Zee had read them many times over and practically had them memorized. There was nothing in them on forging, just as Wanchoo and Aenig had said. Then Zee noticed that the first-year cadet manual was pulled out from the others. Zee recalled Aureosa standing near the shelves and lifting a book out. It had been that handbook.

Zee yanked the book from the shelf and began flipping pages. His stomach grumbled loudly and he realized he hadn't had dinner.

Jessup said, "Zee needs to eat. Grow big and strong like Jessup."

Zee laughed. "I don't know about that last part, but you're right, I do need to eat."

Twenty minutes later, Zee sat at the table with a plate of eggs, plantains, and beans he'd heated on the cookstove, perusing the handbook for anything he might have missed.

"Zee find anything to help with forging?" Jessup asked.

Zee swallowed a mouthful of beans. "Not yet. This book is old and looks like it's had a lot of use. I was hoping there might be notes written in the margins or something."

"Zee will figure it out."

"*We* will figure it out, one way or another." He'd really been hoping the murfolk book Dr. Aenig had given him would be the key, but he'd been working every night on cracking its code, or whatever the symbols were, with no luck at all.

He came to the index at the back of the handbook as he finished dinner but still had found nothing of use. He began to wonder why Aureosa had purposefully left it pulled out farther than the others—unless he hadn't and it was all just a coincidence. Zee tossed the book to the table and rubbed his fists in his eyes in frustration.

Jessup said, "What's that?"

Zee chuckled, remembering how Jessup used to say that when he was little, then pulled his hands from his eyes and stopped. Something was sticking out between the last page and the back cover of the handbook.

Zee snatched the book back up and removed folded sheets of yellowed and stained paper. He unfolded the pages gently, as if they would crumble under his touch. His mouth opened as he read the first page, then hung wider as he scanned the rest.

There were only a dozen sheets or so, rough on one edge from where they'd been torn from a journal, and the handwriting was barely legible, but to Zee they were priceless. A date had been scrawled at the beginning of each day's entry, followed by a set of initials.

"Jessup..." he breathed. "Do you know what these are?"

"How could Jessup know?"

"They're notes taken by a first-year cadet, over eighty years ago." He held the set of pages up for Jessup to see and pointed at the initials. They were hardly more than chicken scratchings, but Zee could make them out. "This says 'PrA.'"

Jessup had learned fast during Zee's reading lessons, and he caught on quick. "Peleus ran Aureosa."

"These are the commandant's personal notes from when he was a cadet—and they're about forging."

"Commandant left them for Zee."

"He left them for *us*."

Jessup grinned. "Jessup told Zee we would figure it out."

All Zee could do was laugh.

* * *

Zee stood before Jessup, clutching sheets of the journal in his hands.

"Aureosa's notes say that forging for the first time is done in groups of pairs and guided by an instructor. Apparently forging together with other pairs can ease the process, having to do with combined wills having more pull on the Empyrean. We're on our own, though, and these notes will have to be our guide."

"Zee and Jessup can do it," his big friend said with confidence.

"They also told us earlier it could be dangerous. I'm not sure what that means, but if Aureosa left these notes for us he must have thought we'd be okay."

Jessup shrugged, which looked oddly comical on a giant sea beast with ten arms and no shoulders. "Jessup not worried if Zee isn't."

"I'm not worried. I've got you."

That brought a smile to the kraken's big face.

Zee climbed up on one of Jessup's front arms and leaned back against his cheek. He had read the pages on forging several times. He'd felt almost ashamed at first, reading someone's private journal, but he was convinced Aureosa had left them for him and Jessup, and that eased his mind. The notes were brief, laying out only the basics of the forging process interspersed with what Aureosa thought were important tips. It was a lot more than they had before, though, and apparently Aureosa thought it would be all they'd need to get started.

"First we have to envision our crucible and core by meditating on it like we did before," he said to Jessup.

"Jessup remembers. Breathe deep. Be calm. See crucible and core."

"That's it," Zee said with a smile. "Ready?"

"Jessup is always ready."

"Of course you are. Okay..." Zee closed his eyes and breathed, calming himself, feeling Jessup do the same. When he felt they were ready, he looked inward. It appeared more quickly and easily this time, but he was still amazed by the spherical space and the cloud of blue motes with a section of yellow that moved within it.

Zee opened his eyes, half expecting the crucible to vanish. He was happily surprised to find he could still see it, as if it hung before them in the cave itself. "These notes are about forging Empyrean, so let's try that. We can try Marisean later."

"Sounds good to Jessup."

"The first step is called mining, but before we do that, we have to envision the Empyreal Plane. According to Aureosa's notes, 'Empyrean exists in the Aether, which is everywhere, but we bodily beings with limited perception only perceive what our finite consciousness can comprehend, a sliver of it called the Empyreal Plane.' Then he added, 'At least that is the philosophy of the ancients.'"

"Skip to good part."

"All right, all right," Zee replied with a chuckle. "I just figured if Aureosa wrote it, it might be important." Zee took a breath and scanned the notes. He was pretty sure he had it memorized, but he didn't want to miss anything.

He explained the process to Jessup. They continued with their meditation, but instead of looking inward like they did to see their crucible, they gazed outward into the Aether with their mind's eye while holding on to the vision of their crucible and core. Their deep breathing quickly fell into sync. Zee focused on the sound of Jessup's heartbeat, then imagined it expanding beyond them.

Sound vanished, bright white light flashed in their mind's eye, then collapsed in on itself. They found themselves floating in an infinite void of darkness, like a starless night sky. Their crucible and core still hung before them, but above in the darkness moved a ribbon of yellow motes of light, like a long narrow cloud that curved away as far as they could see to either side. The yellow motes looked exactly like the ones in Zee and Jessup's core, but here they appeared to be limitless.

Both of them were surprised it happened with so little effort. "This is Empyreal Plane?" Jessup asked.

"I guess so," Zee replied.

"It's pretty."

"Yes, it is." According to Aureosa's notes, Empyrean permeated everything and was regenerative and infinite. Zee didn't tell Jessup that part because he thought it might bore him, but he did explain that the increased strength they felt when together came from the Empyrean ore in their core and probably the Marisean ore as well—and that was unprocessed ore in its natural state. Once they were able to forge it and learned how to use it, their power would grow and they could develop Abilities.

Zee took another breath along with Jessup. "Now we mine, which is collecting more of the particles into our core. Aureosa's notes say it's extremely difficult the first time and is all about strenuous use of willpower. Zepiter rewards the strong, they say. We have to reach into the Empyrean with our will, even imagining using it like a pick and shovel to break the Empyrean ore from the vein and scoop it into our core."

"Sounds simple," said Jessup. "Let's try."

"Really? All right then. Here we go."

While they'd communicated, the vision of the Empyreal Plane had grown dimmer but not gone away entirely. They focused again and it brightened once more. Zee imagined reaching into the vein of yellow ore and chipping at it with his will. At first the motes didn't budge, then they moved but didn't come loose. In a sudden rush the warmth of the bond between him and Jessup grew hotter as the will of the kraken joined with his. It flowed over him, through him, reinforcing his own. Zee concentrated harder and, working as one, they saw motes come free. They floated in a cluster outside the vein but tried to return to it.

Zee groaned at the effort to hold them back. "*We have to make it do what we want. Otherwise it remains just a wild and unruly force of nature.*"

Zee imagined forcing weight and density into his will, then felt Jessup responding in kind. Zee's willpower was strong, but nothing compared to the tremendous force he felt in the will of the kraken. The clusters of motes gained more texture and mass, first like water, then more like earth. The ore moved toward their crucible as they strained, then with a final effort it pressed through the wall of their crucible. Scorching heat tore through Zee's limbs from his hands and feet, and his forehead and chest burned. Jessup grunted. He was feeling it too. Zee groaned but didn't stop until the motes had joined the other Empyrean in their core.

"*More,*" said Jessup.

Now that they'd mined the first time, the process became a little easier, but each scoop was still a tremendous strain and the harsh burning pain of the Empyrean ore moving through them was just this side of unbearable, almost like trying to shove a burning coal down your throat and swallow it into your stomach. Still, they kept going.

How much time passed, Zee didn't know. Both of them felt like their brains had turned into a muscle that burned with the exertion. It was not a pleasant sensation. Throughout his life, Zee had developed a high tolerance for pain and discomfort, but it paled in comparison to what the kraken could bear.

Eventually it felt like their crucible was filling, and neither of them could go on any longer. There still wasn't nearly as much of the yellow Empyrean in their core as there was blue Marisean, but the percentage of it was larger than it had been.

Jessup said, "Enough for now?"

"I think so." Zee shook his head, and took a deep breath. "That's not easy."

"No, it hurts."

"Are you okay?"

"A little hurt doesn't bother Jessup."

"A little? I thought my head would pop."

"Zee said, 'Nothing worthwhile is easy.'"

"I told you that?"

"Yes."

"Then I must have. It's something my da used to say."

Zee pushed down the sadness that tried to rise at the thought of his da. The bond warmed as Jessup comforted him, knowing what Zee was feeling.

"Okay," Zee said, getting his thoughts back on task. He closed his eyes and looked into their core once more. The two colors, oddly enough, each had a different feel to them, a different density and even texture. The yellow felt lighter, more rarefied, than the blue. They'd gathered a good portion, though, which was more than Zee had expected on their first try.

"Next we have to refine it, which is getting it moving and churning it. This mixes the ore with the aura of our bond and makes it our own. That's what the notes say anyway, and I don't think Aureosa would make things up. Anyway, we're supposed to focus on it together and will it to move."

Zee exerted his will on the cloud. His temples throbbed, but the particles wouldn't move. Then he thought about how the motes in their core looked like a cloud slowly moving in the wind. He imagined a breeze blowing through their crucible and the cloud began to move more, ever so slightly. The pain in his head became nearly unbearable. He was about to stop when Jessup's willpower flooded into him once more. It was as if Jessup had been watching, waiting to see what Zee was going to do first, and now he was lending all his will, attention, and even his tolerance for pain, without Zee having to ask. The cloud moved, the colors swirling more energetically within. The magick of the bond, and the power of his friend, never ceased to amaze. The yellow and the blue still didn't mix, but as far as Zee knew, they didn't have to.

Even with Jessup's help, the process was agonizing. Stabbing pain centered in his head, above and between his eyes. Jessup's strength helped, making it just tolerable, but it did not go away. Aureosa's notes said all the steps would become easier as they gained more practice and progressed, but for now it was a grueling business.

The cloud moved faster and changed shape, colors swirling, and the motes began to sparkle. All the while, the yellow and blue remained separate.

When the motes ceased to sparkle brighter or move any faster, they backed off from their efforts. The movement of the cloud lessened, but they were happy to see that the particles continued to sparkle.

"*You're good at this*," Zee told Jessup through their bond while wincing and rubbing his temples.

"We *are good at this*," Jessup replied.

Zee smiled, his eyes still closed. According to the notes, it wasn't necessary to do all of the steps right away. In fact, it was recommended that beginners take a break of a few bells or even a day between them, as each step could be exhausting, even temporarily debilitating, especially for first-timers. Zee was tired, but the pain in his head had diminished to a tolerable ache. Even though he already knew what his friend's answer would be, he asked anyway. Jessup didn't want to wait either.

They didn't move or open their eyes but took a short break to breathe deeply and meditate on the blue-and-yellow cloud in their core. With each breath in, then out, the cloud expanded and contracted slightly, and they felt more refreshed. Zee realized it was the power of the refined ore in their crucible that was rejuvenating them, and though they may be using some of it, it was too small an amount for him to notice.

The final step of forging, called forming, was supposedly the most difficult—which, after what they'd already been through, was saying something. To form their core, they needed to contract their crucible and condense the cloud of particles as much as possible. More advanced pairs could do it once, making more room in their core, then do the whole process over again until either their core felt full or they just wanted to stop. Zee didn't know how much more he could take, and they hadn't even tried forming yet, so they decided they'd give it a try and see how it felt.

Zee focused on their bond and then their crucible. He explored its boundaries, tried to get a sense of its contours, felt out for its edges, but they were extremely vague. The notes said to think of their crucible like another organ in their body, one they could force to contract like a diaphragm, using their willpower to press the motes of ore together, compacting them, which made the core not only more dense, but stronger.

Supposedly, it helped to churn the cloud while compressing it. They pushed hard and could see the walls of their crucible contracting, but it took far more effort than the previous steps, and the cloud resisted. The method of imagining a breeze to get the cloud moving wasn't working in the tighter crucible, and the pain was worse than during the previous steps. They struggled on until it occurred to Zee that their crucible might work much like a chicken's gizzard. The gizzard was where birds temporarily stored what they swallowed, basically a muscle that would squeeze and churn the food, grinding it up with sand and pieces of rock they ate and stored in there. Their core didn't have sand or rocks, but he imagined the wall of their crucible working much the same way. The idea was automatically shared with Jessup, who seemed to naturally understand.

It took a while to figure out how to manipulate their crucible wall, but eventually they got it to undulate, to squeeze from top and bottom, then the sides, and the ore began to churn. More practice and they were able to rotate between churning the ore and contracting their crucible even harder to compress it.

They strained with all their might, physically pushing with their lungs to aid in the visualization, applying as much pressure as possible with all their inner strength, gritting their teeth with the effort. It felt like trying to push a giant boulder up a hill. The cloud continued to resist, as if pushing back. A half dozen times they stopped and rested, then went again, until they were finally able to see, and feel, progress. The cloud was getting smaller and holding together. Encouraged, they kept at it until they'd gotten the amorphous cloud to take on a more spherical shape, then a ball about a quarter of the size it had been.

Slowly, carefully, they eased off, afraid it would spring back, but the core kept its shape and size, glowing brighter than before. Blues still kept to blues, and yellows to yellows, but it looked solid, spinning slowly at the center of their crucible.

They sighed with relief and a great sense of accomplishment, but they weren't done yet. They had to compress the ore until it reached what Aureosa's notes called "critical mass," and a well-formed core should be perfectly round. It wasn't uncommon for the core to spark by itself the first time it was successfully formed, as well.

Bonded pairs could feel when a core was sparked within a hundred yards or so, but Zee figured they would be safe here, well below the dorms and surrounded by stone.

"Ready for the final push?" Zee asked.

"Ready," Jessup replied.

They took a deep breath, squeezed their eyes shut, and pressed inward. It felt like trying to squeeze a rock. All of their muscles tensed, they pushed harder, grunting and groaning with the effort. Zee's head throbbed, veins popped on his forehead, and it felt like his ribs were going to snap. Their groans became cries as they pushed with everything they had. The core gave a little, the motes packing in a smidgeon closer together, then a little more.

Just when Zee was sure they weren't going to be able to do it, there came a distinct feeling of the motes locking into place with a multitude of little clicks. Zee imagined a fire lighting in the middle of the core, and together, they roared, pushing with everything they had. There was a loud snap, then a sound like the lighting of a campfire soaked in highly flammable oil. Their core flared like a small sun, sending a blast of energy through their bodies.

Ceasing their effort was like suddenly letting go of a rope tied to a stone building they'd been trying to pull over. Jessup staggered back and Zee nearly tumbled off his arm. They recovered, gasping for breath and blinking in shock at their sparked core, their own little blue-and-yellow star. It continued to burn steadily.

Zee let out a "Whoop!" of exhilaration and Jessup released a happy groan.

Jessup said, "That was like trying to lift a mountain."

"Yes, it was. Or like me trying to lift a kraken."

Jessup chuckled, tickled by the thought. "Zee lift Jessup…" He laughed so hard he nearly fell over.

His laugh was so infectious it got Zee going too, and he did fall to the floor of the cave. After the bells of exertion, it was a release they must have needed. They'd done it. They'd forged their core as a bonded pair for the very first time, and all in one sitting.

The power of the core continued to course through their bodies, washing away their aches and pains, rejuvenating their minds and shared spirit.

When they'd finally recovered, Jessup wiped tears of laughter from his eyes and observed the slowly spinning core. "Looks like Zee's marble."

Zee chuckled, rubbing his eyes, and stood from where he'd been lying on the floor, curled up in laughter. He recalled the glass marble he'd kept in his little treasure box back home. He'd shown it to Jessup, who had marveled at it, then tried to eat it. The core did look like blue glass with a ribbon of yellow swirling down through it. "It doesn't have as many colors, but you're right."

Zee bathed in the core's power. Though he was visualizing it floating in the air in front of him, its energy flowed from just below his heart. He felt better, stronger and healthier than he ever had in his life. He was practically giddy.

The kraken tightened and curled his tentacles. "Jessup likes sparking core."

"So does Zee," Zee replied.

"Forge again?"

Zee chuckled at his big grinning friend. Of course, he'd been thinking the very same thing.

CHAPTER 30

Bright and early the next morning on the first of their two days off, Zee ate breakfast at his table while reading the pages of notes Commandant Aureosa had hidden in the back of the first-year cadet handbook.

Last night, two more times they'd mined Empyrean, which had floated around the already compacted core like a halo. They'd refined it until it sparkled, then compressed it into what was already there. It was easier after the first time since their forged core made them stronger, but it was still an arduous process. They got to the point where their crucible felt full and they could do no more, then collapsed in exhaustion and slept the whole night right where they were. Not even the extra energy from having a forged core could refresh them fast enough.

Their core was over three feet across when they'd finished. The last time they'd sparked it, they had felt an exhilaration similar to what Tem and Timandra had described when reaching a new class, but they had no idea if that applied to achieving Tin, the first class for bonded pairs. If they had succeeded, though, they should have their first attack Ability, maybe even two.

Zee read Aureosa's notes out loud, running a finger beneath the words while Jessup watched over his shoulder.

"Are you sure you can see these little scribbled words from that far?"

"Jessup has good kraken eyes."

Zee placed the tip of a pencil on the page he was reading. "What's that letter?"

"K, for kraken."

"I guess you do have good kraken eyes."

"Word is 'Keep.'"

Zee twisted around in his chair. "You're a fast learner, too."

"Smart big kraken with good kraken eyes."

Zee laughed, turning back to the notes, then popped the last of a plantain and hunk of bread in his mouth.

"This is all there is about Abilities, just brief notes on how Aureosa and Vandalia developed their Keep, used their first Shield, and tested their aura protection. There's nothing about attack Abilities."

"Zee should not talk with mouth full."

Zee mumbled, "What?"

"Zee heard Jessup."

Zee swallowed his food, nearly choking.

"That's another thing I said to you when you were little, isn't it?"

"Yes."

"You were probably chewing something disgusting and it was falling out of your mouth."

"So?"

Zee laughed again. "You make me sound like my ma." He took a deep breath and sat in silence, thinking about his parents.

"Sorry, Zee."

"No, it's fine. It was funny. I just miss them. I wonder if they would even recognize me now."

"They would. They will."

"Thank you."

"You will see them again."

"*We* will see them."

"Pinky promise?"

Zee chuckled so hard he could barely speak. "You don't have pinkies."

Jessup just shrugged. "Maybe Zee can go see ma and pa now that Zee's not stuck on ship anymore."

"You know, when our boss, Meik, explained our employment contract to me, he said we'll get vacation after we've worked for six months. We can go see them then."

"Zee excited?"

"I am, but scared, too. I wasn't very nice to them the day I got caught on the ship. What if they've been angry with me this whole time?"

"Zee and Jessup will go and find out."

"You're right, of course."

"Jessup excited to see Midge."

"Me too." Domestic pigs could live for decades, so chances were pretty good she'd still be there. "After I learned to write on ship, Dr. Aenig encourage me to write my folks a letter. The captain wouldn't allow it, but Aenig said he'd send it himself, and the captain wouldn't dare confiscate any of his mail. The problem is, my folks can't read, and they never really had any friends that did. Even if they did, I wouldn't know what to write."

"Write that Zee is okay, and he loves them," Jessup said, matter-of-fact. "And Jessup says 'hello.'"

Zee smiled up at him. "I'm just going to do what you say from now on."

"Bad idea."

Both of them laughed.

Zee said, "Who knows, in six months, we might be cadets in the academy. Then we'd really have a story to tell my folks when we finally get to see them."

"And Midge."

Zee grinned, "And Midge."

He sighed and turned back to the notes. "The rest of these pages are random entries. They're dated, but either Aureosa didn't write much after early in his first year as a cadet, or he gave us just these for a reason.

They're amazing to read, though. Mostly because of the enthusiasm he and Vandalia had back then and how much they wanted to progress. It's hard to imagine he was the same age I am when he wrote this." He scanned another page. "There are entries about Slan hai Drogo and Mogon, too."

"Who are Drogo and Mogon?"

"The most famous and powerful dragon and rider pair in recent history. They died a long time ago, but the commandants and the deans of magicks knew them."

"What does it say?"

Zee located the first entry and read it to Jessup.

"Mihir and I just heard that Emir Generals Slan hai Drogo and Mogon are coming to the citadel to take part in the combat exercises scheduled next month with the armed forces of Tosh and our allies. The faculty and staff are just as excited as we are."

The next entry was dated five weeks later.

"The combat exercises were incredible. The cadet wing got to take part, and our first-year flight performed admirably. What an experience. Mogon himself told Venkatarama that he and Mihir had great promise as combat magickers. If dragons could faint, I think Rama would have.

Vandalia and I classed up to mid-level Lead. We both danced with glee when we returned to our dorm. We're also very excited to see the tournament that starts tomorrow. It will last for three days, and Drogo and Mogon are participating. I'm not going to be able to sleep tonight, but I had better at least try."

The last page of notes contained only one entry.

"The tournament was absolutely amazing. Drogo and Mogon beat them all, including two flights of Black Titans from Aldarox and Tur-

reen, each with their own Black Titan combat magicker pair. They have Abilities and tricks I've never even heard of and their opponents had no defense against. It was a spectacle unlike anything Vandalia or I have ever seen. A true inspiration. I am in awe. Vandalia says she's in love with Mogon and wants to have all his babies. She's joking, of course, since she's a Greatwing and Mogon's a Tasarabat and different species of dragons can't interbreed, but I will forever tease her about it.

By the end of the tournament, Drogo and Mogon had progressed to high-level Black Titan. Most amazing is that Drogo is only twenty-six years of age. He just graduated five years ago! Unbelievable."

Zee let out a low whistle. "I'll bet that was incredible to see." He returned his attention to the notes. "There's just one more line."

"Vandalia and I will be Black Titans one day. If there truly is to be a war, I hope sooner rather than later."

"This must have been not long before the war between the alliance of twelve kingdoms, including Tosh, and the Luftoo Empire," Zee said. "They still haven't made it to Black Titan, after all this time…" Somehow, thinking about Aureosa and Vandalia having not yet achieved their dream made Zee sad. It also emphasized just how momentous it was that Drogo and Mogon made Black Titan so young. "Aureosa, Vandalia, Wanchoo, and Venkatarama did fight in that war, survived, and are now commandants and deans at Triumf's Citadel Academy. That's saying something."

Zee stared at the page awhile longer, then flipped back through the notes and stood to face Jessup. "Want to see if we can form our Keep?"

* * *

Three times they repeated how Aureosa described forming a Keep, with no success.

"Is Zee sure we are doing this right?" Jessup asked.

"Unless Aureosa left something out, we're doing what they did." From where he sat on one of Jessup's arms, leaning against him, Zee summarized the notes. "Meditate. Spark our core. Visualize a space in the Aether—you know what, I've been visualizing a space in our crucible and thinking about our core. I'll bet a Keep isn't there but exists somewhere else."

"Where?"

"I don't know. It's magick. I'd think it would be close since it's accessed through a rider's chest. But it couldn't actually be in my chest..." Zee thought a moment. "Maybe it's just kind of anchored to us by our bond or to our core." He tapped his upper lip with a finger. "Let's try not visualizing our crucible at all, just leave our core sparked and look at the space where it normally appears to us and focus on opening a space there."

"Sounds good to Jessup."

They closed their eyes and breathed deeply, allowing the image of their crucible to fade away. After only a few seconds of concentrating on forming their Keep in the Aether alone, a hole appeared in the space before them and grew into a bright rectangle about the size of Mahfouz's shack.

Zee opened his eyes in surprise and found that no matter where he moved them, he could still see the rectangular space if he wanted to. "Jessup, we have a Keep!"

"For keeping things!"

"Let's put something in it."

"A fish!"

"No!" Zee laughed, shaking his head. "I know..." He hopped off Jessup's arm, ran to his wardrobe, and took out his stinger. "This is the only weapon we have, and Dr. Aenig said to keep it a secret."

"Will it poke Zee?"

"Knights put swords and spears in theirs, so I don't think so." He moved the stinger toward his chest. With a thought, it vanished in a flash of blue light.

"Oh..." He looked up. There the stinger was, lying on the floor of the white space. "It worked!" He moved his hand back toward his chest, thinking about the stinger. Another flash of blue light and the stinger was there against his palm. He had to hurry and close his hand before it fell to the floor. He beamed at Jessup. "Now you try. I've never seen a dragon do it, but that doesn't mean they can't." Zee put the stinger back. "See if you can take it out."

Jessup frowned in contemplation, then tapped the tip of an arm against his shell. Nothing happened. He tried touching it to his nose. Still nothing.

Zee stayed silent while Jessup thought, then the kraken took a breath of concentration and moved the tip of his arm to his forehead, just above and between his eyes. Blue light flashed, and the stinger was there. Jessup grunted, fumbling with the pointed metal rod, but it clanged to the stone floor of the cave.

"Oops."

Zee said, "That's okay. It's too little for you to hold, really. But you did it! You can take things out of our Keep, too."

"Like fish," Jessup said with a sly grin.

"Stop it, no fish!"

Zee stepped toward the stinger, but the kraken held out an arm. "Jessup can do it."

Jessup peered at the stinger, then used the stretched and thinned ends of two arms, one of them with its claw folded out, to delicately lift the stinger. The tip of Jessup's tongue stuck out between his big lips as he concentrated on coiling the tip of one arm around the stinger. With a grunt of accomplishment, Jessup moved it toward his forehead. Blue light flashed, and the stinger was back in their Keep.

Zee threw his fists into the air. "Yes! You can use it too!"

"For fish!"

"Argh!"

* * *

They continued practicing putting things in their Keep and retrieving them. Rocks, books, a chair. Jessup even heaved a good-sized boulder in there, just to see how much weight it could take. It didn't feel any different than when it was empty. Jessup also got the bright idea of trying to put Zee in it, but they worried about how that might affect the Keep itself since it was a shared space between the two of them. They also didn't know if live things could go in there. Jessup said they should try it with a fish when they went out later—just as an experiment, of course. Zee just rolled his eyes.

They took everything out but Zee's stinger, which he'd wrapped up in canvas. Zee covered the book Aenig had given him with a towel and put it in as well. During their experimentation they'd found the Keep to be completely watertight, so the wrappings were more to hide what the items were in case others could look in there than to keep them dry.

Next, they sparked their core again and attempted forming a Shield, following Aureosa's notes. It wasn't long before they hit upon the right combination of focus, intent, and visualization, and their Shield of light sprang into shape in front of them, circular and slightly curved. Zee was pleasantly surprised at how thick it was for their first attempt, though still easy to see through, and larger than he'd expected. The bottom edge nearly touched the floor, and the top went just short of the top of Jessup's shell.

With a thought from either of them they could manipulate it to cover them above, go behind them to protect their back, and even go spinning around them. In his excitement, Jessup scurried to slam it against the wall of the cavern, then raised it and bashed the lower edge into the floor, chipping the stone. Zee had to remind him they did actually live there, and they didn't want to bring the whole thing down on their heads.

Zee hopped off and they marveled that they could each summon their own Shield. Jessup's Shield was larger and thicker than Zee's by far, but not as strong as when they formed one together.

Of course that led to them bashing into each other, resulting in Zee being tossed into the air to land flat on his back. His aura pulsed blue, protecting him from injury, and even cushioning the impact.

Zee noted that their Shield and aura were blue, not yellow like everyone else's. The flash of light from using their Keep was blue as well. He didn't plan on them sparking their core where anyone could see or were close enough to sense it, and the commandants, deans, and beastmasters had also remarked that blue Marisean had been unknown until they'd seen it in Zee and Jessup's core. The blue light would draw even more attention, and he and Jessup had more of that than they wanted already.

They couldn't attack each other through their Shields, but they could move them to the side and attack. They took turns hurling rocks they'd found at the far end of the cave at each other's Shields and hitting them with a broomstick. The only thing that affected the Shields at all, though, was Zee's stinger. Hitting it on Jessup's Shield sent sparks flying, and when Zee stabbed the Shield, both the stinger and the Shield flared, electricity shot through the Shield around the impact area, and the stinger point sank in a ways. Afterward, the stinger continued to glow blue for a time, as if it had drawn energy from the Shield itself.

Zee had never really thought about it, but the stinger had always zapped with blue electricity. He'd have to consider that more. It was frustrating they couldn't ask anyone about these kinds of things or for help with figuring out their attack Abilities, but it was what it was. He and Jessup would do their best, regardless.

Some attack Abilities were shared by all types of dragons, such as those having to do with faster flight or moving great quantities of air with their wings or enhancing their roar. Most, however, were augmented versions of their natural projectile. Greatwings and Royals developed more powerful and effective uses of flames, Ice Divers their icy breath, and Rocks their molten dragon ambergris.

The thing was, Jessup didn't really have an attack projectile. They considered his ability to shoot out ink, but that was more defensive than anything, and they couldn't imagine what else ink could do but be ink. The best they could think of was his electric shock. They sparked their core and tested it in the lake in their cavern. The result was incredible. The whole lake flashed like lightning. Zee could feel it where he stood on the dry cavern floor, and his hair stood straight up. Jessup acknowledged that it was much stronger than what he'd been able to do before, and thought he might be able energize it even more than that. They weren't sure if it qualified as a new Ability or if it was just stronger because of their core, but they decided to call it Pulse, just in case.

Their biggest concern then had been that Jessup would zap Zee as well, so they tried another experiment. Zee swam to sit on Jessup's shell, hanging on to the spines, then Jessup very carefully produced a small amount of electricity. When that didn't hurt Zee, Jessup increased it. Zee sat there, watching the blue electricity crackle and leap between Jessup's spines, until Jessup finally loosed a pulse as powerful as before. Zee was able to feel the energy buzzing over and through him, but it didn't bother him at all. All they could figure was that it didn't hurt Zee for the same reason it didn't hurt Jessup. They didn't know what that reason was, since they knew nothing about how bonds really worked, or about electricity other than some marine creatures could generate it and it was what lightning was made of, but it was great news.

That was when Zee had his big idea—maybe Jessup could shoot bolts of lightning.

First they tried Pulse out of the water—not as powerful as the one Jessup had done in the lake, just to make sure Zee still wouldn't be affected. All went well, so Jessup got the arcs of blue light leaping between his spines, and they focused their will and intent on a boulder at the far end of the cave. Jessup fired. The rock remained untouched, but a streak blasted the wall right next to them, spraying them with fragments of shattered stone. Their auras flashed and protected them, but both of them stared at the gouge the lightning had torn in the wall. At least the sheer power of it was promising. Jessup said he hadn't been using anywhere near the energy he could produce, too.

They decided to pull back on the power a little more and tried again. The bolt struck the floor in front of them, causing them to flinch back. It had gone in the general direction, though, which was encouraging. The next try, however, went much worse. Instead of a single bolt, a dozen smaller bolts blasted out all around them, and a small exlposion sounded. They spun to see the table had been knocked over behind them and one of the chairs burst apart and burning.

Zee leapt off Jessup, snatched up the broom, bolted to the chair and beat at the flames, which only accomplished setting the broom on fire as well.

"This! Isn't! Working!" Zee cried, flailing with the burning broom.

Jessup coiled an arm around his waist, picked him up, plucked the broom from his hand with another arm, and tossed it into the lake. Then he swept the burning debris into the water.

Zee watched the charred pieces of wood that had once been a chair hissing and steaming on the surface of the water. "That worked."

* * *

Zee clung to the spines at the back of Jessup's shell near the base, smiling through salty spray thrown up by his friend's shell cutting through the waves. With the protective nictitating lenses of his eyes in place, he didn't even have to blink. The sun was bright above, shining between calm white clouds, but the lenses cut down on the glare as well. He peered out over the sea, and up to the sky. His eyesight was definitely getting better from the strengthening of their bond. The edges of the waves, details of the clouds and birds, were all sharper and more defined. All the better for spotting dragons and riders in the air. He scanned the sea and sky regularly, keeping an eye out for them.

He and Jessup had ventured out to see what more they could do now that they'd forged their core but also because they wanted to practice their nascent attack Abilities without destroying their home.

Zee checked their Keep and found that nothing had moved. No matter how much he or Jessup jostled about, the items stayed right where they were. And there was something new in it. A six-foot-long toona, lying there right in the middle. "Jessup!"

"What?" Jessup asked innocently.

"No fish!"

"It was experiment. It died when Jessup put it in there."

"That's good to know. Good job. Now take it out."

Jessup retrieved the toona. "Jessup just have to eat it." And he did.

Zee shook his head, then realized he could see their Keep even though their core wasn't sparked. And Jessup had been able to take something out of it. He looked over his shoulder. Triumf's Island was a tiny smudge on the horizon. He reached for his stinger and it appeared in his hand with a flash. Being able to use their Keep without their core sparked could definitely come in handy. He put it back just as Jessup dived.

They'd thought about finding a secluded island to practice on, but even a small chance a dragon and rider pair might fly over and feel their core spark or see the flashing blue light of their lightning was too much to risk. They weren't sure it would work underwater, but deep in the sea was the only place they could think of they'd be safe from prying eyes.

Once they were a hundred feet down, Jessup leveled out and they sparked their core. And once again, Zee marveled at the power that surged through them.

Jessup threw back his arms, using his siphon at the same time, and they took off like a loosed arrow. Zee had to hold on tight, but that wasn't a problem with his increased strength. The sea bottom flew by beneath them. They weren't going as fast as a dragon could fly, but Zee wasn't going to tell Jessup that.

Instead, he shouted through their bond, *"You're a speedy kraken!"*

"Super speedy!" Jessup answered. *"Zee swim too!"*

Before Jessup could slow his pace, Zee let go of the spines and leapt up and away. He rolled with the wake, then shot off after Jessup, far faster than he'd ever swum in his life. He shouted in glee. He still wasn't as fast as Jessup, though, so his friend began swimming around him in wide circles.

"Speedy tiny murman!" Jessup said.

"Super speedy!"

"Super-speedy tiny murman."

Zee laughed and almost choked. *"All right, all right. Let's get to work."*

"This is work."

"It is, but we can do more."

According to Aureosa's notes, brief as they were, the idea was to forge as much Empyrean as possible, expend it in training, and keep doing that, packing Empyrean into their core in an effort to stretch their crucible and make it larger, then expending it in training, and doing it again. The process would supposedly become more natural the more a pair did it. For now it was just fun.

They swam for another bell, then spotted the base of an island under the water, strewn with boulders. Eager to try out their lightning again, they started slow, like they had in the cave. Zee had wondered if the salt water would disperse the electricity, but the arcing blue light and bolts worked exactly the same as on land. They figured out how to send either a single more powerful bolt or multiple weaker bolts at a time through what they pictured in their minds and how they focused their concentration, but they still couldn't hit a shaddamn thing they aimed at. After another bell spent exploding rocks at random and without intent and gouging up the seafloor, they took a short break to sit under the water and meditate on their core. They'd used maybe fifty percent of it and were only the slightest bit tired. They were going to have to work harder.

They tested their Shield. It performed just as it had out of the water but was harder to move around, and it slowed their swimming. They pushed power from their core into it, straining to make it thicker and stronger. Each effort was strenuous and caused pressure in their core, like they were holding their breath and running out of oxygen, and it gave Zee a headache. He recovered quickly after each try but found it took a little longer each time.

The two of them made a game of coming up with activities that would help expend their core. Jessup started by shoving huge rocks up the incline of the underwater base of the island. Zee chose rocks that weren't nearly as large, but the effort caused his muscles to burn. They graduated to larger rocks until they couldn't push them any farther, Jessup's at that point the size of a house.

They carried rocks along the bottom of the sea, as big as they could lift. Then they dug into the sand and rocks on the ocean floor with hands and arms, as fast as they could. They burned their core the whole time, Zee checking on its size often to see how much of it they were using. He also realized he could feel the core levels changing without looking at it. With practice, he bet he wouldn't have to look at their core at all to know how fast they were using it up and how much they had left.

Jessup swam up almost to the surface, spun back, and dove straight down, ramming the point of his shell into the silt. Using his arms to grab hold of rocky outcroppings, he began corkscrewing himself into the seabed.

Zee grinned, remembering Jessup doing that to hide when he was small. To see him do it now, with his current power and size, was incredible. *"I'm not doing that!"* he shouted through the bond.

Jessup laughed and his arms slipped off the rocks to flail in the water, the top of his shell stuck in the rocks and sand.

"*Ha!*" Zee teased.

Jessup was undaunted. He curled his arms out in a swirl, then quickly whipped them the other way. Using the resistance of the water and the extra power from the bond, he made a quarter turn, digging deeper.

Zee got an idea. "*Try spinning your arms continuously.*"

Jessup swiveled an eye in Zee's direction. "*What?*"

"*Like this.*" Zee held up his arms and swung them around over his head in a circular motion. With his webbed hand and newly acquired strength, he found the action actually made him turn fairly quickly—and Jessup had ten huge arms, forty feet long when he stretched them out.

The movement was similar to how Jessup would spin himself when swimming, so it only took a little practice to get his arms going correctly and with the proper amount of force. He moved them faster and did indeed begin to screw down deeper.

"*Hurrah!*" Zee cried, then found himself being pulled around his giant friend by the force of the water. Above Jessup, the water spun in a vortex.

"*Keep going!*" he shouted, then swam upward. The vortex broadened all the way to the surface, and when Zee broke the waves he saw that Jessup was creating a whirlpool. Grinning, he swam closer, allowing himself to be drawn into it, around and around, then sucked down.

Not long after he was submerged, the intensity of the whirlpool diminished. Peering down, he saw that Jessup had drilled himself all the way into the ocean floor and was still going, now using his arms to push on the sides of the wide hole he had made.

Zee swam down and peered into the darkness—only it wasn't that dark. Spots on Jessup's arms were glowing blue, casting an eerie light in the hole.

"*Jessup, did you know your arms have lights?*"

"*Yes. Jessup can do it to see better at night or when going very deep in the sea. Parts of shell glow too.*"

"*You can make them glow on purpose?*"

"*Jessup thought Zee might want to come too.*"

Zee laughed. "*That's okay. Maybe you shouldn't go any deeper today. Besides, it's almost time for lunch and I'm starving.*"

"*Okay. Tiny murman needs to eat and get stronger so he can lift Jessup.*" A deep kraken-chuckle rumbled from the hole.

"*I'll do my best,*" Zee replied with a grin. He shook his head, watching Jessup reverse the movement of this arms and unscrew himself. This was all so crazy, like he was in a dream. And after ten years of hardship on the *Krakenfish*, this time it was a good dream.

"*This is good exercise,*" Jessup commented with strain in his voice.

"*I can tell,*" Zee replied. Zee could feel the power from their core being used when Jessup really exerted himself, though not by a lot. Jessup naturally had far better endurance than Zee, but with their shared core, Zee had more than he'd ever had before. The kraken also used more of their core when exercising than Zee alone. These were all things he noted to keep in mind as they learned more and worked toward advancing.

On their way back, they unsparked their core and headed toward the surface. Using his siphon jet, Jessup shot them high into the air. Zee bailed right away and dove, but Jessup's splash was spectacular. They continued back toward the island, both of them flying out of the water, trying to outdo each other with acrobatic flips and spins.

Jessup won the competition with sheer audacity. He'd come rocketing out of the water in a spin, throw his arms out in various patterns, then flip multiple times and throw his arms back to dive perfectly back into the sea. He told Zee he used to do these kinds of things when feeling good, but never with the speed, height, and control he had now, even without their core sparked.

"Now Zee do it like Jessup," the kraken said. He snatched Zee up and flung him as high and far as he could—which was pretty high and far. Zee screeched, tumbling, and barely avoided belly-smacking in the water. Still, he swam back for more. And still, he screeched when Jessup threw him, but now with the thrill of it, flipping and twisting before performing a perfectly executed dive.

* * *

"There's something you don't see every day." Jondon dil Rolio stood heaving for breath in the line of the entire Basic Training cohort, staring out at the kraken and murman frolicking in the surf. They were supposed to be running a rocky trail up into the foothills for a mountain run, but the third-year cadets who were leading them had stopped to gape at the sight.

Next to Jondon, Sallison anh Batcu said, "It's probably something no one has seen in a thousand years."

"Maybe more," said Mehmet can Yasso, leaning forward with hands on his knees, which was no small feat considering his round belly. "I'm just glad for the break."

Not all of the new recruits were as thrilled by the sight. Some grumbled.

Derlick don Donnicky said, "Stupid creatures. Ludicrous and profane." Others grunted in agreement. Sallison wanted very much to introduce her fist to their teeth.

One of the recruits said to Donnicky, "I heard you knew the gilly on ship."

"I did, unfortunately." Derlick replied. "He's small and feebleminded, like all his kind." He snorted in disdain. "And that beast is disgusting. It should be put out of everyone's misery."

Sallison was about to march up to Donnicky and show him the true meaning of misery when a dragon's shout from a distance behind them drew her attention. A little farther inland, a group of twenty duckies were drilling flight formations in the sky. They had straightened their trajectory and were also watching the show out off the coast. Among them, she caught sight of the white Ice Diver with one of his front legs smaller than the other, the foot twisted, turned up and curled, the talons stubby and malformed.

From talk among the instructors, she'd learned his name was Fennix. For a moment she felt something odd, though she didn't know what. Sympathy, maybe, but somehow not. She considered how much determination it must have taken Fennix to make the cut and become accepted into Basic Training in the first place, then get through it, let alone return after failing to make it as a cadet and having to go through it all over again. Even though he trailed at the back of the group, he flew with a swiftness and grace that made the others look awkward.

The Ice Diver glanced at her, then the dragon cadet instructor shouted for them to tighten their formation. He tore his eyes away. For a moment she thought she felt his shame. Somehow that angered her. He shouldn't be ashamed. He should be proud of himself.

"Is everything all right, Sallison anh Batcu?" The voice was deep and pleasant, but Sallison frowned at the sound of it. Up the line of recruits, the tallest of them except for Jondon had stepped forward and was watching her. His name was Inkanyezi ekh Hanyayo, a nephew of the vizier to the king. They didn't come much more highborn than that, and his dark and clear complexion free of any marks, his regal bearing, and his sickening propriety showed it. He also wore a smile that bordered on a smirk—at least it looked that way to her.

"I'm fine, Minny Inkanyezi ekh Hanyayo, no thank you for asking."

Recruits within earshot sucked in breath at her disrespect. Because of his uncle's status, most of them would lick dragon dung off his boots if he asked.

Amusement—or was it good-humored sincerity—glinted in his deep brown eyes. "My friends call me Yezi."

Fastest and strongest, with incredible endurance, already clearly better than all of them with sword, spear, and bow in their early training classes, Hanyayo was Sallison's main competition for top of the cohort. She was determined to beat the others, but Hanyayo would be a real challenge. New recruits had to achieve a minimum individual rating of low-level Sand Class to pass Basic and become a first-year cadet. It would take most of them the full sixteen weeks to achieve it, and some never would. She'd been assessed at mid-level Sand when they first got their assessment badges, but so had Hanyayo. She was determined to reach high level by the end of Basic. If he did too, she'd just have to beat him in the trials.

"Like I said, Minny ekh Hanyayo, I'm doing just fine. Maybe you should focus your concern on someone who needs it, and cares."

Whispers arose around her, but she didn't care what any of them thought. Hanyayo nodded respectfully and stepped back in line. She wondered if she was being too harsh with him, but only for the briefest of moments. She wasn't. He needed to keep his ridiculously noble nose in his own business.

The cadet instructor in the lead finally recovered from her fascination with the kraken and murman and shouted back along the line, "Enough gawking, minnies! We'll do an extra mile to pay for our unexpected entertainment." Recruits groaned. "Make that two!" There were no groans this time.

"No rest for the weak, Yasso," said Chirt sim Nabbit. "And that includes me."

The cadet instructor stationed at the back of the group to keep stragglers moving shouted, "Move out!"

As they proceeded to run again, Sallison looked back to the sea and the murman and kraken, who were oblivious to the attention they'd drawn. She kept watching until they followed the path higher into the wooded foothills and the sea was lost from sight. She hoped her bond with a dragon would be as joyous as theirs. Of course, she had to get through Basic, pass the trials and the acumen test, and get a dragon to accept her for bonding before any of that could happen.

For now, she bore down and ran faster, intent on beating Hanyayo—and maybe even the cadet instructor—to the finish.

CHAPTER 31

After lunch, Zee and Jessup checked their core once more. It was noticeably smaller, but only down to about forty percent. With all that work, they'd used less than Zee had hoped for.

According to Aureosa's notes, greater quantities of their core were used when engaging in combat, simulated or otherwise, particularly when using Abilities. They couldn't really do that, and since they had to keep their forging a secret, they couldn't ask anyone for help, either. All they could really do was practice on their own in secret and forge as much as they could to stretch their crucible and grow their core.

"Then Zee and Jessup should forge," Jessup said brightly. "A lot."

Zee smiled up at his big friend's undampened enthusiasm. "Forging it is, then."

They spent much of the rest of the afternoon filling their crucible with Empyrean ore, refining it and forming their core, then mining more. The process was just as painful but drained them less than it had last night.

When they finished forging for the third time that afternoon, Zee collapsed back against the kraken's cheek. "Sorry, Jessup, I don't think I can do it again right now."

"That's good. Jessup is hungry anyway." Zee slid off of Jessup's arm and the kraken slipped into the cavern lake.

Zee said, "You be careful out there."

"Jessup is always careful," his friend replied, then climbed the rise at the mouth of the cave and leapt into the sea, crying, "Whee!"

Zee rubbed his face, chuckling, then went out for a run to clear his head.

* * *

Zee was tired when he returned from his run, but he set to his regular workout routine. He'd done similar training nearly every night on the ship, but now he'd adapted it to match what the recruits at the academy were made to do—only he did more repetitions than they did. That day he focused on pushers, then crunchers, then started over again and did them four more times.

One thing was for sure, he didn't have nearly the strength or stamina he had when Jessup was around. He'd felt the difference before they'd started forging, but now when they were apart the disparity was even more noticeable.

He knew that both riders and dragons of bonded pairs lost the power of their bond when they weren't together and that it diminished as the distance between them grew greater, until they were back to their normal strength. The distance limit was about a hundred feet, a little longer for each higher class, but not a whole lot. Some bonds were stronger than others, too, and that could add to the distance. Working out away from your bondmate was just as important as training together. Also, if Zee and Jessup were accepted into the academy some day, they'd have to get through Basic separately, without the aid of their bond.

Zee groaned as he stood from his last set of crunchers. Pullers were usually another part of his training, but there wasn't anywhere to do them in the cave. When he and Jessup were staying at Beastmaster Mahfouz's shack, he'd use the rafters. He supposed he could go out and find a suitable tree limb. He looked over the spacious cavern while he got his breathing under control, the burn in his stomach muscles and chest fading, and had an idea. He'd need supplies, but he knew just where to get them. And he had money. It was the weekend, though. It would have to wait until Monday after work.

* * *

Frustrated over his and Jessup's failure to control their attack Abilities, if they even were attack Abilities, Zee sat at the table nibbling on dried banana chips, flipping through books he'd pulled from the shelves, trying to find anything that might help. There was nothing there. All the while, his eyes kept going to the book Dr. Aenig had given him, which he'd taken out of his and Jessup's Keep before Jessup got too far away. He decided to give it another try.

Bells later, the light at the cave entrance was dimming, and Zee still hadn't made any progress with the book. He snatched up his latest sheet of notes, crumpled it, and flung it away, adding it to the many wads on the floor.

He felt Jessup arriving and watched as his friend climbed over the lip at the cavern entrance, swam across the lake, and slid his front arms onto the cavern floor.

Jessup's eyed the mess of paper on the floor. "Zee tear up book?"

Zee ran his fingers through his hair in frustration. "Those are my notes." He set about picking them up and tossing them into a wicker wastebasket. "What did you have for dinner, or do I even want to know?"

Jessup said, "Good dinner. Squids and kelp."

"I remember you chewing on kelp when you were tiny," Zee said with a smile.

"Kelp is good."

"Dragons only eat meat, but my ma used to say, 'Every good boy should eat his vegetables to help him grow big and strong.'"

"Vegetables?"

"Plants. Squids and fish are meat. Kelp is a vegetable." He scratched his chin. "I think, anyway."

A mischievous smirk twisted on Jessup's big rubbery lips. "Zee needs to eat more vegetables."

Zee laughed and threw one of the wads of paper at him. "You are not my mother!"

They laughed together, then Zee returned to his chair and sat in a huff.

Jessup said, "Something is bothering Zee."

"It's nothing, really. Just this book. Dr. Aenig gave it to me for a reason, but I can't figure it out."

"Can Jessup see?"

Zee thought for a second. "Why not? Just be careful with it."

He picked up the book and was about to stand, but Jessup reached to the table, attached small suckers to the book's cover, and took it out of Zee's hand.

Jessup pulled the book to himself and opened it with the tip of another arm, then turned pages with a delicate care Zee wouldn't have imagined possible.

After studying it for a while, Jessup said, "Gibberish."

Zee snorted. "I told you."

Jessup closed the book and inspected the cover. He held it to his nostrils and sniffed, then pressed the tip of his tongue against it.

"What are you doing?"

Jessup held it up. "Murfolk book?"

"That's the idea, I guess."

Jessup dunked it in the water.

"Ahh! Jessup, no!" Zee leapt from the desk, but Jessup still held the book underwater, watching it. Zee skidded to the edge, ready to dive in, but just below the surface the book was emanating blue light, and the webbed hand on the cover glowed bright.

When Jessup lifted it out, the hand imprint still glowed. "Murfolk book." He handed it to Zee.

Amazed, Zee took the book and opened it. The first pages still contained the strange symbols, but they were swirling in odd patterns. He closed the book and placed his palm on the hand stamped into the cover. The light pulsed softly, then dimmed. Opening it again he witnessed the symbols change into a slowly spinning circle with ten arms waving gently. "A krakenbond," he breathed. "Jessup. You're a genius."

Jessup just grinned.

On the following page, the symbols were now uniformly sized and more clearly written in orderly rows at the top of the page and in a column along one side. Zee still couldn't read the language, but a simple color illustration took up most of the page—and it moved in a loop. It looked to Zee like it was about breathing.

Jessup spoke softly. "Magick murfolk book."

The next pages still had the same strange symbols as before. Apparently they'd have to go through it one step at a time, then it would hopefully reveal more.

The illustration was a diagram of a murperson with webbed hands and feet, gills on its neck and along its ribs, and on the left side of its chest was a krakenbond. Just like Zee's. Other than the bond, there was no sign of a kraken. He recalled that during forging, the rider was the conduit for mining ore from the Aether. Could this be the first lesson in forging Marisean?

There was only one way to find out.

At the bottom of the lake, by the light of the book in Zee's lap and from the glowing spots on Jessup's body and tentacles, Zee studied the diagram. Arrows moved in through the murperson's mouth and nose. Some went out through the gills on the neck, but more passed through the lungs and what Zee took as a representation of a small crucible, then out through the gills, all in a repeating, continuous motion.

Zee hadn't thought about it in quite some time, but breathing underwater was more of a continuous process than the in and out of breathing air. He assumed the position of the murperson in the illustration, sitting with legs crossed, hands on knees with palms up, eyes closed, and tried it. The sound under the lake and the circular movement of water flowing in and through him was even more soothing than breathing above.

After twenty minutes, he found that his mind had drifted into a serene state, half conscious, as if in a waking dream. Through his eyelids he caught a pulse of light.

Zee opened his eyes. The diagram had stopped moving, and the page turned all on its own to reveal another diagram. It was similar to the first, but this one showed pathways, or channels, in his body, all connecting to the representation of the crucible in his chest, just below his heart. There were channels that went from the bottoms of his feet, from his palms, and from the center of his forehead, all connecting to the crucible. Zee remembered the burning sensation from mining Empyrean had followed those exact paths. The channels were shown as being constricted in random areas, the walls uneven.

The channels moved in this diagram, slowly expanding, the walls straightening, then repeating, over and over.

Zee closed his eyes and breathed as he had before. When his mind had settled once more, he quested inward, concentrating on the channels in his body, then focused on opening them. It was difficult at first, and he kept having to calm himself and start over, but after several more attempts he could feel the pathways inside him, and they began to clear. As they did, he felt freer, more refreshed. The breathing became even easier. It was as if he'd always been wrapped in something constricting, never knowing it, and was suddenly free of it.

All the while, Jessup had stayed silent, his only sound the soft, deep whoosh of his breathing, like the breaking of distant waves.

Another pulse from the book and Zee opened his eyes in eager anticipation. The murperson was still in the same position but smaller on the page. Behind was a large triangle with round eyes below its base, and ten arms, each looped through the other in a circle around it. The murperson sat on the front loop.

Arrows came out of the center of where the kraken's forehead would be and the center of the murperson's chest, moved up above them, then looped around and down to the openings of the murperson's channels.

"*I'm guessing this is reaching out to see the Marisean, like we did for the*

Empyrean, and maybe mining, too," Zee said through their bond. "*Do you think you can hold your arms like that?*"

"*Jessup will try.*"

Zee pushed himself away from where he'd been sitting on one of Jessup's arms and held the book out for Jessup to see. Studying the diagram with one big eye, Jessup squirmed his arms into the exact position.

"Perfect!" Zee shouted out loud in the water. The sound was different than when he spoke on land, but still comprehensible. Zee was a little surprised his friend didn't make a joking reply. Instead, Jessup sat completely still, eyes closed, breathing deeply. He was taking this seriously. Zee projected appreciation and respect through their bond. Jessup replied with a hum of satisfaction.

Zee climbed up on the loop in one of Jessup's arms and assumed the meditation position shown in the diagram.

Using their combined will, they tried visualizing the Mariseal Plane, but it didn't work. Instead they felt resistance, and Zee realized they'd forgotten to visualize their crucible first. Once they brought their crucible and core into view, Zee concentrated on breathing and opening the channels again, clearing them, expanding them, and without seeking it out or demanding it reveal itself as they had to do with the Empyreal Plane, the Mariseal Plane appeared before their mind's eye.

"Ooh..."

Zee felt his friend's amazement, but he was plenty amazed himself. Unlike the thin vein of yellow they had seen on the Empyreal Plane, a great river of glowing blue particles flowed from dark cosmic horizon to dark cosmic horizon, much wider and denser than the Empyrean had been. And without asking or demanding, the light began to flow toward Zee, through the channels in his hands, feet, head, and chest, into their shared crucible.

The feeling was very different from mining Empyrean. Where they had to exert their will, dig and pull at the golden power of Zepiter and basically shovel it into their crucible, the Marisean ore trickled in like water drawn by a vacuum. And instead of causing pain, it felt cool and refreshing, even cleansing.

"*We're doing it, Jessup,*" Zee whispered through their bond, as if speaking too loudly would scare away the ore. "*We're mining Marisean.*"

"*Jessup likes feeling of mining Empyrean, but this is better.*"

"*It's what we're made for, I guess. We are creatures of the sea.*"

"*You are creature. Jessup is person.*"

Zee chuckled. "*That's fine with me.*" The flow had slowed while they conversed. "*Okay, we need to pay attention.*"

He continued his breathing, thinking on the channels, while Jessup matched his breaths and state of mind.

Marisean ore continued to fill their crucible, floating around their formed core. It took concentration to keep their breathing steady and the channels open, but it was far less arduous than mining Empyrean had been.

They achieved that feeling of fullness in their crucible they'd experienced when mining Empyrean, but it felt more substantial, and the flow began to slow. Zee thought for a moment. "*You know how we contract our crucible when forming? Let's try the opposite. Expanding it, like we would with our lungs when inhaling air.*" Zee felt rather than heard Jessup's assent.

As it turned out, expanding their crucible was more complicated than Zee had thought it would be. It was a lot to think about. Breathing, keeping the channels open and clear, and expanding their crucible was like trying to use a muscle they never knew they had. Their first attempts were akin to trying to rub your stomach and pat your head at the same time and failing miserably. Finally, they could not only feel their crucible expanding, they could see it, the walls thinning as it stretched. More focus on breathing and keeping the channels open, and more Marisean flowed in, slowing to a dribble as they reached their limit. They felt as if they'd inhaled very slowly until they couldn't do it anymore. Zee actually began to feel dizzy.

He allowed the channels to constrict, then purposefully tightened them further. The channels didn't completely close, but Zee was relieved that no Marisean leaked out. The Mariseal Plane faded away, and for both of them it was as if they could finally breathe out again. Though the process had been less strenuous than mining Empyrean, they were still spent.

Zee gasped out, *"We did it!"*

"Best kraken and murman team ever."

Zee watched the mist of blue Marisean ore floating around their core. *"You up for some refining and forming?"*

"For smart tiny murman, Zee asks dumb questions sometimes."

"All right, all right."

Another page in the book had turned. The animated illustration showed their crucible wall moving in an undulating motion, squeezing and relaxing, churning blue light in the pair's crucible, which was now larger and positioned above and beside the murperson and kraken.

"Looks the same as refining Empyrean," Zee said.

While mining Marisean had been easier than mining Empyrean, refining it proved to be more difficult. Zee considered it must be because Marisean was more dense. It took a while, but they managed to infuse it thoroughly with their aura, nearly exhausted from the effort.

The next page the book turned to had a diagram that showed a process much like forming with Empyrean. Once again, the increased density of the Marisean ore particles presented a greater challenge.

They contracted their crucible as much as they could, pushing until Zee felt his head and chest would burst, then rested and did it again. Zee noticed that the blue motes condensed into the blue in their core, leaving the vein of yellow pure, but as they continued forming, the Empyrean grew brighter.

A bell later of what felt like hard labor, they made a final grueling push and the freshly refined motes of Marisean clicked into place with the rest. Exhausted, they stared at their newly forged core. It was closer to perfectly round and now slightly larger than it had been.

Zee asked, *"You ready to give it a spark?"* then sensed Jessup's amusement and corrected himself. *"Forget I said that. Let's spark it and see how it feels—wait..."* The book had flipped to the next page without him noticing.

The illustration was the same as the previous one, but with the core sparking and growing brighter, then repeating. "*Looks the same as what we've been doing.*"

They focused on the center of their core, and it sparked bright. Power shot through them as before but at a greater intensity, and it felt different. It wasn't as hot, and somehow more stable and definitely more powerful. The spark continued to grow brighter, then suddenly burst into flaming blue and gold. Both of them grinned wide at the strength that poured through them.

Zee checked the book and grew excited to discover more pages had been revealed. He flipped through them eagerly, only to be disappointed. The first was obviously a drawing of the kraken and rider forming their Keep, which they had already done. The second depicted them conjuring a Shield, which they already accomplished as well. The third page contained a column of text that Zee couldn't read, with a drawing on the facing page that he interpreted to indeed be about an attack Ability, but all it showed was the pair facing the side of the page with the rider holding an arm forward and an arrow moving away from them to strike a circle with a dot in the middle, which had to be a target.

"That's... not very helpful," Zee muttered. He turned to the next page. There was another column of text, then the same drawing of the pair. This time, though, a half-dozen smaller arrows moved to strike a half-dozen targets. "Neither is that." He blew a breath out through tight lips. "The book's recognizing that we have attack Abilities, but I can't read the text and the drawings are too generic."

"Bad murfolk book," Jessup scolded.

"You know what, though. Now that the symbols have been revealed as an actual language, I might have better luck deciphering them."

"Zee can do it."

"Maybe. I'll give it a try. Meanwhile, we'll just have to keep forging and training, as much and as hard we can."

"Mucher and harder."

"*More* and harder."

"That, too."

They doused their core and were suddenly exhausted. It was a good kind of exhaustion, infused with contentment and a real sense of accomplishment, but exhaustion nonetheless.

The kraken stretched and yawned. "*Jessup is knackered.*"

"*Knackered? Where did you hear that word?*"

"*Robhat Hayes says it at work. It means very tired.*"

Zee had known what the word meant, but all he said was, "*Then I'm knackered too.*"

Jessup surfaced and curled several arms on the edge of the lake. He was asleep by the time Zee had stripped off his swim trunks and crawled into bed.

"Skotadi," Zee uttered, dousing the Empyrean lamps in the cavern, then lay his head on his pillow with a tired smile on his face.

Tomorrow was another whole day off, and he planned on putting it to good use.

CHAPTER 32

Zee was up at fifth bell the next morning, fully awake. He realized he was looking forward to the day more than he had in years. Jessup was still asleep, and the sun hadn't risen, so he ate a cold breakfast while quietly reading a book on the history of Triumf's Citadel Academy until morning light crept through the cavern opening. Jessup groaned and swiped at him sleepily without opening his eyes when Zee told him he was going out for a run.

Zee had been running on the shore of the harbor during the week and decided to see if he could find a path in the forested hills at the base of the mountains for a change of pace. There was a ledge blocked with boulders and rubble that led from the cavern around to the hills. He could dive in the sea and swim around, but running in wet clothes wasn't the most comfortable. He'd have to ask Jessup to help him clear it at some point. For now, he picked his way around, clambering over the rocks.

Once away from the sea, he found a runnable path. It was rough going, up and down the foot of the mountain, through ravines and into the wooded foothills. Zee explored with boyish glee, thoroughly enjoying the opportunity, the first of its kind he'd experienced since he was a boy. Monkeys screeched and hopped through the trees. Colorful birds sang and bobbed their heads. As he jogged past the trunk of a tree covered in vines, his senses tingled. Without thinking, he spun, shooting out his hand, and caught a striking snake behind the head. It hissed, mouth wide with venom dripping from its fangs, and Zee flung it into the underbrush. That sort of thing had been common when he'd been underwater while working on the ship, and he was glad to see he still had a sense of unseen danger on land. His reflexes were also even quicker since he and Jessup had begun forging.

The sounds of cursing, coughing, and laughing came from up ahead. Zee knew he should turn around and head back or take another route, but curiosity got the best of him and he sneaked forward to peer through the low branches of a tree.

On a ledge of rock beneath the thickly leaved branches was a flight of five cadets smoking something from a pipe they were passing around. They wore civilian clothes, apparently enjoying a day off themselves, but Zee recognized them as the third-year cadets who'd sneered at him and Jessup at the tournament. Zee's ire rose, and he had to take several breaths to calm himself.

One of their dragons sniffed the air and turned her head toward where Zee was hiding. "We have company."

The cadets cursed, swiftly hid the pipe, blew out whatever smoke they held in their lungs and wafted at it with their hands.

"Who is it?" one of them asked.

The dragon sniffed the air again, then chuckled. "It's the murman."

There was more cursing, then the tallest of the bunch stood. "Come on out, murman, or we're coming in after you."

Zee considered running away. He might be able to lose them in the rocks and woods, but as threesies they were most likely Bronze Class. He could feel their auras, but without their badges or armor it was hard for him to tell. He wasn't going to run, he decided. He'd been backing down his whole life.

He felt Jessup stir though their bond. "*Zee all right?*" Zee couldn't draw on the strength of the bond at this distance, but the connection was still there.

"*I'm fine*," he said, hoping it was true. "*No need to worry.*"

Jessup grunted, but said no more. Zee stepped out.

The tall cadet said, "What are you doing up here, gilly? Shouldn't you be splashing around in the ocean?"

The other cadets took turns throwing gibes.

"Where's your monster?"

"Look how tiny he is. He's even smaller up close."

"Show us your gills and tail!"

Zee sighed. He'd heard worse, and these were some of the most childish. It might have had something to do with whatever they were smoking. "I don't have a tail."

The tall cadet stepped closer. "Come on, we want to see your fish-face,"

"It doesn't work that way. I have to be in the sea."

"Then you should get back to it. And while you're at it, just swim away. No one wants you here."

With a half smile, Zee said, "Some people do."

Anger replaced the glazed, mocking smile on the cadet's face. He moved closer, a full head taller than Zee, and glared down at him. "Don't talk back to me, gilly."

Zee just gazed up at them.

"Great Zepiter," said the dragon that had spoken first, "just kick his bass-butt, Lukas, and be done with it."

They hadn't sparked their core, but Zee could feel the bond between the cadet and his dragon grow stronger.

Lukas said, "Get out of here, murbrat," and shot out a hand to shove Zee in the chest.

Zee turned and sidestepped, slapping the cadet's hand away as quickly as he had caught the snake. Lukas tumbled forward and nearly fell.

The other cadets guffawed.

"Gilly's got some skills," said another dragon, chuckling.

Keeping his eyes on the fuming cadet, Zee said, "Dame Zara mon Toomsil showed me a few things when she was stationed on ship." That got their attention.

One of the cadets said, "You know Dame Toomsil?"

"I do."

Lukas still fumed but took a breath and straightened his jacket. "Run along then, little murman. You bore me."

One of the others said. "He could tell somebody about... you know."

"What's a gilly's word against five cadet pairs? Who'd believe him, and who'd really care what came out of his fish-face anyway?"

Zee said, "You might be surprised." He backed away, eyeing them all, then spun and left at a comfortable jog.

Once Zee was sure there were no sounds of pursuit, he realized he wasn't even all that angry at them, just himself. What was he thinking? What good would come from fighting? No more than if he'd fought when on ship. He'd get a beating, and for what? His best revenge would be to meet them in combat training one day. Then he and Jessup would humiliate them and show them pain unlike anything they'd ever felt.

He nearly stopped short at the cold calculation and cruelty of his thoughts. It was Jessup's influence, he knew. There was no denying it, Jessup was a predator of the highest order. Zee didn't consider himself meek, but perhaps he needed more of that killer instinct. Though he had killed before, he'd never thought of himself as a killer; never let himself believe that's what he was, deep down. Maybe he should. It's what knights did, after all. That line of thought bothered him, but he had to do something.

Between him and Jessup, Zee was the weak link in their bond. Even without the bond, Jessup was an extremely powerful beast with incredible endurance and fighting skill. He never would have survived all those years in the ocean if he wasn't. Zee himself could barely run well. He had to make more time to work on himself and train even harder. He didn't care what those cadets thought of him. He would do it for himself and for Jessup. He needed no greater driving force than that.

* * *

That evening, after exhausting themselves in the sea as much as they could, Zee and Jessup forged Marisean once more. It was still a lot of work, but easier now that they'd done it before, just like it had been with Empyrean. Zee still kept the book with him, but no new pages had revealed themselves.

As they rested for another forging session within the cavern lake, Zee gazed up to the soft glow on the surface cast by the Empyrean lamps. "*I want to try something else,*" he said through their bond. Unsurprisingly, Jessup was up for anything.

They visualized the Empyreal Plane while underwater and found they could see it just as well, though the vein of Empyrian ore seemed thinner than it had when they'd seen it when sitting on the floor of the cavern.

They climbed out of the lake and positioned themselves to forge there. Zee was glad to see the book still worked out of the water and showed no signs of fading. They'd had to take it underwater today to get the pages to reveal themselves, but apparently the pages would remain visible for some time after a good dunking. They breathed deeply and brought up the Mariseal Plane again. It wasn't quite as dense, and when they tried mining it, it only trickled in through Zee's channels. Maybe it was also because they'd already forged, or, it occurred to Zee, maybe it could be the difference between the circular nature of breathing underwater and the way they breathed air. He recalled one of the sailors on the *Krakenfish* explaining to another how he breathed when playing the sackpipes and had another idea. But it, too, would have to wait until after work on Monday.

Jessup also had an idea. "Zee and Jessup should try forging blue and yellow together. Save time that way."

"You big smart kraken, you."

Jessup chuckled, then they put themselves into their meditative state. They visualized the Empyreal Plane first, then, holding on to it, focused on the Mariseal Plane. To their surprise, it didn't resist. The great river of blue ore appeared in the same endless blackness of the Aether, below the narrower vein of Empyrean. They'd each been beautiful separately, but together they were breathtaking. For a while Zee and Jessup just gazed at them, taking in the splendor of the Aether.

Trying to mine both at once felt like their minds were being split in two. Exerting more will and effort only made it worse, so they focused on the more difficult ore first, Empyrean. Once they got the hot yellow coals to break free of the vein and began forcing it through Zee's channels into their crucible, they tried their technique of expanding their crucible to draw in Marisean—and it worked. It came right along with the Empyrean, only as a dribble at first, but by actively mining the Empyrean, opening Zee's channels, and slowly expanding their core, it flowed in greater quantity.

They realized that mining Marisean with Empyrean tempered the scorching heat and stubborn nature of the yellow ore, making it easier to draw into their crucible. Once they began refining, they also discovered that Empyrean made the Marisean less sluggish. The blue ore became not only easier to refine, but to form as well. That night they forged not just two more times, but three, before they fell fast asleep feeling full, even more powerful than before, and entirely satisfied.

CHAPTER 33

Outside a hardware shop and lumberyard near the docks with Androo Cobbling and a carpenter who also worked for Meik Tabacchi, Zee and Jessup piled building materials into a wagon.

Once it was loaded, Zee said, "There's one more thing. Do you know anyone in town who plays the sackpipes?"

Jessup challenged Zee to pull the wagon himself. Zee decided against it. He didn't want to look stronger than he should for a bonded but unforged pair, and they didn't dare spark their core. Zee took a coil of rope out of the wagon to tie Jessup to it, but Jessup just picked the whole thing up and carried it, leaving Androo and the carpenter shaking their heads.

* * *

Dame Toomsil and Tem sat on their dragons on the harbor wall, watching Zee and Jessup leave the village.

Tem handed Toomsil his spyglass. "What are they doing now?"

She peered through the glass. "Looks to me like the makings of training equipment. Lumber, dowels, posts for pells, rope, sacks and leather, anchor bolts..."

"Seriously?"

She handed the glass back to him. "You know him, Tem. Are you really that surprised?" Tem didn't answer.

* * *

Instead of just following their whims of enthusiasm, flitting from one thing to another in excitement to see what they could do next, Zee and Jessup developed a regimen and routine. Zee had never slept much on ship and found that the extra stamina he gained from having a forged core meant just a few bells of sleep a night was all he needed.

Each morning before work he was up at oh five hundred bells to run on the beach and in the hills, then go back for Jessup and swim five miles in the sea. He also did calisthenics, crunchers, pushers, squatters, and pullers of various types on the bar he set up in the cavern, as well as rotating between sword forms and working the pell and other equipment he built with the supplies he'd purchased. Anything he learned from the various academy manuals and observed the Basic recruits doing, he would do—though he pushed himself to do more. If they did fifty pushers, he did one hundred. If they were running three miles a day, he did five and more than once a day if he could.

In the evenings he'd alternate between more running, swimming, and exercises, but he spent most of his time with Jessup, working on their forging and studying together. Many of the books the commandant and Wanchoo had given them were textbooks used in academy classes.

There were books on the history of the Dragon Corps and the nation of Tosh, military history and strategy, world geography, nautical terminologies, vessel procedures and identification, signaling with flag, bell, and horn, codes of discipline, honor, and leadership, military hierarchy and structure, weather forecasting, dragon types and anatomy, combat training, and more. Some of it was a review of what Zee had learned from his studies with Dr. Aenig or from Dame Toomsil while on ship, but he found it all fascinating. He'd thought it might be tedious for Jessup, but his friend's attention never wandered. Jessup was making great strides with his reading and maths as well.

* * *

Zee ran on a rocky path at the foot of the mountains. Dark clouds rolled in from the west, blocking out the stars and twin moons of Zhera. The air was heavy with moisture, and the wind was picking up. From the looks of the sky, rain would be coming down soon. He considered heading back to the cave, then heard horns and bells from the Basic Training field in the distance below, followed by shouting. He jogged to an outcropping to look down at the field, worried something might have happened.

Instead, cadet instructors had roused the minnies from their long white tent and were marching them out to gather on the muddy field. The duckies they let sleep where they lay in groups on the open ground.

The first drops hit Zee, fat and warm, and he watched as the rain spread over the island to drench the fields. It was pouring, drastically diminishing visibility, but Zee raised the protective lenses over his eyes, something he found he could do even when not in murman form. His night sight had also been getting steadily better as he and Jessup continued to forge.

The recruits set out at a controlled run toward the foothills. An exercise to build stamina and grit, Zee guessed. And if they could do it, so would he. With renewed drive, he set off, but not on the flatter course. He steered upward to steeper paths, running through the rain and over rocks, pushing himself as hard as he could.

A joyous "Whoop!" from the sky caught his attention.

The white Ice Diver recruit with the clubfoot was soaring, swooping, and diving through the rain, and obviously thoroughly enjoying it. He twisted and flipped in the air in an acrobatic display unlike any Zee had seen a dragon do before. He flew straight up, folded his wings and dove, then pulled out of the fall just above the treetops below.

Zee nearly forgot what he was supposed to be doing, so rapt he'd become with the sight. The dragon perched on a ledge, took a deep satisfied breath, and looked out over the training fields in the pouring rain. Zee grinned. The dragon was a kindred spirit, training on his own to compensate for being different. At that moment, the dragon caught sight of Zee standing below on the side of the mountain, watching him. Zee wasn't sure how he'd feel about being spotted, but the dragon nodded to him, then leapt from the ledge and soared off into the rainy night sky.

Inspired further, Zee set off at a greater pace. The path he'd taken came to a steep rock wall where he could either climb to another path or turn around and go back. He decided to climb.

He was over a hundred feet up when water began pouring down the side of the mountain. Fearing he'd made a terrible mistake, he made his way laterally toward a lip in the cliff face where he hoped to wait out the rain. A rock he was using for a handhold came loose and he nearly fell. He watched the rock tumble down the nearly vertical slant and crash into the rocks and trees below. He couldn't help but wonder how badly he'd be hurt if he fell. The only comfort was knowing that Jessup would come if he called and take him to get treated—if Jessup could find him when he was unconscious—and if Zee survived the fall in the first place. This far away from Jessup, he couldn't spark their core to enhance his strength or count on his aura to protect him.

Lightning streaked through the sky as the storm worsened, and the wind blew harder. Cursing himself for being an idiot, he continued toward the ledge, his arms burning and his grip beginning to fail. Jessup's voice came to him. "*Zee?*" Then Zee's hand slipped, then a foot, and he plummeted. "*Zee!*"

Zee bounced down the cliff face, scrabbling for a hold. He slammed on his side onto a jutting rock, which knocked the air out of him, and bounced into a free fall toward the rocks and trees below. "Crabcrap," he wheezed, ribs stinging badly, and tried to mentally prepare himself for impact. "*Jessup!*" he shouted through the bond.

Before Jessup could answer, lightning flashed on white scales, and a powerful claw caught his arm. He was swung so that his legs were held by a shorter, clubfooted arm. Cradled in the dragon's embrace, he gazed up at Fennix.

The white dragon crooked his neck to look down at him. "That was a close one. Are all murfolk this careless?"

Zee winced at the pain in his ribs. It hurt to speak, but he couldn't just stay silent. "I don't know, sir. Maybe. I've never met another."

Fennix chuckled. "Either way, I suggest you be more careful in your training."

"I will. Thank you, sir."

"You're welcome."

"For saving me, I mean."

"Think nothing of it. It's what knight beasts do, is it not? Of course, I'm not a knight beast yet, but I will be."

"I want to be a knight."

"So I've heard."

Zee felt a pang of guilt. Jessup was asking what was wrong and he hadn't responded. "*I'm so sorry, Jessup. I had a scare, but I'm okay. I'll explain when I get back.*" He sensed his friend's relief.

Zee turned to look down. His stomach did a little flip and pain stabbed through his chest, but the view was worth it. There was a brief gap in the rain and the clouds thinned above, allowing faint light from the moons of Zhera to illuminate landscape and sea. "Oh…" he uttered in appreciation.

"It is beautiful, isn't it?" Fennix observed.

"Yeah. Do you ever get used to it?"

"Never." They flew for a time, taking in the sight, before Fennix said, "Do you wish me to take you to town for medical care?"

"I don't think anything is broken, sir. I hate to impose, but could you take me to where I'm staying?"

"Will the kraken be there?" Fennix seemed excited at the prospect.

"Well, yes."

"I would very much like to meet him."

Zee explained to Jessup what had happened and how he would be getting back to the cave so the kraken wouldn't be surprised when a white dragon arrived with Zee in his arms. Jessup was waiting anxiously in the water of their cavern lake when they arrived.

Fennix was the first to speak. "You must be Mr. Jessup. I believe this murman belongs to you."

Jessup blinked in confusion before comprehending Fennix's joke and formal manner of speech. "Yes, that is Jessup's murman. And you are Mr. Fennix. Thank you for helping Zee."

"My great pleasure."

Zee chuckled, then grimaced at the pain. "You know, I'm right here, you two."

Fennix said, "Yes, of course." Fennix held him out as Jessup reached. Jessup swam across the lake, crawled out, and lay Zee on the bed.

Zee pushed himself to sit up against the wall, grimacing as he went. "Please, Mr. Fennix, come in."

Fennix looked around the cave, observing the ceiling was plenty high, then shook himself, sending water from the rain flying, and flapped across the lake. "Thank you. I'm sorry for dripping water on your floor."

Zee and Jessup both snorted. Water was puddling all around the kraken. "You're kidding, right?" Zee said. "You're talking to a murman and a kraken."

"I suppose I am. Which is something I never thought would happen in my entire life. It is truly a delight to meet you both."

Zee sensed no falseness in the young dragon's tone or features and knew already he liked Fennix very much. He could tell that Jessup did too.

Fennix gazed down the length of the cavern. Along the wall was makeshift training equipment lit by pools of light from Empyrean lamps.

With the supplies purchased in town and tools borrowed from his co-workers at the docks, Zee had built the same kind of equipment he'd seen recruits and cadets using in the training fields. There was a wooden man dummy, which was basically a post on a stand with sturdy dowels pounded into augured holes, and a fencing dummy, which was another post with a wooden sword held to it by a hefty steel spring.

He'd also made a pell, a thicker post for hitting with a sword to practice strike placement and edge alignment, and even a pendulum pell, a post with an arm from which hung a bound wad of rags on a rope, used to practice blade control and accuracy. Wooden practice swords of various weights and sizes lay on a workbench, along with an old beat-up metal sword he'd bought at a local shop for use on the pell. A rough shield and a few makeshift spears and javelins he'd fabricated leaned against the wall. He'd purchased a used bow and some arrows as well and had targets set up at the far end of the cavern. There was also a puller bar between two more posts. It might not have looked like much, but Zee was proud of it, and it did the job.

Fennix was duly impressed. "This is quite a well-equipped training facility. Did you make all this, Mr. Tarrow?"

"Most of it, sir. We've been looking for some place with more room for Jessup and for target practice, but we need something that's still private. We haven't had any luck so far."

Fennix tilted his head. "I may know of a place. We wouldn't want to go at night in a storm. I will show you tomorrow, if you like, and you can decide if it's suitable."

"That would be great, thank you. Make yourself comfortable, sir. I mean, unless you have to go."

Fennix glanced out through the cavern opening where the rain was once again coming down hard, and lightning now lit the sky. "I would be glad of the respite, to be honest. Flying and lightning don't always go well together."

"Fennix helped Zee," said Jessup. "You can stay as long as you like." Zee eyed his friend. He did like the dragon, but he was also speaking differently.

Fennix bowed. "You have my sincerest gratitude. I would be honored if you would both call me Fennix. No need for the 'sir' or 'mister' with me."

"Okay," Jessup replied, then said, "I am just Jessup."

"Did you just say 'I'?" Zee asked.

Jessup scowled briefly and gave him a side-eye. "*I* have been practicing my talking."

"That's great! In that case, it's 'I have been practicing my *speech*,' or 'practicing *the way I speak*.'"

"Oh. Okay."

For the first time, Zee sensed that Jessup felt ashamed. "No, Jessup, I mean it. That's truly great. You just surprised me is all."

Fennix looked on with an easy smile. "I would be happy to help in that regard," he said.

"That would be nice," Jessup replied. "You sound fancy."

Fennix grinned. "I suppose I do. I can't help it. I'm a prince of the little tribe from which I come. We're just raised that way. I don't mean that in the way you might think. It's a very small dragon tribe on a very small island of ice, and I am very much an outcast."

"I'm sorry to hear that," said Zee. "If it makes you feel any better, we're pretty much outcasts too."

"The very first time I saw the two of you, I knew we were kindred spirits."

"I thought the same thing just today, when I saw you flying in the rain."

"That proves it then." He sat back and raised his good front foot into the air. "Cheers to the outcasts." Jessup lifted an arm.

Zee shot up his hand. "To the outcasts!" Then he groaned. "Ouch…"

Fennix moved closer and spoke to Jessup. "Now let me instruct you on how to use the power of your bond to aid the healing of Zee's injuries."

"You know we're bonded?" Zee asked.

"Everyone knows. You two are a regular topic of discussion among the recruits and cadet instructors." Seeing the look on Zee's face, he added. "Some of the conversation is not very flattering, I'll admit, but not all of it. Some are watching you with keen interest."

Zee rubbed the back of his neck. "I'm not sure that's better, actually."

"Ignore them all. It's what I do."

CHAPTER 34

The next evening after work, Fennix led Zee and Jessup into the wooded hills at the base of the mountains to a secluded box canyon well away from the running paths, with foliage above from trees that grew along its top edges. Cliffs overhung much of it, and at its center was a huge tree with a trunk that rose above the walls, a hundred feet high. Its canopy, intertwined with vines, concealed the area below even more.

"No one flies low over this part of the island but me," said Fennix, "and nothing can be seen from above, not even a fire, unless someone is looking very carefully. My first year of Basic, two years ago, there was a flight of fourth-year cadets that would come here on occasion, but no one has since."

"It's perfect," Zee replied.

"There's more room than in the cavern," said Jessup. "Very good for a kraken."

Fennix said, "I'm pleased you like it."

While they poked around a bit, Fennix surprised them by asking, "How is your forging going?" Both Zee and Jessup reacted like startled deer.

"We haven't been forging," Zee blurted out much too quickly.

"Please accept my most sincere apologies. I didn't mean to pry. I just assumed it would be the first thing a bonded pair would do."

Jessup spoke to Zee through the bond. *"Can I tell him?"*

Zee turned it over in his mind while still trying to get used to Jessup saying "I" instead of referring to himself in third person. Jessup trusted Fennix, and the kraken seemed to be a great judge of character. Even though Fennix wasn't bonded himself, maybe he could help, too. Zee gave his consent.

"Zee and I have been forging, but not for long."

"Oh..." Fennix took a breath. "I figured as much. You two are terrible at lying."

Zee's cheeks flushed with embarrassment. "I always have been. I think it's because I hate doing it. I was hoping I was getting better at it, though, since it seems to have become more of a necessity around here."

"Only if you're doing naughty things you're not supposed to be doing."

Zee emitted a nervous laugh. "It's not strictly illegal."

"I'm joking. And I promise not to tell anyone."

Jessup, who felt nowhere near as guilty as Zee, grinned and said, "Naughty murman."

Zee gawped "What? Naughty kraken, too!"

They all laughed, then Zee said, "I'm sorry we lied to you, Fennix. We just—"

"Say no more," Fennix cut in. "I understand, believe me. But now that I do know, is there any chance I could see your core?" Zee and Jessup exchanged glances. "Please don't feel obligated, I'm just very curious, you see."

Jessup shrugged. "It's okay with Jessup."

"You should say, 'It's okay with me.'"

"Thank you. It's okay with *me*."

Zee ignored their little speech lesson. They'd been doing it the whole way to the canyon. "Maybe you can tell us how it compares to other classes."

"I will do my best," Fennix replied.

Zee took his position on one of Jessup's arms, they did their deep breathing and meditation, visualized their core, then revealed it.

Fennix hopped up and down on his good front foot. "Is that Marisean?"

"You know about Marisean?" Zee asked.

"We tell many stories in my clan, some of them very old. One mentions the blue power of Postune. We thought it was a fable, but it's true! And your core... Very well shaped, strong crucible walls, and its size! Unless I am a fool and classes don't work the same for murfolk and krakens, I'd say this is Tin class."

A new voice echoed in the canyon. "Maybe even high level."

Then another voice spoke, "Unbelievable."

Zee and Jessup's core vanished and all three of them whirled, seeking who had spoken. They looked straight up. On the edge of the cliff high above, Temothy jal Briggs sat upon his dragon, Timandra, both peering down.

Timandra stepped off and dropped, throwing open her wings at the last minute to arrest their fall, then landed.

Jessup shot out his spines and leaned forward with a growl.

Timandra backed up. "Whoa there, big boy."

Tem held up his hands. "It's okay. We've been asked to check on you two."

"By whom?" Zee asked, his tone touched by panic and a tad defensive.

Tem hesitated. "We'd rather not say, but I think you know."

Zee thought a moment. "There are people who seem to want us here and some people who don't seem to like us very much. Which is it?"

Timandra said, "It's the former. You can ask them when you get a chance."

Zee breathed with relief. He also felt honored that the commandants and the deans were looking after them. He never would have guessed they'd send Temothy jal Briggs, though. "Are you going to help us with forging and training?"

"With what time we can spare from our other duties, yes," Tem answered, "but it must be kept secret."

"A better secret than that you're forging already," Timandra added.

Zee winced. Not only had they shown their forged core to Fennix, they'd forgotten to reveal it only to him. "Right. I'm sorry, ma'am. We promise."

Fennix nearly flinched as her gaze fell on him. "What do you say, Mr. Fennix? We know you can't forge yet, but you're welcome to join us for training."

Fennix was so taken aback by the offer it took him a moment to answer. When he did, it was with a bow of gratitude. "I would consider it a privilege, ma'am, if I may, and time permitting. I will say nothing to anyone. You have my word."

"The word of a prince is good enough for us."

If a dragon could blush, Fennix would have.

Having overcome his shock and worry, Zee said, "This is incredible. Thank you both." He looked up at Jessup. "So much for keeping this place a secret, though."

"It's as private as anywhere on the island," said Tem. "Just don't practice your lightning Ability at night."

Zee slapped his forehead. "You know about that, too?"

"You *do* have a lightning Ability." Timandra exclaimed. She nudged Tem with her shoulder. "You were right, Tem."

Tem held out a hand, a smug smile on his face. "You owe me a silver. Pay up."

"And where would I be keeping a silver? Pay yourself."

Jessup said, "Um, what is going on?"

"We've been keeping an eye on you two when you leave your cavern. Not all the time, of course, and it's been for your own safety as much as anything."

"We were asked to make sure you weren't going to get yourselves into trouble," said Tem.

Zee replied with dismay, "It sounds like we almost already did."

"Not really," Tem added. "We could sense very little of your core when you were in the cavern and felt nothing while you were under the sea, even when you sparked it."

Timandra said, "We saw slight flashes in the deep, though—only because we were watching closely from the sky. Dragons have keen eyesight, even from a great distance, and Tem has a spyglass. He said it was lightning. I said it couldn't be because I didn't want to believe a kraken and murman could have such a devastating Ability, especially at this stage of forging. We made a bet."

Zee realized he still had his hand on his forehead and dropped it to his side. "Okay, first, we do have a lightning Ability. Maybe even two of them. One is a single strike. We've called it Lightning Bolt, and we're terrible at it. The other one is multiple strikes. We called that one Lightning Blast. Each bolt is smaller and weaker but we could hit multiple targets at once if we weren't even worse at that than Lightning Bolt."

"Lightning..." said Timandra softly. She looked up at Jessup. "You become more terrifying by the day, Mr. Jessup."

"Thank you, ma'am," Jessup replied, matter-of-fact.

Timandra chuckled and shook her head.

"We may be able to help you with those," said Tem.

Zee said, "That would be great, thank you. But, second, you've been spying on us?"

Tem raised a finger. "Keeping an eye on you for your own good. There's a difference."

"Not much difference, admittedly," said Timandra. "But a difference nonetheless. And it wasn't our idea."

"Right," Zee acquiesced. "Sorry. It makes sense."

Jessup said, "I would spy on us too."

Tem held a hand to Jessup. "You see?"

"We *are* terrifying," Zee added.

"Jessup is terrifying," the kraken said, then turned up one side of his lips in a crooked smile. "Zee is tiny."

Zee grinned back at him. "I need to eat more vegetables."

Fennix said, "Now I'm the one who doesn't have the faintest idea what's going on."

"It's a silly joke," said Jessup.

"A silly kraken joke," Zee retorted. Jessup snorted. Zee addressed Tem and Timandra more seriously. "You said you sensed our core when we were in the cavern. If you could at Silver Class—"

"Mid-level Silver Class," Tem interjected.

"Right, but that would mean Golds and above would be able to sense it even more strongly, right?"

"In general, yes," said Timandra, "but the sensitivity to cores can be purposefully dampened with time and experience, thankfully. It would become quite annoying otherwise, like everyone was shouting at you all the time. They would have to be fairly close and actively seeking the cores of others to sense yours. Either way, we may be able to help you with that as well."

Tem said, "Did you wonder why you couldn't tell that Timandra and I were right up there?" He motioned to the cliff above.

"It occurred to me," said Zee, " but I was pretty surprised."

"There are passive Abilities used to aid in hiding the power that emanates from the core of a bonded pair, sparked or unsparked."

"Passive Abilities?"

Tem and Timandra looked at each other. Tem said, "We do have a lot to teach them."

Timandra addressed Zee and Jessup. "When would you like to start?"

Zee didn't even have to check with Jessup. "How about now?"

CHAPTER 35

Jessup snapped a log in half and set the pieces for Zee and Tem to sit on. Tem sat with a slight groan, then rubbed his face as he got his thoughts together. "To start, tell us about how your first time processing Empyrean went. We won't ask how you knew how to do it. We already know."

Timandra, who was sitting on her haunches next to Tem, spoke to Fennix without looking at him. "You're not hearing any of this, right, Mr. Fennix?"

"Quite right, ma'am," Fennix answered.

Zee explained how they meditated and used their breathing technique, visualized the Empyreal Plane, then mined, refined, formed, and sparked their core. "It was hard, but we were able to do it two more times that night."

Tem and Timandra were dumbstruck. "All three phases in one night, three times?" she asked.

Jessup replied, "Yes, ma'am."

Zee said, "Why, did we do something wrong?"

"Apparently not," said Timandra, still shaking her head in disbelief. "You're still alive and well, with bond intact."

Tem said, "But no one does that their first time. Most only get through mining before having to quit."

Timandra gazed at Jessup and Zee but spoke to Tem. "I wonder if it's because they were bonded so young."

"But they were separated for ten years and have only seen each other now for, what, three weeks?"

"Maybe the core still strengthens and grows when bonded individuals are apart, even if not nearly as fast as when working on it together?"

"I suppose," said Tem, removing his cap and scratching his head. "Maybe."

He put his cap back on and took a breath. "We got a glimpse of your crucible and core earlier," he said to Zee and Jessup, "but would you mind showing us again?"

"To us only, and Mr. Fennix, if you wish," said Timandra. "Do you know how to do that?"

"Yes, ma'am," Zee replied. "I was just being careless earlier."

"*We* were being careless," Jessup interjected.

"Right." Zee got up from the log and climbed up on one of Jessup's arms. They went through the process of visualizing their core, then felt out for the combined aura of Tem and Timandra's singular bonded aura, as well as Fennix's, and revealed it. Their core had grown over the last couple of weeks and was now closer to three and a half feet in diameter, maybe even a little more. The percentage of Empyrean had also increased in comparison to the Marisean.

The knight rider and dragon got to their feet, gazing at the blue-and-yellow glowing marble.

Timandra said, "It's even more amazing than it was described to us, now that it's forged."

"Yeah..." said Tem.

Zee said, "We've been forging Marisean, too."

"We can do both at the same time now," Jessup added. "It goes faster that way."

Timandra turned her head to Tem. "I think I'm going to need a lie-down."

"You and me both," Tem replied, then asked Zee, "When did you reach Tin Class?"

"The first night we forged. We discovered we could form our Keep and use Shield and the lightning Abilities the next morning."

"And their core has already grown that much," said Timandra. "I'm definitely going to need that lie down."

"Look at the size of their crucible, too," Tem said, "and the thickness and density of its wall."

"I'm looking."

Zee was getting anxious. "Is it weird?"

Timandra said, "Well, yes, but not in a bad way. I know we said you might be high-level Tin Class, but I'm certain of it, now. There's no way way to estimate the other categories, though, accept maybe Aether Capacity. I'd say Lead, maybe even Copper. Either one is terrific for Tin Class."

"With Marisean, though..." said Tem.

Timandra tore her eyes from the core and spoke apologetically. "We honestly just can't tell."

Tem hurried to speak at the sight of Zee and Jessup's disappointment. "The size of a core is the main criteria used for determining class and level ratings, and how close you might be to leveling up to the next class, but that alone isn't enough to know for certain. Leveling up requires increasing mastery of your Abilities as well, and that's especially important for reaching a new class. You're a murman and kraken, too, not human and dragon. It could be very different." He threw up his hands in defeat. "Your levels and classes might not even match ours."

Timandra said, "You might need a larger core for a particular class than we do." Off Zee's look of further disappointment, she added, "Or a smaller one. Again, we just don't know. From what we've been told, nobody does."

Jessup was less disheartened than Zee. "It is what it is."

Fennix said, "That is very sensible, Jessup, and a healthy attitude to have."

"It is," said Zee. He turned to his friend. "You really are a wise kraken."

"I told you."

Zee grinned and the others chuckled.

Tem said, "The only way to really know would be to use the Orb of Assessment, but that's strictly off limits to all but bonded cadet and graduate pairs. I know, I already checked. There would be no way to use it surreptitiously without being seen and the results being recorded, either."

"And we don't know if it can assess Marisean at all," Timandra added.

Tem pointed to his assessment badge, which was silver with two hash marks, representing their mid-level Silver Class threat level. "It could be the same with assessment badges. Even then, ours wouldn't work for you because it's attuned to our bond. As frustrating as that might be, what really matters is continuing to build your core, getting stronger, and mastering your abilities as they manifest." He sighed, then he and Timandra pondered and looked to each other, obviously communicating through their bond. Tem checked his shining silver pocketclock.

"That's pretty," Jessup said.

Tem was taken off guard. "Thank you. I should hope so, for as much as it cost."

Zee said, "Jessup likes shiny things."

"I do," Jessup confirmed.

Zee patted his arm. "He always has. Sometimes he tries to eat them, though." Tem balked, pulling his pocketclock closer.

Jessup said, "Only when I was little. I don't do that anymore."

"I'm glad to hear that," Tem replied, though he stuffed the clock in his pocket rather quickly.

Timandra gazed up at Jessup. "It's hard to imagine you were ever little."

Zee grinned and held his hands just over a foot apart. "He was only this big when I found him."

Keeping her eyes on Jessup, she said, "You grew very fast."

"I eat my vegetables," Jessup replied with a smile.

Timandra snorted and they all chuckled again.

"We have much to cover," said Tem. "It's not late yet, and being Fifth-day, Timandra and I don't have a training session until after noonbell tomorrow. If you have the time, we can cover some basics now."

"We have the time," said Jessup.

Zee said, "We're off work tomorrow, and we don't sleep much anyway."

"I believe it," said Timandra. She turned to the white Ice Diver. "You're welcome to stay, Mr. Fennix, but much of what we're going to be talking about is only relevant to bonded pairs and taught after Basic Training final testing is passed and pairs are chosen for bonding."

"I would very much like to stay, ma'am, if that's all right. I'm going through everything that's taught in Basic for the third time now. It would be wonderful to learn something new."

She directed her next comment to Zee and Jessup. "All right, gentlemen, tell us what you know about forming your Keep."

* * *

Zee and Jessup told them about how they formed their Keep already, then were taught how they could show their Keep to others just like they could their core. And just like when Tem and Timandra had seen their core, they were wowed by their Keep. Apparently newly formed Keeps were usually the size of a footlocker. Zee and Jessup's had been as big as Mahfouz's shack when they'd first formed it, and it had already doubled in size. Tem and Timandra speculated that it could be because Jessup was so large, but again, there was no way to know for sure.

Tem said, "One thing you must keep in mind. Never put anything alive in there if you want it to stay that alive."

"Right," Zee replied. "We already tried that."

"With a fish," Jessup added.

Zee chuckled and shook his head. "As you can see, there are no fish in there now, and never will be again."

Jessup grinned slyly, "I wouldn't say never."

Zee rolled his eyes.

Jessup's expression became more serious. "Could we put an enemy in there and kill them?"

Fennix said, "Now there's a grisly thought, to which even I have the answer. No, you can't."

"We can't, or we shouldn't?"

"You can't," Timandra verified. "No sentient being can be placed in a Keep. It simply won't work."

Jessup frowned. "I am disappointed."

"As many other fresh cadets who've asked the same question have been."

Tem and Timandra explained how Zee and Jessup could mask the power of their core with Abilities called Occlude and Camouflage. Occlude blocked other bonded pairs from feeling the power of their core, sparked or unsparked, but especially sensitive pairs, particularly higher-class magickers, might sense something odd, like an invisible hole in the environment.

Camouflage was like Occlude but also involved wrapping natural energies of the environment with their aura. Hypersensitive magicker pairs could still feel a core through Camouflage, but only if they were very close and actively seeking it out.

Jessup said, "Camouflage. Like this?" His eyes narrowed and he changed color to match the ground beneath him and the cliffs at his back. He could still be seen if you knew he was there and looked closely, but his natural camouflage worked incredibly well. Without focusing on him, and if he sat very still, only his big green eyes stood out clearly.

"Whoa," Zee exclaimed. "That's amazing."

"And scary," said Timandra.

Jessup chuckled.

Zee said, "Is there anything else you can do that you haven't told me about?"

Jessup thought for a moment. "I can fit two of my arms in my mouth at once."

Zee shook his head. "That's not something we'll need to do in battle."

"Enough of that, please, Jessup," said Tem. "You're making me nervous."

Jessup went back to his normal coloring.

"Thank you."

Timandra said, "Anyway, using either Ability will deplete your core, like any other Ability, but not by much. A larger core takes more to Occlude or Camouflage, but only as a percentage of its size, so it won't be depleted considerably faster than a smaller one. Any depletion must be considered, though, which is why pairs usually only do it for short periods, strategically, during battle. Though sometimes letting an enemy feel your power is the best thing to do right up front. It depends on the situation."

"I would recommend Camouflage over Occlude," said Tem. "You'll want to Camouflage only enough to hide the power of your core without completely blocking out your natural auras. Only very sensitive pairs of higher classes, with few exceptions, would be able to tell the difference, but if you had no perceivable aura they could sense you were hiding something. It will take some time to learn to do it properly, but that practice will help you control your other Abilities as well."

Timandra said, "When you use any Ability, you want to make the most efficient use of your core to accomplish the task. The most common error is using too much. More of your core being fed into an Ability makes it more powerful, yes, but it also makes it more difficult to control and can be wasteful. Using far too much can make an attack Ability downright dangerous, for you and for anyone near whom you may not want to harm."

"Later, we'll get into how you can actively sense your flightmates or others you don't want to harm in your vicinity," Tem added.

Zee said, "You said something about passive Abilities earlier."

"Occlude and Camouflage are considered passive Abilities, as are hiding and revealing your core, creating and using your Keep, and even your aura protection, which flares automatically when you're struck. Anything else, for offense or defense, are active Abilities."

Zee, Jessup, and Fennix all nodded. It was a lot to take in, but they were hanging on every word.

Tem and Timandra demonstrated how to Occlude their core, then use Camouflage, and both shook their heads at how quickly Zee and Jessup were able to do them, even if they weren't perfect. Again, they put it down to how long they'd been bonded.

The Silver Class knights then provided a review of how progression in levels and classes was achieved. Bonded pairs progress through a combination of training hard to stay in optimal physical condition, continued forging to enlarge and strengthen their core, engaging in combat, and mastering their Abilities. Zee and Jessup already excelled in training and forging, though Tem and Timandra would help them hone their techniques. Combat was important because it stressed pairs to their limits. The best kind of combat was full combat, either real or virtual. That would be Zee and Jessup's biggest challenge since they weren't allowed to use the virtual combat fields at the academy. There were some things Tem and Timandra could help with, but it wouldn't be the same.

Zee said, "Jessup and I have been bonded for ten years, but Jessup has also been fighting in the sea his whole life. Real combat, very often to the death."

"To the death of my enemies, not me," Jessup said.

Zee chuckled. "Well, yeah."

"You've lived a hard life too, Zee, and had to fight."

"Not like you have, though. My point is, that could be part of the reason he and I have been able to do things with forging and Abilities more quickly than newly bonded human and dragon pairs. It could also be a way to help us progress further."

Timandra said, "Are you suggesting that you and Jessup go out into the sea and fight creatures using your core and Abilities?"

Zee looked to Jessup, who was in agreement, then back. "I am."

"That sounds like good reasoning, but seriously dangerous."

"We'll do what we have to do, but we'll be careful. As careful as we can be, anyway." To Jessup he said, "I don't want to go out and just slaughter things, though. We only fight creatures that attack us. That way we'd also be helping make the nearby waters safer."

"I agree," Jessup replied.

Fennix said, "I'm not sure I like this idea at all."

"Me neither," said Tem. "It makes sense, yes, but I don't approve of the risk."

To Jessup, Zee said, "You're a lot faster now that we've forged our core. Is there anything faster in the sea?"

"Nothing I have seen."

"I know it's not in your nature to run away from a fight, but if we got into trouble, would you be willing to retreat?"

Jessup said, "I would run forever for Zee."

A lump appeared in Zee's throat. He swallowed it down and patted his friend on the arm.

Everyone was quiet for a moment, then Tem said, "I still don't like it, but if you're going to do it, keep a close watch on your core. If it gets below twenty-five percent, I want you to get out of there immediately."

"In fact," Timandra added, "we're going to make that a condition of our training you. Do you swear it?"

Zee and Jessup said, "We swear it," at the same time.

"And never let your core fall below ten percent. That's a safe level, but much below can be dangerous. If your core gets too low, it can burn out. If that happens, you may never be able to reforge it. Your bond could be broken forever."

Zee stiffened. "That's good to know."

Tem said, "It's something we wanted to tell you today anyway, but now it's even more crucial. It's unlikely something like that can happen during practice or training because the core has a tendency to preserve itself. In combat, however, a strong-willed pair can override that tendency."

"We will remember," said Jessup. "Don't break core."

"That takes care of combat, at least to some extent," said Timandra, "which leaves the mastering of Abilities."

As the evening went on, their new mentors told Zee he should think about channeling the power of their sparked core into six different areas: strength, speed, cognition, resilience, sufferance—the capacity to endure pain—and Abilities. Some pairs liked to think of those areas as repositories, almost like smaller, more specialized cores connected to their larger core, and called them "caches." That was only a theory, and you couldn't see caches like you could your core, but whatever technique helped Zee and Jessup use their core's power most efficiently was good. Just like the rider was the conduit through which ore flowed into the crucible during the forging process, the directing of power out of the core was mostly their responsibility as well. Of course they couldn't do either of those things without their beast, and the beast housed the far greater portion of their shared crucible, so it was more of a joint effort than that. The rider didn't have total control of either activity.

The key was to develop control over how much of their core they used for any of the areas mentioned. The more control they had, the more efficiently they would use their core, the more effective their Abilities would be, and the more effective they would be in combat, not to mention their core would last longer. With practice, it would become second nature and take less conscious effort. It was critical to mastering Abilities that manifested with each class-up as well.

Progressing through levels within classes meant not only that their core had grown, which meant they were getting stronger, faster, more resilient, and could heal more quickly, but they had advanced their mastery of the Abilities available to them as well. Progressing to a new class was different. In addition to what a new level represented, a new class added its own additional boost, which could be significant, and a class-up was also when new Abilities would be revealed.

Mastery of an Ability meant achieving proficient stages of accuracy, control, and efficient use of their core for the requisite potency of their Abilities. The only way to master an Ability was through practice, on their own and in combat.

When a pair couldn't progress to the next class, it often had more to do with having reached a plateau in forging than not having mastered an Ability, but that could also cause a pair to become stuck. Since progression got harder as a pair advanced as well, most often a pair would just settle for whatever class they were stuck in.

As it had grown darker, they'd gathered firewood, and Timandra had lit it. It was nearly midnight when Fennix doused the fire with his natural ice expulsion. Tem and Timandra left, promising less talk and more work when they came back in two days. Somehow it sounded to Zee less like a promise and more like a threat. Fennix walked with them to the cavern, he and Jessup chatting all the way, then headed back to the field were the dragon recruits were staying so he could be fresh for Basic training in the morning.

Jessup and Zee were too excited to sleep. They spent the rest of the night moving training equipment from the cavern to the canyon under the cover of night and the trees, then the next day building more equipment for the cavern so Zee could train in both places.

Though they'd be more exposed in the canyon, they both figured it was safer to practice their lightning Abilities and for Jessup to drill fighting with his long arms there than taking the chance of setting everything in the cave on fire with electricity or breaking it. If they did something particularly dumb they might bring the cave right down on their heads.

CHAPTER 36

True to their word, the Silver Class knights came two days later, then kept a schedule of twice each week and one weekend day after that. Two days a week they all worked together on Abilities and forging. Tem and Timandra forged with them regularly. Forging was always easier with others, but they'd been shocked the first time by how forging with Zee and Jessup seemed to cool the Empyrean ore enough to make every step of the process faster and less painful, even though they couldn't see or forge Marisean themselves. They'd been able to forge nearly a third more ore as a result. Zee and Jessup had noticed a difference as well, though nowhere near as dramatic as Tem and Timandra had experienced.

The Silver knight pair also gave them tips on working with their Shield, taught them how to use Deflect, which was a quick flash of flat Shield used to divert strikes and requiring less core power, and a basic Ability called Push, also related to Shield, but more like an invisible pulse that could knock opponents back. They were also shown how to use Burst, which gave them a boost in speed over a short distance. Every lesson involved developing more efficient use of their core.

Apparently, Push, Burst and Deflect usually developed at Lead Class, but advanced pairs at high Tin sometimes were able to do them. Zee figured that could be why they hadn't shown up in the murfolk book, as Jessup continued to call it. Tem and Timandra weren't surprised Zee and Jessup could do them. They just chalked it up to further proof of how exceptional their bond was.

They also tested just how much their protective aura could take and how long their Shield would hold up against attacks from the Silver knights, as well as continued to work on their Lightning Bolt and Lightning Blast Abilities during the day. They got better, but progress was slow. Using just the right amount of core power was proving extremely difficult to master, and they only hit their targets about one out of ten times, which could have been luck as much as anything.

The other two days each week, the beasts and riders trained separately so they wouldn't have the help of their bond strength. Timandra, Jessup, and Fennix, when he could make it, would go to the canyon, while Zee trained with Tem in the cave.

Tem sparred with Zee and instructed him on sword, spear, shield, and archery, as well how to make the most effective use of his sword training equipment, and the proper ways to do pushers, pullers, and crunchers and how they were judged in Basic trials.

Zee threw himself into each lesson with gusto. His favorite was learning the finer points of swordplay, including strategy. Tem was much better than Zee, but away from their beasts, Zee was faster and would score hits far more often than Tem would have liked.

* * *

On a day when riders and beasts were training separately, Zee and Tem retreated to the cavern, leaving the dragons and kraken in the canyon. Both of them pounded at a pell with their swords. Tem had brought Zee a better training sword than the one he'd commissioned from a smith in town, and it helped his accuracy tremendously.

Shoulders and wrist aching, Zee stepped back to watch, as he had many times, just how Tem placed his feet, held his shoulders, moved his arms, and used his wrist to control the blade.

It was still hard to believe this was the same person as that haughty squire who had snubbed him so badly for years on the ship. Now he was here training him, giving up his own time and, in some cases, sleep. Zee had even begun to think of them as friends.

Zee leaned on his sword. "Why are you here, Tem?"

Tem looked over his shoulder and stepped back, surprised at the question and breathing hard. He seemed to think for a second, then turned to lean back on the pell and wipe the sweat from his brow with his sleeve. "It's good for me. To be honest, I was starting to get complacent in my training. Just look at me. I'm sweating like a pig."

"Pigs don't sweat."

"They don't?" Tem's eyes lit as he remembered. "Oh, right. 'The boy on a pig.' You would know."

Zee chuckled but said, "Seriously, it has to be more than that."

The smile was still on Tem's face, but he took a breath and it faded. "I wasn't entirely forthcoming when I told you why we came that first day. We weren't ordered by the commandants or the deans. You have Dame Toomsil to thank for us being here."

"She sent you, then."

"No. Aureosa and Wanchoo had talked to her about it, and she came to me. We discussed it, but she did not ask or order me here. She didn't even suggest it. I agreed to meet with the commandants. Being lead instructors, Zara—Dame Toomsil—and Peloquin are much busier than Timandra and I are, but that's not why I volunteered. I'm here because I believe it's the right thing to do."

Zee was taken aback. "I thought you hated me."

A sly smile curved on Tem's lips. "Maybe I do."

"You can hate me all you want, as long as you keep training me."

Tem chuckled, then it faded too. "I never hated you. Disregarded, had no respect for, maybe, but that's all in the past. The truth is, I owe Zara, and I owe it to myself."

"I don't understand."

Tem's brow furrowed, then he gazed at the light dancing on the water of the lake. "I'm going to tell you something I don't want you to repeat. I only learned of it after I was accepted into the academy."

"All right."

"Zara's mother came from a family of name and status. She fell in love with a woodcutter who did not. Their daughter was raised on the forest slopes of a mountain as Zara Drook."

He paused a moment to let that sink in—which it did. She'd had a lowborn name, just like Zee.

"One day, a Silver Class dragon and rider of the Dragon Corps were caught in a terrible storm and crashed down on the mountain. The knight was badly hurt, and the dragon had a broken wing and leg. Young Zara Drook, only thirteen years old at the time, found them and did what she could to dress the wounds of the rider while the dragon guided her. Her family took them in, fed them, and cared for them. The rider regained consciousness after few days but was still in no shape to move, and the dragon still could not fly. When other knight pairs finally found them, Zara stated that she had always wanted to be a knight. The rider, whose family was quite influential, and the dragon, who came from a highly respected tribe, both put in a good word for her, and she was accepted into a squireship. During that time, she took her mother's name at their recommendation, mon Toomsil. Her parents were later killed in a landslide while she was at the academy."

Tem looked to Zee. "She's not one of the murfolk, of course, but Dame Toomsil has seen much of herself in you since the first day we met you. I know how the higher classes think and behave toward others. It's the way I was raised. I played the game, and watched it play out while I was in the academy. I also watched Dame Zara mon Toomsil, a true knight of the realm. At some point along the way, I realized I wanted to be less like my father, and more like her." His eyes met Zee's. "Does that make sense?"

It took a moment for Zee to process everything. "Yes, it does."

"Timandra has also had a tremendous influence on me. I'm truly lucky to have her."

"Thank you for telling me."

Tem smiled genuinely. "Thank you for listening. And for not telling me to sod off when we came to you in the canyon."

"I could tell you now, if you like."

Tem shrugged. "I wouldn't leave anyway. We both still have a lot to learn." He went back to striking the pell.

Zee watched him for a minute, then stepped to his pell and got back to work.

CHAPTER 37

On the days when Tem and Timandra weren't there, Zee and Jessup focused on their conditioning and core building. They also went out into the sea to fight monsters. They didn't find sufficient opponents every day, but the deeper they went, the better their chances were. Jessup even lit the glowing areas on his shell and arms to attract them. Zee found it more frightening than Jessup, but they handled each beast without much real danger and incurred no significant injuries. In a way, it was disappointing, but a large part of Zee was just as glad they didn't run into a leviathanfish, monstaray, or any of the other truly huge and terrifying beasts he had heard of.

They tried their lightning Abilities against the creatures and missed every time. More often than not their foe would flee after seeing it, and Zee had asked Jessup not to chase a beast that had given up, so they stopped using it for combat entirely.

Overall, the effort was terrific practice for working together, and the strength of their bond and their core benefitted greatly. It gave Zee practical experience with controlling the amount of their core power that was channeled into the areas Tem and Timandra had told them about as well. It also helped push them to their first real class-up.

* * *

One night after a forging session, they were suddenly overcome with a powerful euphoria. Zee and Jessup could barely breathe, so overwhelming were the joyous exhileration and feeling of invincibility that flooded through them. After a few moments, it leveled off and they breathed freely. Their core no longer appeared before them, but it was still sparked.

Zee pushed away from Jessup and spun back to look at him, wide-eyed and grinning like an idiot. Jessup had the same expression.

"What happened, Zee?" Jessup asked.

"I think we just classed up."

"To Lead?"

"It should be." Not knowing for certain was no reason to stop what they were doing, though. "The important thing is we're progressing, and that we keep doing it."

The next day, they told the Silver knights about it and showed them their core. The knights were amazed. They confirmed Zee and Jessup's assumption that they were probably now Lead Class, and already at the high end of low level. That in itself wasn't what had them shaking their heads, though.

Tem said, "You realize you've advanced nearly an entire academy year already."

Zee pondered. "Progression can only begin after Pairing Day and the pair starts forging. That happens at the end of sixteen weeks of Basic, so the year is really only five months."

Tem laughed out loud. "You did it in three weeks!"

"Leave some progression for the rest of us, why don't you," Timandra huffed.

Jessup said, "No, all ours." More laughter and shaking of heads ensued. He gazed at their core, now four feet across, an increase of half a foot since they'd last shown it to Tem and Timandra. "It doesn't look much bigger to me. We need more."

"Don't we all," said Tem. "Even a small increase in diameter represents a significant increase in volume, though, and that applies exponentially as the core grows."

Timandra said, "You've been forging every day?"

"Yes, ma'am." Jessup replied.

"It must be exhausting."

Zee said, "It is, but we like it."

Tem considered their core. "Your ratio of Empyrean to Marisean seems to be remaining the same."

"It has been since we began forging Empyrean and Marisean together. We're thinking its about one fifth of the total core."

"Sounds right to me. Do you have any sense of what new Abilities you might have?"

That was the thing. No more pages in the murfolk book had been revealed when they'd checked last night. They hadn't told their mentors about the book, though, and thought they should still keep it a secret. Tem and Timandra had told them that new Abilities could usually be felt, though, like a potential hiding at the back of their minds, waiting to be found, so Zee didn't have to lie.

"We don't feel anything, but we tried this morning anyway, We don't think we have anything new."

Timandra said, "I'm sorry to hear that. It's not all that common, but a class-up does occur sometimes without any additional Abilities coming with it. In every case, the pair has made progress with their current Abilities but haven't reached enough skill with them. Their core, however, has grown beyond sufficient size, and the progression happens anyway. When you've improved your control of Lightning Bolt and Lightning Blast, or even just one of them, at least one new Ability should become available to you. Before you get down on yourselves, remember, you did develop Burst, Deflect, and Push early."

"And," Tem added, "need I remind you, a years worth of progression in three weeks?"

"Right, thank you," Zee replied. He couldn't help it, though. He wanted more. And there was no doubt Jessup did, too.

After that, they started using their lightning Abilities against beasts of the sea again. Well, trying, anyway. They still couldn't direct the bolts where they wanted them to go. Zee was more philosophical about it, accepting that they just needed to keep working at it and eventually they'd get better. Jessup would get downright angry. His mood would affect Zee as well, and their aim got even worse. He'd have to calm them both down before they had even a chance of coming close to their targets—or began chasing after a fleeing monster, blasting wild lightning all the way, which happened more than once.

* * *

In the little time they had off work and training, and Basic for Fennix, the Ice Diver prince continued to help Jessup with his speaking and reading. One night, Zee entered the cavern with a new purchase.

"Look what I bought!" he announced.

Jessup eyed it. "An octopod doll?"

Zee laughed. "No!"

"It's sackpipes," said Fennix, not looking particularly happy about it.

Zee arranged the pipes on his shoulder. "There was a sailor on the ship who had a set, and I heard him teaching another sailor a technique used to play it called circular breathing. I've been thinking it might be closer to how murfolk breathe underwater with their gills. It might help with Marisean mining when we aren't in the water and maybe even with Empyrean mining."

Jessup said, "Okay..."

"I've taken a few lessons during lunch time at work." He placed the canter in his mouth, inflated the bag, and began to play while keeping a steady flow of air through his lips by alternating between puffing out his cheeks while exhaling and compressing them as he inhaled.

Jessup gritted his teeth at the whining screech of the instrument, and Fennix winced.

Zee stopped after a minute. "Phew. It makes me dizzy."

"Me too," said Jessup.

"I was thinking nauseous, myself."

"All right, you two, I'll go practice somewhere else." Zee headed around the lake on the narrow stone ledge along the wall at this end of the cavern. "You'll both be sorry when I find out circular breathing really does help with forging, and I won't teach it to you."

"If that's the case," said Fennix, "we'll beg for mercy."

"I'm already begging for mercy from that sound."

"Ha!" Zee exclaimed and left the cavern.

Fennix said to Jessup, "Perhaps he's developed a new defensive technique to keep enemies away."

"It would work on me."

Later that evening, Jessup paused in his reading as a long-legged cave spider crawled over the edge of the table and walked slowly across as if it owned the place. When it got to the other side, Fennix turned it around with a nudge of his nose. They studied it closely as it made its way back.

"Are you thinking what I'm thinking?" Fennix asked.

"I might be," Jessup replied. He lifted the tip of a tentacle and reversed the spider's trek once more.

* * *

In the canyon, Zee and Jessup hung a dozen rocks wrapped in rags and rope from the lower branches of the tree, placing them at various heights and distances, roughly in a circle. Jessup used them to practice striking with his arms, which helped with controlling his accuracy and force, and the activity became one of his favorites. It was also one of Zee's favorite things to watch. When Jessup was in particularly good form, he would get them all swinging, then dodge, turn and strike them randomly one after the other, and occasionally get them going in a pattern he'd set in his mind.

During an evening when Tem and Timandra weren't coming, Zee worked at the pell in the canyon, shirtless and with his loose pants rolled up to the knees. He struck the pell again and again with his heaviest metal training sword—which was really just a blade of flat iron roughly ground sharp on both sides, with a handle. In his other arm he held a shield of the size used by knights, but weighted to be considerably heavier.

Sweat dripped into his eyes, glistened on his body, and soaked the waist of his pants. Dr. Aenig had been fascinated by the fact that he perspired, since he was a murman and made for living in the sea. The surgeon had theorized that perhaps sweat glands were latently there in Zee's dermal layer and had developed because he had been raised on the land since infancy. Then again, maybe murfolk perspired in the sea to help regulate the level of salt in their bodies. Who knew.

His arms and shoulders burned, and his wrist was growing weak. Each swing became slower and more inaccurate. When the blade stuck in the wood, each tug to free it was a monumental chore. Which was exactly what he wanted.

Everything he did, if there was time, he continued until he just couldn't do it any longer. Finally, he dropped the sword and shield and leaned on his knees, breathing deeply with satisfaction. He stretched, grimacing, then waved his arms and rolled his wrists to clear the sting and burn. He was satisfied with his progress at the pell so far. When he'd first started, he only lasted ten minutes swinging the heavy sword. Now he could go for bells at a time.

He knew he was particularly strong for his size and was getting stronger, he just wasn't very big. And even after over a month of running every day, he was still slow compared to what he'd seen the minnies doing. By his reckoning, he'd be close to last in a Basic foot race.

All in all, though, everything he and Jessup put themselves through was paying off, and as hard as it was, they enjoyed it very much. Some nights they got so caught up in training, forging, or learning something new, they didn't sleep at all.

Having recovered somewhat, he picked up an old towel and wiped his face, arms, and chest. Craning his head back he looked down, running his fingers over the krakenbond. In just a few weeks, it had grown until it now covered his whole left pectoral, with arms stretching across his ribs and sternum, and up over his collarbone. It had become darker, thicker, and harder as well, particular at the center. He could barely feel the touch of his fingers on it. He wondered just how big it would get and if it would become as hard as Jessup's shell. Somehow he didn't think it would, because it wouldn't make much sense if it began to hinder his movement.

A grunt and a "Ha, HA!" came from the other end of the canyon. Zee strolled to lean on the tree and watch a kraken and a small white dragon with a clubfoot sparring.

Jessup struck out with his arms while Fennix bobbed, weaved, and snapped at them with his teeth, occasionally blocking with a wing or his good front leg or spinning to slap them away with his tail. Fennix used his wings to bound over Jessup and come down behind him. Jessup didn't have to spin around, just turn a little and swivel an eye back.

Jessup's control of his arms out of the water had advanced greatly, but Fennix avoided his strikes and swipes, leaping, tucking his wings to drop to the ground and roll, blocking and dodging away. Of course, both of them knew that Jessup could strike Fennix easily if he really wanted to, even extend his tip claws and sucker spikes. By the same token, Fennix could use his freezing breath on Jessup, though they'd discovered it did little more than make his tentacles sting. This was more about training and discipline than winning, though, and they certainly didn't want anyone to get hurt.

"You are doing good today, Fennix," said Jessup. "I think you're getting better."

While still dodging, Fennix corrected the kraken's speech. "'You are doing *well* today.'"

Jessup repeated, "You are doing *well* today." Then he grinned with mischief. "Much gooder than yesterday."

"Now you're just messing with me, you rascally kraken."

"This rascally kraken is now going to go faster. Try to keep up, tiny dragon."

"Do your worst!"

Jessup swung his arms in scissor attacks and snapped them like whips, but Fennix managed to avoid them, then launched himself into the air to fly over Jessup's shell once more. Jessup threw himself to tip over backward, shaking the ground, and thrust up with multiple arms.

"Gah!" Fennix exclaimed, unable to escape the wall of kraken arms. Jessup grabbed him, wrapped him up, and held him close until he couldn't move. "I concede!" came the dragon's muffled voice.

Jessup let him loose. "Thank you again for helping me with training, Fennix," Jessup said. "I enjoy it very much."

"It's a mutually beneficial arrangement, I assure you."

They made quite a pair, the big sea monster and the small white dragon with a deformed front leg. It warmed Zee's heart that Jessup had another friend. A beast friend. "Are you two done playing?" he said.

"Playing?" the kraken replied. "Jessup doesn't play."

"*I* don't play," Fennix corrected.

"Fennix doesn't play either."

Fennix looked at him askance, then saw he was smiling. "Rascally kraken." To Zee, he said, "I'll have you know, this is serious work."

"I can see that," Zee replied with a smile. He could also see that Fennix had sat back and was rubbing his clubfoot with his other claw.

Jessup noticed too. "Does it hurt, Fennix?"

The dragon realized what he was doing and quickly dropped to his good front foot. "No, no. It's fine." Then he saw the genuine concern in his new friends' eyes. "All right, it aches at times, but it's nothing to worry about."

"It certainly doesn't affect the way you fly," Zee said. "You're amazing."

"Thank you," Fennix replied. "I've learned to compensate for the weight imbalance over the years."

"Years of hard training, from what I've seen."

"I do what I can."

Jessup said, "Is that why you don't have to stay with the dragon recruits all the time and can train on your own?"

"It's not that. You've probably heard this is my third time going through Basic Military Training."

"We have," Zee replied.

"I may fly sufficiently, but I cannot run well. I'm also small, even for my breed, which isn't very large already compared to those Royal brutes and the Greatwings, so I am not very strong. The Rocks aren't particularly long or tall, but they are quite powerful for their size."

He was quiet for a moment. "I failed the final running test and the boulder roll in my first year but stayed here on the island for the summer and trained every day. I passed my second year, just barely, but was unable to find a rider on Pairing Day." Fennix swallowed, as if pushing down the pain of his disappointment, and spoke with determination. "I stayed to train once more, planning to do even better in the Basic trials this year, but this seems to be a stronger cohort of dragon candidates than the last, so I must work even harder. Then I have to find a rider willing to pair with me. This is my last chance." He gazed at the ground. "I pray to Zepiter every night that I may fulfill his will for humans and dragons to bond and grow stronger together."

For the first time Zee saw Fennix allow the full weight of his burden show through. "We'll help any way we can."

"Anything you need," said Jessup.

"Thank you, my friends. I appreciate you more than you can know."

Jessup said. "We appreciate you more."

Fennix looked up at him with a half smile. "Are we going to make this an appreciation competition, now?"

"Yes." Jessup tried to hide a grin, not very successfully, which made Fennix laugh.

Zee said, "Let's get back to work. None of us will achieve our dreams sitting around talking about it and being morose."

"True that, Mr. Tarrow," said Fennix. "True that."

* * *

While they waited for Tem and Timandra to arrive at the canyon, Zee rode Jessup with their core sparked, a training shield on his arm, and a wooden sword in his hand. Fennix leapt from side to side, forward and back, shooting streams of freezing ice particles for them to Deflect or block with their Shield. So far they'd been doing well.

Fennix shot upward on his wings, feinted to the side, then plunged down behind them, firing at their back—but their Shield was already there. At the same time, Jessup spun and lunged forward so swiftly he was a blur, forcing Fennix to jump back. Their Shield dropped, and Zee thrust out a hand. Light pulsed forward, knocking Fennix to tumble away over the ground.

Jessup stopped, and Zee shouted, "Fennix! Are you all right?"

Fennix leapt to his feet and shook off the dust, more excited than upset. "I'm fine, don't you worry. That was wonderful! You just used your Shield blind, then Burst and Push, all in swift succession."

Zee said, "We did, didn't we?"

"And best of all, you didn't have to think about it. Your Abilities are becoming second nature."

They heard clapping from above and looked up to see Tem on Timandra on the cliff above.

Timandra said, "Bravo!"

"I guess we can go home," said Tem. "There's nothing more we can teach them."

"Hey!" Zee shouted up. "There's plenty we still don't know."

"That's true," said Timandra. "I guess we'll stay."

Fennix, Jessup, and Zee all grinned.

* * *

Nearly a month and a half of training with Tem and Timandra passed, Zee and Jessup's skills and core size increasing with each passing week. In spite of their efforts, they couldn't reach Copper Class—their next big goal, and the murfolk book had revealed nothing more. Tem and Timandra scoffed at their impatience, but it had been four weeks since they'd classed up to Lead.

CHAPTER 38

It was the last day of the workweek, and a dozen decrepit old warships were to be decommissioned and sunk, but the Dragon Corps and the academy weren't going to let them go entirely to waste. Zee and Jessup had spent the week helping to salvage anything useful. Jessup lifted cannons like they were toys and set them on carts on a pier. Zee stripped metal, assigned mostly to removing underwater fittings and propellers.

They spent most of the last day helping to tow the ships out of the harbor and anchoring them in the sea where they were to be used for a cadet wing strafing exercise.

Zee rode Jessup as they and several oartugs pulled the last of the ships into position. Jessup could have pulled it himself if he and Zee sparked their core, but as much as they wanted to, it wasn't an option out here where everyone could see. Under the guidance of a Silver Class instructor pair, they positioned the ship in line with the others. Jessup lifted Zee to the deck and held the ship steady while Zee dropped the anchor.

They cruised back toward the island where several Navy ships were anchored with sails furled, along with oartugs and barges, their decks teeming with spectators. With the ships placed, the dockworkers and maintenance crews were to have the rest of the afternoon off to watch.

These exercises were quite a show, Zee had been told, and he and Jessup had been looking forward to it all week. Faculty and instructor pairs soared at ease overhead. High on the cliffs and fortified harbor wall civilians and many of the academy staff and faculty were lining up to watch.

Zee caught sight of a tall bald man he recognized as Androo Cobbling on one of the barges and waved at him. Cobbling waved back, as did the shorter, stockier bald man next to him, Meik Tabacchi. Robhat Hayes nodded, puffing on a pipe, and Mickal rot Fletcher lifted a flask before downing half its contents.

The sound of boots marching on stone floated down to the sea. Zee and Jessup looked up to watch all of the over one hundred Basic Training recruits marching along the wall in formation, two abreast. Cadet instructors shouted, "Left! Left! Left, right, left!" It was a particularly hot and humid day, and the heat pressed upon them like a heavy weight. They had to be uncomfortable in their training aketons and armor, but they marched sharply, and Zee envied them. Directly above them, the Basic dragon recruits flew in a column, flying slowly in serpentine so as to match the speed of the minnies below. Fennix flew toward the back of the column, keeping perfect distance and form.

A cadet dragon instructor roared, "Sing!"

The voices of the minnies and duckies rose together, singing the Dragon Corps Hymn. A sense of pride and longing rose in Zee's heart.

From the isle of Triumf's Citadel
On wings of wrath we soar
To protect our nation's sovereignty
From the skies our might will roar

Through the light and through the darkness
Over sea and over shore
For our king and homes and citizens

Cadet instructors shouted, "Who are we?!"

We're the Kingdom's Dragon Corps!

"Hurrah! Hurrah! Hurrah!"

* * *

Sallison anh Batcu marched smartly in the line of recruits, Jondon dil Rolio clomping along at her side.

The lead cadet instructor shouted, "Minnies, halt! Single file! Left face!" They obeyed and, with only a few awkwardly bumped shoulders to mar their precision, turned to face away from the sea, toward the academy.

On the field below, the full academy wing was assembled. There were no first-years among them since Basic was not yet complete, but the field held over three hundred cadet pairs stood in full battle training armor, organized in four groups with their constituent squadrons and flights.

At the front of each group stood their group leader, and facing them all were Cadet Wing Commanders High Mountain ber Sakai and Saralin. Sallison could hear their voices but couldn't make out what they were saying from that distance.

From where he stood between Sallison and Mehmet can Yasso, Jondon said, "There's your sister, Mehmet."

A tall, powerful-looking, third-year cadet stood out front of one of the groups. "My dear, loving sister."

Beside Mehmet, Chirt said, "May she fall off her dragon in shame."

The four of them chuckled.

As bad luck would have it, or more likely his own surreptitious maneuvering, Inkanyezi ekh Hanyayo stood next to Sallison. He spoke quietly without turning to face her, not wanting to draw the attention of the cadet instructors.

"How is your archery training going, Minny Batcu?"

"Well enough to beat you when the trials come around."

"I look forward to the challenge."

"I look forward to putting an arrow in your rear portal." She'd raised her voice just enough.

"Minny Batpoo!" Sallison winced as a third-year cadet instructor stomped up to her. "You've just earned yourself the privilege of night watch for five days straight!"

"Yes, ma'am! Thank you, ma'am!"

"Don't thank me, thank that ugly pucker of a tortle's under-tail you call a mouth."

"Ma'am, yes, ma'am."

Someone snickered down the line. The cadet instructor glared and marched to scream in Derlick don Donnicky's face, spittle flying. "Did I say something that amuses you, Minny Duckdinky?"

"No, ma'am!"

"Maybe you think I'm sweet on Minny Batcrap because I give her so much loving attention. Is that it?"

"No, ma'am!"

"Maybe I'm sweet on you, too. So sweet, in fact, I'm going to give you five days of scrubbing pots!"

"Ma'am, yes, ma'am! Thank you, ma'am!" She glared up and down the line, then marched off along the wall. Donnicky stared straight ahead, face red and scowling.

Sallison breathed out in relief. Night watch would be awful, especially after training all day, but her punishment could have been worse. Her mouth had gotten her into trouble at least a half dozen times since she'd arrived. This time it was worth it, though, just from the look on Donnicky's face. She chuckled to herself. Docklicker was pretty good, but Duckdinky was even better. She'd have to remember that.

Horns blew on the field below, and the cadet wing commanders took flight. One after the other, each of the groups took to the air and circled over the field.

A cadet instructor on the wall shouted, "About face!" They turned as one toward the sea and "enemy" ships the cadet wing would be attacking.

An odd hum rose in the sky, and a flat disk of yellow light almost twenty yards across floated over the wall. Atop it, three fourth-year magicker cadet pairs stood at the edges at equal distances, their wands glowing, as well as the superintendent, commandant, and academic dean pairs. The disk continued out over the water and rose higher for a better view of the exercises. The Ability was called Platform Disk, one that only magickers could do. Zee had seen it used for observation in cadet training, but he'd heard it was also handy for transporting injured dragons and knights in battle. Magickers could create small ones individually, larger when working together.

A familiar voice sounded across the water. "Zee Tarrow! Mr. Jessup!"

Beastmaster Mahfouz waved him and Jessup over from where he stood at the railing of the nearest Navy ship, Mildrezod and another rider and dragon pair next to him.

They swam to the ship and Mahfouz introduced them to Citadel Tackmasters Sadir sem Samir and Timy, an Ice Diver, who were in charge of all beast harnessing and saddlery.

Mahfouz spoke to Samir loud enough for Zee and Jessup to hear. "There's a challenge for you. How would you saddle that beast?" While Samir and Timy looked over the kraken, Mahfouz said. "Mr. Jessup, would you show them how your shell spikes operate?"

Jessup spoke to Zee through their bond, and Zee hopped off into the water. Jessup retracted the spikes Zee had been holding on to, then extended all of them.

Zee learned something new when Timy whistled. Dragons could whistle. Some of them, anyway.

"You can control them all individually, Mr. Jessup?" Timy asked.

"Yes, ma'am," Jessup answered, then demonstrated, retracting and extending the spikes around his shell. The tackmasters seemed thrilled.

Samir said, "This will make for a great challenge to think about."

"You may have to do more than think about it," said Mildrezod. "These two will be cadets one day, mark my words."

"I don't mean to be rude," said Timy, "but that seems highly unlikely."

Mahfouz said, "Would you care to make a wager? Twenty of my largest pumpkins for a dozen bottles of your best cherberry wine?"

"Thirty pumpkins and you have yourself a wager," Samir replied.

"What do we get?" Timy asked.

"Right," said Mildrezod. She bumped Mahfouz with her snout. "And what are you thinking, wagering away my pumpkins?"

"We'll think of something," said Mahfouz, "right, Sadir?"

"Of course." The dragons grumbled while Mahfouz and Samir shook hands.

Mahfouz grinned at Zee and Jessup. "Don't let us down, lads. Mildrezod does love her pumpkins. She'll never forgive me if I lose."

"We're doing our best, sir," Zee shouted as he climbed to the top of Jessup's shell to watch the exercise.

More horns sounded, this time from buglers on another floating Platform, followed by the roars of three hundred dragons high in the sky.

The first of the four cadet groups came roaring down through the clouds. By their light blue aketons, it was Alpha Group. One squadron after another, they flew high along the line of ships, using bombardment Abilities to drop bombs of fire, ice, and superheated ambergris stones, many of which punched right through the top decks.

Beta Group, in yellow, followed, coming in from a lower angle, the larger Royal Ebons in the front clutching at masts, crushing them in their grips and breaking them in two. Zee noticed that the fourth-year cadet pairs, who had achieved the highest Classes, led each group, followed by third-year pairs, then those in their second year, and each group was made up of roughly an equal number of flights from each year.

The third wave, Gamma Group, came in strafing with flame, freezing rain, and ambergris lava. The wing commander flew at the head of the final group, Delta, and nearly destroyed the first ship with a Comet of fire.

The pairs behind him split to go around the rising flames, but when coming together beyond it, two pairs of second-year cadets collided in the smoke. One of them righted themselves and swooped up, though the dragon was having trouble with one of its wings. The other pair, however, crashed through the deck of the burning ship. Black smoke billowed out of the hole, and spectators cried out.

* * *

Recruits gasped all along the line on the wall, and Sallison cursed.

Bugles blew, bells rang, upper-class pairs with Ice Divers swooped to blast the deck with ice, and magicker pairs leapt from the walls while the ship began to list to one side—but the murman and kraken were already speeding toward the burning ship. The kraken roared to warn the cadet pairs, louder than any dragon she'd ever heard, then the mighty beast of the sea shot out of the water and crashed down on the deck, Zee Tarrow clinging to the spines above his brow. Jessup jammed his arms through the smoking hole in the deck, heedless of the flames, and tore it open. The ship tipped more, and water poured in as it sank.

The murman dove into the smoke and billowing steam, and then the ship was gone, the kraken riding it as it sank beneath the waves. Cadet pairs circled over the boiling patch of sea that was strewn with charred, steaming debris. The Platform carrying the faculty and staff floated closer, as did several smaller Platforms with magickers who specialized in healing. The roiling water settled, and all were silent as tense moments passed.

Zee Tarrow splashed to the surface, holding the limp rider in his arms. Nearby, several kraken arms thrust up, holding the dragon, followed by Jessup's shell and face. The dragon began to cough. The rider did not.

Zee wrapped his arms around the young man's chest from the back and squeezed violently. Water spewed from the rider's mouth and he sucked in air. Both the rider and dragon were scorched but alive.

Seconds passed while everyone just stared. Then came the mighty voice of Beastmaster Mahfouz. "Hurrah! Hurrah!" Others took up the cry, until everyone was cheering.

* * *

Only then did Zee fully realize what he and Jessup had done. They hadn't even thought about it, just decided subconsciously as one to race for the ship. The only words spoken between them in the time it took them to reach the ship was a reminder not to spark their core. They'd had faith the strength of their bond alone would be enough, and it had been.

Each holding the lives they'd saved in their arms, he and Jessup gazed at the cheering crowd, then their eyes met, and they grinned.

A staff magicker pair flew down and took the rider from Zee. More magickers floated a Platform to Jessup, just above the waves. They looked more tentative, but Jessup gently laid the dragon at their feet. One of them tended to the beast as the Platform sped away.

Zee swam to Jessup and climbed onto his shell.

High above, Cadet Wing Commander Beast Saralin roared, "Cadet Wing, form up! Report to Field Three. Now!"

Any pairs who had not already rejoined their groups did so swiftly. The cadet wing commanders hovered as the groups headed back to the island, gazing at Zee and Jessup with expressions Zee couldn't read, then shot off to follow the rest of the wing.

The large Platform with academy faculty and staff floated down to just above the waves.

All of them were silent as they watched Zee and Jessup, making Zee nervous. Dean of Academics Philliam sim Tooker even wore a scowl. Then Zee saw that Aureosa, Vandalia, Wanchoo, and Venkatarama were smiling.

Standing closest to Zee and Jessup at the edge of the Platform, Superintendent Lora aye Hyooz said, "Thank you for your service to the academy and our cadets, Mr. Tarrow, Mr. Jessup."

Zee once more had to suppress the urge to salute. "You're very welcome, ma'am. We only did what we knew was right."

She just looked at them for a short time, then said. "Either way, it was above the call of duty for your position and much appreciated."

Jessup said, "It was fun."

Her brow lifted in amusement, her glasses riding up on her nose, then she looked out to where the ships were anchored. Three of them were still afloat. She turned to Commandant Aureosa. "We'll need to have them scuttled."

Aureosa in turn spoke to a young pair of staffers. "Inform the rear admiral." The rider and dragon saluted and took off back toward the largest of the Navy ships.

Jessup and Zee communicated briefly through their bond, and Zee asked Superintendent Hyooz. "May Jessup do it, ma'am?"

"Scuttle the ships?"

"Yes, ma'am."

She turned to Aureosa, who nodded, then back to Zee. "I don't see why not."

Jessup said, "Thank you, ma'am."

"Be careful, Mr. Jessup," said Vandalia. "We have no one to send to save a kraken." Jessup grinned.

* * *

The recruits walked in step along the wall. They were heading back to the field, but the instructors didn't seem to be in much of a hurry. All eyes were still on the sea. The faculty Platform rose, then Zee and Jessup were swimming toward the ships that hadn't sunk. None of them, including Sallison, said a word as they watched.

As the murman and kraken approached the first ship at high speed, Zee Tarrow leapt from the beast with a "Whoop!" and backflipped into the water. Spikes shot out all over Jessup's shell, and he submerged just before striking the vessel amidships. There was a resounding crunch and the ship lurched sideways, practically broken in half. It was nearly sunk by the time Jessup shot out of the water with a roar to fly in a high arc and hit the deck of the second ship with the point of his shell. He crashed right through. That ship did break in half.

The kraken's underwater roar could be heard by all. If they knew Jessup, they'd know it was a happy roar.

* * *

Meik Tabacchi clapped Androo Cobbling on the shoulder as they watched. "There's our boys."

* * *

Dame Toomsil sat upon Peloquin on the wall next to Tem and Timandra. Through their bond, Timandra said to Tem, "*There's our boys.*"

* * *

Mahfouz grinned while Samir stared in shock. Mahfouz said, "There's our boys, Mil." Mildrezod puffed smoke from her nostrils.

Jessup's arms reached out of the sea to wrap around the last and smallest of the ships. The water below the ship lit up with blue light, then electricity crackled over Jessup's arms and pulsed brightly. The ship burst into even more flames. The arms squeezed, crushing the hull and deck like they were made of twigs.

Samir's Ice Diver dragon, Timy, exclaimed, "Holy Mother of Zepiter."

* * *

Zee and Jessup swam lazily behind the ships as they entered the harbor. Jessup was quite proud of himself. He told Zee he'd always wanted to see what he could do to a ship and explained in detail how he'd used what he'd learned about a ship's construction at the docks to destroy them. Zee clapped him on the shell in encouragement.

Once at the docks, Zee leapt from Jessup to where Tabacchi, Cobbling, Hayes, and Fletcher waited, clapping and whistling, along with many of their work crew.

Zee blushed, and Jessup rose up, a wide grin on his face. "Jessup wants to break more ships."

"Maybe another day, Mr. Jessup," Tabacchi said with a laugh, "but only when they need breaking, all right?" Tabacchi put a hand on Zee's shoulder. "Come, Mr. Tarrow, let's get you and Mr. Jessup paid for the week."

Cobbling added, "And how about we finally have that pint?"

CHAPTER 39

Robhat Hayes raised the toast for their third round. "To Zee and Jessup, the newest heroes of the citadel!" Everyone at the table cheered, mugs were clacked together, and Zee took a sip of his ale, blushing for the third time since they'd sat down at the trestle table in the Blind Pig.

This was Zee's first time at a tavern, and he found that he liked it. The ale and all the attention, however, not so much. He'd tried ale on ship and hadn't liked the taste. It wasn't nearly as bad after two, though. "Jessup's the real hero. I was just along for the ride."

Tabacchi shook his head. "I don't think a single soul in the whole watery world would call jumping into the burning hull of a sinking ship 'along for the ride.'" Zee grinned and watched the bubbles pop on his ale.

"Where is the big fellow, anyway?" Cobbling asked.

"He said he'd cruise the harbor and wait for me, maybe go out and start retrieving the chains and anchors from the scuttled ships."

Tabacchi said, "The lad's a worker, bar none."

Cobbling snorted. "I beg your pardon?"

"Especially barring you, Androo."

Only half hiding that he was pouring liquor from his flask into his ale mug below the table, Fletcher said, "He didn't want to come to the pub?"

Zee chuckled, but when Fletcher looked up, his expression was serious. Fletcher glanced at Hayes, who was staring at him blank-faced. "What?"

Zee pointed behind the bar. "Why is there a door on the wall?"

Meik and Andrew turned to inspect a windowless door of worm-eaten wood, placed within a crooked frame carved with odd runes.

Meik said, "Nobody knows."

Hayes shrugged. Fletcher belched and said, "What door?"

Zee's gaze wandered past Fletcher to a dark corner at the back of the bar where three people sat. One of them had a short beard and a wide-brimmed hat with a feather and spoke closely to a tall woman in a cloak with her hood pulled up. Daggers lined the belt of the man in the hat. He looked dangerous, even with the paunch at his belly. Sitting opposite them with his chair turned so he had a clear view of the bar was the tallest man Zee had ever seen, bald with a scar from the crown of his head down the side of his face to his chin. The sword leaning against the table next to him had to be longer than Zee was tall. If the man in the feathered hat appeared dangerous, this guy looked absolutely deadly.

Tabacchi said softly, "Don't stare, lad."

"Sorry. I didn't realize I was."

"The man in the hat is Shawnnegan tan Kinglehorst, a notorious black marketeer. The tall fella, Tomassi tal Clewsano, is King Shawnnegan's muscle. He's no bonded knight, but still one of the most feared men amongst the rogues and thieves of Tosh."

"King Shawnnegan?"

"That's what folks call him, or he calls himself, who knows how it started. I'm telling you this so you steer clear of them, understand?" Next to Meik, Androo gave Zee a serious nod.

"Thank you. I'll remember that." Still, Zee couldn't help but take another look as he heard a chair slide back in the corner. The woman stuffed a pouch in her cloak and stood. As she walked by, Zee caught the glint of silver scale mail under her cloak. She kept her head down and left the bar, pulling her hood tighter against the rain that had begun after Zee and Meik's crew had arrived.

Zee shot a questioning look at Meik, but the door burst open to loud cursing. Two young men and a young woman entered, flapping the rain off their cloaks. They wore civilian clothes, but Zee recognized them as three of the five third-year cadets he'd had a run-in with while training in the forested hills. One of them was Lukas, the tall cadet who had done most of the talking and taken a swing at him.

The cadet stomped the rain off his expensive boots, grumbling. He peered around the bar with a frown, but Zee looked away before his attention fell on him. The cadet strode to the table in the corner. After a once-over from Clewsano and a wave of King Shawnnegan's hand, he took a seat.

Cobbling said, "You know that cadet, Zee?"

"We met, briefly."

"It wasn't a friendly meeting, I'd wager," Robhat said, ale dripping in his beard.

"Not really, but it's fine." Zee shrugged. He'd been so busy forging, training, and working, he'd honestly forgotten all about it.

"Kid's a piece of work," said Androo.

Meik said, "Name's Lukas tar Tarzian, spoiled brat of the high admiral of His Majesty's Navy, who also owns more land and factories than anyone else in Tosh. The only more powerful people in the kingdom than Admiral tar Tarzian are the king himself, his vizier, and the queen."

"And the brat knows it," Hayes said, then feigned spitting on the floor.

Zee glanced at where Tarzian conversed in low tones with Kinglehorst, who shook his head in disagreement about something.

Meik leaned closer. "Shawnnegan travels about selling all manner of illicit goods, but his most popular wares here on the island are black-market elixirs and pills for bonded pairs. They only enhance the power of a rider and beast for a short time or aid in healing, so they're not strictly illegal for full-fledged knights. It's frowned upon to obtain them in this way, though. If a cadet is found with them, it's grounds for immediate expulsion."

"Kid thinks he's above the law," added Androo. "And he's a bully to boot."

Zee turned to where the other two cadets sat at another table, mugs of ale untouched, eyes nervously roving over the crowd. Looking out for anyone from the citadel, Zee figured. If they'd seen Zee, they either hadn't recognized him or didn't care.

Out of the corner of his eye, Zee saw Tarzian pass a pouch to Kinglehorst and receive one in return. Tarzian put the pouch in his pocket and stood, a satisfied smirk on his face, then turned, and his eyes fell on Zee.

Zee returned Tarzian's gaze squarely. He couldn't help it. There was something about the arrogant sneer on the cadet's face, or maybe Zee was just done with turning away and keeping quiet, as he had for all the years on the HMT *Krakenfish*. It could have had something to do with the two and a half mugs of ale he'd consumed, too.

Zee wondered what might be going through Tarzian's mind. Maybe that no one in the bar would say anything if there was a confrontation. Or maybe he was now aware Zee knew the commandants and was considering the consequences. Tarzian could just ignore him, or nod, maybe even buy him a drink. Instead, he resorted to what bullies always do. Intimidation.

Tarzian sauntered across the tavern and stood sneering down at him.

"What are you looking at, gilly?"

Feet shuffled and chairs scooted as nearby patrons moved away. Zee swallowed, wondering if he'd gone too far.

Androo said, "He's not looking at anything, cadet. We don't want any trouble."

"Shut your fish-hole, peasant," Tarzian spat, his voice oozing with haughty condescension.

Something sparked in Zee—not his core, that would be a very bad idea—but anger. Real anger. He'd once heard a lord governor use that word when talking down to his da.

Tarzian spun back on Zee. "You and your monster think you're heroes, now? We would have saved them. You just wanted the attention, because you're nothing. Lowly sea scum, not worth the filth you spring from."

Meik began to stand from his chair, hands raised in placation. "Gentleman, please, there's no cause for—"

Tarzian reached across the table and shoved Meik in the chest, sending him tumbling back over his chair. Just like he'd tried to shove Zee.

Now Zee was certain he hadn't gone too far. In fact, he hadn't gone far enough. He could take the insults, but he wasn't going to let Lukas push his friends around. Zee'd had no friends for a very long time, and he wanted to keep them.

He stood and pushed between Tarzian and the table, causing the cadet to step back. The two cadets who had entered with Tarzian jumped up from where they sat, but they stayed where they were when they saw Tarzian's hand go to the haft of his sword.

"You draw that weapon in here and we're done, forever."

The voice was King Shawnnegan's, who stood near the back door with Clewsano. The big bald man was even taller standing than Zee had thought when he was sitting.

Rage flashed across Tarzian's features, but his hand moved away from his sword.

Clewsano glared at the cadet, then opened the door, followed Kinglehorst into the rain, and closed it.

Tarzian's sneer returned. "I don't need a sword to teach a gilly a lesson." He snatched Zee by the shirt and hurled him toward the front door with more speed and strength than any normal person could muster.

Patrons leapt out of the way as Zee crashed through a table and chairs. He pushed to his elbows, but paused. Jessup was questing through their bond, having sensed Zee's emotional state.

Zee spoke first. "*It's all right, Jessup, just stay where you are, please. I'll let you know when this is over.*"

He felt Jessup's concern and frustration, but finally his friend answered. "*I understand. You do what you have to do.*"

"*Thank you. I will.*"

Zee checked himself. No serious injuries, just some scrapes and bruises. He'd had worse. Zee hadn't felt Tarzian spark his core. His strength had come strictly from being bonded. His dragon had to be close.

From where he crouched to help a dazed Meik to a sitting position on the floor, Androo shouted up at Tarzian. "Using the strength of a bond on civilians is strictly forbidden. You could be expelled for that."

Tarzian retorted, "And who's going to report me?" No one spoke. Then, to Tarzian's surprise, Zee stood and clapped dirt and debris from his hands. Eyes locked on the arrogant cadet, Zee stepped clear of the debris. Customers near the door exited quickly behind him, leaving the front door open to the pouring rain. The rest of them crowded against the walls. Zee knew what Tarzian was thinking. Zee should have been squirming on the floor with broken bones, been out cold, or worse.

"I won't say a word," Zee said, "but I will answer." It was possibly the first time he'd spoken to someone that way in his life. It felt good. Jessup was having a good influence on him after all. Well, maybe not good, but right.

Tarzian jeered, "Fine. My dragon is right outside."

Power pulsed from the cadet as he sparked his core. No one else in the tavern felt it since they weren't bonded, but Zee did. Zee didn't know what class Tarzian was since he'd never seen him in armor or with a class and level badge, but if he had to guess, he'd say low- to mid-level Bronze. As far as he knew, he and Jessup were still Lead Class, two Classes lower. Zee didn't care, not even when Tarzian thrust his arms down and out to his sides and his right hand burst into flames.

Zee glared at him from beneath his brow. "So is my kraken."

At that moment, lightning flashed outside with a sharp crack, flaring though the windows and the open door behind Zee, followed by a sharp crack and rumbling of thunder. Zee didn't know if Jessup had something to do with it, or if he could even do such a thing, but the timing had been perfect.

Tarzian and his flightmates had been involved in the training exercise today and seen what Zee and Jessup had done, maybe even witnessed Jessup's destruction of the ships.

The warmth of their bond heated and power swelled within Zee. Jessup wasn't coming to the tavern and he hadn't sparked their core, but he was closer. Much closer. Right across the wharf in the harbor. Channeling his strength to Zee. And he was angry.

Zee clenched his fists at his side. Blue light burned in his eyes. His hair rose from his shoulders and waved slowly. Electricity crackled over the krakenbond on his chest, then spread down his arms to flare around his hands. Zee had no idea how it was happening, but he went with it, covering his surprise with a feral grin.

Fear flitted across Tarzian features. He peered through the front door and windows, perhaps imagining the kraken's hulking figure appearing out of the gloom, sizzling with electricity, then tearing the Blind Pig's entire front wall out onto the street before snatching him up with a monstrous arm and eating him.

At least, that's what Zee hoped he was thinking.

Tarzian withdrew the fire from his hands and doused his core. The fight had left him, but the hatred in his eyes remained. The two other cadets joined him.

"We'll see you soon, gilly," Tarzian said through a hateful smirk.

"Not soon enough." Zee concentrated on letting go of the lightning on his fists, and it fizzled out.

Tabacchi got to his feet. "I will keep my mouth shut for now, tar Tarzian, but a word from you about any of this, if there is any hint that you've filed a complaint against a certain young murman, and I will have plenty to say about what you've done, why you come here, and how often, regardless of the consequences."

"And he won't be the only one," Cobbling added. Everyone at the table stood, glaring at Tarzian, including Robhat Hayes, then over half the people in the bar rose or stepped forward.

Mickal rot Fletcher looked around from where he still sat, then groaned. "Oh, fish it." He rose from his chair as well, raised his mug to Tarzian, and chugged his drink.

Tarzian cast a last glaring look at Zee, spat on the floor, and stomped to the back door, the other cadets in tow.

Breath escaped in the wake of the confrontation, and everyone looked at Zee.

Fletcher said, "Next time, we're going to the Bucket."

CHAPTER 40

The following Firstday morning, Zee slid his and Jessup's stamped time cards into slots outside Meik Tabacchi's office and stepped away from the line of workers.

"Mr. Tarrow!" came Meik's familiar voice.

Zee turned to see Meik on the wharf with Kareem eh Mahfouz and Mildrezod. Zee hesitated, wondering if they'd heard what happened at the tavern, but strode over and greeted them.

"You're being assigned a different duty today, at the request of the academy," Meik said.

"Recruits and cadets are going through water survival training today," Mahfouz explained, "and our lead lifeguard is out sick."

Mildrezod said, "After your show of bravery and skill at the strafing exercise, we're hoping you'd fill in."

"I'd be honored," Zee replied, somewhat taken aback, but also relieved this wasn't about the tavern incident. He'd also get a firsthand look at more recruit and cadet training, which he hadn't had much time for lately.

* * *

Having changed into lifeguard's swim trunks, Zee stood on a low diving platform at the edge of the training pool. It was more like a lake than a pool, over a hundred yards wide and twice that in length. Situated at the edge of the island, one side was bounded by a fifty-foot-high breakwall wide enough for two dragons to walk on abreast, two others by sandy beaches, and the far end a rocky slope to a natural ridgeline.

Two groups of twenty-five Basic Training minnies marched in while being berated by their cadet instructors. Among them he spotted Sallison anh Batcu, kitted out in training armor, her helmet under one arm. She looked up at him, but by the time he thought to raise a hand in greeting, she was already eyes-forward and all business.

A squadron of upper-class pairs flew in as well, followed by a group of dragon recruits. Zee grinned up at Fennix, who rocked his wings slightly to acknowledge him without risking the wrath of his instructors.

Zee had been asked to do a safety check of the pool before the exercises. He'd almost laughed when a security officer had offered him a snorkel, and politely declined.

Without taking a deep breath, because he didn't need to, he dove from the platform. It took him little time to check the full length and width of the pool, which was uniformly about twenty feet deep, with a sandy bottom, and surprisingly clean. He inspected the channels that ran through the wall with heavy grates at both ends to allow for water circulation. They were only a foot across, the grate openings not even large enough for a salt-ranha to fit through. Zee tugged at them anyway to make sure they were secure. All the while, he spotted only a few schools of tiny colorful and harmless fish.

Zee climbed out at the end of the pool and gave the security officers a thumbs-up. They stared at his gills and webbed hands and feet as he walked by, but he paid them no mind. By the time he'd taken three more steps the gills had disappeared and his hands and feet had returned to normal.

* * *

Sand shifted in a circle at the bottom of the pool, opening to reveal an eye three feet across, with a pupil in the shape of an X. The eye roved around the pool, unblinking, then closed again, and the creature waited.

* * *

Recruits craned their necks to watch Zee walking behind them, only to be scolded by their instructors. He was still an oddity among them. He'd become just one of the gang among the workers at the docks, for which he was grateful, but with each passing day he felt more like he might never fit in at the academy, even if he did become a cadet. That was okay, though. It would be nice to make friends with some of the cadets, but it didn't really matter. He and Jessup just had to be the best among them.

Zee climbed the rungs to sit atop a twenty-foot-tall watchtower at the corner of the pool. More lifeguards took positions and several fourth-year magicker pairs lounged on benches on the beach. No one looked particularly concerned.

Dragon cadets waded into the water. All of them held their wings in tight, their riders swimming alongside with one hand on the saddle. They swam better than Zee would have imagined, considering. All dragons had hollow bones, so unless they were wearing a lot of armor they didn't have to worry about sinking. They just weren't built all that well for swimming. The Ice Divers were the swiftest, and the Rocks had the hardest time, floating lower in the water than the others, but even they didn't seem to be struggling too terribly.

Zee was happy to see Fennix keeping up with the fastest of the dragon recruits, even the other Ice Divers. He had one less leg to paddle with, but he used his wings efficiently, and Zee knew very well he kept himself in exceptional condition.

The rider recruits had the more difficult task. Wearing full training armor, they were made to climb to thirty-foot diving platforms and jump in. It became clear to Zee they'd trained for this already and this was just practice. That didn't mean they were doing all that well.

They sank as soon as they hit the water and stripped off as much armor as they could before surfacing. Zee watched for signs of panic or telltale bubbles, ready to leap if needed. The cadet instructors paid close attention as well. They might treat the recruits hastily, but they didn't want any of them to drown.

Once the recruits surfaced, they had to swim out to a line of buoys in the middle of the pool, tread water for a quarter bell, then strip their trousers and tie off the ends of the legs to create a makeshift flotation device. Once that was accomplished, they were to swim back. The recruits went one at a time from five platforms, and as soon as one set started swimming out to the buoys, the next five jumped in.

It was Zee's task to watch the recruits, while the other lifeguards kept an eye on the cadets. One of the magicker pairs flew slowly back and forth over the water as well. Zee lifted the protective lenses over his eyes to sharpen his vision in the sun's glare and repeatedly scanned each one of them.

One recruit in particular drew most of his attention, however. Sallison had been one of the first in the water and made it out to the buoys more quickly than any of the others. Zee figured she had to be near the top of the Basic Training cohort. It wasn't just her condition and skill that intrigued him, though. She'd gone out of her way to speak to him his first day on the island, and gotten herself into trouble for it. Other than Dame Toomsil, who'd been more of a mentor—and his mother, he supposed—he'd never had any female friends and certainly never anything more than that. Jessup was right, too. She *was* pretty.

Zee reprimanded himself for letting his mind wander and returned his focus to the pool. Even with all one hundred recruits in the pool, everything was going fine until Zee noticed one recruit out by the buoys was no longer in sight. Then a dragon screamed.

Zee leapt to his feet on the tower.

The dragon of one of the cadet pairs swimming laps thrashed frantically and was tugged beneath the surface, then lifted out of the water, clutched in an enormous, hairy crab's claw.

The pincer snapped shut, cutting the dragon in half. Its rider wailed.

The creature shoved up farther out of the water. Its shell was covered in shaggy fur, as were its pincers and the slim front legs it used to gather one half of the dragon to the tentacles above its wide mouth packed with rows of jagged teeth. A single eye, three feet wide and with an X-shaped pupil, gazed from the center of its shell, and a smaller eye was centered just above its mouth and tentacles. Zee recognized the monster crab from one of Aenig's books on deep-sea fauna. A chasmclaw.

Cadets, recruits, and dragons shrieked, splashing frantically for the nearest shore while instructors screamed for them to hurry.

Zee spoke briefly through his bond, and dove.

* * *

"*Jessup, I need your help.*"

Jessup froze in the middle of lifting a crane mount onto a pier.

He set the mount down roughly, causing workers to jump back, climbed onto the wharf, and shuffled away as fast as he could.

* * *

The surface above Zee churned with frantic swimmers, the water filled with their muffled shouts and the muted roars of dragons. He grabbed a chubby recruit who was floundering beneath the surface and pulled him upward.

The recruit gasped and sputtered in Zee's arms. "Thank you!"

The dragon of a Silver Class knight pair on the breakwall roared an alarm into the sky, then a recruit shouted nearby in the water.

"Mehmet!" It was Sallison, swimming fast toward Zee and the recruit he held.

"Sallison!" Mehmet replied. "It's a chasmclaw!"

"I see it." She took hold of him, then said to Zee, "I've got him." Zee let go and she began swimming away from where the chasmclaw was wreaking havoc on the cadet pairs, dragging the recruit with her. Then she stopped and turned back. "Be careful."

A familiar voice shouted Zee's name from above. He spun to see Fennix hovering near. "What can I do to help?"

Zee shouldn't have been surprised to see him. Ice Divers could plunge into the sea to catch fish, then swim up and thrust with their wings to clear the surface. Of course Fennix would be one of the first out of the water.

Zee scanned the pool, considering how to save as many swimmers as he could, but the monster crab continued to attack the cadets. Even the other Ice Divers were having trouble escaping in the splashing throng. Most of the pairs had sparked their cores for extra strength, but it wasn't helping much.

The cadet magicker pairs scooped recruits up and dropped them on shore as fast as they could, but it wasn't fast enough. The Silver Class knight pair swooped down from the wall and blasted the monster crab with flame, but the beast ducked under the water and leapt back up, stabbed the dragon with the pike-like end of one of its legs right through their aura protection, and jerked them under.

Back to Fennix, Zee said, "Get as many out as you can."

* * *

Sallison, who'd been watching Zee and Fennix and wondering how they knew each other, said, "Take Mehmet, Mr. Fennix. I'll see who else I can help."

When the white dragon looked at her, he paused for a moment, and she got that same odd feeling she'd had when she'd seen him flying while watching Zee and Jessup frolic in the surf.

His voice snapped her out of it. "My pleasure, ma'am." Fennix flapped to them, the downdraft raising waves in the pool. "Hold your arms up, recruit."

Mehmet hesitated a moment, then did what he was told. Sallison helped keep him above water while Fennix gripped his wrists with his hind claws.

Fennix turned to Zee. "What are you going to do?"

"I have to stop that thing."

Fennix gazed at him seriously, said, "Don't die," then hauled Mehmet toward the shore.

Sallison gazed at the chasmclaw as it chased a swimming pair. "What he said."

"I'll do my best," Zee replied with a nervous smile. "You be careful, too." She gave him a curt nod.

Zee narrowed his eyes at the crab-monster and dove beneath the surface.

Even with all her training and martial upbringing, Sallison couldn't imagine going after that monster. And Zee didn't even have a weapon. People could say all they wanted about the young murman, but they couldn't call him a coward. She swam toward a cluster of struggling recruits.

* * *

The best thing Zee could think of was to distract the crab in the hope of giving the swimmers a chance to get out of the lake. He spied the armor shed by the recruits piled at the bottom of the pool, but there were no weapons. Not that a training sword would do much good against this monster. He shot toward the beast.

The chasmclaw was even bigger than he'd thought. Its shell had to be twenty feet wide, its legs thirty feet long. Zee put on speed and slammed into the eye on the top of its shell with his shoulder. The clear covering of the eye barely gave, but it got the creature's attention. It ducked under and spun to glare at Zee with the one eye on its face, pincers held wide. It loosed a shriek, and lunged.

* * *

Jessup clambered over a wall at the edge of the academy training fields. Zee had told him he'd be at the training pool across the island. Jessup had never been there, but he felt Zee's presence and headed straight for it.

* * *

Zee shot in and slapped reaching mouth-tentacles away, then front-flipped over the chasmclaw's shell. The crab was surprisingly fast, but Zee was faster. Even without Jessup being close enough to lend him the strength and speed of their bond, he was able to avoid the monster-crab's pincers and stabbing feet.

Zee kept close, swimming around its legs where it had a harder time keeping track of where he was, then shot out in front of it again. The monster glared at him, then turned and strode toward the splashing dragons. It no longer considered him a threat.

He shouted and tugged at a back leg, then swam over its shell to punch at its frightening eye, but the beast kept going. What Zee needed was his stinger. He could remove it from his Keep without sparking their core, but Jessup had to be closer. He expanded his bond sense and could tell that Jessup was coming but was still too far away. Zee had to do something, and he had to do it now.

He shot beneath the crab as it reached for a swimming dragon and grabbed hold of the lower half of one of its claws with both hands. The beast shoved up out of the water, snapping and waving its claw in the air, trying to dislodge the pesky murman. The pincers didn't close far enough to snip off his fingers, but several of them were nearly crushed. Zee gritted his teeth through the pain and hung on.

* * *

Jessup grunted with Zee's pain. He had to run faster. He could have swum out of the harbor and around the island, but he hadn't thought of that in his rush. There was no guarantee it would be faster, and it was too late for that now.

Cadets and instructors shouted at him as he shuffled straight through training fields, heedless of whatever activity the riders and dragons were engaged in. No one tried to stop him, and anyone in his path parted with haste.

Fennix had been helping Jessup practice walking like a spider, but the technique still evaded him. His failures had been comical, he knew it, but it wasn't funny now. He tightened his arms, pulled eight of them under him while holding the forward two up in front of him. He went slowly, thinking about alternating opposite pairs at a time, then remembered how Fennix had chastised him for thinking too hard about it the last time they'd tried it. He forced himself to breathe slowly and put himself into a state similar to when he and Zee meditated for forging, letting his mind relax while keeping the movement of his legs at the back of his thoughts, pushing himself higher and stepping farther. Before he knew it he had closed his eyes. When he opened them he was running faster than he'd ever thought possible. He almost tripped but caught himself, and ran.

Instructors stopped shouting in mid-sentence. Dragon's nearly collided in the sky. Everyone stared at the kraken, raised up on eight legs, speeding across the fields, stepping over walls ten feet high, even leaping a low storage building, all without slowing or missing a step.

* * *

One of Zee's hands slipped from the chasmclaw's lower pincer just as the beast lifted the other from the water and reached for him. He was about to swing out and drop into the pool when he felt the power of a Red Titan pair sparking their core, heard Dean Mihir han Wanchoo shout, "Viraam!," and lost all ability to move.

Zee hung at an odd angle, frozen still. He couldn't even turn his head. The surface of the pool rippled out from the immobilized crab.

The deans of magicks flew within sight, Wanchoo riding bareback on Venkatarama. They hadn't even had time to saddle the dragon. Zee noticed that Amoxtli was with them this time, holding tight to the deans shoulder and unmoving, like she was a piece of armor. Wanchoo had his wand pointing at the crab, projecting a cone of yellow light.

"Are you all right, Mr. Tarrow?" said Venkatarama.

Zee, of course, couldn't answer.

The commandants circled, Aureosa shouting, "Get everyone out! Get them out!" Gold Class pairs that had accompanied them began retrieving recruits and cadets from the pool. Staff magickers lowered Platforms to the surface of the pool for swimmers to climb onto.

The crab's eyes glowed with crimson light, as did the water beneath it, and the monster began to move. Wanchoo and Rama groaned with effort. The crab's eyes flared. The cone of light failed. The crab lunged, and Zee dropped to the pool.

Zee surfaced to see the deans holding the monster back with their Shield, then the crab's claw smashed through it. Wanchoo and Rama Shifted to the side, avoiding the blow, and conjured a Testudo Globe around the beast. The Globe sizzled and blinked at the water line, then it, too, failed.

There were still too many swimmers in the water, too close for Aureosa and Vandalia to use their most powerful attack Abilities, but they shot a

Beam of fire at the creature that should have punched a hole right through its shell. Shaggy fur caught fire, but the crab shrugged it off and moved toward a group of dragons and their riders still in the water.

Jessup's roar sounded from a distance. The familiar heat of the bond flared, hottest in the krakenbond on Zee's chest. Zee dove, his chest flashed blue, and his stinger was in his hand. He shot upward and out of the water. He reversed his grip on the stinger and gripped it with both hands as he flew, then hit the crab at the center of its big eye, stabbing the stinger deep.

The crab lurched and bucked, shrieking, trying to reach Zee with its enormous claws. Zee's hands erupted in sizzling blue electricity. With a shout, his fists flashed, sending the power down the stinger's shaft and into the beast. The crab jolted, shook, then collapsed into the pool where it floated, steaming.

Zee jerked the stinger free and sat back on the dead creature's back, breathing heavily. Finally he lifted his eyes to find everyone except those still floundering in the water staring at him, including the commandants and deans.

"*I'm here, Zee!*"

Zee spotted his friend come running over the rise that separated the training fields from the pool.

Jessup stopped when he saw Zee sitting on the dead crab-monster. "*Oh... Are you okay?*"

"I'm okay," Zee said. "Wait... *Were you running? Like a spider?*"

Jessup grinned.

Everyone else continued to stare.

CHAPTER 41

Jessup tipped the dead chasmclaw onto its back on the beach, shaking the ground and sending up a cloud of dust. Magickers approached it cautiously, wands aimed, just in case. All recruits and cadets had been cleared from the area, the seriously injured flown to the infirmary. Mahfouz and Mildrezod moved somberly along a line of bodies, cadets and dragons alike, which Zee and Jessup had helped retrieve from the pool. Altogether, one knight pair, three cadet beasts, five cadet riders, and two recruits—a human and a dragon—had been killed. Over twenty had been injured.

Jessup shuffled over to where Zee sat on a stone bench facing Dean Wanchoo, who sat on a second bench carved into a boulder. Amoxtli launched herself from Wanchoo's shoulder and flew toward him. Jessup didn't flinch this time, but his eyes swiveled up, trying to see what she was doing as she landed and scampered up his shell in a spiral to hunker down on the point, seeming perfectly content. Venkatarama stepped to the side to give Jessup room to join them.

Zee leaned out to watch a group of faculty and staff up the beach in a heated discussion with Commandants Aureosa and Vandalia.

Wanchoo spoke, drawing his attention away from the conversation. "That's twice in less than a week you two have saved cadet lives."

Jessup said, "I didn't do anything."

"But you did, didn't you?" said Venkatarama.

Zee couldn't read the dragon's expression, but he feared it might be an accusation. They hadn't sparked their core, though.

Jessup didn't answer.

Zee looked back over his shoulder. The academy's chaplain, Antoon oh Connor, was saying prayers over the dead. The chaplain caught his eye and stared, his expression difficult to read. Zee looked away. "I didn't save all of them."

Rama gazed at the beach as well. "It's a hard truth in the military, learned through painful experience. You can never save everyone."

They sat quietly, then Wanchoo said, "May I see this weapon you used, Zee?"

Zee hesitated, then unwrapped the stinger and handed it to Wanchoo. He hadn't wanted to put it in his Keep while people were watching, but neither could he just have it disappear after everyone saw him use it, so he'd wrapped it in the shirt he'd been wearing when he'd arrived at the pool.

Rama moved closer to inspect it as well, then he and Wanchoo exchanged glances. Zee was pretty sure they were talking through their bond. Wanchoo closed his eyes and waved a hand over it, whispering words Zee didn't understand.

Strange symbols began to glow along its length. Zee held his tongue in spite of his surprise.

Rama said softly, "It's a wand..."

"I believe so," said Wanchoo, not taking his eyes off the stinger. "Though like none I've ever seen."

Zee peered at the symbols. They looked similar to the ones in the book Dr. Aenig had given him, but more like letters of a foreign language. "Can you read the writing, sir?"

Wanchoo shook his head. "I wish I could. I've never seen anything like them." He looked up from the stinger. "Did Dr. Aenig give this to you?"

A moment passed before Zee replied, "The crew found it on a salvage dive. All it did was zap, and not very well. They thought it was junk since it isn't gold or silver, so they gave it to the doctor when he said he'd like to have it."

Wanchoo said, "If it was one of ours, or of an allied nation, we'd have to confiscate it. I can guarantee you, however, it is not." He waved his hand over it again and the symbols disappeared. He handed it back to Zee, who rolled it back up in his shirt, inwardly breathing a sigh of relief.

Wanchoo spoke more softly. "This electrical power you manifested... Neither you nor Jessup sparked your core."

Rama said, "If you did, you are very good at masking its power if even we can't feel it."

Zee spoke softly as well. "We didn't spark it, sir, but we've been practicing Camouflage."

"Good lad."

"Jessup can produce electrical current naturally," said Wanchoo, "just as a Greatwing or Royal can produce fire. That you've become able to do the same is not entirely surprising. It's called a sympathetic Ability. They develop in riders of pairs who have a particularly strong bond, but they do not require a sparked core like other Abilities do. They usually don't manifest in anyone below Copper Class, and even then not for everyone. There are White Titans who don't have one."

Zee wasn't sure how to respond to that, but Venkatarama spoke, saving him the trouble.

"There are names for sympathetic Abilities, just as there are for common Abilities, but we've seen nothing like yours." He turned to Jessup, "What have you called it?"

"Um..."

"Go ahead, Jessup," Zee encouraged him. "You came up with it."

Jessup shuffled a bit. "Lightning Fists."

"I like it," said Rama.

Wanchoo smiled. "Quite appropriate." He leaned closer. "I wouldn't go around showing it off or lighting up the night just for fun, however."

Zee said, "I understand, sir."

Jessup beamed with pride. "Zee wanted to call it Sparky Paws."

"I did not." Zee chuckled, as much from being nervous as amused by Jessup's taunting. "Fennix said that."

Wanchoo said, "We'd heard Recruit Fennix was spending time with you."

Zee winced. Of course they knew. "Yes, sir."

Wanchoo's smile was genuine, though, and Rama was smiling as well when he said, "Young Fennix is well within his accommodations to visit you, as are you to receive him."

The crunch of boots on loose stone alerted them that people were approaching. Wanchoo's smile disappeared and Rama sighed with a deep-throated rumble.

Zee and Wanchoo stood as Aureosa and Vandalia led the group around the boulder. Those that followed lined up in a semicircle. Among them were Superintendent Hyooz and Dean of Academics Philliam sim Tooker.

"How are you holding up, Zee?" Vandalia asked.

"I'm fine, ma'am, thank you for asking." He'd been in similar life-threatening situations on the *Krakenfish*. Just like those times, and when he and Jessup had gone to help the fallen cadet pair, he'd done what he felt had to be done. And just like those times, the true danger to himself hadn't occurred to him until afterward.

Chaplain oh Connor joined the group, steering well clear of Jessup. Mahfouz and Mildrezod weren't far behind.

Dean Tooker cleared his throat. "How did this happen, Mr. Tarrow?"

"I don't understand, sir."

"You checked the pool prior to the beginning of the exercise, did you not?"

"I did, sir." At their silent stares, he added, "So did the other lifeguards."

"They aren't murfolk, though, are they?"

"No, sir."

"How is it that a creature of this size escaped your attention?"

"It must have been buried in the sand, sir." Truth was, Zee had been wondering about that himself. He'd always been able to sense danger when it was near, especially in the water, and that aptitude had only gotten stronger as his bond with Jessup had grown. How had he not sensed a twenty-foot-wide chasmclaw?

Hyooz looked around at the group. "The more pertinent questions are, How did it gain access to the pool, and when?"

"Indeed," said Tooker, though his accusing gaze at Zee didn't abate.

Zee felt Jessup's ire rising but calmed him the best he could.

"A crab that size could have climbed the wall," said Mahfouz.

Superintendent Hyooz replied, "There are always guards on the walls, as well as making rounds in the air."

"As much as I hate to admit it," said Aureosa, "it could be possible. If the sentries have passed by or are looking the other way, there could be a brief window of opportunity."

Tooker said, "To sneak in like that suggests a malicious intelligence the creatures are not known to have."

"Perhaps it tunneled in," said Mahfouz.

"The island is solid rock," said Mildrezod.

Superintendent Hyooz pushed her spectacles up on her nose. "Nonetheless, the base of the island should be checked by divers."

Zee said, "I can do it, ma'am." She glanced at him, but didn't answer.

Tooker said, "Chasmclaws are deep-sea dwellers. Scavengers. They rarely come to the surface, and never to hunt. What brought it here in the first place?" The eyes of the dean of academics fell on Zee once more, and the chaplain continued to stare with that unreadable expression.

Zee didn't know where this was going, but he didn't like it. Hadn't he just killed a monster that was attacking the academy?

Aureosa said, "This is ultimately my responsibility."

"And mine," said Vandalia.

"As commandants of this academy we are charged with not only the training and discipline of cadets, but their safety and the security of the citadel as well. There will be a thorough investigation into the matter and I will deliver a full report. Meanwhile, security details will be doubled."

"Your loyalty to the Dragon Corps and the academy are not in question, Commandants," said Superintendent Hyooz. She turned to gaze at Tooker over her spectacles.

"Of course not," said Tooker. "I have never doubted that you always have the best interest of the corps, the academy, and the kingdom at heart, Peleus." His eyes went to Jessup, then Zee. "As much as I may disagree with some of your courses of action."

"There is also the question of how the beast was able to shrug off the Beam of a Red Titan Class pair," said Vandalia. "Even if it could do such a thing naturally, it also resisted Wanchoo and Venkatarama's Viraam holding Ability and broke free of their Testudo Globe."

Wanchoo said, "The Abilities of even the most powerful magickers do not hold well in water. The beast was mostly submerged, and chasmclaws are naturally extremely powerful. This one is not, however, an entirely natural beast."

"What are you saying?" Hyooz asked.

Wanchoo and Venkatarama shared a look, then led the group to the crab, where Wanchoo climbed up between its splayed legs to its expansive underbelly. Aureosa followed without question. Amoxtli left Jessup and returned to Wanchoo's shoulder. The others hesitated but climbed atop the crab as well. Zee half expected to be told to wait on the beach, but no one said anything, so he joined them.

Wanchoo stared down at the broad plates of the crab's belly, which were devoid of the fur that covered it carapace, legs, and pincers. "It's as I suspected." The dragons came closer, rose on their haunches, and craned their necks to see.

Dozens of glyphs had been carved into the plates. Zee shuddered at the sight of them. They struck him as hideous and profane, though he had no idea why. From the looks on the faces of the rest of the group, they felt the same way. Chaplain oh Connor made the sign of Zepiter over his heart, whispering a prayer. When he looked to Dean Wanchoo, Amoxtli was cowering on his shoulder, ears flat back against her head. She whimpered softly.

Aureosa crouched and reached to one of the glyphs, but stopped with his fingers suspended above it. He pulled his hand back and stood. "What are they, Mihir?"

"I don't recognize the symbols or their configuration, but I assume they are wards, perhaps a spell or enchantment. My guess is there are some of all three. Stealth magick, wards against entrapment Abilities, possibly strength enhancement. We must consider that this beast could have been in thrall to a powerful magicker. Someone who could have sent it here."

"Who?" Hyooz asked.

"I don't know."

"I didn't think anyone practiced this kind of magick anymore," said Tooker.

"Neither did I. Not for hundreds of years, perhaps longer."

"We'll study these thoroughly," said Rama, "and call in our best scholars."

"Do that," Hyooz replied, "but I suggest we keep this on a need-to-know basis. That a wild beast was able to sneak onto Triumf's Island and harm students is bad enough. Word of a planned attack could start a panic."

"Meanwhile," said Vandalia, "we should maintain business as usual but with heightened security. I will see to it immediately."

Aureosa said, "We must inform the king as well. I'll dispatch a confidential letter as soon as I'm back at the citadel."

Zee's head spun as they all stood in silence. Jessup just stared down at the crab's shell. No words were spoken between them, but emotions flowed through their bond. Confusion and worry, but also the warmth of mutual support.

Tooker looked to Superintendent Hyooz. "There is also the matter of a kraken running loose across our training fields."

"No one was harmed, I take it?"

Aureosa shook his head. "Not that I've heard, and I would have heard by now."

Vandalia said, "His bondmate was in danger. I'm sure he can be forgiven this once."

Hyooz considered it, then nodded.

"Perhaps Mr. Tarrow and Mr. Jessup should be placed under watch," said Chaplain oh Connor, "at least temporarily."

"Why is that, Chaplain?" Aureosa asked.

"What if someone drew the creature here, perhaps even signaled when it was safe for it to climb the wall in the night. Chasmclaws, like all sea life, are children of Postune. So are murfolk and krakens. They could have known the creature was there in the pool all along."

Jessup growled, glaring at the chaplain. The man didn't appear frightened, but took the slightest step back. Zee was angry as well, but quelled it to help Jessup calm down.

"And why would they do such a thing?" Vandalia asked.

The chaplain tipped his head in deference. "I'm not trying to stir up trouble, but cadets and recruits have died, Zepiter rest their souls. We should consider all possibilities. I'm only positing one such possibility. Mr. Tarrow and Mr. Jessup wish to become cadets, but have been thwarted. At worst, it could be vengeance that drives them. At best, they wish to elevate themselves in the eyes of the faculty and staff and used the creature for that purpose."

Mahfouz's fists were clenched, but his voice held steady. "Zee was only informed of his appointment to the water survival exercises this morning."

"It could be a coincidence, but does anyone know what's actually wrong with the lifeguard he has replaced?"

No one was backing up the chaplain's theory, but Tooker and the superintendent both looked pensive. Zee couldn't believe this was happening, and he had to reassure Jessup that everything would be all right. Jessup wasn't convinced, but he understood that resorting to violence would only make things worse.

"Twice now, Zee and Jessup have saved lives on this island," said Mildrezod. "Lives that we ourselves, with all the might of the citadel, could not protect and would have been lost if it were not for them. Are you saying they also arranged for cadets to collide and fall into a burning ship?"

The chaplain's brow knitted. "Highly unlikely. It did provide an opportunity for them to prove themselves, however, and they did not hesitate."

"I would call that heroism," said Vandalia.

"Perhaps."

Dean Tooker said, "I propose we conduct an inquiry into the matter."

"This is ridiculous," Mahfouz spat.

Hyooz said, "Let's keep our heads, gentlemen, and our voices down." They glanced around. The attention of several magickers and knights quickly turned away, but they were all at the other end of the beach or high in the air, too far away to have heard the conversation. "We will reconvene in the boardroom at twenty hundred bells this evening. I'll request the presence of anyone else who should be involved in a meeting to discuss an official inquiry."

She took a deep breath. "Meanwhile, there is no evidence of wrongdoing on the part of Mr. Tarrow or Mr. Jessup. They will remain free to go about their business unless further evidence suggests otherwise. What say you, Commandants? Security is ultimately your purview without an official vote of the board to supersede it."

Aureosa and Vandalia answered together. "Agreed."

She looked around the group but none posed an argument.

Chaplain oh Connor simply said, "As you see fit, of course."

"We'll need to address the full student body, faculty, and staff as well. And we must send letters to the families of the deceased. I and my staff will take care of it. For now, I recommend you all attend to the injured and traumatized."

As one, they saluted. She saluted back, climbed to her dragon, and the two of them flew off toward the citadel.

Aureosa said, "Mr. Tarrow, Mr. Jessup, walk with me."

* * *

After speaking to Zee and Jessup, Aureosa and Vandalia flew straight to the citadel, where they landed on a wide balcony on the third floor. Wanchoo and Venkatarama were already there.

"The boy and the kraken?" Rama asked.

Vandalia said, "We don't believe they're going to swim off into the sea, if that's what you mean."

They stood quietly for a time, then Aureosa voiced what he knew to be on all their minds. "There was red light in the eyes of the crab."

Wanchoo said, "The glyphs on their underbelly glowed as well. No one else has spoken of it. In the madness of the attack, I doubt they noticed."

"If they did, they wouldn't know what it could mean," said Vandalia. "They might even assume it was something the crab did naturally."

Rama said, "I would assume the same if not for the terrible surge of power that accompanied it."

"But in a non-sentient beast?" Aureosa asked, then paused, brow furrowed. "Was it brought back?"

"There was no sign of that," said Wanchoo.

"And the glyphs?"

Wanchoo stared at the balcony floor. "I spoke the truth. Those are new to me—but the dread Rama and I felt from them was not." He looked up. "They radiate the same sense of foreboding horror that has haunted our dreams for many months."

CHAPTER 42

The setting sun was painting the horizon red and gold when Fennix winged his way around the mountain, deeply concerned for his newfound friends. If he were to admit it to himself, they were the only friends he had in the world, but he couldn't have asked for better.

He spotted Zee sitting on the ridge of rock that separated the ocean from their lake in the cavern, chin in his hands. Next to him, Jessup floated in the sea, anchoring himself with several arms on the ridge.

Fennix called out as he came in for a landing, "Are you all right, Zee?!"

He lit upon the ridge and strode closer, hopping on his good front leg.

"I'm okay, Fennix," Zee replied. "Thank you for asking."

Jessup said, "Zee is sad."

"I'm not sad. Just frustrated."

"I would have come sooner," said Fennix, "but our instructors wanted to keep us close for a while."

Zee said, "What happened was pretty crazy. I can't blame them."

"You should hear the wild stories that are circulating. Some said a chasmclaw fifty feet wide attacked in the training pool, killing everyone, including Gold and White Titan Class pairs. Others say Jessup ran across the entire island, raised high on his legs like a spider, crushing dragons and shaking the ground with his passing. Then the two of you engaged in a fierce battle with the beast, nearly bringing down the breakwall, and you slew it with an enchanted sword of blue light."

"Sounds about right to me," said Jessup.

Zee snorted, and a weak smile spread on his lips. "It was nothing like that, and you both know it." He blew air out between his lips and slumped. "It was bad, though."

Fennix said, "I'm very sorry this happened, Zee."

"I think everyone is, but thank you. And what about the courageous white Ice Diver prince who swooped from the sky, shining bright as the sun, and saved a hundred cadets and recruits from certain death? I heard he carried ten at a time."

Fennix grinned. "I wish. Though I pulled out quite a few."

"You're a hero," said Jessup.

"Hardly, my friend. I think the recruit Sallison anh Batcu got over a half dozen out."

Zee perked up. "Do you know her?"

"I only know she's among those vying for the top of her class. Do you?"

"No, I just thought you might."

Fennix glimpsed Jessup looking between the two of them in the awkward silence that followed. "Is it true, Jessup?" he asked. "Did you actually run like we've been working on?"

Jessup grinned. "I did, finally. I was fast. Thanks to you."

"The hard work was all yours, my friend. I just offered encouragement."

"I didn't step on any dragons, though."

"I didn't imagine so."

Zee said, "I could hardly believe it when I saw him come over the hill. It was amazing, and kind of scary."

"Even better," Jessup replied.

"How long have you two been working on that?"

Fennix looked to Jessup, who shrugged his okay, then said, "Several weeks. It's been... well, it's been a process, let's leave it at that."

Jessup said, "I tripped and fell down a lot."

"If it had been my vocation to train him, I would have asked for hazard pay." They laughed together.

"How didn't I know?" Zee asked.

"Jessup wanted it to be a surprise."

Zee looked to Jessup, who said, "Surprise!"

When their laughter subsided, Zee took a deep breath. "We might be in some trouble, though, Fennix."

He and Jessup explained what had happened after he'd killed the crab, sharing what Deans Wanchoo and Venkatarama had said, then the conversation with Superintendent Hyooz and the others, the accusations, and the possibility of an inquiry.

"That's preposterous," Fennix exclaimed. Then he sighed. "Though, and I hate to say it, I'm not surprised. Families of the cadets, and the board, will want an explanation and, more than likely, someone to blame."

Zee said, "After everyone left, Vandalia and Aureosa told us the superintendent didn't have a choice. She had to bring the request for an inquiry to the academic board. They're meeting tonight. We'll just have to wait and see how it goes."

After a period of silence, Jessup said. "Commandant Aureosa said if it was up to him and Vandalia, Zee would be getting a medal."

"You deserve one, Mr. Tarrow."

"I don't know about that."

"I also think both of you have much to be thankful for, even in this situation. It appears that the commandants and deans of magicks are firmly on your side. Those are some very powerful allies."

"I just hope it's enough," Zee replied.

"Also, it doesn't sound like anyone suspects that you've been forging."

"Nobody said anything about it." Zee felt bad about lying to Fennix. He and Jessup still hadn't told their Ice Diver friend the commandants and deans had known all along, and were the ones who'd sent Tem and Timandra to help them.

Jessup was taking it all pretty well, but Zee was still somber. Fennix tried to think of a way to cheer him up. Then a dragon roared out over the sea. The three of them watched as a knight pair swooped low then soared up and disappeared behind the mountain, headed toward the interior.

Fennix heaved a dramatic sigh. "I wish I knew what it was like to carry a rider." He glanced at Jessup out of the side of his eyes.

Jessup caught on quickly. "Zee has always wanted to ride a dragon."

"So you've said."

Zee said, "You've never carried a rider, Fennix? Not once?"

Fennix sighed again. "Sadly, no."

Zee looked back and forth between them. "You two do realize I know what you're doing, right?"

Fennix clutched his clubfoot to his chest. "I haven't the foggiest idea what you mean."

"Sure," Zee said. "But are you serious?"

"I am. It's a selfish offer on my part, though. I would be thrilled and honored to take you for a flight, Mr. Tarrow."

Zee turned to Jessup. "Are you sure you wouldn't mind?"

Jessup looked confused by the question. "Why would I mind?"

"I'd be riding someone other than you."

"That little thing? He probably won't be able to carry you for very long, anyway."

"Ho ho!" said Fennix. "That, sir, sounds like a challenge."

"It is. I challenge you to take Zee flying."

Fennix looked to Zee. "I'm sorry, but now we have to. My honor would be tarnished until the end of my days if I did not accept a formal challenge of this nature."

Zee shook his head but couldn't hide the grin that bloomed on his lips. Back to Jessup, he said, "Are you sure you're sure?"

Jessup crossed his two front arms and looked down at Zee. "I am sure."

"Okay, you win. And I win. We have to be careful, though."

Fennix said, "There's nothing in the Dragon Corps code of conduct or laws of Tosh that forbid an unbonded dragon to carry a rider, or a non-cadet to ride one. It's just rarely done."

"You've looked into this, have you?" Zee asked wryly.

Fennix's eyes darted about for a moment. "Perhaps…"

* * *

"I'm riding a dragon!" The thrill Zee'd felt since Fennix first leapt into the air had only grown stronger, and all his worries of the day had faded away.

"I'm carrying a rider!" Fennix shouted beneath him.

They'd waited for darkness, then Zee had climbed upon Fennix's back. Zee had been nervous but settled in much more easily than he'd expected. Memories of riding Midge came back to him, at once happy and sad. Happy for all the time he'd had with her, sad because he hadn't seen her in ten years. Riding a pig wasn't easy, and Zee recalled how he would have to grip with his legs and lean with her when she turned. Of course, a fall from a pig would be nothing compared to a fall from a dragon, but Fennix had assured him he'd be very careful.

So far Fennix had kept his word, not only to make Zee feel safe from falling, but also to avoid the two of them being seen. He'd flown around the base of the mountains, low and close to the water, beneath the view of any guard stations and far below the cadets' quarters, until the mountains blocked even the dim light of the newly risen moons, then straight out over the sea in the mountain shadows.

The waves sped by beneath them. For Zee's sake, Fennix made no tight turns or other sudden moves, but he wasn't holding back on speed. They weren't much higher above the water than Zee would sit when he rode Jessup, but the feeling was much different. There was no spray of the waves, no bouncing or splash, just the wind and gentle rise and fall with the beating of wings. Zee began to think the grin that split his face might be stuck there permanently.

Once they were several miles away from the island, Fennix angled upward toward a low layer of clouds. Zee felt his stomach drop and a strange queasiness as the ocean fell away beneath them. The nausea abated, replaced by a touch of vertigo, but soon that faded as well.

Even in the dark, he could see for miles in every direction. Then they entered the clouds, and he couldn't see a thing. It was very much like sailing through fog, but this fog got brighter as they ascended, until all of the sudden, they broke through into the clear night sky.

If Zee had thought he could see for miles before, here he could see forever. The stars were brighter than he had ever seen, casting light on the surface of the clouds below like moonlight on a rolling gray meadow that spread to the horizon in every direction.

Fennix circled, peering into the distance all around, searching for any other pairs in sight, then slowed to be heard better over the wind. "What do you think so far?!" he shouted.

"Are you kidding? This is fantastic! How is carrying a rider?"

"Every bit as wonderful as I'd imagined. Much easier than I would have thought as well. Entirely natural, if you get my meaning."

"Well, I'm not very heavy."

Fennix laughed. "That is true. Do you want to have some fun?"

"This isn't fun?"

"Of course, but *more* fun. Are you feeling secure back there?"

"I am, surprisingly so. It's actually easier than riding a pig."

"Pardon me?"

"Never mind," Zee said with a laugh. "I'll explain later."

Fennix shook his head, puffing icy mist as he laughed. "Lean farther forward and hold on tight. If I feel you coming unbalanced or slipping in the slightest, I will adjust accordingly."

Zee did as he was told, reaching to grip the spines higher on Fennix's neck and squeezing tighter with his legs.

Fennix flapped harder, increasing their speed, then swerved gently back and forth. When Zee had no problem hanging on and leaning into the turns, Fennix went faster and made the turns tighter.

They practiced like this for a time, climbing and diving as well, until it was clear they each had a good feel for the other. Then the real fun began.

Fennix shot up into the air and dove, spiraled, and even did a few loop de loops, both of them loosing whoops of excitement. Fennix didn't try the crazy aerobatics Zee had seen him do by himself, for which Zee was glad, but he did perform a long twirling dive that made Zee's head spin.

Fennix pulled out of the dive just above the surface of the clouds and flew over it. "How was that?" the dragon asked.

"Amazing. I think I'm a little dizzy, though."

"It used to happen to me all the time. You get used to it." They flew awhile longer, enjoying the view, and Fennix said, "I hate to say it, but we should probably be heading back. Jessup will be waiting, and we'll have to tell him all about it."

"He's going to be jealous. You'll have to give him a ride next."

"Oh, dear!"

They were both still laughing, skimming the starlit surface of the clouds, when Zee felt the sudden tingle of danger.

He just had time to shout Fennix's name when five dragons and riders shot up through the clouds in front of them. Fennix braked wildly with his wings to keep from colliding with them.

Zee recognized them immediately. Lukas tar Tarzian and his cadet flight. The last two meetings Zee'd had with them hadn't gone well. From the looks on the faces of both the riders and the dragons, he had a feeling this was going to be worse.

Tarzian shouted through a predatory sneer. "We thought that was you! The cripple and the freak!" Waves of energy swept over Zee as each of them sparked their cores.

Fire roiled in the maw of Tarzian's Royal Crimson dragon. "Burn!" it hissed, then blasted a column of searing flame. Fennix plunged into the clouds.

Zee hung on for dear life as Fennix dove, far faster than they had flown before. The fire hadn't touched them, but the heat had been incredible. Fennix leveled out in the thick cloud cover but continued flying fast.

Leaning forward as far as he could, Zee shouted, "Are they trying to kill us?!"

"They wouldn't dare!"

"Are you sure?!"

Fennix thought for a moment. "No. This far out, they could incinerate us and sink us with lava if they wanted to."

The back of Zee's neck tingled. "Turn to port!"

Fennix didn't hesitate, rolling to the left as more fire streaked down, vaporizing a swath of mist where they'd just been.

"Starboard!" Zee cried, and they avoided a Stream of ambergris lava from one of the other pairs. A blast of ice made the clouds flurry with snow, and more fire melted it. Zee shouted each time, and they barely avoided the attacks.

Instead of continuing to dive, Fennix swooped swiftly upward and climbed. He stayed below the upper surface of the clouds and sped through them. No more attacks came.

"They will find us," said Fennix. "We need to get back to the citadel. They truly wouldn't dare continue an attack within sight of the island."

"If we make it."

"There is that."

"Then let's see how fast you can really fly."

* * *

Fennix had flown faster but not often. Carrying a rider slowed him less than he would have thought, and Zee was a natural rider. A pang of remorse clutched his heart as he wished he could bond with Zee, but he knew that was impossible. Zee was a murman. There was no feeling of connection between them, and Zee was already bonded. He felt guilty for even thinking such a thing. Jessup was his friend. So was Zee. He forced himself to have faith that he would pass Basic once again, that this time he would find a rider, be bonded, and become a full-fledged cadet. He clung to that, let it fuel his heart, and pushed himself even harder, pumping his wings with everything he had.

Though he could barely see in the mist of the clouds, he didn't question that he was going the right way. Dragons had an innate sense of direction, and he was no exception.

Suddenly the clouds around them lightened, and they shot through the edge into clear sky, lit by the moons to the east and the stars above. Fennix could see the island, but it was still miles away.

Zee had remained silent, most likely to keep them from being heard by their pursuers. Then he spoke. "Don't look back, Fennix, just fly!"

"Are they pursuing?!"

"Yes." The murlad's voice was surprisingly matter-of-fact.

Fennix's mother had often told him he was more intuitive than other dragons. She said it was a gift from Zepiter to compensate for his physical disability. He'd been skeptical when younger, but had later realized she was right. He could sense the emotions of others. Right now there was no fear in Zee. No anger, either. Just a steely resolve.

Fennix kept himself in exceptional shape, but the muscles of his chest and neck ached from the sustained exertion of flying at top speed. He clenched his long jaw, breathed deep, and flew.

Fast as he was, however, no matter how hard he tried, he couldn't keep ahead of bonded pairs for long. Especially bonded pairs with the furnaces of their cores aflame.

Two of the pairs dove to fly in front of Fennix and Zee. At the same time a pair came up on their left and another on their right.

Tarzian's voice roared from above. "Gotcha!"

Fennix dove. Flames, ice, and lava, enhanced by the power of their attackers' cores, rained down around them. Zee shouted no warnings or directions. Tarzian and his flightmates weren't trying to hit them, Fennix presumed, but drive them into the sea. Perhaps they weren't trying to harm them at all, but just wanted to teach them a lesson, whatever that lesson might be in their cruel and twisted minds. The ocean, however, was also the perfect place to dispose of their bodies.

* * *

Sallison rocked up on her toes to ease the ache behind her knees—if anyone caught her moving more than that she'd get into even more trouble—and cursed her unruly tongue once more. She really didn't like nobles, though, with their arrogance toward anyone they deemed lesser than themselves and obsequiousness toward those wealthier and more powerful from whom they wished to curry favor. And it was just so much fun to goad them.

Luckily, she hadn't had to deal with many of them until she'd come to the academy, sequestered as she'd been behind the high gated walls of her home all her life. At least she'd been able to train and squire for one of her father's White Titan guard pairs. Now she was free. Well, more free.

Right now that meant free to serve her third night in a row of watch duty on the highest and coldest guard post on the dorm mounts, facing nothing but the sea. And she wasn't allowed to move. Stay still as a statue, she'd been told. No walking, no sitting, just staring at nothing for six bells straight. To be caught sleeping meant instant expulsion from the academy. No questions, no recourse. You were just out, and for good. It wasn't a problem keeping herself awake, though. Her bad temper and energetic nature took care of that. It was the standing still for so long that was torture. She wanted to scream and jump and run and train—maybe even make fun of more nobles, in spite of the consequences.

That thought brought a smile to Sallison's face, then it disappeared as she spotted something drop from the clouds, miles out over the sea. She squinted, trying to make out what it was. Then more specks came out of the clouds, and dim flashes appeared. She couldn't be certain, but it looked like a dragon was being attacked. Now she was allowed to move.

Sallison leapt to the telescope mounted on a tripod that was bolted to the stone of the ledge, swung it up and peered through it. She still couldn't see great detail, but it looked like a dragon with a rider was being pursued by five other pairs. She also couldn't identify which might be friend of the kingdom and which might be foe. Either way, whatever was happening, she was convinced it shouldn't be.

She'd been dying to ring the bell. She'd even entertained doing it just to see what would happen. This was her chance, and she wouldn't even get into trouble for it. Most likely. She grabbed the rope and yanked, then again, and again.

* * *

Zee yelled, "Watch out!"

Fennix launched into a succession of his swiftest evasive maneuvers—and he'd practiced them often. Their pursuers were trying to hit them now, and though Fennix tried every trick he knew, the flight kept driving them closer to the sea.

"Keep it up as long as you like, freaks!" Tarzian shouted. "You can only go so low!"

* * *

A fourth-year cadet pair swept down to the ledge, the rider wearing a deep scowl.

"This had better be legit, recruit!" he shouted.

Sallison didn't bother saluting, just pointed toward the horizon. "Dragon pairs incoming, sir. It appears to be an aggressive pursuit."

He and his Ebon Royal dragon whipped their heads toward the sea in surprise. The dragon turned back. "I can't identify them. Are they knights or cadets?"

"I can't tell, sir."

The foursies looked confused and appeared to be speaking through their bond.

Sallison grew impatient. "Sirs?"

The rider said, "If they aren't cadets, we have no business going out there."

After another nerve-racking pause, Sallison said. "Then go get someone who does!"

Anger at a recruit giving him orders flitted over the rider's features, then realization that she was right. The dragon leapt and they soared off around the mountain.

* * *

A streak of fire singed Fennix's tail, and a spatter of sprayed lava struck his back. His scales prevented either strike from burning deep, but there was pain. He gritted through it and kept flying. He hadn't worked this hard, for this long, to die this way. And he wouldn't let Zee die either.

In the sky near the mountains ahead, dark clouds approached swiftly, heat lightning flickering through them.

* * *

Sallison peered through the telescope in feverish apprehension. The dragon being pursued was an incredible flier, using swift aerobatic moves to evade a constant barrage of ice, fire, and Rock dragon ambergris.

The ledge grew darker, thunder rumbled overhead, and Sallison was hit by a strong gust of wind. She tore her eyes from the telescope. Where had that storm come from? It was moving fast, out toward where the dragons and riders were, its powerful winds kicking up waves as it advanced. And where was it going?

She pressed an eye back to the telescope. The dragons were closer now. The pursuing riders wore civilian clothing and she couldn't make out their faces. As for the fleeing pair... "Oh no..."

The dragon being chased was Fennix. But he wasn't paired... Who could be on his back, riding low and clinging tight to his neck? Was that the murman, Zee Tarrow?

* * *

Zee leaned even farther forward and spoke only as loud as he had to. "Get down as close to the surface as you can."

A moment of panic seized Fennix. "Are you going to jump?"

"No. Even without carrying my weight, you can't outfly them. I'm not leaving you. Jessup's coming, and we have a plan."

Fennix felt Zee's resolve grow even stronger. Fennix dove as instructed, evading more attacks. They gained a little distance on their pursuers, but not for long. Soon projectiles flew all around them once more.

Zee shouted louder than he had since the attack had begun. "Dive, Fennix, dive!"

* * *

"Well, we survived." Commandant Aureosa strolled to a table at his favorite outdoor café on the wharf and pulled back a chair. It would be good to relax after the somber address at the academy earlier, then the meeting of the Academic Board to discuss whether there would be a formal inquiry into Zee's role in the crab attack. Superintendent Hyooz had done most of the talking at the former, but he and Wanchoo had spoken the most at the latter. The motion for an inquiry had passed, but the vote to proceed would have to wait until the Board of Visitors could convene. Meanwhile, Aureosa had already launched a formal investigation into how the crab might have gotten in.

A flash of gold flew past and Amoxtli settled atop a post that held a string of Empyrean lights. Across from the commandant, Dean Wanchoo pulled back a chair of his own. "'Survived' is the right word, I'm afraid. And barely." He and a group of trusted magickers had removed the plates from the crab's belly, inspected its tissues and taken samples, then transported the plates to one of their academy laboratories to study the strange runes. He nearly shuddered at the feeling of dread they'd conjured within him.

They had just sat when a cadet pair landed in haste on the wharf. The man leapt from his dragon and ran to two Gold Class knight pairs on academy security duty who had been discussing something good-naturedly, side by side.

"Sirs! Ma'ams!" he shouted, addressing the dragons as well as the riders. He caught himself, stood to attention, and saluted. Once they'd saluted back, he blurted, "There's something happening."

"What is it, cadet?" Aureosa heard one of the dragons ask.

"I was informed by a recruit on night watch. We can't tell if it's cadets or knights who are involved. I didn't know who else to come to."

"Just tell us what's happening."

"The recruit used a spotting scope, but they're quite a ways out—"

The cadet's dragon interrupted him, "Sirs, ma'ams, it looks like a flight of pairs are attacking another pair out over the sea."

Aureosa got up from his chair and went to the deck railing. "Where is this happening?"

Both the cadet and his dragon's mouths dropped open at the surprise query from their commandant. The dragon recovered first. "Due west from the mountains, sir!"

Aureosa turned to Wanchoo, who had joined him at the rail. "I was so looking forward to a nice, quiet meal."

By the time he'd finished speaking, Vandalia and Venkatarama had rocketed down to land on the wharf, a great gust of wind sending the café canopies flapping.

* * *

Sallison grunted anxiously, eye pressed to the telescope. Fennix dove straight for the sea, spiraling one way then the other to evade his pursuers. She turned her attention on the attackers. She didn't recognize the riders, but the harnesses and saddlery of the dragons proved it. They were cadets. Her temper flared. Whoever they were, she'd find out, and if they hurt Fennix, she'd make sure they paid dearly. She had the connections to do it, too. No matter who their parents were, they would suffer.

With a jolt of guilt, she realized she hadn't even thought about Tarrow's safety. She didn't want Tarrow to be hurt either, of course, though she wondered if it had been the murman who had convinced Fennix to do something as stupid as taking him for a flight.

* * *

Fennix felt Zee lie flat on his neck and reach his arms around it as the dragon tucked his wings and plunged straight into the sea. Twenty feet down, he swam, using his narrow wings like fins. They stopped and looked up.

Flames roiled over the waves, shot through with globs of molten dragon ambergris. The fire didn't penetrate the surface, but the water boiled and steamed above. The lava quickly cooled and sank harmlessly.

Then the surface began to freeze. Fennix couldn't imagine how cold the breath of the Ice Diver above had to be to freeze salt water that quickly, but it was part of a bonded pair, and they had obviously sparked their core. A thick layer of ice spread out at a shocking rate.

Fennix began swimming to reach the outer perimeter of the ice. He was running out of air when they got to the edge and was forced to surface, blowing out the air in his lungs as he went. He barely had time to gasp another breath and glimpse that the storm was closer and darker before flames descended upon them and he had to dive again.

He looked back at the sound of something plunging into the water above. The Ice Diver had come in after them, its rider no longer on its back. Fennix's maneuverability was more limited in the water, and the other Ice Diver clamped its jaws down on the bone of his wing as he tried to roll away. Then Zee was sitting up, his stinger crackling with blue light in his hand. He stabbed at the dragon's neck. The beast's aura protected it from being skewered, but the stinger penetrated enough to zap it hard. The dragon recoiled, then glared at them with sheer hate, preparing to strike again.

Fennix realized something. He'd trained with the murman and kraken enough to know that if Zee was able to retrieve his stinger, that meant—

His thought wasn't completed when a kraken arm whipped around the attacking dragon and jerked it into the depths.

Fennix broke the surface of the waves, gasping. He tested the wing the other Ice Diver had bitten. It would be sore, but there was no serious injury. Zee surfaced next to him, no longer on his back. Blue light burned behind the murlad's eyes, which Fennix had seen before, but he also wore a feral smile. Fennix turned in the water to follow Zee's gaze.

The cadets circled, searching the water around the wide patch of thick ice, upon which stood the rider of the Ice Diver that had dived in after them.

Tarzian's dragon spotted them. "There they are. Sneaky little freaks!"

One of the other cadets shouted, "Lukas! Don't you think they've had enough?"

Tarzian shot the cadet a glare, then sneered. "No one will miss these two. We're doing Triumf's Island and the Dragon Corps a favor." His dragon's mouth lit with fire.

Black clouds darkened the sky, thunder rumbled overhead, and a deep voice reverberated from beneath the sea. "I AM HERE."

A powerful wind slammed into the dragons and riders, and the ice exploded beneath them in a flash of blue light.

* * *

Sallison gasped as the cadet who'd been standing on the ice went flying, flipping head-over-heels out over the sea. The cadets in the air were battered by broken ice and knocked away by the blast. Even from this distance she heard the dragons shriek as they flapped to right themselves, then finally got their wings under control.

At the epicenter of the exploding ice was the kraken, Jessup. He lifted the Ice Diver who had dived after Fennix and Tarrow and chucked it to flop though the air and splash down again. Then blue electricity arced across the kraken's spines.

* * *

Fennix looked to Zee, whose smile had transformed to an expression of fierce concentration. As relieved as he was that Jessup was here, he also feared they might do something they would regret.

Later, Fennix would be glad he hadn't been watching Jessup at that moment, because everything went blinding blue and white.

* * *

"Ah!" Sallison jerked her head away from the telescope and blinked frantically at the flashing globes that obscured her vision. Even in her distress, her mind tried to make sense of what she'd seen. Whatever the kraken had done, it had to be an Ability of some sort. She'd known that Jessup and Zee were bonded, but now she had no doubt they'd been forging as well. And not only that, they'd been working on attack Abilities.

* * *

The commandants and deans of magicks sped through the night sky, eyes on a cluster of black storm clouds that hung in the air above the sea about a mile away. Lightning flashed in spidery bolts, striking four objects in the sky. Except the lightning hadn't come from the storm. It had come from the sea. Aureosa and Wanchoo exchanged glances, then fed more power into their Streak Ability. They and their dragons shot forward, virtual streaks of golden light.

They slowed at their destination to find a flight of cadet riders floating on the waves among chunks of ice, and Jessup clutching Zee and Fennix close. Four of the cadet riders were groaning, clinging to dragons, who flopped groggily in the water. The fifth rider was swimming to his Ice Diver dragon, who reached out toward him with a wing.

Wanchoo and Venkatarama both eyed the sky above, where the last signs of the storm clouds were dissipating. Rama curved his neck to look back at Wanchoo, both of them struck with wonder.

More pairs arrived from the citadel, including two magicker pairs and the Gold Class MPs.

Aureosa sighed with relief that no one appeared seriously injured, or worse. Then his features became stern. "What is the meaning of this?!"

The cadets gulped and said nothing.

Aureosa turned upon Zee, who gulped as well. "Mr. Tarrow, perhaps you can explain?"

"I..." Zee looked to the cadets, then took a breath. "We were just training, sir. Perhaps we went a little too far."

"Mr. Fennix?"

"That's right, sir. We're very sorry about the trouble."

Aureosa scowled, then waved a hand at the academy pairs. "Get them out of the water. Bring them to the courthouse for questioning. We'll get to the truth of this, one way or another."

* * *

Sallison could see well enough to use the telescope once more, though spots still danced in her eyes. Knights were loading the downed cadet pairs onto Platforms conjured by magickers. To her great relief, Fennix was all right. And the murman too. It struck her as odd that the kraken was holding them both close, keeping them out of the water and safe. Fennix didn't even seem to mind. They must know each other well. She'd have to think on that.

Meanwhile, the others didn't look so good. Whatever shape they were in, they deserved whatever they'd gotten.

She jumped back from the telescope as the foursie pair who had come when she rang the bell suddenly filled her field of view. From the look on the rider's face, he hadn't come to congratulate her diligence. Most likely to reprimand her for disrespecting him earlier.

The dragon settled on the ledge and said, "Minny anh Batcu, we were planning to gather anyone on watch who might have seen what transpired, but when the commandants learned that you had sounded the alarm, they asked for you specifically. We're to take you straightaway."

Instead of being relieved, Sallison winced. This might be worse. Maybe Aureosa and Vandalia knew she was being punished for shooting off her mouth. Again. They might give her a talking-to, which would be bad enough—but they might also tell her parents...

CHAPTER 43

Zee sat in a chair across the desk from Commandant Aureosa, trying not to fidget under the man's unblinking gaze. It didn't help that the collar of the overalls he'd been given to wear itched at his neck.

Finally the commandant spoke. "I know very well what kind of person Lukas tar Tarzian is, and his dragon is as vicious as he is. When it comes to bonding, like is attracted to like more often than not. His flightmates don't have quite the same personalities, but they are loyal to their flight leader. I can't entirely blame them. It's how they're trained."

Zee wasn't sure what reply the man wanted, so he just said, "Yes, sir."

"I'm also aware of a recent incident at a tavern in town. I'm not privy to all the details, but I do know that Tarzian and a certain young murman were involved."

Zee swallowed but stayed silent.

"The recruit on night watch who rang the alarm has testified that you and Fennix were indeed being attacked, and any claims it was a training exercise are false. She used more colorful language than that, but that's how it's been logged. Personally I believe the cadets were in the wrong, and they will be punished accordingly, though what form that will take is not up to me. These kinds of things are decided by an academy tribunal.

It's not strictly illegal for you to have ridden Fennix. The fact remains, however, that your kraken attacked cadets of the citadel."

Zee's anger flared—not at Aureosa, but at Tarzian and his lackeys. "In defense of me and Fen—" Zee cut himself off.

"As I suspected." Aureosa leaned back in his chair. "Regardless of the reason, there are already members of the faculty and the Academic Board crying for your heads—not literally, thank Zepiter. Not yet, anyway. But with the rumors that are spreading about the chasmclaw attack, the possibility of an inquiry, and now very strong evidence that you and Jessup have been forging, we find ourselves in a difficult situation."

Aureosa's expression had changed from stern to worried, even sympathetic. Zee flushed with shame and regret. He felt terrible about putting Aureosa in this position after all the man had done for him and Jessup. He never should have flown out on Fennix. Not today, anyway. "I'm very sorry, sir. If it helps, Jessup held back. He could have killed them, but he didn't."

"I'll do what I can, but since you're a civilian, the township also has jurisdiction in this case. A combined village court and military tribunal are convening now." He pushed up from his chair, then looked as if he was about to say more but decided against it. Instead, he called out, "Next!"

Zee stood as the door opened. A knight security officer entered and led him out.

As he passed through the doorway he found himself face-to-face with Lukas tar Tarzian, who also had a security officer gripping his arm. Tarzian didn't look Zee in the eyes, just scowled at the floor, face flushed and sweating. Zee was pulled away and Tarzian was led inside.

* * *

The handcuffs rattled as Zee tried to twist his wrists into a more comfortable position behind his back. Security officers stood at either side.

Zee had been questioned by the town and military judges together, and now he'd been waiting on the wharf across from the town courthouse for more than two bells.

At the edge of the wharf, Jessup waited as well. A half dozen knight pairs and several magicker pairs had been posted around him, and more circled in the air above. All of them were White Titan Class.

Jessup had also been questioned, and had stuck to Zee's story. After all these years, Zee still felt bad about lying, even if he felt it was the right thing to do. Considering how he and Jessup were already looked down upon, even despised, and may be subject to an inquiry soon, saying that Tarzian and the others had attacked him and Fennix, even intent on killing them, might make people hate him and Jessup even more. Zee had no idea what Fennix may have said when he was questioned, but he trusted their new friend, and Fennix was smart. He wasn't in a much better position than they were. He didn't need enemies either. Regardless, a deep worry passed between Zee and Jessup through their bond.

Zee said, "*However this turns out, Jessup, thank you for coming to help us.*"
"*I'm sorry for doing it the way I did.*"
"*Don't be sorry. I'm sorry for putting you in that position.*"
"*We can both be sorry, then leave it at that.*"
"*You are a wise big kraken,*" Zee said. "*On the bright side, we succeeded in controlling Lightning Blast, and it feels like we finally classed up to Copper.*"

Zee could sense Jessup was smiling inside, though it didn't show on his face. "*I felt it too,*" his friend said. "*Lightning Blast still needs work, though. There were many wasted bolts of lightning.*"
"*We'll work on it when all this is over.*"
"*And we're still terrible at Lightning Bolt.*"

Zee turned at the sound of heavy, clawed footsteps. Fennix came around the side of the courthouse, flanked on both sides by much larger knight dragons. He met Zee's gaze, then nodded slightly. Zee could only assume Fennix had continued to back up Zee's story and mentioned nothing about forging.

Empyrean lamplight spread across the worn wooden planks of the wharf as the courthouse doors opened. To Zee's surprise, Sallison anh Batcu stepped out, holding her helmet in one hand and scratching her shaved head. She seemed just as surprised at seeing Zee between two guards and in handcuffs, and she frowned. Then she saw Fennix guarded closely by two knight dragons, and her frown deepened.

Zee realized she must be the recruit on watch Aureosa had told him about. He wasn't sure what to say to her. She'd told a very different story than he, Jessup, and Fennix had. But it had been the truth. He could never fault anyone for that. "Thank you sounding the alarm, Recruit anh Batcu, and for testifying on our behalf."

She eyed him for a moment. "I didn't do it for you." She tipped her head toward Fennix. "I did it for the dragon."

Zee felt like he'd been punched in the gut. Maybe deservedly so.

* * *

"I don't know what you thought you were doing," Sallison continued, "but you know this is his last chance at Basic, right? The last thing he needs right now is trouble like this." Her temper was rising, and she knew it, but she didn't care. Zee and Fennix appeared to be friends—how that had happened, she had no idea—but friends didn't encourage friends to risk getting kicked out of the citadel and lose everything they'd worked for, everything they dreamed of.

Fennix said, "Sallison, taking Zee for a ride was my idea. I'm the one to blame."

"Not the only one," said Jessup. "I encouraged it."

Sallison didn't know what to think of Jessup, but her temper deflated as she gazed at Fennix, punctured by his words. "Well... you should know better."

The last vestiges of her anger vanished as the little Ice Diver with a clubfoot smiled. "You'd think so, right?" Sallison couldn't help but smile in return. "I told Zee I'd never had the privilege of taking a rider to the sky. That in itself isn't uncommon for a dragon recruit, of course. What I did not tell him, what was truly on my mind and weighing on my heart, was this: if I didn't pass Basic and find a rider to bond with, there was a good chance I never would."

Fennix's smile still lingered, but it was touched with sadness.

Sallison, on the other hand, was on the verge of tears. Zee and the kraken gazed at Fennix with deep sympathy. The three of them were definitely friends. The best of friends.

She was struck with a pang of jealousy. She didn't have friends like that. Plenty of adults looked after her and cared about her, and she had her brother and sister, but that was different. She'd become attached to a few of the other recruits, but she purposefully kept an emotional distance from them. She resolved not to do that so much.

"You will pass, Recruit Fennix," she found herself saying. "And you *will* be paired."

"That is very nice of you to say," Fennix replied.

"I'm not just saying it."

She must have sounded extremely sure of herself. Even the guarding riders and dragons were staring at her. Fennix appeared to be at a loss for words.

The courthouse doors opened once again. Sallison stepped out of the way and found herself standing closer to the small Ice Diver.

* * *

Dean Philliam sim Tooker was first out the door. "There is no denying the kraken attacked our cadets, Peleus." Tooker's voice was even and measured, but he wore a hint of a scowl.

"I don't deny it," Aureosa answered, taking Tooker off guard. "We can't prove it based on the conflicting testimonies, but it's my belief that Mr. Tarrow and Mr. Fennix were being assaulted with deadly force, with no provocation other than the fact they are different."

Vandalia stepped from up the wharf with Venkatarama. "Mr. Jessup did exactly what any dragon would do for its rider."

Tooker had no reply.

In his usual impassive tone, Chaplain Antoon oh Connor said, "From the descriptions of the attack, there may now be enough evidence that they have been forging as well. That should be added to the inquiry proposal."

"We have no proof of that," said Dean Wanchoo. "For all we know, small bursts of lightning are something krakens can project as naturally as a Greatwing breathes fire."

"There is also the question of an unholy storm."

"Are you saying that krakens and murfolk can control the weather?"

The chaplain held up his hands. "We know almost nothing about them."

Venkatarama snorted.

"The inquiry notwithstanding," said Aureosa, "both judges agree, whether they're forging or not has no bearing on this case. The laws against forging outside of the academy specifically name humans and dragons. They say nothing about murfolk and krakens."

Tooker said, "Perhaps the laws need to be changed."

Zee listened to the exchange, but couldn't tell if things had gone well or terribly. The bright side was it sounded like none of the cadets had said anything about feeling Zee and Jessup spark their core, which meant their Ability to Camouflage it had worked perfectly, the cadets had kept it to themselves, hadn't noticed, or, Zee wondered, if perhaps they couldn't feel a core being sparked under the water. He'd have to ask Tem and Timandra if they'd help him and Jessup test that out. That depended, of course, on what happened now.

More faculty and staff came through the door, including Dame Toomsil, followed by Tem. Meik Tabacchi and Androo Cobbling were there as well. They must have been called in to testify as to Zee and Jessup's character. Zee was grateful for that, and felt a little less nervous.

The town judge strode out last, followed by the military judge. The town judge called out, "Mr. Zee Tarrow."

Zee stood straight, trying to hold his nerves in check and keep the anxiety out of his voice. "Yes, Your Honor."

"For your part in the assault on academy cadets by your bonded beast, you are sentenced to thirty days." The judge frowned, then continued. "Your sentence shall be served in the citadel brig instead of the town jail, at the commandants' request."

The military judge stepped forward. "As for Mr. Jessup, since no one was seriously injured, you will be put on probation and continue to work on the docks. Since the two of you are bonded and Mr. Tarrow will be incarcerated, it's expected you'll be on your best behavior. This arrangement has always worked well for bonded riders and dragons. If there is the slightest infraction on your part, another thirty days will be added to Mr. Tarrow's sentence. Is that understood?"

Jessup stared at the group, his feelings difficult for even Zee to read. After a tense few seconds, he said, "No."

Members of the group looked to each other in confusion.

The town judge said, "No, what, Mr. Jessup? What part do you not understand?"

"I understand all of it, ma'am. No, I will not work. Put me in chains. Large chains. I will serve the same sentence as Zee."

Zee's initial reaction was disbelief—but this was Jessup. He should have known his friend would react this way. Still, he pleaded with him. "Please don't do this, Jessup. I'll only feel worse."

"I would feel worse knowing that you were in jail while I was free. I am also aware that I have a short temper. If I were to do anything to lengthen your sentence, I wouldn't be able to forgive myself. It will be better this way, for both of us."

Zee's throat clenched and tears formed in his eyes. His friend was sacrificing his freedom, just for him. With his hands cuffed behind his back, Zee couldn't even wipe his eyes.

He felt a warmth of comfort coming from Jessup. The kraken spoke through the bond, his voice practically cheery. *"Don't worry about me. I can sleep for thirty days. It will be nice to have a rest from all that training you make me do."*

Zee almost laughed but managed to keep it to a soft snort. He turned back to the judges. Most of those watching looked as if they were in shock. Zee wasn't sure if it was at what Jessup had said or because he spoke so well and was obviously not just a dumb beast.

The judges waved Superintendent Hyooz, Commandant Aureosa and the other lead faculty close. After a quick exchange, the military judge cleared his throat and announced that, per Jessup's request, he would be incarcerated as well.

From the smug looks on the faces of some of the faculty and staff, Zee was more convinced there were plenty of people who weren't happy with a murman and a kraken being on the island, in the academy or not. From the expressions of some, the sentence wasn't harsh enough.

"Recruit Beast Fennix," the military judge continued, "you stretched the limits of your special accommodations by flying so far from the island, but we find that you have not broken any specific laws or academy regulations. You will return to Basic Military Training. However, your accommodations to train outside of the regular Basic regimen are hereby revoked, and any infraction will be grounds for immediate dismissal. Is that clear?"

Fennix bowed. "Yes, Your Honors. A wise and fair judgment."

To all gathered, the military judge said, "In addition, while it is not strictly illegal for a murman and kraken to bond or forge and has no bearing on this particular case, we feel it's important to have that information on file. Therefore, we are issuing a court order that Mr. Tarrow and Mr. Jessup be assessed for a bond rating. They are to appear before the Orb of Assessment tomorrow morning at oh nine hundred bells."

Zee caught Aureosa glancing almost imperceptibly at Wanchoo. An assessment would prove beyond a doubt that he and Jessup had been forging. Like the judge had said, it wasn't strictly illegal for them to do so, but the chaplain and Tooker seemed to want to challenge that as part of their inquiry. That worried him less than what proof of their forging might lead to, though—like an investigation into how they learned to forge, and beyond that, maybe even how they developed their Abilities.

That could cause problems for the commandants, deans of magicks, and maybe Tem and Timandra most of all. If the inquiry was made official and they had to appear for a hearing and testify under oath, would he be able to lie to protect them? Would they tell the truth if put in the same position? He just didn't know. In a way, this was worse than being sentenced to the brig.

On the other hand, he wanted badly to know exactly what class and level he and Jessup had achieved, and a real assessment was the only way to accomplish that. Apprehension, guilt, and anticipation all mixed together made for a nauseating emotional state. He took deep breaths to ease the turmoil.

The town judge said. "Thank you for your service today, everyone. This joint court and tribunal is adjourned."

* * *

Sallison wasn't exactly sure why she had stayed, but she was glad she had. What the kraken had done amazed her. That he'd purposely allowed himself to be chained for a month meant his and Tarrow's bond must be incredibly strong. She could only hope to have such a bond one day. And they were going to be assessed tomorrow. She couldn't imagine how that might turn out, but she'd make sure to find out.

Lost in her thoughts, she barely noticed when Zee was lead one way, Jessup the other. In fact, nearly everyone was gone already. Then that odd feeling came over her again, and she turned.

Fennix's guard dragons had left, and he stood watching Jessup shuffling away down the wharf, escorted by the White Titan pairs.

"He'll be all right," she said.

He turned back to her, then smiled. "Walk back with me? I'm quite frightened of the dark, you know."

"Liar."

Both of them laughed, then headed toward the Basic Training fields, chatting all the way.

CHAPTER 44

As soon as Zee was locked in his cell, he reached out to Jessup. *"How is it so far? Are they treating you badly?"*

"The first thing they did was feed me fish. If they keep doing that, I will be happy."

"Maybe I won't worry about you so much then."

"Don't worry about me at all, Zee."

"Maybe just a little? It bothers me that you can't move around or swim."

"Okay, a little. I'm fine, though. You just take care of yourself. If they do bad things, tell me and I will break these chains and come get you."

"Don't you worry about me, either." Zee thought for a second. *"Do you think you could break the chains?"*

"Maybe. They are big chains, though. I think they are enchanted, too."

Zee sighed out loud. Having Jessup being locked up was worse than being in the brig himself. He could feel that his friend was okay, though, and he knew that keeping calm himself would help Jessup, too. *"We're going to be assessed tomorrow."*

"I'm excited."

"Don't get your hopes up. We don't even know for sure if the Orb will be able to assess a murman and a kraken. And if it does, I'm worried about how that will

affect the people who have helped us." He explained his concerns to Jessup, who was less familiar with how inquiries and hearings worked.

"*We should be careful, then,*" Jessup replied. "*I want to know what level we are, too, but not if it gets them into trouble.*"

"*I don't know what we can do, either way. We'll just have to see.*"

"*It will be what it will be.*"

Zee smiled. "*The wise big kraken speaks again.*" He could tell that Jessup was grinning. "*Talk to me anytime you want. See you in the morning.*"

"*I'm looking forward to it.*"

"*Me too.*" They said their goodnights.

* * *

A bell later, Zee was on his fifth set of pushers. Being locked up for a month would be bad enough. The least he could do was try to stay in shape. The bar on the heavy cellblock door clunked as it was lifted on the outside, and the door opened. He stood and swung his arms to work out the burn in his chest. The five cadets filed in, one guard ahead of them, one behind.

There was just one cellblock in the academy brig, twelve cells on either side of a single hall. Until the cadets arrived, he'd been the only one in it. There apparently weren't many disciplinary problems at the academy. Not that resulted in incarceration, anyway.

Tarzian glared briefly at Zee, then went back to scowling at the ground. The others just looked ashamed, even afraid. One by one they had their cuffs removed and were placed in individual cells, three of the cadets across from Zee, two more in cells beside his, including Tarzian. The walls between cells were stone block, for which Zee was glad. At least he wouldn't have to put up with Tarzian glaring at him every day for a month.

The creak of cots being sat on and heavy sighs came from the other cells. The cadet across from Zee looked up but quickly looked away when he saw Zee was watching him. Someone rattled their door, testing it. Probably Tarzian.

One of the cadets said, "How long are you in here, Chandley?"

"Fifteen days," came the reply. "You?"

"Same. Tadcliff?"

"Same here."

All reported they were sentenced to fifteen days, except Tarzian. He'd received thirty.

Zee got down to the floor, wedged his feet under the bars of his cell, and began his fifth set of crunchers.

The cadet directly across the hall said, "How about you, Tarrow?"

Zee was surprised he'd been addressed at all, let alone that it was a question unaccompanied by a derogatory epithet or a gibe. He tried not to let his surprise show and kept doing his crunchers. The name tag on the cadet's overalls read "och Dominick." Zee recognized him as the one who had questioned Tarzian when they were attacking Zee and Fennix.

"Same as Tarzian, thirty days," Zee answered.

Zee couldn't see Tarzian, but he was sure it was him who harrumphed.

Dominick was quiet for a moment, then asked, "What about your kraken?"

"He's not my kraken, any more than your bondmate is your dragon."

"Fair enough."

Zee was inclined to leave it at that but decided to answer the question. "He's chained to pylons in the harbor."

Dominick looked surprised. "Our dragons are back in training. They just have to stay out of trouble."

"Jessup was told the same, but to go back to work. He refused."

"Why?"

"Because he's my friend."

The other cadets were silent while Dominick thought that over.

The cadet in the cell next to Dominick looked up from where she sat on her cot. Her name tag read "en Zendaya." "Couldn't he just break his chains?"

Zee considered how to answer and decided on, "Maybe."

She and Dominick appeared to be worried by that answer, which was just the reaction Zee had hoped for. "He's being guarded by White Titan

Class knights and magickers," he added.

That didn't seem to make them feel any better, which pleased Zee even more.

Dominick came to the front of his cell and rested his hands on the bars. "Why didn't you say anything when you were questioned by the commandant and the judges?"

Zee finished his crunchers and stood. "What makes you think I didn't?"

"You said we'd been training when they first found us, and I was told you gave no testimony of self-defense."

Zee didn't respond.

"The judges can lie during questioning," Dominick continued, "but if they were going to, they'd say the opposite. That you spilled your guts and said we attacked you and Fennix unprovoked. Maybe even tell us they'd understand if we did it. Try to get us to gloat about it or goad us into getting angry and saying something we shouldn't and incriminating ourselves. I know how it works. My mother is a judge, and my father is a barrister."

"I didn't see the point," Zee replied. "Tosh needs riders, especially now. You could have been expelled."

"What do you mean, especially now?"

Zee wasn't sure why he was talking to them at all, but he didn't see the harm in it, and staying that long in a cell without any conversation wouldn't be pleasant. "When I was on ship, before I came here, there was talk about larger and more aggressive monsters in the sea. I hear things while working on the docks, too. The ocean is getting even more dangerous, and there are rumors of pirates in unmarked ships, painted ghostly white and gray, that come out of the fog and take ships. Even knight pair escorts disappear. Supposedly the only survivors are found floating on lengths of timber, babbling crazy."

Zendaya said, "For real?"

"It's hard to tell. Nobody at the academy is saying anything, and you know how sailors are with their tales. They call the pirates Wraiths. Some say they really are wraiths."

"He's just trying to scare us," said the third cadet on the far side. Zee couldn't see her name tag.

"It's working on me," said Zendaya.

Tarzian said, "If any of this is true, we'll just work that much harder to advance when we get out of here."

So would Zee.

* * *

At half past eight bells the next morning, Zee was led out of the brig to find Deans Wanchoo and Venkatarama waiting for him.

Together, the deans of magicks said, "Good morning, Mr. Tarrow."

"Good morning, sirs."

Zee had felt Jessup's presence and now saw him approaching with his White Titan pair escorts. They had already said their good mornings and spoken earlier, so they both just grinned at seeing each other.

Amoxtli perked up at the kraken's approach and flew from where she'd been perched on Rama's head to her favorite place on top of his shell. Jessup just rolled his eyes.

Dean Wanchoo had Zee's handcuffs removed and dismissed the guards. "We'll return them when the assessment is complete."

Once they were away from the brig and headed along a path to the citadel, Zee said, "We're sorry about this, sirs. We don't want to get you into any trouble."

"Don't worry about us," Wanchoo replied, "We've gotten into worse over the years, and we're still here. The inquiry may never materialize. Even if it does, and it comes out that we aided you in your forging, the worst they would do is slap us with a reprimand. We are generals and Red Titans, you know."

Zee thought it was probably more serious than the dean was letting on and he was just trying to make Zee and Jessup feel better, but he appreciated it anyway. "Thank you, sir."

"Temothy and Timandra have told us you're forging both Empyrean and Marisean at the same time," said Venkatarama.

Zee suspected they'd been reporting he and Jessup's progress to the commandants and deans of magicks, so he wasn't surprised. "Yes, sir,"

Wanchoo said, "You found Peleus's notes, I take it?"

"Yes, sir. I assumed he put them there on purpose."

"He did, of course."

"But, why? We know he shouldn't have."

A corner of Wanchoo's lips lifted a touch. "I believe you remind him of himself when he was your age."

"It must be the gills," Jessup interjected.

Rama snorted black smoke and chuckled.

Wanchoo feigned being taken aback. "My goodness, Mr. Jessup, you've made Venkatarama laugh." He held a hand up to his face as if to keep Rama from hearing. "The dragon dean of magicks is not well known for his sense of humor."

Rama frowned, but agreed. "It's true."

Zee grinned at the two of them. The deans of magicks at Triumf's Citadel Academy, joking around in his presence. Who would have thought?

Wanchoo said, "It's the most natural thing in the world for a young bonded pair to forge. You would have figured it out one way or the other. This way you had some early guidance, which is not only more efficient, but safer as well."

"I remember you saying that before. Can forging really be dangerous?"

Wanchoo held up a finger. "I'm glad you asked. That is something we wanted to talk to you about. Early forging can be inefficient, overly difficult, and time-consuming if done without supervision, but it's very rarely harmful. There is, however, something called over-forging. It's rarely brought up at the academy since only pairs with exceptionally strong crucibles, and particularly those who are also a tad overzealous, are at risk. Cadets simply don't develop crucibles strong enough for anyone to worry about it. We believe you two, however, fit both criteria."

Zee wasn't sure if that was a compliment or a reprimand. Maybe both.

Dean Wanchoo continued, "Some bonded pairs get it into their heads that the more compacted their cores are, the more powerful they'll be, and they could also fit more formed Empyrean into their crucible. That is not the case. Once your core is formed, never attempt to form it further without first mining and refining more ore. Undue pressure on the core can cause it to crack, releasing more energy than your crucible can handle. Your crucible can be damaged, your core can spontaneously spark on its own, and your Abilities may even manifest accidentally."

"That would be bad," said Jessup.

"Indeed," said Rama. "Furthermore, if you continue to compress your core, it can detonate in a truly magnificent and devastating fashion. We have seen a cracked core, which can repair itself over time, but never a detonation, which cannot."

Zee said, "You mean, it could kill us?"

"You and everyone else within a quarter mile in every direction."

Jessup said, "Duly noted, sirs. Don't make our core go boom."

Wanchoo chuckled. "I couldn't have said it better myself."

Rama said, "Temothy and Timandra have told you about the dangers of stretching your crucible too far, I assume?"

"Yes, sir, and we try to be careful."

"Good."

Wanchoo said, "Now, there are some things you should be aware of prior to this assessment. Even if the Orb can assess a murman and kraken, it may only be able to rate you for your level of Empyrean."

Zee had expected that might be the case but was disheartened nonetheless. He felt that Jessup was too. They might not learn their true class and level at all.

Then Rama said, "In fact, that's what we're hoping for."

Zee nearly stumbled. "Why, sir?"

Wanchoo said, "For one thing, we should continue to keep your Marisean a secret, if possible. We have enough trouble for now. For another, if there is one thing people fear more than what they don't understand, it's power greater than their own. And fear can make people do drastic and terrible things. We also don't need to give them any more reason to pursue their inquiry than they already have. If your core is as large and your crucible as strong as Tem and Timandra tell us they are, Marisean notwithstanding, a full assessment could cause further resentment against you that you just don't need, even jealousy."

"Jealousy? Of us?"

"Consider it this way," said Venkatarama. "The two of you brought down an entire flight of third-year, Bronze Class cadets quite easily, and with a single strike. Word is already spreading."

Zee and Jessup exchanged glances, then Jessup spoke earnestly and with the proper amount of contrition. "We understand, sirs." Inside, though, Zee knew the kraken was feeling pretty good about himself.

Wanchoo said, "We appreciate that you want to know exactly what your class and level are, and you will. Just not yet."

"When, sir?"

"I wish we could say. Believe me, we would very much like to know ourselves." He flashed Zee a reassuring smile. "Even with an assessment of your Empyrean only, we may be able to make a much closer estimate of your true class and level."

Encouraged, Jessup nudged Zee, nearly knocking him over. Zee chuckled softly while the deans of magicks just looked at them.

"There's one more thing," Wanchoo added. "How well have you two mastered your Camouflage Ability?"

CHAPTER 45

The ranking faculty and staff had already gathered in the courtyard when they arrived. Wanchoo called Amoxtli to his shoulder, then instructed Zee to climb up on Jessup's shell and the two of them to approach the apse-like structure that contained the Orb of Assessment. They did so, standing the same distance from it they'd seen the cadet pair doing when they'd been on their way to the combat exhibition.

They were using Camouflage to just the level they'd practiced while walking along the path to the citadel. Apparently the Orb would see right through it, so it wouldn't affect the assessment, but it would hide the feel of their core's full size. In fear they were Camouflaging their core strength either too much or too little, Zee scanned the faces of the crowd, but no one seemed to suspect anything.

He concentrated on controlling his nerves. Seeing Dame Toomsil, Peloquin, Tem, Timandra, the commandants, and Beastmasters Mahfouz and Mildrezod among the others eased his anxiety a bit. He and Jessup just had to hope this went well, for all of their sakes.

Wanchoo said, "Venerated Orb, we have a bonded pair in need of assessment."

The Orb began to glow with white light, then rose to float above the top of the plinth where it had been sitting. It spoke in the same strange voice Zee had heard before, sounding almost like several voices speaking from a cave at once, and in perfect sync. "Proceed."

"Rider Zee Tarrow and Beast Jessup reporting for bond assessment."

The Orb grew brighter and spoke again as its words were written in the air in flowing cursive.

Rider: Zee Tarrow
Beast: Jessup
Rating: Bond

The Orb began to turn. Then it dimmed, pulsed a few times, and flickered. Murmurs arose in the crowd, and Zee held his breath.

Jessup reached out through their bond. *"What is it doing, Zee?"*

"I don't know," Zee replied nervously. *"It didn't do this when we saw the cadets being assessed."*

He glanced at Wanchoo and Venkatarama, then Commandants Aureosa and Vandalia, but they were all silent, watching the Orb as if nothing was wrong. Still, they seemed to almost imperceptibly relax as the Orb brightened again, the white light that shone through its facets turning to yellow, and it said, "Commencing assessment."

The Orb projected a cone of light, the yellow spots from its facets swarming over Zee and Jessup. Zee shivered under its scrutiny. It wasn't cold, but Dame Toomsil had been right. It was like ants were crawling through him, the colony inspecting every inch of his body, mind, and soul, and particularly their core and crucible, with an otherwordly intelligence.

"It's tickly and prickly," said Jessup.

Before Zee could answer, the results of the assessment began appearing, the lines written one at a time.

Class: Tin
Level: Low

Magick Affinity: Unknown
Aether Capacity: Unknown
Type: Knight
Potential: Unknown

The Orb stopped turning and dimmed, its yellow glow shifting back to white.

Zee wasn't sure what to think of the stats that floated in the air. He'd only seen the one assessment before, and none of the categories had been rated "Unknown." He looked to the crowd to see what their reaction was. There were knitted brows, frowns, and a few smirks of satisfaction at having proof that the murman and kraken had been forging. The deans of magicks and commandants remained as stone-faced as before.

The Orb began to throb again, then brightened. The others were considering the stats and didn't seem to notice, but the deans of magicks' eyes widened slightly.

Wanchoo said, "Thank you, Orb. That will be all."

The light in the Orb went out and it descended to rest on the plinth. As it did so, the stats of the assessment faded from view.

From where he stood next to Superintendent Hyooz, Dean Tooker said, "We would also see their core." Murmurs of agreement rose from some of the gathered faculty.

Commandant Aureosa said, "The revealing of their core is not stipulated in the court's order."

"Then we will order it ourselves," Tooker replied.

Vandalia said, "Perhaps you've forgotten, but Mr. Tarrow and Mr. Jessup are civilians. We haven't the authority to make them do anything not specified by the court. We've complied with their order. Anything more would be a case of overreach, and perhaps necessitate an inquiry in itself."

Tooker narrowed his eyes, preparing a retort. Superintendent Hyooz opened her mouth to weigh in, but it was Chaplain oh Connor who spoke.

"Our esteemed commandants are correct, and either way, we don't need to see their core. There's no question now that the murman and kraken have been forging outside of the academy's purview. The inquiry proposal can now include a question as to whether it should be legal for them to do so under the intent of the law, rather than the letter of the law."

More murmurs arose, but Superintendent Hyooz put an end to the proceedings. "Thank you, Mr. Tarrow and Mr. Jessup. You are dismissed to serve the remainder of your sentences."

* * *

Once they had put some distance between themselves and the citadel, Zee said, "That was close."

"Very close," Dean Wanchoo replied. "It's unlikely that Dean Tooker knows about Marisean or has even heard the term, let alone suspects you have it in your core. Very few do, even among learned scholars of history and lore, and his specialty is mathematics. Most likely he simply wanted to see what a murman and kraken's core looks like. We can't blame him for that. The chaplain on the other hand, may."

"Why wouldn't he want to see it?"

Venkatarama said, "It has long been held that bonding is solely the domain of humans and dragons, the children of Zepiter. That we are most esteemed of all living things in the eyes of Zepiter, and when bonded, practically angelic in nature. The knowledge that a murman and kraken can be bonded in itself poses a threat to the foundational principles of the Church of Zepiter. Now it has been proven that you can also access the Empyreal Plane. This goes against what the Church has taught in their sermons throughout recorded history. If it was also revealed that Marisean exists, and can be forged by murfolk and krakens along with Empyrean, the Church would have to reconsider everything they believe, perhaps even acknowledge that Postune is on a level equal to Zepiter, and her children, you and Jessup among them, every bit as blessed as humans and dragons."

Wanchoo pondered a moment. "What do you know of the teachings of the Church of Zepiter and the Holy Scriptures?"

"Very little, to be honest," said Zee. "My parents evoked Zepiter sometimes, but the prayers my ma would say were to Postune."

"She most certainly considered you a blessing, and you do come from the sea. There are many who still evoke Postune over Zepiter, fisherfolk in particular. They just keep it to themselves since it is looked down upon by the Church and, by extension, the majority of the population."

"In the eyes of the Church, murfolk and krakens are lesser creatures, even wicked," Rama added.

Jessup's broad mouth spread in an impish grin. "I *am* wicked"

"A little wickedness in a knight pair can be a good thing."

Zee said to Wanchoo, "That doesn't surprise me, sir. I've had enough experience as a murman on ship to believe that completely, and we've all heard the stories about krakens being murderous monsters since we were young."

"We had hoped to protect you from this," Wanchoo said, "but not discussing the full extent of it with you may have been a mistake. Once the knowledge of your forging gets out, there may be powerful people who would be happier if you simply did not exist."

"I'm pretty sure there already are."

"That doesn't mean you are in imminent danger. True fundamentalists are in the minority in the Church, as well as in the wider population of Tosh. We meant it when we said you are safe here, and the stronger you become, the safer you will be, even if, one day, you would have to leave."

Jessup said, "We don't want to leave, sir."

"I'm glad to hear that, and we will continue to do everything we can to help you."

Zee asked a question that had been rolling around in his mind since the day they'd arrived on the island. "Why, sirs? Why are you helping us so much if it's such a risk for you?"

Wanchoo smiled. "Because we do not believe you are demons sent by Postune to corrupt the academy, the kingdom, or the world. To us, you are a gift."

Zee and Jessup weren't sure what to think about that, but gratitude swelled between them through the bond. "Thank you, sirs. That means a lot."

Rama said, "Just don't go too far from the island for a while, all right?" They both looked at him, and he cleared his throat. "After you're released from incarceration, that is."

"Yes, sir," Jessup replied.

Zee said, "Is it normal that so many of our stats were rated 'Unknown,' sirs?"

"Not really," said Wanchoo. "It happens on occasion with potential for pairs who are just beginning to forge, but not the other categories. The Orb seemed to be having trouble figuring out how to assess you at the beginning. It could be because you're not human and dragon, but it could also have to do with the Marisean. Did you happen to see the Orb begin to brighten again after the assessment?"

"We did, and I meant to ask about that. Do you think it was going to assess us for Marisean?"

"I've never seen it do that before," said Wanchoo. "It's quite possible, which is why I asked it to stop. There is still very little known about the Orb of Assessment."

"That would be good if we have a chance at a full assessment someday."

"It would indeed. Speaking of which, Temothy and Timandra tell us they'd guess approximately one-fifth of your core is Empyrean, the rest being the much larger quantity of Marisean."

"That's right, sir. We think we may have progressed to Copper Class last night, too."

"Again?" Rama said. "Already?"

Jessup said, "We were stuck at Lead for a while, but we think engaging in combat and using our Lightning Blast somewhat effectively pushed us over the edge."

"Stuck?" Wanchoo grinned. "When did you reach Lead Class?"

"About four weeks ago."

"Most cadets don't advance to Copper until well into their second year. Show us this core of yours, if you would, and only us. You don't need to spark it."

Zee and Jessup revealed their core as they walked. It had grown to almost five and a half feet across.

The deans exchanged glances. Venkatarama said, "Based on your assessment for Empyrean alone, we can indeed give you a better estimate as to your actual class and level, now."

They listened carefully, their smiles growing.

The four of them arrived at a fork in the path to find the White Titan pairs that had escorted Jessup earlier and two brig guards waiting. Zee and Jessup thanked the deans, who then headed back toward the citadel.

Zee said to Jessup. "Have fun in your cozy chains."

"You have fun in your cage."

The White Titans and guards appeared to have no idea what to think of the strange pair.

"Talk to you soon," said Jessup.

"Very soon," Zee replied. Then he spoke through their bond. *"Like now. Or how about now?"*

"Zee is silly."

Zee grinned all the while he was handcuffed and led back to the brig.

* * *

Zee didn't say a word, even after the guards had left and the other cadets had come to the bars of their cells in anticipation. He'd told them the court had ordered that he and Jessup be assessed. They were dying to know the results.

Finally, och Dominick said, "Well? How did it go?"

Zee pretended to just now notice him standing across the hall. "It went fine, I guess. I won't know if we're in trouble for forging until after the inquiry, if there is one."

"You have been forging, then." The voice was Lukas tar Tarzian's, from two cells down. Oddly enough, he sounded more relieved than angry or accusing. Better to be beaten by a forging pair than just a regular old bonded murman and kraken—if there was such a thing.

Zee continued to stretch his legs in preparation for some calisthenics while they waited impatiently to hear more.

In the cell next to Dominick, Zendaya frowned at Zee as if willing him to speak. After an uncomfortable amount of time—for them, not Zee—she asked as casually as she could, "So, what class and level are you two?"

Zee responded even more casually. "Low level, Tin Class,"

Dominick said, "Hmm..." Then his brow furrowed and he said it again, but in a more troubled tone.

Zee held back the smile that tried to spread across his lips. Low-level Tin would be an expected score for any newly bonded pair that had recently begun forging. But no Tin Class pair, whatever the level, should be able to compete with Bronze Class third-year cadets like all of them in Tarzian's flight, let alone beat five pairs at once. Their perplexed expressions proved they were thinking the same thing.

What Zee wasn't going to tell them was that, based on the average volume of bonded pairs' cores, if only a fifth of their core got them assessed at low-level Tin, the deans' estimate confirmed they had indeed classed up to Copper. And not just low level, but medium.

According to Deans Wanchoo and Venkatarama, only Slan hai Drogo and Mogon had advanced as quickly. Zee was still astounded by it all, and remained practically giddy at the thought. He wouldn't let it go to his head, though. If anything, it inspired him to train even harder. He completed the stretches and began his exercizes, pushing himself as hard as he possibly could.

CHAPTER 46

It was after dark on Zee's seventh day in the brig, and he had finished his evening meal, which wasn't terrible and was far from meager. At least he didn't go hungry, had some conversation, if guarded, and was free to train as much he wanted, if limited in scope. He missed Jessup terribly, but they could speak to each other anytime they wanted. He got the feeling the others often spoke to their beasts as well. It had begun to feel like he was one of them but not one of them. Just as good as they were, as deserving, but ostracized because of his name and what he was. His desire to show them all what he was capable of burned brighter every day. Through the bond, he felt the same desire in Jessup.

Jessup was doing well. Zee honestly wasn't surprised. As quickly as his friend could rise to ire, he could also remain incredibly calm, even philosophical. It helped that they meditated together for a few bells a day. Though they were separated by almost a mile, during meditation it was like they were still right next to each other.

Jessup had told him some of the people they worked with had been hired to feed him, including Androo Cobbling, Robhat Hayes, and Mickal rot Fletcher. Zee figured it was because the citadel administrators believed they'd be safer getting that close to the kraken. Apparently they'd toss fish into his mouth from a boat, which amused Jessup greatly.

Zee spent most of his waking time exercising. He couldn't use his equipment or run, but there was plenty he could do, including jumperjacks and running in place. The other cadets had taken to training as well. They had tried to go longer and harder than each other, competing, until they'd realized that none of them could keep up with Zee. Some of them had been solemn about that at first, even angry, but then Dominick and Zendaya asked him for training tips. None of the rest of them said anything, but Zee could tell they were paying attention. Zee was boggled by that. These were threesies. He would have thought they'd be far stronger than he was, but away from their dragons, they were only in as good a shape as they kept themselves in.

Two days earlier, Zee had started doing hand-to-hand-combat techniques against the stone wall as if it was a man dummy like the ones he had in his cave and in the canyon. The others had started doing it as well.

That evening, Zee let his mind go, the blocks and strikes coming automatically, and approached a nearly meditative state. His limbs sped through the techniques, faster and faster. It almost felt like his krakenbond began to tingle, and the area in his abdomen below his heart seemed to warm. He slowed and began punching the wall to strengthen his hands and the skin of his knuckles.

Pride seeped to him though the bond, and Zee heard Jessup's voice. "*Harder.*"

As strange as that was, Zee remained in an almost hypnotic state. He struck the wall with more force, and it didn't hurt. He whispered back to Jessup, "*Harder.*"

Zee punched again and again, he and Jessup repeating the word alternately. Out of the corner of his eye, Zee saw Dominick trying to keep up, but the cadet stopped, shook his hand, and stared at Zee.

Zendaya came to the bars of her cell and glanced down the hall to the door. "Stop it, Tarrow. The guards will hear."

Zee kept punching, then heard a sharp snap. He emerged from his meditative state, fearing he'd broken his hand and expecting the pain to hit any second. But his hands were fine. His knuckles weren't even bruised.

Then he saw cracks in the block of stone he'd been striking. A few chips had even come loose. He turned to Dominick, who was staring, wide-eyed. "I broke the stone."

"Shadcrap," Tarzian called out from his cell down from Zee's.

Dominick said, "I think he did."

The hall door opened and all of them scrambled to their cots except Zee, who stood staring at the cracks in the wall while running a finger over them. He only looked away when someone stepped up to his cell.

Instead of an angry guard, it was Dame Toomsil, with two knight rider security officers. One of the officers shouted, "On your feet!" The cadets all jumped up.

"Mr. Tarrow," said Dame Toomsil. "We're here to escort you to your weekly release to the sea."

Zee was confused. No one had said anything about that. But it somewhat made sense. He was a murman. He still wondered why Dame Toomsil would be sent to oversee such a thing. Her assignment at the academy was as an instructor of the sword.

"You'll then be taken to other accommodations for the remainder of your sentence," Dame Toomsil added.

"Other accommodations?" Zee asked. Behind the knight and the security officers, the other cadets were just as confused as he was.

Dame Toomsil only stepped aside in response and a security officer unlocked his cell.

There was only one guard in the brig offices and processing area, closely inspecting a list of some sort on the wall and paying no attention to them as they strode past.

There was no other security outside, either. In fact, Zee saw no one at all as he was led to a simple horse-drawn carriage. He had a little trouble climbing in beside Dame Toomsil due to his hands being cuffed behind him. There was only room for two, so Zee wasn't sure what the security officers were doing.

As they started moving, Zee asked, "Did you arrange this, ma'am?"

She kept looking straight forward. "I did not."

The wheels left the planks of the wharf and Zee nudged the curtain of his window aside with his forehead. They were skirting the edge of town, away from the main thoroughfare and the water.

"Where are we going?" he asked.

"The less we speak of it now, the better, Zee." Her voice had softened, but Zee was getting worried. Better for whom? Had something happened to Jessup? He reached out to him. Jessup was there, and Zee was sure he'd heard him, but his friend wasn't answering.

Zee's worry became fear. Had the inquiry begun and a judgment reached? Were they going to do something terrible to him and Jessup? Worst of all, why wasn't Jessup answering?

The carriage bumped and rocked, passing over rough ground, then came to a stop. All Zee could tell about where they were was that he could smell seawater very near. Jessup was closer as well, but he still wouldn't speak. Zee didn't get a sense that Jessup was particularly anxious, though. It made no sense.

The carriage door on Zee's side opened and a Silver Class knight helped him down.

In the shadows of the carriage, it took a moment for Zee to recognize the knight. "Tem? What's this all about?"

Tem just turned him around and removed his cuffs, then gestured around the carriage.

Now Zee recognized where they were. They'd come to the more-or-less deserted area of the harbor with the old fishing shacks where he and Jessup had stayed their first week on the island. In fact, the shack in front of them was Mahfouz's.

Off the end of the old dock, Jessup sat in the water between four stout pylons that had once held a heavy pier, long abandoned, disassembled, or rotted away. Lengths of heavy anchor chain of the type used on warships were wound and crisscrossed on his shell, their ends disappearing below the surface. There were no guards on the dock, on the shore, or in the air above. In fact, there was no one to be seen in any direction, there were no lamps, and this area of the harbor was devoid of vessels.

To Dame Toomsil, Zee said, "I don't understand."

"You will." She placed a hand on his shoulder. Zee couldn't tell if it was to let him know everything was all right or out of sympathy.

While they waited—for what, Zee had no idea—he asked Jessup, "What's going on, Jessup? Why didn't you answer?"

"They are setting me free. They said you were coming, and to be quiet until you got here. It is good to see you."

"It's good to see you too, but who's setting you free? Who said I was coming?"

Commandant Aureosa stepped out of the shack onto the rickety dock, conversing with Dean Wanchoo. They looked deeply worried about something. Aureosa saw the new arrivals and waved them over, then he and Wanchoo continued to the end of the dock. As Zee reached them, a creature he recognized as a krisdolphin surfaced near Jessup. Krisdolphins weren't fish, but mammals, over ten feet long, and they breathed through a spout on the top of their heads. Sticking out straight from the creature's snout was a blade of bone with a wave to it, razor sharp. On its back was a rider in a dark gray, tight-fitting suit that looked to be made of sheelskin. The rider also wore an odd helmet with goggles and a hose that connected to a tank strapped to their back. Zee had seen diving suits before, but nothing as sleek and sophisticated as that. There was also a powerful-looking harpoon gun, like a sleek crossbow, in a holster strapped to the krisdolphin's body. The rider deposited a massive lock onto the dock, so large they seemed barely able to lift it. Another krisdolphin and rider surfaced with another lock.

Jessup said, "Thank you." The riders didn't acknowledge him, but the krisdolphins bobbed their heads and responded with a clicking squeak, then submerged again.

Commandant Aureosa observed Zee's expression. "They're members of an elite team of commandos in His Majesty's Navy called SHEELs."

"I've never heard of them, sir."

"Few have, which is as it should be."

Wanchoo said, "Krisdolphins and their riders don't have the telepathic connection that dragon and rider do, but they are extremely intelligent creatures."

"I've seen them in the wild. They're curious and friendly, but I've seen them shred a twenty-foot-long shork when provoked."

"That's another reason the SHEELs use them."

"Pardon me, sirs, but may I ask what this is all about?"

Aureosa said, "All I can tell you now is there are some people who want to meet you and Jessup. They'll explain everything, if you'll come with us."

"Where are we going?"

"To a ship off the island."

Zee considered, then asked Jessup, *What do you think?*

It sounds better than chains and a cell.

Zee trusted the people with them more than anyone, but he couldn't help being nervous. If anything bad happened, at least he and Jessup might be able to spark their core and swim away. In the end, there really wasn't a choice.

"We'll go, sir."

Aureosa smiled. "I knew you would."

"When do we leave?"

The wind kicked up and Zee looked back toward shore at the sound of flapping wings. Vandalia, Venkatarama, Peloquin, and Timandra landed in a row beside the shack.

"Immediately."

* * *

Zee rode Jessup on the dark waves of night. Triumf's Island disappeared in the distance behind them. The four dragon and rider pairs overhead had been joined by others, none below Silver Class.

The krisdolphins with their riders bounded in and out of the waves, leading the way toward a thick bank of fog, then into and through it.

When they emerged on the other side, Zee's breath caught in his throat. The air was clear in a circle over a half mile wide, though a dome of fog surrounded them and blocked the sky above.

Several warships floated in the clearing, including the largest ship Zee had ever seen—though he'd heard of it. It was the HMS *Dragon's Rage*, the high admiral's flagship, the largest ship in the fleet, with four cannon decks, said to be capable of carrying a hundred dragon and rider pairs comfortably. In spite of its size, it was also supposed to be one of the fastest ships in His Majesty's Navy.

Tall, wide openings in the side of the ship, about a third of the way up from the waterline, shone with Empyrean lamplight from within. The pairs that had accompanied them made straight toward these portals and flew in, the dragons barely having to tuck their wings.

The commandos led Zee and Jessup beneath the flagship and proceeded up through a large, round hole in the bottom of the hull.

Jessup stopped at the opening, holding himself in place with his arms as they looked up. The surface shimmered with Empyrean lamplight. The commandos were already climbing ladders, their mounts being lifted out of the water with straps—by what mechanism, Zee couldn't tell.

Jessup said, "*Oh...*"

"It's a moon pool," Zee replied. "*I've heard of them, but I've never seen one.*"

The krisdolphins safely out of the way, they could make out a figure waving them up.

"*Do you think it's safe?*" Zee asked, though he could tell Jessup wasn't worried in the least.

"*I guess we'll find out.*"

Jessup's grin was infectious. "*All right then, let's go.*"

Jessup guided them up the walls of the chute, then reached up with his arms and pulled them above a solid circular rail to peer in. Both of them blinked in awe at the sight.

The entire bottom deck of the ship was a single open space—and it was enormous. The ceiling was high enough for dragons to fly. A few entered openings like the ones they'd seen from the sea, but on the opposite side of the ship. Other than support beams, the only thing that broke up the expanse was a rectangular structure along the starboard side, fifty feet long and fifteen feet high, filled with water and with large glass portholes in its sides. A happily squeaking krisdolphin was being lowered into it from a track-and-pulley system hand operated by more of the SHEEL commandos.

There had to be over a hundred people on the deck, including several dozen knight pairs, though there was room for many more. They were completely silent, and all of them were staring at the kraken and murman perched at the lip of the moon pool.

Having no idea what else to do, Zee waved nervously. "Hello."

Jessup lifted an arm in a tentative wave. The stares became wider.

Zee said, "Permission to come aboard?"

Dame Toomsil and Tem approached on their dragons. If Zee didn't know better, he'd swear both of them were smiling. They were followed by a tall man in a shining blue silk robe and pointed cap, and a woman in a ship captain's uniform.

The woman said, "Mr. Tarrow, Mr. Jessup, I'm Harriette cam Bella, captain of the HMS *Dragon's Rage*. Permission granted, and welcome."

Zee and Jessup just stared.

Timandra said, "Are you just going to sit there all night?"

The tall, regal man in the blue robe said, "I am Davis han Ashura, vice vizier to the Crown. Please, come. We mean you no harm."

Jessup released the water he had in his shell to make himself lighter, then, after briefly inspecting the short wall around the pool, clambered over and onto the deck.

The group parted and Ashura held a hand toward a cluster of twenty or so people and dragons standing around a large table toward the far side of the deck, including Commandant Aureosa and Dean Wanchoo. Wanchoo beckoned them as well.

As they made their way across the deck, Jessup said, "*What is happening, Zee?*"

"*I have no idea. But it looks big, whatever it is.*"

"*Maybe they want to cook us and see what kraken and murman taste like.*"

Zee was taken so off guard by Jessup's ridiculous statement he had to force a cough and clear his throat to cover a blurted-out laugh. Then he wondered if that was actually a possibility. He shook his head to remove the absurd thought.

Approaching the table, Zee recognized one of the men as Lord Governor jal Briggs, a White Titan Class knight. Tem's father. The last time Zee had seen the man, he'd allowed Zee to be taken as a conscript on the *Krakenfish* and was speaking down to his father.

"*What's wrong, Zee?*"

Jessup had of course sensed Zee's change in mood. Zee calmed himself with a deep breath. "*Nothing, it's fine.*" He knew Jessup didn't believe him, but his friend stayed silent. Zee also caught sight of Chaplain Antoon oh Connor standing at the back of the group at one end of the table, watching him with an impassive expression that didn't help ease Zee's mind in the least.

The crowd in front of the table stepped aside to give Zee and Jessup room to approach, prompted by Commandant Aureosa and Dean Wanchoo.

A door in the wall on the other side of the table opened and was held by a Gold Class knight. Another knight came through from what looked like a sitting room and stood to the other side of the door. Apparently Zee had been wrong, there was more to this deck of the ship than the vast open space. The golden armor the knights wore was unfamiliar to Zee as well. It was bulkier and more ornate than regular dragon knights wore.

Next to come through the door was a man with a heavy beard and wearing a fancier uniform than the captain. The high admiral of His Majesty's Navy. His name tag read "tar Tarzian." Zee gulped. He'd forgotten. The high admiral was Lukas tar Tarzian's father.

Zee didn't have much time to worry before the next man stepped through, sleeves rolled up, his midnight hair up in a topknot, peering down at a map in his hands. Though his shirt and breeches were simple, the badge on his breast was that of a Red Titan Class knight, and he wore a slim golden crown in the shape of sleek dragon wings, with a sparkling blue dragon's-eye gem at its center. For the first time in his life, Zee thought he might faint. This was Brevor mon lin Phan, the king of Tosh himself. Was this who wanted to meet him and Jessup?

CHAPTER 47

Without a word, everyone dropped to one knee, one hand held over their hearts. Even the dragons hunkered down and lowered their heads. Everyone but Zee, who stood there in shock. Other than the faint creaking of the ship, there wasn't a sound.

"That will be enough of that," said the king without looking up from the map. "We have a mission to prepare for. There's no time for—"

He had raised his gaze and stood staring up at Jessup.

"Great Zepiter's blaze," he uttered. "I knew it to be true, but did not dare to believe it." The king's shrewd black eyes fell on Zee, who felt as if the world was tipping so acutely he nearly stumbled. "And you must be Zee Tarrow, the young murman."

Recovering his senses, Zee threw himself onto one knee, averting his gaze to the floor. "Your Majesty." He swallowed, trying to wet his throat, which had suddenly gone very dry. "It's a great honor be in your presence." Without looking up, he winced at his fumbled address of the king. Never in Zee's life had he thought he'd meet the man, let alone consider how he would greet him.

Footsteps approached and Zee looked up to find the king staring down at him with an inscrutable expression. "You may rise."

Zee swayed as he got to his feet.

The king gazed up at Jessup again. "Mr. Jessup. I've heard much about you and Mr. Tarrow."

Jessup tipped a bow. "It is an honor to meet you, Your Majesty."

The king studied him briefly, then his expression became firm and he spun back toward the table. "Senior officers and advisers only. Everyone else, back to your business!"

Orders were shouted among the ranks and the crowd dispersed with swift military precision. Some went to the far ends of the deck, which had to be over a thousand feet long. Others marched up stairways. Pairs flew out of the rectangular ports. Soon there were only twenty or so people gathered around the long table, half of them with their dragons—and Zee and Jessup, who had no idea what to do. They exchanged a quick glance and began to back away.

"Not you two," said Vandalia.

They froze as everyone at the table looked up at them.

"Join us," said the king, who was already poring over maps and charts laid out on the table. He didn't look up, but waved a hand toward the side of the table opposite him.

Zee gulped as Dean Wanchoo and Commandant Aureosa moved aside to make room for him. Zee wiped the sweat from his forehead, gathered his comportment, and stepped to the table to stand between them. Jessup followed and stood behind him, Venkatarama and Vandalia at his sides.

Zee forced himself to breathe evenly while everyone waited for the king to speak. To one side of the king was Admiral tar Tarzian, gazing at Zee with an enigmatic expression. Davis han Ashura stood on the other. Beside Ashura was Lord Governor jal Briggs. The rest were other admirals, Navy captains, and several high-ranking White Titan Class knight pairs. At one end stood Dame Toomsil and Tem, with their dragons behind them. Surprisingly, they were the only ones who spared Zee a glance. They nodded, which helped to calm his nerves. A beefy hand was laid on his shoulder, and his heartbeat slowed even more.

Zee looked up to see the hand belonged to Dean Wanchoo, who was also peering at the contents of the table. Wanchoo didn't glance over when he removed his hand, but Zee felt steadier on his feet, and his shoulders had relaxed. Zee wondered if the dean of magicks had cast a calming spell or if merely his serene presence and show of support was enough.

King mon lin Phan moved a chart and peered at another, then sighed and pinched the bridge of his nose.

A deep voice rumbled over the group. It took a moment for Zee to place it, then a Royal Crimson dragon as large as any Royal Ebon Zee had seen stalked from behind other dragons at one end of the table. "Some of you know exactly why we are here, some of you have some idea, others"—his bright green eyes fell on Zee and Jessup—"are completely in the dark."

The dragon wore a crown similar to Brevor mon lin Phan's. He was the king's beast, Norrogaul.

The big Crimson took his place behind the king.

"There is no time to waste," King Phan said. He looked right at Zee. "Mr. Tarrow, I wish to make you and Mr. Jessup an offer that could change your lives, or end them."

Zee nodded weakly, lost for words.

The king continued. "This is a matter of grave importance involving national security and must be kept in complete secrecy."

"We understand, Your Majesty," Zee replied, already knowing through their bond what Jessup's reply would be.

The king gazed around the table. "The same applies to all here, and it must be communicated to everyone under your command. You all must swear a vow of secrecy to the throne." As one, they all agreed. "Then I will get right to it. My son, Crown Prince Talog, has been kidnapped and is being held for ransom."

From the gasps, curses, and shuffling of feet at the table, it was apparent that less than half of them had known the whole truth of the matter.

"As terrible as that is, it's not as simple as it sounds," King Phan continued. "I will turn it over to Ellis si Mauricio, captain of one of the captured ships, to provide details."

Captain Mauricio bowed to the king, then began. "Prince Talog and his dragon, both recent graduates of the citadel and Iron Class knights, were accompanying three Navy frigates on a routine sweep of the Taran Sea when they were attacked on a deathly still night, heavy with fog, by ghostly white ships mottled with gray, with deep red sails but no banners, insignia, or names of any kind. Only one bore a flag, the same ghostly white, with four red blotches, two smaller above and two larger below."

"We have come to know them as Wraiths," Admiral Tarzian interjected. "If you have had any doubt, know now they are very real, and a very serious threat. Their forces wear a motley collection of armor, all appearing as if it has been scavenged rather than of their own manufacture, and all painted the same mottled white as the ships. In spite of their appearance, they are not to be underestimated."

Mauricio continued. "The enemy had a dozen knight pairs, but also sizeable forces of condor riders and petrel riders. The Navy ships and their knight escorts were quickly overcome. Our knight pairs were slain, as were the entire crews of two of the ships, which were burned and sunk. The prince and his dragon fought admirably but were taken down by an overwhelming force. The dragon did not survive."

Everyone stood silent, listening to the grim story, the king scowling as his eyes focused on the table with a faraway gaze.

Captain Mauricio said, "We know these details because the enemy left one ship afloat, with its captain and just enough crew to sail it. I was that captain. We were made to watch as they removed the prince's hand and placed it inside a chest with a foot severed from the prince's dragon. We were then sent to deliver their demands to the king."

Zee was impressed that Captain Mauricio was able to tell the story without pause or any show of emotion until the very end, when his eyes fell to the table, glazed as if he was reliving the terrible events all over again.

The king wore a pained expression as Vice Vizier Ashura placed a wooden chest on the table. With a grimace, the king flipped the hinged box lid open.

Inside was a single dragon's foot, its talons holding a human hand, a golden ring with the royal family's crest on one finger. Both the hand and the talon looked more like they had been torn off than cut with sword or cleaver.

It took a moment for the king to tear his gaze away from the grisly display. When he did, it was with fierce determination in his eyes.

"They have demanded a ransom in gold as well as an artefact, which I will not explain here. I love my son as any father would and I'd pay all the gold in my treasury for his release, but relinquishing the artefact is out of the question. I also do not trust these devils to deliver the prince alive even if we were to meet all of their demands.

"Our mission, then, is to rescue the crown prince by stealth if we can, by force if need be, and, so help me Zepiter, kill every last one of the Wraiths that did this to him."

The expressions of those in attendance ranged from deeply furrowed brows to rage, to a touch of fear.

For Zee, it was mostly disbelief, so many questions and realizations whirling through his mind he didn't know where to start. And the Wraiths were real…

Norrogaul spoke. "In two weeks' time, we are to meet the enemy's ship where the prince is being held in a remote area of the sea far to the north. It will take us that much time to travel the distance. The plan is to send the SHEELs on their krisdolphins to infiltrate the ship and retrieve the prince, but even they would have a difficult time approaching in daylight without being seen. To send them at night, however, especially in that part of the world, would be extremely risky. The creatures of the deep have become even more numerous and aggressive in the north.

"The SHEELs agreed to a night raid regardless—then we received word of incidents involving a young murman and his kraken on Triumf's Island."

Zee swallowed as the big Crimson's eyes fell on him and Jessup.

"If the SHEELs had a bonded kraken and rider with them," Norrogaul continued, "their chances of surviving a night swim would increase dramatically. You would be escorts only and not expected to fight unless necessary. It will be extremely dangerous, nonetheless."

King mon lin Phan said, "What do you say, Mr. Tarrow, Mr. Jessup. Will you help me save my son?"

Zee blinked, trying to take it all in, and glanced at Jessup. His friend just looked back at him, allowing him to decide. It was clear what Jessup wanted to do, though. He looked the king in the eye, as difficult as he found that to be. "Jessup and I are at your service, Your Majesty, whatever form that may take."

The king gazed at him as if assessing his character, then said, "Consider it sworn."

* * *

Zee and Jessup were dismissed, and Vandalia told them she, Aureosa, and the deans would come see them in a bit. Dame Toomsil, Peloquin, Tem, and Timandra led them toward the stern of the ship.

Zee waited until they were out of earshot of the table before saying anything. Dame Toomsil and Tem had their eyebrows raised when he looked at them, and Tem spoke first. "That was something, ay?"

Zee checked again that they were far enough away from the table, but still kept his voice down. "Oh my gods. That's the king of Tosh!"

Dame Toomsil's eyes crinkled at the corners. "Yes, he is."

Zee became pensive, as if just fully realizing what had happened. "Jessup and I are going on a mission for the king..."

"You are, if you're sure you want to."

"There's no doubt in our minds, ma'am. It's just so sudden, and so hard to believe." He turned to Dame Toomsil's former squire. "You could have given me some warning, Tem."

"And disobey a direct order? Not a chance."

"Besides," said Timandra, "then we wouldn't have gotten to see your reaction."

Peloquin said, "It was quite amusing, in spite of the grim circumstances."

"Really?" Zee asked.

"Really," said Tem. Zee groaned.

Timandra said, "Jessup was still as stone, however." To the kraken, she said, "You handled it all with knightly stoicism and aplomb."

"I was in shock," Jessup answered.

All of them laughed, happy for the release of tension after the meeting. There was still the mission ahead, however.

Zee said, "The king mentioned that he'd heard much about us. What has he heard, exactly?"

"Everything," said Tem.

"He knows we've been forging?" Tem nodded. "What about the Marisean? That you and Timandra have been helping us? The chasmclaw attack and the possibility of an inquiry? The troubles with Lukas tar Tarzian and his flight, and the brig?"

"All of it," said Tem, "but also how hard you train, how fast you've progressed, and the high opinions of you held by the commandants, deans of magicks, and your co-workers on the docks."

"And us," said Dame Toomsil.

Zee wasn't sure what to say to that, or if he even deserved it. He settled for, "Thank you." Then he added, "How many people know everything about me and Jessup?"

"Everyone at the table, and before we reach our destination, practically everyone on the task force of ships gathering for this mission will too. They've all been sworn to secrecy by the king himself, or will be before we return, and the penalty for breaking an oath to the throne is quite stiff."

Zee puffed his cheeks and blew out air. "That makes things a little easier on Jessup and me, I guess."

"It will certainly be easier to train when you don't have to hide anything."

"What kind of training?"

"The extreme kind," said Timandra.

Jessup said, "I like the sound of that."

"You say that now."

"Is that why you're here?" Zee asked the knights. "To help us train?"

"In part," Dame Toomsil replied, "but also because Commandant Aureosa requested we come to help put you at ease."

"Dame Toomsil is also familiar with this ship and its command," Tem added. "She and Peloquin were assigned here prior to being transferred to the academy."

Timandra said, "It's quite the honor to serve on the admiral's flagship. One of the highest in the corps."

Zee said, "I'm worried about the admiral. I mean, Jessup and I did knock his son out of the sky with lightning."

"That should be the least of your concerns," said Dame Toomsil. "He's a military man first and foremost, and extremely loyal to the king. He won't do anything to jeopardize the mission."

"What about after?"

"I suppose that depends on how well you behave on his ship, and how the mission goes."

They had paused on the grand expanse of the deck while they spoke. The creak of pullies and gears drew their attention to the moon pool. A foot-thick disk of wood, reinforced and weighted with iron bands and with holes drilled through it, was being lowered from the deckhead into the moon pool. Once it was in place at the bottom, sailors dove in to secure it. Then a circular grate was lowered to be fastened to the opening at the top. Doors were being tipped down over the dragon ports as well, crew on catwalks securing them with latch bolts.

"Looks like they're closing up ship for the night," said Dame Toomsil. "We'll be setting sail soon. Follow me."

They continued toward the stern, other knight pairs and sailors moving away to give them plenty of room. Most stared at Jessup and Zee, but they barely noticed anymore. Zee realized the deck was even longer than he'd thought when sailors slid open two massive doors to another room.

Empyrean lamps lit as they entered. The room extended the full width of the ship, the walls lined with empty shelves. Other than a cot, a chamber pot, and several chairs, the room was bare.

"This has been prepared for you and Jessup for the journey," Dame Toomsil said.

"Just the two of us?" Zee asked.

"It's a big ship."

"Yes, it is."

"There was some concern that Jessup might need to sleep in the water."

"I can sleep anywhere, ma'am," Jessup replied. "This is fine." He swiveled his big eyes, scanning the space. "Plenty of room to stretch out." He spread his ten arms out in all directions, snaking them around the others. Even extended to their full forty feet each, the tips barely went to the bulkheads.

Peloquin eyed Jessup's arms spanning the floor. "That's a little disturbing, I must admit."

Jessup grinned and pulled them back, coiling them close and beneath him.

Timandra said, "You should see him extend his claws and use his arms like barbed whips."

"No, thank you," was Peloquin's adamant reply.

* * *

The six of them sat in casual conversation, which pleased Zee greatly. It was the first time he'd been able to really speak with Dame Toomsil since he'd arrived on the island. None of them brought up the mission, what Zee and Jessup's training would involve, or the Wraiths. Zee wanted to know more, but it was so nice to just sit and talk, the tension of the day draining away as the time passed, he didn't want to ruin it.

He did pose a question to Tem that he knew was a touchy subject, but felt compelled to ask. "I saw your father is here. How are things with you two?"

Tem shrugged. "I wouldn't know. I haven't spoken to him."

"I'm sorry."

"Don't be. It's better that way, believe me."

"Oh, Jessup wanted me to ask, since he hasn't seen her. Did Dean Wanchoo leave Amoxtli at the citadel?"

"I did not ask that at all," Jessup protested.

"You were thinking it."

The kraken gave him a look and shook his head while the others chuckled.

Dame Toomsil said, "She's been left in the care of Superintendent Hyooz, who looks after her on occasion when the dean is away."

"Does the superintendent know what's going on here?", Zee asked.

"That, I don't know."

A knock sounded on the door, and they all got to their feet.

"Come in!" said Dame Toomsil.

The doors slid open and the king swept in, followed by Norrogaul, High Admiral tar Tarzian, the commandants, the deans of magicks, and to Zee's pleasant surprise, Beastmasters Mahfouz and Mildrezod. Behind them came Sadir sim Samir and his dragon Timy, whom Zee had met at the scuttling of the ships and cadet strafing exercise.

A knight and her dragon, whom Zee had never met, came last. She was a small but powerful-looking woman, dressed in leathers with burn marks on them rather than a knight's garb, but her badge and pin marked her as Gold Class with the rank of Knight Commander. She bore an almost amusing resemblance to her Rock dragon, who was slimmer than most Rocks, but heavily muscled.

Zee wasn't sure if he should salute, kneel, or something else. Tem and Dame Toomsil only stood to attention, so he followed their lead.

The king began right away, all business. "Mr. Tarrow, Mr. Jessup, we would see this unique core of yours. We need to have a sense of your strength and capabilities in order to best put you to use."

Norrogaul gave a look to the king, who added, "We would see your krakenbond mark as well."

Zee and Jessup replied together, "Yes, Your Majesty." The group spread out in front of them while Zee pulled off his shirt. He glimpsed grim surprise at the scars that marked nearly every inch of his skin, then solemn curiosity at the krakenbond. The gray patch had continued to grow and now arms reached across his sternum to his right pectoral muscle, down to his abdomen, over his shoulder to his shoulder blade, and two were even beginning to wind their way down his left arm. It was also thicker and darker, textured in a combination of the tough skin of Jessup's arms and his shell. Zee put the attention out of his mind and hopped up onto one of Jessup's arms.

They calmed themselves by syncing deep breaths, and revealed their core to all in the room. Zee took pleasure in the exclamations that came from the group and the looks on their faces, particularly the appreciative smiles of Aureosa and Wanchoo. Zee didn't even feel like a freak. Jessup gave him a mental and figurative clap on the back.

After the members of the group had recovered from their astonishment, comments abounded, some of them talking over each other. They spoke about the size of the core, its nearly perfect shape, the thickness of the crucible, and the shape and progression of Zee's krakenbond, as well as mused on the nature of the blue Marisean and Empyrean together and what his and Jessup's class and level might be.

Zee listened as closely as he could, but the conjecture and differing opinions on how it was all possible and what it could mean was overwhelming. In the end, all the group could do was verbalize observations, posit theories, and guess.

Dean Wanchoo said, "Mr. Tarrow, Mr. Jessup, would you spark it for us? No Camouflage or Occlude, please."

Half the people in the room stepped back when their core flared to life, filling the room with blue and yellow light. Even the commandants and deans seemed surprised. Tem and Timandra just grinned.

The king and his dragon stepped closer, their Red Titan eyes having no problem with the intensity of the light.

"It has the size of a Copper Class pair," said the king, "but it burns brighter."

"It has a different feel as well," Norrogaul added. "Like the core of a pair classes higher, but there is something else…"

Venkatarama said, "We have a theory, Your Majesties. It may be possible there is something about having Empyrean and Marisean together that amplifies the core's power, making it greater than the sum of the two parts."

The king crossed his arms and cocked his head, gazing at the globe of light, but stayed quiet. Finally, he just said, "Thank you, gentlemen. You may extinguish it."

While most of the group conversed further, Zee and Jessup answered a barrage of questions from the tackmasters and armorers, including how thick Jessup's shell was, did it feel pain, if metals would interfere with his electricity, where exactly Zee's gills were, how much did his hands and feet transform when in the water, where Zee rode on Jessup when in the sea, and many more. Ideas about armor, weapons, and saddlery were bandied about. It turned out the knight he'd not met's name was Nanners tan Runoffski, and she and her Rock dragon, Zuki, were the king's own armorers.

The bell was getting late, but that was nothing new to Jessup and Zee, so they had no problem with the group poking, prodding, and inspecting them.

The admiral had only engaged briefly in the conversations, having spent most of the time eyeing Zee and Jessup with an inscrutable expression that made Zee nervous. Zee was relieved, though, that no one asked to look at Zee and Jessup's Keep. The murfolk book and his stinger were in there, which he had placed inside the duffel Dr. Aenig had given him, along with some coin. He still wasn't ready to explain the book if anyone pried.

Finally, King Phan finished a conversation he'd been having with Aureosa and Wanchoo and turned to Zee and Jessup. The others seemed to instinctively know he was preparing to speak and quieted.

All he said was, "Mr. Tarrow, Mr. Jessup, keep forging that magnificent core of yours," then to the others in the room, "We have two weeks before we reach our destination. Make them ready." With that, he strode out, flanked by his royal guard and followed by Norrogaul.

Other than a wink from Mildrezod, the group filed out with no more than a promise they'd be back tomorrow, until Zee, Jessup, Dame Toomsil, Peloquin, and Tem and Timandra were alone once more.

Zee's head was spinning yet again. He really wasn't used to that much attention.

Jessup said, "I feel special."

The others burst out laughing, and Jessup joined them.

"You are special indeed, Mr. Jessup," said Dame Toomsil. "You and Zee both. Never forget that."

They said their good nights and the doors were closed, leaving Zee and Jessup both breathless and exhausted. Zee's life had once again taken a very abrupt turn. Bells ago he'd been in the brig, in fear of a pending inquiry, and now he and Jessup were on the HMS *Dragon's Rage*, recruited by the king of Tosh to help save his son, the crown prince.

Zee resolved not to let the king down, nor any of the others who had helped him and Jessup get here. He recalled another of his da's adages: "No matter the task, give it your all and you will be better for it, whether you succeed or not." Through the deep melancholy that always came when he thought of his parents, Zee wondered if his all would be enough.

It had to be. He wouldn't accept anything less, for himself, for Jessup, or for the king.

PART
FOUR

CHAPTER 48

Early the next day, Zee stretched in preparation for a morning run while Jessup did isometric exercises with his arms—extending and retracting and curling and uncurling them, while resisting in both directions. Jessup alternated those with his own peculiar version of squatters, pushing himself as high as he could and back down. At the height of each, the top of his shell nearly touched the deckhead.

The deck was plenty big enough for Zee to run on, but he looked forward to going topside. He wanted Jessup to go with him, though, and he wasn't sure how he'd get up there.

There came a pounding on the door. Beastmaster Mahfouz's voice thundered from the other side. "Rise and shine!"

The doors slid open and over a dozen people and several dragons bustled in, carrying all manner of tools and craftsperson's bags. Among them were the armorers from last night, the tackmasters, and from their equipment, a carpenter and several Navy smiths, along with a number of assistants. Sailors brought in a small folding table, as well as a very long one for the others to put their wares on. One sailor set a tray of breakfast on the small table for Zee, and another placed a stack of folded training clothes for him on one of the empty shelves against the wall. Two more carried a litter between them, piled with fish.

Jessup's face lit up at the sight of it. "*Zee! They brought me fish!*"

"*See, you are special.*"

"*Special big kraken.*"

Zee chuckled, then chuckled some more at the looks on the sailor's faces when Jessup opened his enormous mouth and pointed at it with the tip of an arm. Once they realized what the kraken wanted, two other sailors ran over to help their mates lift the litter and upend it into the kraken's maw. They retreated hastily, not wishing to stick around while Jessup ate. They didn't even stop when Jessup called after them, "Thank you for the fish!"

The rest of the group didn't wait for Zee to finish his breakfast before they got started. He was stood up by several members of Armorer Nanners tan Runoffski's team, asked to strip to his underpants, and measured in more ways than he'd ever thought possible.

Jessup was asked to demonstrate how he extended and retracted the spikes on his shell, then Tackmaster Sadir sem Samir and his team practically swarmed him, measuring him as thoroughly as Zee was being measured. Zee worried that Jessup might be uncomfortable with having people climbing all over his shell, but his friend had his eyes closed and a contented look on his face.

Zee grinned, then flinched as one of the measurements tickled him.

"Please hold still," said a dour man with a narrow mustache and a tape measure. Zee did his best.

"Sorry about all this, Zee," said Mildrezod. "We haven't much time, and outfitting a murman and a kraken is new to everyone here."

"It's not a problem, ma'am. I think Jessup likes it."

"Hmm...," she said, and moved closer to Jessup, taking in the expression on his face. "Does that feel good, Mr. Jessup?"

Jessup didn't open his eyes, but his smile widened. "Yes."

She snorted a laugh and went to join Mahfouz, who stood with his arms crossed, overseeing the proceedings.

Armorer Runoffski nodded toward Zee's krakenbond. "May I?"

It took a second for Zee to realize she wanted to touch it. No one had done that since Dr. Aenig had when Zee had first been conscripted on the HMT *Krakenfish*. He'd rarely been touched at all other than when he'd been struck or pushed on ship or treated for injuries by the surgeon. He quelled his uneasiness. "Of course, ma'am."

She ran her fingers over it with clinical proficiency and a master craftsperson's inquisitiveness. "Incredible."

Zuki, her Rock dragon, said, "Does it have much feeling?"

"It's sensitive to touch and temperature, sir," Zee replied, "but overall it's much like a thick callus."

Runoffski said, "And extremely tough, from the feel of it. Is there any problem with flexibility? Does it feel tight when stretched?"

"No, ma'am."

"I wouldn't be surprised if it could stop a slash from a sword, in time."

Zee didn't like the idea of being slashed by a sword, but having natural armor wouldn't be a bad thing. He had wondered on occasion how far it would spread, though, but he'd worry about that when the time came. For now, the krakenbond gave him great comfort, and he wore it with pride.

Jessup agreed without reservation when Tackmaster Samir approached him with a Navy metalsmith and carpenter and asked if they could drill a test hole in his shell. He didn't even ask why, just told them it would heal closed within a few days, then pointed out places on his shell above his brow where he believed there to be no cavities where he stored water for deep diving. Even there, though, he thought the shell was probably ten inches thick.

Mahfouz asked, "How do you know all that, Jessup?"

"I can feel them fill with seawater when I dive or flush them with gas for swimming toward the surface." They listened with extreme interest. "Also, a leviathanfish bit me and broke my shell."

Everyone stopped and looked up at that, partly because Jessup was so casual about it, but mostly because few people had ever seen a leviathanfish. Those who had described them as being anywhere from a hundred fifty to two hundred feet long, covered in bronze-colored scales as big as shields, with sharp ridges of scales on their backs, and a head that was all mouth and teeth. They weren't particularly aggressive and rarely came to the surface, but they'd been known to swallow smaller ships after crushing them with one bite if provoked.

Mildrezod said, "I'm glad you're all right, Jessup."

Jessup shrugged, causing people clambering about on his shell to grab hold of his spines. "There was no pain. Not like having an arm bitten off. That hurts."

Timy, Samir's Ice Diver dragon, said, "I... can imagine."

Jessup shrugged again, this time initiating shouts from the people on his shell. "They grow back."

The group exchanged glances, then Samir set a ladder against the front of Jessup's shell, climbed up with a stethoscope, and listened as he rapped on the surface, marking specific areas with chalk. Once satisfied, he took up a brace-and-bit hand drill. The first bit wouldn't penetrate. The second one broke. They marveled at how hard Jessup's shell was, then sent someone to retrieve alchemically manufactured bits made for drilling into steel.

The teams were packing up, including assistants stowing away reams of notes, when Zee pulled his shirt back on and joined the tackmasters and beastmasters.

Samir was grinning up at Jessup as his crew gathered their tools and equipment. "Thank you, Mr. Jessup. This is the most fun I've had in years."

"You have a strange idea of fun, Knight Commander Tackmaster, but you're welcome."

Samir laughed, then reached up and patted Jessup on the shell.

Timy said, "We'll do you and Mr. Tarrow right, Mr. Jessup."

"Thank you, ma'am."

"Excuse me," Zee asked, "but is there a way for Jessup and me to get to the upper deck?"

Mahfouz bobbed his eyebrows. "Follow us."

* * *

Krisdolphins chittered, squeaked, and splashed while a half dozen SHEEL commandos in black swimwear fed them from railed walkways. One commando climbed to the lip of the tank and jumped in.

Mildrezod said, "Would you like to meet your team?"

"Our team?" Zee replied.

"You'll be working with them very closely."

The commandos turned as they approached. A brawny, serious-looking man waved them closer, "Tarrow, Jessup, come on up." He tipped a nod to Mahfouz and Mildrezod. "Commanders."

Mahfouz grinned up at him. "Chief Walster, good to see you. How are those fine beasts of yours?"

"Berrolli and Petrikleo aren't bad. The rest are a pain in in my arse."

Several of the squad members shouted and Walster was hit by a wet sponge thrown from across the tank. "Oh, you mean the krisdolphins? Couldn't be better."

Mildrezod said, "Would you show these lads the way topside when you're done? We've got rounds to make."

"Will do."

Jessup pushed up on his legs to get eye level with the top of the tank while Zee climbed the stairs to the walkway.

"You wouldn't recognize us, Jessup," said Walster, "but Tablert and I removed your chains and escorted you to the ship." He indicated a sleek, muscular woman just down from him on the walkway, who waved curtly.

Zee stepped up onto the walkway and the man offered a hand. "My name's Walster. No need for rank, none of this lot pay attention to that, anyway."

Zee shook Walster's hand. The man had quite a grip. But so did Zee. Walster grinned. "Good lad."

Zee wasn't sure what to make of the SHEELs. No ranks or saluting, and just last names. They also didn't stare at Jessup, or even look like they were trying not to. It was like they saw krakens every day. From their scars and demeanors, Zee figured they'd seen quite a lot in the sea and weren't easily impressed or surprised.

"It's good to meet you, sir."

Another woman, smaller than Tablert but lean with muscle, snorted.

Walster thumbed at her over his shoulder. "See what I mean? We don't go much for the 'sir' and 'ma'am' in the SHEELs."

Or military grooming, Zee thought. Two of the men had beards, and Walster looked like he hadn't shaved in several days.

"Since we'll be working together, let me introduce the gang." He pointed to each as he said their names. They nodded or waved back as they went about their business of scrubbing down the krisdolphins with sponges, feeding them, and generally playing with them. Aside from Tablert, Zee was introduced to Berrolli, Coolbaughm, and Petrikleo, who was astride a krisdolphin, rubbing its head. The woman who had snorted was Chan.

Walster pointed at the various krisdolphins, who were thoroughly enjoying all the attention. "There's Spanky, that one's Tanky, over there is Lanky, and those two are Stanky and Blanky."

The seafaring mammals bobbed their heads and squeaked as their names were called. Another one, whose snout blade was chipped at the end, came up straight out of the water at the edge of the tank near them and turned in circles, keeping itself up by vigorously flapping its tail fins.

Walster said, "There you are. Show-off." It belly-smacked back into the water, splashing them. "That one's mine. His name's Wanky, for good reason."

Zee laughed. "How do they keep from cutting each other with their snout blades in there?"

Wanky shot up and perched at the edge, his blade held up and away from them. Walster scratched him under his snout. "No idea. We wouldn't put them in there if they did, but to be honest, we're more happy they don't skewer us."

Wanky spotted Jessup and let out a stream of clicks and squeaks. Jessup stood higher and, to Zee and everyone else's surprise, emitted clicks and squeaks back. His were deeper in tone and slightly slower, but all the krisdolphins rushed to perch on the tank rim with Wanky, all "talking" to Jessup excitedly. That surprised the commandos again, and Zee as well.

"Can you understand what they're saying, Jessup?" Zee asked.

"Only a little. Mostly that they're happy to meet me."

"That will be incredibly helpful." Walster turned to Zee. "We have to talk through hoses when diving, but the krisdolphins speak to each other constantly. They can communicate directions and distance to a certain extent, but also danger, safety, simple things like that. We've come to recognize most of those verbalizations. They say a lot else we don't understand, though."

"So you don't bond with them."

"No, unfortunately. Certainly not like riders and dragons do. Dragons are the only fully bondable beasts. And krakens, apparently, at least with murfolk. People and drakes can bond to a certain extent. It's called a half bond. They each pick up some strength, speed and endurance from it, and the drake some intelligence, but no special Abilities, and since drakes don't speak, their telepathic communication is limited to the sharing of emotion. Krisdolphins are smarter than most animals, though. We get pretty attached to them."

Zee grinned at the happy creatures. "I can see why. Have you heard anything more about what we'll be doing on the mission?"

"Nothing other than we approach the ship and extract the prince while you and Jessup keep sea beasts off our backs."

Zee petted Wanky, who leaned in for more.

Walster said, "I'm sure something will be scheduled officially, but we're going to sea this afternoon if you and Jessup would like to join."

Zee glanced at Jessup, then responded. "We'd like that very much. Thank you."

A short time later, Walster tugged a rope that ran from a hole in the deckhead down along the wall. After another minute or so, a large bell hanging from the deckhead clanged and the sailors and pairs at the center of the deck moved away. Massive doors folded open in the deckhead, and a square lift, forty feet on a side, lowered through.

"That's how Mr. Jessup can get to the top deck," said Walster. "Just don't use it too often or the sailors get cranky."

* * *

Zee kept up with the other riders for almost a whole lap around the top deck before he started falling back. That bothered him, but he also assumed only the most elite pairs had been chosen for this mission. It was a thrill just to be training among them, even if he was the slowest, weakest, and least advanced.

He continued running along the rail, watching Jessup sprint up and down the center of the deck with Timandra and Peloquin, which was amusing, to say the least. More amusing was watching everyone else watching a kraken run like a spider. The dragons took the lead at the outset of each lap, but Jessup would beat them to the end every time.

Zee found himself flanked by two other runners who slowed to match his pace.

"Quit gawking, Tarrow," said Tem. "You should be ashamed of yourself, letting everyone pass you like that."

Dame Toomsil said to Tem, "How about you two hop over the side and see who swims the fastest?"

Tem glanced over the rail. "I'm not sure I'd even survive the fall."

Zee grinned. "Good morning."

"How was your first night on the ship?"

"A whole lot better than sleeping in the brig." He looked out over the sea. With the dragon ports closed below, he hadn't realized how early it'd been when everyone had arrived at their quarters. Though the magickers' fog still shrouded the ships, he could still see a brighter spot where the sun was only a half bell above the horizon. He breathed deeply of the salty air and watched the rolling waves. The high admiral's ship was so big it sailed incredibly smoothly, but he could still feel movement of the deck beneath his feet. It felt good.

"I never thought I'd say this, but I've missed being on ship."

"It gets in your blood," said Tem. "Almost as much as riding a dragon."

"Almost," said Toomsil.

"Not even close, actually."

"Nope."

Zee chuckled, then took in the expanse of the deck once more. The HMS *Dragon's Rage* had eight enormous masts holding what had to amount to acres of sail. Magicker pairs conjured wind to keep them filled. They didn't even have to stand behind the sails, just wave their wands ever so slightly from wherever they stood.

The deck, over twelve hundred feet long and nearly two hundred feet wide, teemed with activity. Besides the sailing crew on duty and the knights running a circuit around the rails, other knights trained at equipment stations with sword and spear, still more sparred, and some tended to their dragons. There was even a small simulation arena with a ring of floating crystals fifty feet across where two Gold Class knight pairs were practicing close-quarters weapons combat. Above, flights of pairs flew in formation. Several more ships had joined their task force as well. From what Zee could see, their decks were just as busy.

"It's quite a sight, isn't it?" said Dame Toomsil.

"It sure is," Zee replied. "It's nothing like the *Krakenfish*."

"You get used to it."

"I bet you don't."

"Not really, no."

Tem said, "You haven't even seen the swimming pool below."

Zee's jaw dropped open, and he laughed.

Tem checked his pocketclock. "I'm on watch duty in twenty. See you at fourteen hundred for weapons training."

"I should get myself one of those," Zee said. "Are they expensive?"

"Very." Tem hefted the pocketclock in his hand, then tossed it up, caught it, and handed it to Zee. "Take it."

"Seriously?"

"Seriously."

"Tem, I can't—"

"You can, and will. I won't tolerate you being late."

"I... thank you." Zee took the watch. "But now you don't have one."

"I'll get another one at the ship's store."

"The ship has a store? Never mind, of course it does."

"That one's very special, too. It's waterproof."

Tem broke from the line of runners and jogged away.

"He really isn't such a basshole anymore, is he?" Zee asked Dame Toomsil.

"Not as much," Toomsil answered.

Zee laughed.

"You done loafing?"

"Yes, ma'am."

"Try to keep up."

"I'll do my best."

"You always do, Mr. Tarrow."

She shot forward and Zee put on speed to catch her, grinning all the way.

CHAPTER 49

Time on the admiral's glorious ship passed more quickly than Zee would have liked. He and Jessup engaged in intense core building each day by forging with Tem and Timandra. Dame Toomsil and Peloquin even took part in a few sessions.

They went out with the SHEELs that day and every day after. During the sessions, they were taught their hand signs, the best formation for swimming together was worked out and drilled, and Jessup practiced speaking with the krisdolphins. The rest of each day was filled with more weapons, Ability, combat, and physical training, and occasionally there were additional measurements and fittings for tack and armor.

The tackmasters and armorers experimented with different materials and configurations. The ship had a small forge and blacksmithing shop, a machining shop, and an alchemy lab with metalurge magicker and ceramics magicker specialists. Not as extensive as back home, Zee was told, but they were doing their best. Zee and Jessup were both excited to see what they would come up with.

According to Tem, Zee and Jessup were being worked harder than the recruits in their most intense weeks of Basic and the most grueling training undergone by advanced fourth-year cadets, combined. It was nonstop and exhausting, their only real periods of rest when they were slotted time to meditate and forge, and sleep. They were given six bells to sleep, but they only slept four, using the extra time for more core building. To Zee and Jessup, it was only slightly more rigorous than what they would have put themselves through back on the island if they didn't have jobs, but a lot better.

It was also an incredible privilege. Private lessons from seasoned knights and magickers, including the commandants and the deans of magicks themselves, learning things they'd never known or would have thought of. Not only that, the results shocked not only the young murman and kraken, but everyone else as well.

* * *

For the twentieth time, Zee and Jessup powered up Jessup's electrical power. Once they'd fed what they thought was the right amount of energy from their sparked core into it, blue arcs dancing brighter across the spines of Jessup's shell, they focused all their will and intent on the target atop a tall pylon tower at the back of the raft, and let loose. Smaller bolts snapped out in multiple directions, and a larger one zigzagged up into the ceiling of fog that magickally traveled with them to hide the ships.

For the twentieth time, thunder rumbled, and the target remained unscathed.

"Harrumph," said Jessup.

Zee grunted in exasperation. At least they were making the salt air smell nice, like after a thunderstorm. There was no storm this time, however. Just a murman and a kraken who couldn't hit the broad side of a barn with their single-strike Lightning Bolt Ability if their lives depended on it. They'd been able to make their multiple-strike Lightning Blast work against Tarzian's flight, but that was when their lives did depend on it, and they'd used a lot more bolts than needed.

"You produced a fine strike this time," came Commandant Aureosa's voice from behind them. Jessup shuffled through a turn to face the front of the raft. Wanchoo dropped the Shield he'd been using to protect himself,

Venkatarama, the commandants, and Tem and Dame Toomsil and their dragons.

Vandalia said, "It just didn't strike anything."

The raft, over a hundred feet wide and twice as long, was being pulled almost three hundred feet behind the HMS *Dragon's Rage*. It had been lowered to the sea in parts and Zee and Jessup had helped assemble it, which had taken less than a half bell. It was used for any number of things, from carrying extra cargo to transporting more dragons to combat practice. As far as Zee could tell, it didn't slow the massive ship in the slightest, thanks to the ship's sleek hull design and enormous sails boosted by wind from nearly twenty particularly talented magicker pairs.

More warships had joined them on their journey, bringing the count of their task force up to over a dozen of the fastest and most deadly ships Tosh's Navy had to offer. All of them sailed to the sides or in front of the admiral's ship while Zee and Jessup were training, and no knight pairs flew the skies above them, just in case. The rails at the sterns of all the ships in sight were lined with people, though, watching the kraken shoot lightning.

Their group of mentors came closer and Vandalia said, "Remember, Abilities are organic. They grow out of a bonded pair's natural strengths. They cannot be forced upon beast or rider. They are not assigned to you, and there are no absolutes. The best we can do is tease them out and help them grow—and you, and your beast, along with them. These failures are not just yours, they are ours as well. Do not be too hard on yourselves. It can take months, even longer, to master a new Ability."

Aureosa stood with an elbow cupped in one hand while rubbing his chin with the other. "Unfortunately, we don't have months. I'm thinking you're still having trouble with how much of your core's energy to feed into the strike. Vandalia and I can feel it, and in most cases we believe you're using too much, which can affect accuracy more than using too little, and might explain the multiple extraneous bolts." He gazed at the deck of the raft. "Something else seems off as well, though."

"How much energy you feed your strike is also a function of your focus, will, and intent," said Vandalia. "You two have very high levels of all three, which is rare in pairs developing their first attack Abilities. More extraordinary is that you appear to be in perfect sync, most likely due to the fact you've been bonded for so long. It can take pairs years to develop your level of instinctual cooperation through the bond. You are truly exceptional in that regard." She and Aureosa turned to Wanchoo, who stood with his arms crossed, pondering.

"I agree," said Wanchoo. "It will serve you well in your advancement."

Zee felt himself blushing. "Thank you, sir."

Wanchoo smiled and replied with a wave of his hand, "I'm just making an objective observation."

Aureosa tapped his chin. "As far as this Lightning Bolt Ability goes, I'm assuming you're focusing on the object you wish to strike, rather than how to achieve it, correct?"

"Yes, sir." said Zee. "I'm not sure what you mean by 'how to achieve it,' though, other than aiming and building up the charge."

Aureosa glanced at Vandalia, who said, "Instead of thinking about the target of the strike, consider where it's coming from, what you're using to get it there, and what the end result should be."

Jessup said, "I'm sorry, ma'am. I don't understand."

"Think of throwing a spear, "Aureosa replied. "This simple act is not so simple at all, but with practice, you just do it. It involves a complex combination of physical actions and mental activity. How to hold the spear, your stance, your aim, and all the precise movements of breath, muscle, and bone that bring it to fruition. You must also consider the weight of the spear, the distance to the target, and whether you or the target is moving, as well as how fast that movement is and in what direction, all of which require swift adjustments to the actions of your body. That's how an attack Ability works."

Vandalia said, "Some are more like a sword than a spear, and some more akin to shooting a bow. Does that make sense?"

"To a certain extent, ma'am," Zee answered. "But how do we even start?"

"We're making it sound much more complicated than it is in actual practice. Even someone who has never picked up a spear can throw one, just without much accuracy, and most likely the spear will fall short or travel too far, and if it does happen to hit the target, it may not have enough power behind it to stick."

"That makes sense," Zee replied. "I've made all those mistakes when learning spear, javelin, and bow, and that's basically what's happening to us with the lightning. I only got better at spear throwing through instruction on the basics and a lot of practice. I can see how using an attack Ability could be like that. But this is lightning. Is it like an arrow? Maybe a spear?

"I understand the quandary," said Aureosa. "Jessup has always been able to produce electricity, but he's never been able to shoot it, unlike a dragon can with fire, ice, or ambergris lava. It comes naturally to them." He pondered a moment. "What if we think about it this way. The lightning is not the weapon."

Zee furrowed his brow. "Then what is the weapon?"

"You are."

Jessup said, "Oh..."

"The arrow analogy may work best, then. In a way, you two are the bow, but more than that, the archer, the bowstring, and the bow. Think of your mental preparedness—focus, intent, et cetera—as well as your stance, and think of the precise amount of your core you need to channel into the Ability as your draw. Consider aiming as pretty much the same as in archery, and the release of the bowstring at the proper moment is the firing of the bolt."

Zee and Jessup tried Aureosa and Vandalia's method. The first attempt wasn't much better than before, but by the fifth, there weren't nearly as many extraneous bolts flying about, and the main strike passed closer to the target. After another five attempts, though, they still hadn't hit it. However, Zee was glad to see that thinking about not wanting to hit the raft or the pylon tower that held the target was a successful adjustment, and they hadn't damaged them. If only thinking about what they wanted to hit worked as well.

"Rama and I have been discussing it while you practiced, and we may have an idea." Wanchoo lowered his Shield as Jessup turned back toward them again. "Not to disparage Peleus and Van's contributions in the least—the benefits are obvious already—but perhaps we're thinking about aiming the wrong way. And instead of thinking of lightning like an arrow, we propose you imagine it more like a connection."

Jessup said, "Um..."

Zee felt the same way but almost chuckled anyway. Not only because he didn't understand either, but also because Dean Wanchoo had used Aureosa's first name and Vandalia's calling name while talking to him and Jessup, and the commandants didn't seem to mind at all. Not only were Zee and Jessup being personally instructed by such prominent figures from the academy—and Red Titans, no less—they had become surprisingly casual with them. The thought of that alone made him almost giddy. It was a privilege he could never have imagined, and would never forget.

"We know very little about electricity other than some animals can produce it and it's what lightning is made of, or *is*, so to speak," said Rama. "We haven't a clue how it is generated, though experiments continue. There are magicker pairs who have devoted significant amounts of time and effort to studying lightning. It has become accepted that, just prior to a lightning strike, an electrical charge is felt both in the clouds and at the place where it strikes. How this was discovered resulted in more than a few untimely deaths.

"Magickers are particularly sensitive to changes in levels of power, and make no mistake, electricity is one of the greatest natural powers in existence. Mihir and I have felt this charge in the sky and on the ground or sea on numerous occasions. We can feel it in a zap-eel the moment before it zaps, and we can feel it in Jessup, even before the electricity manifests itself on his shell."

"What we propose," said Wanchoo, "is that you consider not aiming your lightning like you would a projectile, but connecting yourselves to your target. In a way, you are not an archer, string, or bow, but the cloud where the initial charge is produced. The trick, of course, will be to produce the proper correlating charge in your target. If you can do that, however, you will never miss."

Zee sat there on Jessup's shell above his brow, trying to soak in what they'd just been told.

Jessup crossed his eyes in an attempt to look at Zee, his mouth open and round. "Zee, I think I know what they mean. Sometimes, in the sea, things that are close to me will be zapped even if I don't touch them. Little lightning bolts just hit them, but I never see it move like an arrow moves. It just blinks and is gone. I thought it was because it was so fast I couldn't see it, but maybe it really is just a blink of light between them."

"So," Zee replied, "we visualize a connection between us and our target, maybe like attaching an invisible string from us to them, then imagine the string as lightning?" The two of them looked to Wanchoo and Rama.

Wanchoo said, "I can't think of a good way to advise you on how to produce the requisite charge in the target, so your theory is as good as any. You might as well give it a try."

"You can do it," said Tem. "We know you can." Timandra nodded in encouragement.

Jessup turned them back toward the target. They each raised the nictitating lenses of their eyes, then took deep breaths to settle their minds. As one, they focused on themselves, on their core, and on Jessup's electrical power, then instead of switching focus to the target, they extended it to the target. It took a few moments to maintain equal focus on both, as well as to visualize a connection between them. It helped that they didn't have to blink while using their nictitating lenses. An ache began to form in Zee's head, but he ignored it. They breathed out, and held it. Jessup's electricity generation engaged, but it hadn't even built up on his shell when lightning flashed and the target exploded.

Both of them stared agape at the burning debris flying through the air and the flames atop of the pylon tower. When they turned around, they still had the same expression.

Tem threw and arm in the air. "Hurrah! I told you!"

Dame Toomsil, Aureosa, and Wanchoo were clapping, shouting "Bravo!"

Then, floating over the waves, came the raucous cheers of the hundreds of sailors and bonded pairs who had been watching from the ships.

* * *

When Zee climbed down off Jessup, he nearly fainted, and as quick as Jessup was, the kraken was also dazed and barely caught him before he hit the deck of the raft. Zee thought it was because of the intense concentration it had taken to finally make their Ability work combined with the excitement of succeeding and the praise of the crowd. Then they'd checked their core. It was about a fifth of the size it had been when they'd started fully forged, and it had been at seventy percent before they successfully performed the strike. They'd used almost fifty percent on that one strike alone.

Wanchoo explained that a single expenditure of a pair's core on that scale often caused dizziness, disorientation, and fatigue. They would get used to it, though, and the effect would fade with more practice. Finding just the right amount of their core to feed into the Ability to achieve their objectives in terms of both accuracy and power would greatly improve efficiency, and they would use less of their core as well.

They were instructed to return to their quarters and rest. The deans would stop by in a while to speak to them about core building. Rest, however, came in the form of conversation about their Lightning Bolt Ability with Tem, Dame Toomsil, Mahfouz, and their dragons, who were waiting on the lower deck when they climbed out of the moon pool to make sure they were okay, then accompanied them to their quarters.

"We don't even know where the strike came from," Zee said.

Timandra said, "We got an inkling that the electrical charge had been induced, then the lightning simply flashed between the arrowhead-shaped point at the top of Jessup's shell and the target."

"That's excellent, strategically," said Mildrezod. "It means your foes will have little to no idea it's coming."

"Excellent and terrifying," said Mahfouz. He looked up at the dragons from the notes he'd been taking. "Who wants to fight them in simulation first?"

Timandra and Mildrezod, who were standing next to Peloquin, glanced at each other and both took a step backward.

It took a second for Peloquin to realize what had happened. "Great." He snorted. "Thanks a lot, you two."

Mildrezod batted her eyes at him. "My hero."

Apparently, dragons could roll their eyes, because Peloquin did.

Dame Toomsil said, "Come on, Pel, we can fry as well as the best of them. Maybe even better."

"That's encouraging."

"Maybe it's painless," said Tem, "like the instant death from Thunderclap."

Peloquin said, "Or it feels like being run through by a White Titan's lance or burned alive with Inferno." They all grimaced.

"I was joking," said Mahfouz. "The commandants will be making those kinds of decisions. Now let's get out of here and let these two rest."

They took their leave, and Zee flopped down on his cot. Arms crossed behind his head, he looked up at Jessup. "How does it make you feel to know that a Gold Class dragon doesn't want to fight us?"

Jessup's grin was slightly evil. "Good."

"They'd probably kill us within seconds."

"Or not."

Zee laughed, then closed his eyes—a respite that lasted all of five minutes before Deans Wanchoo and Venkatarama arrived.

CHAPTER 50

Before we get started," said Dean Wanchoo, "we'd very much like to hear about your forging process. Don't forget, nearly everything you and Jessup are doing is entirely new to us."

"It's very exciting," said Rama, who, as always, didn't look very excited.

"We magickers are an inquisitive lot, and at our age, Rama and I haven't found anything that has captivated us quite like you two have in decades."

Zee was seated on one of Jessup's arms, while Venkatarama was lying on his belly with Wanchoo leaning against his ribs. "I'm glad we could help, sirs." Zee said. "I mean that."

"That you learned to forge Empyrean so quickly from only Peleus's notes is truly amazing. No one would have thought people and beasts of the sea could forge Empyrean at all. But how were you able to see the Mariseal Plane on your own, let alone mine its ore? Is the process the same as with Empyrean?"

Zee grew nervous. As much as he trusted the deans, he still wasn't ready to tell them about the murfolk book. At least not until they'd gotten further with it and revealed more of the secrets it held. "It's similar, but not really the same. We just experimented with techniques and it appeared. We figured out how to forge it on our own from there."

Wanchoo and Rama gazed at him a moment. They didn't look angry or suspicious, but still, he felt guilty for lying.

Jessup said, "*They don't believe us, Zee.*"

"*I know.*"

"I have a book, sirs," Zee blurted out. He wasn't sure why he'd said it, but he did.

"What manner of book?" There was still no ire in Rama's voice.

Zee tapped his chest and the duffel appeared in his hands. He removed the book, then spoke while he unwrapped it. "A very special book, I think. I'm sorry I didn't tell you before. I was asked to keep it secret because people wouldn't understand, and it could get us into trouble." He slid off Jessup's arm and took it to Dean Wanchoo. "We think you'll understand, though."

Wanchoo took the book gingerly. Rama crooked his long neck to look as well.

Wanchoo turned it over, examining it closely, then opened it, brow furrowing at the strange symbols.

Jessup said, "It's a murfolk book. It only works after it's put in seawater and Zee puts his hand on the cover." The deans' intrigue became fascination.

Zee retreived a bucket of seawater from their Keep, which he had taken to storing there in addition to the duffel bag. It had no cover, but no matter what they did, it never spilled a drop while in their Keep. "I'll show you, if you like."

"Yes, please." Wanchoo gave the book back.

Zee put it in the bucket until it began to glow, then unlocked it with his palm and returned it to Wanchoo. The dean flipped pages, both he and Venkatarama captivated by the moving diagrams.

Zee realized this was the first time he'd taken the book out since he and Jessup had reached Copper Class and scooted closer to see the pages as well. The deans didn't even seem to notice.

When they came to the final pages that had been revealed, Zee looked to Jessup and shook his head. "*There's still nothing new,*" he said through their bond.

"I'm not surprised. We've gotten stronger but we still aren't consistent with our lightning Abilities."

"Where did you get this?" Wanchoo asked.

Zee hesitated a moment. "Dr. Aenig, gave it to me."

"Ah, Aenig…"

"Do you know him? I got the feeling that Commandant Aureosa might have."

Wanchoo didn't take his eyes off the book, gently feeling the pages with his fingers. Zee sensed what he thought might be reluctance. When the dean spoke, though, his voice revealed nothing. "I read his recommendation that you and Jessup be accepted into the academy. Peleus said he was an intelligent and trustworthy type who spent much time with you during your service on the ship."

Zee suddenly missed the doctor very much. "He did, sir. I don't know what I would have done without him."

Wanchoo's inquiring gaze met and held Zee's, then he tapped one of the pages with writing. "Can you read this?"

"No, sir. We've just been following the diagrams. It only reveals a new step when we've completed the current one. We're still on the first pages about attack Abilities."

Rama spoke with awe and reverence. "A murfolk and kraken training manual, with moving illustrations…"

Wanchoo said softly, "I feel magick upon it. It's definitely enchanted, but what manner of enchantment, I haven't a clue. The energy imbued to fuel it is similar to that given off by the blue Marisean in your core, as well as what we picked up from your stinger wand. This and your wand are genuine murfolk artefacts, I have no doubt. In certain circles, they would be worth a fortune, but especially this book. Do you know where Aenig got it?"

"I don't, sir. He was always going ashore at foreign ports and buying old books, though. Mostly about murfolk, when he could find them."

"I see…"

Zee was afraid he might have said too much, but Wanchoo looked up with a glad smile and held the book out to him. "This is a real treasure, Zee, and Dr. Aenig was right to warn you about revealing it to anyone. We're honored you would show it to us."

Rama said, "You have our solemn vow we will tell no one of its existence."

Zee had no doubt they were sincere. "Thank you."

He and Jessup exchanged glances, and Jessup said, "You're welcome to study it some time. Maybe you could help us with the language."

"That would be wonderful," said Wanchoo. Rama even smiled. Almost.

Zee wrapped the book, stowed it, the bucket, and the duffel back in his and Jessup's Keep, and climbed back up on Jessup's arm.

Rama said, "Our main purpose here is to use our experience to help you with forging, as well as growing your crucible and core, but we were also wondering..."

Wanchoo continued Rama's thought. "We were wondering if you would not only show us how you forge so we can offer advice, but also do us the honor of allowing us to forge with you."

Zee was surprised they would even ask, let alone so politely.

It was Jessup who answered. "The honor would be ours, sirs."

It tickled Jessup to no end that the Red Titan Class deans of magicks listened like eager cadets while he and Zee explained their process of forging Empyrean and Marisean together. Zee had to elbow him to keep him from giggling.

Rama sighed. "We so wish we could see the Mariseal Plane, but Temothy and Timandra tell us it's impossible."

"We wish you could see it, too," said Jessup. "It's beautiful."

"We can only imagine."

Under Wanchoo and Rama's direction, Zee and Jessup reforged their core using dual forging, but in more controlled steps. Instead of packing as much ore as they could into their crucible before refining and forming it, they were told to only fill it to about seventy-five percent. They found that method to be easier and it went much faster. Only once their core was back to the size it had been before their efforts of the day were they instructed to mine as much as they could take and stretch their core.

Two bells later, the deans said their goodbyes, acknowledging that forging with them had a cooling effect on the Empyrean ore and made the process both more comfortable and efficient, just as Tem and Timandra had claimed.

Once the doors were closed, Zee and Jessup turned to each other and spoke at the same time. "More?" When they'd finished laughing, they forged three more times.

CHAPTER 51

Jessup watched and listened closely while Dame Toomsil gave Zee more pointers on his footwork.

"Now try to hit me again," she said.

Jessup liked the knight. She was tough, strong, and quite pretty, as far as humans went. That was his impression based on things he'd heard humans say about each other, anyway. He'd told Zee he should buy her chocolates because that's what people did so they could kiss them. That's what Robhat Hayes said, anyway, and Mickal rot Fletcher had agreed. Zee had turned red and said don't be ridiculous. Jessup shrugged to himself. People were silly.

Zee moved well and he was very quick, but she was faster. His fists buzzed with blue electricity as he jabbed and swung and pressed toward her. They were back on the raft, testing out what they called Zee's sympathetic Ability, Lightning Fists. Jessup still called it Sparky Paws because it made Zee roll his eyes and reminded him of the grin on Fennix's face when the little Ice Diver had said it the first time.

Jessup worried about his dragon friend, hoping Fennix was okay and not too concerned about him and Zee or where they'd gone. If he was even aware they were gone, that is. For all Jessup knew, Fennix could still think they were incarcerated. Jessup liked that word, "incarcerated." Not what it meant, of course, but how it felt to say it. Human language was fun. How it was put together and all the weird contradicting grammar rules rarely made sense, but it was fun to learn it and use it. "Contradicting." He liked that word too.

Dame Toomsil danced back, side-stepped, dipped, and swayed, avoiding every one of Zee's blows. Peloquin stood beside Jessup, and he and Dame Toomsil had sparked their core. It made her extremely fast. She moved almost in a blur. That didn't seem quite fair, since he and Zee weren't allowed to spark their core for this training, but it would protect her if Zee did land a blow.

Zee threw a punch, but over-extended. Toomsil grabbed his wrist, her aura flashing at the contact with the electricity there, and threw him over her shoulder to land flat on his back. His Lightning Fists fizzled out while she shook the hand she'd grabbed him with.

"I felt that," she said.

Zee pushed himself to a sitting position and rubbed his lower back. "So did I."

"You're projecting too much," said Commandant Aureosa. "You've been well trained and your instincts and reflexes are excellent, but against a bonded pair, especially with their core sparked, they can see what's coming from a mile away. You need to develop your feints more and lean into the element of surprise. A knight must have an agile body, but the best also have an agile mind."

"And don't over-extend a punch like that," Toomsil added. "It comes from frustration and thinking about only that single blow. Have more patience and self-control. Consider what will happen if you miss, and what you'll do about it."

"I know this is important," Zee replied, "and I'm happy to learn boxing and work on my Lightning Fists, but what does this really have to do with fighting knights on dragons?"

"A question asked by every cadet who has ever entered the academy," said Aureosa, "and the answer is always the same. Everything."

Jessup thought about that, and would remind himself to think about it more later.

Zee sat pondering, then hopped up and punched his fists together, gathering the balls of energy once more. "Okay." Without waiting for Dame Toomsil to get into her stance, he attacked.

It didn't help. Though he came on faster and with swifter strikes, her Gold Class reflexes and speed made it easy for her to avoid his blows. Zee over-extended a punch again—but when she grabbed his wrist this time he pushed more power into his fist, causing her to yelp, and when she spun to throw him again, he hooked her legs with his.

They went down in a heap. Zee threw an elbow at her jaw. She blocked it so quickly Jessup almost didn't see her arm move, then she lifted him off her and threw him through the air.

It was Zee's turn to yelp, but he spun in the air, hit the raft with his feet, and backward-rolled to a standing position, facing Dame Toomsil, who was already up.

They stared at each other a moment, then grinned.

"Better," Toomsil said. She shook her hand and rolled her arm. "That stung all the way up to my shoulder."

Tem gazed wide-eyed at Zee, mouth open in the shape of an "O," then grinned also.

Vandalia said, "Not bad for a novice to get the best of a knight of any class, let alone Gold, even for a moment."

"In battle, it only takes a moment to make the difference between victory and defeat," said Aureosa.

"Let's not forget," said Dame Toomsil. "These aren't your ordinary novices. They've been bonded for nearly as long as Pel and I have, Zee has been training in one way or another and doing very dangerous and difficult work since he was seven, and both have had to fight for their lives, Jessup his whole life."

"I like to fight," said Jessup.

Zee said, "Now you do. I bet it wasn't so much fun when you were little."

Jessup lowered his gaze. "Many things wanted to eat me."

They were all quiet for a moment.

Vandalia said, "Jessup still retains the feral ferocity he was forced to develop just to survive, while Zee is more even-keeled and thoughtful. I already see the bond has given each of them some element of the other, and it's for the betterment of both."

Jessup and Zee considered her insight. They'd have to remember that and each make the other even better.

"They're also extremely driven. More so than might be healthy."

Jessup said, "No rest for the wicked."

They all looked at him.

Zee said, "I need to have a talk with Fennix about the things he's teaching you."

Jessup grinned.

Next, they worked on Shield and Deflect with sparked cores, Aureosa and the others imparting their wisdom. Deflect was more core-efficient, but Shield was more versatile. Instead of just pouring power into it, which was wasteful, they were taught how to change its thickness and density, to rechannel energy from its edges to its center, and vice versa. They could also change its shape rather than its size, all of which saved their core. Just like a regular shield, Shield could also be used as a weapon in close quarters. It could even aid in maneuvering in the air for dragons, but they imagined it might be even more useful for that in the water.

At the end of their training session, the deans of magicks, Dame Toomsil and Peloquin, and Tem and Timandra had left the raft for other duties, leaving Zee and Jessup alone with Aureosa and Vandalia.

Zee took advantage of the opportunity. "We know you left your notes in the handbook for us, sir and ma'am. We can't thank you enough."

Commandant Aureosa said, "I'm glad they were helpful. And that reminds me. Now that you've got the basics, and more, I should probably get those back when we have a chance."

"I'll deliver them to you as soon as we get back, sir. Thank you especially for including the entries on Slan hai Drogo and Mogon. They were incredibly inspiring."

Aureosa looked embarrassed but also nostalgic. "Vandalia and I were very young."

"And naïve," said Vandalia. They shook their heads, chuckling softly.

Jessup said, "You will be Black Titans one day, we know it."

They gazed up at him, a hint of despondence in their eyes, then Aureosa climbed to the saddle on Vandalia's back. "The distant dream…" He patted Vandalia on the base of the neck.

Vandalia turned to them, her features soft—or as soft as a dragon's features could be. "For now, we take great solace in helping others reach the peak of their potential." She smiled, then took a deep dragon's breath and leapt to the sky.

Zee and Jessup watched them fly back to the ship.

Jessup groaned. "I shouldn't have said anything."

"If you hadn't, I would have. It's okay."

"I wish there was some way we could help."

"So do I."

* * *

Over the next few days, they spent bells a day working on their Lightning Bolt. Wanchoo and Venkatarama generated floating targets rather than the fixed target they'd first used. They were basically balls of Platform, Wanchoo had explained, which he and Rama could move about any way they wished.

They concentrated on efficiency and aim more than power, starting low then working up in strength. Eventually they could hit over half of their targets, even the moving ones, which was much better than the none they'd been able to hit at the beginning.

Both the magickers and the commandants had seen them manifest multiple bolts during the scuffle with tar Tarzian's flight, so they practiced Lightning Blast as well, the magickers sending up several balls to aim at.

Their hit rate was far worse, which frustrated Jessup more than Zee, to whom every strike felt like a major victory.

Vandalia insisted Jessup show her the arm-whipping technique Timandra kept telling her about. "She says it's absolutely frightening, and she's a dragon."

Aureosa and Vandalia helped them refine it, adapt different methods, and practice feinting and deception—much like they'd been teaching Zee during his boxing lessons—except Jessup had ten arms instead of two, and his had claws.

Some of the lessons Zee enjoyed the most happened between scheduled training sessions.

Sitting on the raft during a break from Lightning training, Aureosa went over the movements of hands and arms to aid in controlling Abilities. "They're an extremely helpful tool at the beginning, but they can also forecast what you're planning to do. With practice and increasing mental acuity, they become entirely unnecessary, except for the most difficult and highest Abilities. Wanchoo still uses his wand for many things, and you saw me use my hands and Vandalia her wings for Thunderclap. Focusing that much core power into a complex Ability can still require tools on every level.

"Those that are more or less amplified lower Abilities, like Beam or Inferno, take no more mental focus, just more power from your core. When you level up, you can activate it more quickly and pour much more power into it."

Vandalia said, "We can fire six Beams at once before reaching the limit of our split focus and, therefore, control. We use hand and wing movements for those. And, of course, the more Beams, the weaker they are, though they still draw quite a bit of our core."

Jessup said, "What if you tried shooting twelve Beams?"

"We can, and we have. We simply can't control where they're going to go. Handy when surrounded by the enemy even with reduced striking power, but it's dangerous to allies if they're near."

"That would be bad," said Jessup.

"That kind of thing happens more than any of us would like to admit, to be honest."

* * *

By the fifth day, the highest priority in their vastly accelerated training program, even ahead of forging and Abilities training, was simulated combat. It was also their favorite.

CHAPTER 52

Zee took a deep breath and blew it out to calm himself. Beneath him, Jessup pushed up a few feet on his arms and leaned forward, glaring at their opponents.

"*Remember, hard and fast,*" Zee said through their bond.

"*Hardest and fastest,*" came Jessup's reply.

A Simulation Artefact, slightly smaller than the one in the stadium at the academy, floated on a magicker's Platform just above one end of the raft, its Simulation Crystals forming a circle of dim light from one side of the raft to the other at the other end. This would be what Aureosa had called a ground bout, removing both Zee and Jessup's advantage in the sea and the other pair's advantage of being able to fly.

Inside the circle, Zee and Jessup faced a Silver Class knight pair, the dragon a Royal Crimson. They didn't know who they were, but the commandants had wanted it that way. The commandants had also chosen Silver Class because that was the lowest class of pair that had been brought on this mission. They would have chosen Copper or Bronze if they could. By all accounts, Zee and Jessup should have no chance against them. They still didn't know exactly what class or level they might be, but even if they had reached Copper Class, there were still Bronze and Iron between them and Silver. With each class being roughly two times stronger than the previous, a Silver Class pair's threat level would be eight times greater, with significantly more powerful attack Abilities.

They'd put that out of their minds as well. The smirk on the Silver Class rider's face only reinforced their resolve. And, as the commandants and deans of magicks had reminded them, Zee and Jessup were not the typical bonded pair. As far as they were concerned, they were capable of anything and had set their minds to proving it.

And while the Crimson dragon stood seven feet at the shoulders, ten feet to the top of its sharply horned head, Jessup's shell reached over twenty-five feet when he was just sitting on the ground. Pushed up slightly as he was, it was closer to thirty. If he stood up fully like he did when running, he towered to over fifty feet.

Vandalia raised her head high from where she stood outside the simulation arena near the Artefact. "Combatants, spark your cores!"

The wave of power from their opponents' core igniting washed over Zee. They hadn't bothered to Occlude or Camouflage it, wanting Zee and Jessup to feel just how much power they had.

Zee and Jessup didn't hide theirs either, and the smirk faded from the opposing rider's face as their core was lit.

"Begin!" Vandalia commanded.

Jessup sprinted, his four forwardmost arms already whipping to full length, cat-like black claws extended at their tips. The dragon took a step back and blasted super-heated flame. Zee and Jessup didn't raise their Shield, nor did they slow or try to evade the fire. Their aura pulsed as the flames hit, and they'd already raised their protective nictitating lenses on their eyes. Still, the heat felt like standing too close to the open door of a blast furnace. Zee wore only academy training armor since his wasn't yet completed, and, because he had no saddle, a waist strap attached between spines on Jessup's shell and Zee's feet planted against lower spines were all that held him in place. At least the rig left his hands free to hold the alchemically ceramic-coated shield in front of him. Jessup didn't flinch at the blisters that formed on his face and arms or the steam that rose from his flesh, but attacked with even greater ferocity.

The flames stopped coming as their opponents were forced to raise their Shield against Jessup's onslaught, just as Zee and Jessup had hoped. So far, their strategy was working. If the Silver Class knights had their Shield up and in front of them, they couldn't attack. Now to put the next phase of what Aureosa and the others had taught them into effect, using feints and misdirection.

Jessup's arms slammed into the Shield one after the other from the front, top, and both sides while he maintained just enough distance to strike with the greatest speed and impact, then he snapped out three arms at once from the left. The knights' Shield instantly moved to that side to block the strikes and they Shifted away, only to have another of Jessup's arms whip in from the opposite side, coil around the rider, and snatch him out of the saddle.

The dragon gaped in shock and the rider screamed as Jessup flung him out of the arena to splash into the sea.

Jessup stood tall, breathing in aggressive huffs, towering over the dragon and glaring at him. Only the waves and cries of distant gulls could be heard as Zee took in the expressions on the faces of those gathered on the raft, then looked over the spectators on the ships around them and glanced at those flying in the sky above.

"End match!" cried Vandalia. "Victory goes to Mr. Tarrow and Mr. Jessup!"

Tentative clapping rose from those gathered on the raft and from the ships. Zee wasn't sure if it was because they were shocked, or angry that a kraken and murman had defeated a knight pair. It may have been both, but the only reactions he cared about were those of the commandants, deans, Tem and Dame Toomsil, and their dragons. Each one of them was grinning.

* * *

The soaking-wet rider was dumped from a Platform onto the raft beside his dragon, healed from any injuries by the Simulation Artefact. He stood, water pouring from beneath his armor, and attempted to maintain his dignity while Commandant Aureosa spoke to him and his dragon. The man shook the commandant's hand sheepishly, then climbed upon his dragon, where he sat straight and saluted Zee and Jessup.

Zee nodded cordially.

Jessup said, "Thank you for the fight."

The rider stared, then shook his head and they took off back toward the ship.

Tem clapped Zee on the back. "You've won your first simulated combat match. How does it feel?"

"Weird?"

"And you didn't even have to use lightning," Dame Toomsil added.

Zee said, "We thought we'd save that for a surprise."

Jessup said, "And we were afraid they'd Shift, and we'd miss."

Aureosa stepped up. "Victory, against a mid-level Silver Class pair, no less. This will set tongues wagging."

"Let them talk," Jessup replied.

"Don't get too confident," said Vandalia. "You'll be up against a Gold Class pair next."

"Gold Class?" Zee asked. "Now?"

"After a short rest. We have to find your limits as quickly as possible so we know what to focus on in your training. It will also help your progression."

Dean Wanchoo said, "How are your core levels?"

"About ninety percent. We pushed a lot into speed, but we didn't use any Abilities."

Rama said, "Good. You'll probably need it all."

Zee gazed at the Simulation Crystals floating in a circle over the raft. "When we were in Triumf's Theatrum, the Orb of Assessment was able to assess pairs after each match. Could we do that here?"

"Unfortunately not," Wanchoo replied. "The Orbs of every nation with a Dragon Corps can communicate with one another, but we are at too far a distance for ours to assess through the Artefact."

Jessup said, "Don't worry, Zee. What matters is how many knight pairs we beat."

"How many do you think we can beat?"

A devilish grin spread across the kraken's broad lips. "All of them."

Zee chuckled and shook his head.

Vandalia's grin was as devilish as Jessup's. "We shall see, Mr. Jessup. We shall see."

Jessup's grin faltered, and Zee laughed.

* * *

The Gold Class pair looked serious indeed. Older than the young Silver Class pair, and the scars they bore told of experience in real combat.

The dragon, a Royal Ebon, pawed at the raft deck, its claws cutting deep gouges in the wood, while thick black smoke shot out of its nostrils.

Zee and Jessup had come up with a plan of sorts, but Zee was anxious. By the time Vandalia shouted for the match to begin, though, deep breathing and the confidence Jessup exuded had settled Zee's nerves.

* * *

Arms crossed across his chest, Peleus ran Aureosa blinked as lightning split the air between the kraken-murman pair and their foes. In that blink, the golden Shield of the Gold Class knights had already materialized.

From the size and brightness of the flash, the commandant guessed that Zee and Jessup had poured nearly twenty-five percent of their core into that one strike. That was half of what they'd expended the first time they'd successfully used Lightning, but as a result of their training in core-use efficiency it packed far more punch. The knights were knocked back and shaken, but their Shield held. In the next instant, they'd dropped their Shield and a flood of white-hot flame engulfed Zee and Jessup and most of the area of the arena, blocking out sight. The dragon had released Inferno.

A great thump sounded and the raft shook beneath Aureosa's feet. He feared Jessup had fallen and Zee with him. Then rumbling rose from within the Inferno, the raft vibrating with it, and Jessup came rolling fast through the flames. He was on his side, shell spines retracted, and due to the cone shape of his shell, rolling in a half circle, arcing toward the knights. His arms, though steaming and charred, propelled him at incredible speed, his face tucked up into his shell.

The Inferno snuffed out and the knights leapt into the air to avoid the juggernaut of a beast. Jessup adjusted his roll and threw his arms out high.

The knights' Shield flared to life, but arm after kraken arm wrapped them, hooking them with clawed ends and the spikes that protruded from the suckers. The dragon tried to beat its wings, but they too were caught and the kraken dragged them down, Shield and all. In seconds, every one of Jessup's ten arms had hold of them. He pushed his face out of his shell to glare with blue flames in his eyes and a grimace of extreme effort on his face. Aureosa had the sudden realization that this was true life or death for the kraken. He was giving it his all, and more. All simulation combat was supposed to be like that, but for Jessup, it was different. He had fought for his life in the sea too many times to do anything but kill, or die.

The dragon dropped their Shield and fired a Beam at Jessup's face. The kraken's aura flared, but the heat still seared into his cheek. Jessup slapped the dragon's head so hard it sounded like a tree dropping on a boulder. The Ebon's aura flashed, yet he still looked dazed. He bit, sinking his teeth into one of Jessup's arms, but the arm wrapped his snout and locked his mouth closed.

Meanwhile, the rider retrieved a sword and hacked deep gashes into Jessup's arms, until the kraken squeezed both knight and dragon too close for him to wield his sword, enveloping them in a knot of arms. Jessup's wicked spines shot out from his shell, and he pulled them inexorably closer, groaning with the effort.

Still they fought, and they were strong. Jessup pulsed with electricity, Shocking them. His foe's aura flared, but they shook from the attack. They tried to call up their Shield again, but it blinked out in such close proximity. The dragon raked at Jessup's burned cheek with a hind foot, but he let it do its damage. It got a front foot braced against Jessup's shell, but even its Gold Class strength could only resist the pull of that many monstrous octopod arms for so long.

Jessup snarled with the strain, and the light on the raft began to dim. Overhead, dark storm clouds were forming, lightning flashing within them. Spectators gaped up at the sight, then were torn between where to keep their eyes, on the unnatural storm or the kraken grappling with a Gold Class knight pair. Jessup Shocked them again.

Aureosa was so enthralled by the fight, then the storm, he'd nearly forgotten about Zee. He spotted the murlad in the swirling smoke and steam, out where he and Jessup had stood at the beginning of the match, kneeling behind his blackened and deformed shield, peering over it. His hair was nearly burned away, his skin reddened and charred. When he stood, most of his body looked the same. The blue flame of their core, as well as what Aureosa now assumed was the kraken's conviction, burned in his eyes. Zee dropped the shield and ran.

The knights' aura of yellow was dimming. As powerful as a Gold pair's aura was, it could not provide sustained protection. It worked in pulses, which were stronger and lasted longer in higher classes and could be used more often, but every aura had its limits.

Jessup growled through gritted teeth as he squeezed with all his might. The clouds above grew darker and more ominous. Lightning shrieked through them, booming out rolling thunder.

The knights' aura failed and Jessup jerked them onto his spikes. The dragon screeched and writhed and the rider bellowed as they struggled. They both still lived, but couldn't escape. Unless they yielded, the match still wasn't over.

Zee touched his chest as he leapt high onto Jessup's shell. Blue light flared and his stinger appeared in his hand. He clambered onto the knot of Jessup's arms and cocked his arm back, aiming the point of his stinger at the face of the rider pinned within. "Yield!" he roared in a voice the commandant had never heard him use before. If Aureosa didn't know better, he thought he felt a chill from Vandalia at the sound of it.

The knight shouted back, "We will not!"

Zee stabbed the stinger through the man's open mouth.

Even from where he stood, Aureosa heard the rider gurgle, then the final death rasps of both him and his dragon.

Jessup unwrapped his arms, letting the bodies of their foes flop to the deck of the raft. The clouds above shrank in on themselves and disappeared as swiftly as they had formed. Jessup pushed himself upright and shoved the bodies away. Zee leaned back against him and the kraken put the end of an arm around him. Burned and badly injured, they gazed at Aureosa and the others on the raft. Zee's chest rose and fell as he heaved in rasping breaths. Then he grinned.

Standing near Aureosa and Vandalia, Peloquin said, "The old rhymes have truth to them, then. 'When the kraken comes arising, even dragons flee.'"

Vandalia said, "I'd say that goes for murfolk as well."

* * *

Vandalia ended the match, announced Zee and Jessup the victors, and the white light of the simulation arena washed over them, rendering all as good as new. The Gold Class knights got up slowly, obviously stunned. Zee wasn't sure if it was by the loss itself or the manner of their loss. Then he saw that their armor was no longer gold. It was white.

Not only had Zee and Jessup defeated a pair of high-level Gold Class knights, they'd help them break through to White Titan. As surprised and elated as Zee was, he felt remorse over having killed the rider so brutally. He could say he didn't know what had come over him, but he did. Jessup had gotten angry, and his rage had infected him. Through the bond, Zee could tell that Jessup was happy about their victory, but he wasn't surprised like Zee. For him, it was simply what had to be done.

"We did it, Jessup," he said to his big friend.

Jessup smiled. "Best kraken and murman team, ever."

Zee smiled back and tilted his head toward the knights. "Come on."

The rider and dragon eyed them warily as they approached. Zee held out a hand to the rider. "Thank you for helping us train, sir. I'm sorry for how I ended it."

The man looked shocked. "Sorry?" He laughed. "Not in all my years has an opponent said they were sorry for defeating us." He shook his head, then Zee's hand.

Taking Zee's lead, Jessup said to the dragon, "It was an honor to fight you, sir."

The dragon stared at him, then snorted flame. "I have been told that before, but not by someone who beat us so soundly, and never by a kraken."

"I am happy to be the first."

"We should be thanking you," said the rider. "We've been trying for two years to level up to White Titan Class."

"I'm glad we could help," Jessup replied. "I look forward to fighting you again sometime."

The knight said, "Maybe let us take to the air next time."

"And we'll take to the sea," said Zee.

"Deal." They shook again, then the rider turned Zee toward the commandants with a hand on his shoulder, walked him to them, and saluted.

Aureosa saluted back, and the rider said, "Thank you for this opportunity, Daimyo General Commandant."

"My pleasure, Lord Commander."

Zee gaped up at the man. He hadn't bothered to check the pair's rank before the match. Lord Commander was three ranks above Dame Toomsil's Knight Commander rank, and only one away from Earl General.

"You've got quite a find in these two," said the Royal Ebon. "I'm feeling more confident in this mission knowing they're with us."

The rider took to the saddle, and the two flew off.

Tem said, "What the shells, Zee? Do you know who that was?"

"Um... no?"

"Jeram ee Goblers and Potterus." No recognition registered on Zee's face. "The Terrors of Whitecaps Isle?"

"Oh... Oh!" He watched them soar toward one of the other ships.

"They wiped out the entire Randoma Pirate Enclave with only three flights. Weren't they credited for over half the kills themselves?"

"That's them," said Dame Toomsil.

"Holy shadcrap..."

"Still just a little man and little dragon," Jessup observed.

Everyone laughed and Aureosa said, "Mr. Jessup, your confidence will either bear you to uncountable victories or be the death of you."

Jessup shrugged, then grinned. Zee shook his head, grinning back.

"Now," said Vandalia, "we have much to discuss."

CHAPTER 53

Zee and Jessup strode from the moon pool with Tem and Timandra, who had met them there after returning from the matches. None of them spoke, all considering the day.

The commandants had interrogated Zee and Jessup thoroughly after the match. They all wanted to know how they had managed their core in each match. Zee and Jessup had explained as best they could when exactly they directed power into Abilities, strength, speed, resilience, cognition, and sufferance, and approximately how much. Zee had a high sufferance level naturally, but it was nothing compared to Jessup's. He benefited from Jessup's by virtue of their bond, but he'd still had to pump a lot of core energy into it to keep from shrieking and leaping crazed into the sea from the unbelievable heat of Inferno during the match with the Gold Class knights.

From behind his ruined shield, he'd focused on the bond and directed core power to where he'd known Jessup needed it most so Jessup could concentrate on the fight. Most of what Zee'd done had been subconscious or by instinct, initiated by a kind of natural feedback loop that passed between the two of them through their bond.

All had commented on how both fights went, step by step, and offered advice. Lastly, Dean Wanchoo had asked about the storm that had formed overhead during the last match, saying he and Rama and the commandants had seen the same phenomenon during their confrontation with Cadet tar Tarzian's flight. Zee had seen it then, too, but with everything else happening, he'd thought it could have just been a fluke and put it back of mind. Jessup had said it happened when he got angry, which made him fight harder. The group had theorized about this for a bit, then left it at that.

The magickers had dismantled and removed the Simulation Artefact long before they'd finished, and the sun sinking below the horizon.

Zee collapsed on his back on the cot in his and Jessup's quarters, throwing an arm over his eyes. He was tired deep in his bones but also invigorated at the same time. Part of it had to be that their core was down to almost ten percent, but his energy was bolstered by what they had accomplished against all reasonable odds. He still couldn't believe it. He was also still haunted by how he had shrieked at the knight trapped in Jessup's arms, the rage he'd felt at how they'd hurt Jessup, and how it had felt to stab his stinger through the man's face.

"Are you feeling all right, Zee?" Timandra asked.

He forced himself to sit up, where he rubbed his face with his hands. "I'm okay." He affected a smile. "I mean, what a day, right? We beat a Silver Class pair and a Gold Class pair in our first matches ever."

"The Terrors of Whitecaps Isle, no less," Tem interjected.

Zee gazed at the floor. "It feels like a dream." But also a nightmare.

After a pause, Tem said, "You didn't really hurt him, Zee. They're both fine, and better for the match." After all the time they'd spent together, Tem knew him too well.

Zee said, "But there might come a time when I really have to do something like that, in a real battle."

"You've done it before." Tem's voice was serious but with a touch of empathy.

"I know, but my life, or anyone's I cared about, didn't really depend on it today."

Timandra said, "In a real battle, you can't take the time to ask every enemy to yield. Even if they do, not all knights are honorable enough not to return to battle and hurt someone else."

"I could leave them there if they were injured enough," Zee replied.

"That's true, and in your case, they'd probably already be in the sea, anyway."

Tem said, "Simulated combat is about more than exercise, practicing technique, and working your core. It's about developing a battle-ready mind."

Zee remained silent, but nodded.

Timandra tipped her head toward Jessup. "This big fellow already has it, and you two have a powerful bond. You'll get there."

Zee snorted. "He's just mean."

Jessup grinned. "Big mean kraken."

Tem said, "And that's why we love you."

Jessup blinked, taken off guard, and everybody laughed.

"Okay," Tem interrupted, "enough morbid talk. Let's get forging. You two have a lot of Empyrean and Marisean to shove into that big mean core of yours."

* * *

The day got even better when, after forging their core back to where it had been and then some, Zee and Jessup tensed as a sudden flood of power washed over them, through them, bringing the now familiar intoxicating sense of indestructibility and euphoria. It receded more quickly than the previous times it had happened, but like then, they were left feeling as if yet more weight had been shed from their bodies, another layer of gauze peeled back from their senses, and more fog cleared from their minds.

Not only that, Tem and Timandra reached high-level Silver Class. They left cheerful and energetic.

Zee couldn't quiet his mind enough to sleep. Meditation and breathing exercises would probably do it, but some part of him didn't want to sleep. Then he realized why. They'd classed up, and he hadn't checked the murfolk book.

He fetched the bucket of seawater and book out of their Keep and dunked it, evoking the blue glow of its pages. When he put his hand on the cover this time, instead of brightening and dimming once, the light pulsed twice before fading. When Zee opened the book, Jessup looking over his shoulder, the pages turned all by themselves until they came to the chapter on attack Abilities that had been revealed before—but now the diagram had changed. The kraken and murperson were still depicted gesturing forward, but instead of the repeated movement of generic arrows moving away from them, the attack was clearly lightning.

More astounding, the unknown letters below the diagram changed before his eyes to settle on a new configuration, and a glyph appeared below them. The glyph looked much like the triangular illustration of the kraken in the diagrams, but simpler, and there was a bumpy circle centered on the kraken's shell above its face with a jagged line angling down through.

"What's that?" Jessup asked.

"I wish I knew," Zee replied. He also wished now more than ever he could read the language. He moved his fingers over the diagram. "But it's like the book knows what our attack Ability is now."

Zee flipped to the next page. It was no longer blank. Neither were several of the one's that followed. Zee's heart beat faster as he studied the diagrams in glee and wonder.

"Oh, Zee," Jessup exclaimed, "we have more work to do."

CHAPTER 54

Jessup and Zee climbed aboard the raft at sunrise, just as Tem and Timandra flew down to join the deans, commandants, and Dame Toomsil and Peloquin, who had already arrived.

"Sorry we're late," Tem apologized.

Zee said, "Is it because you gave me your watch?"

"No, I have a new one."

"He had breakfast with his father," said Timandra.

Zee asked tentatively, "How was it?"

"Wonderful," Tem replied. "Mostly he asked about you and Jessup, but he wanted to know everything I'd been doing, and to talk politics and my future, of course."

"That doesn't sound terrible," said Dame Toomsil.

"He even gave me a hug at the end."

"Really?" Zee asked.

"No. Can you imagine?"

Everyone laughed.

Tem's face grew dour. "He did apologize for not paying closer attention to my career, though."

"That's nice," said Jessup.

"It makes me nervous, is what it does."

Commandant Aureosa said, "Lord Commander jal Briggs is a fine knight and governor. He's served the Dragon Corps and his province well for many years."

Tem shrugged, then caught himself. There'd been no admonishment in the commandant's tone, but he was the commandant, and a Daimyo General. "Yes, sir. Of course, sir."

Vandalia turned to Zee and Jessup. "You two have caused quite a stir." Her expression was unreadable, but it felt like an accusation.

"Oh...," Zee uttered.

"Everyone wants to fight you now. They're practically clambering over each other for a chance to prove themselves or level up, everyone from Silver Class knights to White Titan generals. The vice admiral has had to organize a lottery. They'll be pulling names from a hat, though we get to choose what classes you're matched with."

"Bring them all," Jessup said through a mischievous grin.

Dame Toomsil said, "Wagers are being made. Not so many on who will win, kraken and murman or knights, but which knight pairs will last the longest."

Zee said, "I'm not sure how I should take that."

"Take it well, I would say," said Aureosa. "Though it does place more weight on your performance. We need to get you stronger and further refine your Abilities. Standing around chatting won't do it."

Zee's brow furrowed. "Speaking of that, Jessup and I think we classed up last night, and we want to show you something."

"Another class-up?" Vandalia asked. "That would bring you to Bronze. How long have you been forging, again?"

Zee did the mental calculations. "We forged for the first time the night of the exhibition match at the academy, then for a couple more weeks before Tem and Timandra started helping us. We trained with them for three weeks, spent a week in the brig, and we've been on the ship for most of a week. About ten weeks, total?"

Timandra said, "And they classed up to Copper less than two weeks ago."

Vandalia gazed at the two of them. "Phenomenal."

Jessup said, "Thank you, ma'am."

Zee retrieved the murfolk book from their Keep and began to unwrap it. "Deans Wanchoo and Venkatarama have seen this, but we want to show it to the rest of you as well."

Everyone watched closely as Zee handed the book to Jessup, who took it with a small sucker at the end of one of his arms then reached to the edge of the raft and put it in the water. After a few seconds, he brought it back, the pages emanating soft blue light. Zee placed his hand on the imprint on the cover. This time it only brightened once before fading. He handed the book to Commandant Aureosa, who looked to Wanchoo.

"It's quite safe," the dean replied. Aureosa took the book. "Probably."

Aureosa raised his eyebrows at Wanchoo, who grinned. Aureosa opened it to the first page.

Vandalia asked, "What is it?"

Jessup said, "A magick training manual for bonded murfolk and krakens." Aureosa's eyebrows raised again.

By the time Zee finished explaining the book, how it worked, and where he got it, they were all crowded close, riders in front, their beasts behind them. After Zee had shown them the new pages that had been revealed, Aureosa looked to Zee. "This changes everything."

* * *

Aureosa and Vandalia led them out into the fog away from prying eyes—which Aureosa said was in itself a strategy. The others, including Dame Toomsil, Tem, and their dragons, rode on a rescue barge lowered from the ship, large enough to fit four pairs comfortably and pulled by Jessup.

There they worked on the new Abilities that had been revealed in the book. The first involved raising water out of the sea in a spout, which they called Water Spout. The second they called Fusilade, which was the shooting of multiple bolts of lightning in quick succession, each having as much power as the single Lightning Bolt. They also had a defensive Ability where their Shield was formed of spinning water drawn from the sea or air and mixed with their aura. They named that, of course, Water Shield.

* * *

Each day they trained and engaged in more simulated combat until their core was nearly spent, then forged, and did it all again the next day. Their opponents, all having witnessed the previous matches, did better against them as they learned how the murman and kraken fought and what they could do. Zee and Jessup had to work harder because of it, think faster, and come up with new strategies and techniques.

On the ships, sailors would groan or cheer after each match, and coin changed hands.

* * *

The day after Zee and Jessup had beaten the Silver Class and the first Gold Class pair, they were pitted against a Gold Class Ice Diver pair. Their Water Shield had already proved to block attacks better than their regular Shield, but it was even more impenetrable when frozen. Once frozen, though, they couldn't see through it or change its size, and it was heavy and slow to move. It made a great ram, though.

At one point in the match, they dropped their frozen Water Shield and made a new one, much larger and thicker. The Ice Diver froze it as well, then coated the raft with a slippery Ice Sheet. Zee scrambled up Jessup's shell to peer over their Shield and spot where their foes were. Jessup reached out, gripping the ice with his claws and sucker spikes, then yanked himself forward with Burst. They engaged Push at the same time they struck their foes with their frozen Water Shield and knocked them out of the ring.

* * *

In their next training session, the commandants went in depth about feeling out for others, enemy and otherwise. Bonded pairs had a natural sense of those around them and learned to know where their flightmates were at all times, whether they could see them or not.

Going beyond that was a passive Ability called Tracking. Vandalia explained that by directing more core power into cognition, which heightened their perception, and feeling out for auras of other pairs like they would when revealing their core, they should be able to see phantoms of gold light against a black background. She also told them it would help at first if they closed their eyes.

Tem and Dame Toomsil flew into the fog on their dragons to act as targets—Zee and Jessup just had to promise to use very weak Lightning Bolts if they were actually going to fire at them. The phantom images were flickering and weak at first, but after a few bells of practice, Jessup and Zee could see them more clearly and target them in the fog, even with their eyes open. Apparently it had taken Tem and Timandra weeks to develop their Tracking Ability, and they still had difficulty with it. Aureosa said that as Zee and Jessup progressed, they'd be able to see greater numbers, and by combining it with their uncanny sense of impending danger, even be able to discern between friend and foe. In the Titan Classes, it would become second nature. Even then, attempting to see too many caused the Ability to become weak and unreliable. As with all Abilities, it would take practice.

* * *

Their next match came in the morning, with Zee and Jessup facing off against a Gold Class Rock dragon pair. Their foes attacked immediately. The spinning Water Shield worked even better than expected to block and cool the flying lava, causing it to drop to the raft, but the blows still sucked up core power and knocked them back. Then the Rock sprayed a Lava Flow that sped toward Zee and Jessup, over a foot deep and too wide for the murman and kraken to escape. Having nowhere else to go and not wanting to wade through the molten dragon ambergris, Zee poured core power into Abilities and they used Burst to leap high toward their foes, Jessup doing a forward flip in the air with his arms tucked. It looked like they were going to fall short, right into the Lava Flow. At the last second, however, Jessup threw his arms out at full extension. The Gold Class pair tried to evade, but Jessup snatched and Shocked them. Zee and Jessup hadn't used too much of their core so far, so they kept Shocking. To their great relief, their opponents yielded just as Zee and Jessup's core was becoming dangerously low.

* * *

That evening, after a forging session, the commandants pitted them against three pairs at once, a Silver Royal Ebon pair, a Gold Rock pair, and a White Titan Ice Diver pair. Jessup whipped his arms and they fired Lightning Blast wildly in an attempt to make their opponents keep their Shields up so they wouldn't be able to attack until he and Zee could get close enough to grab them. They held them off for quite some time, but finally the White Titan pair Streaked in, dropping their Shield at the last second. Zee and Jessup engaged their Shield too late. The rider skewered Jessup between the eyes with a lance, and the Ice Diver speared Zee through his aura and normal shield with an Ice Spike that pinned him to Jessup's shell.

Jessup didn't like losing and adamantly recommended they not do that again.

* * *

Their first sea bout was against four Silver Class pairs, including Tem and Timandra, which began with some good natured taunts.

The simulation arena projected from the back edge of the raft out over the waves, larger than it had been on the raft, the walls of light rising high into the sky and down deep into the sea. The ship didn't slow, so they also had to swim to stay within the ring, and the knights had to keep pace in the air.

Zee and Jessup managed to bring one particularly aggressive pair down with a Water Spout, then the others with a Fusilade of three lightning bolts in quick succession. The pairs struggled in the water but weren't terribly injured. The closest pair were Tem and Timandra. Jessup crept toward them, he and Zee both wearing vicious grins.

Floundering in an attempt to get away, the dragon cried back over her shoulder, "Get away, you beasts!"

They grinned wider, then saw that the other pairs were spread out around them—and two of the dragons were Ice Divers attempting to get out of the water before Jessup could get to them. Zee shared an idea with Jessup, who flipped over, dove below the surface, and began spinning, head down, while Zee focused power into strength and speed. With their core sparked and quite a bit larger than it had been when Jessup had first tried it, a prodigious vortex of water spun up, creating a whirlpool that pulled their foes spiraling down into its center. Zee channeled all the power they could muster into Abilities as Jessup snatched them all into his arms. The resulting Shock was blinding.

They surfaced and Jessup shouted, "Done!"

Afterward, being able to create a whirlpool with that much force was deemed an Ability, and they named it Vortex.

* * *

In further matches, they found that a Fusilade of three quick bolts of lightning could take down a Gold Class pair, but it took up a lot of their core. The first or second strike would destroy an opponent's Shield or weaken it enough that the next one or two dropped them from the sky. Their foes also couldn't escape the strikes once targeted, even with Shift or Streak. They wouldn't be killed, but once in the water with a kraken, they were done for.

White Titans, especially more than one, proved much more of a challenge. They were incredibly fast and their Shields and auras too strong even for Fusilade.

In their first match against three White Titans, spears pierced Zee and Jessup's Water Shield and aura and stuck into Jessup's shell, face, and arms. Zee took arrow wounds and a spear thrust. Jessup surprised an Ice Diver that got too close and caught it with the hook of a stretched-out arm. He yanked the pair into the water and Shocked them, but they used Blast, a more advanced version of Push, and escaped back into the air. No one came that close to Zee and Jessup again.

Their advancing Water Spout technique came in handy but only as a distraction. The Titans pounded attacks into their Shield again and again, draining their core. One of the Titans had mastered Slice as well, a devastating attack where a blinding swing of the rider's sword sent out an arc of cutting power that sheered through their Water Shield and carved a deep furrow in Jessup's shell.

Zee and Jessup had found they could target their Lightning Bolts while their Water Shield was up using the Tracking technique Aureosa had shown them. It worked for Fusilade as well, and they could lock in on one pair or up to three different pairs for successive strikes. They still had to drop their Shield to strike, but it exposed them to attack for only a fraction of a second. They'd also discovered they could Track and target from underwater. They weren't able to fire their Lightning from under the sea to the sky, though, and had to surface to strike.

From beneath the waves, they targeted the strongest of their opponents, then shot to the surface, dropped their shield, fired, and dove immediately, taking only a spear to Jessup's shell.

A shadow flickered over the surface twenty yards away, then a Greatwing splashed into the waves. Zee and Jessup's core was dangerously low, so they just watched as it swam toward the edge of the arena, not wanting to take the risk of trying to drag it below the surface. If the pair still had enough of their core left to use Blast or any number of other close-combat Abilities, Zee and Jessup might not be able to hang on to them, let alone survive. They considered their predicament and decided to just stay under.

* * *

After a few minutes, everyone on the raft glanced at each other, wondering what the murman and kraken were up to. Out in the arena, a Royal Crimson pair flew close to an Ice Diver pair and pointed down. The rider peered into the water, and the Ice Diver shook its head. There was no way it was going in after the kraken.

Shortly thereafter, one of Jessup's arms waved above the surface, then was pulled back under.

Vandalia said, "Are they yielding?"

"I don't know," Aureosa replied. He stepped to the edge of the raft where the SHEELs sat on their krisdolphins watching the match. "Chief

Walster, go see what those two are up to, if you would."

A short time later, Walster surfaced next to the raft and removed his breathing mask. "They're forging, sir. They say they're not coming up."

Vandalia said, "It looks as if our mad murman and kraken are learning. If you can't win, at least don't lose." She called the match a stalemate.

After that, all of the White Titan sea battles ended the same way. Zee and Jessup could hide underwater when their core got low, and if the Titans were weakening, they could fly so high it was difficult for Zee and Jessup to target them even if they did have enough core left to power a strong Lightning Bolt.

Then the commandants and deans decided it was time to show the formidable young pair what real defeat felt like.

* * *

The bout took place on the raft, and Aureosa, Vandalia, Wanchoo and Venkatarama had given themselves permission to start the match in the air. It wasn't fair, but that was the point. Not all combat was fair. Zee and Jessup knew they didn't have a chance but were excited by the challenge. They planned to jump straight up with Burst and use Lightning Bolt as fast as they could, then throw up their strongest Water Shield. They hadn't planned ahead any more than that, which was fine because they didn't even make it that far.

"Begin!"

As soon as they leapt, Lightning Bolt charged and target acquired, they bounced off a Shield conjured by Wanchoo and Rama and dropped like a very large rock. They recovered quickly, throwing up their Water Shield while Jessup shoved himself upright—just as the commandants flared golden, Aureosa slammed his hands together, and Vandalia clapped her wings.

Zee heard a muffled whump, it felt like he ignited from the inside, and they were slammed to the deck by what had to be the white-hot hand of a god. Ten yards away, two Jessups staggered in Zee's double vision, steaming, his shell crushed in on one side and flaming. Most of his spines were broken and several arms had been smashed. Zee's fuzzy gaze fell along his own mangled and charred body. He pumped what little core power they had left into resilience and sufferance.

* * *

Dame Toomsil said, "They're still alive? After Thunderclap?"

"How is that even possible?" said Tem.

Timandra said. "What are they made of? Steel?"

Peloquin just gawped.

* * *

Jessup spun and tipped in what looked like slow motion, dropping heavily to the deck. It reminded Zee of when baby Jessup would fall over and Zee would have to tip him back up. He grinned through what was left of his lips, and Jessup began to laugh, a loud croaking cough. Zee joined him, both of them choking and in pain, but they couldn't stop.

* * *

Aureosa's eyes whipped to Wanchoo's while their dragons just stared.

Vandalia said, "I think we've created a monster."

Aureosa shook his head. "Two monsters."

Rama said, "At least they're our monsters, thank Zepiter."

Wanchoo lowered his wand to his lap. "Or perhaps we should say, 'thank Postune.'"

Still laughing, the young murman and kraken shouted simultaneously, "Again!"

* * *

Jessup's tendency toward frustration and anger became more tempered as the matches went on. He didn't exactly fight with more restraint, but he did manage a more practiced mindset. Gone was the kraken who fought only with fury and reckless abandon, a more shrewd beast of battle taking its place.

CHAPTER 55

For the last two days of their journey, the task force purposely sailed into a storm and traveled under its cover. The prevailing trade winds blew straight toward their destination, a rugged atoll forty miles from the position where the Wraiths would be waiting. Magickers kept them Shielded from the strongest wind and maintained a steady fill of the sails, but the effect was unsettling.

All simulated combat was suspended, and the raft was disassembled and stowed. Zee and Jessup continued to train and forge just as hard as before, going so far as to run and exercise in the driving rain on deck for bells a day.

The mood on the ship grew more somber, but the knight pairs were an inspiration, remaining resolute in their mission to save the prince, and they maintained their military bearing at all times. Zee and Jessup saw less of the commandants, deans of magicks, and Dame Toomsil and Peloquin. Even Tem and Timandra could only join them for a single daily forging session, explaining that plans were being refined, and flights and squadrons were being configured.

Zee and Jessup spent more time with the SHEELs. Mostly they ran drills under the sea where the weather didn't affect them, but they also went over their infiltration and hostage rescue plan and the possible variables.

A four-person fire team of commandos would leave the ship on their krisdolphins the night before the king was expected to deliver the ransom for his son. As had been established earlier, Zee and Jessup's task was to protect them from sea beasts. Beneath the surface, they would swim the forty miles to where the Wraith ships awaited. Once there, Zee and Jessup would stay beneath the ship while the SHEELs snuck aboard and rescued the prince. They even had breach-blasters to blow through the hull in case they became trapped. As soon as they had the prince safely off the ship, they would fire a flare into the sky to alert the task force and head toward them.

While that was happening, the task force would creep out from behind the atoll under the most complete Cloak that Wanchoo, Rama, and the other magickers could muster and sail toward the enemy ships. It would take some time to reach them, but as soon as the magickers saw the flare they would drop the Cloak and divert all their efforts to speed. The squadrons of knight and combat magicker pairs would cross the distance much faster and engage the enemy within minutes. Zee and Jessup and the commandos would intercept the admiral's ship and enter the moon pool with the ship moving at full speed, which they had already practiced a dozen times.

If all went well, the Dragon Corps and Navy task force together would wipe out the enemy completely.

In theory the plan was simple, but the variables were many. Zee was amazed at the professionalism and detail with which the SHEELs ran through the possibilities. It was obvious they'd done this kind of thing before, or something similar, and more than once. If anyone could pull this off, it was them. Zee felt the same about the Dragon Corps and Navy commands.

Zee had to admit he was nervous. Oddly enough, not about the danger, but that he might fail in some way. He was honored that they believed he and Jessup could be of help on such an important mission. A small, bitter part of him also embraced this as a chance to prove to the academy's board they were wrong for not accepting him and Jessup, but everyone on the mission had been sworn to secrecy. Other than Aureosa, Wanchoo, Vice Vizier Ashura, and Lord Commander Governor jal Briggs, the rest of the board might never know.

One day, he and Jessup would show them. Zee took comfort in that, as petty as it might be. Jessup's fierce confidence was a godsend. When the kraken sensed Zee's anxiety, it flowed from him through their bond like the soothing, radiant heat of a hearth.

* * *

First thing in the morning on the day of the mission, Zee went up for physical training on deck. Sometime in the night, the task force had reached its destination and settled into a foggy bay, snug against the sharp, misty atoll. Other than the shuffle of feet of other knights running and sailors moving about on deck, it was eerily quiet. No orders were shouted. Anyone who spoke did so in hushed tones, and even the bell that sounded the time of day remained silent.

Dean Wanchoo sat upon Venkatarama with eyes closed and wand raised, concealing the entire task force with Cloak, a magickers' Ability that functioned much like Camouflage but was used to mask others and, in this case, and entire task force of Navy ships. A dozen White Titan magicker pairs circled Wanchoo and Rama, facing outward. Zee could feel the power of their cores burning steadily. As it had been explained to Zee, only Wanchoo and Rama could conjure Cloak on that level, and the other magickers were boosting its power to both enhance the concealment and keep the deans from collapsing under the strain on their own.

The rest of the morning passed quickly, with more run-throughs with the SHEELs, and a long forging session.

They took lunch in their quarters with Tem and Dame Toomsil and their dragons. Little was said but small talk, words of encouragement, and lighthearted jokes. Tem and Toomsil with Timandra and Peloquin would take part in the assault on the enemy ships, but as was Dragon Corps protocol, the highest-class pairs would take the lead: a squadron of White Titan knight pairs accompanied by combat magickers, with Tosh's Red Titan knight pairs—King mon lin Phan and Norrogaul and Commandants Aureosa and Vandalia—accompanied by Red Titan Deans of Magicks Wanchoo and Venkatarama to protect them at the vanguard.

In the afternoon, Zee and Jessup trained lightly again up top. They were supposed to be resting for the mission, but neither of them could sit still. Wanchoo and Rama and the other magickers were still there, in the exact same position they'd been in the morning. Zee could endure a lot, but he was sure standing still for that long would drive him mad.

* * *

The sun had finally set when nearly twenty people flooded their quarters with tools, ladders, and some rather bizarre-looking apparatuses.

"Time to saddle up," said Tackmaster Sadir sem Samir, keeping his voice down even this deep in the ship.

Armorer Nanners tan Runoffski beckoned Zee over. "Mr. Tarrow, to me."

Assistants and craftspersons descended upon him and Jessup with precision and fervor that felt like an all-out assault.

* * *

Two bells later, Dame Toomsil was waiting in the lower deck with Peloquin, Tem, and Timandra when the doors to Zee and Jessup's quarters finally slid open. The tackmasters and armorers and their teams filed out with their gear. When Zee stepped out behind them, she barely recognized him.

He wore a high-necked body suit of black, subtly striped in gray, similar to the ones the SHEEL commandos wore, but with silver-black scales that glistened like fish scales sewn to it on his torso and upper arms, streamlined pauldrons on his shoulders, scales sewn in like tassets on his thighs, and metallic bracers on his forearms. Gloves of the same material as the suit covered his hands, though his feet were bare except for pieces of scale mail that covered the tops, strapped around the soles. On his head was a smooth black helmet. The helmet had no visor, but there was a short nose guard and the sides curved in to protect his cheekbones. Altogether, it was far more sleek and formfitting than a dragon rider's armor.

Though Dame Toomsil could only see Zee's eyes and mouth, she would recognize his wide grin anywhere.

Zee moved aside to make room for Jessup. The kraken had no armor, but a strange contraption was attached to his shell above his brow. It had to be a saddle, but unlike any she had seen before.

"What do you think?" Zee asked.

"Terrifying," said Timandra.

Jessup said, "Terrifying is good."

"Not you. Zee. What is that thing stuck to your shell?"

"It's a kraken battle-saddle," Zee said cheerily.

Though their teams had left, the tackmasters and armorers had stayed behind. Sadir sem Samir said, "He called it that. We came up with no such name."

There was a seat between two vertical rails bolted to Jessup's shell. Above and below it were half ovals of domed gray steel, the open ends facing each other, with oblong windows of clear crystal that appeared to be three inches thick between ridges of sawlike teeth.

Zee strode over and put a hand on it. "You have to see how it works."

The SHEELs had taken notice and approached as well. Zee climbed onto one of Jessup's arms and pulled himself up. Jessup watched cross-eyed as he moved. Zee sat on the seat and strapped in at the waist, then reached down, pulled a lever, and slid the bottom half of the capsule up on the track and over his legs. Next he reclined the seat back and reached up to the top half of the capsule.

"Watch this." Another pull of a lever and the top part released to slide down over him, then lock into place against the lower. Zee waved at them through the window in the top half of the capsule.

Peloquin said, "It looks like he's inside a beetlebug."

There was a clunk from inside the chamber, and the top slid back up to lock into place, then Zee slid the bottom back down as well. "This is even better." He pull a handle beneath the seat, swiveled it one hundred eighty degrees, then repeated the process of closing the capsule, now upside down.

Jessup said, "That's for when I smash through ships so Zee doesn't have to jump off." That raised some eyebrows.

Zee opened the capsule and swiveled back to an upright position, grinning wide.

"It's brilliant," said Dame Toomsil, coming closer. She ran a hand over the metal of the capsule, inspecting the lag bolts that held it all to Jessup's shell.

Dragon Tackmaster Timy said, "The parts are made of alchemical steel, the surfaces fused with anti-corrosion and heat-resistant ceramic, like your own armor, Knight Commander Toomsil."

Samir said, "It was a team effort between us and the armorers. The design was a challenge, but we did the best we could with limited time and resources."

"It's amazing work," Tem replied.

"There's a seat on the back, too," said Zee. "No capsule, but perfect for riding when Jessup's swimming point first and I should be on top, above the surface or below." Zee spoke as he unbuckled from the seat and clambered out of the saddle. "I have a sword, dagger, rondel dagger, and shield too, but you really have to see this armor." He hopped down and pointed at various pieces as he explained. "The suit is sheelskin, which is super tough anyway, but it's also alchemically infused with ceramic particles. The pauldrons, helmet, braces, and scales of the mail are high-tensile alchemical ceramic instead of steel, so they're much lighter weight and just as strong."

"Stronger," said Armorer Runoffski. At the expressions of curiosity from Toomsil and Tem, she added, "We've been working on it for a while. This will be the first time it's tested in the field."

Zee said, "It's designed for as much freedom of movement and as little drag in the water as possible. I can take the gloves off and store them in my Keep for swimming, and there are flaps in the sides of the suit and in the neck for my gills."

"Does it work?" Dame Toomsil asked.

"I'm going to find out right now," he said, gesturing toward the krisdolphin tank. "But if there's a problem, I can unsnap panels along my ribs and remove the sheelskin gorget on my neck."

He headed toward the tank, but Walster stepped in his way, scowling down at him, muscular arms crossed. "I don't like it." Zee frowned. "We can't have you looking better than we do."

Jessup said, "I think he looks like a bug."

Zee glared at him in mock disapproval. "Hey!"

Walster grinned and thumbed over his shoulder toward the tank. "Hop in."

Dame Toomsil strode beside Armorer Runoffski. "This all had to be very expensive."

"Zee said the same thing. I think he was worried we were going to make him pay for it. It's being covered under our research-and-development budget. King Phan signed off on it himself."

* * *

The test went fine. Zee swam, twisting and turning in the tank, with the armor causing no impediment to his movement or breathing. The krisdolphins enjoyed it as well, squeaking and swimming with him the whole time. When he climbed out, Zee was happy to see the armor drained quickly, too.

Walster said, "You might as well leave it on. We're going to suit up now."

Zee took a steadying breath and pulled off his helmet. "Okay."

Jessup said, "It's a good thing your armor works."

"I know, right?"

Dame Toomsil said, "We have to go. Be safe out there."

"You too, ma'am."

Timandra looked up at Jessup. "Take care of your kraken-self and our murman. You're the only ones we've got."

"I will, ma'am. We'll see you when the prince is safe and victory is ours."

She smiled. Tem put a hand on Zee's shoulder, gave him an encouraging nod, and strode away.

Zee watched them go. He knew he and Jessup were as ready for the mission as they could be, but he still had to quell the thought that this could be the last time he'd see them.

Out of the corner of his eye, he caught movement and a white robe with a red sash. Dean Wanchoo stood in the tall doorway to the room behind the table, waving him over.

Zee had never seen Dean Wanchoo look tired, but he did so then. There were circles under his eyes, and his movements were slow, as if his limbs carried too much weight. Venkatarama lay on a carpet nearby, his head hung low. Keeping up the Cloak for an entire task force for a whole day must have really been taking it out of them, even with the help of the other magickers.

"We can be spared for a bell or two," said Wanchoo. "Fresh magickers have been rotated in. They can keep the concealment up by themselves for that long."

They sat in comfortable chairs at a low table, the only people in the room, with the door closed. Wanchoo poured tea for both of them. He downed nearly all of his, in spite of its heat, then set the cup on a stand next to his chair and folded his hands in his lap, gazing at a beautifully engraved and inlaid box on the table.

Zee sipped his tea and waited silently. He and Jessup didn't know why the deans wanted to speak to them, but Wanchoo looked so exhausted, he didn't want to push it.

Finally, Wanchoo spoke. "You two will be leaving with the SHEELs on a very dangerous mission shortly, this we know, but there are some things we want you to be aware of before you go."

Wanchoo still hadn't looked up at him, so Zee stayed quiet.

When his eyes met Zee's, he said, "You are aware of the two types of bonded pairs, knights and magickers."

"Yes, sir," Zee replied. "Knight pairs are naturally suited to fighting and attack, magickers to defense and healing and, well, magick. They have a greater magick affinity by virtue of how their unique auras mix with

Empyrean during the refining phase of forging."

"Exactly right. There is also, however, a third type."

Zee brow creased. "A third type of pair?"

"Cadets learn of it in second-year courses at the academy, but only in passing and when the exploits of Slan hai Drogo and Mogon are covered in history courses. Drogo and Mogon were the first to be assessed as this type in a hundred years, and there have been none since. It's called a sorcerer."

"Sorcerer..." Zee rolled the word on his tongue. "I'd never heard that about Drogo and Mogon."

"It isn't spoken of often."

Then Zee remembered when Dame Toomsil had shown him and Jessup the assessments taking place at the Orb of Assessment. "I've seen the type badge on Drogo's statue in the citadel courtyard. It had both a wand and a sword."

"That is the emblem of the sorcerer type. You have a good eye. Very few ever notice it."

After a pause, Rama said, "Sorcerers have the affinities of both knights and magickers. All the attack Abilities of knight pairs, but also the defensive Abilities of magickers, including their greater magick affinity, healing Abilities, and talents to create enchantments, potions, wards, and spells. Like other magickers, they tend to specialize, but they can use one affinity to enhance the other."

"It gives them significant advantages in battle," Wanchoo added.

"Do you think there may be some among the Wraiths?"

"We have no way to know, we just don't want you to be surprised if you run into one."

Jessup said, "Thank you for the warning, sirs."

Wanchoo seemed to shrink farther into his chair. "There is another thing." He pondered a moment, then said, "All magick leaves a trace, some more than others, and Rama and I feel a lingering dread in the air. It has come to us for some time, like a foul smoke on the wind, there and then gone again. We've sensed it more often in the last few years, but it has grown ever stronger as we've approached our destination. This close to the enemy, it is constant and cloying. It wears upon us." He took another deep breath with a hint of a shudder. "Please keep this to yourselves, gentlemen, but there is darker Aethereal ore from which to forge than is found in the Empyreal and Mariseal Planes. I shall not speak its name, but I, we, fear that the Wraiths, some of them at least, have somehow gained access to it."

Zee didn't know what to say.

"Peleus and the king are aware of this, and they will be on their guard, but we want you to be as well. The feeling of dread I mentioned when we stood upon the belly of the chasmclaw is the same that we have now, only here it is a hundredfold stronger. We sensed it on the hand of the prince and foot of his dragon as well."

He looked up at Zee once more. "If the aura, Shields, or Abilities of any of the enemy manifest red instead of the yellow of Empyrean, we want you and Jessup to dive as deep and swim as far as you can. Leave the fighting to the Titans."

Zee couldn't believe it, but Dean Wanchoo and Venkatarama, the deans of magicks and mid-level Red Titans, were afraid. He looked to Jessup, who felt it too.

"We're not telling you these things to frighten you," said Rama. "Just be on your guard for more than your usual foe."

Zee still didn't know what to say, but uttered, "We will, sirs."

Wanchoo sat up in his chair. "There is one more thing." Off Zee's reaction, he added, "It's nothing so dreadful as what we've just told you. I promise."

"That's good. I mean, thank you, sir."

Wanchoo leaned forward, spun the finely carved box toward Zee, then lifted the hinged lid. The bottom of the box had square dividers that held small, corked bottles. In the box's top half, more bottles sat on hinged shelves that swung vertical as the lid was lifted, except these bottles were of different sizes, shapes, and colors. Some in the lid were beautifully designed and shimmered with metallic tints like colored oils on water.

Zee had seen similar boxes in the apothecaries back home and on Triumf's Island, but they weren't as fancy as this one, and the bottles had always just been clear or dark amber—and none of those had exuded the intoxicating power Zee and Jessup felt from these. The effect was almost heady, and it took a few seconds for Zee's mind to clear.

Wanchoo said, "These are pills for boosting core power and increasing bond strength, produced by pharmaceutical magickers at the academy and in the capital by the king's own. Some have been dispensed to other pairs for the battle to come, but by regulation, only to those who can afford them."

"We're not fans of that regulation," said Rama, "but it is extremely time-consuming and expensive to produce them, so I suppose there is some logic in it."

"The effects are temporary," Wanchoo continued, "but they can mean the difference between life and death in battle. Even the least potent among them could be dangerous to any pair under Silver Class. More than one could harm even a Red Titan's core. What they would do to a bonded murman and kraken, we do not know."

After another pause, Rama said. "There are knight pairs who refuse to take them at all, out of pride or fear, it's difficult to tell, but their choice is always respected. Nonetheless, we would like to offer one to you."

Zee stared at the bottles, then lifted his eyes to Wanchoo. "How much do they cost, sir?"

It was Rama who answered. "My apologies. When I said offer, we mean at no cost to you."

"That is… very kind."

"It should be swallowed by the rider since they are the natural conduit during forging."

Wanchoo spoke more sternly. "Even if you take one, do not swallow it unless as a last resort, at the moment of most extreme need, understood?"

"We understand, sir," said Jessup.

Zee inspected the bottles, conversing with Jessup. There was no question they wanted one. They'd take any advantage they could get, even with the risk, and the opportunity to be stronger if they needed it was too much to resist. The only question was, "Which should we take?"

"None of them would be harmed if submerged in water, so there is no worry there. Otherwise, they increase in potency from bottom to top."

Zee scanned the bottles, feeling the gazes of Wanchoo and Rama upon him. His eyes, his whole being, through a sensation rising from his and Jessup's core, were drawn to a squat bottle of unremarkable color or design on a shelf in the top of the box. Zee glanced at Jessup, who tipped a nod.

Zee pointed at the bottle. "What's this one?"

Wanchoo exhaled in an almost undetectable sigh, then pulled the bottle from the shelf and uncorked it. The power Zee had sensed earlier wafted over and through him again, only stronger, then was gone. Wanchoo tipped the bottle and a round white pill dropped to his palm.

Rama said, "You have powerful instincts, Mr. Tarrow. That is the single most potent pill in the box."

"Which also makes it the most risky for you to take," said Wanchoo. "But it's yours if you and Mr. Jessup are certain you want it."

"We're certain, sir."

"So be it." He replaced the pill in the bottle and held it out to Zee.

Zee's palms were sweating for some reason. He rubbed them on the thighs of his sheelskin armor and tentatively took the bottle. It was warm and soothing in his hand, but he would swear it throbbed with tremendous potential energy.

"Place it in your Keep," said Rama. "It will be perfectly safe."

Zee did so, and the sense of vitality was gone.

"Remember, only use it if you absolutely must."

"Yes, sir. Thank you both. We'll bring it back to you if we don't need it."

"Now—" Wanchoo placed his hand on his knees and pushed himself up from his chair—"Rama and I need to engage in a quick forging session and get back to work." Zee stood as well. Wanchoo placed a hand on Zee's shoulder, and his mouth curved in a weary smile. "We'll see you back here on the ship, safe and sound with the crown prince, yes?"

Zee smiled back and saluted. He knew he didn't have to salute, but it felt like the right thing to do. "Yes, sir." Jessup saluted as well, bringing a broader smile to Wanchoo's lips.

Wanchoo saluted casually back. "Be safe."

* * *

Watching the young murman and kraken move out into the main area of the deck, Rama spoke through his and Wanchoo's bond. *"They made their choice. It was obviously drawn to them, and they to it."*

"I just hope we've done the right thing."

"It wasn't our idea."

"That doesn't absolve us."

"No, it doesn't." Rama considered a moment. *"Perhaps we should have told them if it were to be sold, it would fetch a price equal to that of an entire battleship."*

Wanchoo snorted, then shook his head and closed the door.

* * *

Jessup said, "That was... something."

Zee's face was drawn in contemplation. "Yes, it was."

A low whistle caught their attention. Walster, who stood across the deck next to the moon pool with Coolbaughm and Chan, tipped his head for them to come over.

The last of the krisdolphins was being lowered into the moon pool as they crossed the deck, fabric bands holding small kit bags and a quiver of short harpoons wrapping its body three-quarters of the way back.

Other than a half dozen sailors to operate the winches and watch the moonpool, the deck was empty, making it feel even larger and more intimidating.

Walster was completely geared up, Chan behind him adjusting the harpoon crossbow and air tank on his back. "It's go time."

"We're ready, sir."

Coolbaughm and Chan were staying behind as backups, but would be waiting in the moon pool with their krisdolphins in case they were needed. Walster climbed up and was straddling the lip of the pool when a half dozen dragon and rider pairs flew into one of the dragonports and alighted on the deck. The pairs stepped to them, the riders in full armor, the dragons kitted out for battle. King mon lin Phan led the group in gleaming, blood-red armor. The others were all White Titans. The banner of Tosh hung on a pole attached to the back of the saddle of one of the dragons. Another held the banner of the Dragon Corps.

Zee snapped to attention, as did Jessup. They hadn't seen the king much at all on the trip. The expression on his face was inscrutable as ever.

Walster didn't climb down to kneel but sat straight and saluted along with Coolbaughm and Chan.

The king saluted back, then inspected Zee and Jessup. When he seemed satisfied, he said, "Be strong. Be brave." His stern expression softened a touch, and he addressed them and Walster. "Bring my son back to me."

The SHEEL commandos put hands to hearts. "For king and kingdom's call."

Phan's gaze went back to Zee and Jessup. "Zepiterspeed to you all."

CHAPTER 56

Fifty feet down in the dark waters, Petrikleo's krisdolphin dispatched yet another overly large and aggressive sheel, driving its wavy nose blade through the killer fish's gills, then returned to formation. Berrolli shot a harpoon bolt to spear yet another overly long and vicious cooda.

Zee sat belted into the seat on Jessup's back as they sped through the sea at the center of the group, the four commandos at equidistant points, above, below, and on each side. All watched the water and listened with supreme vigilance. Zee's eyesight had continued to improve as he and Jessup forged, especially his night vision. He could see as far now in the dark sea as he ever could with the sun shining bright above. His hearing had also been boosted, especially beneath the waves. It didn't come close to Jessup's though. His and Jessup's sense of impending danger had become even more uncanny as well.

The krisdolphins, however, were in a whole other class. They'd dart off before he or Jessup felt anything, sometimes two at a time, clicking signals to the others, take out crabsharks, shorks, and tigerfish with brutal swiftness, then return just as quickly. The four of them had already slaughtered a pack of hammerhead orcapods with far more efficiency than Zee and Jessup had when they'd been attacked on their way to Triumf's Island.

Between their surprising swiftness, calculated maneuvers learned from years of training, the krisdolphins' swordlike nose blades, and the dead-eye aim of the commandos, the SHEELs were a truly deadly force.

Zee and Jessup had only risen to action once, when a scyllacanth almost half Jessup's size shot up from the depths with the speed of a harpoon cannon's projectile and caught hold of a krisdolphin with the mouths at the ends of its tentacles. Jessup had snatched the squidlike creature, freed the krisdolphin, and shoved the scyllacanth's head into his mouth, spines and all, then sucked its screaming legs in like noodles. That got looks from the commandos, but the krisdolphins squeaked and clicked with approval.

The attacks had been practically nonstop since they'd rounded the atoll, but the largest predator so far had been the scyllacanth. More sizable sea beasts piqued Zee and Jessup's senses outside of their view, and the krisdolphins would become quiet, but the monsters either weren't hungry or were smart enough to know the dangers of approaching a kraken.

Tablert checked her Empyrean-lit compass once more to keep them on course, and Zee realized they hadn't been attacked for a while. In fact, they'd come across no sea animals of any kind.

Tablert tapped her compass and pointed ahead. Walster held up a fist for them to halt. Berrolli pulled a telescoping periscope from where it was stowed on his krisdolphin, and the two of them swam toward the surface.

Zee and the others waited in silence. Zee closed his eyes and listened. Other than the soft rush of the commandos' breathing within their masks, the sea itself was eerily silent. Too silent. Jessup was thinking the same thing.

Berrolli and his mount returned, stowing his periscope as they came. He pointed ahead, then used his fingers to indicate the distance of the enemy ships. Three hundred yards. They were almost there.

They moved more slowly going forward, commandos circling above and below Jessup as they went and still no fish in sight. Zee heard the faint slapping of waves on the ships' hulls before he saw them. The twin moons of Zhera cast them as wavering silhouettes on the surface, arranged in a circle with approximately eighty feet between them.

The closest ship was a third the size of the HMS *Dragon's Rage*, but still a sizable vessel and the largest of the Wraith ships. Noticeably absent were chains dropping into the depth for anchorages, which could only mean they had magickers keeping them in place. Below, a vast field of odd ropy kelp waved lazily in the current.

Berrolli crept to the surface with his periscope again. He returned shortly, having identified the larger ship as the one bearing the mottled white flag with four red blotches, the ship the Wraiths had instructed the king to meet for the exchange. Following signals from Walster, they maintained their depth and swam to directly below the ship.

The back of Zee's neck tingled and he looked down at the waving kelp. It was beginning to rise. Jessup spoke through the bond, his voice urgent. "*Zee, that's not kelp.*"

Zee shouted, "Rapid enemy advance from below. Evade and retreat!"

Their reaction was instantaneous but not fast enough. Dozens of tentacles exploded upward, snatched the krisdolphins and riders, wrapped up Jessup, and yanked them into the deep.

Two of the krisdolphins escaped, their skin raised in red welts where the tentacles had held them, their commando riders drawing short sword and combat hatchet. They dove, cutting at tentacles to free their team members, but were caught again and pulled downward.

Jessup extended the spines on his shell, spun and ripped the tentacles that held him with the spikes and claws of his arms, and bit at them with his teeth. Zee slashed with his sword and stabbed with his stinger. With a quick pulse of electricity from Jessup and a blast from his siphon they almost fought free, but the tentacles were countless and unrelenting.

They continued to struggle as they were drawn inexorably deeper, the krisdolphins and commandos bound and helpless around them.

Below, the gaping shell of a monstrous clamlike creature came into view, its open shell with toothed edges plenty large to fit all of them, including Jessup, with room to spare. Inside, a great lump of muscle rippled and clenched, a mouth with concentric rows of teeth gnashing at its center.

The tentacles sprouted from all around it. On its surface, dozens of eyes glared, malevolence personified, and they glowed red.

Jessup thrashed with fury and pulsed with electricity once more, but couldn't escape before the clam-monster's shell slammed close upon him. As strong as the monster was, it couldn't break Jessup's shell. Luckily for Zee, Jessup had been turned when the clam shell closed, or he would have been crushed.

Jessup pressed his arms against both sides of the shell and pushed. The shell barely budged. They had to spark their core.

Power rushed through them as their core ignited. Zee channeled all the power he could into strength, and Jessup pushed again. They focused on the mouth of the beast and blasted it with a Lightning Bolt. Much of the electricity ran off down the tentacles that held them, but the strike caused the muscle to convulse. It didn't, however, die, or make any sign of letting go. The mouthed-and-eyed muscle writhed with the strain, and the shell nearly closed on them again. With a mighty groan, Jessup shoved, extending his arms and spreading the shell open as far as he could. The mouth gibbered and something snapped in the hinge of the monstrous shell, then all the creature's resistance failed as the muscle tore in half. The tentacles went limp, and the glow of the red eyes of the beast faded to black.

Zee and Jessup wasted no time thinking about what they'd done, but tore the tentacles away from them and spun, casting about for the commandos. There were none to be seen. Zee did see something, though, and it gave him pause. Hideous glyphs, carved into the smooth inside of the monster's shell.

They doused their core, backed out of the creature's maw, and turned to find Walster and Tablert upon their krisdolphins. Tablert was leaned forward, clutching her ribs. Walster's right arm hung unnaturally from the shoulder socket. The kit belts of Tablert's krisdolphin had been torn away. Only one of Walster's remained. Riders and mounts had red welts from the stinging tentacles. But they were alive.

"Petrikleo and Berrolli?" Zee asked.

Walster shook his head, then thrust the hand of his good arm upward.

Thirty feet below the main Wraith ship, Walster retrieved the SHEEL communication device from his kit. He attached the cup to his mask, then handed the other to Zee, who held it to his ear.

When Walster spoke, the sound traveled through a wire between them. His voice was thin and far away. "That was a quahogtomb. I've only heard of them, but they weren't described as being that big. How was it you and Jessup didn't sense it?" There was a touch of anger in his tone.

Zee didn't have to use the cup to speak, but he kept his voice down this close to the ship. "Did you see the glyphs carved inside its shell? We've seen them before, on a chasmclaw. I couldn't sense it either."

Walster gazed at him through the crystal of his mask, then sighed.

"What do we do now?" Zee asked.

"Tablert and I go aboard and retrieve the prince."

Tablert forced herself to sit up straight, her face set in a determined grimace.

Zee and Jessup conversed briefly through their bond.

"No," said Jessup, his voice rumbling in water. "You're injured."

"We're not giving up on the mission."

Zee said, "I'll go."

"I can't allow that."

"I have some experience sneaking around on ships without being seen, and I don't see that you have a choice."

Walster looked to Tablert, who met his gaze, then looked down and petted her krisdolphin, which had been stung badly by the quahogtomb's tentacles.

Walster considered, his expression conflicted, then slung the harpoon crossbow off his shoulder and handed it to Zee. "We still have the flare and a spare air tank, but we've lost the breach-blasters. You'll have to get the prince out through a cannon port or from the top deck."

Zee secured the crossbow on his back. "If it comes to having to escape through the hull, I won't need breach-blasters."

* * *

Zee rose from the sea in the shadow of the hull, lifted by one of Jessup's arms. Away from the Dragon Corps magickers' fog cover, the sky was clear, with stars and Zhera's twin moons shining bright. The ship was painted a ghostly white with shades of gray, just as Captain Mauricio had described. Other than that, it bore no markings, name, or designation. He almost reconsidered his task when he looked up. Dangling from the rail all along the ship were dead bodies, strung on rope like laundry hung to dry. Sailors and knights, their uniforms tattered, armor torn open or ripped away. Zee steeled his nerve, signaled Jessup through their bond, and was lifted higher.

The stench of the rotting dead was nearly overpowering. Zee tried not to look, but he couldn't help it. What kind of people would do this?

He held his breath, almost to the height of the rail, peering between eyeless sailors. The bodies blocked much of the view, but he adjusted to look between them. There were only three Wraith sailors on deck, dressed all in mottled white. No others on watch, nor anyone in the crow's nest. And no dragons or magickers. Zee thought that was odd, but then again, the decks below could be filled with them.

This close to the ship, he and Jessup hadn't wanted to spark their core to seek out the auras of any riders and dragons present, even if they tried to Camouflage it. If a particularly sensitive Wraith magicker somehow sensed them, they would raise the alarm. He and Jessup had used Camouflage when they'd sparked their core while fighting the quahogtomb. They hadn't yet mastered the Ability completely, but by the lack of activity on the Wraith ships, it must have been enough. They'd also been pretty deep at the time.

Zee asked Jessup to move him closer to the bow where the moons cast inky shadows onto the deck along the forecastle. His arm brushed the dead sailor in front of him, and the corpse came alive.

It clawed at him with manic fury, red fire burning in the empty sockets of its eyes, gasping gurgles escaping from its gaping mouth. Its jostling awakened the bodies next to it, which hissed and grabbed at him as well.

Zee was yanked down into the sea, the string of the dead with him.

* * *

At the sound of the splash, the Wraith sailors drew swords and ran to peer over the rail. Behind them, the arm of a kraken lifted a murman in dark skintight armor over the opposite rail and deposited him in the shadows.

* * *

One the Wraiths shouted, his voice gruff and deep, "Check the captive!"

"Should we sound the alarm?" one of the others asked.

"Not yet, it could have been a sheel or a loose knot. Check the captive and report!"

Two of the sailors ran only feet from where Zee crouched in the shadows, whipped open the door to the stairs, further concealing Zee, and trampled down.

The man with the gruff voice stalked over, glared down the stairs and slammed the door with a grunt.

Zee gave the man no time to see him or shout an alarm. Instead, Zee threw an arm around his neck and ran him through with his sword. Zee dragged the body into the shadows and lay it down gently, then eyed the dead man. The Wraiths were not demonic phantoms. They were people, like everyone else. And they could die like them.

Heart pumping with adrenaline, Zee took deep, practiced breaths, putting the fact he'd just killed a man out of his thoughts. There might be plenty more killing to be done. He couldn't hesitate. Guilt and remorse could be processed later. He strengthened his resolve with a thought—what would Jessup do? And more, with the knowledge of what the Wraiths had done to the prince and his dragon and to those people strung up on the ship's rails. People who were dead but not dead. The images of the quahogtomb's red glowing eyes and the crimson flames in the dead sailors' flashed through his mind. This is what Deans Wanchoo and Venkatarama had warned them about—only worse. This was necromancy. Zee shuddered at the thought, reported to Jessup, then rolled his neck and descended.

Other than the drip of seawater from his armor, there was little sound below, making it easy for Zee to follow the sounds of the sailors' clomping boots and curses. His old habits of sneaking out of the berth on the HMT *Krakenfish* at night to train returned to him in an instant. Dim oil lamps provided weak pools of light. He moved swiftly, his bare feet making nary a sound, from shadow to shadow, down stairs and ladders, and saw no one.

A door clattered open on the bottom deck and shouts of surprise came from the end of a hall. How many voices there were, Zee didn't know, but it sounded like half a dozen.

Their voices would cover any sound he might make. He and Jessup agreed. The time for stealth was over. He returned the crossbow to his back and drew his sword, then bolted down the hall. Their core sparked as he went, and he pulled his shield from their Keep.

There weren't six Wraiths in the room, but nine. They may have been battle-hardened ex-marines or pirates for all Zee knew, and all had swords or axes in hand, but they weren't bonded knights, and none had armor quite like Zee's.

The first two died before any of them knew he was in the room. The others barely had time to react. He glided from one to the other like a swift shadow, sword a blur, shocked at his own speed and strength. Their mail offered little resistance to his blade, and he took those with breastplates from the side or through the neck. Only the last got a good swing at him with his axe, but Zee slipped under it and slid his sword through the man's ribs.

It had only been moments, but all lay dead at his feet. None had even touched him, so quickly and efficiently had he moved. Zee stood there, chest heaving, amazed at what he'd been able to do.

Only then did he see a young man gaping at him, as stunned as Zee, sitting on the floor with one hand tied to a beam and legs bound. The stump at the end of his other arm was wrapped in filthy bandages. He looked starved, and his clothes were covered in grime. He must have been only five or six years older than Zee.

Zee dropped to one knee. "Prince Talog mon lin Phan, Your Highness, my name is Zee Tarrow. Your father sent me. I'm here get you out."

The prince swallowed, his mouth dry. "Okay." Zee cut his bindings and helped him up. The prince was barely able to stand. "Are you a SHEEL?" he asked.

"No, Your Highness. I'm a hull scrubber." The prince had no reply.

Zee pulled an arm over his shoulder and they made their way out of the room.

The prince suddenly pulled up. "Wait! We have to save Addrian."

"Who?"

"My dragon."

"We were told he was killed when you were taken."

"No, he's here, at the other end of the ship."

"Are you sure?"

"Yes! The distance is too great between us to forge or spark our core, but I can speak to him. I'll tell him we're coming."

Zee balked. Getting one man off the ship was one thing, but a dragon was something else entirely. It wasn't a decision he should make on his own. *Jessup, I have the prince, but he says his dragon is alive and on the ship.*

It only took a moment to receive an answer. *Then we should save it as well.*

Agreed.

Zee spoke to the prince. "Let's get your dragon." By the time they were halfway down the hall, he and Jessup had come up with a plan. Not a great plan, but it was something.

Banging doors, shouts, and the pounding of dozens of boots reached them from the decks above. Where had they come from? Unless they'd been hidden in the stockrooms he'd passed, concealed by more foul magick... Heavy footfalls descended the stairs at both ends of the ship. And there were a lot of them.

It was no use hiding now. He and Jessup sparked their core, then Zee lifted the prince into his arms and ran.

Several feral-looking Wraiths burst into the hall ahead of them. Zee threw up his Shield without slowing, shaping it to fit the hall while tipping it forward, and plowed right over them, leaping so as not to trip on their crumpling bodies. He didn't look back as shouting and stomping boots filled the hall behind him, but felt the sparking of an Empyrean core. He flung his Shield behind him just in time to block a blast of ice. It shoved him forward, but he did not fall. Still, he felt the cold of the attack. So there were bonded pairs on the ship after all, or one rider with an Ice Diver, anyway.

Zee sprinted toward a set of doors at the end of the hall. Almost there. The doors flew open and a large Wraith with a spear roared. Zee kept going, threw himself onto his back at the last moment, and slid beneath the point of the spear, the prince still in his arms. He kicked the man in the knee and took his legs out from under him as they slid, then dug a heel in and spun, pushing the prince to roll away from him, and leapt to his feet. A quick survey of the room revealed no other guards.

The Wraith was up on one knee, trying to rise. Zee front-kicked him out into the hall, where almost thirty Wraiths were barreling toward them. At the lead was a knight in mottled white armor, her frightening helmet in the shape of a dragon's mouth shining gold. She pressed her hands together in front of her and a spiked ball of ice formed. She shoved her hands forward, sending the ice-ball straight at Zee.

Zee grunted as it struck, nearly penetrating his Shield, then grabbed the doors and slammed them shut. At least the knight's dragon wasn't present. That was something to be thankful for. He was also thankful for the heavy crossbar, which he slammed down into place. With that many enemies in the hall, and what Zee assumed was a Gold Class knight with a sympathetic ice Ability among them, it wouldn't hold for long.

Standing back, he grimaced at the sight of dreadful glyphs in strange patterns splashed across the door and walls in red paint—or something red. Zee didn't want to think about what, but he had an idea.

When he spun back to the room, the prince was holding the head of a Greatwing, weeping. The dragon lay on the deck, wrapped in chain, its mouth bound closed with heavy rope. By its appearance, it had not been treated well, and the clawed foot of one front leg was gone, with only a cord tourniquet cinched around the ragged stump.

The Wraiths pounded on the door. Zee hurried to the dragon, pulled his dagger from its sheath on his leg, and cut the rope that bound its mouth.

"Addrian," the prince said tenderly, "this is Zee Tarrow. Father sent him to help us."

Addrian snorted and barely glanced at Zee. Zee recognized his expression not as anger or fear, but shame. "Thank you, Zee Tarrow."

"We're not out yet," Zee replied.

The pounding continued, joined by the chop of axes, and the door began to split.

Zee rushed to check the chains that wrapped the dragon's body and legs. A large lock held them together, too strong for Zee to break, and there were no keys in sight. The guard with the spear may have had them, but Zee had kicked him into the hall. Zee shook his head, chastising himself. That was some good thinking right there. The door bowed and cracked.

"Where is your dragon?" Prince Talog asked.

Zee answered curtly while speaking with Jessup through their bond.

"I don't have a dragon."

"But you're bonded."

"I have a kraken."

The prince took a swift intake of breath. "You're the murman."

"That's me."

Ice grew in the cracks of the door. Wood snapped and the hinges groaned.

"Prince Talog, Addrian, can you spark your core?"

"There isn't much left of it," Talog replied. "But..." They closed their eyes, straining, and their core lit.

"Shield the door, and get down. Whatever happens, don't be afraid."

The prince began to speak. "What—"

The door burst open, the prince and his dragon throwing up their Shield just in time to protect them from flying ice and splintered wood.

Zee crouched next to them and conjured his Shield between them and the back corner of the room. Wraiths came pouring in with a roar.

"*Now, Jessup!*" he cried through the bond, then out loud, "Hang on!"

With a mighty crunch the ship lurched and the hull exploded inward, the point of Jessup's shell having bashed a gaping hole. Wraiths cried out and lost their footing, tumbling against one another. The shell was pulled out like a plug. The sea rushed in, along with the arms of a kraken. Wraiths screamed, crawling over each other in an attempt to escape.

"Addrian!" Zee shouted. "Fire!"

The dragon didn't need any more encouragement than that. He and the prince dropped their Shield, Addrian's eyes gleamed with golden wrath, and he drenched his torturers with flame. From amid the tangle of bodies, the enemy knight tried using her Shield, but she was too late.

Jessup's arms wrapped the dragon. Zee threw one arm around the prince, grabbed Addrian's chains with the other, and the kraken tugged them all into the sea.

CHAPTER 57

The ocean's surface blazed with fire above. The roar of flames, snap of burning timber, groans and cracks of the collapsing hull came muted through the water. Tablert outfitted Prince Talog with a breathing mask and tank, and they sped away, the ship sinking behind them.

Jessup rolled the dragon in his arms as they went, found the lock, bit through it, and removed the chains.

As fast as they were moving, they only made it a hundred yards before they had to surface for the dragon to breathe. The eerie silence of before was gone. Only the bow of the main ship remained above the water, spouting flames. Bells rang on the other Wraith ships, orders were shouted, cannons were run out, and sails were set. All of the ships were painted like the main ship, a ghostly mottled white. Pairs were taking to the air by the dozens, and not just dragons and riders, but petrel riders and condor riders as well, the birds screeching and croaking as they soared. Zee had heard they were used in faraway countries, but in all his travels aboard the HMT *Krakenfish*, he'd never seen one. The birds weren't as large as dragons, and like the krisdolphins, couldn't be bonded with, but they were big, swift, and vicious, and the petrels could dive as deep and swim as fast as Ice Divers. Beacon lamps scoured the surface of the sea.

It would only be moments before they were spotted.

Zee pushed water from his lungs and asked Addrian, who was cradled in Jessup's arms, "How long can you hold your breath?"

It was all Addrian could do to answer, as weak as he was and shocked to be held in the arms of a kraken. "I... long enough."

The prince, wedged below the saddle with his legs jammed into the lower half of the capsule, shouted from behind his mask. "I'll let you know when we need to surface!"

They dropped to just below the waves. Walster had the flare canister out and raised it toward the surface. Before he could pull the string to ignite it, a petrel shot down into the water, its rider hunkered low over its back, and snatched the commando away from his krisdolphin. A swift flap of its long pointed wings and they were gone through the waves above.

They all sat stunned, Wanky squeaking in anguish. Zee spotted the flare sinking and leapt to retrieve it. Once he had it in hand, he shot to the surface, swinging the crossbow from his back. With the weight of the SHEEL in its claws, the petrel hadn't gone far. Walster punched its beak as it tore at his sheelskin armor. Zee aimed and fired. The bolt caught the bird in the throat. It lurched, crying out, and dropped its prize.

Zee heard a krisdolphin's squeak from below and glimpsed Wanky streaking beneath the waves toward his rider.

Having used the only harpoon bolt he had, Zee dropped the crossbow, aimed the flare canister high, and pulled the string. The flare flew high and bright, leaving a colorful trail of sparks behind it.

His Majesty's Dragon Corps and Navy would be coming soon. Unfortunately, lamp beacons pinpointed Zee's location, the ships began to move, and the Wraith forces in the air spotted him. He flipped and dove.

Jessup swam on his back, Addrian held below his chin. With his swiveling eyes and uniform shape, it made little difference to his range of view and none to his speed. He wasn't as fast as he would be without holding the dragon, but with their core sparked, eight arms still available, and the jet of his siphon, he shot through the water with tremendous speed.

More petrel riders dove in after them, driving them deeper, but just when they reached a safe depth, Addrian convulsed. Prince Talog reached up and slapped Zee's leg, then jabbed a finger to the surface.

They had no choice. The dragon would drown if they didn't surface. Jessup lunged out of the water. The dragon gasped in his arms, coughed, then lay still.

The prince jerked forward to peer down at Addrian, tearing the breathing mask from his face. His shoulders relaxed. "He's alive, but our bond is growing weak. We must get him back to the healers."

If they submerged, the dragon would drown. Jessup paddled as fast as he could on the surface, the krisdolphins and their riders having caught up with them and sticking close. The enemy fleet was coming fast, their fell magickers giving them speed, leaving the main ship sinking and burning in the distance behind them.

Condor riders, petrel riders, and enemy dragon riders swarmed the air and dove. Zee and Jessup threw up their Water Shield, protecting them from above, but petrel riders plunged into the water beyond its perimeter to get below. Jessup crushed them in his arms and slashed them with his claws, and the krisdolphins and Tablert fought them off with nose blades and sword. Walster was in bad shape and could only cling to Wanky where Tablert had strapped him to his mount.

A dragon blasted searing flame, but no heat reached them through the incredible density of their Water Shield.

The roar of hundreds of dragons sounded in the opposite direction of the enemy ships. The flaming attack against their Shield ceased and the beasts of the air soared back into the sky. Jessup turned around for them to look.

The Dragon Corps pairs came shockingly fast. The three Red Titans Streaked by overhead, leaving a comet trail of gold light at their backs, flights of White Titans right behind them.

Zee watched in fascination as the king and commandants fired Beams and concussive blasts of fire that seared and scattered aerial attackers, then pummeled the leading ships with long-range fireball Missiles.

Though they weren't knights, Wanchoo and Venkatarama proved to be nearly as deadly. They conjured a massive Shield at full speed, knocking any flying beast and rider in their path from the air. They dove, and with a wave of Wanchoo's wand and a flap of Rama's wings, two ships crashed against a wall of golden light, stopped dead in the water.

The remaining flights of the Dragon Corps arrived. Golds first, then the Silvers, and more battles ensued in the air. Auras and shields flashed yellow, and flames soaked the sky, lighting the crystals of Ice Divers' attacks all colors of the rainbow. Streams and Bombs of molten dragon ambergris flew from the mouths of Rocks, searing orange and gold. The enemy ships' cannons and harpoon guns boomed, sending their projectiles into the sky. It occurred to Zee that Dame Toomsil and Peloquin and Tem and Timandra were up there. He prayed to both Zepiter and Postune they would be safe.

In the noise and bright mayhem, neither Zee nor Jessup felt the swift diving attack of a condor until the beast and rider were already upon them.

The rider leapt from the monster-bird, swinging his axe at Zee. The condor went for the prince's dragon, clawing at Jessup's face and arms, croaking fiercely.

Zee ducked the axe and the blade thunked into Jessup's shell, where it stuck. The man landed on Zee and they grappled violently. Even with Zee and Jessup's core sparked, the Wraith condor rider was incredibly strong. He cursed in a language Zee didn't know and spit in his face. He wore a squat helmet with a spike at the top and leather armor with feathers on his shoulders, all painted the same white with faint gray mottling as the other Wraiths.

Zee tried for his dagger but couldn't break the man's grip on his wrist. He poured more core power into strength, but the man seemed to only get stronger. Blue light danced on Zee's hands, shocking the condor rider, he still did not let go. How was this possible from someone without a bond? Then Zee saw red light burning behind the man's eyes. Not dead and brought back to life, but enhanced by whatever had powered the chasmclaw and quahogtomb. A frigid terror almost overtook him as he thought about what Wanchoo and Venkatarama had told him and Jessup.

"If the aura, Shields, or Abilities of any of the enemy manifest red instead of the yellow of Empyrean, we want you and Jessup to dive as deep and swim as far as you can. Leave the fighting to the Titans."

They'd said nothing about eyes, but this was somehow worse.

Jessup must have felt his trepidation. The kraken poured his courage and will to fight into Zee through the bond, even as he swatted at the condor, which was swift and agile for such an ungainly creature. It flew out of reach, dodging Jessup's strikes, then dove back in with wicked curved beak and claws. Wanky shot out of the water in an attempt to spear the condor in the belly, but the beast banked and raked claws along his side.

In a brief glimpse, Zee saw that the creature's eyes glowed red as well, and on its wicked beak were carved more of the hideous glyphs, which shone crimson as well.

Zee and Jessup's aura flared with each strike, but up close, it did little to help Zee unless the man punched him—which he did, multiple times. Zee's armor and aura absorbed most of the force, but he began to feel the blows.

Prince Talog tried to help, but jammed as he was into the lower half of the capsule, he could only grasp at the Wraith's legs with his one good hand. The man aimed a brutal kick at the side of his head, and the prince fell limp.

The Wraith pulled a short seax from his belt and swung. Zee ducked his head, caught the blow on his helmet, then grabbed the man's wrist. It would be a dirty trick, but Zee wished he could put the rider in their Keep and be done with him. With a grimace, he tried it anyway. It didn't work. Zee's fear had vanished with Jessup's support through the bond, and he did the only thing he could think of. If the man broke free, it would take but one strike to kill the prince. Zee let go of the man's arm that didn't hold the seax, unbuckled his belt, and threw them both into the sea.

Jessup called his name through their bond.

"*It's all right,*" Zee replied. "*Protect the prince and Addrian. Tell the kris-*

dolphins to stay there and help."

Down they went, Zee's gills opening, web forming between his fingers, the toes of his feet spreading wide and webbed as well. Holding tight to his foe, Zee kicked and drove them deeper. The man's red eyes went wide as he realized what Zee was. The Wraith was out of his element now, in the domain of a murman.

He struggled frantically, struck Zee with his knees, and even tried to bite. Zee lost hold of the man's arm but snatched at his leather breastplate and pulled. The breastplate tore free, revealing a chest branded in more glyphs, which also shone with dim red light. Zee dropped the leathers and threw his arm around the man, hugging him close, all the while swimming deeper into the darkness.

The man dropped his seax, twisted his hand out of Zee's grip, and grabbed Zee by the neck. Baring yellowed and ragged teeth, he pushed, attempting to break Zee's grip on him, and tried to dig his fingers through the flaps in Zee's gorget and into his gills. Zee held on, refusing to feel the pain, glaring into the man's red eyes.

Panic took the Wraith, bubbles burst from his mouth, and he sucked in salty water. Twice more the man tried to breathe. His eyes bulged, then the crimson glow within them dimmed and went out. His struggles ceased, but his dead eyes still stared at Zee.

Zee shoved him away, watched him sink slowly, then clenched his fists and roared down at him.

"Zee, are you all right?" came Jessup's voice.

Zee regained his senses. *"All good. I'm on my way."* He sped toward the surface.

* * *

Zee broke the surface in time to see a Greatwing slam into the condor, spearing it with its talons, then crush the bird's neck in its powerful jaws. It flung the monster bird to be torched by a Royal Crimson.

Dame Toomsil shouted, "Mr. Tarrow!" She sat upon Peloquin, her golden armor scorched but whole, while the dragon hovered. Her eyes went to the limp prince, then the dragon.

Before she could ask, Jessup said, "They're alive."

Tem flew closer on Timandra. "You did it!"

Zee climbed onto Jessup. "They're not safe yet. Where are the ships?"

Dame Toomsil's gaze moved away from the battle. "There."

Zee turned and breathed a sigh of relief at the sight of the task force cutting through the waves at top speed, the admiral's ship in the lead.

Four magicker pairs flew ahead of the ships, swooped down, and conjured a Platform. The riders hopped off their dragons, and Zee helped them lift the prince onto it. Jessup lifted Addrian and laid him gently next to him.

A Gold Class healing magicker said, "We'll take good care of them. Well done."

Jessup said, "Take the SHEELs and the krisdolphins as well. They've been injured."

The magicker hesitated, then saw the state of the commandos and their mounts. "All right."

Jessup lifted them to the Platform. Walster was unconscious, but Tablert saluted Zee. The krisdolphins squeaked their thanks as the Platform rose, then floated away toward the admiral's ship.

The pride in Dame Toomsil's eyes was unmistakable, though there was a touch of sadness at what Zee and Jessup had been through. "Well done, Mr. Tarrow, Mr. Jessup."

"Thank you, ma'am," Zee replied.

A Red Titan pair Streaked from the battle to the magicker's Platform, circled twice, then sped to where Zee, Jessup, and the knight pairs waited. Norrogaul hovered, King Phan perched on his back, gazing at Jessup and Zee. "Stay put, you two, your job here is done." To the knights he said, "Toomsil, Briggs, with me." He drew his sword. "We have Wraiths to kill."

Zee shouted, "Your Majesty!" The king paused and turned back to him. By Zepiter, it was impossible to read the man's mood. "The red, sire. We saw it."

"I have seen it. So far, it's nothing we can't handle."

"And dead sailors and knights, Sire, brought back to life."

Toomsil, Tem, and their dragons looked as if they'd been knocked back. Even Norrogaul's head turned. Finally the king's face held a readable expression. Shock and horror.

Norrogaul said, "Necromancy. Are you absolutely certain?"

Jessup said, "Yes, Sire. They were strung from the main ship's rails."

"Where is this ship?" said King Phan.

Zee replied, "Addrian set it afire, and we sank it."

The king pondered deeply, probably speaking with Norrogaul. When he looked up, his eyes gleamed with even greater determination. "Then we must burn them all, now more than ever." He raised his sword. "To battle!"

He and Norrogaul Streaked away, leaving a visible trace of their Red Titan aura hanging in the air.

The knight pairs sparked their cores and followed.

The HMS *Dragon's Rage* passed not a hundred feet away, speeding to the thick of the battle. Along the rails high above, sailors waved their arms and shouted. It took a moment for Zee to realize they were cheering for him and Jessup.

The murman and kraken floated there, bobbing in the waves, and watched them pass.

Zee's adrenaline drained away, and he was suddenly exhausted. Jessup sighed. When they'd doused their core, there had been less than half of it left.

The admiral's ship speared straight toward the enemy task force while the other Navy ships split to either side. Cannons blared in a thunderous rolling boom and kept firing, wave after wave. Masts and bridges splintered on the first of the Wraith ships, and great holes blew open in their topsides. The enemy ships returned fire, but more sporadically, their cannons sounding like popping fireworks compared to the big guns of the *Dragon's Rage*. Combat still raged in the sky, but not as intensely.

The forces of Tosh were winning.

Jessup said, "We should fight."

"You heard the king," Zee replied. "Our job is done." He patted Jessup on the shell. "We saved the prince and his dragon."

Jessup grunted. "SHEELs died."

"I know," Zee responded softly. He'd been thinking about that too.

A foul and terrible chill descended upon them. The hair stood up on Zee's neck. Jessup's spikes shot out on his shell, and he spun back.

A half mile away, a massive wall of fog sped toward them, dark, foreboding, tinged with purple and green like a horrid bruise. Then it stopped.

The fog swirled from waterline to high in the sky, opening an expansive spinning vortex to blackness. Out of it poured a great fleet of the ghostly painted Wraith ships, three times the number of the Navy task force. The air above the fleet teemed with riders and beasts, at least five complete wings of riders upon dragons and hundreds more condor and petrel riders. The knights' armor was a motley mix of designs, but all were painted the identical mottled white, except for the riders' helmets, which gleamed in the metallic sheen of their Class.

The king's Navy was caught between two enemy forces. The whole kidnapping and demand for ransom had been a trap. And the only thing between the Navy and the oncoming force were Zee and Jessup. Jessup spun and roared a warning to the king's forces, then turned back.

Approaching through the vortex was a red glow, low above the ships. Flying Wraith forces scattered from its path. An umbral shape with massive wings cleared the vortex and fog, dropping to fly low over the waves. A dragon—or something like a dragon.

Its head was a dragon's skull with red flames wreathed in black shadow gushing from the empty sockets of its eyes. Six legs of various sizes were tucked up under its length, and three long tails whipped behind, one tipped with a sharp bony point like the blade of a spear, another like the spiked head of a mace, the third slim and lashing. Its scales may once have been gray, but now they were dull and peeling. It was also far larger than the largest beast in the Dragon Corps, its body alone sixty feet long.

At the base of its neck rode a man who appeared to be wrapped in strips of white rags, except for his breastplate, which gleamed white, the Wraith's insignia of four red blotches on his chest. He wore no helmet, and his face was gaunt, long white hair trailing behind his head, his eyes circled in black. They seemed to be in no hurry, their forces passing them above.

"*That pair must be their generals,*" Zee said to himself as much as to Jessup. "*Who are these people?*"

Five more Wraith bonded pairs swooped down to join the generals, the dragons of regular size, the riders in helmets of gold.

"*Bad people,*" Jessup replied. "*That's all we need to know.*"

Zee reminded himself they were just humans and beasts. But these Wraiths, especially the general and the monster he rode upon, emanated a cold and menacing power.

Enemy bonded pairs and other beast riders zoomed by overhead. Blasts of fire and ice, flashing Shields, and the roars of dragons marked the clash of the two forces.

Three flights of the Dragon Corps rear guard descended on the Wraith general rider and beast pair and their escort of Golds. The Gold Wraiths spread out from their leader and sparked their cores. Zee recoiled at the fell power that washed over him. When he looked back, the eyes of the dragons and riders burned red.

The Dragon Corps knights fired as they dove: spears, javelins, arrows, ice, lava, and flames. Dame Toomsil and Tem were among them. Dread filled Zee's heart.

Jessup uttered, "No..."

The Wraith generals sparked their core. Crimson light gleamed from the rider's eyes, far brighter than the other Wraith knights, and the red flames in the sockets of the dragon's skull became bonfires.

Zee nearly fell out of his saddle. The power of their core struck him like the spray of a skunkcat and being hit in the gut with a heavy plank at the same time. Nausea clutched his stomach, and his mind reeled in horror. Jessup groaned.

The Wraith general rider thrust out the fingers of one bony hand and red Shields formed in front of his flight of Gold knights. Then he waved his hand, sending multiple tendrils of red light whipping out, shrieking in the air to strike the Dragon Corps knights, scattering them like chaff.

Toomsil, Peloquin, Tem, and Timandra tumbled through the air. To Zee's relief, they got their wings under them. For a moment, they fluttered there in shock. Others splashed to the waves. Some swam helplessly. Others lay still.

Zee gaped. The Wraith general had Shielded the knights of his guard, then struck with an attack like Zee had never seen.

At the same time, he and Jessup said, "A sorcerer…"

"Make way!" came the thunderous voice of Norrogaul. The rear guard sped out of the way as the three Red Titans came Streaking in.

Wanchoo stabbed forward with his wand. It flashed yellow and a Testudo Globe much larger and with walls thicker than Zee had seen him use before surrounded the Wraith general and undead dragon. The dragon shrugged, pulsed with red light, and the globe shattered. Venkatarama reeled back, flapping his wings, his long mouth agape.

The commandants' aura flared, Vandalia lurched back, drew her wings back, and flapped. The air exploded like thunder. Hurricane winds rocked the general's dragon up and back.

Norrogaul opened his great mouth wide and roared a golden Beam that split the air like lightning, striking the dragon's exposed underbelly. The Wraith's red aura flared, but the commandants and king did not relent.

The Wraith generals' aura expanded, pushing the Beam away and blocking the Hurricane winds. The dragon roared, deep, juddering, unearthly, then clapped its wings, the sound like cannon fire.

Shields appeared before the king and commandants, then another in front of those, conjured by the deans of magicks. The blast broke right through the Shields and slammed into the Red Titans, knocking them back. They managed to catch themselves, then hovered in the sky, steam rising from armor and dragon scales.

The Wraith general rider laughed, the sound of it chilling Zee to the bone.

"*We have to help them,*" came Jessup's voice.

Together, Zee and Jessup breathed deeply, slowing Zee's racing heart. Jessup's will to battle and determination poured into him, turning his resolve into absolute certainty.

"*Yes, we do.*" They sparked their core.

The general rider retrieved a wicked curved sword from his Keep. Glyphs burned red along its blade, and he swung it. Red flame slammed into the Red Titans. Their Shields did not help them. If Zee had blinked, he'd have missed it.

King Phan and Norrogaul shot backward, flaming, to crash through the deck of a Navy ship. Aureosa and Vandalia streaked like a burning meteor into the sea, sending up a geyser of water and steam. Wanchoo and Venkatarama were hurled high, a fiery pinwheel, out over the battling ships behind them, and dropped out of sight. Dragon Corps knight pairs and magickers shot from the sky to their aid.

Zee's resolve did not break. "*Everything we've got, Jessup.*"

"*Everything.*"

The air screamed as a Lightning Bolt struck the demon dragon with more power than Zee and Jessup had ever used before. Red aura flashed. Thunder cracked. The dragon rolled through the air, blasted sideways, shrieking, wings beating helplessly.

Zee almost collapsed from the effort. Jessup breathed out beneath him like a punctured floatbladder. When Zee looked up, the dragon flashed red and stopped toppling. It beat its expansive wings, hovering thirty feet above the water, then slowly turned. The fire in the eyes of dragon and rider alike burned brighter, the inky shadows that accompanied the crimson flames swirling like black smoke.

The sorcerer rider's voice came slithering into Zee's mind. The sound of it brought a deathly chill. "*There you are...*"

He'd spoken to them just like Zee and Jessup spoke through their bond.

Zee's mind recoiled. *"How...?"*

The voice came again. *"How, indeed."* Zee's jaw bobbed wordlessly. The sorcerers could hear them, too.

The demon dragon flapped toward them.

"Don't speak!" Jessup shouted out loud, then dove.

Zee's panic washed away as his and Jessup's bond heated to full force. He focused on their bond and the bond alone. His and Jessup's will, their very souls and minds, became one.

They'd expended nearly half of their remaining core on the most powerful Lightning Bolt they'd ever summoned. And the enemy was still flying.

They had to make the remaining twenty-five percent of their core count. The thought of retreat never entered their minds. Zee went to pull his sword from their Keep but retrieved his stinger instead, then drew out his shield. They sped toward the oncoming enemy.

A shadow and a red glow snaked on the waves above. Jessup fired his siphon, using Burst at the same time, and shot out of the water, straight at the monster dragon's head, Zee channeling core power into strength, resilience, and their Shock Ability.

The peak of the kraken's shell struck the beast's jaw with the force of a speeding ship, Zee and Jessup loosing a blinding pulse of blue electricity at the same time. The dragon's aura flashed red, but that didn't prevent its head from being snapped upward. Massive teeth broke as its mouth jammed shut, bones cracked, and its enormous jaw dislocated.

It screamed and reeled, the hooked tip of a wing carving the water as it fought to stay in the air. Red fire gouted from its broken mouth, spraying the sea and sky. But it didn't go down, and the rider remained seated on its back.

Zee and Jessup plunged back into the sea, then circled up and back around. Zee released the bottom of his saddle capsule and pulled it up to lock into place over his legs while keeping his eye on the enemy dragon above the surface, which began to climb into the air.

Jessup rocketed out of the water, shooting out the spines of his shell.

Instead of colliding with the beast, he landed on its back just above the tails. Red aura flashed, but Jessup's arms wrapped the dragon, claws and sucker spikes hooking onto its great, rough scales. The dragon dropped with a roar, but beat its wings with greater force and climbed once more.

The sorcerer rider turned in his saddle and hurled a red Fireball. Zee raised his shield while conjuring Deflect. The strike slammed him back in his saddle, cracking his helmeted head against Jessup's shell, and his arm went numb, but the ball of flame ricocheted away.

The sorcerer rider appeared shocked, then his eyes narrowed. Zee's whole body clenched as what felt like a phantom hand of ice reached right into him.

The sorcerer's mouth widened in a cadaverous grin. *"I see..."*

The statement seemed to portend much more than the meaning of the words themselves. A frigid dread sent a shiver down Zee's spine and pain shooting through his brain.

Jessup tried to reach the sorcerer with a whipping tentacle, but with the massive length of the dragon, it was too far.

The spikes of a great chitinous mace pierced Zee and Jessup's flashing blue aura and thunked into the kraken's shell to Zee's left, then was torn free. A spear point three feet long struck to his right. The undead dragon was attacking with its tails.

A scaled whip wound around the point of Jessup's shell and pulled. Jessup groaned, digging his claws in deeper. Blue lightning arced across his spines and he pulsed with electricity. The dragon shrieked and its whip-tail withdrew.

Gold and Silver knights of the Dragon Corps soared in, flinging javelins and firing arrows at the dragon's head and neck. They bounced off the bony skull and heavy ridged scales or were incinerated by the red flames of its eyes. Its aura flashed, stopping many others, but one knight pair broke through and drove a lance into its chest. One snap of its enormous jaws and dragon and rider were crushed.

The squadron of White Titans descended, twenty-five knight pairs strong. The sorcerer rider waved a hand. Tendrils of crimson lashed them away, their Shields blinking out, and several plummeted to crash into the sea.

Jessup roared and detonated another mighty Shock into the dragon, then tore at the dragon's scaled hide while also reaching to foul the beast's wings, Shocking it again. The dragon lurched with each pulse of electricity, aura flaring, but continued to fly inexorably upward. Zee threw a ball of electricity at the sorcerer rider's back with all his might. It merely glanced off the man's aura.

Bitter cold enveloped them as a foot of ice coated Jessup's shell and froze his arms into place on one side. Jessup tugged to free himself, to no avail. Electricity swarmed over his shell. With a roar, he released another Shock. The ice exploded from his shell and the dragon spasmed, shrieking.

Zee caught a flash of gold and swung his stinger. Sparks flew as its tip scraped on the scales of a Wraith Ice Diver. A claw tore through his sheelskin armor and gashed his upper arm, then a sword struck a mighty blow to his helmet. Zee's head rang. He didn't want to waste their core on sufferance, but adrenaline pumped through his veins and he barely felt the pain of the strike or the cut on his arm anyway.

A gout of fire poured over Zee. He covered his upper body with his shield, his legs protected by the bottom half of the capsule. His shield glowed with the searing heat. Even with his blue aura flaring, he gasped for breath, feeling as if he was being boiled in a pot. He and Jessup threw out a Lightning Blast in all directions. The attacks kept coming. Their aura winked out and they called upon their Shield—but it wouldn't come. With a thought, Zee saw their core was down to ten percent.

A Gold Class knight pair of the sorcerer's guard shot in through the flames, the dragon with its wings tucked. The rider grabbed the edge of Zee's red-hot shield and yanked it away, dislocating Zee's shoulder in the process. Zee stabbed out with his stinger and heard the dragon squeal. He covered his face from the flames with his good arm. The sheelskin of his armor curled and smoked in the heat, yet Zee's skin only blistered.

Jessup roared and whipped out with one of his arms. A dragon shrieked and the flames stopped. Jessup struck again, missed, and another of the sorcerer's guard swooped passed Zee. This time the rider stabbed him through the shoulder of the dislocated arm with a thrust of her spear, right through Zee's weakened aura. Zee screamed, and Jessup roared. Jessup lashed at the sorcerer dragon with fury, ripping off scales and tearing out hunks of living-dead flesh. The dragon screamed, high and keening.

In the sky above, a dark storm roiled to life, lightning shrieking through the clouds. The sorcerer rider looked up in wonder, then laughed his hideous laugh.

Zee groaned and sat up, one arm dangling and useless, one hand clutched over the wound in his shoulder. Steam rose from his body and from Jessup's shell. The pain was terrible, but it should have been excruciating. He forced himself to breathe, drawing on their bond but not their core, forcing the agony down even further. Still, he felt light-headed, his thoughts were muddled. Then he knew why. Their core was dangerously low, now less than ten percent.

He had no time to consider their predicament, however. Dame Toomsil and Tem were soaring down, only two other Golds and a Silver with them.

The sorcerer lifted his wicked sword and ignited it.

Zee shouted in the voice that was his but not his, "No!" He threw out his hand just as the sorcerer attacked with the same Ability that had knocked the Red Titans from the sky. A massive Water Shield appeared between the sorcerer and the oncoming force. The Dragon Corps dragons pulled up frantically to avoid a collision. The arc of red flame struck the Water Shield. Both Shield and flame blew apart, but Toomsil and Peloquin, Tem, Timandra, and the others, were unharmed.

Jessup sucked in a deep, exhausted breath, and roared. "Fly away!"

They hesitated, eyes wide and mouths agape, then took off into the sky.

The Wraith sorcerers had no interest in them, however. The rider twisted in his saddle to gaze back at Zee and Jessup. Zee had to shake his head to clear his blurred vision, which nearly caused him to swoon.

Flames raged in the Wraith general's eyes, but he wore an expression of malicious glee. He pointed at them with a crooked finger. "Sorcerers!"

Zee barely had time to register that he and Jessup had conjured a Shield to protect others—or the word the man had roared—before the Wraith general rider drew his arm back, gathered smoking red flame in his palm, and hurled it at them.

Zee and Jessup were hit with an impossible force. The claws and spikes of Jessup's arms tore free; they flew back, toppling, and dropped.

CHAPTER 58

A dragon's claw caught hold of Commandant Aureosa's arm and hauled him out of the sea. He flopped onto the Platform and rolled to his back, staring up into the eyes of Vandalia, whose great chest rose and fell with the effort of lifting one man. The Ability the Wraith sorcerer had hit them with looked like a form of Slice, but had struck like a hammer of the sun and somehow drained nearly all of their prodigious Red Titans' core. It felt like their life force itself had been sucked out of them. His bond with Vandalia was still strong, but that was about all he could say for the sum of their strength.

The Platform rose, four magickers powering a Testudo Globe around them, and deposited them on the deck of a Navy ship.

"Are you all right, Daimyo General Commandants?" said a concerned healing magicker dragon.

Vandalia shoved him away in a surge of frustration. "We're fine."

Aureosa felt it too. Frustration, awe, and he had to admit, fear. He wanted to scream out orders, rally his forces, but all around cannons blared, ship sides splintered, and his knights were already doing all they could. Even against an overwhelming force, they fought on with all they had. He was proud of them. Deep remorse clenched his heart. Perhaps they should have just paid the ransom and been done with it. But that wouldn't have been the end of it. This trap had been planned from the very beginning.

His mind boggled at the kind of power that could teleport a fleet through fog. The Wraith's resources had to be far more vast than anyone had suspected. And where did they come from? One thing was certain. These were no mere pirates. It would take the strength of a kingdom to muster such a force. They'd need shipyards, supplies, training, and mountains of coin, things only a nation could provide. He had the sinking feeling that even this was just a taste of their military might.

He wondered if he should call a retreat, but only the king could do that. If Phan and Norrogaul had truly fallen, it would be the choice of the admiral or vice vizier. But where would they retreat to? An enemy force of this size and strength could pursue them to their deaths and the destruction of even the admiral's ship. They had knights and even other beasts and riders with red light in their eyes. And they had a sorcerer pair.

Aureosa and Wanchoo had seen the power of the red only once before, in a battle long ago. It had been awesome and terrifying then, but at least that pair had been on their side. This was worse, and the sorcerer dragon was risen from the dead. He shook his head, gathered his strength, and pushed to his feet, where he leaned with a hand on Vandalia.

"I cannot fight, Peleus," Vandalia said in weary defeat. One of her wings hung crooked and broken.

Aureosa patted her neck. "I know."

"Look!"

Jessup shot out of the sea and landed hard on the back of the undead dragon's back. They watched, helpless and amazed, at the fight that ensued. From this distance it was difficult to tell exactly what was happening. Flames, blasts of electricity, flailing kraken arms and dragon's tails, swooping enemy dragons, and mighty roars. The king's forces attacked as they could to help, but the sorcerers swept them away with ease. Somehow, the young murman and kraken continued to fight.

"They could be our only hope, now," said Aureosa. "We're nearly undone, and no pill or elixir can help us."

Vandalia said, "Those two have surprised us before."

"They face a sorcerer pair gorged on the power of death itself."

"And yet, Zee and Jessup still stand against them. They are a true force of nature." As if in answer, cool wind gusted over them and the moons and stars were blocked from the sky. A storm blacker than night roiled above, seething with lightning.

The unmistakable roar of Norrogaul sounded from a ship alongside them. King Phan and the mighty dragon staggered to the broken rail, Norrogaul dragging a limp wing, hopping on one front leg to favor the other, which was twisted at a terrible angle.

Both commandants breathed a sigh of relief. Vandalia said, "They're no better off than we are, but they live, thank Zepiter."

"I fear for the deans."

"Venkatarama is tougher than I am. If we live, so do they."

The undead dragon's roar drew their gaze back to the fight. A single flight of Gold and Silver Dragon Corps pairs sped to Zee and Jessup's aid. The sorcerer raised his flaming sword.

Vandalia uttered, "No..."

Then a Water Shield nearly a hundred feet wide appeared. It exploded as the aberrant Slice struck it—but so did the Slice. Even as far away as they were, they were staggered by the force of the blow.

Aureosa's mouth opened and closed without words.

The Wraith general rider's amplified voice carried the word he'd been trying to say over the waves.

"Sorcerers!"

Then Zee and Jessup were blasted off the back of the dragon and fell to the sea.

Red light glowed inside the undead dragon. The lance that stuck in its chest was forced out to splash in the waves below. The light flared, occluding the pair entirely. When it faded, the dragon was healed of all wounds. It beat its wings, circling, eyeing the water, then dove with tremendous speed, tucked its wings at the last moment, and plunged into the sea.

* * *

Beneath the waves, Zee's head swam and ached, his stomach convulsed with nausea, and his whole body throbbed with pain. Jessup flopped, rotating in circles, directionless. Worst of all, their core was nearly spent. Zee consciously doused it, then gritted his teeth and groaned as the pain increased tenfold.

Jessup's voice was weak, distant, tinged with anger and alarm. "*Zee...*"

"*Jessup...*"

Their bond was fraying. If their core went out, they'd lose their bond forever. Zee didn't think they even had the strength to forge.

Still, the fire of the kraken's will remained. Lightning blinked from the raging storm high above, flickering across the waves, the bizarre manifestation of his wrath.

"*Last resort, Zee.*"

It took Zee's befuddled mind a second to grasp what he'd said. The pill that Wanchoo and Venkatarama had given them. It was dangerous, but what choice did they have? And the sorcerers were still up there—but he and Jessup were sorcerers, too. He nearly lost his train of thought, bewildered as he was by the sudden understanding. Both knight and magicker. Who knew what wonders they could perform? If they survived.

Zee couldn't move his left arm, and his right felt as if it weighed a hundred pounds as he reached for their Keep and retrieved the pill. He uncorked the bottle and tipped the pill into his palm. The waves of power it gave off were intoxicating, hypnotic, resounding. The trumpets of salvation, or the siren song of death?

The water darkened around them, then the surface exploded. Zee flinched and the pill dropped from his hand. He swatted at it feebly as it sank, only managing to move it farther out of reach with the eddies created by his webbed hand. "*Jessup!*"

Then suddenly, they couldn't move.

The evil-dead dragon floated down into sight, head tucked back on its long neck. It suspended itself with its wings, facing them. Bubbles rose from its skull and scales, and somehow the crimson flames still burned in the empty sockets of its eyes, wreathed in black shadow. Over its horned skull, the Wraith general rider gazed at them with his gleaming red eyes.

The sorcerer rider spoke. "*Murman...*" Zee couldn't even wince at the pain that lanced through his brain.

"*Kraken...*" It was the dragon speaking. The pain stabbed fresh with every word.

"Thunder *kraken*," the sorcerer uttered. If Zee wasn't mistaken, there was wonder in his tone.

"*We will have a piece for the master.*" Slowly, deliberately, the dragon reached with its front legs and clutched one of Jessup's arms in its talons, then opened its cavernous maw.

Zee couldn't speak. He couldn't even scream. Jessup raged in silence and stillness. Lightning flashed over the sea with his fury.

The dragon bit, then chomped again, wrenching its head back and forth until half of Jessup's arm tore free.

Zee wailed in his mind at Jessup's searing agony. In moments it subsided, but the heat of Jessup's wrath had become an inferno.

The sorcerer dragon and rider watched, their very gaze an attack on Zee and Jessup's souls. With a great beat of the dragon-monster's wings, they shot upward, out of the sea to the sky, Jessup's severed arm flopping in the clutch of the dragon's claw. Even there, under the sea, Zee would swear he heard the sorcerer rider laughing.

And they still couldn't move. They sank slowly, inevitably. Jessup couldn't even fill the cavity in his shell with gases to float them to the surface. Their bond was frighteningly weak. Was this to be their end?

The answer was a resounding "no" that resonated through their bodies and minds. The parting words of Dr. Aenig came back to Zee. "Reach deeper than you could possibly imagine. Farther than you ever have before. Only at the bell of most dire need will more power come to you. The greatest potential lies with those closest to defeat." It was as if the surgeon knew this day would come.

A mad rage rose between them, and their core sparked to life. Nearly spent as it was, it banished all exhaustion and pain, and their rage and determination burned bright as ever. They didn't have to speak, their minds connected as one through the bond. Their friends were up there. Dame Toomsil and Peloquin, Tem and Timandra. The commandants, the deans of magicks, and the king. The prince as well, and they had been given a task to save him. That demonic pair of Wraith sorcerers would kill them all. They couldn't let that happen.

Zee sensed Jessup straining harder than he'd ever felt before, then blinked as the curled tip of a kraken's arm raised itself toward Zee, inch by inch. Their core was guttering, nearly spent, when it came within reach and opened slowly. Zee would have gaped if he could at the sight of the pill he'd dropped lying in the center of a small sucker.

Jessup's voice sounded in his mind, forced, as if every bit of his effort was poured into it, and far, far away. *"Last resort."*

Zee mentally clenched his jaw, roared in his mind, and reached with everything he had. Veins stood out on his forehead, his mind in agony, but his hand and the kraken's arm grew closer together. Their core was a guttering ember. Agony shot through their very beings.

With more effort than Zee had ever given anything in his life, Zee clutched the pill, pulled it to him, and forced his mouth to open. Their core dimmed faint blue and gold, disappearing in the dark void of their crucible.

Zee swallowed. A star exploded, reality broke, and agony reigned.

* * *

Aureosa reeled back, throwing an arm up to shield his eyes. Vandalia jerked her head back on her long neck and turned away. If their core was sparked, they might have been able to gaze directly at the ball of white light that blazed beneath the sea. But now, it was absolutely blinding.

The screams of the kraken and murman shook the sea and trembled the sky. It sounded as if they were being tortured beyond all thresholds of pain, yet could not faint or die. Their wails of agony cut through cannon fire and dragon roars. All on both sides, in the air and on the ships, recoiled at the sheer intensity of it. Even the cannons quieted.

Black thunderclouds, denser, darker, churning with rage, roiled out to cover the entire battle, lightning shrieking through them, echoing the kraken and murman's cries.

The Wraith sorcerer pair halted and hovered while they gazed at the bright light below.

"What did they do to them?" Vandalia asked, to herself as much to Aureosa.

Wind gusted behind them. "Not them." Venkatarama stepped up beside Aureosa, Wanchoo upon his back. "Us."

Both were soaking wet and charred. Wanchoo's robe was torn. A few of Rama's scales had been ripped away by the sorcerers' blast. Otherwise, they didn't appear seriously injured.

Aureosa and Vandalia stared at them. Vandalia said, "You gave them the Pearl..." It wasn't a question, but a statement of disbelief.

The deans of magicks stared at the light beneath the sea, expressions softened with remorse.

Wanchoo spoke softly. "They were drawn to it. But more so, it to them."

"They chose each other," Rama added.

A Platform of golden light descended behind them. Boots and dragon claws scraped the deck. King Phan and Norrogaul limped to the rail.

"What's happening?" the king demanded, though there was wonder in his voice.

Aureosa did not take his eyes from the light. "We shall see..."

The white light shrank to a brilliant swirling sphere of blues and golds. The screams faded and died.

No one spoke. No clash of battle sounded. The sphere rose, then broke the surface. Within were Zee and Jessup, ethereal, barely visible, and completely still. Blue electricity crackled over Jessup's shell, arcing between the wicked spines, many of which were broken.

The yellow and blue of the sphere emanated from their very center.

When they opened their eyes, cerulean light blazed brighter than the sphere itself.

* * *

Their minds melded completely, Zee and Jessup had no need to speak. They would give it everything they had, but none of their own could be hurt.

Their awareness was heightened far beyond normal senses. In their mind's eye was every rider, every crew member on the ships, and every beast. It was like the commandants had taught them, but each image was brighter, clearer, sharp silhouettes of gold, red, and the grayish light of unbonded pairs. And they could see them all. Intuitively, their perception absolute, there was no question as to which were friend and which were foe. They focused on the enemy sorcerer pair most of all, the brightest scarlet in their three-hundred-sixty-degree view, then his Gold Knight guards.

Power cycled between them, through them, of them, their sparked core now bloated beyond recognition and spinning wildly. They turned their eyes to the sorcerers high above, and Zee felt the rage of a kraken. Together, they roared.

The Wraith sorcerers reared back, flashing red to Streak away.

They weren't fast enough. Nothing could outrun lightning.

A pillar of electricity blasted straight from Jessup's shell to the undead dragon beast. Night became brighter than day. The sorcerers' red Shield flared, then failed, and they were engulfed in a sphere of crackling, sparking power. They screamed.

Bolts of lightning shot from the sphere to strike the generals' escorts. Shield Abilities shattered, auras failed, weapons and armor melted, and they fried.

Zee and Jessup roared louder. Power pulsed from them up through the pillar of lightning to the sorcerers. More lightning bolts erupted from the sphere, seeking out and striking more of the enemy.

How long their attack went on, Zee and Jessup didn't know. Finally it blinked out. Thunder pounded through the atmosphere.

Zee slumped back against Jessup's shell. The pain of his injuries returned, but it was more remote and distant now. Jessup's arms squirmed sluggishly beneath him, barely able to keep them above the surface. Steam rose from their bodies, and the sea boiled around them.

Zee squeezed his eyes shut. When he opened them, his vision had ceased to swim. Wraith beasts and riders fell from the sky all around, spinning, smoking, burning. The nearest enemy ships blazed, splintered, and sinking.

The great fell dragon and its rider spiraled afire down toward the sea. Scarlet motes of light gathered to them out of the air as they fell. They flared with red light. The dragon thrust out its wings, halting their freefall. It hovered there, barely able to stay in the air. The sorcerer rider surveyed the ruined Wraith forces from where he sat slumped in his ruined saddle, holding his chest, then he turned his gaze upon Zee and Jessup. The crimson fire had dimmed in his eyes, but his glare of hatred was unmistakable.

The rider drove his heels into the dragon. It flapped away at a limping pace. In its claws, it still gripped the arm it had severed from Jessup.

Wraith riders and beasts that had survived raced to their sorcerer generals in panicked retreat. Dragon Corps pairs shook themselves out of their astonishment and pursued.

The dark wall of fog in the distance swirled to a black pit, the vortex the Wraiths had come through opening once more. In its depths were burning red eyes, gazing through. Two smaller eyes above, two below, enormous, far larger than the those of the Wraith sorcerer dragon. To Zee, it felt like they were looking right at him and Jessup. His soul quaked. A great toothy maw opened below the eyes, large enough to swallow a ship, a gigantic furnace of crimson fire burning within.

Vaporous tentacles of red light shot out behind the sorcerers, dragging many of their force with them. They flew faster, faster, until they became a red smear, leaving any pursuers, and some of their own, far behind. They shot into the hole in the fog and disappeared past the floating embodiments of horror. The phantom beast's mouth snapped shut, the vortex closed, and the mountainous range of fog evaporated.

Above, the storm dissolved, leaving a clear night sky. As far as Zee could tell, none of the king's forces or ships had been struck by their attack.

Jessup's faint voice came to him. *"Did we do it?"*

Barely able to hang onto consciousness, Zee replied, *"We did it."*

Suddenly, he and Jessup went rigid and gasped as the now familier sensation of euphoria and boundless power overwhelmed them, more intensely than ever. When it passed, they were left feeling utterly fatigued but whole, if not entirely well.

They peered into their core. It was at less than five percent of what it had been when they left fully forged for the mission, but brighter and denser, perfectly round, its surface so smooth it gleamed. It looked... perfect. And their bond felt stronger than ever.

The condition of their crucible, however, was another story. It had taken everything they had to contain the power that had poured into their core from the pill. What kind of power it had been, they had no idea. White, hot, and blinding. The pain had been excruciating. Somehow they'd kept their crucible from rupturing, but its wall was stretched far beyond where it had been, wavy, thin, and weak. And it hurt.

Jessup's consciousness faded and they began to sink. Zee could barely keep his eyes open and his vision was blurring once more, but he made out Wanchoo approaching upon Venkatarama; the commandants, King Phan and Norrogaul on a Platform beside them. All with scorched and dented armor and visible injuries, but alive. All three pairs were shouting orders, rallying dragon knights and magickers to them, the sounds muted and far away.

As they sank below the waves, Zee heard the clicks and squeaks of krisdolphins. He repeated, *"We did it,"* and succumbed to oblivion.

CHAPTER 59

Zee gritted his teeth as he strode along a lower hall of the ship, following Dame Toomsil and Tem. He kept his head up and back straight, but the pain of his injuries still lingered. Zee felt bad thinking it, but he was glad of the slower pace set by Tem due to the splint on his leg. Dame Toomsil had her arm in a sling. Both had suffered from broken bones in the battle, now two days past. Magickers had sped their healing tremendously. In another few days they would lose the splint and sling altogether.

Zee had been injured worse than he'd thought, suffering from burns, a broken clavicle, stab wounds, and internal bruising. Wanchoo had aided the healing process himself but told Zee the pill he'd taken had begun mending him and Jessup as soon as he took it. Zee hadn't stepped foot out of the cabin where they put him after Wanky had retrieved him from the sea, and he'd just woken this morning. Apparently the backup SHEEL commandos Chan and Coolbaughm had come on their krisdolphins and descended into the depths to attach ropes to Jessup. It had taken five dragons to pull him up and to the ship, then a heavy winch and chain to raise him through the moon pool.

Speaking with Zee through their bond, Jessup had said he felt fine, if a little sore, and the missing part of his arm had already started growing back. He told Zee it had happened to him before. It itched, but the arm would renew itself, slightly shorter than before, but this time far more quickly because of the pill, help from the healing magickers, and their bond. Zee was headed down to see Jessup for the first time since the battle.

They had indeed spared the forces of Tosh from the power of the Ability they'd unleashed—whatever that was—but some had been injured. Zee had been struggling with that since he'd heard. He hated the idea they'd harmed any of their own. They would be fine, but one of them had been Lord Governor jal Briggs, along with a few of his men. Zee wasn't particularly fond of the man, but he *was* Tem's father.

Aureosa and Vandalia had mused that the strike Zee and Jessup had used was at minimum a high-level Red Titan Class Ability due to the amount of widespread damage it could do, most likely Black Titan Class. They wouldn't be able to do it again until they advanced greatly, and even then it wasn't a guarantee. Not without the pill, anyway, and Wanchoo had said that was the only one. It was, in fact, an artefact called the Pearl, brought from the citadel vault. None had ever been able to take it, its aura causing them such discomfort they hadn't the strength. Not even Slan hai Drogo and Mogon. Yet, it had been drawn to Zee and Jessup and they to it. What that meant, Wanchoo didn't know, but he and Rama had expressed their amazement at his and Jessup's reaction to the pill and what they had accomplished.

Wanchoo had said, "Most surprising is that you lived through it, and didn't kill us all." He'd warned Zee there was a chance their crucible could be permanently damaged, but if it had ruptured, their bond would be broken, which it wasn't. He wouldn't know the true extent of the damage until Zee and Jessup were together and revealed their core to him.

They descended the final flight of steps to the expansive bottom deck. Tem and Dame Toomsil stepped to either side of the door at the bottom and waited for Zee to enter, which confused him. His sight line cleared the top of the doorway, and he slowed.

There must have been much nicer rooms on the ship for the king to work, but he sat at the long table facing the door, writing with a quill. Mingling before him were the highest-ranking officers of the Navy fleet and the Dragon Corps, including their dragons. Beyond that, it looked like every pair that had come on the mission were crowded onto the deck.

Among them were the commandants and deans of magicks. Aureosa's shoulder was bandaged, and he wore a sling, but he looked hale and hearty otherwise. Off to the side, in a discussion with Tablert and several Navy officers, sat Jessup.

Jessup sensed Zee's approach and grinned his big rubbery grin. Zee grinned as well and was about to go to his friend when Vandalia shouted, "Attention!"

Wherever they stood, those gathered turned toward Zee, straightened to attention, and as one, saluted. Zee looked behind him, thinking someone important must have followed them down the stairs. To his surprise, no one was there, and Tem and Dame Toomsil were saluting as well.

Saluting him.

Dame Toomsil gave him a tiny nod. Dumbstruck, he turned back to the group.

The king stood, clasping his hands behind his back. "This is for you, Mr. Tarrow, and your faithful beast, Mr. Jessup."

Jessup was as stunned as Zee was.

"Come," said the king, waving a hand. In the moment it took for Zee to find his legs, the king added, "And Mr. Jessup."

Vandalia shouted, "As you were!"

All moved out of their way as Zee approached the table and Jessup shuffled up on his arms, towering over everyone. Zee saw Lord Governor Briggs standing with several of his men in the crowd. They didn't look quite as pleased with him as the others. Zee couldn't blame them. One of the governor's hands was wrapped in gauze, and the greased burn on his neck looked painful. His men looked to have been treated for burns as well. It took Zee a moment to recognize one of them as the knight who had cuffed his da on the pier so many years ago. The man's head was wrapped in bandages and he held his helmet under his arm. If Zee and Jessup were responsible for his injuries, Zee didn't feel so bad about that. In fact, he kind of hoped they had.

The king sat and resumed writing as Zee arrived. Zee was about to go to one knee, but the king raised a finger without looking up. "Don't kneel."

"Yes, Your Majesty," Zee replied, his voice cracking. Silence followed, a very awkward one for Zee, as the king continued scratching away with his quill.

Prince Talog came around from behind the table in a wheelchair, pushed by an attendant. He still looked gaunt, but the color of his skin was better and the dark circles under his eyes had lightened. He reached out and shook Zee's hand—with his left, since his right had been removed by his captors, the stump held in his lap, wrapped with clean bandages. "I owe you my life, Mr. Tarrow"—he gave a regal nod to the kraken—"Mr. Jessup. I shall not forget it."

"Nor shall I," the prince's dragon said from behind the table. "Thank you, from the bottom of my dragon's heart."

Zee's head felt like it was filled with aloishus goo, but he finally put the words together to speak. "My pleasure, Your Highness, sir. Just doing my duty."

The prince smiled. "For such a young man, a civilian, a hull scrubber, for that matter, from a remote village at the far end of the island, it was far more than that."

"My sentiments exactly," said the king, setting down his quill. Vice Vizier Davis han Ashura powdered the ink and affixed the royal seal to the document. Only then did King mon lin Phan look up at Zee. "You will long be held as a hero in the hearts and minds of all here, but no one else must know of what has transpired on this mission, not even of the mission itself. Not the kidnapping of the prince, the mysterious enemy who nearly defeated us, or the role you and Mr. Jessup played in overcoming them. Do you understand?"

Together, Zee and Jessup said, "Yes, Your Majesty."

He took the scroll from Ashura, who had rolled it and tied it with a ribbon. "At the academy, you will simply be cadets like any other."

"Yes, Your Majesty," Zee replied. "I... Pardon me?"

"By royal decree, you and Mr. Jessup are hereby admitted to Triumf's Citadel Academy." He slapped the scroll into the waiting hand of Commandant Aureosa. "Effective immediately."

* * *

"I know what you must be thinking, Zee," said King Phan.

Zee himself didn't know what he was thinking, so he had no idea how the king could. He was still shocked that he and Jessup had been accepted into the academy. And they were sitting in the same room where Deans Wanchoo and Venkatarama had told them about the red power of the Wraiths and sorcerers, and given them the pill that had helped them save the day in battle. Only now the king of Tosh sat where Wanchoo had been, sipping a glass of wine, talking to Zee like he'd known him for years.

King Phan continued, "You're thinking that being granted acceptance into the academy isn't enough for everything you and Jessup have done for your king, your kingdom, the Dragon Corps, and the Navy."

Zee hadn't been thinking any of those things. He glanced at Jessup, who shrugged slightly. "Well, I—"

"I thought as much, and I agree, which is why we're also granting you a generous annual stipend for life. In addition, all of your past infractions are forgiven, the time on your sentences is considered served, and there will be no inquiry."

Zee wasn't sure what he was going to say, but he opened his mouth to say something. The king silenced him with the wave of a hand.

"While you two are incredibly strong, your power is erratic and not well controlled. The best place for you to advance is at the academy."

"Yes, Sire."

"Good, but I can understand if you feel that you're beyond Basic Training." He tipped a hand toward Aureosa, who sat nearby. "I and the commandants agree. I'm waiving that requirement. There are only a few weeks left in Basic for this year, as it is."

"Instead, we'd like you to visit the castle," said the prince, who sat in his wheelchair next to the king. "We can't celebrate your accomplishments on this mission publicly, but there we can grant you the pomp and circumstance you're due in private." He looked from Zee to Jessup, seeking a reaction. When they had none, he said, "Is that not acceptable?"

Zee gazed at Jessup and they spoke through their bond.

Though it all still hadn't sunk in, Zee felt he'd been able to gather his wits enough to answer, and he and Jessup were in agreement.

"That's all very kind and generous, Your Highness, and Your Majesty. If we may be so bold, though, we do have some requests."

Instead of becoming angry at their presumptuousness, the king chuckled. "Let's hear them, then."

"Would it be possible for our stipend to be sent to my parents?"

King Phan turned to Davis han Ashura, who sat at a small desk, quill in hand. "Can you arrange for that, Vice Vizier?"

"Of course, Sire."

"Thank you, sir," Zee said to Ashura.

Jessup said, "We also want to complete Basic Training and go through the trials like everyone else."

"We don't want any special treatment in that regard," Zee added.

"I see." The king looked to Aureosa, who sat next to Dean Wanchoo. Their dragons lounged on rugs behind them.

Aureosa held his hands up in consent. "I don't see why not, if that's what they wish."

Vandalia said, "You'll be thrown in near the end of Basic, which will be disorienting, to say the least." She smiled and added, "Honestly, having gotten to know the two of you a bit, I'm not the least surprised it's what you want."

Jessup said, "Thank you, ma'am."

"And the third stipulation?" the king asked.

Zee said, "We'd very much like to be fully assessed for our bond rating when we return to Triumf's Island."

For that, the king turned to Dean Wanchoo, who smiled and said, "That will most certainly cause a stir, especially if we discover the Orb truly can assess Marisean, but perhaps a stir of that nature is what we need right now."

King Phan said, "Request granted," then glanced over them both. "Anything else?"

Together, they replied, "No, Your Majesty."

He slapped his hands on his knees. "Then I call this meeting to a close."

* * *

Zee grinned up at Jessup while Vice Vizier Ashura wrote down the information needed to deliver their annual stipend to Zee's parents. And not only would the stipend be sent by courier knight as soon as they returned to Tosh, the vice vizier had also agreed to have something else sent with it. Zee was a little anxious about it, but he couldn't be happier. Neither could Jessup. "Thank you for giving your half of the stipend to my ma and da," he said to his big friend.

"What do I need coin for?" Jessup replied. "New clothes?"

Zee laughed out loud but covered his mouth so as not to embarrass himself. Then he noticed that the vice vizier was chuckling to the point he had to stop writing.

They laughed together, then Ashura blew out a breath. "Thank you, gentlemen. I needed a good laugh after these last few weeks." To Jessup, he said, "You're quite the comedian, Mr. Jessup."

"Big funny kraken," Jessup said with a straight face. "That's what they call me."

It wasn't until Jessup grinned that Ashura realized he was joking. He chuckled again and pointed his quill at the kraken, then went back to writing.

Zee still couldn't believe everything that had just happened.

Jessup, on the other hand, was taking it all in stride. "*Zee deserves all of it.*"

"We *deserve all of it.*"

Jessup looked to the back of the room. "*The chaplain is still watching us.*"

"*I know,*" Zee replied, trying not to look, and failing. Chaplain oh Connor had been there for the meeting, sitting with that inscrutable expression of his. Now he stood with Lord Governor jal Briggs, who had also been in the room, speaking in hushed tones.

"*What do you think they're talking about?*" Jessup asked.

"*Who knows, but honestly, I don't really care right now.*"

Zee felt a presence over his shoulder and turned to find High Admiral tar Tarzian staring down at him.

"Mr. Tarrow, may I have a word?" The man's voice rumbled through his prodigious beard and mustache.

Zee forced himself not to gulp. That, he might care about.

* * *

Nearly everyone had left the room by the time Zee settled into a chair in a back corner, facing Lukas tar Tarzian's father across a low table. The high admiral sat at ease, though he wore a slight frown.

Jessup thought the whole situation was funny, and Zee had to silently shush him through their bond. "*You're not helping.*"

"*But he has so much beard. It looks like a bib.*"

"*How do you even know what a bib is?*"

"*Fennix is teaching me human etiquette.*"

"*What? Why would a dragon or a kraken need to know anything about bibs?*"

"*It's part of learning what he calls 'silly things people do.'*"

Zee tried not to chuckle out loud.

"*Like, when a man likes a woman, they sometimes—*"

"*Shh!*"

The admiral chose that moment to speak. "I'm not happy about losing two of my SHEELs, Mr. Tarrow. You and Mr. Jessup were supposed to be protecting them."

Zee couldn't argue. He still felt terrible about the loss of Petrikleo and Berrolli. "We're very sorry about that, sir. We just couldn't save them all."

Jessup said, "They were good soldiers and good people."

Tarzian's eyes darted to the kraken, surprised by the comment. "On the other hand, its quite a feat you were able to save any of them. You fought and killed a *quahogtomb*, of all things. Few have seen one, even from a distance, and lived to speak of it." He sat forward, hands on his knees. "Tell me, how did you do it?"

They told the admiral the story from first seeing the kelplike tentacles of the creature to their escape, though they left out the part about the profane glyphs carved into its shell. Wanchoo and Venkatarama were the only ones they'd told about that.

The admiral sat back, shaking his head. "You know, there's been some discussion that you be asked to join the Navy if it didn't work out with the Dragon Corps, but we have no instruction for bonded pairs. The citadel is the best place for you. I see that now, especially."

Zee was taken off guard by that information, but replied, "Thank you, sir."

The man waved off the comment as if it was nothing, then frowned and sat quietly for a time, gazing at his hands in his lap. Finally, he said, "I'm fully aware of what my son, Lukas, can be like, Mr. Tarrow. As far as I'm concerned, he deserves the punishment he's been given. I just hope it will be a learning experience for him and he can live up to the potential I and his mother see in him."

Zee groaned inwardly. This is what he'd been worried about, but the admiral continued before he could respond.

"It's my fault, to be honest. I haven't been the best father, even when I was at home, which was never very often." The admiral met Zee's gaze. There was no anger or command in his voice. "Speaking not as the high admiral of His Majesty's Navy, but as a father, I'd ask that you not hold his past actions against him, or think of him too harshly. And if he gives you any more trouble, please don't hurt him too severely. He's the only son I've got."

It took Zee a moment to respond. "I understand, sir."

"It's important to clear the air, and I've waited too long to do so out of pride. Now perhaps you see where Lukas gets some of his attitude." At that, he actually smiled, as much of a smile as he was capable.

"I greatly appreciate it, sir."

"If you ever need anything from His Majesty's Navy, you contact me directly and I'll see what we can do."

"I..."

"You are dismissed."

After shaking hands with the man and leaving the room, Zee turned to Jessup. "That wasn't at all what I expected."

"Is anything that happens to us?"

Zee laughed. "Definitely not."

CHAPTER 60

Zee sat upon one of Jessup's arms at the rail of the HMS *Dragon's Rage*, gazing out over the passing sea. Jessup's saddle rig had been removed. It just wouldn't do for him to have it in Basic. The holes from the lag bolts were still visible, but had already begun to close. His torn arm was healing as well and even regrowing itself.

The sun warmed their faces and aching bodies, the breeze refreshingly cool. It was the first time they'd seen the sun in weeks, it having been blocked by the Shroud of fog conjured by the magickers for the trip to rendezvous with the Wraiths. Zee shuddered at the thought of them.

After the enemy sorcerer had retreated, the remaining Wraith forces in the air had made a frantic retreat in all directions, and their ships had broken off and made a run for it. The king's forces had chased down, killed, captured, and destroyed all they could. Of the twenty ships of the Navy task force, only twelve remained sailable. Five had been sunk by the enemy, three were being towed, while the sailable Wraith ships that had been seized were being piloted by Navy crews.

Zee and Jessup hadn't been told how many sailors or Dragon Corps rider and dragon pairs had been lost. Zee didn't think he wanted to know. Having known the SHEELs and lost two of them had been bad enough.

At least Tablert was doing fine, and Chief Walster would recover well enough to return to service, which was his wish.

"We did it, Zee," said Jessup. "We're going to the academy." He always knew Zee's mood and just the right thing to say.

Zee still couldn't believe it. Part of him almost wouldn't allow him to. It had always been a crazy dream. Still, it was one he'd never given up on.

He smiled, the warmth of Jessup's good cheer and the sunshine making it impossible not to. "We still have to pass Basic Training."

Jessup made a flatulent noise with his big rubbery lips. "Piece of fishcake. We are Zee and Jessup. We are *sorcerers*."

"A sorcerer-type pair…" Zee shook his head. "Can you believe it?"

"Why not?"

"There haven't been any sorcerer types since Drogo and Mogon, not in all the allied kingdoms and beyond, as far as anyone knows. And they were the first in a century before that."

"So?"

Zee shook with laughter. When it passed, he said, "The Wraiths have a sorcerer pair. They're necromancers too. Using whatever that horrid red power is." He shuddered again, remembering the dreadful chill of it, the pain inflicted upon them, the utter violation of the sorcerers speaking in their minds.

"We beat them once. We'll beat them again."

"We almost died."

"Almost dead is not dead."

Zee chuckled, shaking his head. "You are the most confident beast or person I have ever met."

"I am a kraken."

"Yes, you are, my friend."

"Best friend Jessup."

"Best friend Zee." Jessup held him closer, the warmth of their bond heartening them both.

Zee sat up with a thought. "Sorcerers!"

"We said that."

"I know, but..." He retrieved the murfolk book from their Keep.

"Oh..." Jessup uttered, realizing what Zee meant. They hadn't looked at the book since the battle.

Zee also pulled out the bucket. He set it on Jessup's arm, retrieved the book, and dunked it. This time when he placed his palm on the cover it throbbed with blue light three times, then glowed brightly for several seconds before fading.

Jessup said, "That's different."

Zee watched eagerly as the pages flipped to the page where the bumpy circle with the jagged line angling down through it had appeared centered on the kraken's shell above its face.

Zee pointed at it, brow knitted. "Remember what the Wraith general called you?"

"Um... a Thunder kraken."

"I think that's what this symbol means."

"Because of the storms and lightning Abilities?"

"I guess. I wonder what other kinds of krakens there are."

"Or were." A slight sadness drifted to Zee through the bond.

"I told you, if there are any, we'll find them. If there's one, there have to be more."

"I believe you."

"You'd better," Zee jested. Jessup's sadness retreated.

There had been another symbol below the kraken and murman, but now it had changed as well—and it was the same as the one he'd seen on the type badge on the statue of Drogo and Mogon. "Jessup, this means sorcerer type. The book knows! And this is crazy, but it's the same as what the Dragon Corps uses."

"Murfolk and krakens use the same symbol as humans and dragons? How?"

"I don't know. We'll have to show this to Deans Wanchoo and Venkatarama." He flipped pages to find more chapters had been revealed, with diagrams of more Abilities.

Together, both of them emitted an "Oooh..." of excitement and wonder.

Zee said, "We won't be able to do anything about any of this until we heal our crucible, and Dean Wanchoo ordered us to rest for a few days. No training. No forging. No sparking our core."

"That never stopped us before."

A sly smile crept over Zee's lips. He put the book and bucket away, then closed his eyes and breathed deeply.

Jessup joined him. "Time to forge."

* * *

Morning light was leaking into the sky to the east when Jondon dil Rolio threw one log of a leg over the bench and sat with his breakfast tray piled high next to Chirt sim Nabbit and across from Mehmet can Yasso. As Sallison anh Batcu approached the table, a courier knight came striding through the outdoor Basic Training chow area, calling her name.

Conflicted emotions flickered over her features before she answered. "Here, sir!"

She set down her tray as the knight marched over and handed her a letter. "Personal and confidential. Eyes only." He spun and marched away.

Jondon raised his eyebrows. "Hand-delivered?"

Chirt said, "Aren't we special."

Sallison stared at the letter, her expression unreadable. "It's from my father." She strode toward the barracks tent and disappeared around its corner.

The three recruits shared a look of concern, then waited as long as they could.

Chirt peeked around the tent, then Mehmet above her, then Jondon, well above them both.

Standing alone, facing away from them, Sallison gazed down at the letter.

"Sorry to pry," Mehmet said timidly, "but are you all right, Sallison? You've been very quiet lately."

"Sullen," said Chirt, not so timidly. "Brooding, even."

Jondon said, "We're worried about you." Sallison gave no answer, then they saw that her hands were trembling and her shoulders were shaking. They stepped closer.

Jondon asked softly, "Is it bad news?"

"No, it's good news." She turned and looked up, beaming through happy tears. "Very good news." She gazed back at the letter. "Strange, but…"

She grinned again and threw her arms around Jondon's prodigious girth. He gaped in surprise. Sallison didn't hug. Ever.

She released him, then grabbed Mehmet and squeezed, making him grunt. Chirt backed away, eyes wide, but there was no escape. Sallison snatched her off her feet. Chirt squeaked.

Sallison set Chirt down, then wiped the tears from her eyes as she grinned at them all. "Everything's great. Don't you worry about me."

They stared at her as she strode away, lighter in step than she'd been in weeks.

* * *

Sallison rounded the corner of the tent to find everyone on their feet, murmuring, shouting, abandoning their morning chow and crowding toward the path that led from the harbor beach. Jondon, Chirt, and Mehmet came up behind her.

"What's going on?" Chirt asked.

"Let's find out," Sallison replied, then took off at a fast jog around the crowd. As she pushed to the front, she spied several second-year cadet instructors and wondered why they weren't screaming at everyone. Then she saw what had captured their attention.

Jessup, raised high on eight of his legs, striding up the path, with Zee Tarrow in civilian clothing perched on the shell above his brow. The kraken appeared to be walking leisurely, but he moved faster than a person could run. His two foremost legs he held coiled in the air, though one looked to be smaller than the other.

Above them flew the commandants, deans of magicks, and the beastmasters. Everyone knew the three pairs had been gone for over a month. They'd been told the reason was none of their business, but rumors abounded, from negotiations with allied kingdoms to an urgent battle and even to hunt down Wraiths. Sallison paid no attention to any of them and didn't engage when asked her opinion.

As far as they knew regarding Tarrow and Jessup, they'd been serving their sentence, though rumors that they'd vanished or escaped had been spreading as well.

Everyone hushed when they passed, the kraken towering over all. Zee glanced down only briefly, a serious look on his face, then they had passed, on their way toward the citadel.

A frenzy of murmurs arose among the recruits. The instructors spoke among themselves, then one of them announced, "Form up for drill, you rabble!" It took less than a minute for everyone to take their places. "Forward, march!"

It was no coincidence they headed in the direction of the citadel. The instructors wanted to see what was happening as much as the recruits.

* * *

As they grew closer to the citadel, Zee asked Jessup to stop by the statue of Sky Marshalls Slan hai Drogo and Mogon.

He spoke through their bond so as not to draw more attention. *"See their badge? It's the same as the symbol in the murfolk book, like I said."*

"Sorcerers," Jessup replied. *"Soon we'll be sky marshalls, too."*

Zee snorted. *"Let's worry about getting through this assessment and Basic, first."*

Ahead, the commandants and deans landed in the courtyard where twenty-five fourth-year cadet pairs were gathered and Cadet Wing Commanders High Mountain ber Sakai and Saralin were just stepping up to the Orb of Assessment. All stopped and saluted, then caught sight of the murman and kraken approaching.

The Gold Class magicker who stood near the Orb hesitated until Dean Wanchoo said, "Please proceed, Thaumaturge ca Hill."

"Yes, sir," ca Hill responded, then presented the wing commanders to the Orb for a bond assessment.

The Orb spoke as words were written in the air.

Rider: High Mountain ber Sakai
Beast: Saralin
Rating: Bond

Zee recalled the pair had been mid-level Iron Class at the exhibition match, a rare feat for so early in their fourth year.

They were scanned with dappled yellow light, and their stats appeared.

Class: Iron
Level: High

Magick Affinity: Lead
Aether Capacity: Silver
Type: Knight
Potential: Red Titan

The foursies cheered. They'd leveled up to high-level Iron, an excellent rating even for the end of fourth year. They had a good chance of reaching Silver by the time they graduated, which would be truly exceptional.

The Orb said, "You may reveal your core."

Their core materialized, perfectly round and smooth, a dim golden sun about nine feet in diameter.

The fourth-years chanted, "Spark it! Spark it!"

The power of their core washed over Zee as it ignited. He would be impressed if he didn't already know what his and Jessup's looked like. A smile of satisfaction rose on his lips.

"*Not bad, for a little man and dragon,*" said Jessup.

Zee laughed softly, then frowned. Their core might be remarkable, especially for the short time they'd been forging, but they still didn't know if the Orb could assess for Marisean.

An academy assistant hurried across the lawn of the courtyard carrying a folding table. Behind him came more faculty and staff, including Dean sim Tooker, Chaplain oh Connor, and Superintendent Hyooz with Amoxtli held in one arm like a cat. The little creature perked up at the sight of Dean Wanchoo and flew to his shoulder, where she licked his cheek. He smiled and scratched her under the chin.

The fourth-year cadets were dismissed but were curious and did not go far.

Jessup lowered himself to a reasonable height for Zee to dismount and they made their way to where Commandant Aureosa stood behind the table, speaking to the superintendent.

As they approached, Hyooz handed Aureosa a set of papers and Zee heard her say, "I hope you and King Phan know what you're doing, Peleus." At least she didn't sound angry.

Aureosa glanced at Zee with a barely hidden smile. "So do I."

The superintendent stepped back to join the others while Aureosa flipped through the papers, Vandalia peering over his shoulder.

Aureosa set the document on the table and tapped it. "These are the enlistment papers drawn up by the board. They could not refuse the king's proclamation, but they've made your acceptance probationary based on your recent infraction. Abide by all regulations and you'll be fine."

Together, Zee and Jessup said, "Understood, sir."

"Jessup's acceptance is verbal, but you need to sign here, Zee." He paused while handing him a quill. "Are you sure you want to go through with this?"

Zee was shocked by the question. "Absolutely, sir, more than anything."

"What Zee said," Jessup agreed.

Aureosa said, "I had no doubt, but I had to ask."

Zee looked over the faculty, administration and staff that had gathered to witness the rather irregular proceedings. He took a deep breath and signed the document.

Vandalia said, "Assemblies will be held shortly where you'll be introduced to your cohorts, and the order of business from now until the end of Basic will be explained. We and the deans of magicks will see you with the rest of the recruits from time to time, but from now on, you and Jessup are on your own, understood?"

Jessup answered for both of them. "Yes, ma'am."

"All that's left is the swearing in," said Aureosa, "then you'll officially be recruits in His Majesty's Dragon Corps, with all the rights and privileges, as well as the substantial obligations and expectations, that entails."

Zee and Jessup shared ridiculously wide grins.

* * *

Sallison anh Batcu leaned forward where she sat in the grass, reaching for her toes in a stretch and watching as Zee Tarrow raised a right hand, then Jessup an arm. She'd been right, one of the kraken's arms was significantly shorter than the other. It looked as if it had been bitten off but was healing well.

She and the others had been ordered to halt on a rise at the edge of the training fields in sight of the courtyard and engage in stretching exercises. It was an obvious excuse to see what the murman and kraken were up to, but no one was shooing them off.

"They're being sworn in," said Jondon.

Chirt said, "They've been accepted? Now?"

"But Basic is almost over," added Mehmet.

Behind them, Derlick don Donnicky groused, "If this is real, I'll tell my father and he'll file a formal complaint."

"You may want to hold off on that," Inkanyezi ekh Hanyayo interjected, seated next to him. "There's only one way I can think of that this could happen."

Sallison glanced over her shoulder at him, then turned back to gaze at Zee through narrowed eyes.

* * *

"Are you ready?" Dean Wanchoo asked.

Zee looked to the man, then past him to the crowd that had gathered at the edge of the courtyard and on the training fields. There were far more than the group of fourth-years now, and he spied Sallison anh Batcu among the recruits. With a surge of joy, he spotted Fennix as well, hurrying through the fields with the dragon recruits. He wanted to wave, but the Ice Diver was pretty far away and Zee didn't want anyone else to think he was waving at them.

Jessup had no such reservation. He raised an arm and wagged it vigorously. People did look around, wondering, but at least Fennix grinned.

Zee turned back and gazed over the faculty and staff, many of whom looked angry. For once, though, he wasn't the least bit nervous. He wasn't just ready, he'd been ready. "Yes, sir."

Tem, who had been waiting in the courtyard with Timandra, Dame Toomsil, and Peloquin when Zee and Jessup arrived, indicated to the recruits and instructors that had unofficially gathered and said to Commandant Aureosa, "Should we clear the crowd, sir?"

Aureosa looked to the bystanders, considering. "Let them watch."

Jessup positioned himself in front of the Orb, and Zee climbed onto one of his arms.

Wanchoo said, "Venerated Orb, Rider Zee Tarrow and Beast Jessup reporting for bond assessment."

The Orb spoke and the words appeared.

Rider: Zee Tarrow
Beast: Jessup
Rating: Bond

The Orb glowed brighter white, but flickered and seemed to hesitate, causing a wave of susurration among the cadets and recruits.

* * *

Sallison had heard the Orb acted oddly when Zee and Jessup were assessed after they'd been sentenced, and now she saw it with her own eyes. Word had spread quickly they'd been rated low-level Tin, but other than knight type, all of the other categories had been Unknown, which was strange. There'd been as much speculation about it as there'd been about where they were being secreted away for a month—the same amount of time the commandants, deans of magicks, and beastmasters had been gone.

Then the Orb became yellow, and everyone quieted. Dapples of light projected from its facets as it turned, scanning the murman and kraken. The scan took longer than Sallison had seen before, but finally the stats began to appear.

Class: Copper
Level: Low

Magick Affinity: Bronze
Aether Capacity: Unknown
Type: Knight
Potential: Unknown

Eyes went wide as recruits gasped.

Mehmet said, "That's an early-second-year score."

"Unbelievable," Chirt exclaimed.

Jondon said, "What does it mean that their Aether capacity and potential are unknown?"

They were even more confused when the Orb stopped spinning, throbbed slowly, and stayed silent instead of prompting Zee and Jessup to reveal their core.

Then the Orb said, "Please wait," and everyone hushed. It had never done that before.

* * *

Zee's chest clenched with worry. This was it. What if it couldn't assess Marisean? He looked to Wanchoo, who gazed at the Orb, as if willing it to work.

The Orb said, "Awakening," drawing more gasps. Its light reverted to white and it once more began to turn. "Recalibrating."

Zee held his breath.

Dean Tooker crossed his arms where he stood between Superintendent Hyooz and Chaplain oh Connor. "What are you up to, Wanchoo?"

It was Venkatarama who replied. "We have no control over the Orb, Dean Tooker, as you well know."

The Orb said, "Reassessing," ending any further conversation. The light in the crystal brightened and turned blue.

Zee heard murmurs in the crowd and felt the intensity of their collective scrutiny, but he could breathe again while the Orb scanned them with the blue light of Marisean.

The categories remained hanging in the air, but all the ratings were erased, the letters being deleted backward, then rewritten.

Class: Iron
Level: Low

Magick Affinity: Silver
Aether Capacity: Unknown
Type: Magicker
Potential: Unknown

* * *

Sallison leapt to her feet, followed by the other recruits. All pretense had been forgotten. The whispered comments of earlier were replaced by downright exclamations.

"What the shells?"

"Impossible…"

"And magickers?"

"Blue light?"

"What is with all the 'Unknowns'?"

Jondon blinked down at Sallison. "What's going on?"

* * *

Zee saw the dean of academics wearing a scowl of consternation. The chaplain just gazed at the stats, expressionless as ever.

Zee had been told by Wanchoo and Rama to be prepared for a rating like this if the Orb could read Marisean, but the reality of it hit him hard. "*We really do have a fourth year score.*"

"*Of course,*" Jessup replied.

But the Orb wasn't finished.

* * *

Once more, the Orb stopped turning, slowly pulsated, and stayed silent, then once more it changed back to white, resumed turning, and said, "Recalibrating."

Mehmet said, "A third time?"

After an anxious pause, some of the crystal's facets turned yellow, then the remainder of them changed to blue.

The Orb spoke. "Reassessing."

All watched in stunned silence as the murman and kraken were scanned with both blue and yellow light. Again, ratings were deleted and replaced.

Class: Iron
Level: Medium

Magick Affinity: Gold
Aether Capacity: White Titan

After the type rating of magicker was deleted, there was a pause while the Orb continued to scan. Then the rating was written in the Orb's flowing cursive.

Type: Sorcerer

Sallison could only stare while others gasped and spoke in feverish whispers. Then the potential rating was erased. Again there was a pause. When the rating began with "Un," Sallison expected another Unknown. Instead, it said,

Potential: Unlimited

No one said a word. Other than a few exchanged glances, they all stared in shock.

Sallison gaped, trying to make sense of what she was seeing. To reach mid-level Iron Class alone was excellent even for a graduating cadet. As far as she knew, they'd progressed that far from low-level Tin in, what, five weeks? And sorcerers, with White Titan aether capacity and unlimited potential?

Sallison couldn't help but wonder—what in Zhera's name were they capable of? She looked to the instructors, then ber Sakai and Saralin. From their expressions, they were wondering the same thing.

The crowd began to chatter and shout.

Then the Orb spoke again, shocking everyone even further—including the faculty. "Quiet please. Assessment in progress."

All went silent. Never before had the Orb addressed spectators like that.

"Zee Tarrow and Jessup," it said, "you may reveal your core."

Sallison watched as the pair looked to Dean Wanchoo, then took a deep breath, and their core appeared.

"Good gods..."

"What is that?"

Sallison's hand went to the letter in her pocket. She'd suspected there would be blue in their core. Seeing it was something else entirely. Marisean was real. Not only that, there was Empyrean with it.

Zee and Jessup's core was slightly smaller than ber Sakai and Saralin's had been, but it looked more solid, and it gleamed as if polished.

Then she noticed their crucible. The wing commanders' had been normal for a pair of their class and level, the wall thick and strong, and its ring floating a couple of feet away from their core all around, about fourteen feet in diameter.

The wall of Zee and Jessup's crucible was of irregular thickness, but it had to be over twenty feet across.

Dean Wanchoo said, "Spark your core, gentlemen."

It ignited, and all but the highest-class pairs in attendance had to shield their eyes at its brightness. Bonded cadet pairs and faculty alike recoiled, amazed at the pulse of power that struck them.

* * *

Where she stood near Aureosa, Wanchoo, and Venkatarama, Vandalia said to her rider, "*It feels like the core of a White Titan, Pel.*"

Aureosa just looked at her, then turned back to the core and stats.

* * *

Sallison had never seen bonded pairs react like that to the sparking of an Iron Class core, and she wished with all her heart she could feel it as well. But she would, and soon. There were only a couple of weeks left in Basic. She had no doubt she would pass. Then Pairing Day would come, and she would find a dragon to bond with.

A strange feeling drew her eye away from the murman and kraken's extraordinary core. Peering through the crowd, she caught sight of the dragon recruits, and Fennix among them. He wore an enormous toothy grin. He seemed to feel her eyes upon him and looked her way. His grin faded to a smile.

No one complained or tried to stop Sallison as she pushed her way to him, they were so enthralled by the shining Marisean and Empyrean core. She stepped up beside him and turned back to the sight in the courtyard.

"Did you know about this?" she asked.

It took him a moment to respond, but his answer was firm. "I did not." Then he asked, "Do you know where they've been?"

She also hesitated, but her answer was just as firm. "I do not."

They eyed each other suspiciously until Fennix snorted. "Keep your secrets, then."

"What secrets do you think I have?"

"How should I know? That's the very nature of secrets, is it not?"

Both of them cracked a grin.

* * *

Zee had hoped, even expected, their assessment to be good, but nothing like this. He knew they had classed up in the fight with the Wraiths, but before then they'd been estimated at low level Bronze. If that estimate was accurate, their near-death experience and the pill they'd taken had pushed them through mid and high Bronze, to low Iron Class, and a whole additional level, all in one fell swoop. And the rest of the ratings... He wasn't even sure what they all meant.

The Orb turned back to white, then dimmed. They unsparked their core, which faded from sight. Zee climbed off Jessup and they looked at each other, Zee in amazement, Jessup with a wide crooked grin.

Jessup said, "We said we'd show them."

"Yes, we did."

Zee gazed over the gathered cadets. Some did not look happy. All had been outshone, and some were still stunned. Others stared, leery of the strange recruits in their midst or trying to calculate just what this meant to their own positions and advancement. Zee and Jessup had suddenly become far more than an oddity or frightening monsters. Now they were competition.

Zee turned to the faculty and staff. They wore mixed expressions. Dean sim Tooker and Chaplain oh Connor had moved away from the group and were conversing quietly. About what, Zee wasn't sure he wanted to know.

Beastmaster Mahfouz gave him and Jessup an enthusiastic thumbs-up, and Mildrezod was grinning. Mahfouz nudged Tackmaster Samir. Zee couldn't hear what was said over the buzz of the crowd, but by the roll of Samir's eyes, he guessed the beastmaster was reminding him of the bet they had made.

Aureosa stared at the stats, which still hung in the air, and shook his head. "Unlimited potential..."

"Is that good, sir?" Zee asked.

Vandalia said, "It's unheard of, is what it is."

Jessup shuffled closer. "What does it mean?"

"Honestly, we have no idea."

Aureosa said, "Black Titan is the highest potential we've ever seen, and not very often, at that."

Zee stood to attention as Superintendent Hyooz, Dean Tooker, and the chaplain approached.

"I don't know what to say," said Hyooz, "other than, Welcome to the academy."

"Thank you, ma'am."

Tooker spoke to Commandant Aureosa. "It looks like your little gamble is paying off so far, Peleus, but only time will tell."

The chaplain gazed at Jessup, then Zee. "The Church will be watching." From the man's expression and tone of voice, Zee couldn't tell if that was a threat or a compliment. Either way, it sounded ominous.

The three walked away, leaving Zee and Jessup with the commandants and deans of magicks.

Wanchoo said, "You have much to live up to now, and still much work to do."

"Your crucible has healed tremendously," Venkatarama added, "but it's still weaker than it should be. And you have those new Abilities to work on."

Vandalia said, "All of that will have to wait until you pass Basic, however. Without being able to draw on your bond, that alone could prove challenging."

"That's the way we like it, ma'am," said Jessup.

He met Zee's gaze. With a smile, they both said, "Time to get our heads back in the dirt."

*　*　*

Vandalia watched as senior instructors spoke to the newest recruits, preparing to split them into their respective rider and beast cohorts. *Perhaps it's time we told them the truth of the last sky marshalls.*

Aureosa sighed. *"We will. For now, let's let them enjoy themselves, and focus on passing Basic."*

EPILOGUES

Captain Ion Bomba scowled across the table. "Out with it, surgeon." He tore at the chicken leg in his hand and spoke with his mouth full. "If you've taken the time to come to my quarters, I can't imagine it's good news."

"That depends," said Dr. Drall tak Aenig, leaned back in his chair, half smiling at the captain. "You might be just as happy to be rid of me."

Bomba stopped chewing, and swallowed. "Rid of you?"

Aenig pulled a letter from his coat pocket. "I can't go into details at this time, but I've received an offer for employment elsewhere. One I have already accepted."

Bomba sucked at his teeth. "Can you tell me what ship you'll be joining?"

"I won't be working on a ship, and I'll no longer be a surgeon."

"Not a surgeon? What else can you do?"

"Something I should have done long ago."

The captain looked downright disappointed. Aenig almost felt bad for the man. Almost.

"I see," said Bomba. He took a deep swallow of his mead. "When will you be leaving the *Krakenfish*?"

"As soon as we return to port in Tosh."

The captain breathed a growling sigh. "I still have to tolerate you for a few weeks, then."

"And I, you."

Bomba snorted, then shook his head. He poured two drams of whisky and handed one to the surgeon. "Here's to mutual tolerance, then."

Aenig took the glass and lifted it. "Hear, hear." They drained the drinks and slammed the glasses upside down on the table.

Aenig left the captain's quarters with something he hadn't felt in many years. A feeling that had been kindled when a young murman had been conscripted onto the ship a decade ago, grown hotter when he'd learned of the boy's remarkable childhood friend, and now, beyond all expectations, had ignited into a fiery blaze.

That feeling was hope.

* * *

Seela Tarrow was just coming out of the house to do some evening weeding in her herb garden when a dragon landed in her yard. She froze for a moment, then smoothed down her dress and went to stand close to her husband, who'd stopped short while working on a new picnic table.

She held onto Jad's arm as the rider dismounted and came striding toward them.

"Is this the Tarrow residence?" the man called out.

Jad cleared his throat. "It is, sir."

"Jad and Seela Tarrow?"

When Jad didn't answer, Seela said, "Yes, sir."

"I have a delivery for you from His Majesty, Brevor mon lin Phan." He retrieved a hefty pouch from a satchel at his side. When he set it on the table, it made the unmistakable sound of jangling coin. Seela and Jad just stared.

The knight continued while he reached into his satchel once more. "It's the first payment of a stipend you will receive on this date every year." He laid a sheet of paper on the table, then uncorked a bottle of ink, held out a quill and pointed to a line at the bottom of the sheet. "I'll need you to sign here for proof of delivery."

Seela nudged Jad. He didn't know how to write, but he had made his mark on documents a few times. He stared at the paper then back at the knight. "I don't understand, sir."

"It's all above board, I swear on my honor as a knight of the realm." When they still didn't seem convinced, he added, "I don't know much more about it, but the stipend has been arranged for by a Zee Tarrow. I'm assuming he's your son?"

At the mention of Zee's name, a large pig lifted her head from where she'd been nosing through the dirt by the shed, oinked loudly, and trotted to the table as fast as her old legs could carry her.

It was a good thing, too. Seela's knees nearly buckled, and her husband wasn't much help. A pitiful sound escaped his lips and he almost fell. Between the two of them, they barely stayed standing, Jad holding the edge the tabletop, Seela with a hand on Midge's head.

Seela breathed the word, "Zee..."

If the knight was surprised by the nearly fainting couple and curious hog, he didn't show it. "Yes, ma'am."

With great effort, Jad forced himself to speak. "How is he?"

The knight pulled an envelope from his satchel and held it up. "He's written you a letter. I've been instructed to read it to you."

Seela could barely breathe, but managed to gather herself. "Where are my manners. Please, sit."

Now the knight was surprised, but he took a seat on the bench while she and Jad sat opposite. He even removed his helmet.

Seela said, "Would you like something to drink?", and moved to get back up.

The knight held up a hand. "No ma'am, I'm fine, but thank you."

Seela settled back on the bench, then leaned forward and put both hands on one of the knight's. The man was only slighty taken aback, and didn't pull his hand away. "Have you seen him? Zee, I mean."

"I haven't, ma'am, but from what I've heard, he's now a recruit at Triumf's Citadel Academy. And he's riding a strange and mighty beast indeed. It's all anyone is talking about."

It took Jad a moment to recover, a day forever etched in his memory rushing straight to the front of his mind. "What sort of beast?"

"A kraken, sir, of all things. Goes by the name of 'Jessup.'"

Midge oinked again, then squealed with delight.

THE END
of Book One

ACKNOWLEDGMENTS

Thank you for reading *Kraken Rider Z*! I'm incredibly grateful. It was an absolute blast to write, and I hope that showed through in the story. While I'm at it, there are some other people to whom I owe a deep debt of gratitude as well.

I would not have been able to complete this book without the undying support and enthusiasm of David Estes, my co-author, and Bryce O'Connor, the head of Wraithmarked Creative. It's been a trying couple of years, and they stuck by me every step of the way. Thank you, fellas, from the bottom of my heart.

I also want to thank my Beta readers. It doesn't matter how many notes you gave me or how far you got through the manuscript, everything you did helped. Thank you Sadir Samir, Parzival Bach, Kara Lea, Taylon Pruett, Shazzie, Luis Dall, Mike Voss, Beth Tabler, and Michael Abbott! A special thanks to Mihir Wanchoo, who has not only been a great reader, but a rousing cheerleader and a wonderful friend. More special thanks to John Bierce, Sarah Lin, Phil Tucker, and Davis Ashura. I took all of your sage comments to heart, and they made this a far better book than I could ever have done on my own.

All the readers and reviewers who enjoyed *Paternus* and kept telling me they couldn't wait to see what I came up with next, yet were never pushy and always positive and encouraging, thank you!

Also Don Billmaier, John Hoot, and Joe Shumski, tireless supporters and best of friends. You all are the best. And huge thanks to John Hoot again, an ex-Marine and my military consultant, who helped keep me from sounding completely ignorant and foolish. Any ignorance and foolishness that remains is entirely my fault, either for ignoring his advice or simply not asking the right questions.

Thank you to my family, Harriette Ashton, Richard Ashton, Daphne Early, Dianna Ashton, Dillon and Irina, Drew Ashton, Simon and Chelsea, Sasha and Liz, Maggie, Donovan, Wyatt and Weston, and extended family Polina, Lera, and Nica. You keep me going every day, whether you know it or not.

The Terrible Ten, who keep me focused, connected, laughing when things are rough, and my head above water. You know who you are.

Last but in no way least, the rest of the Wraithmarked team, Eira Brand, Shawn T. King, Ben Doran, and Taya Latham. I love you all!

All the very best,
Dyrk

Made in the USA
Monee, IL
07 January 2024

50142027R00344